A Life Loved

A Life Singular
Book 6

Lorraine Pestell

Paperback ISBN: 978-1-925151-08-4
E-book ISBN: 978-1-925151-09-1
Amazon ASIN: B071KTJDCV

Other books in the "A Life Singular" series:
Book 1 – A Life Singular
Book 2 – A Life Found
Book 3 – A Life Entwined
Book 4 – A Life Lived
Book 5 – A Life Tested
Book 7 – A Life After

Author's website: http://lorrainepestell.com
Twitter handle: @LorrainePestell
Facebook fanpage: http://www.facebook.com/ALifeSingular
Goodreads profile: https://www.goodreads.com/LorrainePestell

For Professor Susan Stefan,
who acknowledges my reality

The author supports two not-for-profit organisations providing invaluable
assistance to Australian children in need:

EdConnect Australia (formerly the School Volunteer Program)
(http://EdConnetAustralia.org.au) *"Training and mobilising an impressive
nationwide army of volunteers to deliver the life-changing mentoring and
learning support in schools to young people and assist them in fulfilling their
education potential."*

The Smith Family (www.thesmithfamily.com.au). *"The Smith Family, the
national children's charity helping young Australians in need to get the most
out of their education, so they can create better futures for themselves."*

Prologue

'I'm not that good with words,' Freya lamented, 'except after the fact.'

Dan smiled into the telephone. 'You're an introvert, like me. It's a pain, isn't it? Thinking on our feet's just not natural.'

Last year's winner of The Good School's scholarship was beginning to relax. She always shied away from using the telephone, and the more important the conversation, the harder it was for her to initiate. Why was that? Things usually worked out fine.

'Oh, I agree!' she chuckled. 'And for me, it's also because I think more in pictures than words. I guess that's why I'm an artist.'

'And a real good one,' the Scot jumped in. 'And I'm not just suckin' up to *ya*! Thanks for all the info', by the way. I can't wait to get started, and I hope you'll stay around for a wee while to help me out.'

Freya glowed inside. There was something very appealing about Dan Finley's accent, or was it his sense of humour? His apparent vulnerability or his empathetic turn of phrase? What had got into her? Relationships weren't her thing.

'Sure. I haven't decided where I'm heading when my year's up,' the Queenslander replied. 'My mum's expecting me back in Brisbane by Christmas. My brother's finishing high school, and she wants us to go on holidays together. Haven't really thought about it though; accommodation, a job, you know…'

A cough burst through her earpiece. 'It's fine, Freya. Just wonderin'. No bother.'

'Sorry. I was rambling, wasn't I? I do that all the time. Go off into a daydream and leave everyone else behind. Sorry about that.'

Dan inhaled, his heart rate out of control. 'It's fine. Now I know you've got a mam and a wee brother, so that's two new things I've learned about you today. I read what happened to your dad too. Must've been awful. Do you think about him much?'

'No,' the young woman steadied her nerves. 'Well, yes. More than he deserves probably. That's what a psychologist said to me once. How about you? Your family, I mean…'

The Glaswegian student, whose application had stood head-and-shoulders above the rest in this year's shortlist, came to Ryan and Kierney Diamond's notice during a recent Childlight Board meeting. With precious few resources and significant entrepreneurial spirit, he had established three youth drop-in centres in his hometown's poorer districts.

One particular sentence in the press release issued by the Diamond Celebration Foundation's media machine to announce Dan's acceptance of the bursary made the siblings jump to attention. Not only had he based the model for his clubs on The Fellowship, a charity sustained by their parents since their early days together, but he also hinted at similar facilities for younger children. "Confusion is a killer" had been highlighted in bold.

'My dad's not part of my life the now,' this year's winner answered. 'He left us when I was a baby. He didn't understand stuff. Couldn't cope, I reckon. I think about him a lot though. Much more than he deserves, just like you said!'

'Oh... That's sad too. Sorry to hear that,' Freya said. 'Living through that made you a stronger person though. That's something for us both to be grateful for. Do you remember the bit in Act Two of "ALS" that talked about that?'

'"ALS"? Hey, that's great! Do you call it "ALS" too?'

The painter laughed aloud. 'Yes! I got it from Kierney actually. She's become like my big sister. You'll love her. No, she's not like my big sister at all. Sorry. That was a stupid thing to say. But she's so friendly and helpful. Anyway, there I go again...'

Dan chuckled. 'Fine, whatever! Which bit? Are you thinking of when Jeff's talking about arriving in the next life with a brain already full of knowledge?'

'Yes, exactly! Oh, wow! It's so cool that you know the book so well. I loved when he wrote about how some people don't learn how to do anything during their lives, so they start from Square One again next time round. I feel that way too. I find it amazing that some people aren't interested in stuff. Why not learn as much as you can while you're here, to give yourself a head-start in your next life?'

Suddenly light-headed, the sociology undergraduate forced himself to take a few deep breaths. He stood up and opened his lungs to ingest more oxygen, but this only made matters worse. Sitting back down, he rested his elbow on the desk and let his chin drop into the cup of his free hand. Had he read "A Life Singular" so many times that he could hear the prose in his own mind?

'I'd really like to talk to you some more about this. Can we Skype next week, please? My ID's on my auto-signature. I've got exams this week, but next week's much freer.'

'OK,' the young woman responded. 'I'd like that too. Not Thursday, but any other day at this time'd be good. It's great to speak to you, Dan. Congratulations again! And good luck with your exams.'

'*Ta!* I should be studying the now, but can I ask one more thing?'

'Yes. What?'

'This is going to sound weird, but if you could paint your experience of The Good School, what would the picture be of? I was going to ask you for three words to sum it up, but you said you weren't a words person.'

Freya giggled. 'No, I'm not, and I need time to think about it. My gut-feel says something like I've grown in every dimension, but that sounds as if I've just put on heaps of weight. Can I e-mail you later? I'm an introvert too, remember?'

Bathurst Bar Mitzvah

Quite a crowd had gathered while the outside broadcast crew set the stage. Ryan and Kierney were to be interviewed in the foyer of Her Majesty's Theatre on Exhibition Street, where a new season of "The Black Sheep" was opening. Five months had passed since their dad's suicide, and Melbourne was hungry for good news from the Dyson-Diamond stable.

Penny Reid, a veteran ABC journalist, was all smiles, seated opposite two of the town's best loved Generation Ys. 'Welcome, everybody, to a very special programme. Tonight must be bittersweet for our guests, who need absolutely no introduction. Please join me in thanking Jet and Kierney Diamond for stopping off on their way into the show.'

To polite applause, the brother and sister sat tall in their chairs and acknowledged the smiling faces. 'Thanks, Penny,' they responded in unison.

'It's great to be here,' Ryan added, reaching for his sister's hand. 'Thanks to everyone for supporting the new cast.'

The pair had been warned to expect some intrusive questions about their father's unexpected exit, wondering what sort of reception their frank answers might engender from the locals. Stonebridge Music staff had fielded the full spectrum of public opinion, from abusive telephone calls to compassionate letters, disbelief and sadness being uppermost in people's minds.

From the change in her facial expression, the teenagers presumed Penny had exhausted her stock of pleasantries. 'I read in your dad's autobiography that your parents had you kidnapped,' she stated in a somewhat condescending tone. 'What was that like? How did you feel about them putting you through something like that?'

Remnants of grief bubbled in the pit of Kierney's stomach as she prepared to answer, determined to remain even-tempered. 'Oh, that was years ago! I can hardly remember, to be honest. I can see how some people might think it was unnecessary, but Mum and Dad understood what it takes to be resilient. And people in the public eye certainly need to be resilient and prepared for anything.'

Her brother leaned forward, also feeling a little defensive. 'Yes, it was a horrible experience at the time,' he forced a grin, picking out an attractive brunette in the crowd to steady his nerves. 'I was pretty angry when we found out it'd been a set-up all along, but at least we then had the confidence of knowing what it feels like to be in that situation, and how we'd cope if it ever happened for real.'

'Our parents believed a person can get through almost any hardship if they're loved,' the Sydney University student chipped in. 'We were unbelievably well loved. End of story, as *Papá* would've said.'

A tentative ripple of applause broke out behind the cameras. No-one could ever doubt the celebrity couple's dedication to their children prior to Lynn's fatal shooting. Then, in the aftermath of this tragedy, their father's mature adjustment to the loss of his professed soul-mate had been publicly admired and privately sobbed over, as the sackfuls of fan-mail still pouring into their management company's offices bore testament.

However, since the showman's final statement-to-end-all-statements, views expressed from all quarters were polarising to say the least. Twenty years of blissful marriage brought to such a sudden and unfair conclusion was bound to take its toll, said some. Many others wondered what sort of man deserted his own children in their hour of need?

'So how can you rationalise your father taking his own life and leaving you without that love?' Penny posed the question on everyone's lips.

Ryan was ready for it. 'Oh, we're still loved. Just from a long way off. We believe the way you're treated as a child sets you up for life, for better or for worse. We had the best childhood anyone could possibly ask for, and already knew about Mum and Dad's pact not to stick around if one of them died. It was very tough, of course, but we talked everything through beforehand. I know it's hard to believe, but not even we expected to recover as quickly as we did!

'Children are supposed to outlive their parents. It's the natural way of things,' the sportsman continued, sounding more like his dad every day. 'We had come through losing Mum, and there's no way of telling if we'd have found it harder to lose him too so soon than if he'd stuck around for another ten years or so. No-one knows the answer to that conundrum, and there's nothing we can do about it anyway. *Ergo*, let's just all move on, shall we?'

Penny scowled at the shouts of encouragement booming from over her producer's shoulder. 'That's one way of rationalising it, I suppose. I hope it doesn't creep up on you in the future.'

'It's possible, I agree,' Kierney acceded. 'But I'm pretty sure we're safe from any ill effects. I think they would've been evident by now. We have a lot of help from psychologists and counsellors. We're bearing up as well as can be expected so far. For example, it was *Papá*'s forty-fifth birthday yesterday.'

A few people cried out in dismay, startling the young woman. Whether these were ardent fans mindful of the significant date or stickybeaks uncovering this showbusiness nugget for the first time, she couldn't be sure. Her elder brother beside her, strong, handsome and smiling, boosted her confidence. She ought not to doubt herself. Her parents brought her up with the courage of her convictions. There was no shame in showing them now, objectionable public opinion notwithstanding.

'So we took a bottle of his favourite wine up to the dam at the Dysons' Benloch farm, to the spot where *Papá* re-joined *Mamá*. Their special place. We were definitely a bit nervous, but it was great. We feel close to them all the time. I know it sounds weird, but we've always been comfortable with weird.

'He was confident we'd be fine, and he was right. I remember a conversation we had on the day I got my driver's licence. It was the day before *Mamá* died, in fact. *Papá* joked that their parenting days were over because I didn't need driving around anymore and because Ry was already living overseas quite independently. Jet you were then, I guess...'

The cricketer nodded. 'Yeah. I was still Jet at that point. We'd become more like mates than father and son, so it made sense to leave us to our own devices.'

***

Ryan "Jet" Diamond sailed through his first year at Melbourne Academy without drawing breath. Gregarious and interested in everything, he had jumped at the offer made by his proud parents to become a weekly boarder at the start of Year Eight, following in his Uncle Junior's footsteps. He couldn't wait to immerse himself in after-school activities and the inevitable *camaraderie* which such a diverse range of ages and backgrounds was bound to generate. Endowed with endless physical and mental capacity and an incurable zest for fun, he threw himself into life with courage and determination every single day.

The man who had sworn repeatedly that no child of his would ever be sent away to school had no choice but to eat his words when he saw how well their son was thriving in this new mode. Since his travel schedule continued at a ridiculous pace, and Lynn's career had been relaunched now that their kids' demands on her were greatly reduced, the reluctant concessionaire into the moneyed set admitted to his father-in-law that the arrangement was by far the best option for all concerned.

By contrast, Kierney was fast becoming the invisible child. Happy to amuse herself for hours, either in her bedroom reading or writing, or in the gymnasium training or dancing with the music turned up as high as the mirrored wall would tolerate. More recently, she had discovered new inspiration in the studio, experimenting with recordings, and would invariably emerge at dinner-time spoiling for a fight.

There was nothing the young girl enjoyed more than fierce arguments and wide-ranging debates which often lasted well into the evening, challenged but never thwarted by her parents' *penchant* for playing devil's advocate. No topic was off-limits, the celebrity couple only too happy for her to test the boundaries of childhood in such a safe and supportive environment. They hadn't forgotten their own desperation to discover whether treasures currently beyond their reach were worth having.

Although their firstborn was outwardly every bit a Dyson and his sister was the dark, sultry spitting image of her father, as each child grew, it became obvious to everyone that both were a perfect combination of traditional dynasty and *radicale nouvelle*. Younger than most of their classmates, the Diamond progeny presented to the world as happy, mature and autonomous products of their well-rounded upbringing.

Weekends at *Escondido* were sacrosanct though. Whenever they were in Australia, all four Diamonds gravitated to Mount Eliza on Friday nights with few exceptions, keen to share their news and collaborate on all manner of projects *en famille*. The Polish Jew in Jeff now appreciated the pull of the Sabbath, and with it the feeling of security which came from knowing that everyone he held dear was under one roof by sundown.

This awakening had nothing to do with religion, as true for many social customs. It had everything to do with love.

Most nights spent in the city would see the family fending for themselves, but on the occasions when the influential couple invited locals and visitors over for dinner, or if they foresaw a particularly hectic day, certain extra members of household also made their way to the apartment to help out.

Nannies long forsaken in favour of occasional childminding, nineteen-ninety had seen this role scratched from the famous family's payroll. Taking their place, a retired non-commissioned army officer and his wife were employed as housekeepers. Ross and June Monroe, accompanied by two lively Jack Russell terriers, took up residence in one of the modest cottages on the property in time for the new school year.

Lynn had spent the majority of the last twelve months producing and promoting the success of various albums, both her own and those of others. From outside *Escondido*'s serene and homely walled courtyard, the new arrivals found themselves rubbing shoulders with the "A List", who all considered the Diamonds' luxurious Mornington Peninsula hideaway a home-away-from-home while working on their forthcoming offerings.

'Are we going to give Jet a *bar mitzvah*?' the worldly woman asked one morning, lying in bed listening to a summer rainstorm lashing against the French windows.

Jeff turned over and stroked his wife's shoulder, massaging it while he considered her question. '*Bar mitzvah*? Never even thought about it. Cool idea though. He is getting pretty horny these days.'

'Horny?' his wife yelped. 'Whatever's that got to do with anything?'

'Yeah, horny! What d'you mean? It's got everything to do with it, angel! A *bar mitzvah* heralds your passage to manhood. You know that.'

'OK. Sure. But in that case, why did your grandmother feed you cake? She didn't make it about sex. I reckon you're making that part up for your own benefit. It's supposed to be when boys are responsible for their own actions, isn't it?'

His bluff called yet again, the billionnaire rolled onto his back and issued a laboured sigh of defeat. 'Yeah, yeah, yeah...' he moaned. 'Spoilsport. It's also meant to be a religious thing, and not a cake-eating thing. So my *Bubshka* was just as much of a heretic as I am.'

'Hmm... Anyway,' Lynn reached over and hugged the man she loved so much. 'Whatever the reason, I think he should have one. Don't you?'

For the rest of the day, Jeff's normally unswerving concentration sprang regular leaks; thought-bubbles of their son's impending transition from child to adolescent. What might be the best way to recognise this milestone? Turning thirteen had seen his own first watershed, flanked by his father's imprisonment and his mother's violent death. However, the doting dad was less keen to hurry his obstreperous upstart into adulthood. "The Boy Who Would Be King" was living up to every expectation his family had set for him. Why exert additional pressure for no good reason?

Teenaged years, the boy from Canley Vale recalled, were for the most part troublesome and confusing. He was pretty sure Jet didn't equate turning thirteen with becoming a man. If his empathetic powers were reading his son right, his current manly ideals were defined more as driving fast cars or motorcycles, neither of which were legal until much further into his second decade. The lad was surrounded by strong role models, and hence he also recognised working hard and playing even harder as vital measures on life's scorecard. His grandfather and uncle lived this way, clinically and empirically. And so did his father, although with virtues far less puritan.

It wasn't until the songwriter was behind the Aston Martin's steering wheel, heading home on the Nepean Highway, that the breakthrough came. With an R.E.M. compact disc turned up loud and an autumn fog sticking to the windscreen, the black sports car cut a swathe through the south-eastern suburbs, spiriting its *incognito* occupant to his beloved family. A plan for a boys' weekend away was now brewing, the supreme proportions of which he couldn't wait to test on his dream girl.

Lynn was tucked up in bed by the time her husband turned the key in the courtyard door. Janey had given him a soaking wet welcome home, requiring him to shed his outer clothing in the laundry before climbing the stairs in his boxer shorts.

Stopping first to check on Kierney, whose sound sleep floated in dreamy imagery above her head, fenced in by a stockpile of paperbacks and notebooks containing her mysterious compositions, he then paused in his son's bedroom doorway and smiled. Even though the night was chilly, there lay Jet, out cold and stark naked atop the bedclothes, one hand casually behind his head and the other defending an erect, pre-teen penis.

Yes! the proud *lothario* hissed under his breath. Like father, like son... Some things in life were non-negotiable, and the confluence of Diamonds and sex was one such unassailable truth. He crawled into bed beside his wife, revelling in the warmth of her resplendent body.

'Hey,' she whispered, the contrary sensations of warm breath on her neck and cold skin on her back penetrating her subconscious. 'What time is it?'

'Late,' his lips purred, close to her ear. *'Je t'adore.* Sorry to wake you.'

'No, you're not,' the Olympian grinned, twisting around and cupping a roasting hand against the new arrival's face.

Jeff sniffed. 'Yeah, no. OK. You may be right. I'm not sorry. But to compensate, I've had a bloody good idea.'

'Really? I can tell,' Lynn replied, her fingers gripping round his taut shaft as it pressed against her abdomen.

The world's greatest lover kissed the most beautiful woman on Earth with all the passion he could muster. His saviour would at some point wise up to the overindulgence she lavished on him. Hearing her breath quicken, he begged his day of reckoning to hold off until tomorrow at the soonest.

His left hand loitered in the small of her back, urging her ever closer, and the deft fingers of his right hand slipped along the walls of her vagina. 'I didn't mean sex, by the way,' the poet answered, eliciting an enticing whimper of submission. 'I meant I had a good idea about Jetto's *bar mitzvah.*'

'Oh,' the singer moaned. 'Do we have to talk about this now?'

'Yep. We do,' her tormenter chuckled. 'I can't wait to make you come and I can't wait to tell you my idea, so they'll just have to cohabit for a while. I've been waiting for this moment all fucking day, angel. And I love you so much for planting the seed. You're the absolute best, Lynn Dyson Diamond.'

Jeff rolled his lover over without missing a stroke. She inhaled sharply as he entered her, and an orgasm broke free right on cue. She kissed her husband's chest, covering his "JL" tattoo.

'Oh, wow! That was so amazing,' she sighed, staring into a pair of demanding brown eyes. 'Will you do that again?'

'You bet!' the master responded in mock arrogance. 'How many would you like, madam? Ten? Twenty?'

Another wave of pleasure engulfed them, making the writhing woman cry out. Putting his hand over her mouth, her husband warned her about waking the children.

'So what's this bloody good idea that can't wait?'

'Bathurst,' Jeff gasped, rising above her and sinking further inside with each drive. 'With Don and Dawson.'

'Bathurst? Motor-racing, you mean? When?'

'October. It'll be his rite of passage. I'm going to teach him everything I know.'

Lynn moved faster to match his pace with her own undulations, bringing him ever closer to climax. 'That'll take way longer than one race,' she whispered, her teeth nipping his wrist while loving fingers stroked her face.

'Christ Almighty,' the songwriter growled. 'See what happens when you feed my ego?'

Holding each other close, the forever couple lay in the dark and willed the ecstatic sensations to take their sweet time in subsiding. Although she had no real idea what a boys' weekend at Bathurst might entail, the notion of the fathers and sons being together for such an event appealed to the blonde musician. She imagined the foursome surrounded by roaring engines and myriad acrid odours of petrol, burning tyres and mechanics toiling away. This particular manly image suited their new teenager down to the ground, with or without the sex education syllabus appended to the weekend's itinerary.

'Oh, I love you so much, Jeff. So much... It sounds like a fantastic idea. He'll really love it. Are you going to tell him in advance or leave it as a surprise?'

'We should tell him on his birthday, I reckon. And I'll sound Don out over the next few days.'

'OK. Do you plan to teach Dawson everything you know too?' the impish woman grinned. 'Don and Sue might not be so keen on that part.'

Rolling over and sliding out of bed, the former tearaway smirked. 'Yeah. Most likely more Sue's reservations than his. I'll speak to him next week. This October might see a changing of the guard, teams-wise, which'd be great to witness in close-up.'

Enjoying her husband's newfound animation, Lynn let him head into the bathroom without requesting clarification of this last, cryptic sentence. Motor-racing was far from her favourite sport, and she was too sleepy to be fussed about finding out why the guards were changing. The metaphor seemed apt regardless, and its mystique added extra intrigue.

***

'They've signed the agreement, angel.'

Pouring two cups of coffee from the *cafetière*, adding milk into both and a liberal dose of sugar for himself, Jeff sat down at the breakfast table where his beautiful best friend was engrossed in a newspaper article. She glanced up, her eyes meeting a wide smile that was still a rare commodity for this early in the day. She assumed he had been checking inbound faxes in the office for the last half-hour, anxious for word on one of DCF's notable projects.

'Thanks,' his wife replied, still a little distracted by an opinion piece in the sports section. 'Signed? Which agreement?'

Was her vibrant news-hound referring to another product acquisition which Paragon Holdings would take from garage to consumer with its venture capital program? Or was this a new Non-Government Organisation hitching its wagon to their unstoppable philanthropic locomotive?

Noting the apparent lack of concern, the handsome man opted to keep the industrious woman guessing, planting a kiss on her head and squeezing her shoulder. At thirty-four years old, Lynn Dyson Diamond remained the hottest property known to man, and no amount of inattention could diminish his love for her.

'They're on the last straight. Letters are being drafted as we speak; heads are nodding, and hands are shaking. All hell's about to break loose, I reckon.'

'Oh. Merehtu, you mean?' Lynn whispered as her lips were drawn into a meaningful kiss.

'The very same. Toast?'

The athlete slipped off the breakfast bar stool until her feet touched the flagstone floor of *Escondido*'s kitchen. She followed her magic-man's muscular, bare-chested frame across to the refrigerator, lacing her arms around his waist and kissing his tattoo, the shape of their shared "JL" symbol hard to decipher through a damp mass of greying hair.

'We ought to,' she grinned. 'Congratulations. That's huge.'

'Why, thank you,' the comic responded, pressing his crotch against her hip and stealing gratuitous access to her breasts through her bikini top. 'You're not so small yourself.'

Lynn groaned, powerless to resist her husband's charms. 'Oh, for God's sake. Shut up, you sex-mad brute! Leave me alone for one second. I thought this was serious... Can't you concentrate on something else for a bit? Will there be a change of government too?'

'Looks like it. It is serious, and I am serious. And get this...'

A stern index finger traced a line from his wife's pouting lips, over the curve of her chin and down her neck until it came to rest on her sternum. His right hand curled behind the base of her skull, encouraging their faces closer together.

'What?'

'It might even happen on Kizzy's birthday. Wouldn't that be amazing? Freedom on Freedom's birthday. Serendipity, *regala mía*.'

'Wow! I'm so happy for you,' the Diamond double-act's supreme organisational powerhouse told her passionate front-man. 'For the whole team. Does everyone know already? You guys've worked so hard for this. It'd be perfect if the dates coincide. And I hope you're going to take some credit somewhere along the way.'

The peacemaker sighed. 'Thanks, gorgeous. I'm not sure who knows yet. My name'll be up in lights at some point, I don't doubt, but it's really not important right now. Harnessing the momentum when they make the official announcement's what matters. Africa'll be front and centre on the global stage for a month or two. We can't afford to sit back and smoke cigars while all that's going on.'

'No, I suppose not. Wouldn't be a good look to gloat before anything positive comes out of it.'

'And I wouldn't be surprised if violence were to escalate if the transition's not managed properly,' Jeff leaned over and kissed his wife's cheek. 'You OK if I go over there again?'

Lynn raised her hands, butter knife readied for their toast. 'Not particularly. But how can I say no?'

Her opponent backed away, eyes wide in mock fear. 'I don't know. 'Cause you're the one with the weapon?' he offered.

The clown's foolish banter never failed to melt his dream girl's heart, even after nearly fifteen years of marriage. He dared to make another approach, kissing the sensitive hub of nerves at the corner of her mouth.

Using the lightning reflexes honed over years of athletic excellence, the Olympian sidestepped her opponent's mounting advances and managed to smear butter down his cheek with one deft flick of her wrist. 'Violence may escalate,' she threatened, watching his fingers whip across his jaw in wonder, 'so you'd better manage it properly, Mister Diamond.'

'Whoa! *Gotcha*, loud and clear!' the pacifist laughed, ripping a sheet of kitchen paper from the roll to clean a greasy mixture of butter and marmalade out of his overnight beard. 'Loud and clear, Ms Double- D. Anything you say.'

Despite the campaigners' long-awaited good fortune, the mood in the apartment that day turned fraught with unexpressed angst once news of the Derg's capitulation had been sufficiently sliced and diced. They made a decision the previous night to shelve a project on which they had collaborated for almost six months; a screenplay with the working title of "When You're Gone" and inspired by their Ethiopian hostage experience.

The movie's theme explored the fears and uncertainties of being left to carry on alone without the ability to say goodbye, told from a grieving partner's point of view. In fact, this was the second time its development had been deferred. Earlier suppositions that the couple had expunged enough of their own disquietude to allow a return to the screenplay's dark plot proved misguided. The emotions it stirred up were no less raw and controversial than before, rendering it a bridge too far for public consumption at this time.

The lovers admitted a temporary defeat, unable to understand why their individual instincts were so at odds. Although shared memories of the tense few days spent in an information drought drew them ever closer, the subject matter engendered an esoteric fissure which frightened them both. Anxious to protect their precious family's happiness at all costs, they threw in the final towel after an argument about the story's *dénouement* turned vicious.

If one of them were to die, how might life unfold for the other left behind as truly singular? With no prospect of being together for the rest of this lifetime, would the remaining human embodiment move on or would he or she grieve until the bitter end? Even once the script had been dusted off to resume the creative process, the screenwriting pair soon acknowledged that another two years of maturity had done little to answer these questions with a clear conscience.

In broad daylight, and after a restless night, it was as if the mournful cloud had been lifted from above the pair's heads. Lynn had mixed feelings on sealing the package a courier would deliver to the family's safe deposit box later this morning. These heretofore unarticulated ambitions were set to join the vast array of copyrighted materials already in the bank's custody. Ethereal memes speaking of undying and unquantifiable love took the screenplay's place, infusing the kitchen with a comforting optimism to complement the aromas of toast and fresh coffee to perfection.

Jeff's instincts had been right on the money concerning the many interwoven political schemes across Africa. Missing Kierney's birthday by one day, a reversal of the ban on the Tigrayan People's Liberation Front and other anti-Derg organisations promised repercussions across the whole continent. Within a fortnight, President de Klerk announced Nelson Mandela's release from prison after serving twenty-seven years behind bars for violent activism against *Apartheid*.

A shiver ran down the negotiator's spine as he watched his peacemaking colleague, Jemal Merehtu, addressing the international media contingent beside the much taller South African. The influential, grey-haired lawyer described an era only too familiar to the thirty-seven-year-old, when the military wing known as the Ethiopian People's Revolutionary Party had been formed as a defensive action against the ruling force's iron fist. He and his loyal team had trodden the narrowest of paths between right and wrong for longer than he cared to remember.

The former Robben Island prisoner stopped short of issuing a direct threat, instead choosing to stress to their attentive audience that the grounds for initiating combat insurgencies in the nineteen-sixties were no less rampant today. Despite the fact that they had all grown into reasonable men, the celebrity philosopher remained suspicious that his role in future peace talks would become no less challenging as long as Mandela and his cronies held the ascendancy.

The newly-installed leaders were conciliatory however, expressing their desire for a climate conducive to lasting settlement, sharing the world's hope for an end to armed struggles. Digesting their televised speeches sentence by sentence, the delegation's inner circle maintained a respectful silence from their hideaway in the south of France. Upon reflection, the only rock star at the table felt relief that the innocence of his gorgeous gipsy girl's eleventh birthday had not been sullied by this postulating nonsense.

'Good call,' Jeff muttered to the Zimbabwean mediator to his right, pushing back his chair and accepting a handshake. 'That'll do, gents, eh? Mission accomplished for now.'

Despite the party atmosphere, the billionnaire still harboured an underlying unease. After hours of serious deliberation with their insurers and security advisers, he managed to persuade Lynn to be present for the auspicious occasion. She had accepted the invitation amid equal reservation but replete with enthusiastic pride. The couple arranged to fly out of Melbourne late the following night, with the children safely in their bedrooms after Kierney's birthday dinner.

Arriving at Tullamarine at one o'clock on Sunday morning, the concourse was mostly deserted when the Diamonds strode through the check-in area and were whisked away through Passport Control by three uniformed security guards. And less than a day later, the Diamonds and the Engelbrechts feasted on rare *Chateaubriands* and savoured aged *liqueurs*, making good on the commitment the former university colleagues had made four years prior. The years peeled away with each unearthed memory, their partners a study in contrasts who enjoyed renewing acquaintances and celebrating their husbands' astonishing achievement until the bohemian retrospective decanted into mellow equilibrium.

Jeff held his wine glass aloft, preparing to toast his professorial buddy. 'To you, mate! I'll never forget the time I looked out the window of *la grande maison provençale* to see you and Mehretu meandering across the lawn with your hands in your pockets. The two of you talking in the grounds like you'd been friends for years. That's as close as a heathen like me gets to a miracle.'

Pieter nodded to the pretentious court jester whom he had come to respect with the utmost humility. 'Indeed, sir. I had the sense that we'd make headway that day too. I *carpe*d the *diem,* as a certain drunken Aussie used to say.'

'Ha! I always was a dumb fuck. It was the beginnings of trust,' the younger man explained to the brace of radiant smiles across the table. 'It was an amazing sight. And then the moment when Jemal signalled they were ready to sign a new constitution... Jesus Christ! That's got to be my proudest moment in the whole damned campaign, even though I really hadn't done anything to make it happen.'

'What? Yeah, right,' Lynn shrugged at the others. 'You never do anything to make things happen. Just light the blue touch paper and retire. Take responsibility for something for once in your life, why don't you?'

The dark knight's eyes drilled into hers as he angled down for a kiss, their hands clasped together under the table. 'Harsh words, angel, *comme d'habitude*. But seriously... I just forced some mutual understanding. That's all it took.'

'You make it sound so simple,' Mathilde Engelbrecht swooned.

'Perseverance and patience,' Jeff smiled at the homely South African. 'And those, I believe, are qualities I learned from my exquisite guardian angel. But Jeez, Piet! I remember standing at the empty table after it was all over and taking stock of the enormity of reaching an agreement. That was an effing trip too. Vital vindication of all the hours spent on the 'phone and on 'planes, thumping tables and tearing up drafts, *et cetera*. Preaching the bleeding obvious and banging my aching head against a brick wall.'

Later the same week, an ecstatic and vociferous crowd gathered outside London's Houses of Parliament to watch Jeff Diamond taking overdue credit with his *regala* by his side. Britain's Prime Minister had invited both halves of the peacemaking pantomime horse to address a roomful of society figures at a state dinner given in their honour. An apprentice television journalist, who managed to find himself on the steps leading to the hotel lobby at the same time as the idols' car drew up, jumped at the chance to scoop a spontaneous interview.

The magnetic entertainers, as gracious as ever, obliged with a selection of priceless sound-bytes summarising the Diamond Celebration Foundation's progress towards stamping out sickness in the aftermath of the North African famine, and how Teachers for Peace projects were empowering displaced communities through education and economic grants in the region. Good, bad or ugly, all were related from a highly personal standpoint, albeit without fanfare, sending the reporter's credibility rating skyward on the evening's prime-time news broadcasts.

When asked about his part in Nelson Mandela's release, the great man became far more circumspect. 'I was one cog in a gigantic wheel, Derek. I can't claim much credit for what's happening in South Africa. All I can tell you is it took five years of endless hounding: meetings, 'phone calls, letters and hours and hours of lost sleep. Regardless though, it was still amazing when it happened, wasn't it, angel?'

The blonde Olympian flashed her photogenic smile into the camera's lens. 'Certainly was! To see Mister Mandela walking away from that prison was a special moment, for sure. But for me, watching the expressions on these guys' faces when the Ethiopian treaty was signed tops everything. This was the culmination of some heavy-duty blood, sweat and tears.'

'Professor Engelbrecht,' Derek Wilson interrupted, 'as I understand, paid you the ultimate tribute, Mister Diamond.'

'He was very generous,' the reluctant hero acknowledged.

The young man continued, reading from a crumpled sheet of paper pulled from his jacket pocket. 'I cut out a quote from an article in The Guardian from a few days ago: "Pieter Engelbrecht, who counts himself as neutral politically but who clearly represents the white establishment, has gone on record to say that Africa as a whole owes a huge debt of gratitude to Jeff Diamond. Without his focus on replacing war with peace and wrong with right, I doubt we would have moved forward much at all."'

Sensing her husband retreat from the overt self-aggrandisement necessary to respond to this excerpt, Lynn answered on his behalf. 'Yes. Thanks! Pieter also said these kind words to us directly,' she confirmed. 'He had been reluctant to get involved to begin with. He didn't think peace was possible in the region, and no-one wants to be associated with a failed operation. Afterwards however, he told me privately that being part of the Ethiopian delegation was the highlight of his career.'

'And the highlight of yours too, Jeff?'

'Well, yeah. Of course. One of so many,' the songwriter chuckled, stuffing his hands deep in his pockets as embarrassment prevailed. 'My life's turned out to be one long highlights package. I'm not going to put this ahead of the pack, but it's up there. No question.'

'So what now?' the interviewer quipped. 'How do you top this? "Addis Ababa, the Musical"?'

Lynn laughed. 'Hmm… Could work! Not a bad idea, Derek.'

The humble showman shook his head, reaching long arms across to block his wife's ears. 'Please, no! Don't put such thoughts into her head,' he warned with a sexy half-smile designed to send female audience members into raptures. 'I don't anticipate there'll be any quick fix in negotiations for the foreseeable future. This stunning taskmaster won't let me ease up, for one thing.

'And they're already preparing for elections in Ethiopia, and a planned referendum aimed at forming an autonomous nation for the South Sudanese. I expect this crusade'll trudge along for another few years at least, and we have to divide our time across plenty of domestic issues too. The world's not yet perfect, but it's crawling in the right direction. Our immediate goal is just to keep the momentum going.'

That night, after kicking back in the corner of a Neal Street restaurant to share the best in food, wine and conversation with the production team from a rival television station, Jeff and Lynn finally locked themselves into their hotel room and left their game-faces on the chest of drawers next to the key. Exhausted from being the centre of attention, they tumbled onto the bed, wrapped in each other's arms and exhaling in unison.

'Who was it who said, "Stop the world. I want to get off"?' Lynn asked. 'Wasn't that from a Broadway show?'

'Hmm… Think so,' came a half-hearted reply. 'Sounds appealing right about now. What d'you reckon to that Eleanor woman tonight?'

'She was OK. So serious.'

Her husband chuckled. 'You're not wrong. She forgot to bring her personality. I don't think she'd even have cracked a smile if we'd engaged in foreplay at the dinner table.'

The tennis champion began to undo her man's shirt buttons one by one, tickling the hairy skin covering his tattoo. 'Like this, you mean?'

'No,' he growled, pushing her backwards until he straddled her slim hips. 'More like this.'

Giant, caring hands made their way from the beauty's waist, past her breasts until they cradled her tired head. She curled her mouth sideways to kiss the knuckle of his thumb, moaning quietly as his mass smothered her entire body. This man was passion personified, no matter how many hours he had worked or which of his many and varied duties he had discharged during those hours.

'You're gorgeous,' she whispered. 'I need you so much. You were magnificent tonight, my noble warrior.'

'Noble warrior?' Jeff repeated, sitting up to unfasten his pants and allowing his lover to undress in front of covetous eyes. *'Gracias, mi amor.* You inspire me, as always. Next time, I shan't hold back in front of frigid stage assistants if this is what it does to you! I need you too. And without a second to spare...'

Lynn giggled, being gathered up into strong arms and turned over to face the headboard. 'Hey! Steady with all the inspiration! How come you were never a supporter of Lech Wałęsa, given your Polish background?'

'Lech Wałęsa? Jesus, woman! What made you bring him up at this precise moment?'

'Just wondering, after Harry commented on your wide coverage of world affairs. You still steer clear of Eastern Europe, don't you?'

'Who says I didn't support him?' the dark-haired man slapped her bare behind and brushed the tip of his penis across her pale buttocks.

'Did you?' the woman reeled back, catching his hand and hauling him down onto the mattress. 'You never spoke about it.'

'Not openly, no.'

'But does that mean you did?'

The enigmatic star cocked his head, his saviour's undivided attention recharging his flagging batteries as usual. 'I might've. I didn't like him, but I sympathised with what he was doing. That's all I'll say.'

Feeling the force of his erection begin to fill her, his Number One fan changed the subject. Her instincts told her to mind her own business and trust his reasons would become clear in good time. Given the Sydneysider's experiences as a youth with the Polish gangs menacing the western suburbs with their bloodthirsty stand-over tactics, perhaps endorsing a product of the same culture was simply a bridge too far. As his warmth engulfed her, moving her to tears with its intensity, she chose to remind him instead of their recent exploration of souls and reincarnation with the children.

To the breathless singer's delight, Jeff's eyes lit up, confirming she had saved the lost boy's complex mind from a date with Gravity the troll. Once they reached the dizzy heights of orgasm and started on the floating journey back to Earth, he prised himself free of her grip, slipped off the bed and fetched a bottle of *Shiraz* and two glasses from the dressing table.

The long-limbed nymph rolled off the bed too, threading her arms into a silk robe to take the chill off her tingling skin. Her spent companion didn't make a sound. She returned from the bathroom a few minutes later to find him in the same position, still erect and with his eyes firmly shut. Today had been a momentous day, and tonight was clearly more than a one-climax night!

The adoring wife began to caress his muscular legs, watching the fibres of his quadriceps twitch and tremble with each circle. A move towards his upper arms elicited a similar reaction, this time accompanied by a smirk and a slow, satisfied exhalation. Although his straight penis flinched as she swallowed its head and began to suck in purposeful strokes, there was no sign of life from the rest of his bulk.

'Are you still with us?'

'Nope,' her husband muttered out of the corner of his mouth. 'It's just you and him tonight, baby. No need to wake me up when you're done. I'll see you in the morning.'

'Oh, OK. That's fine,' Lynn laughed. 'Nice and easy. I was about to tell you how sexy you were tonight, and how much you turned me on in the restaurant when you were running your hand down my back while attempting a sensible conversation. Shall we arrange for a late check-out in the morning?'

'Hmm... *Une idée excellente, mon amie*,' the intellectual broke his silence. 'These last few days've been a welcome oasis for our souls, *n'est-ce pas*?'

'*Mais oui*,' the nubile nude replied, batting his errant hand from her backside. '*Bien sûr*. How is your soul tonight, mate?'

'*La Lutte* is proceeding to plan. *Santé*, you most wonderful of wonders. Y'know... I was thinking about the whole two-dimensional souls thing while you were in the bathroom.'

'The essence and the ego? Was I that long?'

'Yeah,' the rocker chuckled. 'Whether it's our kids or African stuff, or even making a record or performing on stage, good only comes about when there's balance between the two.'

'Really? That's an interesting observation. Please explain, prof', while I do my best to distract you.'

The intellectual grimaced, not fancying his chances. 'Jeez! Game on, lady, if I must. Anyway... The essence is outward-looking, concerned with everything being connected properly. The ego focusses inwards, making sure we each have what it takes to play our part in the interconnected world. Does that make sense?'

Lynn giggled, herself unable to concentrate on the soft tissue massage she had deployed as her treatment of choice. 'Maybe. Not sure where you're going with this, but it makes sense so far.'

'*Bueno*. So as we live through the various episodes in our life, our attention waxes and wanes between these two aspects. Much like yours is now...'

'Shut up and get on with the story,' the athlete sighed, renewing her efforts.

'It's what leads us to strive further; to test ourselves and recalibrate our direction. Universal concerns and personal concerns always compete when we take account of stuff happening around us. Deciding how we need to react to everything, y'know... We should always be mindful of the journey other people are on and that it might affect the way they behave too. There's usually a perfectly good reason for doing what they do or say, if only we're open to accepting it.'

'So that's *La Lutte*, in a nutshell?' his muse crooned, now having given up her attempts to derail the vehement orator. 'Realising everyone's course is motivated by their own essence and ego, and there's stuff-all we can do about it unless we put pressure on them to question their motives.'

Her husband's heart soared. '*Exactement, Regala*. Bloody well said! I love you so much,' he shouted, lunging for her waist and locking their lips in a deep kiss for several seconds. 'The eternal struggle that manifests within us at each moment of truth also endures throughout time, lazing on the back porch until it's needed again.

'It's a combination of old learnings we carried forward from the past and new ones we'll take with us into the future. There was a great quote from Rabbi Harold Kushner I read not so long ago: "The mirror never changes, but everybody who looks at it sees something different."'

Lynn caught her breath. 'Looks at it or looks in it? That's what you mean, isn't it?'

'Aha! *Bravo*, gorgeous,' Jeff cried out again, swooping his arm over in a wide arc to reach his wine glass. 'Exactly my point. If you understand the difference between looking at the surface of something and seeing the complexities inside it, you're ninety-nine percent of the way there.'

'The way where?'

'Wherever you want to go. Rabbi Kushner's mirror was a metaphor for God. But I prefer to think of it as the soul, which means maybe, therefore, they're the same thing after all. Who knows, but I'm keeping my soul well separate from a God of the masses.'

The fading princess smiled, nestling her face against his mass of soft chest hair. 'Oh, I love you so much, you wise, old man. I can't believe we've been talking about this for so long and it's still such a mystery. A mystery that binds us together.'

'Wait a minute! Less of the old man, if you don't mind,' the songwriter begged, relishing his penis hardening again in his dream girl's hand. 'The evolution of language has misled us.'

'Has it?' she couldn't hide a sigh. 'What do you mean?'

'Christ, that feels so good. Don't stop. I mean when theologians talk about religiosity and saving souls, they often attribute masculine or feminine to behaviours, like languages that make objects or even abstract things either masc' or fem'.'

'Which varies between languages anyway,' his student interjected.

26

'Sure does,' Jeff inhaled as a surge of desire welled up from his nether regions. 'Listen, you minx... That's precisely what I mean. For example, a chair's female in France but male in Germany, so how can a trait designated as one or the other be used to explain ethereal stuff? Utter crap, I tell you!'

Issued a temporary reprieve once more, the red-blooded lover stretched himself on top of the mattress while his partner switched spots to focus on his satisfaction again. He grinned when he spied a pair of raised eyebrows begging him to carry on.

'Therefore, in my presently violated opinion...'

'Pleasantly violated, I hope,' she countered.

'Oh, for fuck's sake! You are the absolute fucking best, Lynn. Let me finish, and then I'll finish you off once and for all.'

Feeling sorry for this intrepid explorer so torn between feeding their brains and assuaging their carnal needs, the thirty-four-year-old desisted. She flopped down onto the sheet and propped her head on her hand to concentrate on his latest essential lesson.

'Go on, please. Enlighten me.'

The orator chuckled. 'Thank you, you disobedient temptress! I'll enlighten you alright... What I'm trying to say is that it's totally unhelpful to use the words "essence" and "ego" to describe the two sides of a soul. I'm going to write about it when we get home. "*Yin*" and "*yang*" might be better? They don't divide us down gender lines and unleash some of those negative responses Jetto mentioned from the girls in his class.'

His wife nodded. 'Oh, yes. I know what you mean. Girls can be so cruel sometimes. They're the first to get upset when a boy insults them, but then they're bitchy to everyone behind their backs.'

'Yeah. Works both ways, I assure you. And this game of picking sides based on pre-conceived biases sets us in unhealthy competition with each other, hence all the violence in the world... Competition, as you Dysons understand so well, is a team sport. It's using both *yin* and *yang* capabilities in all people to their best advantage, rather than denigrating particular behaviour.

'We need to stop labelling everything like we're running wild with a supermarket price-gun. This has to be our new message, angel. Can we? Like, think about what you want to achieve, then look around you to see who and what's at your disposal without focussing on the labels they have stuck on them. And use everything wisely.'

Lynn sat back on her haunches beside her fervent but inanimate bedfellow, taking hold of his last remaining moving part and working its entire length with urgency. With his eyes closed, Jeff could sense her vagina so close to his face. The need to partake in the awaiting nectar overpowered any further cranial cogitation, particularly when combined with her hand's rapid stimulation.

'Resistance proving utterly impossible,' he admitted defeat, turning his head leftwards and tugging her hips in close.

'Oh, thank God!' the kind woman groaned, squirming as his tongue set her clitoris on edge in an instant. 'I was beginning to wonder if you'd forgotten I'm here.'

The adoring husband roared at the top of his lungs, flipping them both over with crazed eyes and pinning the glistening woman down. Shaking his arms free of his open shirt, it twirled in a few rhythmic circles in the air above his head before he tossed it across the room like a *matador*'s cape. Lynn arched her back and reclined on the bed, with her head at its foot, and admired the tanned, lithe form of her beautiful black stallion.

'Forgotten you're here?' Jeff repeated. 'Angel, I cannot possibly forget you're here. Even when you're not here, I imagine you here. You don't have to touch me to drive me to absolute distraction. Are you going to let me make you scream?'

Aquamarine eyes flashed their assent, and Olympic-strength hands reached up to grab her man's waist, spinning round to a kneeling position on the edge of the bed. With her hands caressing his genitals, his mouth engaged hers, the kiss' force tipping them both over.

Lust overrode their exhaustion, and the long-time lovers pleased each other until his climax could no longer be restrained. Emitting a long moan, the commanding rock star seized control with a heart-stopping kiss until his orgasm reached its peak.

'Good?' the athlete enquired, seeing contentment creep across his face and hearing a desperate play for oxygen, her hand massaging his neck while he rode out the powerful sensation.

'Oh, yeah. About as good as it gets,' the poet confirmed. 'You are the best. That was truly amazing.'

The bedroom had darkened during the romantic lesson, and the couple had barely regained their composure when the telephone rang on Jeff's bedside table. Groaning now for a quite different reason, he unwrapped himself from their drowsy tangle and rolled over to deal with the brutal assault on their blissful seclusion.

Who dared to disturb them well after midnight? It had better be worth it. Both parents' thoughts sprang to concern for Jet and Kierney at home in Melbourne. Their eyes met, exchanging worried looks as the father's hand lifted the receiver.

'Hello?'

Lynn could hear a man's voice, though unable to discern individual words. Her husband paused while the caller identified himself. The longer the silence, the more apprehensive she became.

'Yeah. Hi. This is Jeff Diamond. OK, Oliver. I'm well, thanks. Right,' the head of the family waved a reassuring hand while endeavouring to interpret the other man's tone. 'Sure. I guess so. That's very cool. Sure. Please go ahead.'

Winding his hand in circles in the air, he smiled at the quizzical expression from the other pillow. 'On and on and on and on...' he mouthed.

'Who is it?'

Jeff held his hand up, indicating that he would put her out of her misery as soon as the conversation concluded. The inquisitive woman nodded, running to the bathroom to freshen up after their recent romp, relieved no harm had come to their children.

The billionnaire carried on listening to the rambling messenger. From what he could make out, he was calling from a public relations firm in Boston, Massachusetts. It appeared there had been an announcement that nine divisions within the Paragon Holdings group had won awards in a prestigious technology and innovation competition.

'Sorry? Yeah. Very good news, thanks,' the Chief Executive Officer answered, following every move as his saviour returned and slid under the crisp white sheet. 'It's just that it's pretty late, and I'm here trying to enjoy the rare and sublime company of my wife.'

Lynn frowned and pointed at the clock. Jeff nodded, complaining again under his breath at the ability of this nervous employee to waffle on. She cuddled into his side to warm up, and he placed an affectionate arm around her frame.

'No, Oliver,' the celebrity scoffed, losing patience. 'You've dialled a hotel in London. Forty-four's the UK. Yes. It would indeed be Thursday in Australia if we were in Australia. No worries. I don't have working hours, to be honest, so it's my fault. Tell you what... Would you mind sending me the list through on a fax? I need to think about a response. Don't want to give you something off the cuff, mate. You'll have it in a couple of hours. No, I don't have the number. Sorry. If you ring the hotel back on whichever number you dialled, I'm sure someone'll be able to give you one for their fax machine. Ask them to slip the fax under our door, and I'll get onto it as soon as it arrives. Cheers, mate.'

The comedian moved the receiver away from his ear and scanned it over his naked body, as if to reinforce the need to terminate the call. The sleepy blonde giggled, lifting the sheet so he could do the same with her exposed flesh. The possessive husband shook his head. There was no way on Earth he would give this timezone-challenged PR guy a glimpse of her stunning physique.

'Yeah. Sure thing,' Jeff laughed when he had to pull out of a kiss at the last minute. 'Sorry, mate. I have to go. Get back to Gerry Blake or Matt Newcastle if you need any stats about the company. I don't have that kind of info' with me here. Thanks heaps, Oliver. G'night. Yeah, thanks. *Adiós.*'

The receiver rocked as it settled back onto its cradle. The rock star let out a long sigh and extinguished the bedside light.

'Who was that?' his wife asked, lifting the sheet to cover his shoulders. 'Oliver who?'

'Oliver from Masters in Communications in the North End,' the frustrated man responded in a passable New England accent. 'MIT's media guy.'

'Did he think he was ringing Australia? How weird! How did he even get this number?'

'Hannah,' the billionnaire sighed. 'Gerry told him to 'phone Cath, who wasn't there, so he spoke to Hannah. She gave him this number 'cause she was sure I'd want to hear the good news.'

'Oh, OK. She meant well. Anyway, what good news? And at this time of night?'

'Jesus, angel!' her bedfellow yelped. 'Gimme a break! I've answered enough questions tonight, without you peppering me with more. You know what it's like over there. Americans don't consider anywhere to be outside their range of timezones. He thought he was ringing Australia anyway.'

Lynn ran an elegant index finger along the line of her man's pursed lips to calm him down. 'Let's get some sleep. You can tell me all about the good news in the morning.'

'Sounds perfect, if only I didn't have to prepare a statement for their imminent media release. He's sending a good news fax, which is likely about to be slid under the door any minute now. I told him I'd work on it and shoot it straight back.'

'But why do you need to turn it round so quickly?' the project manager *extraordinaire* persisted. 'Tomorrow US time or London time?'

The showman shrugged, exposed again. 'You're right. I don't have to do it, but I'm compelled to do it 'cause it boosts my *ego*.'

'Even though your essence needs a rest?'

'Yeah, yeah, yeah,' her imperfect stranger sneered. 'I'm gagging to find out the details now. You know damned well I can't resist a dose of compulsion every now and again.'

As always, Lynn understood his impulses only too well. She kissed him goodnight, urging him to hurry back to stock up on some sleep. The couple was flying back to Sydney the following morning, after one more press conference. Their children would be waiting at the airport as a surprise for their father, before he and Jet set off for Bathurst and the boy's elaborate *bar mitzvah*.

***

Jeff groped around in the dark for his clothes and dressed in the bathroom. Slipping on his shoes and picking up one of the keys, he let himself out of their room and descended in the lift to the ground floor. Heads turned in the busy *foyer* as he waited his turn at the *concièrge*'s desk, signing autographs and posing for photographs in his dishevelled state.

Oliver's fax arrived in the time it took for the superstar to explain himself to a pretty, young receptionist. He then signed yet another scrap of paper which was immediately folded over several times and slotted into her pocket. Once in possession of the ten-page document, he made his way to a quiet corner of the hotel bar to review the analysis, starting with the list of patents and resulting solutions his company had developed. He ordered a whisky on ice and an *espresso* before settling in to compose a suitable Chief Executive's response.

The "information superhighway", the invention credited to Tim Berners-Lee, had been the catalyst which had unleashed untold potential. Several technological advances designed by companies funded through Paragon Holdings over the last ten years were now on the cusp of mainstream supply. The celebrities' vast incomes had been turned into seed funding for a whole host of winning enterprises on the MIT innovation hit parade.

A grateful sense of pride coursed through the rock star's veins as he scanned down the list of achievements, all attributed to entrepreneurs who profited from songwriting and performing royalties. Humble in triumph, he spent a few moments dreaming of how he and Lynn were making a difference to the world in so many indirect ways, quite independent from the influence they exerted as public figures.

Wrestling with a reinvigorated Gravity, these feelings of accomplishment were tempered with a deep-seated and somewhat disconcerting sense of charlatanism. Was it right that his brainchild, built entirely from showbusiness royalties, should receive the recognition of its peers on the back of other people's inventiveness? Jeff Diamond was nothing more than a catchy brand name made available to these visionaries for realising their dreams.

Yet what was so wrong in this? The lost boy who had recently celebrated his thirty-eighth birthday did his best to convince himself it was only right and proper that his easy money and elevated profile should open doors, allowing himself to count this as a skill in and of itself. The nobody from New South Wales had brought masterminds together to achieve great things. He could hear his beautiful best friend's voice scolding his negativity. He had nothing to be ashamed of. As they had written in Sarah Friedman's latest volume of psychiatric research, celebrating success was fundamental to sound mental health.

The renowned wordsmith scrawled a few lines of commentary about his draft press release on a blank piece of hotel notepaper. Not dissimilar to writing the bridge in a song lyric, once he found the hook, the rest flowed with minimal effort. He downed what remained of his tepid coffee, content with the night's work, and chased the bitterness away with a mouthful of whisky.

Returning to to the young staff member on the reception desk, the celebrity made another request. 'Hi, again. Is there somewhere I could go to make a private 'phone call, please?'

'Certainly. I can find you a room, sir,' the shy woman replied, flustered by a second visitation from her handsome idol.

'I already have a room, thanks,' Jeff made her blush. 'My wife's sleeping in it.'

'Oh, I see,' she smiled. 'So sorry. Of course, sir. Let me ask one of my colleagues.'

'Thank you.'

The hotel employee vanished behind a wooden panel, leaving her famous client to survey the establishment's comings and goings. His fingers played with the lid of his cigarette packet, craving a shot of nicotine to counteract the turmoil generated by his cerebral washing machine as it churned with new ideas.

A porter arrived after a few moments to usher him backstage to a small office equipped with a telephone. Jeff tipped him, and the door closed with a resounding click.

'Gez,' he said, hearing his manager's voice on the other end of the line. 'How're *ya* going, mate? Yeah. Thanks. You too. Still in London. Too right. Can't wait actually! Tomorrow morning. One o'clock or so, I guess. Hey, look... Can you ring me back on this number, please?'

Chief Officers Executive and Financial of one of Australia's largest private corporations sat twelve thousand kilometres apart and discussed the statement they wished to enter into the annals of time. The two close friends then moved on to other matters, some business and some personal, before the celebrity resolved to sign off and make the most of the remaining night-time hours.

His beautiful best friend slept on undisturbed in their ninth-floor suite. He stood in the bedroom doorway, gazing at the heavenly creature who had made this phenomenal level of success possible in the first place. He had a fair idea where his life might have gone if she hadn't risked everything and chosen him over her father. Where would he be without his two greatest allies? Would Gerry have taken their burgeoning empire to such heights without him? And would Lynn have faced into another future with as much commitment and determination as she had shown in the last fifteen years?

Fifteen years! In another six months' time, the couple with the matching tattoos were to notch up yet another milestone. Disrobing at the end of the bed, the Sydneysider doubted his ability to slide in under the covers without waking his Melbourne aristocrat, picture-perfect from every perspective. What a life singular the soul-mates had spun from their endless golden thread! And how complete had she and the children made him!

As expected, Lynn stirred when a hundred kilograms of after-hours philosophy sank onto the mattress. The preoccupied world-changer lay on his back and stared at the ceiling, rolling his various thoughts over and over.

As if the judicious gymnastics taking place on the other side of the bed was permeating her own brain, she turned over and opened her eyes. 'Still awake?'

'Hey, angel,' Jeff replied. 'Yeah. Can't relax. I started to get sleepier when the music stopped. But as usual, as soon as my head hit the pillow, the symphony fired up again, back with a vengeance. Sorry. I was trying not to wake you.'

'That's alright. Can I help?'

'You already did.'

'Not enough obviously,' the caring woman suggested, propping her head up on her elbow.

Beckoning her face towards his, the songwriter hugged his muse in closer, a heartfelt kiss pressed into her forehead. She rested her cheek on his sternum and listened to his thumping heartbeat. Never had someone exuded such genuine gratitude as this man, she was sure. Despite conquering the worst of his fears, her lost boy remained cursed by his hyperactive, overanalytical mind; for the most part his greatest asset, and yet on occasion, also his most burdensome liability.

'It's my fault. I can't find the "Pause" button,' he rued. 'There's a million things running round my head, all jockeying for pole position.'

'Open the door and let 'em run out. That's what you'd tell the kids.'

The intellectual chuckled. 'Yeah. Probably would! They'd never run out of their own accord.'

'Won't they?' Lynn's wry smile tunnelled into his brain.

'Oh, I get it. Have I ever opened the door?'

'Well, have you?'

'Nope. I'm scared we're going to get so caught up in all this high-tech' crap and the aftermath of Ethiopia that we're in danger of losing what we have. Losing each other, I mean.'

'Really? Why? I'm not going anywhere,' the singer teased. 'Where are you going?'

'Nowhere,' her husband groaned. 'This life of ours is just a little teeny bit, slightly, totally overwhelming at the moment. Things aren't going to slow down, angel. I want us all to take advantage of every opportunity, but I also don't want to neglect you or the kids.'

A sigh of pure dismay blew a gossamer stream of air through the hairs covering his tattoos, making Jeff shudder.

'Since when've you done that?' the sportswoman asked.

'Cheers,' he sniffed, smiling at her shocked expression. 'Yeah, I know. I love you so much. I already feel calmer, so thanks.'

'All good,' the drowsy woman replied. 'You're welcome, and I love you too. You're like one of those plastic handheld games you get in Christmas crackers... You know, the ones with all the little metal bearings, where you have to tilt and rock and shake it until you get the balls in the right indentations.'

Happy to hear her enervated partner chuckle at the analogy, Lynn continued. 'When you're all strung out like this, you just need nudging back into place.'

'What'*ya* talkin' about? My balls are already in the right indentations, baby. You saw to that earlier,' Jeff claimed, hugging her tightly. 'It's the rest of me that's not so shit-hot.'

The rear-end of the Diamond pantomime horse heaved herself up to a sitting position and pointed to the telephone. It was lunchtime in Melbourne, and the children were on school holidays. She remembered their son would be in town, at cricket training until late afternoon, but their daughter would most likely be at home under the housekeepers' watchful eye.

'Why don't you ring Kizzy? She'll be at *Escondido*.'

Her partner's sombre outlook dispersed a little, his chameleon instincts kicking in. He dialled the number and waited for the call to connect, picturing a string of idyllic scenes from their custom-built Mexican *hacienda*.

'Hello?'

'June, hi. It's Jeff. How're you going? We're great, thanks. Is Kierney there, please?'

The traveller heard the elderly woman's sensible shoes scurrying across the hallway's marble tiles, imagining the eleven-year-old having run down the stairs at the sound of the main telephone. Sure enough, her sweet voice called out in answer to the summons, and more footsteps, lighter this time, tripped closer and closer. He also heard something not meant for his ears...

'*¡Olá, Papá!*' the breathless youngster greeted him, hopping onto one of the armchairs against the staircase wall and tucking her feet underneath her. 'Where are you? *¿Está la mamá allí?*'

'*Sí,*' her dad replied, overjoyed to hear such impetuous affection in her voice. 'London still. We're in our hotel, in bed. It's two in the morning, and I couldn't sleep. Are you having fun, gorgeous?'

'*Sí, gracias. Mucho, mucho,*' the girl affirmed. 'Did you hear what June said just now?'

The energy had deserted Kierney's voice, suddenly hushed and hesitant. Jeff smiled at a quizzical look from his wife. Secrets were being given away too readily, treating each to a different piece of the puzzle at the same time; a delectable situation the empath vowed to relish while he could.

'June? No. *¿Por qué? ¿Qué te dijo?*'

'*¡Papá!*' his daughter squealed. 'You *did* hear her. You must have. I can't tell you what she said 'cause it's meant to be a surprise.'

By now, Lynn had cottoned on to what had happened and let out an exasperated sigh. She had hoped to avert the usual deep depression her favourite man encountered every time he returned from an overseas trip by organising a special homecoming. The accolades bestowed upon their organisations were bound to deliver an extra shot of darkness into the mix, and now it appeared their therapeutic subterfuge had been blown wide open.

The peacemaker held out his right hand, inviting his saviour to cuddle in. '*Mamá*'s disappointed too, gorgeous,' he relayed. 'Are you guys meeting us in Sydney on Friday?'

'Yes,' Kierney whined. 'I can't believe we gave it away. Sorry, *Papá*.'

'You don't have to be sorry?' her dad insisted. 'It was a slip of the tongue. *Mamá*'s sorry, you're sorry, and I'm sorry. The only one who's not sorry is June, and that's only because she doesn't know.'

The child laughed. 'June does know. As soon as she said it, she slapped her hand over her mouth and stared at me like a cornered possum.'

'A cornered possum? ¡*Muy buen*'! That's so cool. Clever simile, *pequeñita*. Well, I'm looking forward to seeing you anyway. You still gave me a nice surprise. Just a couple of days early. And now I've got the whole flight to dream about how good it'll be. Please tell June it doesn't matter.'

Jeff gave his dream girl a tender kiss, knowing the plan had been spoiled for her most of all since she would have taken equal pleasure from his reaction. Their grown-up little girl wouldn't understand the significance of bringing the family together in Sydney prior to Jet's *bar mitzvah*, but her dad certainly did.

'Listen, angel. Speak to your *mamá* for a minute,' he invited, searching the beauty's eyes. 'We'll see you and Jetto on Friday. Have a good time 'til then.'

'OK, *Papá*,' Kierney reverted to her previous, carefree tone. 'Have a fun time there too. *Te amo*.'

'*Te amo también, KLF. Adiós.*'

Her father handed the receiver over, opting to make himself appropriately scarce. He ducked into the *en suite* to allow his leading ladies to lament the loose-lipped Scotswoman's unfortunate disclosure.

The musician stared at his reflection, his eyes taking some time to adjust to the unnecessary brilliance delivered by the two banks of lighting, one on each side of the mirror. So the lyric for "Roads of Stones" was about to be played out for real. He and Lynn had discussed it from time to time, but no definite plans had been made before.

The pleasing concept also filled him with a huge sense of foreboding. How might he cope with returning to the Canley Vale flat with his thirteen-year-old son, bringing the second verse of the nineteen-seventies' hit to life? And to cap it all, his gorgeous gipsy girl would see his childhood home too. She hadn't made an appearance in the song, yet her presence to share in the experience was appropriate.

Lynn had finished the telephone call by the time her husband opened the bathroom door. Laying her head down onto the pillow, she turned to greet him with a glint in her enquiring eyes, dying to gauge his reaction.

'It's an amazing surprise,' Jeff assured her, climbing back into bed and switching off the light. 'I'm sorry it was messed up. It doesn't matter at all.'

'It does matter,' the Olympian contradicted. 'Now you definitely won't sleep, and I'm scared you might even have a nightmare.'

'Yeah. It's possible, you're right,' the songwriter agreed, realising the room was too dark to communicate via nods and shakes of the head. 'But it's all good. An awesome idea to line it up with our motor-racing trip. And I meant what I said to Kizzy about it being a good thing to look forward to with twenty-two hours in the air. We're booked into Business Class, aren't we, this leg? So we'll get there quicker anyway.'

His wife laughed out loud. 'Will we? How do you make such ridiculous statements sound so logical? I'm glad you're not derailed further. I didn't know how you'd feel about having the visit sprung on you. You're definitely worried about it. You wouldn't be telling these awful jokes otherwise.'

'Oh, shut the fuck up, wench! Me, worried? Now it's you who's making ridiculous statements. Go to sleep, OK?'

The new Jeff Diamond reached for the remote control, and the television sprang into action, crackling and spitting until the display settled down. Reliving memories of the early nineteen-seventies, his old self tapped the arrowed button until the volume was as low as it would go. This well-worn *scenario* came straight from their pre-London days and served to warm both hearts.

Lynn kissed her perfectly imperfect stranger goodnight and rolled over, shielding her eyes from the picture's dancing lights. She fell fast asleep within a few minutes, leaving him to distract himself with late-night programmes. Or not, as it turned out.

Testing Times

'Hey, *Papá*! Did you read this one?'

Kierney's voice punctured the widower's thought-bubble. While she leafed through Lynn's diary entries for nineteen-ninety, his mind had drifted off on a pleasant time-warp. He languished with great fondness in the era when pop music was a global currency, when a handheld telephone weighed more than a pint of beer, and when they were still the Four of Diamonds.

'This one,' the seventeen-year-old flapped the black, leather-bound volume, index finger keeping her page as she crossed from the couch to the desk. 'Sorry. Were you asleep?'

Rubbing the unyielding muscles on the back of his neck, Jeff coughed and twisted his chair round to face his smiling daughter. 'Yeah. Must've been. What've you found now?'

The passage in question was written a week before his beautiful best friend's thirty-fifth birthday and a week after she had won an eleventh US Open tennis championship. The globe-trotting couple had met up for a weekend in London, mid-way between the European and US legs of the rock star's latest world tour. At the pinnacle of their performing careers, they were allocated top billing at the season's Royal Variety Performance, playing to an adoring crowd of the city's A-list and tugging their forelocks to the House of Windsor.

'"Today I was gazumped by Miss Piggy!"' the dark-haired gipsy girl had tears in her eyes as she read aloud. 'Do we still have that on video? I'd love to see it again.'

Jeff's mouth broke into a smile, having no trouble remembering the act which had brought the curtain down before the show's intermission. He had stumbled upon the self-same memory only a few days earlier while poring over old newspaper cuttings and magazine articles with Cathy and two members of the Stonebridge Music team, preparing collateral for his autobiography's latest chapter.

'Whoa! Let's have a look, please?' he replied, so keen to capture more of his wife's innermost thoughts that he almost snatched the journal from his daughter's hands. 'It was such a pain in the arse to do, that stunt. I reckon your *mamá*'s account of the pink pig and the pyromaniacs'd pull no punches. She got burned; nearly set her dress on fire.'

'On fire?' Kierney yelped. 'Shit! How come?'

Her father's eyes scanned down the page of leisurely, handwritten prose, accepting a cigarette purloined from his own packet. He chuckled as his carbon-copy next snaffled his lighter and held it in front of his nose.

'Cheers, *pequeñita*. Don't mind if you do? Please go right ahead. No worries, *Papá*. Plenty more where these came from.'

'Oh, shut up. You pinch mine too,' the young woman defended herself. 'What happened? How did *Mamá* get burned?'

The songwriter filled his lungs with smoke and rested the cigarette on the side of the ashtray while he reached an arm around his loyal housemate. 'Here, look...

> '"I'm relieved the tennis season's already over because I sustained an injury to my wrist after Jeff left me for a stuffed puppet. I knew it would happen sooner or later, but a stuffed puppet? Poets, pyrotechnics and pork clearly don't mix!"

'See what I mean?'

The classic snippet of television footage had captivated fans across the globe and even earned a slot on the Australian evening news at the time, and the Diamond children had seen it replayed many times in the intervening years. The scene started with the handsome rock star at the keyboard, serenading Lynn with one of their platinum-selling hits from the late nineteen-seventies, "Reborn".

The superstars' sizzling stage presence translated equally well to the small screen, sweeping the audience away on their romantic melody until a booming explosion unleased fiery flashes and a large quantity of dry ice. Jeff was left sitting at the piano, singing to the Muppets' Miss Piggy when the smoke cleared. The more his puppet princess swooned, the more he had hammed it up, leaning in to steal kisses and having his hair messed up by amorous trotters.

Recounting the story from the present day was more difficult than the widower expected, given what had befallen the love of his life some five years later. 'I knew things hadn't gone quite according to plan, 'cause I could hear people frantically asking if *Mamá* was alright. But the show must go on, and all that, so Miss Piggy and I had to carry on getting down and dirty like we had in rehearsals.'

Kierney's face was a picture of concern, both for the backstage accident and for her father's painful recollection. The fact of their mother almost going up in flames had never been made public before, even to her or her brother. Lynn had been patched up during the interval, ready for their two remaining appearances of the night.

'But didn't I do "These Boots Are Meant For Walking" with *Mamá* afterwards?' the teenager asked. 'I don't remember her having burns on her arm.'

'The wonders of make-up, I'm guessing,' her father smiled. 'You guys were too far away to see anything, thank Christ. It would've been hard to keep singing if you'd been freaked out. Whatever… It wasn't that serious, except the show's producers were shitting themselves that we'd sue for damages. They offered to pay for our hotel accommodation, dinners, *et cetera*. Got all out of proportion at that point. *C'est domage, mais c'est la vie.*'

His daughter frowned. 'Yeah. Guess so. Was that the same night we all did "Mack The Knife" too, with the "Crocodile Dundee" moment?'

'Sure was. That was a good skit, I have to admit. You guys did well to keep straight faces.'

To cap off a unique evening of entertainment, the Diamonds had delivered a choreographed rendition of the Bobby Darin favourite, dividing the verses between family members. Jet had taken great pleasure acting out the body "just oozing life", much to everyone's amusement. The spellbound crowd had laughed again when Lynn pulled out a Stanley knife and the kids countered with packets of white plastic airline cutlery.

Jeff produced an enormous *machete* blade from nowhere, bringing the number to a fitting close. With the background music edited to a tee, the opportunity to reprise Paul Hogan's immortal line was too perfect to cut from rehearsals.

'Now this…' the swashbuckling showman brandished his weapon until it glinted into the camera, reenacting the memorable Hollywood gem. '*This* is a knife.'

'Look out, Old Mack, he is back!' father and daughter brought the piece to its conclusion in unison, their *staccato* enunciation timed to professional perfection.

The *duo* chuckled to one another, a little awkward at how easily they slipped back into the old routine. Skipping fifty or so of the diary's pages, in search of other beauteous secrets she had unearthed, Kierney settled down to read more of her mother's *memoires*. Her legs crumpled underneath her, depositing her in a tidy heap on the rug at the writer's feet, eager to share more magical passages of text.

'Did you see what *Mamá* wrote about you ringing her with your first mobile?'

The author paused, distracted by an e-mail arriving in his Inbox. 'What? First mobile 'phone?'

'Yes,' his daughter answered. 'It's very romantic. You need to read it, if you haven't already. Here…'

The entry in question was from the tail-end of May. A rare break in Jeff Diamond's tour had bisected the tennis calendar, finding both parents in the same country at the same time. Thinking her husband was still away on a business trip, Lynn had answered the telephone at their city apartment, overjoyed to hear his voice.

The seventeen-year-old impersonated her mother's voice with an eerie likeness. 'Listen, *Papá*:

> '"Jeff asked me if the kids were asleep, which they were. 'Good. More 'phone sex? Which room are you in?' I said I was in the office and let him whisk me away to paradise as he always could. He asked, 'Are you thinking of me while you work?' I told him I hadn't been able to think about anything else, especially since he'd started down this path!
>
> 'Let's do it some more then,' he said, using his sexiest tone. 'I'd rather have you here,' I said in reply. 'It's so much better when you're here.'
>
> To my surprise, his next words were, 'Come into the bedroom then. I'm waiting for you.'
>
> I love this man. I really love this man. I will always love this man."

'Had you seen that before? It's so amazing. I love how she's so honest.'

The grieving man's face had twisted into an expression not quite resembling a smile but which had struggled to advance much further than a frown. Rivulets traced down his cheeks from eyes squeezed shut, and the fingers of his right hand scratched the front of his shirt; out of habit, out of blind faith or out of genuine irritation?

'Jesus! I remember that night like it was yesterday. Fuck, I wish it were yesterday, and we could go to the apartment and find you in the office, angel. Happy to meet you there anytime. Just say when.'

Kierney scrambled to her feet and into her father's waiting embrace. Words were superfluous between them, both missing their dearly departed relative's steadfast guiding hand and limitless capacity for love.

Their grief was less raw these days, now five months after García had taken Lynn from their perfectly imperfect family. The tears were no less meaningful for the teenager's determination to move on to bigger and better achievements, and no less agonising for her parasitic front-man in his quest to put their life singular in order in time to meet her for their next adventure.

***

Jeff groaned, slamming the driver's door and taking an accentuated deep breath. Passers-by could hardly believe their eyes as, one by one, Australia's most famous family climbed out of a nondescript Holden and blinked in the shimmering sunrise. Such a contrast to the last time he had stood in this spot, when he and his dream girl had braved the Boxing Day barbarians lurking behind the front door of this lowly abode, intent on tormenting the world-changer during his protracted apprenticeship.

'Ah, Canley-Vale-on-Sea. So good to be back.'

Lynn rolled her eyes at the blatant lie, her husband's fake smile and imperious *persona* not fooling her for one second. She and the children had a pretty good idea how many challenges this morning would throw up, trusting the closure he was to experience at its end would do more than cancel them out. All four had practised visualisation techniques in the airline lounge, waiting to be called for their flight, until the sight of the Stones Road disappearing in a rear-view mirror was etched on their collective psyche.

Politely deflecting a snatch of joyous whoops of recognition from residents whose community facilities received regular facelifts and injections of cash for redevelopment courtesy of the district's most prodigious son, Jet, Kierney and their mother stood on the footpath beside the anonymous rented sedan they had collected that morning from Sydney's Kingsford Smith Airport.

The Diamond family stalled for a few minutes, gazing up at the three-storey tenement building which spanned a whole block of the downtrodden neighbourhood. With her arm firmly around the lost boy's waist, inside the leather jacket he so seldom left behind, the blonde stalwart studied the lines on his face. What was he thinking?

Was the fear of whatever lay behind Door Number Four as great at thirty-eight as it had been at twenty-two? She hoped not but expected otherwise. After all their research into trauma's stubborn legacy, she doubted this impressive man, whose all-encompassing career had turned him into such a phenomenal role model for young and old, would ever be free of his childhood scars.

'Wonder where that delightful gent', Joe, is now...' Jeff smiled at his wife's concern. 'In the ground, with any luck. That'd have to be a bloody big mother of a coffin.'

Joe Cafici was the proprietor of the hardware store next to the stairwell entry; a local businessman with links to the western suburbs' gangs. It had also been rumoured that he acted as a police informant from time to time, leading to most adolescents in the area despising him. For Jeff, this hatred was amplified yet further by the portly Italian's habit of preying on his desperate mother and under-aged sister for sexual favours. He never had managed to discover how significant a part this scandal-merchant played in Paul Diamond's conviction, only certain of the rewards which flowed thereafter.

Although the old man had retired a decade ago, the shop still traded under his name. Business looked to be booming, which made the homecoming boy feel sick. Sharing a joke with his son about the lengths of *salami* hanging in the window of the delicatessen on the other side of the alley, he shunted the children forwards with sudden hostile resolve. Several customers were forced into double-takes as the celebrity quartet marched in lockstep towards the glass door that would take them upstairs to the scene of these and countless other atrocities.

Lynn took her man's trembling hand, eagerly clasped as four pairs of feet covered the short stretch of littered footpath. Searching his eyes for clues as to his mental state, she received a playful wink. The telepathic throwback to nineteen-seventy-four made them both glow inside; remembering the last time they had lingered in this same spot. The recently reconnected lovers had been full of trepidation that morning too, pausing while he smoked an extra cigarette and hoping it would deliver the stamina required to climb six flights of stairs and confront his darkest demons.

The youngsters were several paces closer to the entrance than their parents, necks crooked upwards to the top floor. Despite being spared the most graphic of details, they understood the terrible memories their father had lived with for so long.

'Is that your room?' Jet asked, spinning round and pointing to the leftmost of the dual-paned windows. 'The one with the guitar sign in the bottom corner? Did you put that there?'

'Yep. That's it, mate,' his dad confirmed, his own finger directing their eyes a little further to the right. 'The guitar's nothing to do with me. Must've been stuck there well after I left. They've got flyscreens these days. Flash, eh? Never had those when we lived here. And that one was our lounge room.'

'So, kids,' his wife added, referring to the first window again. 'That's where you have to stand and look out, in order to make the story come true.'

The youngsters sang the pertinent verse on cue, seldom embarrassed to break into song. Customers clutching plastic bags of shopping stopped to tune in, searching the pavement for television cameras.

'Press the doorbell, please, Jetto,' Lynn requested, drawing their attention to a brass *plaque* screwed into the brickwork. '"Sing and Play". Is that the name of their school? Cute!'

Jeff shrugged, his complexion becoming greyer with each step. Since serving its primary purpose of exorcising ghosts from his nightmares, he had had as little as possible to do with this property. It had been leased back to the council for the past ten years, on the *proviso* its anointed landmark status would be used for the benefit of present-day Stones Road natives.

The Diamonds had been pleased to hear that a modest music school now operated out of the apartment where The Australian Elvis lived as a boy. Once the plans for Jet's Bathurst *Bar Mitzvah* solidified, Lynn had approached the teachers to arrange a time for the family to drop by before the day's classes began.

No sound came from the entry-phone when Jet pressed it, and his mother quickly whisked his hand away before he had a chance to repeat his action with more boisterous ambition. After a second or two, a red light flashed twice and the crackly tones of a female voice burst through the tiny speaker, so faint that the visitors could scarcely make it out.

The teenager announced their arrival with his customary self-possession, and the door into the stairwell released with a buzz from upstairs. Jet pulled it open, inviting the rest of his clan to file past. Signalling approval of a job well done, the proud dad ruffled his son's hair in thanks for a gesture befitting a young man on the cusp of his coming-of-age weekend.

'You OK?' his *regala* whispered.

A nervous Kierney turned round, hoping the answer would be positive. Slipping her fingers into her *papá*'s free hand, she saw his face had tarnished to a deathly white. She had no idea what to expect inside the modest dwelling which had been the subject of many mysterious conversations, only knowing that event descriptions were becoming far less sanitised with each birthday she and her brother celebrated.

Their mother smiled in encouragement, then tutted as the athletic lad sprinted ahead and bounded up four flights of stairs, no doubt trying to produce as much noise from his flat-footed strides as possible in the tall, narrow echo-chamber.

'Wait for us, Jet,' she shouted up to the landing between the first and second levels. 'Take it slowly, please.'

She oughtn't to have been surprised when her husband released their hands without a word and gave chase, rocketing up the steps two at a time. He soon caught up with his son, who was now leaning over the railing at the very top. Out of breath, the impetuous pair watched on as their womenfolk climbed the remaining flights in a much more decorous fashion.

'I said, "Take it slowly,"' the distinguished woman frowned, wagging an index finger at the leather-clad overgrown child. 'Especially you.'

Exactly as he had done in the same spot sixteen years before, Jeff merely smiled and lit himself a cigarette. 'Sorry, angel. All good.'

Lynn was sure that all was not good but let his comment slide with the children in earshot. Too easily identified were the tell-tale signs of mental torment: the sweat on his brow, the tension in his jaw and the dark, sunken eyes no doubt dreading the re-appearance of phantom enemies from his past. Moreover, racked with sympathy, she recognised his need to remain strong for Jet and Kierney, not only as a classic competitive statement in front of his son and heir, but also to signal that this former den of ill-repute held no danger for them.

A slight man in his mid-thirties, not much taller than the budding cricketer, opened the door before the family unit had a chance to re-assemble itself. He stepped out onto the landing, closely followed by a woman who dwarfed him in all dimensions.

'Welcome, welcome!' the teacher cried out, casting his arms in dramatic arcs. 'It's such a pleasure to meet you, and we're so privileged to have you on the premises. Come on in! I'm Tristan, and this is my partner, Leanne.'

Jeff hung back, apprehension shielded in his usual chivalry, ensuring his wife's hand was the first to be shaken. 'Thanks, Tristan. This is Lynn, as you well know. And these are our daughter, Kierney, and our son, Jet.'

The veins on the extrovert music teacher's forehead looked like they were about to burst. 'Hello, one and all! Wonderful to meet you at last. Please come inside. We've got some tea and coffee ready. Have you already had breakfast?'

The tall, slender Olympian ushered her offspring through the door before inviting their hosts to lead the way. Apart from being the well-mannered thing to do, her main objective was to give the apartment's former occupant plenty of space to cross the threshold in his own time.

True enough, she felt a sticky hand slide into hers. The songwriter had requested she make no reference to their previous visit or to the nasty memories held therein. On no account were Tristan and Leanne to know of the difficulties he faced in returning to his childhood home.

'Fuck!' Jeff mouthed to his beautiful best friend, managing at the last minute to pluck a neutral disguise from somewhere.

Enquiring blue eyes allowed the lost boy a short interval to absorb his new situation and beat an orderly retreat if the panic rose to unbearable levels. To her delight, he transmitted a nervous message to carry on, and she wasted no time in yanking his hand forward and propel him inside until all six bodies stood huddled in the cramped kitchen area.

'So, Jet and Kierney! Would you like tea or coffee, or would you prefer a juice?' their Amazonian host asked, her bulk having trouble navigating the small space without bumping into everyone else.

'Oh, yes. I'll have juice, please, Leanne,' the youngest Diamond answered, stealing a glance past her brother and in the direction of the door.

The girl's expression changed from one of curiosity to abject dismay, anxious to interpret the distress on her father's face. She was witnessing firsthand the meticulous sketch of blind fear which her mother had often provided; the outer manifestation of the oppressive clouds under which her hero had grown up. She tried to imagine him as a young adult, standing welded to the doormat and unable to summon the courage to open the front door. Authenticity notwithstanding, this reality check was still a shock to behold in person.

Her brother, on the other hand, remained oblivious to his dad's internal suffering and the others' tender responses. 'I'll have a juice too, please, Leanne,' he replied, diverting momentarily from his path into the lounge room.

'No worries,' the bubbly woman smiled. 'And for Mum and Dad?'

'Coffee, please, Leanne,' Lynn chimed in, 'for both of us. White, and two sugars for Jeff. Just milk for me, thanks.'

The only response the billionnaire could muster was a moronic nod, thankful that he had been relieved of his duties as head of the family while he pulled himself together. His head swam with a frenzy of wayward thoughts, the magnolia-coloured walls closing in around him and daring him to take a step in any direction. Looking behind, he noticed Tristan had closed the front door, leaving the struggling man feeling trapped and confused.

'OK! Thank you,' the esteemed record producer began, letting her man's hand drop while she accepted two mugs of steaming coffee. 'You'd better give us the tour, or your students'll arrive before we're finished.'

Knowing it was unsafe to give Jeff responsibility for his drink yet, the elegant sportswoman walked into the longer side of the L-shaped space which had been the Diamond family's lounge room. A collection of musical instruments lay strewn over two trestle tables against the wall, alongside an upright piano. Another table on the opposite side was piled high with a variety of books, well-worn scores and manuscript paper, next to a tray of pencils and erasers.

'Old habits die hard,' she laughed, attracting Kierney's gaze. 'Reusing the sheets by rubbing your dots out at the end of the class. Do you still do that at school, Kizzy?'

Distracted from her examination of a motley assortment of electric and acoustic guitars, some on stands and some leaning at precarious angles, the young girl skipped over to her mother's side. 'Yes!' she answered in happy familiarity. 'Do you do that too, Leanne?'

Tristan took the lead, offering a potted history of the couple's private music school: who taught which instruments; the types of students currently enrolled; and a few autobiographical details of their individual, decidedly non-stellar careers. The Melbourne Academy starlets were at their attentive best, smiling and chuckling at each appropriate moment and fielding the many questions posed of their own musical predilections.

Gradually, Jeff's reverberating nerves ceased to dominate his consciousness. Hoping their hosts hadn't construed his uncharacteristic social reticence as rudeness, he held a hand out for his coffee, which was transferred into his keeping with a furtive kiss. He winked at his daughter, who grinned back in relief.

An obsessive need planted by his trollish nemesis wanted so much to launch into a tirade of past afflictions. The tortured soul fought back a compelling desire that his offspring confide in his private recollections; how this meagre home had been furnished, the uses it had been put to, and the awful sights and sounds its walls had kept secret before its conversion into a wholesome place of learning. He gave thanks, as Lynn would later, that his tongue was not yet ready to play.

His guardian angel, as always, displayed far more patience with these situations than the former tearaway ever could. She sauntered across to the front window, beckoning the children to follow her and look out. Realising something was amiss, Jet span round to check on his father, guilt and shame splattered all over his face.

The rock star cleared his throat. 'That's where we used to sit, guys,' he explained, sweeping his left arm from one end of the room to the other, 'surrounded by boxes of all kinds of stuff, stretching all the way back to this window.'

'What sort of stuff?' Tristan asked, fascinated to hear the celebrity's account of living here.

'Stuff to sell,' the songwriter remained as cryptic as the situation demanded. 'You name it, my dad sold it. There was a small table here where Auntie Lena… my sister, Madalena… and I used to eat.'

'Dining table?' Leanne prompted.

Jeff sniffed. 'No. Not really. Nothing that organised.'

Figuring out the reason the music teachers weren't being fed the whole story, Kierney broke away from the rest to accompany her father back into the kitchenette. She leaned into his side as he propped himself up against a breakfast bar which had been added since his time, and he put a loving arm around her shoulders. She did her best to transfer positive energy to her beloved *papá*, predicting their passage into the remaining two rooms would only inflate his dread.

Tristan joined the dark-haired pair and lifted a selection of muffins and *croissants* out of a box onto waiting platters. He held them up as an offering to their godlike visitors, beaming as the eleven-year-old helped herself before her brother had time to claim the lion's share.

'Mmm…' the girl said. '*Pain au chocolat.* My favourite. Thank you very much.'

Jeff declined, nausea bubbling on the brink of restraint. He watched his son deliberating over which sugar-filled item he might tackle first. Ever predictable, the boy picked a gooey chocolate muffin and began to peel the corners of greaseproof paper away so he could minimise the mess when breaking it apart. Filled with gratitude that their children were far removed from the ratbags of Sydney's outer west, he caught his wife's gaze and allowed himself to gloat for a second or two.

'Thanks, Tristan,' the thirteen-year-old grinned, making eye contact with their host as if he were aware his gentility rating was being judged. 'Too many goodies here! May I come back for seconds, please?'

The short man burst out laughing in theatrical volume, nodding in an exaggerated motion. In comparison to his partner, his personality more than made up for his lack of stature.

'Of course you may, young sir. And thirds, if you're lucky.'

'Thanks, mate. This one's always starving,' Jeff reported. 'Who've you got coming this morning? Must be pretty quiet on weekdays.'

The other half of the teaching cohort invited Lynn to partake in the breakfast fare, begging forgiveness for her slow reaction. The tennis champion dismissed the apology as unnecessary and helped herself to something she could share with her son, who accepted a generous portion of a *croissant* without hesitation.

'Indeed. We're thinking of asking the local primary schools if their curriculum could include off-site music lessons to fill a few gaps during term-time. We usually have some keen beans in the school holidays, but mostly mums and uni' students during the week,' Leanne told their guests. 'A clarinet, a singer and two guitarists today, if I remember correctly. And a barber's shop choir rehearsal this evening. They're coming along nicely actually. It's a shame you're not going to be able to watch any of them.'

Preparing yet another white lie, Jeff smiled at the quaint expressions which continued to roll off their hosts' tongues. 'Sorry, guys. We'd have loved to stay longer, but Jet and I've got to get across to Bathurst this afternoon.'

'Oh, really? Mount Panorama? How excellent!' Tristan gushed in false excitement. 'That'll be heaps of fun, won't it, young man?'

As "The Boy Who Would Be King" nodded without cracking a smile, the Diamond parents' locked eyes once more to share a covert aside. One white lie deserved another! It was clear this delicate musician was totally unimpressed by anything to do with thrumming engines and smoking tyres.

Accepting a refill of coffee, Jeff again rested a hand on his daughter's shoulder, steering her towards the other end of the apartment. 'Come this way, guys, please,' he requested, inviting her brother to join them. 'We came here so you could see my old bedroom, so let's do it. Yeah?'

The superstar felt his blood pressure take an immediate skyward hike in spite of a supportive smile from his dream girl. Both children, anxious to make the morning easier for their dad, fell into line beside him with commensurate unease. Lynn stayed seated in the classroom with teachers large and small, tasked with holding their attention until the dastardly deed was done.

All three doors at the end of the short corridor were propped open, to the great man's relief, and he steeled himself to enter each in turn. 'Go left,' he instructed the children, fixing his eyes on the streams of daylight entering into the passageway from the front window. 'This was Auntie Lena's and my room.'

It took only the most transitory of glances at the cluttered studio on the street side of the apartment for the lost boy to zoom back through time. Now firmly grounded inside his childhood refuge, his older self noticed both youngsters appeared somewhat mesmerised by the door opposite; the one leading to the rear-facing room. They knew the bare bones of what had taken place therein, although it would be many more years before they were deemed ready to hear the whole truth.

Having his precious gems in close proximity had an unexpected calming effect on the tormented soul, feeling controlled and almost pleased to discharge this ill-fated but obligatory chore. Mental agitation prevailed as expected, along with the abiding physical symptoms of cramping legs and a consistent, blinding throb behind his temples. Unlike the previous time he and Lynn had stood in this room, no visual onslaught threatened to knock him to his knees, and Gravity and his demonic mates had so far failed to wield their furious force.

'I have to say I expected you to make a lot more noise than you do,' Leanne stuttered, left alone with one of the world's most prominent stars. 'Much more gregarious... Somehow we tend to think all showbusiness people are attention-seeking. You're just like a normal family really.'

Lynn chuckled. 'Thanks! We try to be a normal family as far as we can, whatever that really means... We do have our noisy moments too. Probably a bit jet-lagged today. Jeff and I've just got off a 'plane from London, and to tell you the truth, this place doesn't hold happy memories for him. He wants to show it to the kids now they're old enough to appreciate it, and then basically forget it.'

The other woman nodded in sympathy. 'I see. Of course I've read about your husband's mental problems, and the work you both do to help sufferers is truly inspiring. That explains the pained look on his face. I wondered if he was hung-over, and now I feel embarrassed that I stereotyped him.'

The guest sat her empty coffee mug on the table, idly leafing through the score of a Gilbert and Sullivan operetta. 'That's fine. He is often hung-over,' she laughed. 'We have this odd need to give Jet and Kierney the experience of hardship without them actually having to go through it. Does that make sense?'

'I suppose so,' Leanne agreed. 'It's still a rough neighbourhood round here, but we like it. Most people are friendly enough, and the Stones Road's so well-known because of Jeff Diamond. Our link with you certainly generates a lot of interest.'

Meanwhile, in the second music studio otherwise known as Jeff Diamond's boyhood bedroom, Jet and Kierney took great pleasure in examining the collection of posters of their family which had been framed and hung on the wall. It was odd to see their own faces adorning someone else's place of work and gratifying to know their parents' generosity was valued so highly.

The children took their places at the window, re-enacting one of the many lyrics they had been able to recite more-or-less from the moment they could speak. Their father brought the verses to life as they stared out over the infamous suburb, finally understanding his motivation to rise above his unfortunate circumstances and forge a path to Lynn Dyson's door. Neither was convinced by the concept of soul-mates, yet both celebrated being the product of unending love.

The songwriter filmed the amusing *cameo* performances for posterity, sensing the same disassociation as last time ridding his body of tension. He couldn't wait to share the home video footage with his saviour, knowing she had been the architect of this edifying diversion. Almost jealous that she would run through these mini-memories without him, while he and their *bar mitzvah* boy were having their eardrums assaulted by Fords and Holdens, it was wholly appropriate that she be rewarded for the healing they dispensed.

Snapping the camera's screen back into its resting position, Jeff turned away from the window and pointed first to the right-hand wall. 'Over there was Lena's side, guys. Her bed was here, with a wardrobe in that corner. She had posters of anyone and everyone on her side. I'm not even sure if she even knew who half of them were. She wasn't fussy, as long as they looked hot.'

'And so that was yours,' Kierney continued the commentary, seeing his tentative gaze swap to the opposite side. 'Where was your bed?'

'Here,' her father pointed to the front corner. 'Y'see that square patch in the ceiling?'

Both children nodded, botched repairs visible in the plasterboard joints overhead.

'There must've been a tile missing on the roof, or a blocked gutter or something,' the nostalgic man went on, ''cause whenever it rained heavily, water would build up and then drip steadily through the ceiling and down the wall. The first time it happened, my bed was pushed right into the corner, and I came home to sleep in a bloody great puddle.'

Jet let out an unsympathetic snort, while his sister screwed up her face at the uncomfortable image.

'And then one day, obviously long after it should've been fixed, a whole section collapsed.'

'Oh, my God!' the lad screeched. 'Were you in bed?'

'No!' the indignant man snapped back. 'Jeez, where did that come from, mate? I thought you teenagers had your voices broken in and under control by now. Anyway, give me some credit... I'd had the sense to move the bed by then, but it was still an almighty mess. That up there's not the original patch-up though. I did a reasonable job, but it's been done again since. And painted too, which I could never be arsed to do.'

'Do you think I could fix a ceiling, Dad?' his son asked, anxious to restore his manhood.

Jeff smirked. 'Sure you could. No sweat. You're a pretty good handyman. Not like Gerry... He wouldn't have a clue.'

Both children laughed, having a fair idea how successful their parents' indomitable manager might be at hands-on work. The small room's atmosphere had been lifted by the *ad hoc* injection of humour, and it occurred to its former occupant that he was faring better than expected without his *regala*'s assistance.

Before the healing patriarch had a chance to reap the benefit of this illuminating fact, the young sportsman lunged at him, landing a punch squarely in his gut. Apparently none was immune to the portent of today's engineered therapeutic fix. The tall, muscular man braced himself to retaliate, well accustomed to such ambushes. He flicked a foot behind his son's left knee and almost sent him crashing into a ramshackle collection of music stands.

'Hey!' Jet whined, brushing dust off his new black jeans. 'Your song doesn't say anything about kids getting attacked in your room. Just wait 'til we get to Bathurst... Daws and I'll have your guts for garters.'

The artist scoffed. 'Oh, will you? We'll see about that. But you're right. Humble apologies, you *oik*. So what d'you think about coming here after all? Kiz?'

'Weird, a bit,' the eleven-year-old looked up from a piece of sheet music she had been examining. 'It's not like we had any photos to know what it was like when you lived here or anything, is it? Hard to see the "before" and "after". Not like Benloch, with all the pictures of *Mamá* and Uncle Junior as kids.'

'True enough,' Jeff agreed.

'Yeah, but it is good to be here,' her brother's voice became more subdued. 'Just like I thought actually. Much brighter and far less grungy than you said. The view's what I imagined too: rooftops and the street; loud with all the cars going by... Did you hear it all the time?'

'Don't remember,' their father mused. 'Must've.'

'So where did you keep bikes and stuff?' Jet continued. 'If you didn't have a garage or garden shed or whatever?'

The billionnaire smiled at this innocent question, posed by a young man surrounded by the finer things in life. A *frisson* of satisfaction ran down his spine, recalling the many quiet resolutions made with his pregnant wife before their firstborn arrived, determined that any child of theirs should enjoy a much improved standard of living compared to the one he had known.

These maturing little gems had everything they needed, and no opportunity was out of reach as long as they strove for it. By no means did they have everything they wanted however, as he and his privileged better half were used to hearing; a complaint all four accepted as healthy and perfectly normal. What they lacked in material possessions was compensated through being spoiled for choice in terms of amazing experiences, having travelled to every corner of the globe as Lynn Dyson and Jeff Diamond's human baggage. A regulated upbringing kept their feet on the ground and their hearts open to life's inequalities.

'I never had a bike, mate,' Jeff responded after his moment of reflection. 'When I told my dad I wanted to get one, d'you know what he said to me?'

'No.'

'He said, "Just pick one up off the street. Find one you like and bring it 'ome. I've got cutters if it's got a chain."'

The young man's mouth fell open. 'He told you to steal one?'

His father chuckled. 'Yep. We *are* talking about your granddad, remember? He didn't exactly respect the concept of personal property. In his world, if you wanted something that someone else had, just go and effin'-well nick it. No worries, mate!'

Not wishing to labour the point too far, the Sydney native focussed the youngsters' attention outside, telling them which aspects of the view had changed. Describing his regular commute to high school, they took an imaginary journey through the poorly lit streets and dangerous parks. Kierney sidled up beside the storyteller, staring into the distance towards Fairfield.

50

'*Qué pasa, pequeñita*?' the empath asked, disturbed by her glum demeanour. 'Don't want to be here?'

The youngest Diamond straightened herself up. 'Sorry, *Papá*. Yes, I do. Well, sort of... It's not that I don't want to be here. I just don't know *why* I'm here.'

Intrigued rather than disappointed, the philosopher slouched against the windowsill and fixed his daughter's gipsy eyes in his own. 'Why don't you know why? Because I said so! What d'you want to know?'

She giggled. 'Oh, *nada, nada. N'sais pas vraiment.* I mean, I know why we're all here, and I'm glad to have seen your flat. But I don't feel anything. Like my heart and soul don't know why they're here.'

'Ah, yeah? Interesting observation. And good, in a way,' Jeff reassured both children, hearing his son confess to a similar sentiment. 'You too, mate? Now you mention it, that makes me feel vindicated in a weird way. Bringing you here's not some kind of emotional blackmail to make you appreciate what you've got, or anything like that. You guys don't need to be saddled with my shit. You just need to know where you come from, to inform where you're going. Make sense?'

The young lady's bottom lip quivered as if she were about to cry, causing her dad to take a pace forward and hug her close. Anticipating the onset of girly waterworks, Jet decided to seek out extra breakfast and offered his excuses.

Kierney rested her head against her favourite *confidant*'s solid chest, and the matching pair stood in silence to let the mood resolve itself. 'I wish our family started from you and *Mamá*,' she admitted. 'I don't need to know about your *mamá and papá*. I can't bring myself to miss them 'cause they were so horrible to you. Is that a mean thing to say?'

'Not if it's your honest opinion. You can choose not to think about them, but we shouldn't deny previous generations existed just because the memories aren't cool. You're happy to have "G" and "G" in your life, aren't you?'

'Yes,' the youngster hissed, her shoulders drooping. 'It *is* mean then. I'm sorry, *Papá*. I should get over it.'

Jeff smiled. 'It's fine, gorgeous. You're not alone with these unhelpful thoughts. I often used to wish my family'd started with me too. I could do without Auntie Lena still, half the time.'

His daughter grinned back, wiping tears from her eyes with the sleeve of her dress. 'Hmm... Maybe you shouldn't have told me that.'

'Maybe not. The truth is that our family didn't start from me and your *mamá*, as distasteful as it may seem,' the intellectual assured her. 'It's important for all of us to know whom we're descended from, even if they weren't people you can relate to or admire. No-one gets to choose their ancestors, but you can make sure you choose a future full of people you're proud to be associated with.'

The student nodded her head, this time with tears of pride brimming in her eyes. '*Gracias, Papá. Eso es excelente.* Sorry for being so nasty. I didn't mean to say what I said.'

'Oh, yeah? I hope you did,' Jeff raised a quizzical eyebrow, applying gentle pressure on her sagging shoulders. 'Now you're going to plead a split personality? You're entitled to your opinion, so stick to your guns. I won't be angry or upset. I hated my parents' guts when I was your age, and I still rarely want to think about them. What *Mamá* and I'd be heartbroken about is if you guys turn your backs on us.'

'What?' Kierney yelped. 'No way! We'll never turn our backs on you. Never, ever, ever!'

Jeff lifted his guard as a barrage of feeble blows were directed at his torso, gathering the fighter into his arms to save his bruises. 'Hey! Enough already. Let's leave *la abuela* and Granddad behind today then. Only speak about them when absolutely necessary. And to be honest, that's precisely the point of coming today. We'll be out of here in ten minutes' time, never to return if we play our cards right.'

Misgivings out of her system, the thoughtful girl relaxed. She stepped out of her father's embrace and twirled round to the window as if she were floating on a magic carpet of happiness, breathing on the clean pane of glass and drawing a smiley face before rubbing it off with her coat-sleeve. Her co-conspirator dealt her a scolding glare on behalf of her mother, and she couldn't help but laugh.

'Sounds like a plan, Stan! So is that why you always use the Spanish word for grandmother when you talk to us about your *mamá*?' the trainee philosopher blurted out. 'Because we never met her?'

'Never thought about it. What d'you mean?'

'Well, "G" and "G" are Grandma and Grandpa. We called Granddad "Granddad" to his face, but didn't...'

'Yeah, we did, baby,' Jeff cut her short, realising she had lost a step somewhere along her brief timeline.

A pang of guilt coursed through his veins for having expected too much of one so untainted and accepting.

'We gave my *mamá* a name for you two. You must've been too young to remember. After Granddad died, we went to *Abuela*'s grave. Jetto read her name out, but you were too little. You've come quite a way since then, kiddo! And after that, we went to New York to scatter Granddad's ashes? Do you remember?'

Kierney shook her head. 'No. Did we?'

Her father nodded. 'Yep. Auntie Lena came with us. It was bloody awful! *No importa, pequeñita.* Let's all talk about it later on, away from here. Time to go? You've seen enough, methinks. Captain Marvellous is clearly only interested in the food, and I've definitely had a gutful. That only leaves *Mamá*, and I bet she's hanging out to be rescued from the theatrical thespians.'

Hand in hand, the pair of dark Diamonds left the remodelled bedroom and its obliterated horrors to join the others. The smaller of the two hesitated outside the remaining door, wondering if she ought to suggest looking inside. The songwriter kept going, without so much as a cursory glance in its direction.

Jet was playing the piano when the wanderers re-appeared in the main room. He had exceeded his sugar *quota*, banging out a boisterous tune with vigour. Above the twelve-bar chords, Australia's highest selling female recording artist held court with the spellbound teachers, furnishing highlights of a recent tour and giving away tips for musical arrangements.

Pleased to see her black knight in reasonably good spirits, Lynn rose to her feet and prepared the children for an orderly exit. Jeff's relief was palpable, and it took every ounce of her Dyson fortitude not to rush into his arms. Such public shows of affection were unwise in their current setting, both lovers having learned not to pander to his emotional frailty.

Nevertheless, the singer felt the tug of their invisible elastic connection as if it were trying to fell her to the floor, using its momentum instead to throw herself into enthusiastic hugs for their hosts. 'Thank you for your hospitality, Leanne. And you too, Tristan. Are we ready to go, people?'

'Yes, ma'am. We should hit the road,' her husband affirmed. 'Thanks heaps for letting us trespass on your private property. Mission accomplished, eh, guys?'

The cricketer nodded, bringing his rock'n'roll massacre to its *coda* with a flourish before ending with a deliberate bum note. To a chorus of groans from his kith and kin, Tristan and Leanne clapped like true sycophants, a regular occurrence for the talented family.

The billionnaire requested an all-important envelope from Lynn's handbag, suddenly drained of all energy. 'Well, thanks again,' he began, shaking both their hands. 'We're stoked you guys've built this great little business up here. As I was just saying to Kizzy, our work here is done. We'd like to leave you with some paperwork our solicitors have drawn up to transfer the title into your names.'

The confused couple's eyes travelled from the thick, white envelope to its statuesque postman. Jet and Kierney looked at each other, fascinated by the whole scene. Their mother urged the music teachers to open the package, which they did, as yet unsure what it contained.

'It's *kosher,* but you're under no obligation,' their landlord explained. 'It's yours if you want it. And if you don't, we'll sell it with you as sitting tenants with the same length of lease as remains on the existing one.'

'Title? You're giving us...' Leanne stammered, sniffing back tears. 'Have I got that right?'

'No,' her partner gushed. 'You can't possibly do that!'

'You can try and stop him,' the smiling blonde laughed, 'but he's deadly serious. Jeff doesn't want to see this place again, and you're doing so well here. Take it, please. It's our pleasure.'

Grinning from ear to ear, Tristan wrapped his arms as far around his effusive partner's waist as common decency would allow. The fateful documents tumbled out of the envelope and onto the floor, the children pouncing to retrieve them while their parents made sure they hadn't left anything behind. Leanne then adjusted her course to engulf the celebrities, who had to catch her before she fell over.

'Jeez! Careful!' Jeff shouted. 'Hope your insurance is up-to-date. Have a think about it anyway... You don't have to decide now. The legals can be done whenever. Just let our office know. All the details are in there.'

Clutching the reconstructed packet, an awkward silence descended while the stunned couple thought of a suitable response.

Tristan took the rock star's right hand in both of his. 'Well, this is a huge shock. But a nice one, of course! I can't believe you'd be this generous,' he crooned. 'We'd never dreamed of owning our own studios. I'm sure we'd love to take you up on it. Thank you so much, all of you.'

'You're welcome,' Lynn replied, smiling at the sight of her handsome man towering over the featherweight. 'Ask as many questions as you like. Everything's negotiable. Our staff can walk you through it, but it's not that complicated. Christian von Wehrden's the best person to talk to about the nitty gritty.'

'Nitty gritty,' Jet murmured in embarrassment, gritting his teeth. 'Mum! Can't you think of something cooler to say than nitty gritty?'

'Shhh,' his sister scolded, jabbing the thirteen-year-old in the ribs.

The world-changer shot his son a stern look. 'What was that? Mate, I hear Bathurst's nice this time of year,' he cocked his head towards the front window. 'Such a shame you won't get to see it. I'll have fun with Don and Dawson, don't you worry.'

The cheeky smile vanished from his son's face in a brief moment of self-doubt. Was his father serious? Leaving them all wondering for as long as he could bear, the comic's right hand winged its way past Lynn's ear to skim the scalp of the boy's curly, blond head.

'Alright! Please excuse us,' his wife begged their hosts' indulgence. 'You were saying something about not being gregarious, Leanne? I think things are about to change. Thanks very much for our breakfast and for showing us around. It's been fantastic to see inside after all this time.'

The flat's residents leaned in to give Lynn and Kierney farewell hugs. The raucous pair of holidaymakers were already heading for the door, only to reel back around in the opening to wave before rounding the corner into the chilly concrete passageway.

Steeling himself for any tenacious demons who might take the opportunity to rain on their parade, Jeff grabbed Tristan's hand to seal the deal. Once the deed was done, the strong teenager nudged him sideways into the railing. Almost toppling for a second time, the big kid righted himself only to fall into Leanne's parting embrace.

'Watch it, you idiot,' he snarled. 'Very nice to meet you, Leanne. Good luck. This world needs all the music teachers it can get, so thanks again. *Adiós.*'

'Thank you. And we will,' the beaming woman said. 'Thanks a million. We'll be in touch soon.'

The boy from Canley Vale stepped across the threshold of his childhood home and onto the landing for the final time. Having counted his lucky stars only a minute earlier, he cursed aloud when a panic attack seized his every sense. Had it been laying in wait since they had entered, held at bay by Gravity and Miss Irony for maximum impact?

The stairwell rose up to swallow his legs. He let forth a thunderous roar and launched himself down the six levels as soon as he heard Door Number Four click shut. Unaware of the crippling mental minefield his dad had encountered, Jet was quick off the mark in pursuit.

Kierney sighed and tutted with her mother as they watched unleashed male hormones propel the male cyclones down the stairs. With no thought for the neighbours, the demob'-happy ruffians shouted their heads off the entire way down, attempting to knock each other into the wall at every turn. Evidently, the emotional release was more powerful when shared, and Lynn felt the young girl cuddle into her on their sedate descent to the carnage below.

'Are you OK?' she asked her daughter.

'I'm fine, thank you,' she answered. 'A bit scared for *Papá.*'

'Are you? Me too actually. He'll be OK. That's why we did this before they go off and do stupid boy things for the weekend. He'll have forgotten the worst bits by the time they get home.'

The eleven-year-old nodded. 'Yes. I know. It's nice to see *Papá* clowning around. I am glad we came, but he shouldn't come again.'

'No,' her mother chuckled at the wise words. 'You're not wrong there, *pequeñita*. We shan't be coming here again. Did you go into the back bedroom?'

'No. The door was open, but we just walked past. It looked like another music room. Nothing special. *Papá* didn't even sneak a peek.'

Lynn was relieved. 'Probably a good thing. He did pretty well, don't you think?'

'Oh, yes. Very well.'

When the girls reached the ground-floor exit, the boys were already waiting at their car, red-faced and out of breath. Jeff dipped his hand into his pants pocket and pulled out a set of keys, dangling them at arm's length towards his wife. Knowing her husband rarely surrendered the steering wheel, Lynn accepted them without objection. Such an abdication of responsibility was understandable under the circumstances.

Accompanying his *chauffeuse* the short distance from kerb to driver's door, the tortured soul tugged the beauty against his tired body and kissed her, paying no regard to the risk of having their privacy breached by a member of the public. 'Whoa! Thanks, angel,' he gasped. 'That's much better. I needed to taste you so badly. And thanks to you guys too. I'm bloody glad it's over. Come along, keen beans. Let's get going.'

With a car full of laughter, Lynn steered the Statesman's nose away from the kerb and joined the Friday morning traffic. The foursome was lulled into silence after a few minutes, each processing their individual perspectives on the tiny apartment which had been surrendered not a moment too soon. Although the ordeal had been a breeze in comparison with the first time she had set foot inside, at least no-one had been any the wiser to untoward behaviour.

Taking her eyes off the road ahead to check her drowsy passenger, the caring woman noticed his facial muscles had relaxed somewhat. 'Feel better? You didn't go into the other room?'

'Beginning to, yeah, thanks,' he replied. 'And no, I didn't. No need.'

'Sure?'

'Yep. Coward's answer, but so be it.'

'Hey, Mum?' Jet chimed in from the rear seat. 'Can we stop somewhere for the toilet, please? I really need to go.'

'Christ, mate!' his father laughed. 'So do I. That's the best bloody idea you've had for weeks.'

'Me three!' Kierney registered her interest also. 'Too much juice.'

With the cabin's ambiance replaced by pressure of an entirely different nature, the former local directed Lynn to a park where he used to hang out as a boy. Within minutes, they were motoring back to the airport, whence the womenfolk would soon board a flight to Melbourne, crossing lofty paths with Don and Dawson Jenner, who were on their way north for their long-awaited boys' weekend.

***

Driving the hundred and sixty kilometres from Sydney to Bathurst gave father and son ample opportunity to unwind from their frenetic morning, crammed into a rented car with their *bar mitzvah* companions. Their route took them close to the Canley Vale flat for a second time, but Jeff chose not to mention it. He had closed another chapter of his life for good, content with the way things had worked out. And now his duty was to help everyone make the most of his son's celebratory *jamboree*.

The cross-country jaunt wound this way and that, speeding up once they were through the busy commercial centre of Penrith and soon finding the bitumen flanked by dense woodland on both sides. The afternoon traffic was light for a Friday, the absence of heavy vehicles enabling those bound for the Mount Panorama circuit to navigate without obstruction or delay.

After stopping for drinks at Blackheath, in the foothills of the Blue Mountains, the accomplished rally driver put his foot down along the Great Western Highway, with the boys counting off farms and yet more woodland all the way to Kelso. Cathy had booked them into a bed and breakfast in the small town, far enough away from the main event that the celebrities were unlikely to be followed home from the racing venue at the end of each day.

The staff at their accommodation were keen to meet their special guests, mollycoddling them with mandatory meets and greets. Soon done with the associated autographs and photographs, a necessary evil which the Jenners accepted without batting an eyelid since being admitted into the stars' circle, the quartet unloaded the car into their respective twin rooms.

The teenagers grew more hyperactive the closer they got to their destination, eager to steal a march on the track and check out the teams and this year's cars. No-one could deny that their elders were any less excited, though more circumspect by virtue of their role as responsible parents.

'When were you last here?' Don asked his famous neighbour.

'Two years ago.'

'Dad won the celebrity driver's race,' Jet interjected.

The architect nodded his approval. 'Did you? Nice one. Congrats. Are you entering again this year?'

Jeff shook his head. 'Hadn't planned to. This is a private weekend.'

'Right!' his son sneered. 'What's that when it's at home?'

'What's that when it's at home?' the superstar repeated. 'Is that the most intelligent retort you can come back with? A private weekend's one where no-one's looking and I can finally maim you sufficiently that you'll never hit the low notes again.'

The older boy cackled, crossing his legs at the thought of his friend's vulnerable body parts being crushed by Uncle Jeff's gargantuan strength. Don cringed in the passenger seat along with the youngsters, and the comedian checked out the queasy reflections in the mirror.

A series of strange pulsing sounds burst through the chatter, making them all jump out of their skins. The driver opened the sedan's centre console to reveal a portable gadget which looked as if it had been stolen from a James Bond film set. Until then, no-one else had noticed the power cord strung from the cigarette lighter into the box between the two front seats.

'Jetto, please could you answer that?'

'Sure!' the lad replied with glee, lifting out a brick-like, black base unit and stretching the tangled curls of its cable into the rear passenger area. 'Hello? Oh, hi, Gerry! I mean Uncle Gerry. Sorry! How are you?'

'Hey, Luke, my boy!' they heard the Blake & Partners Chief Executive Officer's familiar haughty accent booming through the handset's loudspeaker. 'Is Obi-wan there?'

Jet passed the telephone through the gap for his dad to take over. 'Blake-san!' he shouted over the commotion and engine noise. '*Wie gehts?*'

'Wow! I didn't know you guys had a car-phone,' Don marvelled. 'Amazing! Can you see this, Daws?'

The venture capitalist drove on at full speed with the bulky plastic receiver stuck to his left ear, his shoulder hunched to hold it in place whenever he needed to change gear. In truth, the ability to make telephone calls while on the move was still every bit as wondrous for the celebrity *entrepreneur*. He played it cool in front of their buddies, chatting away to his business manager in Melbourne until the line dropped out.

'*Adiós*, mate,' the comedian frowned at the sudden vacuum of dead air, blowing a kiss into the receiver and handing it back to his son for stowing on its cradle. 'Still not too reliable, but they're getting there. Twelve more months, I reckon, and everyone'll have one.'

The car park at Mount Panorama was enormous, hectares of attended paddocks waiting for the hordes to arrive. The capacious, white Holden, an updated model from the family's own luxury vehicle, prowled up and down a couple of rows before the passengers spied a vacant spot. All four enthusiastic patrons jumped out, stretching their legs and raising their arms above their heads to kick-start their dormant circulatory systems.

Friday afternoon's crowd was building up in preparation for the opening ceremony, and the group's passage to the concourse was impeded by the inevitable attention the Diamonds received. Jeff apologised to his guests, but there was nothing anyone could do about it.

'Beer?' he suggested.

'Yes!' came a reply from the teenagers.

'Ahem! Don, beer?'

'Oh,' Jet whined. 'That's not fair. I'm a man now.'

'You wish! Not according to the law, kiddo,' the doting dad lamented, putting an arm around his shoulder and hugging him into his side as they strode towards a beer tent. 'Sorry, mate. Not this weekend. If you're good, I'll let you snort a line of coke tonight back in the room.'

The Jenners gaped at the rock star in their midst, eventually exploding into laughter once they realised he was only joking. They never quite knew how literally to take the larger-than-life Mister Diamond, often bewildered by his flamboyant lifestyle.

The foursome chose a table overlooking the pit straight and settled down for a pre-dinner history lesson proffered by the knowledgeable rev-head. He had always been an ardent fan of the Bathurst tradition and the race that topped off the weekend, the One Thousand. He told them how the Ford Sierra had been dominant for the previous two years, admitting to a hunch that the Holden Racing Team might come up trumps this year.

The Melbourne Academy best friends were transfixed by stories of spectacular crashes and engines blowing up after fast starts, and the man with the photographic memory outlined the emergence of the Nissan team as worthy opponents to the perennial Ford-Holden rivalry. Jet had a particular fondness for the Skyline flagship of the Japanese stable, and grabbed every opportunity to ride co-driver with his Uncle Junior in his tamer, road-tuned model. He couldn't wait to see the R32 four-wheel drive version up close.

The crowd saw their first piece of action during the support car race, which gave enthusiasts a chance to select the best vantage points for the next couple of days. The teenagers fancied Conrod Straight, where car-shaped blurs flew past at speeds in excess of two hundred and fifty kilometres per hour. Eager to learn though, they changed their minds when the expert convinced them to contrast this with a stint at Forrest's Elbow, where the winding hill would sort the men from the boys in gear selection and positioning for the downhill section.

Washed out after their pre-dawn start and by the anticipation of a thrilling weekend, the friends drove back to their accommodation after a quiet dinner. The adults were as tired as their sons, opting for an early night before the following day's fun unloaded in earnest.

Don had been working long hours on a construction project in Jakarta for the last few months, and the musician-turned-businessman did his best to maintain the inbound flow of information, lapping up the rarity of immersing himself in someone else's life. The unlikely pair, one nudging forty years old and the other on the other side by a similar margin, enjoyed a few quick stubbies on the verandah of their two-bedroomed cottage, swapping motoring escapades from their youth while their respective firstborns scored a head-start on sleep.

The architect decided to turn in when the clock struck ten. All too aware of his likely pattern at the end of a stressful day, Jeff knew there was no point in doing the same. He would only lie in the dark for hours, listening to his son snoring while his mind ruminated on the day's anxieties.

The songwriter grabbed his coat, cigarettes and wallet and let himself out of the cottage, leaving a note scribbled on the back of one of the leaflets they had picked up earlier. His fingers felt at home whenever they were in touch with the worn cowhide of "Dad's comfort blanket", as the trusty jacket had come to be known between Lynn and the kids. The first ever birthday gift the twenty-year-old nobody had received from a certain Miss Dyson had covered almost as many miles as he had in this crazy life of his. Summer or winter, it travelled with him as an essential link to those he loved.

While he worked his way through a litany of calls left in his message-bank, the fingers of the star's right hand fiddled with a worn spot in the lazy black fabric. It was as if they knew there was a cigarette packet in the pocket underneath, inaccessible within the confines of their cottage. Afer eighteen years as a lost boy's favourite thing on an endless, trailblazing odyssey, who knew what else had accumulated between leather and lining?

Jeff lit up, impatient for the nicotine to hit the spot. The rental car all but drove itself back to the racetrack, so preoccupied was its driver. He brought it to a full stop in a dark lay-by on the deserted, tree-lined road, wondering whether the car-phone would manage to latch onto a signal so far from civilisation. It felt almost shameful to be this keen to make contact with his women so soon into the male-oriented getaway.

Reception was stronger than usual, as it turned out, connecting the billionnaire with his *pied-à-terre* in the city. The answering machine activated after four rings, triggering a vague memory that Lynn and Kierney had tickets for the ballet tonight. He cursed under his breath. Leaving a quick message, the bored intellectual levered his tall frame out of the car and began to meander along the highway under the stars.

Jeff was glad of his globetrotting coat after all, fastening it against the night wind. His mind's revolutions tipped regularly into the red zone as he decided what he should say to his son tomorrow evening at their official *bar mitzvah* dinner. Which pieces of advice did he wish someone had given him about growing up? Things he would rather not have learned the hard way...

One theme stuck out straightaway: not to let youthful arrogance assume he already knew all the answers. It had taken the so-called genius, who blitzed every examination and grasped every new concept within seconds, much too long to stop jumping to conclusions. Would Ryan Jeffrey Blake Dyson Diamond be street-wise enough to go it alone? Was he equipped with the wherewithal to make sound decisions? As the boy's most active mentor so far, he liked to think so, but was this merely vain paternal pride?

Leaning on a robust farm gate and ingesting a perfume of damp sheep and fertiliser, the philosopher lit another cigarette. He tried to remember the words to Rudyard Kipling's iconic poem, "If". Its power had inspired him as a wayward adolescent many a time, when his sense of purpose had been compromised by forces beyond his control. As he pieced together all four verses, New South Wales' most influential village idiot appreciated its beauty and simplicity even more as a weary traveller.

The erstwhile conflicted teenaged rebel fantasised, indeed as much now as then, that Kipling must have invaded his soul and composed these lines from the mess he found within. Yet as the red tip of ash crept ever nearer to his fingers, the metaphor mutated into crystal clear wisdom: Kipling had helped him see inside his own soul.

Despite the wealth of information Jeff had consumed in the intervening years, he was not a single step closer to determining who or what controlled one's destiny. Such universal truths were not up for debate, and no words the award-winning lyricist might string together to proclaim his son's future triumphs would sound half as eloquent as this timeless ode to majority. It was not possible to conquer uncertainty by projecting the same diffidence on an opponent, however noble the chosen cause may seem.

"'If you can bear to hear the truth you've spoken twisted by knaves to make a trap for fools,'" the singer recited into the darkness. "'If you can talk with crowds and keep your virtue, or walk with kings, nor lose the common touch… Yours is the Earth and everything that's in it. And, which is more, you'll be a man, my son!'"

"The Boy Who Would Be King" was now well on his way. He had been dubbed thus as a toddler by parents drunk on ambition and with a powerful sense of irony, since no impediment was likely to block the path of Bart Dyson's eldest grandchild. Barring serious injury, he was set to captain the Victorian state cricket team in the Sheffield Shield next year. Then by his sixteenth Dyson assessment day, if all went according to plan, he should be reporting his appointment to the country's test match squad.

The father smiled to himself, remembering a comical exchange he and Jet had recently shared. In sport and in every other field of endeavour, the young scholar excelled by dint of hard work and a keen intellect. A strong "IQ" would undoubtedly take him far, tagged with a corresponding "PQ" to afford him mastery of the practical skills about which the family's business manager could only dream.

An adequate measure of emotional intelligence was the only remaining ingredient needed to turn Ryan Diamond into a great man. Kierney had been blessed with a high "EQ" from an early age, whereas her brother would require some coaching to acquire these sixty missing degrees.

Jet had learned the same famous poem during the previous school term, probably better able to recite it than his dad. But did the youngster understand its significance? Diamond Senior had been to hell and back a number of times before his own bizarre *bar mitzvah*, with a collection of invisible souvenirs to prove it. In his way, the cricketer had also accomplished plenty in his short life; he had enjoyed success and experienced some character-building personal failures. It was not beyond the realms of possibility that some of these subtle lessons had seeped into his sponge-like brain.

The world-changer and his stunning horse's arse had long concluded that merely hearing or reading about life's struggles second- or even third-hand could never be enough for their children to gain a true appreciation of how hard life could be, yet they had vetoed any ridiculous attempts to simulate an authentic gruesome event. Why subject their privileged loved ones to hardship on this basis? All the dedicated parents had to do was encourage the youthful, porous hearts and minds to digest all input and then test their ability to see things from other people's perspectives.

Sending a plume of white smoke into the still air, Jeff sighed as tears welled over his lower eyelids. How swiftly a generation had passed! Reinforced by their trip back to his Stones Road flat this morning, his spirits were now galvanised to launch his son into manhood over the coming days.

And how damned clever was that guardian angel of his? The rock star approaching his forties steeled himself against any lurking demonic backlash and visualised his thirteen-year-old self standing at the street-facing bedroom window, staring up at a leaky ceiling and inventing a future far away with the girl of his dreams. This degree of mental clarity gave him immense confidence to stand in Jet's shoes too.

Whichever path this fortunate son might take through life, it was entirely his own choice to make. All he need ask of his father were sage guidance for moving forwards and a friendly reception whenever he felt the urge for a retrospective.

The celebrity pressed the button on the side of his watch to illuminate its screen: after eleven o'clock. The girls should be back in the apartment by now, so he wandered round to the car and composed the number for a second time. This was perhaps the only weekend in the year when a telephone call from these woods would be possible, since a fair proportion of the eastern states' communications technology had been trucked to Mount Panorama for the big race.

'Hey, Lynn. It's me,' he said, a tide of relief soaking his mind. 'Did you guys have a good night?'

'Hello! Oh, yes, thanks. It was beautiful; sparkling and gloriously colourful, and our seats were up high enough to see the whole stage in one go. How about you two? Are you OK?'

Her husband sniffed. 'Ah, yeah. We're good. Not quite so sparkling, but fine, thanks. Jet and Dawson went to bed pretty early. They were knackered, and he's a bit too Vladimir Chestikov for his own liking.'

The compassionate mother laughed at the lad's cruel nickname, a recent head-cold having accentuated the unpredictability of his extending vocal cords. 'Poor kid. Don't tease him too much.'

'I'm not. It's cold here, which isn't helping. Don's asleep too.'

'And you? Sleeping, I mean?'

'Clearly not,' Jeff sniggered. 'Ten out of ten. But hey! Get this, angel… I'm calling you from the car, in the pitch blackness, miles from anywhere. Fuckin' amazing, isn't it?'

Despite the humorous banter and obvious geeky satisfaction, the Olympian detected a deep-seated melancholy in her man's voice. She sensed he was none too keen to return to the accommodation and face the prospect of falling asleep within a stones throw of the Jenners.

'Are you? It's very clear. Certainly is amazing. Are you alright though? How are you feeling about this morning?'

'Ah, y'know…' the billionnaire answered with one of the audible half-smiles he knew his dream girl appreciated. 'Wish you were here. Want your sweet lovin'. All the same bullshit I deal you when I'm lonely. And you thought I was going to surprise you with something different.'

It was his wife's turn to sigh. 'No. Not really. You're not doing well at all, are you? Cut the crap, JMD. Wake Jet up if you need some company. He can handle it.'

'No, angel. I'm cool. Just wired about the next couple of days and in need of a release of pent-up energy, if you know what I mean. Ignore me. I'll have you know I've been doing some outdoor planning for what I'm going to say to The Great Sorprendo tomorrow.'

'Oh, great,' Lynn perked up. 'Birthday dinner? That's better.'

'Yep. I've got my speech pretty much figured out, tempered with the fact that I don't want to embarrass him in front of his mate. My head's in a good space, angel. Peaceful, considering...'

'Honestly?'

The lost boy groaned in jest. 'Honestly. Stop worrying about me, OK? How's Kizzo?'

This latest batch of levelheaded, carefully chosen words brought tears to the tennis champion's eyes. The pair were so well tuned in to each other's emotions that her absent lover could almost taste the salt water. They sat nursing dead air for a few seconds, with only love travelling up and down the virtual telephone line.

Finally, Lynn broke the spell. 'I love you, you know that? Kizzy's fine too, thanks. Full of questions on the flight home earlier. Some I could answer, and the rest you're the only one who can. So beware when you get back!'

Jeff chuckled. '*Bueno*. Thanks for the warning. I love you so much too. I really appreciate what you did for us today. Flawlessly planned, *genia*.'

'You're welcome, and I'm happy with how it went. You seemed to get through it pretty easily, but then I could sense you'd reached your limit towards the end too. At least you never have to think about that place again now. It's served its purpose. It was a good investment after all.'

'Indeed. *Sorta kinda*.'

'But as I said to Kierney on the 'plane, I wouldn't want to be learning the double bass; having to cart it up all those stairs every lesson,' the singer mused, hoping to steady the caller's nerves in case the call cut out. 'They'd have to rig up one of those pulleys you installed for your neighbour.'

'Whoa!' her lover called out, midway through a yawn. 'How d'you know about that? Did I tell you? I hardly remembered what you were talking about myself.'

'Yes! Of course you told me. How else would I know something like that, you idiot? You pointed out the ruts in the bannister when we were there on

Boxing Day, while we were working up to turning the front door key. Don't you remember?'

'Yeah. I do now. Infallible memory, as usual,' the grateful man praised. 'And another positive thought for me to take to bed. You are too good to me, *Regala*. Remind me to bang you rigid when I return.'

'Okey dokey. I'll make a note of it. Are you likely to need reminding?'

'Who knows?' Jeff teased. 'Once I've passed on all my sexual secrets on to Jetto, I won't have a clue what I'm doing anymore. You'll have to teach me.'

The long-legged blonde giggled. 'Right! You may live to regret that. Chance to get my own back after all these years.'

'Oh, for fuck's sake! Get off the damned 'phone,' her husband ordered. 'I can't sit in the woods wanking all night. I'll catch my death. Time to drive these thoughts home and attempt to sleep in the same room as our son with your metaphysical fingers playing with my dick all night.'

'Shut up. Just recite "If" a few more times. That'll soon take your mind off sex.'

The songwriter sniggered. 'Not a chance, baby. Not a hope in hell. I need to be raging tomorrow anyway. I have an important message to pass on. My loins need to be stirring, or it won't come across well enough.'

'OK! I dread to think. *Buenas noches, Don Juan*,' Lynn mocked the horny poet. 'Have fun, whatever you end up doing. Say hi to the others from us.'

***

The Saturday before each year's Bathurst One Thousand presented fans with ample opportunity for observation, analysis and inhaling incendiary odours. All four red-blooded males woke in high spirits, with oil in their veins and anticipating the petrol fumes lining their nostrils while they cooked up a barbecued breakfast.

Bearing no resemblance whatsoever to the billionnaire rock star who had stripped his assets the previous morning, Jeff flipped bacon with one hand and cracked eggs onto the griddle with the other. Cigarette pendulous over the spitting selection of food, he wore a fetching combination of leather jacket, boxer shorts and a pair of fashionable, brown Chelsea boots.

If his housemates even noticed, no-one thought to say anything. The boys boosted their appetite by wrestling all-out on the living room floor, sending the rug skimming from under their feet whenever they grappled for another shoulder throw. For a whole windfall weekend, they didn't have to worry about offending their female family members' more delicate sensibilities, free to dole out protracted bouts of raucous, slapstick comedy and douse each other with harmless profanities.

Here was Lesson Number One for Jet and Dawson, a slam dunk for the tong-wielding champion of diversity: understand your audience; and treat everyone with respect. To earn a place at the long-overdue plenary on gender equality, even when on the cusp of adulthood, it was essential for a real man to acknowledge the points of similarity and difference for each sex and to remedy his actions accordingly.

The two fathers conjured up scenario after ridiculous scenario as the day progressed, compelling their sons into snap decisions on how to behave in all circumstances, only interrupted by another noisy batch of V8s screaming round the bend and shattering their concentration.

Jeff was fascinated to discover his son was less of a spur-of-the-moment decisionmaker than his older friend and stood ready to apply extra encouragement for thinking on his feet. Lesson Number Two: real men didn't always have the time to deliberate.

The third lesson involved the celebrity removing Jet's wallet from his backpack and secreting it in Dawson's coat pocket. Jenner Senior was affronted at first, never having contemplated testing his children's integrity. It wasn't until quite a while later, when the young guest of honour was asked to pay for the next round of drinks, that the plot moved on, and with no objection to volunteering his own money, the elders observed the *bar mitzvah* boy digging around in his bag and checking his pockets.

Agitated and somewhat humiliated, the cricketer turned to his father. 'My wallet's not here. It was in my bag. I'm sure it was.'

'Yeah? Sly way of skipping your shout. Are you sure you haven't dropped it somewhere?' the actor pressed. 'Pretty careless, mate. When did you last have it?'

Jeff presumed Don to be unaware of an incident which had occurred at *Escondido* a couple of years earlier, when he and Lynn had caught the regular sleepover buddy stealing from their son's room. The singer had confronted Dawson after their suspicions were aroused, a selection of toys and small amounts of cash going walkabout each time the lads spent the weekend together.

Sure enough, a collection of items at the bottom of the older boy's schoolbag betrayed his guilt, and both teenagers had been treated to a spontaneous lecture on jealousy and theft. The issue had never arisen again, since the patient woman had threatened a mortified Dawson that his parents would be informed if anything else were to disappear.

The peacemaker was also bullish that the brief breach of trust imposed on their friendship had not slipped Jet's mind either. Helping him work out what may have happened to his wallet, the foursome retraced their steps, forced to ignore the practice races which carried on booming and whizzing around the track. Ending up where their search had commenced, the missing artefact had failed to come to light.

'Maybe someone stole it?' Don suggested, tumbling into the orchestrator's snare. 'Did you leave your backpack anywhere where you couldn't see it?'

'No. How would people have known my wallet was in there? They'd have had to be quick.'

Jeff was satisfied with this initial response. The thirteen-year-old had not jumped to the obvious conclusion, even though he was sure the lad's mind was processing the possibilities. How would he challenge his friend, if indeed he suspected him at all? Several more leading questions were posed to the increasingly enlightened sportsman, who never once considered his dad could have set the pair up.

'Did you put it in yours, Daws?' the boy asked out of the blue, framing his question with care. 'After we paid for our chips?'

The student sneered. 'No. I haven't got it. See for yourself...'

The amateur psychologist would have rubbed his hands together in glee at this priceless *vignette*, except for the fact that it would have given the game away. The next lesson was revealing itself as planned, the older teenager becoming defensive. With any luck, both kids would get a chance to show their mettle in this exercise.

'Are you going to search me too?' the celebrity teased. 'You haven't thought to check *my* jacket.'

Laughing at first, Jet fell for the dummy and began to rummage through his father's pants and jacket pockets. 'It's not here. What's going on, Dad? Did you take it?'

His father shrugged. 'You need to figure it out, mate. It's your wallet; your responsibility to recover it. What would you do if I weren't here?'

'Have *you* got it, Don?' the youngest holidaymaker became more circumspect. 'Did Dad give it to you?'

'No!' the architect replied, shocked by the accusation. 'What would I want with your wallet? You must've left it somewhere. I think it's gone, Jet. Let's forget about it, or we'll miss everything. I'll buy the drinks.'

'Wait a minute. How much money did you have in there?' Jeff asked, letting the test ride for a little longer.

'Everything,' the lad moaned. 'All my cash. And my school pass, tram ticket and 'phone card. Everything.'

The superstar raised his hand. 'OK. Don't stress, mate. That stuff's all replaceable. We'll head down to the corner and see if it's been handed in at the shop. Then we'll check out the pit lane. Don't let it ruin the weekend. I'll sub' *ya.*'

He peeled off a twenty-dollar note from his own wad of cash, passing it to his son. 'Guys, go and buy us some coffees and hot chocolates. Whatever you want. It'll all sort itself out.'

Accepting the money, two sets of eyes met, and all became clear. The new leader was being sent to have a heart-to-heart conversation with his comrade to establish his property's whereabouts, knowing he shouldn't spoil the rest of the weekend ahead.

The wise man noticed the boy's Adam's apple gulp. A protective urge rose up inside, wondering if he was asking too much, only to see him turn and slap Dawson on the shoulder. The pair tore off at full pelt, leaving their dads leaning on the fence.

Jeff lit a cigarette and made small-talk with Don and a couple of inquisitive fans who had been stalking them for half an hour. He checked his watch from time to time. Their sons stayed away for a long while, and he was itching to find out how the situation had been tackled.

Would Jet come back triumphant, either with the truth or with a concocted excuse to cover for his mate, or would he choose not to mention it at all?

And how might Dawson react? Would the older lad come running to his own father, ranting and raving about being framed? Or might he feel compelled to come clean about his prior indiscretions?

After fifteen minutes or so, the pair returned, armed with four full cups with ill-fitting lids and several packets of lollies. The younger of the two strode tall and proud, while the other was doing his best to emulate his friend.

Mission accomplished, the intellectual rejoiced.

'Good man,' he smiled, taking hold of a steaming cup of coffee and five sachets of sugar. 'Cheers. You were a long time.'

Don detected some disquiet, judging by the insolent scowl on his son's face. 'What's the matter with you?'

'Nothing,' Dawson stared into the middle-distance, dunking marshmallows in his hot chocolate.

Meanwhile, Jet had squeezed up so close to his father that he was almost treading on his toes, laughing and pointing at the tidal waves of foamy milk cascading over the lip of his mate's takeaway cup. There was no malice in this act, the philosopher noticed. The lifelong friendship remained intact.

'So... All sorted?' Jeff asked.

Nodding, the younger teenager stepped aside and stood tall again.

With a public apology to the Jenners owing, to be dispensed over lunch, the blatant bond between the Diamond men compounded hour by hour as the day went on. Value judgements had passed from father to son like a dependable toolkit from master to apprentice.

Everyone's attention turned to the track when, as if on demand, the starter's gun fired to signal another practice race. The superstar directed his pride and joy toward the fence, where Dawson had laid claim to a decent view. Jet did as he was told, and it soon became clear that any awkwardness had been left behind. They were clowning around again, beyond of their fathers' earshot, picking out specific cars they liked the look of and sniggering at a group of scantily clad showgirls shivering in the pits.

Enough experimentation for one day, the intellectual concluded. He was itching to find out what had transpired between the two friends, wondering how he and Gerry would have fared in the same situation. The quartet sprinted to their car as soon as the day's timetable had finished, in an effort to escape from the packed car park before the rush. *Pizza* was voted the all-round favourite for dinner. Once inside the cottage, while their fathers showered and changed, the young men's respective maturities were given another, invisible and far less onerous nudge with task of choosing a restaurant and making a reservation.

Run Your Own Race

Squashed into a booth in an unassuming Italian *trattoria*, the Jenners and the Diamonds wasted no time in ordering beers and soft drinks, vital accompaniments for examining the menu's culinary delights. They exchanged initial impressions of the Bathurst field and placed imaginary bets on which car and driver would win tomorrow.

One of the Holden Racing Team officials, who chased down the celebrities during the afternoon for his fifteen minutes of fame, had let slip that the competition's rules were due to change the following year. The time between placing an order and receiving their meals passed in furious debate as to how these new constraints might affect future races.

'Nissan won't be able to compete if they ban the turbo',' Jet lamented. 'The Skyline's my favourite car, and it'll be crap if we're stuck with boring old Fords and Holdens.'

'It makes it more Australian though,' Don argued. 'We've got to stay good at something!'

Jeff frowned. 'You raise a valid point, mate. We haven't got the resources here to compete with the Japs. Interesting to see which wins out in the race for technical supremacy: small island with huge population or huge island with tiny population. My money's on people-power generating the momentum and revenue. Your grandpa doesn't agree though, does he, Jetto?'

'No. But don't both of you think anyone can be great?' the sporting youngster shot back.

'Sure, mate. Individually great, yeah. But enough to beat other countries who have more people, more facilities, more universities? More everything? Hard ask, I reckon.'

His son paused, unsure whose side to pick. 'But Aussies are good at heaps of things. Cricket, for example. Tennis and rugby. Swimming.'

'Absolutely,' his father agreed, lifting his beer bottle to his lips and tipping it up to drain the last mouthful. 'But most of those depend on people performing as individuals, even if it's a team-based sport, rather than something like motor-racing, which is more like a factory of moving parts all having to perform as one.

Anyway, this is getting way too serious for a Saturday night. Let's talk about sex... That's an individual team sport, if ever there was one.'

'Sex isn't a sport!' Dawson shouted at the top of his voice, attracting the attention of almost every other diner.

The Diamonds cracked up at the fifteen-year-old's outburst, leaving the others basking in their embarrassment. Diffusing the redness, Jeff requested another round of drinks and began to tell a story from his first visit to Mount Panorama. Gerald Blake Senior had succumbed to many months of pestering by the inseparable pair, eventually agreeing to take his son and three friends to Bathurst as a treat for Gerry's eighteenth birthday.

The year in question, in the "dark ages", as Jet was at pains to point out, motor-racing fans had been looking forward to the introduction of the Holden Monaro GTS, which was his Skyline equivalent. It had been scratched at the last minute however, to the fans' immense disappointment. The big race's lap-count had increased since those days too, measured in miles instead of kilometres.

As he relayed his high-octane memories to the next generation, the famous father realised the importance of recognising the relentless passage of time. 'It was bloody amazing,' he waxed lyrical about his first trip to a race-track. 'I was in heaven. The smells, incessant noise, the sights... Everything was exactly how I'd imagined it for years, and to be there in person was like a dream come true.'

'Yeah. It is for me too,' the flagging thirteen-year-old interjected, leaning into his father's side to feed off his enthusiasm. 'I love the buzz around me all the time, even now. Thanks for bringing me.'

'And me,' Dawson echoed. 'Thanks, Uncle Jeff.'

The celebrity raised his beer bottle to the youngsters. '¡Excelente! Cheers, guys. You don't have to call me "Uncle" these days. Just Jeff's fine, as long as it's OK with you, Don.'

His neighbour shrugged. 'Fine by me. Wouldn't be with Sue, but what the heck.'

'Ha! Yeah. Lynn neither! Anyway, back to 'sixty-seven... Gerry's dad was pretty well connected with some of the sponsors, so we got to go into a few team workshops. We drove a practice lap then too. All the things we've done today. The only difference was that Gerry and his school-friends already had their licences. I was only your age, Daws, so guess where I spent the weekend?'

'In the back seat,' the architect butted in, chuckling. 'How frustrating!'

'You're not wrong, mate,' Jeff grinned. 'I was spewin'. I fancied myself as the best driver in the world at that point, and I was the only one who wasn't getting a guernsey.'

'The best driver in the world?' the older boy teased. 'How did you think you were the best driver in the world if you were only fifteen?'

'You've driven out at Benloch, haven't you?' the rock star answered, hoping Don was not opposed to the activities the Dysons allowed his son to participate in when he went away with the famous foursome.

Dawson nodded. 'Yes. But that's not racing.'

'True, but it could be if you set yourselves up right. My mates and I used to practice driving in the street. Drag racing, taking fast corners, handbrake turns, *et cetera*. All highly illegal, and you guys mustn't try it on the open road, but it was the way life rolled where I grew up.'

Jet's eyes were wide with envy, anxious to hear more of this story. 'Oh, wow! That's ace! Can we do another practice lap tomorrow, please? What was it like?'

'We'll see,' his father replied. 'Might be able to if we get there early. Everyone'll be flat-out tomorrow. That practice lap was just as amazing, mate. I sat in the back, as Don said, being thrown from side to side.'

'Dad!' the boy objected, being knocked sideways by a crash simulation which sent him flying. 'Lucky I wasn't drinking.'

The larrikin smiled at the tone of his son's reprimand, a dead ringer for Lynn's. 'Sorry, son,' he said, not in the least bit sincere. 'Paid attention's what I did, while the others were posing and eyeing up the chicks. I listened to the instructor and watched his feet switch from pedal to pedal, getting a feel for the timing of when the car slowed down and accelerated. It taught me heaps about listening to the sound of the engine and working out the best time to change gear, 'cause obviously I couldn't pick up any practical skills by lurching backwards and forwards in the seat.'

Taking them all by surprise, the orator's hand slammed into his son's shoulder blade, sending his stunned face hurtling towards his half-eaten *pizza*. The Jenners gasped, then burst out laughing when the frustrated youngster tried to neutralise his father's onslaught without causing another scene.

Jeff smiled, grabbing the flailing fists and casting his eyes around the restaurant. '*C'est fini*. You OK, mate? Get the picture? Quite a ride, huh?'

'Bastard,' the thirteen-year-old cursed under his breath.

'And so… After that weekend, I spent every spare dollar for the next few weeks at amusement arcades, learning how to race the machines. Absolutely obsessed I was! I got so *aggro* at Bathurst with not being able to drive that I ended up hooking up with the best-looking glamour girl I could find. On her ciggie break! Compensation, y'know…'

'Oh, really?' Don's interest piqued for a second, before thinking better of it in front of the impressionable adolescents.

To no avail, of course! The lads were all ears, and the world's greatest lover was once more in his element.

'Oh, yeah!' he declared. 'Much more stimulating way to pass the time. I finally got something the others didn't. Short-lived though, as it turned out, 'cause we were sprung in a compromising position by her supervisor. She got fired on the spot!'

'Oh, my God! Did she?' his son frowned. 'That wasn't fair. Didn't you come to her defence? You should've told him it was your fault.'

'My fault? It was only half my fault,' Jeff leaped to his own defence. 'I did try, mate, I assure you. Perhaps she wasn't a very good worker, and he was just looking for an excuse to get rid of her. That bloke wasn't going to listen to someone like me. Wanted to exercise his authority, maybe.'

Gravity dealt the lost boy a swift boot in the gut when his billionnaire alter-ego noticed a graceless air of disapproval on Don's face.

'I'm not sure the boys should be hearing this, Jeff.'

'Mate, I disagree,' he countered. 'In my opinion, it's precisely what boys should hear. This weekend's all about teaching these guys how to behave like good men, and that micro-adventure was one hell of a learning experience. We all have to make our share of mistakes, and then do our best to learn from them. If you learn early, your journey to manhood's over faster.'

The architect backed off, smarting into his beer bottle. He was ashamed that his conservative intellect couldn't compete with the great man's quick wit. He refused to make eye contact with Dawson, who was fascinated by the direction the conversation had taken.

'So what did you learn from that?' the cricketer probed further. 'How did you convince one of those girls to have sex with you? How old was she?'

The evening's third beer loosening his tongue, the former reprobate was chuffed at the confidence his son exuded when asking these questions in front of others. 'Ah, y'know... Just turned on the charm, mate. Showed a bit of interest,' he boasted, 'Nineteen or twenty, I'd guess. Hot and available. Those were my only criteria in those days, I'm afraid. *C'est la vie.*'

Jet chuckled. '*Tómelo or déjelo.* Right, Dad?'

'Abso-flaming-lutely! I asked her why she was working there, what she did the other fifty-one weekends of the year, *et cetera*. Found out she was a student at Sydney Uni', so talked to her a bit about that. One thing led to another, as it does, and I found myself inside her undies.'

'Excuse me?' the man opposite hissed. 'Keep your bloody voice down. This is all very titilating, but there are children present.'

Dawson shrunk down into his chair, wishing his dad would stop interfering. He sucked hard on his straw, draining the last of his Coca-Cola, snickering in boyish pleasure at the stupid raspberry noises the ice cubes made when clamped to the end of his straw. His friend failed to see the funny side, annoyed to have the story censored.

The charismatic showman was ready with his rebuttal, as always. 'Children, yeah. Children who're on the springboard, all set to dive into our murky adult world. Don't kid yourself they're not fantasising about doing what we're talking about, mate. Didn't you?'

Watching the upright Melbourne professional demur for a second time, Jeff cocked his head and grinned to indicate no hard feelings. 'Guys, where getting your leg over's concerned, you need to be honest with yourself, first and foremost. What are you after? Don't say one thing and do another. If you're upfront with yourself, it helps you be honest with the girl. *¿Comprende?*'

Admitting defeat, Don relaxed a little and joined in the conversation. He had to admire this influential personality's ability to speak frankly in front of his family. In front of anyone, truth be told. The bloke was nothing if not genuine, which was why the Jenners had been so keen to pursue a friendship with their city neighbours in the first place.

'So this all happened when you were fifteen? Bloody hell! I was seventeen, and I was still one of the first in my class.'

'Did you meet Mum when you were seventeen?' his naïve son asked.

The architect coughed, put well and truly on the spot. 'No,' he replied, struggling to match the level of honesty their exemplar had set. 'I had a few other girlfriends before I met Mum.'

Clearly, Dawson was on his own voyage of discovery this weekend. Jet appeared by far the more knowledgeable on this riveting subject, despite their parallel paths through school and their many common interests. Increasing his father's satisfaction, the thirteen-year-old seemed to be exercising the same mature discretion which he and Lynn had cultivated when sharing intimate matters with relative strangers.

Sensing the young athlete cuddle into him again, the superstar knew time remaining for this type of paternal closeness was dwindling. He didn't have the heart to douse his friends' fire, seeing no point in coming clean that his own *début* had in fact been two years earlier than Don thought.

How long would it be before this ambitious, sports-mad kid who was more than half Dyson had his own sexual escapades to recount? For now, he seemed content to live vicariously through his dad's many and varied exploits.

Unease prevailed on the far side of the table, prompting the empathetic star to swerve the conversation into other automotive capers for some respite. He launched into another amazing tale about the first time he had been invited to drive the Mount Panorama circuit. This memory took them back to nineteen-seventy-seven, shortly after Jet was born.

The authorities had declared Jeff ineligible for the celebrity race since he and Gerry had won the Lombard RAC rally in the UK the previous year. Not to be outdone, he had managed to one-up the organisers by posting a faster practice lap time than the entire professional field clocked on the day.

All four holidaymakers were dog-tired by eight o'clock. Having eaten their fill of *pizza, pasta* and sticky desserts, and with the majority of families having departed, the celebrity ordered a round of hot chocolates for the teenagers and coffee and brandy for himself and his conservative companion.

The lads had begun to fidget on the rickety wooden chairs, and the adults were finding it hard not to do the same. Their host prepared to bring the coming-of-age meal to a fitting end. He didn't bother seeking permission to return to the topic which would perk them all up, primed to override Don's protestations if necessary.

'OK, gents! Where were we?' the storyteller thumped the table with his usual mastery, dark-ringed eyes scanning from Jet to Dawson and back again. 'When you see a girl on the street and you think, "Man, I *gotta* have me *summa dat*," what's that all about?'

'Making babies,' the coy fifteen-year-old sniggered.

'Yeah, partly. But that's just a symptom of the real cause. The root cause, if you pardon the pun. Not every man wants to have kids, especially young blokes.'

'Power!' Jet proclaimed, shaking a triumphant fist.

'Right, kiddo. Fulfilling your destiny,' the peacekeeper softened the message when he sensed his neighbour retreating again. 'Feeling worthy... All that jazz. Make sense?'

Neither boy felt qualified to offer an opinion, fascinated nonetheless.

The wise man continued. 'Sexual maturity marks the transition from powerless to powerful. Teachers and other adult figures, like priests and rabbis, tend to try and convince kids that sex is only for procreation.'

'Why?' his son whined.

'To put them off? Who knows? My guess is it stems from moral and religious doctrines designed to tell you you don't need sex 'til you're ready to be a responsible two-up, two-down family. Population control, reducing the burden on society of accidental kids... But as we all know, that's bullshit, *innit*?'

'Sex is a primary need for everyone,' Jet chimed in. 'Is that what you mean? Like Maslow's hierarchy: food, shelter, water and basic bodily functions, including sex. It's one of the non-negotiables.'

'*Exactamente, chico*,' his dad smiled. 'Non-negotiables is right, for most people anyway. But what I'd like to pass on to you tonight, as the ultimate gift from your visit to my new theme park, "Mount *Bar Mitzvah* World", is that sex is not like singles tennis. Sex is a team game, me hearties.'

Don expelled a lungful of air, chair creaking under his shifting weight. This was indeed a valuable lesson to teach a youngster, yet he felt ill-equipped to have a forthright conversation. He envied how unaffected the renowned communicator was by the level of expectancy at the junior end of the table.

'*Par exemple*, since forever, sex has always been a way for animals, including pre-historic man, to feel like they were invincible, so they could go out bold and courageous the next day and kill a sabre-toothed tiger or two.'

The two virgins smirked at the silly image, and Don breathed a sigh of relief. This was not the angle from which he expected the issue to be tackled.

'And it continued through the centuries, pretty much,' Jeff went on, 'while physical fighting was society's negotiation technique of choice. But none of that's necessary so much now, is it?'

'No,' his son shook his head. 'I s'pose not.'

'Not to the same extent at least,' the younger father grinned. 'We have to temper our natural urges to beat the shit out of each other to suit the way our lives roll these days. You can feel powerful without being the all-conquering hero, with the heel of your boot grinding into the other bloke's balls as he lays writhing on the ground.'

While his audience squirmed in their seats, laughing at the grizzly image, the peacemaker raised his left hand and screwed the tip of his index finger against his temple. 'What you have to remember at all times, guys, is that true power doesn't come from winning by yourself. Good power's when everyone wins. Sex is like cricket or football. You get it already, I know, Jetto. Not like boxing, where it's just you against the other bloke. Or girl, in this case. Entirely up to you whether your opponent's male or female, but let's assume we're heterosexual for the purposes of this weekend. Yep?'

Jeff felt the warmth of bone and sinew pressing against his side, the boy's sense of belonging deepening. 'And the point is, guys...' he insisted. 'You have to understand that the way you feel often isn't the same as how the girl feels. If you can't connect the two sets of feelings in the moment, you'll never feel the magic.'

Don leaned back in his chair, swirling his brandy schooner in idle circles. Only now was he starting to appreciate his famous friend's intentions. Indeed, he and Sue couldn't think of a happier couple among their wide circle of friends than Lynn and Jeff Diamond. Why not provide such role modelling at an early age, rather than focussing on protecting curious minds from the unsavoury aspects of this grown-up activity?

'For women, sex is as much about fulfilling their destiny as it is for men, but they're motivated by different forces: by feelings of inclusion and community, and by finding someone who's going to ward off sabre-toothed tigers.'

The teacher veered ninety degrees to his right and growled with surprising realism, causing the unsuspecting youngsters to jump. Out of pure reflex, the cricketer's hands leaped kangaroo-style into a boxer's guard.

His father backed away. 'Whoa! Cool it, mate. Don't go on the attack straightaway. You need to measure your opponent faster, but we'll talk about that another time. When you pick a girl to have sex with, she won't want someone who's going to shove her down on the ground and rip her clothes off within five minutes of meeting. She most likely wants someone who'll treat her with kindness and provide an environment that nurtures affection first. That's because, instinctively, women who plan to be mothers at some stage want their kids to be raised right. If you can't treat *her* well, she's not likely to trust you with her kids, is she?'

The thirteen-year-old baulked. 'Even if it's only the first date? There's no way either of you know if there's going to be a second one. Never mind about having kids!'

'Sure. Even then,' Jeff nodded, wiping the smile off his face in an instant. 'It's a principle. Another non-negotiable. Guys, you should at least know if you like each other before you get your kit off.'

'*You* didn't,' his son taunted, being privy to many tawdry accounts of the rascal rock star's early love-life. 'You told me you wanted to feel invincible.'

'Yeah, but that's me, mate. You're not me, thank Christ. And the whole purpose of this weekend is for me to warn you not to do what I did. My teenaged years weren't healthy. You don't need to fuck any damned female who crosses your path simply because it makes you feel invincible. You're way better than that. That's why we're having this conversation today: to get a head-start on growing up well.'

'Alright,' Jet promised. 'I won't, Dad. Thanks. I do know this already.'

Admiration shone from both youngsters' eyes, while Don slouched incredulous as the impressive orator in front of him turned from authoritarian to vulnerable in one fateful sentence. What had he meant by his teenage years not being healthy?

The battle-weary celebrity sat taller in his chair, engaging his voice of reason for the rest of the lesson. 'The nurturing stuff that women are programmed with isn't too relevant these days either, to be honest, 'cause there are fewer gender-based boundaries. In past centuries, there was no way a woman... 'specially a mother... could've survived without a man's financial or physical assistance.

'Nowadays, it's getting gradually more equal. It's possible for women to earn enough money to raise a family on their own, or for men to stay at home and look after the kids while mothers have a meaningful career. That's why we're working with Childlight to change the stereotypes, guys. So that daughters of helpless mums don't end up becoming helpless mums themselves. You can do anything with your life, and so can the girls you go out with. Remember this when you're grappling with your invincibility, mate, please.'

The boy with the door-opening pedigree inhaled, exuding pride and not put off in the least by this speech. His best friend's dad watched the young sportsman lock into each person's gaze without flinching, as nonchalant as if they were still discussing Ford *versus* Holden.

'But remember, when you meet a girl and want to have sex with her,' the world-changer redoubled, 'just like you feel like you want to conquer her, she feels as if she wants you to protect her. It's inbuilt, so don't try and deny these gut feelings. Use 'em wisely, Jetto. Make 'em relevant to who you both are. Schoolboy and schoolgirl, not caveboy and cavegirl. Cool?'

'Yeah. Way cool!' Jet snarled, beating his majestic chest. 'But we can still have sex then? We don't have to wait 'til we know each other really well, or I've met her parents or something?'

His dad grinned. 'What? Who told you you should wait 'til you've met her parents?'

'Oh, just one of the girls at school.'

'Melissa?' Dawson volunteered, his expression giving everything away. 'She fancies Jet heaps. She writes his name everywhere and gives him her lunch.'

'Ah, yeah? Good work, son. Keep an eye on her. She'll come in handy one day.'

'When I'm horny?'

'Indeed,' Jeff confirmed, locked in the same hormonal vice. 'As all hell, mate.'

The consummate negotiator read the Jenners' awkward glances and proceeded to reel them in. 'So listen, lads,' he joked with a piercing glare. 'If there's one thing that sets the man apart from the boy, it's using his brain during sex.'

'Eh?' Dawson shouted. 'His brain?'

A whole new sitting of late-night patrons turned in unison to eavesdrop on Jeff Diamond's table. His presence at Bathurst was scarcely the world's best-kept secret, and it was futile to expect word not to spread about their chosen dinner venue.

'I've been told a man's dick and his brain are the same thing,' Don opined out of the blue, adding to the table's mirth.

'That what Sue tells you?' the songwriter grinned. 'Must be true in that case! What I mean is all our various pieces of raw material are pretty much the same. Y'know, boys' bits and girls' bits... Big dicks and big tits are not what makes sex good or bad. It's like sport again, kiddies. You win if you use them raw materials wisely. If you can't, you lose. *Ker-boom!* End of a beautiful friendship.'

Jeff held an imaginary gun to his son's head and pretended to shoot. 'Make sense, Captain Marvellous?'

The lad nodded, once again leaning in a touch closer and snapping a quick salute. 'Makes sense, General Knowledge, sir!'

'Cheers, mate. Stand easy. The other myth about sex in the animal world is that there's no affection. No love. Well, stop the presses... There bloody well is! That's been debunked now too. Animals spend ages in foreplay, creating a comfortable environment, all for the same reasons as for humans. Not quite romance as we know it, but there's a basic need in us all to be loved and physically worshipped. If you're up for it, we should take another trip to the

Night Zoo in Singapore. It's one of the best places to see how touchy-feely animal sex is.

'Your mum taught me everything about affection, Jetto. Before we met, I didn't see the point of holding hands or anything,' the lost boy re-appeared, much to the others' consternation. 'Sex was sex. Do enough to get my rocks off; nothing more, nothing less. But that's not how it needs to be for you guys. Not in a real relationship.

'The whole idea of partners always being one male and one female is crap too. Who says sex has to be one-on-one? Group sex can be fine, as is bi-sexual sex or gay sex. Nothing's wrong or right. It all depends on who you are and what you like, provided you're not forcing anyone into anything they're not up for doing. So don't judge, OK?'

'Have you and Mum had group sex?' Jet asked in a voice so unaffected that even his dad was left a little discomfited that his answer may be overheard in the restaurant.

'A couple of times, yeah.'

'Really? Wow! I didn't know. Awesome!'

The rock star shook his head, shooting a half-smile in his neighbour's direction, having shared these stories with him one drunken evening a few years prior. 'Neither of us enjoyed it, to be honest, mate,' he recounted. 'What Mum and I have is very special and best done in private. I don't need anyone else, and neither does she. Some people get off on it though. Each to his or her own.

'Living in a pack has its advantages too, if you like that kind of thing. How d'you want to raise the next generation? There's a fair amount of research saying kids who grow up in communes are better adjusted mentally than kids with the traditional set-up of one mum and one dad. Many different species of animal use sex as entertainment, by the way: group sex, homosexual sex and even incest.'

'Is incest brothers and sisters?' Dawson checked.

'Incest is any family *combo*, mate. That's illegal and a discussion for another day, at this late hour. I don't want to talk about any seedy stuff this weekend,' the showman lowered his voice. 'And neither do I want to talk about rape or sexual assault with you. For two reasons: one, because tonight's a happy night, and I'm supposed to be giving you an idea of an optimistic future; and two, because you need to experience the basics before you're able to take in that kind of shit properly. You should know more about yourself and how you deal with the fundamentals before you tackle the subtleties of these dangerous variations.'

'But why? Why's it dangerous for us to know about rape?' Jet countered, disappointed to find out there were still things for which he was considered too young.

'Mainly 'cause the effect of something so traumatic on victims, like rape, stays with them for a bloody long time. Forever, sometimes.'

'Oh, I know. Like...' the blond sportsman began, on the brink of spilling the beans about his auntie while not *en famille*.

'Spot on, mate,' Jeff winked. 'Good man. Anyway... Back to animal sex.'

Inappropriate diversion averted, the others groaned. The celebrity caught a waitress' eye, signalling for the bill and ordering a final round of drinks.

'For example, dolphins are arguably the closest to man with regard to reasoning,' he reminded the boys. 'You know that, don't you? Dolphin sex is described as rampant but orderly, i.e. they go at it hammer and tongs, but it has a repeatable pattern. There's a right way to do it. Foreplay with dolphins apparently can last for days.'

'Phew! Days?' Don hissed.

'Yeah, man. I'm with you!' his friend laughed, lowering his voice. 'I don't know how they can hang on. I'd be climbing the effin' walls! And dolphin sex is a whole body experience, just like it is for women. So, guys, when you're with a girl, don't just zero in on her boobs and vagina, even though they're what your instincts are telling you to go for. Make her feel good first. Touch her all over. Not rough, like you're forcing her to like it. Ask her what feels good and what doesn't. With dolphins, the male won't go for full-on sex until the female asks for it, and therein lies a good lesson for us too. If you treat your girlfriends well enough, they'll ask for it. So, mate, what's the moral of the story?'

'That it's up to us how good we make sex?' Jet replied without hesitation, 'as a couple.'

'*Sí, señor. Exactamente,*' the proud father drummed the table with both sets of fingers. 'Run your own race, Jetto. Find a compatible partner and go for your life. Don't stick around with incompatible ones. It'll hurt to say goodbye, but it's always for the best if the chemistry's not going on. Have partners in series preferably, but anything that works for the interested parties is fine. And once you find someone you love, keep it fresh and stay together, especially if you have kids.'

The big man's voice cracked as the emotion grew with his soliloquy's *crescendo*. 'There's absolutely nothing good in abandoning kids,' he insisted. 'Nothing, guys. *Nada, nada.*'

Their final round of drinks arrived at an opportune time for a break in proceedings, and the handsome grandstander excused himself from the table and headed to the restroom. The enlightened *trio* stretched back in their seats in a mellow silence, each ruminating on the pearls of wisdom so amiably dispersed.

A few minutes later, having been bailed up by a bunch of rowdy motoring enthusiasts who had come in for a late dinner, their chief stooge returned to find his weekend companions stirring their drinks in an absentminded stupour. Giving his son the evil eye, he sat down and began to copy them. His antics made Jet laugh, doling out a playful slap on the forearm in the same way Lynn would have done. Life was good.

'Right, kids!' Jeff shocked them out of their lethargy. 'Last sermon for tonight... Very important, you guys. Don't underestimate the significance of making a human being. As a matter of fact, both making one and not making one. Don't want one, don't make one. Simple enough?'

Both boys laughed, nodding in earnest.

'If you don't want to be a dad, use contraception. Every fucking time.'

'Literally!' Don interjected, all hope of keeping the conversation on an even keel now abandoned to the brandy and their combined tiredness.

'Quite, mate,' the musician raised his eyebrows. 'Remember, even if the girl says she's got it covered, still use a condom 'cause you never know when someone might lie to you. Not everyone's honest. And if you're going to be the greatest cricketer in the history of time, mate, have a guess at how many women are *gonna* want to have Ryan Diamond's baby...'

Jeff could almost feel gusts of air expelling from his compadres' lungs, as this indisputable fact tapped all three on the forehead. Another *leçon à-propos* for a teenager whose entire life had been spent in the public eye, destined for a very bright future. Dawson was no slouch when it came to sports either, and they both looked forward to emulating their heroes in attracting fair maidens.

Dazed, the Dyson aristocrat stared first at his friend and then at his father. 'Oh, my God! I never thought of that. Shit! Did girls want to have your baby, Dad? Did they pretend to be on the pill or something?'

'Jesus! I don't know if they pretended. It's not something you go around accusing people of, mate,' the songwriter groaned, suddenly more serious. 'But yeah, I'd guess some of them did. It's not worth taking the risk. You never know where on the spectrum on intention the other person is. Some didn't care, but others gave me an uneasy feeling, like I should be extra-careful.

'Jet, I never once went to bed with anyone except your mum without using a condom. Promise us you won't be careless about this either... There's way too much pain and anguish for all concerned when you have to decide what to do about an unexpected pregnancy. Let's not go through that, OK?'

'No. Like Gerry, you mean?' the boy blurted out before he could stop himself.

'Yep. Exactly like Gerry,' his dad nodded. 'And Auntie Lena. It's a terrible decision to have to make, believe me.'

'Wait a second... Gerry Blake? Has he got a child?' the architect piped up, having met the jovial businessman many times at Diamond functions. 'I never knew.'

The compassionate philanthropist sighed. 'Yeah, no. You wouldn't, mate. He never talks about her. Jenna was born a few months before Lynn and I got married. She's gorgeous, isn't she, Jetto? Lives with her mum.'

The blond lad blushed, much to his friend's delight. A mutual curiosity had developed between him and their business manager's accidental daughter, who was more than two years older. Over before it began, the fleeting affair had been dismissed as a harmless crush as soon as their parents cottoned on.

Winking at the uncharacteristic shyness on display, Jeff moved on. 'And so, when you think you're ready to have kids, you need to enter into the kingdom of parenthood with both eyes open. Eh, Don?'

'Ha! How did it go? Abso-flaming-lutely?'

'Halleluja! Don't stumble into it in a drunken haze. Understand what it means and whether you think a kid'd be happy in your world. And make sure your partner wants the same thing as you do, and for the right reasons. Talk about it before you let your swim-team loose in the luscious lane of *lurve...*'

'Dad!' Jet cried out. 'That's revolting! I can't believe you said that.'

The Jenners fell about laughing. Sex education in the style of Jeff Diamond was an elective worth taking!

'What's revolting?' the comic sneered. 'If you can't describe it, you shouldn't do it. Am I being factually incorrect?'

'How should I know?' his son shot back. 'Finish the sermon, vicar, 'cause I'm dying for the toilet.'

'Sure. We'll go in a minute. It's getting late. I'm hoping to plant a few seeds in your testosterone-infested brains. Family planning, to give it its nicey-nicey, official euphemism, are two words that go together for a damned good reason. Talk about it, OK? Preferably *ad nauseam*... There ain't no turning back. Think about the sort of world you want to bring your kids into? Mate, your *mamá* and I only ever disagreed on a few things, as you know. It's a nightmare to get through, but totally worth it. Keep talking all the time. Don't leave anything unsaid. *Capisce?*'

Jet tipped his cup to the ceiling in childish defiance, draining the dregs of tepid hot chocolate into his mouth and smacking his lips. 'Loud and clear, boss!'

'Hey! I'm serious, son. 'There's no more important thing, as an individual or as a couple, than to do the right thing by your children. So humour me, please. I know you're nowhere near having kids yet, but take this as a warning shot across your bows from someone who gives a shit. Don't have 'em if you don't want the obligations that go with 'em.'

'Dad?' the inquisitive student looked up.

'Mate?'

'How often are you supposed to have sex?'

'Every five minutes,' Dawson mocked, causing his father's coffee to go down the wrong way.

The world's greatest lover frowned, scratching his head. 'Jesus! You OK, Don? Slap him, Daws, please. Every five minutes? I bloody well hope not. You'd want it to last a bit longer than five minutes, numb-nuts! There's no right answer to that question. As often as you both want, and you can always make up any shortfall on your own.'

Don exhaled again. 'Oh-*kay*! Time to go. Drink up, boys.'

Reaching for the leather jacket which was slung over the back of his chair, Jeff fished into an inside pocket to retrieve his wallet. 'We'll get the bill. So many things affect how much a person needs sex, or wants it. You have to be sensitive to what your partner wants too. If she's someone who only wants it once a week, and you need it six times a day, there's an incompatibility looking for a resolution right there.'

'How?'

'Well... Either you come to a compromise and stay together, or you agree to split up so you can both find someone better aligned. Stress can make you need more or less. So can being tired.'

'And oysters,' the architect offered.

The songwriter smirked. 'So they say... It's all about communication again, at the end of the day. The better we communicate, the better we'll fornicate.'

This rhyming play on words made Don and Jet laugh, but poor Dawson failed to see the joke.

'Fornication means having sex,' the younger celebrity clarified.

'It's alright for you, Diamond,' the envious man opposite complained. 'You're so full of self-confidence, and you look like the archetypal red-hot *Romeo*. What about the rest of us, who don't have your smouldering good looks and charm? It's not so easy to have girls falling at your feet when you're Mister Ordinary.'

The celebrity shrugged. 'Why thanks, darling. But, mate, that's why we've all come away for this weekend. We're here to build our sons' confidence by taking away as many unknowns as we can, so when they're in a situation for the first time, they've got the basics covered. Confidence comes easier when we can focus on our strengths, knowing everything else is under control.'

'Oh, I see,' Don puffed out his cheeks and blew through pursed lips. 'And there was I thinking we'd come to watch the V8s! I wish my dad'd talked to me like this. That's all I have to say.'

'Me too,' the Sydney native shook his head. 'Plenty of time for everything. I don't want my kids to learn about life the way I did. End of story. Shall we head back to *casa nuestra*?'

The quartet rose to its feet, commenting on how inhospitable the weather looked outside, the roadside trees bending over on spindly trunks. They stretched stiff legs and slotted arms through coat-sleeves amid a veil of whispers and a flurry of furtive fingers from the restaurant's second sitting.

Don approached the counter with his famous friend while the youngsters disappeared to the lavatories in a hurry. Chatting to the awestruck manager, the men expressed surprise that the small town's streets were all but deserted at ten-thirty on the eve of the big race. They meandered back to the car, peering in shop windows and stopping to admire or deride the rows of collectors' cars which had converged on Bathurst.

For the first time in over twelve months, the thirteen-year-old slipped his hand into his father's while they walked along the footpath. Jeff's heart swelled with joy, convinced this odd scheme was already paying dividends. Putting a benevolent arm around the solid young frame instead, the pair of Diamonds matched each other stride for stride, taking it in turns to set the pace.

'Hey, another thing, guys…' the soothsayer attracted the Jenners' attention. 'When you're ready for your first real sexual experience, my advice is to choose someone you don't know too well. Not someone from school. Someone you're pretty sure you'll never see again, and someone who won't bitch about you to her friends. Then, if you screw up, if you pardon the pun, you won't have to live with the consequences.'

By the look on Don's face, this dilemma rang true. The empath dared to hope these secrets might seep out of their own accord at a later date, as Dawson headed towards manhood. And how would each set of parents celebrate their daughters' ascension?

'Mum didn't practice on someone else first,' Jet dispelled his dad's pleasant introspection.

'Nope. She didn't,' he grinned. 'I got there too quick. But she did get some time to experiment when she lived in the US. In fact, we always joke about that, because when she came back, she kept comparing me to "everyone else."'

'Everyone else?'

'Yeah. You get what I mean!' the rocker laughed aloud. 'Not good for anyone's self-confidence now, is it?'

Don fastened his coat high around his throat, remaining tight-lipped. The travellers had reached their car and waited for the billionnaire to produce the set of keys. He stubbed out his cigarette, a long spray of smoke condensing in the freezing temperatures, while two muted squeaks from the remote central locking added to the evening's surreality.

'Don't look at me!' the Diamonds' longstanding friend scoffed, piling into the front passenger seat. 'Not quite everyone else. That would've been a bloody miracle.'

The headstrong *lothario* made a grab for his rival's genitals. 'Oh, yeah?' he chided. 'Don't even go there if you value your life. Anyway, faithfulness or exclusivity is another interesting idea, guys. How far do you have to go with someone else to be unfaithful to your girlfriend?'

'I don't know,' Dawson moaned.

Looking in the rear view mirror, Jeff engaged with both boys' confused stares. 'Have a guess.'

'Full-on sex,' his son ventured.

'Yeah, ultimately. But what if you kiss someone else? Your girlfriend's not going to be happy about that either.'

Jet growled, throwing his back against the seat in frustration. 'True.'

'Chill, mate. Life is complicated. Get used to it! So Don, what does faithfulness mean to you and Sue?'

'Never talked about it,' the older man batted yet another awkward question away.

'Why not?'

'No idea. Anything that makes her jealous, I suppose,' he replied, glaring at the driver's tall frame.

The questionmaster reverted to his rear passengers. 'OK then... How about this for a hypothetical? What if you're having sex with someone else but you're fantasising about your girlfriend? To whom are you being unfaithful?'

'Both,' his son responded in a heartbeat, giving the rock star a scorching cattleprod of *déjà-vu*.

'Christ! Have you spoken about this with Mum?'

'Yes!'

Jeff chuckled, whipping the car around a sharp corner off the main street and fishtailing under slippery acceleration. 'Hmm... Spooky! I'm clearly on dangerous ground here! I agree now, mate. But when I was in my teens, I didn't believe it.'

An accurate bowling arm flashed from behind the driver's seat to clip his father's left ear. The former sexual mercenary's punishment stung, its sweetness rendered still more acute by the strain on his invisible elastic connection. His beautiful best friend was watching over them both, and he reached up to rub the shirt in front of his "JL" tattoo.

'That's from Mum,' the teenager cackled. 'It depends who's going to be hurt, doesn't it?'

'Yes, mate. It does indeed. She taught you well.'

'So how do you stop the other person from getting hurt?' Jet continued. 'Keep it a secret?'

'Maybe,' Jeff replied, 'but that's deception. Lying by omission is still lying. Y'know... "I promise to tell the truth, the whole truth and nothing but the truth."'

'Yeah. Of course it is.'

'Alright, know-all, riddle me this...' the patient father twisted his head round. 'If someone tells your girlfriend you were out with another girl at a nightclub on Chapel Street on Saturday, when it was really Church Street on Friday, you can deny it quite truthfully, can't you.'

'Yes. Well, sort of,' the impish student grinned. 'But it's not the whole truth.'

'*Exactamente, hijo mío,*' Jeff said, giving his son a thumbs-up sign. 'And if you know she went to the pub with one of your mates because she wanted to get her own back, does it mean you're entitled to go to the nightclub with another girl? What's that?'

'One good turn deserves another?' Don chimed in.

The peacebroker laughed. 'Not bad, mate. Not bad. It's trying to absolve your sins by pointing out her own. You've still done wrong, regardless of what she might have done. They're two separate issues, and we can only and must only be held responsible for our own actions.'

Despite the animation in the car, Dawson had fallen asleep with the noise of the rain on the roof and the steady motion of their homeward journey. Jet leaned across to tap the other boy's father on the shoulder, his finger raised in front of his mouth and pointing with the other hand.

Without warning, the exuberant teenager bellowed into his friend's ear. 'Eyes right, Jenner! Tits ahoy!'

The fifteen-year-old jumped out of his skin, turning on his tormentor with clumsy limbs. The car shook and swayed with the weight of two bulky adolescents wrestling on the rear seat, first shoes and then hands flying close to the driver's shoulders.

'Guys, stop, please,' an unusually stern voice commanded. 'Enough. It's too late for this reckless shit. High on hot chocolate and ice-cream, anyone'd mistake you for children. Now, Jetto... Look at Gerry, for example. If he ever gets married, he'll be one hundred percent faithful because he's done everything else. He's got rampant but orderly out of his system.'

The lad let out a breathless laugh, settling down for the last five minutes of their trip. 'Guess so. He won't be a dolphin anymore.'

'Yep. He'll go from dolphin to swan. They mate for life.'

'Like you and Mum. You're swans.'

'We are, yeah. And I'm damned lucky too, 'cause I got playtime out of my system very young.'

The white Statesman pulled up outside their darkened cottage, headlights illuminating the line of trees behind. Cutting the engine, Jeff urged the boys to keep quiet as they went inside. He locked the doors and followed the others up the narrow, overgrown path, gripped by the predictable fear of bedtime without his beautiful best friend. Nevertheless, he was pleased with how the weekend was turning out, and even more so with the mature way his son engaged in the contrary adult subject matter.

A moment of self-doubt, brought on by the sound of the key unlocking the front door, made the devoted father wonder if he was overdoing the emphasis on sex, relieved to have it diffused by Jet's very next question.

'So, Dad, do women always look for the strongest, most good-looking man?'

'Yes and no,' the celebrity's hackneyed answer took the lad by surprise, as it did every time. 'I'm sure they want that kind of man. Some give up because they don't have the self-belief to go after him.'

'Same as us?' the teenager offered, struggling with a coat he was growing out of and making a meal of throwing it onto a hook in the hallway, where it hung lopsided like a punctured basketball.

'Pretty much,' Jeff nodded. 'The only difference is that women still like to be asked out, not the other way round. But they'll ask *you* out, mate. Goes with the territory, whether you like it or not!'

The junior sportsman puffed his chest out a little at the compliment. 'But if women choose the strongest, how come small, weedy men still get girlfriends?'

'Depends how you define strong, mate. There are heaps of features about a person you could describe as strong. Like standing up for people, being kind or smart. Good manners... All sorts. D'you want to talk about this now, or shall we leave it 'til tomorrow?'

'Now, Dad,' Jet insisted. 'Please? I'm not tired. Are you, Daws?'

'Much!' Don scoffed, watching his own son disguising a yawn.

'Sit down, comrades,' the teacher beckoned to the couches in the cottage's cosy lounge room. 'Just a few more minutes, then lights out. Strength doesn't have to be physical. It's about character and fortitude, by which I mean mental and emotional strength too. A good catch for a woman can be any combination of the traits she values: his ability to get a good job, to earn good money, to stand up for himself and his family in an argument or other sticky situation. Reliability is a type of strength. Man or woman, we tend to consider someone weak if he or she caves in and does things we were depending on them not to do.'

The boys looked confused, and the architect was beginning to nod off, propped up in an armchair.

'Like what?' Dawson asked.

Jeff lifted his gaze to the ceiling, trying to think of an example. 'Giving into peer pressure. You know what that's all about, as leaders at school. Or breaking promises. Say, if your girlfriend wants you to go to a movie with her on Friday night, and you say you will. Then one of your mates invites you to a party. What do you do?'

'Letting someone down?' the younger teenager offered. 'I'd ask her if we could go to the movies another night, and then maybe we could both go to the party. Win-win situation.'

The proud father raised his son a high-five. 'Cool, mate! A win-win's exactly what a strong person should aim for. Excellent solution,' he praised. 'And what's that an example of?'

'Negotiation?' Jet hazarded. 'Good communication.'

'Spot on. You've got it. Strength is whatever your partner thinks is important, and not necessarily what *you* think is important. Coming home and saying you bench-pressed a hundred and fifty kilos isn't going to impress most women all that much, whereas coming home and using your well-honed muscles to carry her to the bedroom and make her feel like a million dollars...'

All three laughed.

'Thank God for that,' Don murmured, flexing a drowsy arm to track down his long-forgotten biceps.

'So why do you train so hard then, Uncle Jeff?' Dawson goaded his friend's dad, aware that he spent a large number of hours every week running and working out in the gymnasium.

The wise man lit a cigarette, disappointed at the older boy's mean streak. '*Touché!* Cheers, Daws. It comes back to what we were talking about earlier; about making the most of your raw materials.'

'If you've got it, flaunt it,' Jet chuckled as he rattled off one of his mother's favourite platitudes. 'Use it intelligently.'

'You, sir, are on fire tonight!' the handsome man grinned, stabbing his finger in the air in line with his boy's ruddy face. 'And what d'you mean by that exactly?'

'If people are impressed with what you look like, they'll be more likely to listen to what you have to say? Good on the outside, good on the inside.'

The world-changer nodded. 'Yep. Being who we are, mate, is a package deal. Much of what your mum and I do depends on who we can get on-side. Charisma only gets you so far, guys. You've got to have the integrity to be credible as a leader. The real deal, as they say. If you want to be known as strong, it's helpful if you can show strength in as many ways as possible. By looking and behaving a certain way, you appeal to the widest possible constituency.'

A snore turned into a cough as Don realised he had nodded off during another vital lesson. 'Constituency? What are you talking about? Are you going into politics now?'

Jeff sniffed. 'Jeez. No, thanks! We've always taught our kids to project forward, mate. What you do today is important, but not half as important as what you'll do tomorrow. Think before you act, but don't let it stop you acting. Analysis paralysis, as Gerry says. Every choice you make will matter at some point. D'you want to be like Auntie Lena or like Mum?'

Stifling a yawn of his own, the storyteller wheeled round and faced his son with a terrified expression.

'Like Mum,' Jet yelped.

'Are you Grandpa or Granddad?' his father persisted. 'Make the choice every day, mate.'

'I need you to send me more effin' money,' Jet whined, doing his best impersonation of his whacky aunt. 'You never send me enough fuckin' money, *chico*.'

The untimely reminder made the star's blood boil. 'Oh, very funny. You're lucky Mum's not here to hear you swear so proficiently. All I'm trying to say is that you want everything in a relationship to be symbiotic.'

'Feed off each other,' the snoozing architect mumbled. 'That's actually a good way of expressing it.'

'Cheers, Don,' Jeff smiled. 'Providing it's not a lose-lose situation. I'll eat your arm, and you can eat mine. That's not quite what I meant.'

The boys laughed and then rubbed their eyes, tittering when they spotted each other's mirrored action. An old-fashioned carriage clock on the mantelpiece struck eleven times, emitting a dose of sleeping potion for the foursome.

'Bed?' the songwriter suggested. 'Good call. The upshot of this lecture is, Jetto, that now you're a man... And as your father, I'd like you to take sex as a metaphor for the rest of your life. These ideas work just as well for captaining the under-sixteens cricket squad as they do behind the bike sheds. Use the same decision-making process for every part of your life. Sound ethics, empathy and decent behaviour are as much as anyone can ask of you, mate. If you can prove that you're acting in everyone's best interest, you've done the right thing. Put that in your pipe and smoke it, Rudyard Kipling.'

Feeling spent, the father held out his left hand to his firstborn, who walked into a manly hug.

''Night, Daws, Don,' the boy made his way towards the door. 'Thanks for a fantastic day. See you in the morning.'

Outside the Diamonds' quarters, Jeff placed his hands on the blond upstart's shoulders. They stood staring at each other for a long time, a comfortable silence easing them into the night. If he had been criticised for spending a disproportionate amount of time with his broody, dark-haired gipsy girl, this epic triumph of masculine advancement was well on its way to redressing the balance.

'You're a star, mate. Don't anyone try and tell you otherwise.'

'Thanks. I feel bad for Dawson though. His dad's got the shits with him because he's struggling to hold his own.'

The billionnaire stood back, opening the door for the youngster to enter. 'Don't stress. In that case, they're both suffering from the same condition. I'm sorry about the wallet exercise, and I'll speak to Don. He's a good dad. He'll get over it. Keep doing what you're doing.'

'OK. You were awesome at dinner, by the way. I really love talking about this stuff. About growing up well. Dawson said he wishes you were his dad.'

'Yeah?' the celebrity grinned. 'Cheers, but that's not so good. I need to speak to Don some more then. I hoped you'd appreciate the sentiment. The same principles apply everywhere, mate. At work, you could be the corporate psychopath and take everyone down on your way to the top, or you could bring everyone on the upward journey with you. The choice is yours, as it is with sex, and it's your leadership style that'll be counted. Get ready for bed. I won't be long after you.'

'Thanks, Dad,' Jet said, standing on tiptoe to give him a quick kiss on the lips. 'I love you. This is the best weekend. You're amazing. I'm so glad you're my dad.'

Jeff was overcome by the teenager's private expression of emotion. He couldn't remember the last time his son had kissed him. A long time ago.

'Thanks, mate. It's very special for me too. You've handled yourself like a king today, make no mistake. There's nothing you can't do. Never forget it. I love you so much, and so do Mum and Kizzy. We're a good team. And tomorrow will be more about cars, I promise.'

'Don't care. I like hearing all these stories. But I am looking forward to the race too.'

'G'night, mate. *Dors bien,*' the tall man leaned over and tried to sneak another kiss, but this time he was pushed away.

'Hey. Don't get greedy,' his son taunted, before sprinting into the bathroom for sanctuary. '*Toi aussi,* you pooftah.'

After the lads had gone to bed, the dads sat smoking cigars on the tiny porch, soaking up the silence after a demanding yet satisfying day. Privately, Jeff mulled over the implications of the *bar mitzvah* boy's heartfelt opinions. Displays of affection would henceforth manifest only on the young man's terms, which was fine. Had his father been around to be welcomed or spurned at will, no doubt he would have been no different.

The celebrity's hunch that Don was troubled by falling short in the "cool dad" stakes didn't remain a secret for too long either. Discharging his frustrations, he ground the stub of a luxurious Honduran into the ashtray.

'I appreciate what you're doing, now I understand more.'

'Yeah? Cheers, mate.'

'I'm jealous though. You guys are so close. I can never think of anything worthwhile to say to my kids, apart from "Tidy your room."'

Feeling sorry for his friend, the songwriter laughed. 'Hey, don't get me wrong,' he reassured. 'There's plenty of that shit going on in our house too. Lynn takes the brunt of the hard stuff mostly, while I come home to enjoy the good times. We've always encouraged Jet and Kierney to critique their own life choices and to understand their places in this huge, breathtaking and inhospitable jungle we live in. How they can control it to their advantage, *et cetera.*'

'Oh, is that all?' the conservative architect jeered.

Jeff shook his head, knowing full well the serve was warranted. 'Fuck you! Pretentious, I grant you. But people are going to want to shoot our guys down at every turn. We want them to be prepared for anything.'

'Yes, I see,' Don shrugged. 'It's just that it always feels sort of too personal to talk about. Fake, almost.'

'We started early,' the philosopher explained. 'It'd be pretty tough to have to start on the deep-and-meaningfuls now; from nothing, I mean. Probably still worth it, if you can get over the weirdness. Dawson's a good kid. He'll have no problem becoming a good man. Leading by example's a powerful thing. You and Sue are successful, so Daws and Mai'll notice and want to emulate you. Nothing to worry about, sir.'

The older father lifted his mug to his lips, forgetting he had finished his tea a few minutes ago. 'Shit! Bloody empty! Anyway, thank you,' he acknowledged the endorsement. 'You know, I never smoke unless I'm with you. I hope you're right. But the difference is your kids'll be great. Ours might be successful, but yours'll be super-successful.'

'That's the plan,' Jeff laughed, crossing the room to switch off a chintzy lamp on the sideboard. 'World domination, here we come!'

Fathers And Sons

The next morning, Jet was up bright and early. The sound of the bathroom door clicking shut woke his father too, although part of him had already been awake for a while, judging by its size and the attendant sense of urgency. The last thing he remembered was soliciting a type of mechanical meditation from the light, rhythmical snoring on the other side of the bedroom. Sharing quarters with his son was an agreeable novelty these days, but also somewhat awkward. He reached a hand over the edge of the mattress and scooped his boxer shorts under the quilt.

'Dad! Sweet. You're awake,' the early bird yelled, bounding across the floor and taking a flying leap onto the bed. 'Are we going for a run?'

'Jesus Christ,' Jeff moaned, rolling over in his single bed to face the wall and avoid full body contact first thing in the morning. 'Where the hell d'you get your energy from? You're as cheery as your bloody mother, but with none of the perks.'

The thirteen-year-old squatted on the end of the bed and waited for his father to crawl out of the habitual dawn-time chasm. He wavered back and forth, flexing his ankles and lifting his arms in an effort to keep his balance before allowing himself to face-plant into the bedclothes.

Feeling close to sixty kilograms of solid man-child land prostrate beside him, the songwriter considered it safe enough to turn around and sit up. 'Where's my cup of tea?' he asked, holding out an expectant hand. 'This weekend's not all about you, you know.'

'Isn't it? It was last night.'

Jeff flung the covers back and swang his legs over the side before Gravity had the chance to deafen him with screams of "Bad idea!" Grimacing as his feet found Sunday morning's cold floor, he bent down and grabbed Saturday night's T-shirt, threading it over his head and standing up.

'What's that?' the teenager exclaimed, pointing at his dad's crotch.

The superstar smiled in mock arrogance. He had renounced all licence to be embarrassed, given the rough ground they had traversed over dinner the previous evening.

'You don't know what this is?' he grabbed his drooping erection. 'Big is what it is. Bigger than yours, boy-oh, especially first thing in the morning. Eat your heart out. Let me go and piss. Get dressed, and we'll head out into the fresh air.'

Father and son cracked on at a steady pace through the satellite town's empty streets, revisiting parts of last night's conversation. They rehashed how the youngster had dealt with Dawson having his wallet, and the peacemaker told him how proud he was of the way both boys had behaved. He also confided that he hoped the fifteen-year-old might own up to some of his past indiscretions by the end of the weekend.

'May I ask you another sex question?' Jet asked in a hushed voice.

'Sure,' the billionnaire grinned, gazing around the broad, tree-lined avenue. 'No-one can hear you.'

'How do you know?' the lad laughed. 'Dad, how often should you masturbate?'

Ever the epitome of cool, Jeff extended an arm and hooked his fingers into the neck of his son's singlet. The loss of momentum slowed their stride for a few seconds before he let go and watched the cricketer lurch and stumble until he corrected his balance.

Annoyed he had fallen for this old trick, Jet pulled up and rounded on his father. 'Fuck off and answer me, you bastard!'

'Whenever, mate. As often as you need to. There's nothing wrong with it. You just need to pick your moments carefully. Be private about it, y'know.'

The pair jogged on, waving at a farm vehicle full of men who had recognised them and were determined to make it known. Once free of the brief *fracas*, Jet nodded, finding noticeable relief in his dad's answer.

The teacher carried on. 'It's perfectly natural, and as soon as you have sex with a woman you'll realise that it's nowhere near as good as the real thing.'

'What does that mean?'

'Well, an orgasm's an orgasm, whether you're on your own or not, but we're still driven to have sex with a third party.'

The boy snorted. 'Hi. This is Lynn. She's my third party.'

'Yeah,' Jeff whined. 'Your mum is my third party, and there's none better in the world, so lay off and concentrate.'

'So does it feel better with a third party?'

'You really have to ask this question? Yeah, sure it does. I don't fully understand why though, so there's something for us to work on together. Obviously, it's to push us to partner up and procreate on many psychological and practical levels, but the physiological reason's a complete mystery to me. Some blokes choose not to have a third party because wanking makes them feel good enough without the complication of having to deal with another human being in their life. Some people aren't interested in putting themselves in anyone else's shoes.'

Jet groaned. 'What does *that* mean? What's that got to do with orgasms?'

'Not a lot,' his father chuckled. 'I mean some guys don't want to to be bothered with interpreting and reacting to someone else's alien feelings. I can understand where they're coming from, to a certain extent. It's much easier to be selfish than not, so I hope you're not one of those blokes. You'll be missing out on a whole host of other dimensions of life if you are.'

'And I won't have kids.'

'No. That'd be a tad miraculous,' Jeff smiled, crossing the road without warning and leaving his son behind.

Jet lined up behind the unsuspecting rock star and delivered a *karate* kick to his backside. 'Take that! Unless they invent some way of men making babies on their own.'

'Not likely, mate! Nice try. Although having said that, I reckon it won't be long before we can make babies with neither parent involved. Great for people who want kids but can't have them, but where's the fun in that for the rest of us? But hey, Jetto. Listen… What'd be useful, when you're milking the *salami*, is to take yourself right to the brink and then back off. Learn how to stop and start again. You need to be able to stop if your girlfriend says stop.'

'Stop having sex?'

'Yep,' his father affirmed. 'This is important, mate. If a woman tells you to stop, even if you're feeling like there's no turning back, you have to stop. It'll kill you. Your balls'll do everything in their power to stop you from stopping, so practise how to handle that feeling. Take a break for ten minutes or half an hour, and then get back on it. The feeling'll be more intense, I promise you.'

'Like getting a reward for patience?' the teenager sniggered.

'Yeah. Something like that. I could never do it at your age. It took me ages to control myself. I was filled with fucked-up compulsion. You won't be that way though, mate. You're strong as an ox mentally, but practise all the same.'

An energetic wire-haired terrier raced out from a front yard, taking the runners by surprise. It barked like a maniac, not the kindest way to signal to the neighbourhood that there were celebrities on the loose. The commotion set off at least two other dogs nearby, and the Diamonds had little choice but to stop and make a fuss of the noisy culprit until he calmed down.

Once they had left the yappy meteor behind, Jeff was soon playing catch-up with the young pretender. Spying a sports oval after the next side-street, he acted out a quirky scene of picking up the dog and dropping it onto the toe of his boot for an elegant, slow-motion kick at goal. His son added howling sound effects as both shaded their eyes as if they were tracking the animal-shaped missile as it soared towards the goalposts for a six-pointer.

Reaching the pristine local football ground, the billionnaire nudged Jet's shoulder and darted across the road again, hurdling the low fence with ease. They raced towards the line of four white posts, both players' eyes scouring the sky for the invisible furry ball to come hurtling down from above. Jostling each other for position, the teenager yelled at the top of his voice and bumped his dad out of the way of the contested mark.

Jeff was about to take Flying Fido safely on the chest when a sharp pain shot through him. The toe of his son's running shoe impaled his left kidney and landed on his hip bone to lever the sportsman up for a *specky*. The frolicsome pair fell in a pile of arms and legs onto the soggy ground, continuing to emit muffled yelping noises as if the poor dog was caught in the scrum.

Brushing the grass and soil off his clothes, the thirteen-year-old jumped to his feet and offered a hand to pull his father up into a hug. 'This is still a fantastic weekend, Dad. I'm having the best time.'

'Very cool, mate. Me too. Happy *bar mitzvah*, Ryanovitz.'

The game of "Mark the Dog" continued to entertain the ruffians for several more minutes, until the absence of an actual ball made their industry a little too futile even for the morning's juvenile pleasure. They set off again to complete their fast-paced circuit, turning a corner and heading in the direction of the cottage and breakfast with those lazy Jenners.

'Hey, Dad?'

'Yeah?'

'How come you don't ask me if I've masturbated?'

''Cause it's none of my business,' Jeff answered without hesitation. 'It's between you and your gear-stick, unless and until you want to share it with me.'

'Gear-stick!' Jet screeched. 'That's even a bit funny, seeing where we are. Not bad, for a change.'

The songwriter sniggered, tweaking the top of the lad's ear until he apologised. 'Whoa! High praise indeed. Did I tell you Don and I were going to the race on our own today? Sorry, mate. Must've slipped my mind...'

His son laughed louder. 'Sure. That's even funnier. Ha, ha, bloody ha!'

'Whatever. But seriously, some things are up to you to tell me. I'm not going to confront you about whether you've had sex either. It'll be between you and the girl.'

The boy's canter became a trot, and then a walk, clearly aiming to get something off his chest. 'I've tried, but I don't think it's working.'

'Ah, yeah? No worries,' Jeff smiled, stopping to put his arm around his son's shoulder and pulling him close. 'Doesn't sound like you're ready. I assure you, you'll know if it's working!'

Tension slipped from Jet's jawline. 'Oh, OK. Cool. It does feel good for a while. But then my erection goes away, and it's just sore after that.'

The kind man ruffled the boy's hair. 'Don't force it, mate. Give it time. You're only thirteen, Jetto. If it's still the same when you're twenty-three, we'll need to talk. That's when it'll be time to intervene!'

'Shit, yeah!' the boy shouted. 'You know what's weird about us being here together?'

'No. What's that?'

'I miss Kizzy.'

'Do you? *Muy buen*,' his father smiled at the abrupt change of tack. 'You wouldn't have said that last year.'

'Yes, I would,' Jet whined. 'You and Mum are away heaps, so it's never strange when you're not around. No offence.'

'None taken, much!'

'I don't miss Kiz when I'm staying at school. But when I'm with either of you, it's like I expect her to be there too. It's weird, 'cause most kids say, "Wouldn't you rather have a brother than a sister?" I never wish I had a brother. Dawson's like my brother.'

Jeff's heart soared, hoping his brain was recording these snippets of conversation well enough for him to replay them to his dream girl. 'Jeez, mate. You're going great guns this morning. It's not weird at all. Well, how should I know? I never had a brother either. Gerry was my Dawson. We felt a sort of fraternity. I don't know how much closer I would've felt towards a blood-brother.'

'Sisternity,' the youngster played with the word on his tongue. 'Sounds like a social club for dunnies!'

'Sisternity?' his dad laughed. 'That's actually pretty good. Better than sibling rivalry. Make sure you tell Kiz about your toilet fetish when you get home, mate. I'm sure she feels the same way.'

Don and Dawson were up and about when the athletes arrived back at the cottage, and Jet took great pleasure in recounting "Mark the Dog" as a monologue, complete with canine colloquia. After another of the rock star's signature "breakfasts of *champignons*", and while the lads had completed a second sweep of their rooms to ensure nothing was left behind, he picked up the receiver to check in with the Melbourne apartment. The sweet sunlight from Kierney's voice pushed his spirits higher still.

'*¡Olá, señorita bellissima! ¿Todos OK allí? Muy bien. Oyes. ¿Puedo hablar rapidamente con la mamá?*'

Handing Don the car keys while he waited for his wife to come to the telephone, Jeff smiled at the sounds of happiness in the background at both ends. Miss Irony's whispers always niggled at his conscience during these moments, reminding him that familial bliss was more than the lost boy deserved, but they were drowned out in no time by his guardian angel's warm greeting.

'Hey!' he crooned. 'Christ, I miss you so much. Thanks, angel. I love you too. Everything OK down south? Exactly. Euphemisms are all the rage here, baby. Ah, yeah... The best night. *Mission accomplie, mon amie.* Yeah. Tell *ya* later. Soon, hopefully. Listen... Will you guys be in town or at *Escondido* tonight? Nice. No, it's perfect. Just cooking up a bit of a plan, that's all. Did last night go well? Great. Sure. Can't wait. Thanks. You too. *Adiós,* gorgeous.'

The foursome sped back to Mount Panorama, eager to secure the best vantage point for the day's racing. They chose a spot halfway up Conrod Straight, and were plagued with autograph hunters for a good half-hour before being left alone in a rather deafening peace.

With the Diamond *duo*'s secret men's business binding them yet closer together, the event's thunderous build-up took on an almost incidental air in comparison to their private milestones. It was as if the teenager had fastened himself to his father's sleeve, choosing coffee over hot chocolate and making an ineffectual play for a cigarette!

Never had Jeff felt so much *simpatico* with this rambunctious rascal, tempted to suggest the pair try to make contact with the supposed extra uncle whose existence the boy's grandfather had let slip on his death-bed. He realised too, with a modicum of spiteful reproach, that any guilt he once harboured for favouring his gorgeous gipsy girl was now expunged.

How delighted Lynn would be at this news! The couple had forsaken their usual telephone *liaison* the night before, and the doting dad's *libido* spiked as he visualised her face. Quite apart from knowing she would be working, they had agreed to reserve Saturday night as a "men only" night. Nothing was to come between her two favourite boys, and indeed nothing had.

The race got underway amid great fanfare. Television cameras from several channels had picked the celebrities out in the crowd during the warm-up and zeroed in for interviews, before eventually allowing them to merge back into the backdrop. Early laps saw the field stretch out, giving the wise father a chance to instigate a few more challenges for Jet and Dawson.

With each test passed with flying colours, Jeff watched his boy's self-assurance grow within a matter of hours until his transformation into outright leader was well on its way. 'You can and must make a few mistakes, guys,' he told the school-friends, 'as long as you own up when it happens and take responsibility to fix the consequences. And you can change your mind too. Your mum and I defy stereotype in that respect; she's naturally stubborn, and I change with the wind. We've taught each other so much over the years about when to be flexible and when to hold our course.'

'What about?' Jet asked.

The intellectual stared into the air, formulating a concise explanation. 'Like being big enough to admit when something you just found out causes you to rethink your point of view. It's important to use your principles when you make a decision. But then it's equally important to make sure your principles are still valid as things around you change. I used to think I stuck to my principles, but it became very clear, with a little nudging here and there, that a lot of the time I didn't.'

The thirteen-year-old chuckled at the great man's shameful expression. 'How come?'

'Ah, y'know... I used them when I felt like it, and sometimes even made 'em up as I went along. Usually for self-serving motives,' the father admitted. 'I was way more of a control freak when I was young, mate. And that's not good.'

'But you always say Mum's a control freak too,' Jet teased. 'Worse than you were?'

'No way,' Jeff smiled. 'Not in a million years. She had her moments. Still does... But we've both mellowed with age; better at knowing how to get what we want from situations. Guys, have you heard the term "due diligence"?'

'Due diligence?' Dawson repeated, turning to his friend. 'What's that?'

'It means you should always do your homework,' Don interjected.

'Homework?' the older boy cried out. 'What's homework got to do with anything?'

The lead pack of souped-up touring cars flashed past, their engines straining as they accelerated out of the bend. Adults and children alike craned their necks to see who was in front, unable to hear the commentary delivered over the tannoy.

'Mobil, I think,' the superstar cupped his ear against the noise. 'Go Brocky! The Skyline's way back, Jetto, sorry to say. Anyway, where was I? Due diligence... Not school homework! It's a figure of speech, guys. Bit like "Don't jump to conclusions." Do your research and find out all the info' you can about something before you make a decision. Risk mitigation. You've heard us talk about that, mate.'

'Yeah. A gazillion times,' Jet groaned. '*Ad* nauseous, or whatever you always say...'

His father sniffed. '*Ad nauseam*. Go on then, fruit of my brainwashing loins, tell us what it means.'

'It means all the stuff you can do so nothing bad happens, to prevent something or avoid it.'

'*Eggzackerly* right, Einstein,' Jeff shook his head. 'And it's about the only thing *Mamá* and Gerry have in common. They're built for being duly diligent. I'm not. I'm crap at it. Way too impulsive.'

'Don't trust what anyone tells you,' Dawson ventured, 'in case they're lying?'

'Yeah, Daws. Pretty much. Or at least learn whom you can trust and whom you can't, and never take things at face value. There's always a back-story, kids. The truth is never quite as obvious as you might think.'

The marathon race concluded under a blanket of thick cloud, deteriorating weather no match for the electric atmosphere of Ford versus Holden. The imported British driver, Win Percy, along with veteran Australian champion, Allan Grice, won the day in their SS Commodore VL, and the *bar mitzvah* crew were plunged into V8 heaven when a Holden Racing Team executive ushered them into prime position to watch the cars cross the finish-line. This was the first General Motors victory in the history of the Bathurst 1000, which engendered mixed reactions in the crowd.

As soon as the winners' presentation was over, with all the usual glitz and glamour of champagne showers and half-naked, leggy blondes, Jeff thanked the sponsors for their hospitality and whisked the others away to the car park. His personal assistant had booked an alternative means of transport to speed the celebrity and his party to Canberra airport, not only to avoid the inevitable crush of everyone trying to leave Sydney at once, but also to give the boys one last treat before they returned to normality the next morning.

'Where are we going?' Dawson asked when they reached their rental car, unsure why he was being handed his suitcase and told to hurry up.

'Surprise!' his mate's dad grinned. 'Wait and see. Got everything, guys?'

He slammed the boot down hard and checked all the doors were locked. The tired but elated band of merry men followed the modern-day Robin Hood through a door marked "VIP", coming face to face with a bank of security guards. Once inside, the Diamonds paused their brief *sojourn* in the real world, leaving the Jenners to chase after them open-mouthed. With fawning officials flanking their path, they marched through the building and out to a waiting helicopter, sleek and black, rotors already whirring and cabin bouncing on its skids.

'Wow!' Jet's breathy utterance spoke for all three. 'Is this for us? Thanks, Dad! This is awesome.'

His father grinned, raising a hand to invite everyone to climb inside. 'No worries, mate. Thought you'd like it. Beats being stuck in traffic for four hours. It's Cathy's fault, so you'll need to thank her next time you see her.'

'Sure! I shall,' the cricketer nodded. 'Abso-fucking-lutely.'

Jeff clipped his son's head of blond hair with strong, musician's fingers. Don listened in, not knowing whether to be amused, angry or offended by this new level of ostentation. Secretly in awe, his grown-up self ought to guard against such measures which would only create more envy in his own children.

'How long does it take to get home in this?' Dawson asked.

His school friend scoffed. 'Ages. We're not going all the way to Melbourne in the chopper, are we, Dad?'

'Nope. We're flying home from Canberra Airport. Getting up to Kingsford Smith'll be a bloody nightmare tonight, so Cath booked us back from there. And I thought we might do a Bowral fly-past in honour of Sir Don.'

'Very sensible,' the other Don approved. 'Thanks for inviting me to your birthday weekend, Jetto! I've never been in a helicopter before, and I've never seen Bradman's old oval either.'

'Dad's just got his licence,' the excitable lad boasted.

The pilot finished his control tower checks and clipped the radio microphone back next to a complicated bank of instrumentation. As the tail lifted, all four passengers' stomachs pitched groundward. Jet's hand slipped into his father's, who pursed his lips and gave the chilled forehead a furtive kiss.

'Are we near Bowral? Wow! I never knew.'

'Have you?' the fifteen-year-old gaped. 'Have you got your own chopper, Uncle Jeff?'

A fleeting self-satisfied fat cat moment gave way to a suggestive grin. 'Abso-fucking-lutely. It's our way of sneaking into the city from the coast. Cool, isn't it, Jetto?'

The helicopter performed a precipitous reverse *pirouette* while ascending into a strong sideways gust and left the ground behind at a most unsettling angle. Hovering for a few seconds about twenty metres above the roof, it executed a sudden clockwise twist and levelled out. The occupants could no longer make out the amazed looks on people's faces down below.

'How come I've never seen your helicopter?' Dawson asked, clutching his belly. 'Where is it?'

'Hidden away from the likes of you two mad gadget fiends,' Jeff scoffed, shaking his head. 'Too tempting, mate. Can't afford to take any risks. I'll take you for a spin one day, maybe in the summer holidays. Or we could go to Phillip Island for the "Moto GP", if you like.'

'Awesome!' the boys shouted in unison.

A weather report showing heavy rain making landfall on the southern New South Wales coast put paid to their *détour* to Donald Bradman's birthplace, nestled in the highlands to the west of Wollongong. The future captain of the national cricket side had visited the country only a few months ago, with its quaint pavillion reminiscent of the sport's motherland and a museum which kept fans fascinated for hours.

Australia's greatest ever batsman was the perfect role model for a child of Lynn Dyson and Jeff Diamond; part thoroughbred and part mongrel. "The Don" was a man who maintained a parallel career as a stockbroker, who never lost his nerve in a crisis and who led the post-war team known as "The Invincibles" to an unbeaten test series against England under a shroud of depression.

Neither boy was too disappointed by the news that their aerial pilgrimage had to be cancelled. There would be plenty more opportunities in the years to come, and their energy levels were dropping fast. Backpacks had been emptied of all remaining grubaceous matter, with Jeff joking that they could land in the car park of a "KFC" or "Hungry Jacks" if they were starving.

The star treatment continued when the travellers reached Canberra. Safely transferred to the Qantas lounge, the Jenners disappeared on a jaunt round the terminal, leaving the Diamonds to while away the last thirty minutes before their flight, exchanging experiences and opinions about the big race in an effort not to fall asleep.

Before too long, their companions returned and presented their host with a gift bag containing an expensive malt whisky.

'Awesome!' Jeff impersonated the teenagers, removing the glossy box and turning it round in his hands. 'You didn't have to get me anything, guys. Thanks heaps though. This'll slip down a treat.'

'Yes, it will,' his son chimed in, snatching the bottle from his father's unsuspecting fingers.

'Oh, no, you don't! This is for real men, not wannabe men,' Jeff extended his right hand towards Dawson. 'It's been fun, and great you could join us on our kooky boys-to-men journey.'

The older lad fumbled, grasping for the large hand. 'Thanks for a great weekend, Jeff.'

'No worries. Thanks to you too, Daws,' the superstar said, before turning his attention to the architect. 'And you, Don. Let's make a date to start this off.'

'You're welcome,' Don replied. 'And you're on! It's pretty cool to get a glimpse of what your life's like. You are really something special, man.'

His neighbour smiled, shrugging off the excessive compliments. 'We're all the same. Better get our shit together. Our substitute brains'll be coming in two minutes.'

'Substitute brains?' Dawson repeated. 'What's that?'

'The airport security dudes,' his friend explained while the teenaged pair headed for the gentlemen's toilets. 'Mum always thinks they treat us like we're not capable of remembering anything ourselves.'

As expected, two uniformed guards turned up a few minutes later, ready to escort their honoured guests to the departure lounge. The national capital's airport being so small, there couldn't have been more than fifty paces between the door of the Qantas Club and the line of ground staff checking passengers' boarding passes. The brevity was almost a disappointment for Don, who was beginning to enjoy being held in such high esteem by his fellow citizens.

Jet and Dawson had a row to themselves, seated behind their fathers. They put on headphones as soon as they had fastened their seatbelts, a trustworthy indication of tiredness. Stooping underneath the overhead locker, Jeff turned round to check on them before the seatbelt sign illuminated.

'You guys OK?' he asked. 'Anything on?'

'Music,' his son's friend shouted.

The celebrity shot an apologetic frown in the direction of the flight attendants, who had been distracted from their checklists. He reached forward and swiped the headphones off the lad's head. Don jumped up too, wondering what his son had done to incur the famous man's ire this time. Jet caught the architect's eye, much more used to controlling the volume of his voice.

'Shhh,' his dad hissed. 'If you want to say something, take these off, please. We're not here to entertain the other passengers, Daws, mate.'

'Can we eat our meal, or are we meeting Mum and Kiz for dinner?' the younger boy asked.

'Sure. Eat if you want. I'm not sure what we're doing tonight. It'll be a while, so *bon appetit*. Now listen, guys... I'd like to say one more thing to you before our weekend's over. Well, two, actually.'

Their shoulders drooping with the idea of having to absorb yet more wisdom, the boys sucked in their frustration and perked up.

'One...' Jeff began. 'I've had an amazing and very rewarding time with you two this weekend. You're great company, and you've impressed me big-time. Both of you.'

'Thanks, Dad,' his firstborn grinned. 'And two?'

Snarling under his breath, the tall musician tilted over the back of his seat and grabbed the metal span of the cricketer's earphones, taking a few strands of hair with it. Jet gritted his teeth, accustomed to his parents' rules for aeroplane *decorum* and knowing full well he was about to be clonked on the head with the puny piece of audio equipment.

'Insolence will get you nowhere,' the comic grimaced when he saw how many blond sacrifices were trapped in his pinched fingertips. 'And two... There's no doubt in my mind that both of you are going to be successful at whatever you decide to do for a job, because you've never had any problem applying yourself. Managing your time across sport, music, school, whatever... What I hope is that you'll do more than apply yourselves. I hope you'll take stock every now and again. Y'know, stop and have a bloody good think about what you're doing and what you're achieving from time to time. Life changes so fast, guys. Keep on top of it. Always be ready to recalibrate if you need to.'

Although a consistent theme with the rest of the weekend, Dawson was not wholly on the same page. This was not Jeff's concern however. The older boy's maturity was Don's problem and none of his business. He would grow into it in his own time. More disconcerting, however, was the shock of seeing himself staring back out of the aquamarine eyes his son had inherited from his mother.

'Thanks, Dad,' the boy smiled. 'I'll remember. All of it. So what are we doing for my eighteenth?'

'Far out! Your eighteenth? Jeez, Jet! *Gimme* a chance to get over this one. Eighteen's a long way off. Don't grow up too fast. Your mum and I can't handle thinking of you as an adult just yet. That'd do my head in.'

The aircraft began to edge slowly backwards, away from the departure gate. Jeff gave the boys a thumbs-up sign and slumped back down into his seat, pleased to be handed a small can of beer by his companion.

Pouring the cold, golden liquid and smacking his lips in anticipation, the philosopher raised his glass. 'To our kids' futures,' he declared, 'wherever they may take them.'

'To our kids' futures,' Don chanted. 'Thanks again for a great weekend.'

'*De nada*, mate,' the humble man replied. 'I've enjoyed it as much as you. More probably.'

Cruising high above the Blue Mountains, the passengers winged their way towards the Victorian border. Jeff unclipped his seatbelt and stood up as soon as the signal was issued. He opened the bulkhead door and delved into his carry-on luggage, reaching down a folder of paperwork and a copy of the recent novel by Gabriel García Márquez, entitled "The General In His Labyrinth".

Don raised his eyebrows as the weighty volume dropped onto the seat beside him. In contrast, he passed the time by leafing through a golf magazine, picked up while shopping for Jeff's whisky. The pair sat in silence until their dinner arrived, the long-haired, unshaven rock star as industrious as ever, and the conservative city slicker chilling out.

'Whoa. Fuckin' 'ell,' Jeff exhaled, pouring a some red wine from the small bottle which accompanied his foil-wrapped delicacies. 'I *gotta* break it to you, mate... All this talk of sex has left me uncontrollably horny.'

Surprised at having been let into this sort of confidence, Don raised his glass again. 'I'll drink to that,' he laughed. 'Me too. You have a very descriptive way with words.'

The songwriter winked. 'Works wonders, doesn't it?'

'What was it? You have to communicate well to fornicate well?'

'Absolutely! All this training's put me in mind of a refresher. Crash course. Will Sue be home when you get back?'

'Yes,' the older man nodded. 'The girls'll have cooked something, I expect. Sue likes to get Mairi cooking. Why? Did you want to do dinner? You could come down to ours.'

'No, mate. That's not exactly what I was getting at,' the larrikin smirked. 'Cheers anyway... My plan is to send the kids out for an hour or two, so that we adults can... Well, y'know...'

'Ah,' Don cottoned on. 'That's an interesting idea. You really practise what you preach, don't you? Does Lynn drop everything for you whenever you ask for it? Lucky bugger!'

'Yes and no,' Jeff shook his head. 'She doesn't drop everything. She used to, before I learned how to restrain my inner wildebeest. Not now though. Far from it. But we never miss a genuine, drop-in-your-lap chance, that's for sure. And tonight presents one hell of a golden opportunity. You OK with the kids going to the movies at Greater Union with Mariette, if we pick them up?'

'All four? I doubt Sue'd be too keen. She'll want Dawson to go to bed early.'

'OK,' the negotiator backed off, raising his hand in a promise not to force the issue. 'You guys work it out. I'll walk our three round to Russell Street and collect them afterwards, so it's up to you.'

The men could hear no sound from the boys behind. They discussed their upcoming working weeks and how Australia might fare against England in The Ashes this coming season. The home team had been in devastating form, and neither thought they were in danger of losing the series.

'You know what, Mister Diamond, sir?' the architect opened, after another lengthy pause. 'I've learned a lot about who I am this weekend, thanks to you.'

'That right? All good then, cheers. Hope it's not too confronting.'

Don let out a caustic laugh. 'Well, yeah... I'm not too sure, to be truthful. I'm beginning to wonder if I'm turning gay, spending all this time with you and liking it.'

The ancient soul smiled. 'That's the Bathurst *bar mitzvah* working its magic, mate,' he offered. 'You're waking up to yourself. I'm sure you'll remember which side you bat for when you find your wife in bed later.'

The Princess And The Warrior

'Thanks, Sue. Delicious as usual. D'you mind if I take a break for a ciggie on the balcony?'

The Jenners had been nervous beyond belief in advance of their old friends' arrival this evening, checking and double-checking with each other on topics which should be tolerable to the widower and his daughter. In fact, they had been surprised to have their latest invitation accepted, what with the murder trial and all the razzamatazz surrounding Jeff's apparent sympathy for the man who extinguished his wife's breath.

'No. You go too, Donny,' the gracious woman replied. 'I'd like to talk to the girls on our own for a second. I'll bring some coffee out in a mo'. There's more dessert too, if you'd like some. Hope it's not still raining.'

Jeff pushed his chair back from the table and went in search of his leather jacket. Slotting one arm into its sleeve and then the other, his nerves steadied as soon as his fingers closed around the cigarette packet and lighter, deep in the left-hand pocket. Kierney was such a polite guest, he smiled to himself. She and Mairi had never had much in common, and no doubt the seventeen-year-old would rather have joined the men outside than face another inevitable inquisition on her father's state of mind.

'You OK?' he asked, leaning over to place a kiss on his daughter's head. 'Come out in a minute, if you want. I'll save you a spot.'

The young woman giggled. 'Cool. I might, thanks. Can I help you take these things out, Sue?'

'Let's put some music on. It's too quiet in here,' Mairi blurted out.

The Jenners' second child made no effort to assist with clearing the table, scraping her chair clumsily across the floorboards without waiting for her mother's permission. The Diamonds shared a sympathetic glance. With Dawson given a leave pass to attend a party at one of his Melbourne University friends' houses, his sister had been churlish all evening.

'Careful! You'll scratch the floor!' Sue snapped. 'Alright, but something decent. And not too loud. Then come and stack the dishwasher, please.'

'Mum! Get off my case! I wouldn't even be here if Aaron's parents hadn't forced him to go to Daylesford with them. For God's sake!'

Kierney locked eyes with her host, both sets of arms laden with dirty plates and cutlery. She crinkled her nose in subtle amusement, unwilling to take sides in the familiar angst-ridden tussle. A Bon Jovi opening guitar riff swept through the apartment in a stroke of pure defiance before the volume was reduced to a more tolerable level.

'I'm sure you don't behave like that in front of guests, do you?' Sue tutted. 'It's not my fault Aaron's out of town. We can leave all this here. We'll do it later. Let's make some coffee and relax. Your boyfriend sounds like an interesting man.'

The student smiled, nodding. 'He is. Very possessive though. I'm in the opposite situation to Mairi. I stood him up tonight!'

Fighting back tears, Kierney thought better of casting herself as whiter than white. What she wanted to say was that witnessing her neighbour's daughter being so rude to her parents made her realise how lucky she was to have a clear conscience in this regard. Mairi might think differently if she were to lose her mother after displaying such antagonism.

'How long's Aaron been on the scene?' she asked instead.

'Oh, not long. Four months or so,' the architect answered. 'Are you alright? Did I say something wrong? You look a bit upset all of a sudden.'

The nimble teenager turned back from placing the condiments into a high cupboard. 'I'm fine, thanks. It sneaks up on me every now and again. Missing mum. All good though. Where does this one go?'

Sue's eyes filled with tears too, sprinting across the kitchen to relieve the youngster of a bottle of olive oil. She slotted it onto a shelf beside the stove-top and pointed her guest towards a laden tray. Kierney picked it up and waited until they were both ready to return to the dining room. Another bout of raucous laughter erupted through the open window, making her feel better. The charismatic showman was on song.

'That's what I wanted to talk to you about,' the motherly woman said. 'Are you having coffee?'

'Yes, please. I'll take Don's and *Papá*'s out to them.'

'Thank you. You're an angel. Mairi, come and sit up, please. Don't just sit there like the world's ending.'

The seventeen-year-old focussed on filling two mugs with steaming coffee while the older girl hauled her backside off the rug as if she had put on thirty kilograms since dessert. Sue patted the surface of the dining table next to her, encouraging her fractious daughter to join them.

'So...' she opened. 'Tell us how you're doing. And how's your brother? Dawson never tells us whether he's heard from him.'

'And not the version you say in front of your dad,' Mairi added, almost scornful, as if she had been primed to ask the question against her will.

Kierney winced. 'It's the same version. Jetto's great, thanks. I spoke to him yesterday. He's swatting for exams, or so he says. It's very cold over there. They've had snow already, apparently.'

Sue chuckled. 'Yes, I've heard that one before. Snow in November? It still sounds so weird for us. And how about you?'

'I'm fine too. Thanks for asking. The worst of the grief's over, I think, and I'm so busy with this uni' project. Only the occasional thing catches me out.'

'Good. We were wondering if you needed some more excuses to get out of the house or anything.'

The well-mannered teenager gulped a mouthful of coffee down, pretending her reaction was brought on by the drink's high temperature. Why did everyone insist she shouldn't spend so much time with her grieving father? She had always loved being in his company when her mother was alive, and they had been admonished by the general public then too. It was doubly annoying that people still considered their bond unhealthy after February's tragedy, when it felt like the most natural thing in the world to cling together.

'I'm out of the house all the time,' she replied with a bright smile. 'And we've got Indie now, so we share the load of dog-walking and everything. *Papá*'s so busy with the book that we often don't see each other for hours, even when we're both at home.'

'You're mates with Nat Svensson, aren't you?' Mairi interrupted. 'She went to my school.'

'Yes. And Paula Hind-McNab. They've been friends since primary school, I think. Nat's so funny. She cracks me up. Do you still see them?'

'Na, not much. Not since I left. Did you see my dad's face when Mum called him "Donny"? He's such a sook around your dad.'

'Mai,' Sue scolded her daughter. 'Stop being so critical all the time. Every family uses pet names for each other. Isn't that right, snuggle-bum?'

Embarrassed, a pathetic growl emerged from the back of the petulant young woman's throat, and she stormed out of the room.

'Good-oh! That's got rid of her,' the mother chided. 'What a wet blanket she is these days. Love! I don't remember being so bent out of shape when I was her age. Anyway... Please let us know if you need any help, Kizzy. We can't begin to imagine how things are. Don't feel you can't ring us, OK?'

'Thanks. I shall. We're coping pretty well, considering... You knew *Papá* was in New York for the last few weeks, didn't you? And he's got his best man duties for Gerry and Fiona lined up too. There's heaps going on. How's work for you? Are you busy?'

Sue's gaze lifted from her drink, unsure whether the seventeen-year-old's level-headedness was contrived. She was her father's daughter after all. Lynn had confided in her years ago that Jeff was a master of manipulation when he chose to be, and they had seen such duplicity many times since her death. Face to face, he certainly wore his heart on his sleeve. She couldn't help but wonder if he and Kierney hadn't schemed up a fraudulent *charade* to hide their anger.

'Me, busy? Yes. Always. I've got a particularly grumpy key stakeholder at the moment.'

The student frowned. 'Oh, that's not very constructive. What sort of project is it?'

'A three-storey office block in Kew. Not too far from the junction,' the architect replied. 'But good try, Miss. I'm not here to talk about my work.'

'Why not? I'm interested. Honestly!'

Sue bit her lip. 'Oh, you're so like your mother. She would've said that too, in exactly the same way. Is your dad really going to write an autobiography for both of them? So soon, I mean? Don't you think it'll be all doom and gloom?'

Kierney chuckled. 'No. Yes, I mean. It's the autobiography *Mamá* never got the chance to write. And it's got way more happy chapters than sad ones. I'm reading bits as he finishes a draft, and I love it. So many great memories. He's having to leave out heaps, otherwise it'd be a thousand pages long!'

'Oh, wow! Everyone'll buy it, I'm sure.'

'I expect so.'

'But is he really ready to write about it all?'

'Am I really ready to write about what all?'

Jeff's tall frame appeared in the dining room doorway, dwarfing his longtime friend. Sue and Kierney jumped, collecting themselves and welcoming their men back to the table. How much had he overheard? Not much, both hoped.

'As ready as I'll ever be,' the philosopher smiled, applying a kiss to his daughter's worried forehead. 'Too much to expect you'd be poring over glossy mags, I s'pose. Or sinking your sixth glass of shampoo behind my back.'

While Sue disappeared to refill the coffee pot, her husband opened the sideboard and pulled out a selection of *liqueurs*. He handed a varied assortment of bottles to the celebrities, who placed them and four tumblers onto coasters swiftly dealt across the polished jarrah.

'We were talking about writing too,' Don teased. 'Shampoo? Fuckin' idiot! Outside in the freezing cold. Roll on summer, eh, Kierney?'

'Oh, yes. I'd be up for a ray or two of sunshine. You sound happy, or are you just off your faces? Did you smoke something?'

Feigning horror that his carbon-copy would suggest such a thing, Jeff raised his index finger to his lips. The lady of the house wasn't to know. She rejoiced in silence, guessing a top-up might be on offer once they returned home. If only Mairi understood the benefits of staying in her parents' good books!

The inebriated host poured whiskies for himself and the impressive rock star whose acquaintance he coveted, before pouring a *Cointreau* for his wife. Looking from father to daughter, his hand hovering over her dearly departed mother's favourite, he was assaulted by his own attack of anguish when both southpaws picked the Bailey's Irish Cream.

'Bloody hell, you guys,' the architect moaned. 'What a fucking travesty! I still can't believe what happened. She's the last person we'd want this world to be without.'

The grieving husband reached a long right arm over to pat his friend's shoulder. 'Well said, mate. Can't argue with that. To Lynn! See you soon, angel.'

While the others toasted the absent star, Kierney watched her father's fingers disappear inside his shirt, slipping between two buttons. 'To *Mamá!*' she whispered, leaning to rub the spot where she imagined his tattoo itching.

Jeff coughed, sitting straight and taking his daughter's hand. He winked at her, cherishing her acceptance of the bizarre ritual which sustained him day after eternal day.

'Where's Mai?' he asked.

'In her room,' Sue responded. 'Sorry she was in such a foul mood. Your young lady is a breath of fresh air. So what were you laughing about out there?'

Both men sniggered like boy scouts hiding pornographic contraband.

'Our trip to Bathurst for Jet's *bar mitzvah,*' the billionaire replied. 'I'm writing about it at the moment. Wanted to make sure I get the facts right.'

'Although neither of us can really remember,' added his partner-in-crime, rocking back on his chair. 'Only that I learned as much as the boys, I think. And the bloody whirly-bird at the end... That was a ripper, mate.'

Kierney was well aware of her father's ambitions for this dinner party, having read the initial paragraphs of the particular episode. She had participated in a three-way telephone call the other day, to capture the essence of her brother's account of this character-building weekend, too young to understand its significance at the time.

'Dawson talks about that trip all the time,' Sue told them. 'Something about playing footy with a dog?'

'Yeah,' Jeff laughed. 'He wasn't even there for that! Jetto's Oscar-winning performance must've been pretty good. I'm stoked he enjoyed it. We set him up a *doozie* on the Saturday, which I still feel guilty about.'

Don shook his head. 'Don't, mate. It taught him a good lesson. Everyone needs to know how to handle themselves when they're falsely accused of something. Happens all the time with customers, doesn't it, Sue?'

'No,' his wife frowned, sarcasm rife in her voice. 'I don't know what you're talking about. Don't remind me about that excuse for a man. What did you do for your *bat mitzvah*, Kierney? That's right, isn't it? *Bat mitzvah* for girls?'

'We made her stand up through twenty-four hours of motor-racing too,' the doting dad joked, pouring himself a second cup of coffee. 'You loved it, didn't you, baby?'

The graceful teenager stifled a yawn, shielding her mouth. Her thirteenth year had been a stormy period indeed. If she were honest, she didn't much care to recall many aspects of attaining her Jewish majority; arguing with everyone, suffering through prejudice and being denied opportunities for all the wrong reasons. Throughout the turmoil, both then and now, her birthday gift had been one of a few highlights which had more than made up for these disappointments.

'I had the best *bat mitzvah* present ever,' she countered. 'And a whole year to enjoy it.'

'Enjoy it?' Don's curiosity was piqued. 'What delights came your way? I dread to think, knowing this man's inventiveness.'

Kierney chuckled. 'Nothing to do with sex, Uncle Don. Sorry to disappoint you. I got to spend a lot of money without getting anything in return. One of many great learning experiences.'

***

'Shit!' Jeff swore, picking up his half-finished glass of grapefruit juice and emptying it down his throat in one go. 'Bloody woman.'

Kierney lifted her nose out of a book. 'What's going on?'

'Sorry, gorgeous,' her father replied. 'She's so effortlessly infuriating, your adorable Auntie Lena.'

The family had been enjoying breakfast together on a quiet Mount Eliza Saturday morning when the rock star's older sister had rung out of the blue. Jet answered the telephone and had been swapping anecdotes with the caller for at least five minutes before his dad saw fit to rescue him. The boy had walked back to the *patio* table looking bemused, shaking his head as he tried to make sense of the bizarre conversation he had shared with his aunt.

There followed a strained, stilted dialogue between brother and sister, in their usual mixture of Spanish and English, one side of which echoed around *Escondido*'s ground floor within full earshot of the rest of the family. Once a certain seriousness of purpose became apparent, Jeff decided he had better retreat to the office to use the kind of language reserved for such a discussion.

'She only wants to sell the apartment to two of her friends and then rent it back off 'em,' he seethed with frustration on his return to the table. 'As a matter of fact, I think she thinks she's already done it.'

'Sold her apartment?' Lynn asked. 'Can she do that?'

'No! Thank Christ for small mercies! She says she *needs* a lump sum to go on a cruise, and she reckons she needs a cruise more than she needs to own the roof over her head,' the songwriter lamented. 'Can you believe it? She's completely clueless. Where's the logic in that? I said, "D'you really think I'd agree to paying rent on a place I've already paid for?" Jesus!'

'And what did she say to that?' the sympathetic woman asked.

110

Jeff roared in a mixture of anger and disbelief. 'Oh, you can probably guess what she said, angel. She said, "You could buy me another one." Sure, Lena. Anytime. What a joke, eh, kids?'

'How much is the cruise?' his son interjected. 'Nowhere near as much as an apartment. Can't be!'

Kierney whistled. 'Some cruise! Round the world six times. Hope she doesn't get seasick.'

The world-changer stood up to fetch his cigarettes from the bench-top. Opening the sliding glass door in advance of lighting up, he doubled back to his children instead, with his hands in a strangling pose. He made straight for the blond teenager's exposed neck, then diverted towards Kierney at the last minute and wrapped her up in a bear-hug.

'So how did you leave it?' his wife smiled at the happy scene. 'What did you mean by "She thinks she's already done it"?'

'Who knows, angel? I'm not sure, to be honest,' her husband turned back from the doorway to reply, cigarette shoved between pursed lips. 'All I know is she saw this cruise advertised somewhere, and that she and a girlfriend want to go on it. Of course, neither of them has enough money. Any money, to be more accurate, I reckon. Then someone called Trim or Trin told her he and his wife'd buy the flat if she's willing to sell it. Hence two and two making forty-nine...'

Lynn chuckled, shaking her head. 'Unrelated? Was it a coincidence?'

'Can't be a coincidence. I bet a few links in the chain've conveniently slipped her mind. Lena's as transparent as they come, and dumb as dog's when it comes to buying and selling stuff. He would've seen how desperate she was to go on this cruise and thought, "Cool! Good bargain to be had here."'

The Diamonds' children stared at each other, having no difficulty envisioning their aunt in a heated discussion with this mysterious trickster. They also knew how hard their father had tried to set his sister up with a comfortable lifestyle and that she rarely showed any gratitude. Even now, after almost two decades of generous fraternal subsidy, she still only made contact if she wanted something.

'The apartment's in Paragon's name, isn't it?' Lynn asked, convinced the billionnaire would have ensured he retained some form of security on the property.

'Certainly is. That's what she's so pissed off about. She thought she had a deal, so she booked the holiday. Now the bloke's come back and said his solicitor's having problems with the title search. Surprise, surprise!'

Janey lumbered in from the sunshine, seeking out a shady spot to rest her weary bones. All four gravitated towards her, Jeff catching both children by the shoulder and keeping them at bay while their mother moved the dog's bed so their beloved pet could see into the garden.

'Don't crowd her,' he crooned. 'She knows we love her. She can hear it in our voices. Good girl, Janey. More coffee, angel?'

'Good girl, Janey,' the youngsters echoed, concern written all over their faces.

Lynn accepted a fresh, piping hot brew, sitting on the floor next to the huge, affectionate ball of white fur. Losing Merak had been tough on the family and George, his rightful owner. When this fully-grown rescued *albina* German Shepherd crossbreed came into their life quite by accident, they had no idea how old she was or what she had been through during her puppyhood. Now approaching the tenth anniversary of her arrival at *Escondido*, the former farm-girl and her sentimental black stallion were prepared for the worst.

Said dark horse slumped down on a kitchen chair and gazed out of the window with tears in his eyes. '"I thought it was *my* effin' apartment, you bastard!"' he whined in an irate, high-pitched impersonation. '"Why d'*ya* say it was mine if it ain't? You better sort it out, *chico*."'

'She didn't say "effing" to me,' Jet laughed, muscling in on the theatrics. 'I got "Your dad's a bloody arsehole. He better bloody well be there."'

The mother dealt their son a kindhearted glare. 'Enough, Jetto,' she warned, before reverting her attention to the annoyed benefactor. 'So Lena wants you to pay for the cruise instead, I'm guessing?'

'Not yet!' Jeff's laugh was laced with mock hysteria. 'It hasn't occurred to her that there might be a "Plan B". She just wants me to let the apartment go for half its value.'

This frightening fact secured Kierney's attention. 'Half?' she piped up. 'That's not a bargain. It's a steal.'

Both parents laughed aloud at the adult turn of phrase.

'You're not wrong there, *pequeñita*,' her father praised.

'Trim gave the price a haircut,' Jet didn't want to miss out on an opportunity for a pun.

Hearing his wife groan, the Sydneysider repeated his earlier intention, this time placing his hands around the lad's neck and pretending to squeeze. 'You're not going to make your fourteenth birthday at this rate, mate.'

'At this rate, mate,' Jet chanted, pleased to find his fingers gaining the strength these days to fight back. 'This rate, mate. This rate, mate.'

'Jesus! I'm surrounded by lunatics,' their dad said through gritted teeth, releasing his hands. 'Janey, save me! I get much more sense from you than I do out of these guys.'

The old girl's tail gave a single appreciative thump, to a round of applause. She lifted her head as if taking a bow. Lynn picked up a piece of bacon rind left on her plate after their breakfast and bent down to feed it to the ailing dog.

'There you go, beautiful. So are you going to pay for the cruise to restore normality, or are you going to make her sweat?' she asked.

'I feel like ignoring her altogether,' Jeff smiled. 'See what happens. Why should I bail her out again? She got herself into this mess. Whoever this Trin guy is, he's already paid for survey reports and all the legal fees. He'll be looking for some redress, no doubt. I'd be none too happy either. He thought it was a done deal. Wasn't 'til the bank recovered the title… or so she says… that anyone noticed the company name on it. It all came tumbling down at this point.'

Three human sympathisers and one loyal canine remained agog, waiting for the story's conclusion. The storyteller abandoned his chair and went to sit on the floor next to his wife, taking her outstretched hand and kissing it.

Fondling the dog's jowls with the other hand, his fingers travelling round her neck and behind her ears, Jeff issued a new set of orders. 'Janey, *écoute-moi…* Your mission is to find Madalena "moronic" Moreno and lick her into submission. *D'accord?* No more Miss Nice-Dog. I mean it. She's cactus, old girl. Cact-*us*!'

'Well, for what it's worth, she's lucky you didn't put it in her name,' the blonde singer told her husband. 'It'd already be gone by now if you had. Did you tell her that?'

'No point. She wasn't in the mood for listening. I said I'd ring her back tomorrow. "But I need the money, *chico*." *Sayonara*, Lena. Click, *brrrrr…*'

The latest shrill characterisation made everyone dissolve into laughter once more. Kierney put her hands over her ears, and Lynn did the same for Janey.

'You hung up on her?'

***

Jeff knocked on his daughter's bedroom door, holding the piece of paper Lynn had handed him as soon as he returned home. 'Kizzy, may I come in, please?'

'*Bien sûr, Papá,*' a cheerful voice answered.

The traveller surveyed the large space, which became more and more like a fortune teller's caravan every time he entered its inner *sanctum*. There were swathes of heavy fabric in earthy tones looped from each cornice, lamps with bulbs of different colours everywhere and flickering candles on most surfaces.

Books, records and a plethora of dark-coloured clothing were artfully housed all in the correct places, and myriad pictures adorned the walls: pop stars, sporting heroes, Greek and Egyptian gods, a number of African figures and Indian *yogi*. What kind of new age, cosmopolitan global citizen were they raising in this peaceful house by the seaside?

The eleven-year-old was in the middle of her homework, with a rock radio station playing right next to her ear. The visitor sat down on the bed and leaned over to check out some of the text books which were strewn all over the *duvet*.

'Sorry to interrupt,' the adoring father began, flicking through a copy of Molière's play, "Tartouffe". '*Celle-là te plaît?*'

'*Ah, oui,*' Kierney replied. 'It's hilarious. Cheeky. Did you do it at school too?'

'No, but I borrowed it from the library on someone's recommendation. It is funny, and there are some sound messages in it too. I wouldn't mind reading it again. D'you need it tonight?'

'No. Take it,' the girl invited. '*Whassat* you got?'

Her dad smiled at the childish expression their children refused to leave behind. 'This 'ere's why I'm interrupting you. *Mamá* gave it to me just now, when I got home. It's a letter from school.'

'Oh, sugar!' she pulled a frightened face. 'What've I done?'

'I don't know. What have you done? You sure look guilty all of a sudden,' Jeff laughed, wiping a kiss across her flushed cheek. 'Time to confess your sins, my child.'

The conscientious student giggled and held her hand out to see the letter, pouting when it was snatched from her grasp before she could take hold.

'*Pas encore,*' her father shook his head. 'I want to talk to you first, then I'll let you read it.'

Becoming suspicious, the youngster shrugged. 'Whatever… Talk away.'

The negotiator had flown in from another round of peace talks in the south of France, excited to be back *en famille* after a fortnight overseas. He made himself comfortable on his daughter's bed and patted the mattress beside him. With minimal hesitation, Kierney sprang from her chair, sitting cross-legged and cuddling into her beloved *papá*, pretend guilty conscience having vanished without a trace.

'It's from Missus Nash,' Jeff announced.

'English.'

'*Sí. Cierto.* And it's a heart-warming letter written about a heart-wrenching poem.'

Kierney inhaled in immediate recognition. '"The Princess and the Warrior",' she guessed. 'Missus Nash told me she loved it. I got a high mark for it too.'

'Yeah. You don't say!' the songwriter said, squeezing her shoulder. '*Mamá* and I both cried when we read it. It's a masterpiece. I am so proud of you, Kizzo. It's a work of art, as a poem or a song. Truly.'

'*Muchas gracias.* I'm stoked you like it.'

'Oh, I like it. Love it. But I do have a question. Several questions, in fact.'

'Mmm?' Kierney impersonated her grandmother with pitch-perfect accuracy.

The quadruple Grammy winner laughed aloud. 'First question is, "Are these the same princess and warrior you brought me when I had malaria?"'

'Yes!' she answered, thrilled her dad remembered. 'I thought you fell asleep on me that day.'

'I did, *pequeñita*,' Jeff admitted, 'but not as soon as you think. You slunk away a few minutes after you finished singing. I remember hearing the bedclothes rustle. I must've been right on the edge of consciousness, otherwise I would've stopped you and asked you to read it again.'

Tears welled up in the girl's eyes, her mind transporting her back to the Christmas her father had come home from Africa with more than his usual post-trip blues. She had been determined to cheer him up, turning to her mother for ideas. Lynn responded in her typical encouraging way, suggesting she tell their idealist and invalid insomniac a fable of all-conquering love.

'The lyric's changed a bit since then, but yes. Basically the same. *¿Por qué, Papá?*'

'*¿Por qué?*' he echoed, raising his voice. '*Porque,* my fifty-two-year old angel, you told me this story eighty years ago.'

Kierney nodded, slapping her fingers to her cheeks in delight. She always loved when her intrepid aeronaut played with temporal numbers this way. From as early as her childhood memories would take her trekking through her own time-span, she had been mesmerised by her parents' rocky road to romance. Only one idea sprang to mind when her teacher set them a poetry assignment, and the verses had tumbled through her in a surge of artistic productivity.

'Yes, I did. Second question?'

'Not yet,' Jeff shook his head, receiving a peck on the lips from his favourite schoolgirl. 'I want to know how much the back-story morphed since the original?'

Kierney's eyes focussed on the bedroom wall as she tried to remember. 'Not too much. The language obviously, 'cause I know way more interesting words now. But not the main theme. I've been tweaking it at the edges for ages.'

'*¡Excelente!* That's mind-blowing,' her dad sighed, shaking his head, ''cause *Mamá* remembered me describing your first rendition, and it freaked her out that you had such dark thoughts going on at such a young age. And that you captured our moods from that time so perfectly despite not even being conceived yet.'

The poem in question was submitted as part of a creative writing assignment after spending more than five years fermenting. A fusion of both her parents' songwriting techniques, the girl's unconventional style comprised most of her father's passion and little of his impulsiveness, married with her mother's perfectionist engineering.

Its verses spoke of pre-destined love pitched head-to-head with conflicting positions in society, symbolised in modern-day Australian folklore by the immortal, class-spanning romance. With the famous child's inside scoop adding the spice of ages past, the pain which leeched from between the lines was intoxicating.

'Dark thoughts? Oh, not again... I wondered if this might be the real issue,' Kierney half-smiled. 'There must be more than *"Bravo, pequeñita,"* to make you come up here instead of waiting 'til dinner or something.'

'Right,' her father nodded. 'Well, *bravo, pequeñita*, by the way... And that's such a Lynn Dyson thing to say. There's no issue, Kiz, if you think there's no issue. We're not worried about you.'

'But?'

The superstar's gaze burrowed into his daughter's mind, followed by a hand raised in warning. 'You know what the "but" is... At least, I hope you do. *Mamá* and I'd be pretty lousy parents if we constantly assume we know what's going on with you guys while you're growing up. D'you know what I mean?'

Kierney shuffled sideways over the sheets until the pair was no longer touching. 'I know what you mean, but why can't you just tell the school to leave us alone?'

'I will, baby!' her greatest ally insisted. 'I came up here to talk to you about how great the lyric is.'

'OK. Thanks, *Papá*, but that's not all you're here for, is it? School doesn't need to check up on me. You *do* know it's make-believe? So what if it's dark for a kid? It's not the first time, and I don't want to write normal stuff; all puppies and kittens and happily ever after.'

Jeff couldn't help laughing. 'Hey! Hold your horses, Joan of Arc!' he said, keen to diffuse her ire. 'This is me you're shouting at. I get it. Completely, alright? Don't get all hyped up. I love this lyric, and your *mamá* does too. We just need to make sure no ghosts and ghouls are lurking inside you that we need to help you vanquish.'

'Trolls, you mean.'

'Sure. Trolls too. If you can tell me this imagery isn't masking any harmful stuff that's troubling you, I'm done. One of us'll ring Missus Nash tomorrow and stick it to her.'

The eleven-year-old shook her head, giggling at the silly expression. 'No! There aren't,' she groaned. 'I love being me. I love you and *Mamá*, and even Jetto. Well, usually... They need to know I like dreaming up fantasy stories, that's all. They should expect it with an ancestor like you.'

'Ancestor? Jeez! Makes me sound way too old, but I know what you mean.'

'It's just like the news,' the impassioned artist reasoned. 'Some bits are happy, and then other stuff's sad or makes you angry. I promise I'll write a happy poem for Missus Nash next week, to stop her worrying and writing you letters that look like a gold star at first, but then end up being evil meddling when you get into them.'

Jeff raised both hands in front of his face as if he thought he were about to receive a slap across the face, before tipping over to curl his fingers around his daughter's waist. 'Now *basta, basta, señorita crítica!* It's not evil to care about someone's state of mind,' he said, kissing her forehead. 'But I do know what you mean. My school did the same to me, heaps of times, so it's weird for me to hear this coming from you.'

'So why *"basta, basta"*?'

'Because you need to give people the benefit of the doubt.'

'Why? They don't give me the benefit of the doubt.'

Her dad sighed, the lost boy inside screaming through the young woman's words. 'Come on... You know why. And that's me giving *you* the benefit of the doubt while I'm listening to your obstinacy. You can't expect people to know what makes you tick. We all make our best guess about others until we know better. I understand your frustration. That's what I said to *Mamá* and how we'll respond to Missus Nash. We're on your side, Kizzy, but it doesn't hurt to check. Her or us, eh?'

The girl murmured her agreement.

'And hey, who knows? One day, you might be grateful for people interfering in your life... What if something happened to you at school that you can't tell us, like bullying? Or worse? I hope we never get to the stage where you can't tell us stuff, but sometimes things happen that we internalise. They keep growing and festering inside us until life gets out of control. Jesus, baby... It happened to me often enough, and I don't want to see you in those dark places.'

The tears in her father's eyes persuaded Kierney to give the world a second chance. 'I'm sorry, *Papá*. I didn't mean to get angry. I know what you're saying, but that won't happen to me.'

'I hope to hell it doesn't,' Jeff replied, 'but it could if we're not careful. We can't protect you twenty-four seven, can we? Even between *Mamá* and me, Jetto, and all the "G"s and everyone else... I hate having to say this to you, but we can't guarantee any if our safety a hundred percent. *Mamá* and I need to be able to rely on others watching over you.'

'You didn't have anyone to watch over you,' the eleven-year-old said, cuddling into his bulky frame. 'That's why you kept things inside, I know. I can't think of anything I wouldn't be able to talk to you about.'

'*Bueno*,' Jeff smiled. 'That's perfect. So what are you buying me for Christmas?'

'*Argh!* I'm not telling you that,' the girl groaned, trying to wriggle out of his grip. 'I promise I'll tell you everything except what I'm buying you for Christmas, OK? You have to go now. There's homework to do. I don't have time to chat.'

Jeff released his trainee temptress, watching her slither off the bed and straighten her clothes. Pre-teen conflict was evident in her every act, resisting an inherited natural inclination towards grace and similitude. His heart's vacillations alternately filled with pride and flushed by protectiveness, he knew they hadn't even crossed the start-line of her race for independence.

If today's dilemma was typical of the emotional overload a father faced before a daughter's puberty, he had a steep hill in front of him. He must increase his capacity to deal with a whole lot more angst in years to come; both hers and his! And although Jet's journey to greatness would be far more straightforward than his sister's, the parents were awakening to the need for supplementing the usual vigilance with an element of clairvoyance.

'You've got some nerve,' the musician teased. 'What homework've you got?'

'History,' Kierney replied, turning back to her desk and retrieving her school diary. 'Really interesting... How the women's rights movement started in Australia.'

'Great! Any particular angle?'

The studious child handed her notebook over, sitting down and sipping from a glass of water. She hoped the man who valued learning so highly might stay and dispense some of his limitless knowledge on social justice issues. The likelihood was low today, since he had only recently arrived home and was due to fly out again the following afternoon. She remembered her mother mentioning a conference call with an African aid agency after dinner too.

'Y'know...' Jeff finished reading the discussion brief, his face lined with thoughtfulness. 'I reckon I did pretty much the exact same essay back in the dark ages.'

The eleven-year-old's eyes lit up. '*Mamá* told me. Have you still got it?'

''Xpect so, yeah. I remember being intrigued by where the word "suffrage" came from. D'you want me to see if I can find it?'

'Oh, yes, please! That'd be fantastic. Only if you've got time.'

'We've got some time before we eat, *pequeñita*. Half an hour'll get you started anyway, I'm sure. Wait there...'

Kierney would have jumped up and hugged her dad if he hadn't turned tail and legged it down to the storeroom. Serendipity at work, she imagined him thinking; a chance to dispel any residual negativity from the original purpose of his visit and make them both feel better about the world.

Sure enough, Lynn's enquiring eyes met an impish grin and a thumbs-up from her husband as he flashed past the study doorway. What was he up to now? The conversation with their precocious poet must have gone well. She decided to ignore his industry, curious to hear the sound of filing cabinets opening and closing in quick succession. An update served with dinner and a glass of red was always worth the wait with her matching brace of scheming savants.

Stopping on the way for a kiss, Jeff patted his dream girl on the head with a beige exercise book sporting bent corners and with half its spine peeling back. 'You remembered this?' he breathed against her cheek. '*Je t'aime, mon amie.*'

Father and daughter spent the following forty-five minutes in tempestuous discourse, one minute in compassionate agreement and the next locking horns as the intellectual advocated for the devil in the face of his opponent's storming *naïvetée*. Paragraphs were written and re-written through tears, and a page of notes was torn out and abandoned amid whoops of joy until the essay was complete. She took great care in transcribing the escapades of such luminaries as Mary Lee, who had migrated from Ireland to South Australia to push her adopted state to give the female population a voice at the political table.

The young artist, herself no stranger to publicity by dint of her birth, was charmed to discover her hometown had also been significant in securing Australian women the right to vote. Melbourne's heroines were Henrietta Dugdale, pioneer of the "Woman Movement" in eighteen-seventies' Victoria, and Donna Dexter, famous for bringing bloomers from the UK to Australia to wear under her scandalous trousers.

Kierney also marvelled at the courage of Vida Goldstein and her Sydney counterpart, Louisa Lawson, two more inspiring figures who were writ large. She recounted their stance during Federation, and anger simmered within her heart that it had taken a further six decades for Aboriginal people of either gender to enjoy the same rights.

'"*Suffrigium*",' Jeff rolled his best comic Latin accent. 'It was originally a verb: to support. And I think it can also mean you're eligible to be a political candidate.'

'Run for Parliament?'

'Yep. Active rather than passive suffrage. Does that make sense? You can passively vote or actively campaign for a cause or a party. Same verb, endless confusion. Welcome to the crystal-clear world of adulthood, *pequeñita*! And I need a cigarette while you finish it off.'

Kierney shook her head and sighed. 'So do I.'

'Ah, yeah? Nice try, but I think not. I'll leave you in peace now, but I just wanted to say one more thing about Missus Nash's letter.'

'Mmm?' Marianna Dyson made another *cameo* appearance in the evening's performance.

Laughing involuntarily for a second time and making for the hallway, the exasperated teacher dropped his left hand until the offending article slapped across the leg of his pants. '"She crashed through a door that she'd slammed in her own face only moments ago,"' he recited, pointing to the end of the third verse. 'D'you know how powerful an image that is?'

Kierney erased her cheeky grin and nodded in gratitude.

'Them's potent words, *pequeñita*. And "in love with the solitude that scared her half to death,"' Jeff added. 'This lyric's the work of a great writer, Kizzo. Really it is. Don't lose that compelling sense of urgency, and don't ever stop expressing yourself honestly. We'll back you, baby. Every way we can.'

'Thanks, *Papá*. I shan't,' the youngster vowed. 'I'm glad you like it. I'll turn it into a song. I already have a melody idea.'

The chart-topper shifted to one side and picked up a pen from his daughter's desk, placing it into her outstretched left hand. 'Cool. Get on with your homework,' he ordered, kissing her forehead, 'then get dressed in your polka-dot skirt and pink slippers and come down for dinner. We'll help you write that song on the weekend. *Te amo.*'

'*Te amo, Papá.*'

***

Christmas nineteen-ninety saw "Diamond Fever" reach its highest pitch yet. On top of their incessant concert tours, Lynn and Jeff were inundated with offers of work, public appearances, after-dinner speeches and photo-opportunities galore. Such was the call for their presence that they regularly vied with each other for the fans' attention, popping up on rival channels at the same time.

Furthermore, their workload yielded gratuitous benefits for the many artists whose careers had been given wings from within the Stonebridge fold. Often too busy to record and tour with their own musical material, the prolific composers donated part-baked offerings to other singers and songwriters around the world, furthering their aim of charitable symbiosis.

Nothing could dilute the magic in the Midas couple's relationship. Absences were habitual these days, sometimes stretching further into the future than either deemed bearable, and yet the all-consuming joy of reunion nourished their bodies and souls back to full health at every opportunity. Friends and family peppered conversations with commentary on the superstars' enduring intimacy, and the odd wisecrack found its way into the newspapers from showbusiness associates wondering if their happiness was nothing but an elaborate, money-grabbing scam.

Even the lovers themselves were enchanted by the ease with which their two complicated careers melded with the demands of a plethora of commercial interests and charitable causes, not to mention the children's diverse pursuits, to form a most unique and extraordinary life. Fulfilled beyond measure, spending the festive season at Benloch gave the ancient souls ample opportunity to deposit Jet and Kierney with their cousins and steal away for some Coldwater Creek revitalisation.

Jeff had racked his brains during the months preceding the couple's fifteenth wedding anniversary, determined to find a unique and extraordinary way to celebrate. With the way their marriage had gathered pace and climbed from initial high to ever higher, it would be a challenge to present his beautiful best friend with an adequate testament to their love.

Celebrating in full view of their adoring public, the superstars sought special dispensation to miss the Dysons' New Year's Eve party, usually a convenient occasion to encapsulate their anniversary with minimal fuss. Instead, they arranged their own shindig at a Melbourne hotel.

The showman decided on a ten-course *dégustation à deux*, crafted from his wife's favourite dishes by a chef of international repute. He even went as far as designing a formal invitation. The wording was chosen with equal care by the leading man and his loyal office manager, who had waxed lyrical at the idea, telling her boss and the rest of the team that she wished her husband were half as romantic.

Cathy's unfailing efficiency delivered the printed summons in a weighty gilded and embossed envelope, tucked between the usual aggregation of fan-mail and official correspondence. Opened two days later, the gesture elicited the desired response from its recipient, observed from a safe distance by its orchestrator.

'What's this?' he heard her ask Janey, as if the ailing dog would have a clue.

The family were on borrowed time with their faithful rescued white Shepherd, and Lynn had taken to working in the kitchen to minimise the number of times the animal had to be disturbed. Incontinent and no longer able to eat standing up, Jet and Kierney took turns at holding her food or drink bowl under her chin.

'Looks posh, doesn't it, Janey-girl?' the lady of the house said again, flipping the envelope over and tearing it open with care.

Smoking on the deck, Jeff's mind was cast back to their getaway weekend in Edinburgh in nineteen-seventy-five, when a hung-over, healing rock star had proposed to a sexy, blonde tennis player upon her return from winning the US Open.

Now, as they had then, the sportswoman's eyes filled with tears as she scanned the invitation's simple message.

"31st December 1991, Lynch's restaurant at 7pm,

Jeff Diamond

passionately, lasciviously and affectionately requests

an evening of ultimate pleasure with the intoxicating company of

Lynn Dyson Diamond

to celebrate the fact that I have only been married to the world's
most beautiful woman for fifteen years, and feel this is not nearly long
enough to know you or to love you completely.

And afterwards for breakfast at the Grand Hyatt Hotel with our
wonderful children, who have made this marriage into a family beyond
my wildest dreams.

RSVP in whichever way you see fit, angel."

Lynn said nothing more to the dog, nor to the man loitering on the verandah. Leaning on the railing by the steps down into the pool, he watched as the invitation was slotted back into its envelope and placed on the table among the piles of pending paperwork. Moments later, after downing what remained of a cup of tea, she left her seat and gave Janey a gentle scratch behind the ears.

Had she forgotten he had nipped out for a cigarette? The old dog lifted her head as her master entered through the sliding doors, and he bent down to make a fuss of her too. Nimble footsteps made light work of the staircase, causing his blood pressure to rise. His body wanted to follow, but his mind persuaded him to stay downstairs.

Fifteen years ago, such an offhand reaction to one of his so-called statements would have thrown the lost boy into a whirlpool of panic and insecurity. Not today however. The industrious renegade had been found by his *regala*, and the wise man she helped him become had seen her moved to tears by a love letter. Her neutral attitude surely foreshadowed a response under construction.

Already aroused, spurred on by fantasies of the morning's training attire being substituted by lacy *lingerie* or less. He knew his former anxiety-ridden self should have paid more attention to his lower brain than the one in his head in those testing times. Following judgement's obstinate lead in baby steps, he had learned to trust in their relationship beyond all doubt, and he was consumed instead by a yearning impossible to ignore.

But ignore it he must, Jeff decided. He poured a fresh cup of coffee and installed himself in the office to deal with papers submitted for an upcoming Paragon Holdings Board meeting, pressing a button on his new, hi-tech telephone to activate the speaker. He hoped that a few minutes spent discussing pros and cons hidden between the lines of numbered paragraphs would restore his sexual equilibrium to a level worthy of someone about to celebrate fifteen years of marriage. He made a vain attempt to concentrate while Gerry outlined cost-benefit analyses of the companies' various ventures, interspersed with unpalatable but instrumental dollar signs and the liberal application of trailing zeros.

All to no avail! When his manager signed off with a typically distasteful joke, the "Pause" button on the Chairman's *libido* automatically released, putting him right back where he had started. His wandering imagination had encouraged Lynn to join him in the Diamonds' Mission Control, whence she had remained tantalisingly close and oblivious to his presence.

After another five minutes had gone by with no sign of his aloof goddess, today's game of cat and mouse lost its appeal. There was only so much anticipation a red-blooded male could withstand, and he had long since admitted defeat in the face of limits set by a siren whose whole life had been controlled by stretch targets. Jeff climbed Escondido's magnificent curved staircase, heartbeat echoing in his ears.

Jet and Kierney were both down on the beach with friends, making the most of a perfect surfing day. The house was empty barring Janey and the family's three inscrutable felines, who padded around like ghostly inspectors. He gave the door to the master bedroom a gentle push, expecting to find Lynn inside.

Wrong again! The only clue as to his lover's whereabouts came from a small, yellow sticky-note on his pillow: "Showtime."

'Yes,' Jeff hissed through pursed lips, kissing the piece of paper and feeling his insides surge with renewed energy. '*Gracias, Regala.*'

Rubbing his erection through his jeans to stoke the fire, the thirty-eight-year-old teenager ducked into the *en suite*. He shook a few drops of after-shave onto his palms and watched the man in the mirror slap his beaming face before cantering down the stairs again. His son's patented socks with sliding superpowers spirited him across the entrance hall's white marble tiles, stopping to catch his breath at the doors to the function room.

The boy from Sydney's downtrodden south-west was still regularly amazed that he could afford to own such a luxurious home, and crossing the threshold of this spacious *salon* during the day felt somewhat out-of-bounds. Since the children graduated from primary school and no longer entertained their parents with childish plays and musical *extravaganzas*, the Diamonds had all but annexed this impressive room from their everyday life.

This morning was beginning to live up to decidedly abnormal expectations, the billionnaire smiled as he glanced at his watch. How long did they have before a telephone call, a visitor or a returning child would disturb them? Long enough for what he had in mind!

The grand piano's dust-cover had been turfed off into an ugly red-brown, tarpaulin sculpture of *Uluru*, and stirring chords added to the surreal atmosphere. He slipped through the half-open door and feasted his eyes on the sights and sounds of his dream girl making sweet music in her own effortless style, wearing a black, silk teddy with tiny red roses, the skin of her slender arms and legs tanned and radiant, and thick waves of blonde hair loose over her shoulders.

Lynn looked up and smiled when she sensed his presence. 'What took you so long?' she asked. 'I almost outsourced.'

Her husband leaned against the piano, determined to take their time. His eyes transfixed in hers, he lost himself in a melodious babbling brook evoked by his very own *virtuosa*. With both upper and lower brains focussed on actions rather than words, all he could do was shrug, unable to conjure an appropriate retort.

Grinning, the pianist tossed her hair back off her face, changed to a minor key and slowed the *tempo* to introduce a new ballad. She began to sing, beckoning for her handsome audience to sit beside her. No longer so impatient now the seductive reply to his invitation was underway, he took a seat on the piano stool and slipped his right hand between her naked thighs.

Lynn leaned leftward against her man's strong torso and accepted a kiss, giggling as her words disappeared down his throat. 'Thanks. Lynch's for dinner on Monday. I love you so much, Jeff.'

'I love you too,' he whispered, running tingling fingertips along the line of her bra strap, pausing as he entered the valley between her soft, supple breasts before inching back up the left-hand side until he could lift her chin and lock their mouths together.

The words of this particular song had been written six months ago but saved for their special occasion. They spoke of never-ending passion in a life which got better and better with every passing day, sentiments often uttered by both musicians and woven into the fabric of their partnership.

To her delight, the rock star lifted his wife's hands off the keys and began to play a variation on her theme, a complementary lyric materialising as they sang. She unbuttoned his shirt and slipped her hand inside to fondle the hairy skin over his tattoos, eliciting a groan of absolute pleasure.

Jeff Diamond told Lynn Dyson how he had forgotten what loneliness felt like and that it had been replaced by a jet-stream of inspiration which pushed him ever upward. The song made them both cry until the front of his shirt looked as if it had been caught in a spring shower.

'Thank you,' the world-changer whispered once their combined emotional vocabulary was exhausted. 'That's quite an RSVP. Couldn't you have tried a little harder?'

Leaning back and frowning, Lynn objected. 'Not good enough? Do you want it in writing?'

'No. I want it in bed.'

'Oh, OK,' came a flirtatious reply. 'What, now? Be my guest! But make it snappy 'cause I'm cold in the air-con'.'

His own body temperature well into the red zone, the caring man noticed goosebumps on his beautiful best friend's arms. Standing up, he offered a chivalrous hand to help her to her feet, lifting her shimmering black robe off the lid of the piano and holding it out like a matador's cape. She paused in front of him, pressing her tattooed left shoulder against his chest until their "JL" symbols fused together until the satin shivered its way in between.

'Oh, that feels amazing,' she murmured, succumbing to the delights of his arms wrapping the cloak around her and his hemmed-in erection thick and stiff against her buttocks. 'How come you're always so warm? Take me upstairs. I want you as much as you want me.'

'Impossible,' Jeff chuckled. 'And it's "hot", baby. Less "warm", more "hot".'

The couple sprinted across the hall and bounded up the steps two at a time, reaching the top in a breathless dead heat. To her astonishment, instead of coaxing her onto the bed, Lynn's efforts to undress her muscular companion were thwarted by his endeavours to position the electric keyboard for another recital.

'What are you doing?' she gasped. 'See? I want you *more* than you want me!'

The athlete forced her way between musician and instrument, tugging his jeans down to his angles and threading his penis through the fly of his shorts. His conviction sorely tested, he uttered a low moan when her tongue wrapped around the engorged tip, pulling her jaw backwards until her mouth let go and the huge organ flicked the end of her nose.

Both musicians dissolved into laughter, grateful for the momentary lapse in lovemaking fury. The lace-clad blonde stood behind her balladeer while his dark chocolate baritone coughed into action. Deft fingers did their best to mask excessive treble from the outdated keyboard which had serenaded many a poignant private encounter.

'This one's called "Original",' he announced. 'I started writing it while we were in Rio.'

'At the *Mardi Gras*? Oh, wow. That was a while ago.'

Jeff nodded, expanding his chest and giving into a relaxing shoulder massage. He had been waiting so long to sing this song and, grimacing each time the tinny bass notes spoiled the allusion, delivered it with all the fervour of a Mississippi Baptist minister.

Before he could finish the last chorus, Lynn twisted the volume knob in a slow fade, took her minstrel's hands off the keys and enticed him towards the bed. Her satin robe slithered to the floor on command, and they fell in a happy heap onto the sheet, sharing memories of their trip to the Brazilian *festa* while they treated each other's senses in delirious raptures.

Twice interrupted by the telephone ringing next to their heads, first Lynn and then Jeff denied the distraction, expecting to hear their housekeeper come through the front door at any moment.

'Jesus, this is so damned good. We should do this more often, angel.'

LORRAINE PESTELL

Ahead Of Our Time

Dan sat back for a second, his spine aching after ten minutes of Facetime with Freya. She seemed pleased to hear from him, and he wished he had summoned the courage before now. Three weeks had passed since he received confirmation of his scholarship to The Good School. Last year's winner was eager to help, giving him ideas for his speech and tips on cheap places to stay in Boston.

The young artist had been nervous too, reverting to cold Massachusetts winters and the layout of MIT's campus whenever their conversation faltered. Little did either student know about the secrets they kept close to their hearts. Did she feel as drawn to open up as he did? Was he game to tell this mysterious woman the truth?

'Are both your parents Scottish?' the Brisbane native asked.

'*Auch, aye,*' the shy social worker laughed in the broadest brogue he could muster. 'Me mam's from a town called Cumbernauld, which is north-east o' Glasgow, about halfway to Stirling. We live in Partick, in the dumpiest district, quite a long way from the university. And I think Dad stays in Dundee now. He's not been in our lives since I was real wee. Young, I mean.'

'Oh, I see. I love your accent. I haven't spoken to many Scottish people. Americans aren't very good at understanding strong accents, by the way. You'll be frustrated when you get here, always having to repeat yourself.'

'Ha! Kierney told me that too,' Dan replied. 'I get blank looks even wi' English folk. It's fine. I speak quietly too, so I'm kind o' used to it. Your dad was from Sri Lanka, was he no'? Have you been there? Sounds pretty exotic.'

Freya paused. Certain details of her past were common knowledge since her art began to appear on gallery walls, yet she still found these truths difficult to acknowledge. When she first saw a picture of the the boy to whom she was handing over The Good School's reins next month, it gave her the impression that he was a kind soul. Maybe he wouldn't jump to such inconsiderate conclusions about her father.

'*Auch, aye!*' she repeated, her face reddening again. 'No, I've never been there. He was a refugee; came to Australia by boat. Really dangerous, and he nearly died getting there. Sri Lanka was more dangerous though. He was a Tamil and grew up in a war zone basically.'

'God, that's enough to make anyone... Well, I know he took his own life. I hope you don't mind me sayin'.'

'No, I don't mind. It saves me from telling you. People... you know... He never recovered from the time he spent at sea, and later in a detention centre for asylum seekers. My mum used to be sympathetic, before they got married. She's a social worker too, like you, but without a degree and all the other amazing stuff you've done. But then he got too violent, and she despised him after a while. But you don't want to hear all this. How about your mum? What does she do?'

'Oh, not much,' the ambitious Glaswegian answered. 'I *do* want to hear it. Ev'ry fam'ly's got its problems. Mines definitely does! Mam's just got a boring cleaning job. She's bitter about *ma* dad too, so we've got that in common. Is your connection dodgy? My screen keeps flickerin' on and off.'

Freya felt a little nauseated as she watched Dan's face wobble up and down and from side to side as he fiddled with his iPad. 'You're making me sea-sick. It's fine at my end. Have you got a partner?'

'No!' the young man dropped his tablet computer onto the desk in fright. 'Have you?'

'No. I mean, that's good,' she snapped. 'You won't have to leave anyone behind then. You won't be broken-hearted like Lynn and Jeff were when you come to the US. Do you like Dan or Danny? Not Daniel?'

An eerie atmosphere had descended on the student's bedroom, as if someone had crept in and was hovering over his shoulder. Was the Queenslander suggesting what he had wondered all along? Either they were both totally insane or...

'Either's fine. My first name's not Daniel actually,' he heard himself say. 'It's a long story.'

'OK. That's cool. I like long stories. Sorry if I embarrassed you. I'm interested in people who aren't like me.'

'Me too. It's alright. I'm not used to talkin' about mysel'. Try to avoid it, honestly. Way too complicated for most people. Anyway... Have you been to Melbourne? Been on the "ALS" tour?'

Current and future worldly scholars, both funded at the expense of the Diamonds' legacy, burst out laughing at the reference to their shared obsession. Kierney had joked during a recent three-way conference call that unofficial meet-ups happened on a regular basis on her parents' old turf; sometimes a diversion from the normal winery stops in the Mornington Peninsula to peer through the gates of *Escondido*, or otherwise a pilgrimage to Benloch, only to be turned away by security guards stationed outside Bart and Marianna Dyson's homestead.

'Totally!' Freya rocked forward and almost bumped her nose on the screen by mistake. 'No. Seriously, I haven't. I'd like to, maybe when I get back. I did go to Sydney a day early before I flew out here. I got the train to Fairfield and went to the Stones Road.'

'Oh, wow! Did *ya*? That's fantastic. What'd *ya* see?'

Through the video connection, Dan saw the impressionable painter's index finger zoom towards the screen, obliterating her face for a couple of seconds. Scrolling through photographs, he guessed. He heard soft mutterings away from the microphone, and a Messenger notification rang at his end.

'Did you get anything yet?'

'*Aye.* Hold on.'

The Scot opened the message and tapped on one attachment at a time. He recognised the flat above the hardware store from pictures in Jeff Diamond's autobiography, feeling his chest tighten. The next showed a street corner he couldn't place at first, until he enlarged a section to reveal a red neon sign over the door.

'Alberto's boxing club,' he exhaled. 'Oh, my God. You were there? I'm so jealous!'

'Thought you'd like them. There's more, if you like.'

Dan flipped back to Facetime and the young woman's wide smile. 'Cheers. These are great. Hope I get to go one day. And to Melbourne. D'*ya* think, after my year's up, we'd be able to convince Kierney to let us visit the dam?'

Once again, the air became turgid with a sudden tension. Freya's expression was hard to read. Too far? Invisible elastic connection? Together, forever, wherever?

Don't be so bloody stupid, the nineteen-year-old chastised himself. 'What's your favourite line from "ALS"?' he asked, anxious to know if the same outrageous idea was whizzing around the Australian's digs overlooking the Charles River.

'One line?' Freya yelped, then covered her mouth. 'How the hell could you pick one line?'

'Yeah. Sorry 'bout that. One of your favourites then…'

'Hmm… Let me see… One that makes me laugh every time is when Jeff was making his speech at their fifteenth wedding anniversary party, in front of "Big D". Do you know the line I mean?'

'*Cierto*,' Dan replied without thinking.

'What did you say?'

Shit, he cringed. Had he been about to append "angel" to his response? The colours of his fantasy were running into reality, and it would be impossible to separate them if he went any further.

'*Aye.* I know the one. You go first.'

Freya's eyes were shining, as if moved to tears. 'I'm not sure I'll get it word-perfect, but something like "He paid me to take her off his hands, you know... Pitiful it was. How could I refuse? I needed the money."'

Her fellow *aficionado* chuckled. 'That's pretty accurate, I think,' he said, having refrained from mouthing along with her. 'The one I like from that time is "Gipsy Jack saw my future." Remember that one?'

'Something about Jeff having kids at private school?'

'Yeah. So you *are* as sad as me! It's when he sent Jacinta a picture of Jet and Kierney in their MA uniform, after she teased him that he'd never be rich enough for Lynn to want to go out with him and that she'd never go with someone with socialist ideals.'

The daughter of a Sri Lankan refugee smiled, pondering her own future. Not-Daniel Finley seemed like a nice guy. He would never have been selected for next year's leadership bursary if his character was dubious. Was he who she thought he was? And was she what he expected? This in itself presented a fundamental problem.

'I'd better go, Dan,' Freya straightened up. 'It's late here. I should get some sleep. It was great talking to you.'

'Oh, OK. Same to you. Hope we can talk again soon.'

'Sure! Look forward to it. Good luck with all your packing and stuff.'

***

Lynch's was a regular haunt, one of many fine restaurants in Melbourne's inner suburbs. Indeed, it had been the venue of the first decent meal the soul-mates had eaten together, along with Gerry and Suzanne, way back in March nineteen-seventy-two. Dressed for their glamorous party later on, they stood out in the crowd, worth every million of their billion-plus dollars. Seated in a quiet corner as requested, the staff protected their special guests from the rest of the high-classed New Year's Eve revellers.

'Well! Fifteen years,' Lynn smiled, holding her hand out across the table. 'That's a bloody long time.'

'You're not wrong,' the thirty-eight-year-old agreed. 'Too long for you? Feel like a change?'

The stunning blonde picked up the menu. Her companion chuckled at the affectation, lifting his fork and using it to lower the top edge of the leather-bound folder. His heart skipped a beat when lashes elongated by dark brown mascara fluttered in front of subtly-shaded eyelids, and then again when the temporary shield snapped back *in situ*.

'I said, "Do you feel like a change, Missus Diamond?"' he repeated, loud enough to turn nearby heads.

This time, the menu was replaced on the empty dinner plate with obedient grace. The playful rogue could never resist a scandalous scene. This habit had aggravated his well-bred companion in their early years together, but she now had to admit to quite enjoying it.

'Sorry?' she feigned distraction. 'Did you ask me something?'

'You heard. Looking for something new?'

Lynn nodded. 'Oh, yes. I suppose I am. Every day, in fact. Aren't you?'

'You bet... If I show you mine, will you show me yours?'

'*Bien sûr, mon ami.* Isn't that what friends are for?'

The rock star sighed, reaching for the whisky and dry ginger he had been served as an *apéritif*. He, as the master negotiator, could not have explained his own state of mind any better than this. With another year of triumphs, trials and tribulations at an end, a new half-decade of bliss with this amazing woman was nothing short of a miracle.

'*A mi regala,*' he toasted. 'You are still my dream girl. Always were, always will be.'

'And to my beautiful black stallion,' his wife replied, clinking her glass against his and taking a sip with lips painted a rich blood red. 'You make me the happiest person in the world, Jeff. Every day. I love you more now than I did fifteen years ago, and that's saying something! So here's to the next fifteen.'

Only pausing their natural non-stop dialogue to fill up on mouth-watering seafood and a delicate *Chardonnay*, followed by rare *Châteaubriand* and the obligatory smooth *Tempranillo*, the anniversary couple stretched their celebratory *tête-à-tête* for as long as possible, despite being under the constant scrutiny of every other patron.

Melburnians loved the fact that these high-profile celebrities continued to call Victoria's state capital home. And in return, said celebrities no longer worried about the following morning's scuttlebutt. Newspapers predicted an impending shipwreck whenever a photographer captured either star in close proximity to a person of the opposite sex. Each local fan for whom the Diamonds could do no wrong had an opposite number ready to cast aspersions at their every word or move.

Cathy Lane and the staff at Stonebridge Music had clipped and filed countless editorials, interview transcripts and magazine articles pertaining to the famous foursome, and had even devised a humorous scoring system which they shared with the self-effacing celebrities on a monthly basis. It evaluated each passage against a checklist of positives and negatives, marked up the truths and the myths, and plotted the many scandalous fictional earnings estimates on a rolling graph.

It was not uncommon to read about divorce settlements larger than a small country's Gross Domestic Product being mediated behind closed doors, usually linked to reports of one or other party sighted in the throes of unfaithfulness. Neither was it unknown for the couple to play along with an artless journalist;

or else, with considerable regret, they would go so far as to honour such injustices with the cold shoulder, much to the consternation of whichever publication had advanced the opinion.

To remedy the imbalance however, Blake & Partners would engage a lawyer or ten to seek a retraction, particularly if the lies risked damaging the children's mental state. The Diamond Celebration Foundation's coffers were invariably a little fuller after these minor incursions!

The lovers' conversation turned to a more delicate avenue of enquiry while perusing the dessert menu, having depleted most light-hearted and nostalgic topics. For some years now, the press persisted like a dog with a bone that Jeff's relationship with his daughter was unsavoury.

No-one was brave enough to suggest incest, but busybodies and self-righteous do-gooders laid consistent accusations of an improper closeness, often accompanied by *paparazzi* pictures of the pair hugging and kissing. Lynn knew full well that her husband had no case to answer, yet the endless speculation was beginning to wear them both down.

'What d'you want me to do?' the doting dad asked, placing his knife and fork down on an empty plate. 'I'm sick of it too, angel, but it's a zero-sum game. Deny it, and it'll enflame the situation; back off, and we're publicly admitting to something dodgy.'

The Olympian sighed. 'Then do nothing. Whatever you do, there'll always be someone who thinks the worst. You'd go from alleged kiddy-fiddler to a neglectful dead-beat dad. No-one notices the ones who're doing the right thing when it comes to amateur child protection.'

Her husband let out a sarcastic laugh. Despite the healthy dose of facetious cynicism in these words, they left a bitter taste on their palates. Transported back to their favourite pub in Covent Garden, prior to their non-engagement, the unforeseen troll versus angel moment took them by surprise.

Australia's darling reached for the unworthy pretender's hand. 'I'm sorry. I went too far. That wasn't meant to sound quite as damning as it did.'

'I know, *Regala*,' Jeff smirked. 'I thought we'd swapped brains for a second there.'

'Oh, that's a scary thought! Glad you can see the funny side.'

'D'*you* think I'm too close to her? Gerry does. I know that for a fact.'

'No, I don't,' his wife insisted. 'We know the truth. Kierney loves you to bits; idolises you. Both kids do. And there's no way anyone could prove anything untoward was going on.'

The end of Lynn's sentence was delivered in a whisper, her eyes directed beyond the peacemaker's left shoulder, where a waiter was making his approach. Under the table, her skin tingled as the smooth surface of a new leather shoe stroked her calf muscle. The acute sensation travelled all the way to her throat, causing her to gasp into her tumbler of water.

Engaging the hotel employee in animated French while a cheeseboard and Lynn's dessert were delivered and positioned with meticulous pride on their table, the empathetic superstar winked and lifted his wine glass.

'To the many untoward things I'd like to do with you tonight.'

The sportswoman chuckled and raised her eyebrows, distracted by a bonus accessory on her plate. As was customary when preparing for a Grand Slam tournament, she had passed up a selection of sticky sweets in favour of a more austere *affogato*.

Cutting a triangle of stilton and eating it off the side of his cheese knife, Jeff imbibed her joy at spying a small, square parcel wrapped in glossy crimson paper lodged between the glass of *crème de cacao* and the shot of *espresso*. 'That bloke fancies you. He told me just then.'

'Oh, really?' the playful woman replied, lifting her hand as if to wave the young man back to their table.

'Open it,' he growled.

Raising her eyebrows and grinning to herself, Lynn upturned the two shot glasses, tipping coffee and *liqueur* in a synchronised downpour over the vanilla ice-cream. She had presented her expert purveyor of romance with an anniversary present before they left home for dinner: an oil painting of the Four of Diamonds, created from a photograph that captured their happiness in a charming composition of light and shadow.

'Thank you. You shouldn't have.'

Her husband scoffed at the deliberate platitude. Watching his wife unwrap special gifts was one of his best-loved pastimes. And, even by his own admission, he had outdone himself on this occasion. Painted fingernails peeled the slithers of double-sided tape away from the paper, liberated the box and cracked it open.

'Oh!' Lynn looked up from the most exquisite piece of jewellery she had ever seen. 'Oh, my God. This is…'

Her fingers made light work of prising two fused circles of gold out of their slot in a midnight blue velvet pad, one yellow and one white woven around each other, elegant and weighty and studded at intervals with rubies and diamonds.

The thirty-four-year-old rotated the piece along every possible axis. 'Eternity?'

'Twice, if I could,' the charmer nodded. 'It's for your finger.'

'Oh, thank you, professor. Lucky you're here,' she laughed. 'It's so perfect that I can't even tell you to stick your advice up your…'

Jeff dropped the cheese knife onto his plate and reached for the ring. 'Just put the damned thing on, will you?'

Four of the world's hardest-working and most valuable hands engaged in table-top combat until Lynn saw reason and extended her left straight out towards her chivalrous playmate. He twisted the stunning dual band onto her annular finger until it came in contact with her engagement and wedding rings.

'Wow!' the recipient pulled her hand back and held it up to catch the light. 'It's exquisite. Absolutely stunning! I love the way it's part *matte* and part polished. So subtle. You spoil me so much, and I love it!'

Her husband chuckled. 'Yeah. Subtle in an ostentatious kind o' way. Custom-made for the only woman I shall ever love, for the rest of our life singular. You're welcome, angel. It and you look beautiful.'

'It does. And I love the way it's just the tiniest bit broader than the other two.'

'Jesus! You noticed,' the schemer blanched. 'Christ, I love you so much. That was my first criterion when we designed it: it had to be wider, brighter and heavier than the others, but not so much as to make it stand out.'

Lynn choked back tears. 'Well, it works. It's gorgeous, Jeff. Just gorgeous. Thanks again. I feel eternally loved, and I hope you know I love you in all the same ways.'

The emotional man jumped to his feet, sending his chair scooting backwards into the wall and drawing the attention of their fellow diners. His wife stood too, eager for the warmth of his arms around her. After first kissing the latest symbol of their perfectly imperfect partnership, Jeff anointed the delicate skin under her left ear with his passion before lingering for much longer at her mouth.

Surrounded by polite applause and a chorus of anniversary wishes, the showman fetched each wine glass in turn so they could acknowledge the kindness with a toast.

'Thank you,' Lynn smiled. 'Sorry to disturb you.'

Ever the gentleman, her husband stepped aside and invited her to sit down again. He paused for another moment, with his hand woven around her neck behind a curtain of silky golden hair. They both laughed at the murky beige soup which had started out as an *affogato*.

'We can get another one,' Jeff offered.

'No. It's nice. A little warmer than usual, but tastes just as good. So where were we with you and Kizzy?'

Napkin suspended in mid-air, the superstar frowned, disappointed to revert to serious matters so soon. Disregarding all uninvited social commentary was the only justifiable course of action, in his opinion. Kierney was fine, he had Lynn's full support and, with the exception of the conservative, part-time Roman Catholic who managed his business affairs, no-one of any true significance had voiced an objection.

'No change,' he replied. 'What d'you think, angel? What if you were her?'

Australia's darling was caught tipping the last centimetre of her dessert into her mouth, this question forcing her to swallow it down in a hurry. 'Oh, God. I don't know. It's hard to compare my relationship with Dad and you two. A whole different baseline. I'd have been totally grossed out if he was more demonstrative, but I love seeing you and Kierney together.'

'So we just live with the back-chat 'til she's sixteen? Eighteen even?' the peacemaker ventured. 'If not, what are we prepared to submit to? To clear my name. Jesus! The very thought makes me feel sick. I mean... It's got to impact on Kizzy's view of the adult world, hasn't it?'

Lynn grimaced. 'It won't come to that. They'd need pretty strong evidence to back you into a corner. Order a coffee and change the subject.'

Considering the idea's merits, Jeff sat back and cupped his wine glass in both hands. All at once, the pressure inside intensified, squeezing tears from his eyes, raising his heart rate to an audible level and pumping blood below the belt.

'Can I take you home?'

'No!' the elegant singer answered, laughing out loud. 'I genuinely *have* got a better offer. And so've you!'

'Damn!' he cursed, catching the eye of a middle-aged lady on the next table and winking. 'You're no fun. *Gonna* make me wait again... Better offer, eh? You'll pay for that.'

'I expect I shall. What's the running order for Anna's wedding music?' Lynn asked, conscious of the excitement her outspoken *beau* continually caused for people around them.

In the Grand Hyatt's ballroom later the same evening, the lovers unveiled their "Fifteen-Love" anniversary theme, at a gigantic function for the Diamond Celebration Foundation's combined charities. The fundraising campaign was to run through to the conclusion of the Australian Open tennis tournament, where Jet and Kierney were playing in the Juniors and Anna threatened to steal the women's singles crown from her older sister.

The party was a joyous opportunity for promoting valuable messages to encourage people to stick together through adversity. This was also the first New Year's Eve the entertainers had spent away from their children, who had accepted invitations from school-friends' families keen to show off their connections.

Initially, the famous parents had been impressed that both offspring were old enough for independent social lives. Now the evening was upon him however, Jeff felt a little bereft. Still, he couldn't pull rank at this late stage, and they only had to wait until breakfast to see them.

***

Jet and Kierney were already seated at a table in the hotel restaurant, surrounded by starched white linen and silver cutlery, when their parents emerged from the lift. Their heads were buried in books, not only because they were voracious readers but also to discourage other guests from bothering them this early on New Year's morning. It was eight-thirty, and none had slept for more than four hours. There would be little time to relax over breakfast either, since the family needed to be on the road to Benloch soon, bound for the annual Dyson weigh-in.

All heads turned to witness the attractive celebrity couple reunite with their children after their independent nights out. The youngsters, well-mannered as ever, stood up to give each parent a hug, wishing them a happy anniversary. A vibrant *bouquet* of mixed pink and white lilies lay on a separate table, over which the kids competed to present to their mother. Ceding the flowers to his sister, the young man extended his right hand to his father.

'Well, you two look very respectable,' Lynn praised. 'You must be tired. We are anyway! Thanks so much for these. How long have you been here?'

Kierney yawned on cue, rushing to cover her open mouth. 'Oh, thanks, *Mamá*. Only ten minutes or so. How was your party?'

'*¡Fantastico!*' Jeff declared, cupping his daughter's cheeks in his hands and kissing her forehead. 'I agree with *Mamá*... Seeing you here, all *schmick* and under your own steam, makes me so proud of you. *Gracias a los dos.* D'*ya* get blind drunk last night, mate?'

Jet turned ninety degrees to his right to avoid the gaze of an inquisitive elderly couple at the next table. 'We were allowed one stubby each.'

'Were you? Did you like it?' Lynn asked, indicating for them to sit down.

'Not much,' the boy replied, pulling a face. 'I couldn't finish it. We didn't get to bed until after three o'clock. I'm scared how badly I'll do today, Mum.'

'Oh, well,' the Olympian grinned. 'Nothing we can do about it now. And it won't be the first time a Dyson's rocked up on New Year's Day with a hangover. I've always thought it was a pretty sadistic day to put us through our paces, but you know Grandpa...'

'Yeah,' Jeff shook his head. 'We know Grandpa. I've never understood that logic either. It's not as if he's a quaker himself when it comes to the demon drink. Maybe it's a case of if he has to suffer, so must everyone else.'''

'Be quiet, you!' his wife hissed, slapping her own control freak's arm. 'What about you, Kizzy? How was Kelli's party?'

Kierney accepted a glass of freshly-squeezed orange juice from a waitress and had to crunch down an icy mouthful before she could answer. 'It was great, thanks. Wow! That's cold! Piraea and Olympia didn't turn up 'til really late because their 'plane was delayed. The girls all stuck together, dancing and listening to music. No boys allowed.'

The thirteen-year-old scowled. 'Thank God! No boys'd want to go anyway.'

'Oh, yeah? D'you *wanna* reconsider that statement?' his dad chimed in. 'Your face gives you away, mate.'

'Shut up, *Nacho*-man,' the dark-haired girl gave her brother a playful nudge. 'So... You guys are "Fifteen-Love" now. Does it feel different?'

Lynn smiled at the gipsy's dreamy air. She was so like her father, and romance suited her right down to her Doc Marten boots. Expressing herself in these terms was a relatively new habit, previously preferring to dwell in more meditative and macabre worlds.

'We are,' the happy woman affirmed, placing her left hand on the tablecloth next to the centrepiece. 'Look at this. Isn't it beautiful?'

Kierney's jaw dropped. 'Oh, my God! That's *gorgeissimo*, *Papá*! I didn't know you were getting *Mamá* a ring.'

'No. It was a spur of the six-month decision,' the billionnaire laughed.

Four cooked breakfasts arrived, and Lynn slipped her hand out of view, where it was snaffled into her grateful man's grasp. They were all hungry after their long nights. Jet smothered his food with tomato sauce, sharing a silent joke with his father when they spotted Lynn's customary maternal glare.

'Ugh! Gross, Jetto. Can you taste anything else with all that?'

'Vampire juice,' the boy jumped in. 'Go on... Tell me it's not what you wanted to say. I dare you!'

The dignified athlete growled under her breath. 'Enough, you insolent child. *Papá*'s speech to kick the fundraiser off was wonderful; a real tear-jerker. And we had the longest dance together, didn't we? Probably even longer than on our wedding day. Exhausting!'

The teenager groaned. 'Oh, please! What's all this slushy, gushy, mushy stuff? Why are girls so obsessed with how romantic everything is?'

He closed his eyes and pretended to waltz with an invisible partner, swaying from side to side with one hand in the air. His sister thumped his thigh under the table, reminding Jeff of the way the Blakes used to carry on a whole generation ago.

The amused Sydneysider gave Kierney a stern look, before facing his son to stir things up a little more. 'Oh, yeah? So what are you obsessed with these days, mate?'

'Which girls look the hottest,' the thirteen-year-old jeered. 'I know, I know. It comes to the same thing. Just sex on each other's terms.'

'That's right,' Lynn laughed, seeing the expression on her husband's face. 'Don't get your dad started! It was a magical evening, whether slushy, gushy, mushy or hot, hot, hot. We raised a lot of money and haven't had much more sleep than you guys.'

'*Muy buen*'. So will you tell us how you and *Mamá* met, *Papá*?' Kierney changed the subject. 'Please?'

'Again? You know the story already,' he replied.

'I know, but only from *Mamá*'s side.'

'From the slushy, gushy, mushy side,' the sportswoman qualified, grinning at their son.

'Oh, cool!' Jet thumped the table. 'So this is going to be the hot, hot, hot version then? *Allons-y*, folks!'

'Sure. Let's get some coffee first,' Jeff decided, removing the napkin from his lap and flagging down one of the staff. 'Hey, Greg!'

The family's attention was drawn to the restaurant's reception desk, where their long-time driver and his new Thai wife were booking in. He was tasked with picking them up and deliver them to the Dyson homestead for lunch prior to the assessment meeting, and the anniversary couple were overjoyed to see him and Tuyet making the most of their morning off.

Even though the diminutive woman was no longer a newcomer in their extended *Escondido* household, it had taken the retired soldier nearly a year to feel comfortable enough to mix business with pleasure. After a brief, cheerful exchange of New Year's Eve exploits, the Diamonds encouraged the newlyweds to enjoy a private breakfast, watching them head to the buffet and fill their plates.

Resuming their disrupted conversation, Jeff and Lynn regaled various stories about their first few weeks together, some of which were already staples for their children, while they tucked into muffins and *croissants* as fuel for the demanding day ahead. Too young for some of the racier tales until now, Kierney was captivated by the thought of her father as a nineteen-year-old, driving all the way down from Sydney in his rattly, blue Ford Fairlane in the hope of bumping into the girl of his dreams.

Pointing a sticky finger at the wordsmith, Jet couldn't hide his curiosity. 'So how did you convince Mum to go out with you?' he asked. 'How many times did you have to ask her out before she said yes?'

'Only once, mate,' the thirty-eight-year-old answered, angling his head at a cavalier angle towards his wife and winking. 'Only once.'

'He really took me by surprise,' the blonde explained, smiling at the disbelief on the boy's face. 'But I would've said yes anyway. He sort of drew me in.'

'Hypnotised you,' her husband nodded.

'Plus he was much better looking than anyone I'd ever met before.'

Kierney giggled at the way her larrikin father pointed to his handsome countenance with both index fingers, and then again when her mother grabbed his closer hand and pushed it into his lap. Grunting and picking up his half-finished coffee, he proceeded wrap his fingers around hers until their hands were clasped under the table.

'What's going on down there?' their daughter's voice sounded accusatory. 'Keep it clean, please. Not in front of the children.'

'You prude!' Jeff matched her tone. 'Don't jump to conclusions, *pequeñita*. You're just jealous. Now, d'you want to hear the story or not?'

'Yes! Course I do. *Por favor, señor.*'

The songwriter released his beautiful best friend's hand, which snaked back onto the table as if it were trying not to be noticed. His breath stolen by the sight of her new eternity ring, he caught the others' eyes and gave in to an enormous rush of happiness. The youngsters both leaned forward on their chairs, hanging out to hear the rest of their father's story.

'Well, it might've taken us by surprise at the time,' he stared into his partner's deep, blue pools of heavenly promise, 'but I'd been planning it for weeks. You know that.'

'I do,' Lynn replied, inclining sideways to kiss his cheek. '*Sigue, señor.*'

Jeff coughed, feeling the same mysterious obstruction in his throat every time he recalled these early days. 'I can't remember whether it was the day after I arrived in Melbourne, or maybe it was the next day...' he continued. 'I bought two tickets to "A Streetcar Named Desire" by Tennessee Williams.'

'I know this part,' the fanciful eleven-year-old said.

'Then you can tell us,' her dad scoffed. 'Were you there? Spying on me?'

'Perhaps I was,' the youngster teased. 'In my former life.'

The philosopher shook his head, his bluff called yet again by his precocious miniature. 'Anyway... I decided to buy the tickets without the faintest bloody clue how I was actually going to meet your *mamá*. I wasn't so *naïf* to think it'd be easy to get close to a sixteen-year-old superstar protected by a formidable dude like Bart Dyson. Nobodies from Canley Vale on Sea don't figure too highly on the eligible bachelor polls.'

'Canley Vale on Sea,' Jet repeated with a chuckle. 'I love it when you call it that. It's so not true!'

'No kidding,' the comic moaned. 'But as luck would have it, when I started work at the uni' a couple of weeks later, I saw something on one of the noticeboards that was to change the course of history.'

'Oh, Jeff! Don't exaggerate,' his wife giggled.

'I'm not, angel! It did change the course of history. For me anyway. It was the MA students due to attend a Year Twelve Open Day, and I scanned down the names, hoping I'd find the one I was looking for. I can still feel the brain-freeze from when I saw your name written there, angel.'

Jeff's left index finger traced down an imaginary roll-call in mid-air, coming to a sudden stop at the invisible name which made his eyes pop out of his head. He drummed the fingers of his right hand against his chest, denoting his quickening heartbeat. His spellbound audience laughed out loud.

'And then I thought, "Holy crap!" Now what the hell do I do? Just walk up to her after the lecture, tap her on the shoulder and ask her to go to the theatre with me? Such a simple task became a whole lot more complicated than I'd ever imagined in all those years fantasising about meeting you. I mean... She was Lynn Dyson, and I was...'

'A nobody from Canley Vale on Sea!' the children chanted in unison, before dissolving into another surreptitious fit of giggles as a snooty waiter glared in their direction.

Their father nodded. 'Precisely. You see my problem?'

Agreeing *con gusto*, the couple's progeny turned to check their mother's reaction this time.

'Don't look at me!' Lynn feigned innocence. 'My character hasn't even made an entrance yet.'

Jeff smiled, reaching his arm around his wife's shoulders and brushing her temple with loving lips. Although his own lengthy list of achievements had elevated him to a more than deserving match for this chart-topping musician and multiple Olympic medallist, Gravity the troll still nagged at his ingrained sense of inadequacy at times like these.

'So what did you do?' Jet asked, having abandoned his former disinterest. 'Go home and shut your bedroom door for a while?'

'Excuse me?' Lynn hissed. 'Keep your voice down, please. That's disgusting! I suppose you learned that in Bathurst too?'

The storyteller scowled. 'Mate, you're letting the side down. What happens on tour stays on tour, remember? Besides, I lived on my own so no need to shut any doors.'

The boy nodded, trying not to smile. On balance, Lynn had been impressed by the increased maturity their son was demonstrating since his *bar mitzvah* weekend, rippling with self-assurance in adult company. His tact filter required finer calibration however, prone to over-excitement a little too frequently.

'But yeah,' Jeff confirmed the lad's suspicions. 'Several times, in fact.'

The dignified thirty-five-year-old's eyes widened, like any good mother's should on hearing such a suggestive comment. 'You can shut up too!' she said through gritted teeth, jogging her husband's upper arm with all her force. 'Be quiet, for God's sake!'

'Yeah, *Papá*,' Kierney joined in. '"Not in front of the children," I said! What happened next?'

'Jesus Christ! Ladies, please…' the celebrity declared, relishing the attention and keen to give the story his best shot. 'I'm trying to deliver a balanced account of our first encounter, to satisfy the diversity in my audience. Will you please leave it to me?'

'Very well,' Lynn snapped in jest. 'Pray, continue, Don Juan.'

Jet whined. 'Oh, God. Now we're deep in enemy territory. Dad, hurry up. When's the hot part?'

'Sorry, son,' his father sympathised. 'I know. Painful, isn't it? Anyway, that's exactly what happened. *Mamá* was with Auntie Michelle and a few other girls, and Lloyd de l'Enseigne had a broken leg. He was on crutches, wasn't he, gorgeous?'

'Oh, yes!' Lynn exclaimed. 'I'd forgotten about that. He broke his ankle over the summer, that's right. He and Nick dropped me off at the Uni' Club as well, didn't he, a few days later?'

'Indeed,' Jeff nodded, absorbing his wife's warmth and letting it flow through his system like a drug. 'Many, many days later. An intolerable number of days, if I'm allowed to admit it. But you're fast-forwarding past the good stuff.'

'Sorry,' the object of his affection said, placing two fingers over her mouth to prevent it from uttering any further secrets.

'*Merci, mon amie. Alors*, where was I?'

'With girls and Lloyd on crutches,' his daughter recapped, on tenterhooks.

'*Merci, mon autre amie.* I caught up with them all after the class filed out of the lecture theatre. I'd been lurking in the room behind, between the classroom and the computer lab'. Your *mamá*'d been eyeing me up through the window for a while.'

'Excuse me? I was not eyeing you up,' the indignant woman refuted.

'You absolutely were!' the man next to her insisted, kissing her pouting lips. 'But never mind. Have it your way.'

Making the children laugh once more, he continued. 'Once I drew alongside the gaggle of girls, I thought, "It's now or never, mate." I introduced myself and told *mamá* that I had two tickets for the play and that she was coming with me.'

The quartet of relaxed diners all burst out laughing at the audacity of the superstar's biased recollection. Regardless of the outcome's origins and the players' intentions for that morning, none could deny this crucial juncture had changed Australian popular culture forever.

'*Told* her she was coming with me?' Lynn repeated, emphasising the erroneous choice of verb. 'Funny... I don't quite remember it that way.'

'Oh, really?' her lover frowned. 'Poor thing. Must be your age. Let's face it, darling... Your memory's not what it used to be.'

'*Papá!*' Kierney yelped, hearing her brother guffaw.

'*Whaddya* mean, *pequeñita*? You doubt me? Looking back on it though, it was a bloody surreal experience. It was like I'd gone back to school; girls in uniform walking down a long corridor. Like I was in my past, present and future all at once.'

His wife swooned. 'Oh, that's a lovely image. I remember it as clear as day too. Something struck a chord deep inside me, although I didn't understand it at the time. My friends were amazed I said yes, and so was I.'

'And so were you, *Papá*,' their daughter hazarded. 'Weren't you?'

'Damned straight, I was! That's what I mean about hypnotism. I told your *mamá* I hypnotised her, so maybe I did. Who knows? Whatever forces were at play that day, it worked, against all probability. So...'

Jet and Kierney both took a deep breath in response to the musician's raised hands, chiming in with invisible conductor's *batons*. 'So the rest is history!'

'Jesus! I'm utterly predictable. No, wait! Don't answer that. Irrespective, I was bloody amazed that the date actually took place. I had every expectation of being booted down the steps of Dyson Administration when I turned up. All that time agonising over how the hell I'd manage to convince Lynn Dyson to go out with me, and it just happens like magic...'

Said Lynn Dyson, who had also been wallowing in these fond memories, leaned over and gave the joyful man's cheek a chaste kiss. 'Well, from my side, it never once crossed my mind to cancel,' she added, 'despite the fact I already had a ticket to the same show on the same night. One of the *flukiest* coincidences of all time! I still find it so unbelievable, by the way...'

'Oh, yes,' their daughter cried out. 'That was amazing.'

'When your dad asked me out,' the singer went on, 'it felt like my chance to act like a real grown-up. A proper date with an enigmatic stranger. And we never had any problem finding things to talk about, did we? Even from that first day.'

Jeff shook his head. 'Nope. You made it very easy.'

'Because...' Kierney took over as if undergoing some sort of enlightenment and glanced across at her brother, 'it was all pre-arranged. I believe *we* made you two get together so we could choose you as our parents.'

Lynn inhaled, her eyes brimming with spontaneous tears. 'Oh, darling! That's such a beautiful thing to say. Thank you.'

'Actually, Kiz,' Jet stifled an involuntary groan which he realised was unjustified. 'It is a pretty nice idea. Stupid but sweet too.'

The man known for galvanising people's emotions was floored by the girl's innocent remark, and yet more so by its endorsement by the young cricketer. He echoed his beautiful best friend's commendation, anxious not to cause a scene in the hotel restaurant.

'Is this a deliberate ploy to get more pocket money, guys?' he joked in the most authoritative tone he could muster.

The children gave each other a high-five, their father's insinuation inciting them to reel off as many compliments as possible, in the hope of yielding further financial fruits. Humouring them as always, Jeff reached into the back pocket of his pants to retrieve his wallet, miming the counting out of several notes with a pained expression.

Meanwhile, a woman stopped next to the Diamonds' table on her way out with her husband, eager to mention how lovely it was to see the family getting on so well. The humble world-changer looked over his shoulder to where their driver and his wife were bearing enjoyable witness to the perpetual spotlight which saturated their employers. On cue, Greg offered a light-hearted mock salute.

'Thanks, but it's all for show,' the songwriter lied with a glint in his eye, scrawling his autograph on two business cards and passing them to his co-star for countersigning. 'We hate spending time with each other. Happy New Year.'

'You're such a bastard,' Lynn muttered as the guests turned to leave. 'No wonder people write nasty things about us.'

'Yeah, Dad. You're such a bastard,' Jet stole his chance for gratuitous foul language.

'Now, before we go,' the mother slapped both hands on the edge of the table to attract the others' attention. 'Remember to go easy on Uncle Junior today, kids.'

'Because of his knee?' Kierney checked.

The tennis champion nodded, turning to her husband to fill him in on news she had received the previous day. 'Yes. He's been advised to stop playing footy altogether. I don't think he's made the decision yet, but he will, I'm sure.'

'Career-ending injury,' Jeff sighed, disappointed for the amiable midfielder. 'Bummer. No other option? I'm guessing they've already been through all that. Jesus, that's shit for him.'

Again, the youngest Diamonds showed a similar level of compassion, blessed with so much but preferring not to take anything for granted. Seeing his son's shoulders shake, he imagined him rubbing his own hard-working knees in sympathy.

'He's having one more go at surgery,' Lynn told them. 'He's going to concentrate on athletics now, and give football away. He's quite interested in coaching too, so Mum says.'

'Last time he and I spoke,' her husband added, 'he was talking about some deal to set up a Melbourne-based NRL team.'

Jet's interest had been sparked. 'Rugby? In Victoria? Wow!'

'Yeah, mate. We might be buying into it. Nothing certain yet, but it'd be great. Anyway, also before we go, can I just say something to you fabulous wonders?'

Kierney giggled, seeing her mother's eyes scan the immediate vicinity in search of people answering to this description. 'Us, *Mamá*. *Papá* means us. You do, don't you?'

'Sure do, *pequeñita*. I want to say thanks to you, angel, for sticking with me, and cheers to you guys for being here today to share this anniversary with us. I love the fact that our story means so much to us all. I hope the magic never diminishes.'

'Hear, hear!' Lynn chimed, raising her empty juice glass. 'Thank you for being here too. I love you. All of you.'

'While I was writing my New Year letters to you yesterday afternoon,' Jeff continued, his eyes requesting his wife's hand to be placed on his own and then for the children to add theirs on top, 'I got thinking about our shared history and how it's getting longer and more complicated.'

Kierney's *visage* was a study in anticipation while Jet's contorted to disguise a yawn. Their mother waited for the inevitable missive of profound wisdom which reinforced the foundations of their perfectly imperfect family on every special occasion.

The philosopher didn't let them down. 'I'd like us to revisit these moments more regularly, now you guys are building your own histories independent of ours. *Mamá* and I are locked together in our life singular, and up 'til recently, you two were part and parcel of that one life. From here on, I want you guys to take control of your lives.'

'Oh, I agree,' his wife added. 'Your dad and I've talked about this for the last few weeks. We don't want you to feel like I felt with Grandma and Grandpa dictating my whole life. Of course, we're still here a hundred percent to answer questions and help you make the right decisions, but we'd like you to feel you have the freedom to explore whatever you want to explore.'

Neither youngster possessed sufficient insight to interpret their parents' intangible anniversary gift in practical terms, yet their smiles betrayed an underlying comfort with the concept. Jet pulled his hand clear of the pile and scratched his nose, embarrassed by the earnest atmosphere which had descended over their table.

'And the other thing I'd like to get more into is developing song-lines,' the passionate man added.

Lynn turned her gaze away from the children at the germination of an idea she had sowed in his mind a few days ago. 'Song-lines? You are such an introvert! I love it when these things suddenly bubble up to the top of your brain. Yes, there's no reason why we can't create song-lines to pass stories down the generations.'

'Like aboriginal clans?' Jet asked.

'*Exactamente*, mate. What we all need... not just we here,' the father's arms expanded out from the four-person table they occupied, 'but we everywhere... to understand is that history changes a little bit each time a different person tells the story. Stands to reason really, 'cause it's the origin of the word: his story. Or her story or their story... History and truth are two very different and equally impossible things to verify, so never be afraid to stand by your own true story.'

'Truth according to whom?' Lynn mused, leaning her head on her wise man's arm.

The thirteen-year-old huffed. 'According to what you see and hear.'

'D'you reckon, mate?'

'Why not?'

'No. I don't agree, Jetto,' his sister puffed out her chest. 'What about stuff you couldn't see or hear? If it happened but you didn't see it, does that mean it's not true?'

The ecstatic father pointed an all-knowing finger towards the dark-haired gipsy girl before turning around and giving Greg a subtle signal. 'On your feet, *familia mía*! Time for torture town.'

Pausing at the front desk to pay for their overnight stay and both sets of breakfasts, the forever couple collected the trolley bearing their luggage and sauntered through the lobby towards the lift. Once in the basement car park, Jeff put an arm around each child and hugged them close.

Lynn went ahead of them with the intention of updating Tuyet on the plans for Anna's upcoming marriage to her Canadian research fellow, Brandon Everett-Vincent. The youngest of her generation, the gymnast and her *fiancé*, both scientists with a passion for finding the cure for various cancers, were to be wed on the first of February. Far less fond of the spotlight than her elder sister and the popular showman, the younger couple had opted for a quiet wedding at Benloch.

'I want to be taken for granted,' she heard the songwriter wax lyrical a few steps behind. 'I can't steer the rough seas without my lighthouse. Are you getting this, *Regala*?'

The elegant woman span round and blew her poet a kiss. 'Yes. Thank you. And no alcohol involved!'

'Bloody cheek, eh, kids? You are my peace and contemplation and my thundering reckless abandon, and I'll never tire of either. And you gems are my compass. As long as I've got you to come home to, my sense of direction can't fail. Got that?'

'Got it,' Kierney giggled, swinging her free hand. 'Yes. Thank you.'

***

Shortly after the new term began, Kierney came home with a note for her parents about the Year Eight *discothèque*. Jet's class was also included, but a school dance wasn't something to figure highly on the sports-mad boy's social calendar. His sister, however, had concocted a grand plan to defy critics of her special relationship with one of the greatest performers of contemporary times.

'*Papá*, will you come with me, please?' she asked over dinner.

'To the school disco'? Are you asking me out on a date?' Jeff beamed. 'Thanks heaps. I'm flattered, but have you run this past your *mamá*?'

'No!' the girl screeched, looking from one parent to the other. 'Please, *Papá*. I want to dance with you in front of all my friends and teachers, *et cetera*. It'd be way cool.'

'Way cool,' he sighed with a rueful smile. '*Et cetera*. Jeez, you're growing up too fast. I can't. Sorry, Kizzy. I'd love to, but I can't, can I? I'm too old to go to a school dance, and it's just not appropriate. You know that really. Yeah?'

Heartbroken at her dark-haired family members' *chagrin*, Lynn placed a sympathetic hand on the musician's wrist. She could only imagine the conflicting emotions swimming in his mind. Kierney inserted another forkful of food into her mouth, determined not to give up without a fight.

The cricketer had his own news to impart, jumping into the lull in conversation with a summary of the day's training accomplishments while his sister formulated arguments for her follow-on. Their parents exchanged furtive glances, both knowing the subject was unlikely to remain closed for long.

'But why isn't going to the dance together appropriate?' Kierney asked once the discourse paused again.

'Come on, darling. You know why. These events are meant for you kids to get to know each other at the start of the new school year,' her mother explained. 'They're not for parents or any other adults. I'm sure none of your friends is taking her dad?'

The bright student shook her head. 'But none of their dads can dance like *Papá* can. They *want* me to bring him.'

'Him?' the songwriter laughed. 'Excuse me! I am still sitting here, y'know.'

Jet guffawed. 'Hey! Who said that? Oh, it's him, Kizzo.'

'My friends want me to bring *Papá*,' his sister giggled. 'Sorry.'

'You guys crack me up,' Jeff groaned. 'Very funny. But seriously, *pequeñita*, if you're going to ask someone to go with you, it'll need to be someone from school.'

'You'll enjoy yourself more with your friends and dancing together,' Lynn advised. 'You'll have a great time.'

'And anyway, *Mamá*'ll be jealous. Won't you, angel? She won't talk to you for a week.'

'You wouldn't be jealous,' Kierney objected, subjecting her mother to a death-stare worthy of a supreme court lawyer's cross-examination. 'Would you, *Mamá*?'

The seasoned negotiator put down his cutlery and raised his hand to the young girl. She needed to know she was on a hiding to nothing by pursuing this line of attack, even though he admired her tenacity. Their demure, angelic daughter, in her trademarked long, floral skirts and lace-up boots, was no push-over when it came to stating her case. It was incumbent upon him and his beautiful best friend to teach her how to pick only battles worth winning.

'Miss Diamond, *tais-toi para un momentito*, OK?' he called a time-out. 'Overruled, I'm afraid. Pure and simple. It's not appropriate for me to go to the dance with you because of all the stupid talk about us being too close. You know about that. Go with your mates and stop trying to make a point. You'll get plenty of other opportunities, don't worry. Why don't you teach your mates to dance?'

'Great idea!' Lynn agreed. 'Thanks, *Papá.*'

Not convinced, Kierney still wasn't ready to surrender. 'Hmm... Yeah. *Gracias, Papá.* But we should be allowed to love each other like we do,' she persisted. 'I thought it was healthy for families to be close. People criticise families when they're not close, and now they criticise us 'cause we're *too* close.

Make up your mind, everybody! It's not like you're going to feel me up or whatever...'

'Feel you up?' both adults shouted at once.

'Christ, Kizzo,' Jeff grumbled. 'Where did you hear that? I hate the thought of you even understanding what "feel me up" means.'

The girl's shoulders drooped, knowing she had hurt her parents. 'I'm sorry, but I'm not a little kid anymore. It's when someone touches you in private places, like sexual assault. *Argh!* Now you're going to stop letting me read the 'paper or watch the news, I s'pose, in case I learn about real life before I'm old enough. Jet knows about these things, don't you?'

Her brother nodded, an additional eighteen months of maturity having taught him greater circumspection around adults. Before her husband let forth his full wrath and ruined their peaceful dinner, Lynn smiled, encouraging them all to finish their meals.

'Calm down, everyone. I know you're fed up with this, Kierney, darling. It is incredibly frustrating. Please believe that it's especially frustrating for *him* here,' she chuckled, nodding to her outspoken social justice advocate.

Shooting metaphysical daggers at his wife, Jeff turned to his daughter. 'You bet. Thanks, angel. *He*,' he asserted with a sickly grin, 'is bloody pissed off with the whole sordid matter, if you forgive my language. But we're not going to change the way people think on this topic. You're a child, *angelissima*, albeit an inordinately clever one. And I'm a man who makes a living from expressing bestial urges. Sex, in other words. The two don't mix. You can see that, can't you?'

Seeing the eleven-year-old's bottom lip quiver at having upset her dad, the patient teacher took over. 'People jump to conclusions too quickly, Kizzy, and the law's on their side, unfortunately in our case, because *Papá*'d never dream of doing anything nasty to you. But the law's there to protect us from men who do prey on women and girls.'

'I get that, *Mamá*. And I agree with the law. I wish people could see who the good ones are.'

'Jesus, *pequeñita*. Me too! Amen to that!'

'Excellent, darling. Imagine if they accused *Papá* of sexually assaulting you, and a judge found him guilty... We'd be forbidden to spend time together as a family after that. *Papá*'d most likely go to prison, everyone would hate him for what they'd been told he did, and we'd all be devastated, wouldn't we? It'd wreck everything.'

The youngsters were quick to acknowledge how terrible this fate would be to their happy unit, not to mention their parents' stupendous endeavours. Now thoroughly thwarted, Kierney cleared the last few morsels left on her plate and excused herself from the table. Lynn let her go. She could tell she was on the verge of a tearful meltdown.

With much the same turmoil going on inside his own heart, the clan chief kissed the well-balanced disciplinarian beside him and cursed the inescapable bond he shared with their second-born. They gave Jet special dispensation to take his dessert into the lounge room to watch some television while they floundered in the solemn aftermath of his sister's admirable fight.

Lynn embraced the man who had made a career out of standing for right over wrong, locked in a restorative kiss. She reiterated her unerring support, telling him she adored him more every day. It was entirely their doing that their offspring were ready and willing to uphold their rights against slander and libel. Yet there was such a fine line between helping them to maintain a level of authenticity and instilling enough prudence to serve them well into adulthood.

At its essence, Kierney's desire to thumb her nose at their detractors wasn't wrong, but both celebrities knew how powerful perception could be when one lived in the public eye. Had they become so much part of the establishment that their actions were driven by perception rather than reality?

The couple opted to give the young girl half an hour to mull over their verdict, goading a reluctant boy away from a comedy show to assist with loading the dishwasher. Any concern they had for Jet's take on their discussion was dismissed as unfounded, being treated to a graphic account of a presentation he and a classmate had given to their peers on being vigilant for predators.

Lynn left her two men laughing about Sean's role-play antics and climbed the stairs to their daughter's bedroom. Knocking on the door, she nudged it open and found her lying on the bed and reading a book.

'Can I come in, please?'

Sitting up, Kierney nodded and patted the mattress beside her. Grateful for such an amenable response, the dignified woman slid across the bed until the pair were cuddled up against the wall.

'Are you OK?'

'Yes. I s'pose so,' the girl murmured. 'I just don't think it's right.'

'Good, because it's not right. And that's the problem in a nutshell. *Papá* and I agree with you wholeheartedly. If we could ignore the harm it might do, we'd parade through the streets with you, holding up banners saying, "Dads can cuddle their kids!" But we need to be realistic about which risks we accept and which we shouldn't. Does that make sense?'

'Yes, *Mamá.*'

'Thank you, beautiful,' Lynn stroked Kierney's smooth forehead. 'We can't afford to upset too many people because we'd like them to continue helping us and listening to all the important messages. Just because your dad's Jeff Diamond and he dances like a *tornado* isn't really a good enough reason to put our family and all that goes with it in danger.'

'I know,' the youngster nodded, giggling at the silly image. 'But I'm sure people wouldn't complain if Piraea's dad came with her to the disco'. Just because *Papá*'s Jeff Diamond, dances like a *tornado* and we love each other, why does that make it wrong for him to dance with me?'

At face value, the argument was hard for the showbusiness stalwart to refute. 'You're right. It's not logical. No-one knows anything about Piraea's dad, and that's the difference. Everyone knows your *papá*, and he built a reputation on living dangerously. Even if we know none of that old scandalous stuff's true anymore, once certain busybodies get an impression into their heads about someone well-known, especially if it's about drugs or drinking or sex, they assume the person always behaves the same way.'

'But *Papá* never did anything horrible to kids, did he?'

Lynn hugged the burgeoning human rights activist in close. 'Absolutely not, no. Not to adults or kids. *Papá*'s never done anything to hurt anyone, and we wouldn't hide something like that from you and Jet if he had. Heaps of adults still don't understand the difference between love and sex.'

Kierney looked shocked. 'Why? Even I know that!'

'*Even you*?' her mother trilled. 'Only the theory, I hope! Some people think being a rock musician means your dad takes advantage of women; gets them drunk and feeds them drugs to get his kicks. He might've done a long time ago, but he never forced anyone into anything. And certainly not since we were married. Sadly, with the media always hungry for front page news, it's often "Once a bad boy, always a bad boy." But *Papá*'s really the best boy as far as we're concerned.'

Kierney sniggered at the stage-show reference she had heard before. 'He *is* the best boy. I'm still going to ask him to dances when I'm at uni', like you when you first met. No-one can do anything if I'm an adult.'

'Oh, that's not fair either,' Lynn frowned. 'He wasn't my dad, and I was only sixteen, so technically still a minor. I don't want you to wish your childhood away so soon purely to get your own back on the do-gooders. It's important not to blow things out of proportion, Kizzy. That's the real lesson. We're only talking about a school dance here. And we'll use other opportunities to make the point that if someone likes to have fun, it doesn't mean he or she's a bad person. Behaviour's only bad if it has a harmful effect on others.'

***

Cathy and Ryan startled themselves more than each other when the nineteen-year-old looked up from the page he was reading and saw Stonebridge Music's office manager standing right next to him. She had expected to find her boss in the room she had booked for an early meeting, hoping to capitalise on some quiet time before the rest of the staff arrived to proof a list of tracks to complement the Diamonds' autobiography.

'Jet!' the red-faced woman cried out, depositing two full mugs of *cappuccino* on the table before they slipped through her fingers. 'I didn't know you were home. Hi! Where's your dad?'

'Hey, Cath! Don't know. Ciggie or loo? Hello! Nice to meet you. I'm Ryan.'

Six feet and four inches of brawn, topped with a darkening mop of curls, embraced the family's long-suffering publicist. "The queen of all things administrative", as the lad was known to describe her, marvelled at where the years had gone and how much of a man he had become.

'Oh, yes. Ryan, I'm sorry. I still think of you as Jetto. How are you? Did you want a coffee too?'

'I'm great, thanks,' the Cambridge undergraduate replied. 'I'll help myself in the kitchen. That's fine. I got home yesterday. All ready for Gerry's wedding. Yippee!'

The middle-aged woman let out a high-pitched giggle, as if she had inhaled from a helium balloon. 'Ooh, listen to your accent! A proper English gent' you are now. Is Kizzy here too?'

'No. She's busy with a uni' project. What's this?'

The teenager picked up a playlist he had been scanning, waving it in front of Cathy's eyes. His dad had been melancholy the previous evening, desperate to unload his woes on someone other than Kierney for a change. They had switched topics as soon as the student thought fit, preferring the persecution of Gerry and Fiona's marriage plans to delving into the morbid underbelly of his father's grief.

'It's the songs your dad wants to feature as significant for the book. We're supposed to be finalising them today, so we can send audio and video tracks to the studio. What do you think of the rundown?'

Ryan was about to provide a facetious response regarding adding a legend based on the number of tissue boxes required for each song when his father's frame appeared in the doorway. Deciding to chart a more seemly course, it felt somewhat ironic that the bereaved man would find this observation funny. A good deal funnier than his employee would tolerate at any rate…

'Classics,' he said instead. 'Is there going to be a clip for every one? A CD stuck to the inside cover or something?'

'Yep. Cheers, Cath,' Jeff toasted his loyal marketing guru with his cup. 'This machine's much better than the old one, isn't it? Actually tastes a bit like coffee. Want one, mate?'

'I'll get it myself, thanks.'

'DVD,' Cathy answered the young man's question. 'And yes, in a plastic cover affixed to the jacket's interior.'

'Very technical,' Ryan chuckled. 'Which version of "Original" are you using?'

The superstar pulled a chair out and slumped onto it, energy discharging from his body at the prospect of wading through the five or six award-winning videos made for this hit alone. He was thankful to have his son join them this morning, giving him and his faithful colleague an incentive not to dissolve into blubbering pools of wretchedness during the looming exercise.

'That's something we need to decide today,' he replied. 'Stay and help us. We value your opinion, sir. Which one d'you think your mum'd pick?'

His son blanched, turning tail to fetch a drink. 'God! I have no clue. Don't make this all up to me. Back in a min'. May I pinch some bickies?'

'Go ahead,' Cathy laughed. 'He's doing well, isn't he? Getting more like you every time I see him, wisecracks and all.'

With the list of chart-toppers on the left and the autobiography's table of contents on the right, the threesome debated whether to order the playlist to strict chronology or to build to an emotional *crescendo*. The result of a focus group comprising twenty of the couple's biggest fans had come out at fifty-fifty; a most unhelpful outcome!

'I think the original "Original"'s the best one,' Ryan offered, having traced eight different versions in Stonebridge's archives. 'It puts it into the right context for the book, as opposed to being solely about you guys. It'd be good to remember it this way rather than from the memorial service.'

The sensitivity in the cricketer's comments took his father by surprise. 'Yeah. I like that, son. See? It's a good thing you're here. *Whaddya* reckon, Cath? *Mardi Gras* version?'

'Oh, I love them all,' she said, wiping a tear from the corner of her eye. 'My favourite's the one you recorded at Palm Springs for your anniversary in 'ninety-four. But I agree with Jet... Ryan, I mean... The *Mardi Gras* footage puts it in the right light for the reader. Do we have to use the same audio track as video clip?'

'No. Guess not,' Jeff shrugged. 'Not for any of them. Doesn't really matter. No-one'll listen to the audio at the same time as watching the video. Whatever... You decide. I'm going down for a cigarette. Coming, Ry? Join me in the car park while the ladies put the show together.'

Cathy laughed at the youngster's grudging obedience. 'Ooh! A trip to the car park. There's an offer you can't refuse, you lucky boy!'

She felt sorry for her two favourite men, their movements restricted by Melbourne's suffocating affection for the bereaved family. Before Lynn's shooting, her handsome billionaire employer had revelled in the company he always drew when smoking on the steps of their Collins Street office building, holding court with supporters and critics alike and posing for photographs with astonished tourists.

These days, the attention the gaunt celebrity attracted tended to fall into two quite distinct categories: either angry fans baying for blood in revenge for his wife's untimely demise or a stream of opportunistic women hell-bent on becoming the next Missus Jeff Diamond.

At least having the popular sportsman by his side might make people think twice about airing their less savoury opinions, yet she understood why the lonely man preferred the basement's seclusion, quite apart from being able to admire the string of expensive vehicles parked there while their executive owners toiled away on the floors above.

'What was it like on Copa Cabana beach that day?' Ryan asked, squatting on the kerb a few paces from the lift doors. 'Gay Pride was still pretty marginal in 'ninety-one, wasn't it? Not like now?'

Jeff scratched his chin, in dire need of a shave. 'Safety in numbers, mate,' he replied, taking a long drag on his cigarette and gulping the smoke down into his lungs. 'The Rio carnival's about much more than Gay Pride. It's a mainstream carnival, celebrating hedonism of all varieties. We were invited down there because of our connection with South American HIV and AIDS charities, so everyone automatically assumed we were there for Gay Pride. It all kind of snowballed from there.'

'So what was it like in such a huge crowd?' his son pulled the conversation back from the nostalgic rhetoric to which his dad was prone.

'Ah, y'know... Nuts! Hard to breathe sometimes, especially after dark, when all the incense burners were lit. I remember one of the cameramen fell off the truck, he got so doped up by the dense air.'

'Really?' the younger man chuckled. 'How long did it take you to notice?'

His father grinned. 'About four hundred metres! He hitched a lift on a scooter. Caught us up just as we were bringing the song down. Lynn spotted him being *hoiked* up; six beefy brutes heaving his buttocks in the air.'

'Was he gay?'

'Nope. At least he wasn't before that. Maybe he found himself in Rio.'

'So can I ask you a soul-mate question?' Ryan veered off on a sudden tangent.

'Sure. Ask anything you want.'

'What I'm struggling to understand is, if you and Mum have been soul-mates for generations, how come you think she's a much younger soul than you?'

'No idea,' Jeff shook his head, stubbing his cigarette out on the side of the litter bin. 'It always felt as if I'd been round a few more times than she had. Like I'd learned from a far broader set of experiences. Another good question as yet unanswered. Why d'you ask?'

'No reason,' the sportsman responded. 'Just wondering whether it's all feasible, this reincarnation business. Or whether it's all in your head, and we're never going to know you again.'

The forty-four-year-old let the door into the lift lobby rock on its hinges, pulling his son's chest towards his. He was asking a great deal of his two amazing children, and they seldom fought back against his idealistic exit plan.

'Whoa, mate. Let's talk about this when we get home. I know it's a fucking huge leap of faith for you guys. Did you talk about this with Kizzo?'

'Yeah. Her take's that she's decided to let you run with it, but I'm not so sure. Do you really know what you're doing, Dad?'

'Nope. Of course not. Do *you* know what's going to happen every time a bouncer leaves your hand? Or every time you sweep an in-swinger?'

'Most of the time,' the lad scoffed. 'Your point being?'

The lift bell sounded, and the pair of Diamonds stood aside to let four Japanese businessmen out, accompanied by a secretary whose make-up would have been more suited to the *Mardi Gras* than to the Boardroom. They exchanged matching scowls of distaste, gave respectful bows and stepped into the emptied chamber.

'My point being that we all have to take chances; leave some things to fate. If the alternative is to exist somewhere my soul no longer belongs, I'd rather give it a red-hot go at starting again. No science behind it. Blind, dumb faith and unassuaged lust.'

***

'Happy birthday, Kierney!' Lynn announced, heralding the family's arrival at her bedroom door. 'May we come in?'

'Too late!' her brother burst in, arms laden with colourful gift-wrapped packages. 'We're here, like it or not!'

The popular refrain sung in three-part harmony brought the lazy Sunday morning at *Escondido* to a standstill. Violent storms over Indonesia had threatened to derail the family's celebrations, with Jeff's flight first diverting to Singapore before taking the long way around the enormous Australasian land mass. The aeroplane carrying three hundred and fifty passengers had eventually touched down at Tullamarine in the early hours of the morning, with at least one of this significant number impatient for the doors to release.

Disrupted airline schedules always put the housebound mother on edge too, and the wanderer was not surprised to find her on the treadmill when he timed his homecoming with the sunrise. They made their fevered reacquaintance in the study, not wishing their tryst to be interrupted by excitable early risers.

'Come in!' Kierney shouted, delighted to see everyone. 'What time is it?'

'Eight-thirty,' her mother answered. '*Papá* nearly didn't make it in time.'

Jeff sat down on the edge of the single bed with its covers bunched up at one end due to the steamy night temperature, leaning in to receive a hug to welcome him home. 'Happy birthday, *pequeñita*,' he said, kissing her with tears in his eyes. 'Today is a very special day.'

'Thanks, everyone. All these prezzies! For me? It is a special day!'

'You need to come downstairs,' Jet commanded. 'This room's too much of a mess to do the opening thing in here. You won't be able to tell what's new and what's old.'

'No, mate,' the father cut his bossy son off. 'Kizzy decides. Here or downstairs, baby?'

'*I* decide?' Kierney couldn't believe her luck. 'Wow! That's good. It really *is* a special day!'

Lynn's eyes were full of wonder, eager for the morning's adventure to be underway. Her husband had been looking forward to this day for months now, with many hours of consultation having been devoted to it. Now the day had finally arrived, she realised he wasn't alone in his eagerness for the magic to unfold.

'*Sí, señorita*,' the great man affirmed, winking at his dream girl. 'Today, *nuestra hija hermosa, llena de promesas*, you make all the decisions. Today is your *bat mitzvah*.'

'No, it's not,' Kierney giggled. '*Papá*, you're a year early. I'm only twelve today. You didn't go away for that long.'

Jet had plonked himself down on the floor next to the pile of presents, none the wiser to their parents' secret. Lynn perched on the edge of the mattress beside the dark-haired half of her family. It was a pleasure to see the troubled soul reshape his appalling childhood through their pair of little gems, and she had difficulty making up her mind as to who was the more excited.

During his research prior to their son's thirteenth birthday, Jeff had been surprised to discover that, according to Jewish tradition, girls attained adulthood at twelve; a year earlier than boys. It presented a rare lucky break for his wife, able to exercise superiority over her competent world-changer, who had long refuted the myth of girls maturing at a younger age than boys.

'Oh, but it is,' her dad countered. 'I didn't know it either until last year, when I was digging around for information for Jetto's *bar mitzvah*. I'm pretty sure we never had one for Auntie Lena, so I had no idea it was twelve and not thirteen. We decided to leave it as a surprise when we found out.'

'So where are you taking Kizzy for her *bat mitzvah* weekend?' the big brother asked. 'What's the equivalent of Bathurst for girls?'

'The United Nations?' the earnest youngster offered.

The intellectual smiled. 'Not yet, but you'll get there soon enough. We've got a much different strategy for your entry into womanhood, gorgeous.'

'Really? What?'

'Hold your horses! Nothing happens 'til we get showered and dressed. Let's open all these presents first, and then we'll explain,' Lynn suggested. 'Down or up?'

'Down,' the birthday girl stated, springing up to a standing position on her bed and raising triumphant arms towards the ceiling. 'I decide... No! Wait... I proclaim that Kierney Diamond's *bat mitzvah* shall begin in the lounge room in twenty minutes! Is that enough time?'

'Splendid, splendid!' her father impersonated their grandpa, seizing the girl under the armpits and twirling her off the mattress and round in a circle before letting her feet drop onto the carpet. 'Alright, already, *meyn mentshn. Vamanos.*'

The others left the gleeful twelve-year-old to her own devices, adjourning to a breakfast hurriedly relocated from the deck to the lounge room owing to a sudden summer drenching. While his mother laid everything out picnic-style on the floor next to the white grand piano, Jet arranged his sister's gifts in a precarious tower.

Jeff stole into the kitchen and wrapped his arms around the stunning blonde who made his life so perfect, anxious to expel some of the pent-up verve which was so foreign to him this early in the day. When she sent him packing for impeding her progress once too often, he did his best to sabotage his son's efforts by pulling a vital package from the bottom of the colourful structure, much to the boy's annoyance.

When the littlest Diamond graced the doorway, her father ran to escort her to breakfast like a bride to the altar. The playful chaperone twisted and turned several times on their way through the room, eventually inviting the birthday girl to sit down on a cushion in pride of place next to her favourite pancakes.

After proposing a toast with orange juice, Jet began to dispense presents from his wobbly display. Each item was unwrapped with the utmost care, testing everyone else's patience, and greeted with a squeal of delight followed by vociferous thanks. Once the full splendour and generosity were revealed, the family took turns to pose for happy snaps.

'OK!' Lynn called out to her husband, who jumped up to relieve her of a tray of teas and coffees. 'You'd better tell Kierney your plan, or "G" and "G"'ll arrive and we'll still be sitting in here!'

The excited girl looked up from a book which had captivated her already. 'What plan, *Papá*? I've never had a birthday plan before. This is a lovely *bat mitzvah. Gracias a todos.*'

'You're welcome, *pequeñita*. Very welcome,' Jeff grinned. 'It's the only *bat mitzvah* you'll ever have. Once in a lifetime experience. And I need to give thanks too, 'cause I no longer have to take responsibility for any of your sins. We're off the hook, angel.'

Lynn pouted, her hands egging him on. 'It makes me feel old though.'

'What's the damned plan?' Jet teased, stamping his foot. 'Stop focussing on yourselves, grown-ups.'

'Bloody cheek, Jetto!' his father exclaimed, walking across the room to flip the lid off the piano's keyboard. 'That's an accusation and a half... Thanks heaps for the vote of confidence! OK. Kierney Lynn Freedom Diamond, come over here, *s'il te plaît.*'

Eyes wide with intrigue, the youngest family member tiptoed towards him, with her brother hot on her heels. Resting on the highest-pitched piano keys, hidden from view all night, was a white envelope enscribed with her name and the date. While his wife took over photographic duties, Jeff handed it to the slender girl in the flowing dress.

Was it his imagination, or had she started to look more womanly since this morning? Her face was lengthening, its features becoming finer, and her hands sported longer, shapely fingernails. With bare feet and her hair tied back off her face in an untidy ponytail, it was as if she had arrived at the cusp of adulthood. A lump formed in the old soul's throat at how unready he was to let his children go. With their childhoods went his, and this frightened him more than he cared to acknowledge.

'Now, looks can deceive,' the comic regrouped, placing a heavy hand on Kierney's shoulder and staring into his wife's shining blue eyes. 'We all know you've been an adult for a few years already, but happy coming of age, Kierney. This is from *Mamá* and me.'

Jeff felt his skin tingle as the birthday girl leaned her full weight against his hip in a gratifyingly familiar way. He breathed a sigh of relief, pleased she felt like the same child he had farewelled last week. He cupped his left hand around hers, tugging it against his ribs to maximise the warmth of her friendliness.

'What is it, *Papá?*'

'*Abrirlo,*' he replied. 'It's a decision for you to make before you're thirteen.'

Kierney looked puzzled, almost too scared to break the seal. 'A decision?'

Her mother nodded, camera poised to capture her opening the gift and finding out what it contained. The twelve-year-old slid her left index finger under the edge of the flap and tore the envelope open centimetre by centimetre, her legs juddering with nervous energy.

Inside were two pieces of paper, one larger and folded in half around its smaller counterpart. She removed them, flattening them out, and began to read the handwritten message on the topmost sheet.

"Kierney Lynn Freedom Diamond, happy twelfth birthday from *Mamá*, Jet and me.

The future is all yours, beautiful *bat mitzvah* girl. You will soon be a huge success, and from today you're in control of the journey. Here's something we'd like you to use wisely. Make thoughtful choices. Seek as much advice as you need, but you decide.

Te amamos, Kierney. *Te amamos mucho, mucho. Papá* xxxx"

The gipsy girl's dark eyes filled first with amazement and then with tears, flipping over to the second piece of paper. It was a cheque made out in her name. Catching her breath and almost falling over with incredulity, her eyes searched upwards for her beloved *papá*'s sanction.

'A million dollars? To spend on useful things. *O, gracias tanto, tanto, Papá,*' she cried, hugging his waist and rocking him from side to side. '*Te amo.* I love you too, *Mamá.*'

Kierney tore over to Lynn, who braced herself to receive the full force of the girl's gratitude. 'I love you too too, darling! We know you'll do the right thing with this money.'

'Oh, *Mamá,*' she wept without inhibition. 'I shall, I shall! This is the best birthday ever. How can I learn how to spend a million dollars?'

'We'll help you,' her dad answered from the piano stool, where he had collapsed under the weight of his own joy. 'But that question's an excellent start.'

'You need to think about it very carefully, now you're an adult,' Jet added, asserting the vast amount of knowledge he had gained since the previous July.

LORRAINE PESTELL

Spread Your Wings

As an antidote to all the hype surrounding the Diamond family and to the grim and sometimes demoralising nature of their humanitarian work, the quartet set about writing a movie screenplay together. A plot took shape over a lazy Sunday lunch on the *patio* at *Escondido*, and sketch after sketch was incorporated as each bizarre idea took shape. Jet and Kierney were keen and productive participants, eager to learn the science behind creative arts. It was also the perfect way to delve into aspects of life with which the youngsters were coming to grips.

'I can't believe I'm having a dispute with my daughter about the definition of masturbation,' Jeff laughed, shaking his head and reaching for the dictionary.

Kierney shrugged and smiled a saccharine smile, saying nothing.

'Y'know...' her father continued. 'Strangely, it gives me a certain thrill of pride, to be perfectly honest. Not only did we create baby humans, but now we're making you into a couple of adults. Does this mean I've graduated as a parent?'

'You graduated as a parent a long time ago,' his daughter countered. 'This is your Masters.'

'Shit!' Jeff laughed. 'Y'think? What do I have to do for my PhD? Become a grandfather?'

'Yes, I do think! A granddad bouncing our kids on your knee and teaching them about sex.'

'Jesus Christ! That doesn't bear thinking about on so many levels. Where were we again?'

With his daughter peering over his shoulder, breathy giggles warming his ear, the intellectual flicked through page after page of the family's well-worn Macquarie hardback until he reached the entry for their *mot du jour*. Their eyes met over the dual definition.

'It's both!' Kierney said, pumping her fist and raising a hand for a high-five. 'Perfect. We were both right. That doesn't happen very often.'

'Well done, brain-box,' her dad completed the gesture and slammed the dictionary shut. 'The tide is turning. Did you get the results back for your chemistry test?'

The twelve-year-old nodded. 'I did OK. Eighty-eight.'

'Eighty-eight percent? Pretty good for a subject you don't like. Well done for that too. Does *Mamá* know?'

'Yes. The paper's downstairs, in the kitchen, if you want to see it. I can't get interested in chemistry. It won't serve any purpose in my life.'

Jeff laughed aloud. 'No. No real purpose except for the physical composition of just about everything!'

'No!' his adorable rebel whined, ramming her hands onto her hips. 'No purpose for my career. You know what I mean.'

'Yes, I do know exactly what you mean, *pequeñita*, because I never got fired up about chemistry either. But you need to put your career on hold for a while. Even lawyers and judges can benefit from knowing how stuff's put together.'

'Oh, OK,' Kierney batted her eyelids. 'I came second in the class. Did you see the T-shirt I had printed?'

Lynn had warned the maligned father that their butter-wouldn't-melt daughter had taken matters into her own hands after the debunked school dance idea. The youngster pulled the new item of clothing out of a plastic bag and held it up against her body, plain white except for a linear design on the chest, saying, "I ♥ MY DAD".

Her broad grin vanished as soon as she clocked the despair on Jeff's face. 'What's the matter? Don't you like it?' she asked. 'It's meant to be funny. I thought you'd like getting one over on those idiotic critics.'

The superstar held his hand out for the T-shirt, holding it up to examine the slogan before screwing it into a ball on his lap. Suppressing his first response, only to have the void supplanted with a potent nicotine craving, he struggled to understand why he had taken this series of actions. Why the need for such a sensory connection to this inflammatory piece of clothing? And furthermore, at whom or what was he so angry?

'Kiz, *I* love it. Of course I do. I love the sentiment and I love that you want to flaunt it, but it won't work out the way you think,' the wise man began to explain, realising his *bat mitzvah* girl was not quite as mature as she claimed. 'Sit down, gorgeous, please.'

'But why?' Kierney moaned, disgruntled. 'What do you mean by "won't work out the way I think"?'

''Cause it won't be taken as a joke,' Jeff replied. 'You're not yet in a position to say "Up yours" to people who think they're protecting you. Plus it puts me in a worse position too. People'll think you're having a go at their prudishness.'

'I am!' she dared to laugh. 'It's ridiculous. You always say so.'

'I know, but you can't do this. It's one thing to speak out *en famille*, but not in public. Not so brazen, if you know what that means... I'm sure *Mamá* told you something similar.'

160

The twelve-year-old blushed, snatching the offending article back. 'I haven't shown her yet. I wanted to show you first. I thought you'd be rapt.'

Jeff sighed, sitting on his hands to prevent their incessant fidgeting. 'Jeez, baby, I would be rapt if it wasn't likely to put us in the shit even more than we already are! The situation *is* ridiculous, for sure, but we can't afford to alienate anyone; press, fans, y'know... Believe it or not, most of the people who object to the way I behave around you are only trying to protect you. Or rather, they think they are. Your laudable campaign for our civil liberties will fail, Kizzy, this time. I guarantee it.'

'It won't! I don't agree,' Kierney pouted. 'Why shouldn't I tell people that I'm perfectly happy with how things are between us? If they see I'm happy, maybe they won't keep banging on about it. They'll see they're making a fuss over nothing.'

The billionnaire shook his head. Motioning for his daughter to follow him, he led her out of the office, down the corridor and through the kitchen, collecting a packet of cigarettes and his lighter on the way through to the verandah. He pulled a chair out and invited her to sit down while he stretched his spine and sedated his mixed-up emotions.

'Your argument sounds logical, *pequeñita.*'

'That's 'cause it *is* logical,' the cheeky girl shrugged, mimicking his pose.

'Don't push it,' her father warned. 'It's logical for you and me, and for *Mamá* and Jet and most people who know us well, which is why I'm flattered that you designed the T-shirt. I'd love to see you wearing it at home. Every day. But you have to trust me and *Mamá* on this... If you wear this in public, it'll backfire on you. On all of us.'

'It won't. I'm sure it won't. It's for a magazine interview, and it'll work, *Papá.*'

'No, Kizzo. You can defy me all you like, but I'm telling you you'll suffer the consequences. No, make that "We'll suffer the consequences," in fact. Who's doing the interview? Next you're going to tell me it's "Playboy" or "Penthouse" or something... Jesus Christ!'

'What's "Playboy" and "Penthouse"?' Kierney asked, having a fairly good idea. 'Porno'?'

Jeff chuckled. 'Porno'?'

'Hey, stop! Why are you laughing at me? That's not fair, *Papá.* You always tell Jet not to tease me.'

'Oh, I don't mean to tease you, angel. I really don't,' the doting dad stroked the youngster's cheek. 'You are so beautiful when you're all riled up, and the word "porno"' just sounds so incongruous coming out of your mouth. They're men's mags, yes. Soft porn'. Forget I even mentioned them, OK?'

The dark-haired girl stood up and hugged her frazzled mentor, beginning to doubt herself. Her parents, especially this maverick of a man whom so many revered for his courage in the face of outdated conventions, never normally opposed her ideas with quite so much conviction. Perhaps she ought to pay closer attention.

'OK. So tell me why it's not going to work.'

'It'll piss them off, for one thing. You know what *Mamá* says about keeping the customers happy… Or else they'll assume you're too *naïve*, or even that I put you up to it. There are heaps of child abuse cases where the kid doesn't realise there's anything untoward going on. It's called "grooming". They'll put us in the same bracket, angel, and neither of us wants that to happen, do we? Do either of us? Does we?'

'Does we? I love how you take liberties with grammar! It's so nerdily daring. But no, there's nothing wrong with the way you treat me,' the young girl insisted.

Her father shook his head. 'We know that, sure. Daringly nerdy, even… You may well genuinely believe there's nothing wrong with how we are together, but the law's purpose is to cater for the possibility that there might be something dodgy going on that you're unaware of. So which is it? Sheila Average-Magazine-Reader doesn't know what our life's really like. And is there not even the slightest chance you might be ignorant about perverted adult stuff at only twelve years old?'

Kierney shrugged, her eyeballs tracking her finger's progress while it traced abstract patterns in the layer of dust and leaves which had settled on the *patio* table after the night's coastal gales. Her silence divulged a certain concession that these persuasive analyses were at least worth further consideration, though she was still not prepared to admit to sailing uncharted waters.

Jeff continued, his tone kinder this time. 'In many ways, I hope you are ignorant about these things.'

'I know what you mean,' she said, 'but I thought you didn't believe in keeping information from kids.'

'I don't. Doesn't mean I want you to hear this stuff and start filling your brain with fear and negativity before you need to. It's called "protecting your innocence". It's what dads do. People don't always react the way you expect them to, *pequeñita*. You know that already.'

The young girl remained adamant, reaching across to snatch the T-shirt back again from her father's lap and hugging it close to her chest. 'No, *Papá*. I don't care about all that. I just wanted to have my photo' taken in this and do an interview about our family. Just like you and *Mamá* do when you've got something to say.'

'Sure, baby. But to achieve what? Explain to me where you think that'd get us?'

'It'll tell everyone I love you and that they should mind their own business.'

Jeff smiled at her vehemence. 'Clever switch away from the conditional, gorgeous. You're listening very carefully. I like your style a whole lot, but I can't let you do this.'

'Oh, why not?' Kierney blasted, clenching both fists and thumping her knees. 'I thought you'd be proud of my independence. One minute you're *bat mitzvah*ing me, and then you tape my mouth.'

The showman exhaled in surprise. 'Tape your mouth! Very nice, my little drama queen. You see me taping your mouth? I would be proud of you if I wasn't so damned sure you'll end up looking like a dork. Look at this...'

Pointing at the white bundle in his daughter's lap, he invited her to stand up and hold it in front of her body. She obliged, first reading the slogan upside-down and then staring back at her unusually obstinate alter-ego.

'Kizzy, you're a twelve-year-old girl,' he clarified, rubbing the T-shirt's sleeve between his thumb and forefinger. 'Still four years away from the age of consent. You know what that is, don't you?'

'Yes. Legal age for having sex.'

'*Bueno*. I'm nearly forty, and this could easily be a nightdress. It could, couldn't it?'

Kierney nodded, unperturbed. Inwardly, the teacher rejoiced. He and Lynn had raised resilient children who were prepared to stand up and be counted. Now their job was to teach them how to apply this useful attribute to their advantage rather than becoming its victim.

Jeff carried on. 'Think about it... If I saw a picture of a beautiful young woman in a magazine wearing nothing but a nightshirt, in no matter how innocent a pose, my mind would instantly turn to sex.'

'I know,' his daughter laughed. 'But that's you.'

'No. That's most adults, baby,' her father insisted, resisting the temptation to smile. 'Believe me. Adults' brains work differently to kids'. Once we hit puberty, we're programmed to think about sex. I'm not even sure why, to be honest... Even prudes and puritans who'd prefer to deny sex even happens at all, their minds still work that way mostly. If they didn't, why else d'you think they kick up such an unholy fuss about this sort of thing?'

Hearing her beloved *papá* plead a strong case for the opposite point of view, Kierney began to appreciate his perspective. She knew he wouldn't lie to her. If he thought this was an issue worth contesting, he would support her, wouldn't he? This must be a bad move after all.

'OK,' she sighed. 'It's just not fair, that's all. I'm so powerless. So much for being in control of my own destiny.'

The compassionate man laughed, offering the plaintiff a hug. 'Oh, no! Not you as well.'

'As well? What do you mean?'

'Sorry, angel. I'm not laughing at you.'

His daughter gritted her teeth. 'Sounds like it.'

'I'm laughing about something you reminded me of, and it's lovely. You sound just like your *mamá* when she and I first met. Being powerless is a kid's lot in life, gorgeous. And for good reason, 'cause you need to learn how to use power sensibly before we let you have it and use it in anger. And in this particular instance, I'm bloody glad you're powerless. Is the power to make a fool of yourself something you crave?'

'No. Course not! I won't make a fool of myself. I'm going to make a fool of Sheila Average-Magazine-Reader,' the girl snarled, unable to stop giggling at the convoluted moniker.

'Kizzy, you *will*. Listen to me! If you're lucky, the protection your youth affords'll probably save your neck. I hope it'll help us stay out of trouble. That doesn't happen too often, I assure you.'

Kierney sunk back onto the poolside chair, deflated and glum. Noticing how uncomfortable she had become, her father swore he could feel her body temperature rise.

'You're not going to be proud of me then,' the Melbourne Academy student muttered, unwilling to make eye contact.

'*¿Qué tal?*' Jeff asked, the penny not taking long to drop. 'Jesus, *pequeñita*. You've already done the interview. Is that why you've wilted like yesterday's spinach?'

The youngster nodded, tears spilling down her cheeks. 'Sorry, *Papá*,' she whispered. 'I did it yesterday, while you and *Mamá* were in Sydney.'

The celebrity was determined not to let his daughter understand the extent of his disappointment. 'Does *Mamá* know?'

'Yes and no,' the dark-haired gipsy chanced, a little more defiant again. 'She knows I did an interview, but she doesn't know about the T-shirt or being photographed in it.'

Her father lowered his tall frame into an empty chair, the familiar, stale taste of panic filling his mouth and all enthusiasm for the day running to ground. Kierney moved to sit on his knee for a cuddle. At the last minute, her instincts made her recoil, taking his hand instead.

Annoyed that the youngster had thought twice about seeking refuge in his lap, Jeff allowed her some latitude. He understood only too well the importance of keeping one's distance. Growing up was hard for everyone, no matter how old or young.

'Good,' he frowned. 'Although you should've told her the whole story. Please trust us, Kizzo. We need to know what's likely to hit the press if you're intent on paving your own path to notoriety, and so do Cathy and the guys in the office. They're the ones who get to listen to the prude squad's gripes. It's only fair to tell them what's coming their way, isn't it, angel? And we all need to help them front up to the consequences on your behalf.'

Kierney cringed. 'Yes. I'm really sorry, *Papá*.'

The billionnaire's stomach felt uneasy, and he coughed his windpipe clear while lighting another cigarette. 'Hmm... I think you will be. Do you know when it's released? Which magazine is it?'

Shaking her apologetic head, the twelve-year-old began to cry, this time giving in to the desire for paternal comfort. Jeff accepted her with open arms and a kiss on her perspiring temple. A salutary lesson to be learned for him and his beautiful best friend too, he acknowledged. Could the Diamond parents trust Stonebridge Music's employees to exercise a duty of care towards Jet and Kierney on their behalf? Obviously not.

As the full account became evident, pouring forth from repentant lips, it turned out that Cathy had failed to assign someone to oversee an interview with the minor celebrity. This was a serious breach of protocol in itself, about which Lynn would be furious. However, even if another adult had been in attendance when the girl presented for the photographer dressed only in a T-shirt, he wondered whether he or she would have objected or paused proceedings to seek counsel.

'Don't stress,' he said, cupping her head against his chest. 'We'll deal with it. D'you want to tell *Mamá*, or shall I?'

Kierney sniffed, lifting her chin. 'I'm surprised you're letting me choose,' she smiled. '*Mamá* wouldn't.'

'Probably not. You're right. You need to do it.'

'Oh! Do you think she'll be angry? I shouldn't have said anything. Damn!'

'No,' Jeff shook his head, grinning at her kittenish audacity under pressure. 'Think before you speak, baby! *Mamá* won't be angry. She'll be worried about what people are going to say when they read the article. We both understand why you did it. It wasn't so long ago that *la mamá* was but a powerless child. She won't have forgotten the oppression of youth.'

A smile spread across the girl's tanned face, shifting her weight until she sat upright, high enough yo give her dad a kiss. 'You're so good at cheering us up. *Gracias, amigo*.'

***

The tale of the indecorous nightdress unfolded as predicted over the ensuing week. A two-page article appeared in a popular women's magazine, featuring three inserts showing the confident youngster proclaiming love for her precious *papá*. The measured piece had been fashioned with Kierney's best interests in mind, yet conjecture abounded as soon as copies left newsagents' shelves. Daily newspapers rushed to cover the fallout, which even featured on the television evening news in Australia's eastern states.

'Cath, hi,' the songwriter opened, hearing his chief publicist take the call. 'I'm guessing you've seen it?'

'Yes. I'm sorry, Jeff. Has Lynn seen it too?'

'Not yet,' her boss answered. 'She's in the US. I'll ring her later on. Anything happened over there?'

'Apart from some very red faces and another resignation offer, no, not much,' the office manager dared to joke. 'Nicole and I feel terrible. I'm so sorry we didn't supervise Kierney. We should've stayed in the room with her.'

'Yeah,' the headstrong star sighed. 'She's still learning, guys. Not old enough to lose the training wheels just yet, eh? We'll know for next time. No-one's to blame, and we're all to blame. Lynn and I feel plenty guilty too. We should've counselled her or found out what she was planning. She's determined, I'll give her that. D'you know how she managed to order the T-shirt with that slogan in the first place?'

'No. I suspect she cornered Minnow. You know how easy he is to manipulate.'

'Minnow?' Jeff echoed. 'Who's Minnow? That shy trainee ad' guy?'

'Yes. He's the one who offered to resign first. It's a sweet article actually, don't you think?' Cathy added, hoping she wasn't overstepping the mark. 'Everything would've been fine If she hadn't insisted on being photographed in the T-shirt. Jeff Diamond's daughter wants people to treat him fairly and not make him out to be someone he's not. She reminds me of you when you first started out, if you don't mind me saying so.'

'I know. Tell me about it! Jesus Christ! Lynn's not about to let me forget this either. Amen for freedom, beauty, truth and love. Now our daddy-daughter love's bloody well out there in all its free and beautiful truth, I have no choice but to back her up.'

'Really?' the marketing specialist was astonished. 'Is that wise?'

'Wise? Who gives a toss about wisdom? This is my daughter we're talking about. What choice do I have? Fuckin' independent women! Watch this space 'cause I'm *gonna* have to go all out. The conniving little fox played me as much as the rest of us, but I love her for it all the same.'

The Diamonds' loyal assistant giggled. 'Wow! She's going to be a handful as she gets older. We'll need to have a strategy. You will, I mean.'

'Yep. *We* shall, Cath. Right first time! Don't stress about it now. Lynn's more philosophical about it than I am,' the rock star explained. 'Well... She was before it was published. Might change her mind when she experiences the aftershocks, but I doubt it. Lynn's not often the mind-changing type.'

'That's true! I'm sorry it's got this far without me stepping in, Jeff. Let me know if I can help.'

Australia's bad-boy-turned-good sighed. 'Yeah. Anyway, thanks. It's not your fault. All we can do is protect Kierney. There's no point trying to gag her now. She's slapped the topic fairly and squarely on the table. Forced the issue in true Diamond style. If she wants freedom of speech as a minor, she needs to learn to live and die by what she says, so let's hope she asks for advice in the future.'

'Do you think she will?' Cathy asked, mindful of her hot-headed employer's outspoken past.

'Yep,' he affirmed. 'She's been burned. And she's getting heaps from her bro', who for a change looks like a saint.'

The mother of two laughed louder this time. 'I can imagine! Jet'd never speak out about something he felt was unjust, would he? Is it "unjust" or "injust"?'

'"Injust" sounds right, but I don't think it is,' Jeff smiled at their shared *penchant* for dissecting the English language. 'Don't distract me with lexical *conundra*, Missus Lane.'

'Apologies, sir,' Cathy flashed back, hoping the great man was only kidding. 'Did you want me to arrange a press conference?'

'Yeah,' he sighed. 'Guess so. Tomorrow morning soon enough? No point panicking, is there? It'd be like we're admitting there's something to hide.'

'Hmm... Alright. Will Kierney be there?'

'Absolutely not,' the celebrity snapped. 'She'll be at school. We'll do something together one evening towards the end of the week if we have to. Depends what happens. Showing up tomorrow'll tease out whether anyone's interested, but I doubt we'll hose it down in one session.'

'I doubt it too.'

'The inner-east leotard and leggings brigade'll be huddled over their skinny *latte*s as we speak,' the Sydney native scoffed. 'Lynn came up with that expression the other day, by the way. I like it. It's an apt caricature to see us through this current crisis. But who gives a fuck, Cath, really?'

'I know,' the couple's loyal assistant agreed. 'People should worry about something important for a change. Just think of all the blokes... rock stars especially... who father children and never even play a part in their lives? They're the ones they should be complaining about. You're the best parent any kid could have, boy or girl. You both are, I should say.'

Jeff paused for a few seconds before responding, reflecting on his own origins and waiting for Gravity to knock him to his knees. It was a pleasant irony indeed for the product of such bad parents to receive a vote of confidence from the middle-classed Melbourne mother, herself partial to the odd communal coffee between early-bird aerobics and her uptown working day.

'Thanks, Cath. Cool of you to say so. We're pretty relaxed within ourselves, but the thunder's going to strike in unexpected places, I reckon. Either it blows up and over in a few days, or someone'll feel compelled to conduct some prolonged examination of our private life. None of us has the time or the appetite for that sort of scrutiny.'

The public relations specialist groaned in sympathy, also mindful of the impact on the Stonebridge Music crew. Her team comprised fourteen permanent staff at the present moment, augmented when necessary by a retainer of willing casuals called upon to respond to the deluges of extra correspondence during each world tour or fundraising campaign. The law of averages would suggest at least a handful of these might not subscribe to the same parenting manual as their charismatic celebrity bosses.

'Well, they won't find anything, so it'll be a waste of time if they do,' she said. 'How's Kierney anyway?'

'Contrite,' Jeff chuckled. 'Embarrassed and maybe even a little ashamed. All constructive emotional reactions. Shows she's heading in the right direction, and we're proud of her for that. She knows it was one almighty error of judgement. We all have to make a few mistakes in life, so why not start counting now, while we're here to bail her out?'

***

Father and daughter ate dinner together that night in their city apartment, having slipped unnoticed into a movie theatre after school to watch "Home Alone" for the second time. The hilarious family comedy provided a welcome diversion, replenishing the dark-haired *duo*'s stamina sufficiently to pick apart the fateful piece of journalism together and undisturbed.

An hour later, Jeff ruled the subject closed and sent Kierney to bring her homework into the lounge room. She was grateful for this subtle show of solidarity, the usual tranquillity found in her bedroom less appealing tonight. There had been no word from Jet, squirrelled away at school where none of his friends would be tempted to turn the cover of a women's glossy magazine.

Hard lessons and their ensuing promises were analysed anew during a long-distance telephone call made at opposite ends of her parents' respective days. They agreed a strategy for tackling the inevitable backlash; an unapologetic allegiance to the end, regardless of who said what about whom. Since their united front's near-fatal schism over something as trivial as their son's cricket training, almost half a marriage ago, the couple had ceased to take each other's opinion for granted. This was not the time to test for exceptions to prove the rule.

The country's media collective descended on Melbourne the following morning, bright and early as predicted, gathering in a conference centre auditorium. Some were keen to satisfy while others sharpened their quills to placate and provoke their various consumers' curiosity. The relationship between The Australian Elvis and his fresh-faced yet precocious gipsy child monopolised the headlines around the world.

From his table in front of the row of cameras, the rock star smiled up at the stunning blonde on screen. 'Morning, angel,' he said. 'I half expected you to be in your nightwear too. Shame.'

Titters of laughter drifted upwards from the press *corps* while the wire's delay took its time to transmit the *risqué* comment from husband to wife. Lynn smiled when it filtered through her earpiece and shook her head as if warning him to tone down the humour.

Melbourne's favourite society figure's resplendent image was beamed into the makeshift television studio from Los Angeles, where she was directing a film. This oversized two-dimensional rendition of his dream girl set her husband's pulse racing while the stage-hands hooked a microphone onto his shirt and tested the sound levels. The forever friends bantered back and forth with the production team, ready to answer any question and defend all accusations sent their way.

And those who came spoiling for a fight were rewarded in spades. First came several questions about the whereabouts of Kierney Lynn Freedom Diamond, which her patient father answered by sticking to the facts. Pleasantries soon over however, the inquisition's depth and divergence shocked even the seasoned crusaders themselves.

Tugging on their invisible elastic connection for moral support, Jeff's unspoken wish to be the one sitting on the other side of the planet was echoed back to him several times during the interview by his empathetic dream girl, who resorted to uncharacteristic bad language on more than one occasion in response to unnecessarily invasive questioning.

Had Jeff Diamond put his daughter up to this stunt?

How dare he use his little girl to further his infamy?

Did Lynn turn a blind eye whenever she left the country?

What unthinkable depravities did their children witness as part of a showbusiness family?

'Please, everyone. Stop!' Lynn's voice rang out through the loudspeakers. 'We've agreed Kierney went too far this time, as Jeff said at the very beginning. We're not perfect. None of us is.'

What sort of mother travelled overseas when her children were in school?

How could they allow their children to conduct interviews unaccompanied?

Didn't they supervise how their daughter spent her pocket money?

A twelve-year-old child should not be given the means to design and print her own T-shirt.

'Edward, this is something Kierney feels very strongly about,' the dignified woman replied to a right-wing journalist known for his disdain of popular culture and its protagonists. 'She wanted to speak up about how unfair some of the opinions are about her father. She loves him, in the same way most girls love their dads. I love mine too. I idolised my dad at that age, just like Jet and Kierney look up to us. That's what's behind the T-shirt's slogan. There's absolutely nothing sexual about this in her mind. She's not old enough to think in those terms.'

No matter how calm and measured the stars' answers, the self-righteous contingent remained up in arms. Cathy Lane and her assistant publicist blanched and winced as vicious vitriol was hurled at their idols, more accustomed to batting away hyperbolic praise and accolades.

How did the couple deal with the subject of sex education?

Shouldn't they be trying to protect their children from these adult concepts?

Did they think it appropriate for their daughter to be photographed in a nightdress?

'OK, OK!' Jeff shouted, raising his hands to silence this next volley of biting questions. 'Now wait a minute, please. Kierney didn't understand the connotations you and I might put on "I heart my dad" when she did this. She sure as hell does now, and we have you guys to thank for that. None of us brought sex into this. You lot did! We're prepared to answer any relevant questions. You're wandering off-topic, and you're not going to like my answers unless we move on.

'Whatever you might think's happening behind the gates of our house, we're a normal family whom you choose to invite into your homes through the TV. You don't have to have us in your faces. Don't like what you read? Read something else! Imagine if I were learning about your private life over my Weetbix each morning? How'd you feel about that?'

An awkward hush descended on the assembled throng, and the famous orator saw Cathy give him a thumbs-up sign. With the added weight of his wife live on trans-Pacific television, the tables were about to be turned. A Diamond press conference seldom tarnished the celebrities' profiles, and she was confident the crowd was in for a treat.

'Lynn and I,' the master communicator regrouped, lifting his gaze to the screen. 'That's her up there, in case you hadn't caught on.'

Hearing laughter ripple through the pack of subdued hounds, Jeff winked into the camera, trusting his beautiful best friend to pick up on his telepathy. 'Gorgeous, isn't she? Anyway... We took the decision when our kids were first born that we wouldn't shut them away, either for your sake or for theirs. We're in the business of raising awareness on some pretty serious issues that affect families everywhere, and keeping our public life segregated from our private life serves no purpose in this arena. Consequently, when Jet and Kierney become involved in our public life, it's inevitable that they're exposed to adult-rated material. They are. No doubt about it. But we work through all that together, and they're fine with it.'

The Olympic gold-medallist nodded from her elevated position, sending shivers running down her outspoken husband's spine. When it was clear she had nothing to add, he continued, gauging room's temperature as its occupants responded to his loosely rehearsed speech.

'Now, for those of you who're convinced I'm committing a whole slew of despicable sins, banging my twelve-year-old daughter, being unfaithful to the world's most beautiful woman, *et cetera, et cetera…* Well, bloody well think again, please. Have you seen the lady up there?' he pointed to the large screen to his right. 'There's where a hundred and ten percent of my sexual energy goes. Not hard to imagine, is it?'

Jeff paused, glaring at a number of reporters whom he knew liked nothing better than to stir up trouble. 'Lynn and I, whether we like it or not, are sex objects. Pure and simple. And actually, we do like it. Sex sells stories, as we're seeing today, and we have stories that need selling. Am I right, angel?'

The world-changer again looked up at the Californian broadcast, impatient for his words to be relayed into the earpiece his dream girl wore. After a few seconds, she nodded and smiled.

'You are right. What we ask people to believe is that Jeff's one of the most loving and compassionate people who ever lived. We're very demonstrative as a couple and as parents, and obviously this has transferred to our children too. They expect us to behave in a certain way. It's how we validate each other. It's fine for some people not to like physical contact, as long as we're free to enjoy it. Please accept our ability to differentiate between showing affection to a child and to each other.'

From his spiny hotel chair in Melbourne, busy carving grooves in his numb buttocks, the songwriter glowed inside. He could always count on his goddess' support, even when asked to turn on her own kind. Fleetingly, he allowed his mind to ponder the type of woman she would have turned into if she had fallen in love with the type of man her father had sought for her.

His blood stirring with a timely reminder of the resistance they had met as young lovers, Jeff spoke out again. 'Thanks heaps, baby. So, if I like to walk down the street hand-in-hand with my daughter, or cuddle her when we're watching TV, or dance with her on stage, it doesn't mean I'm doing anything inappropriate with her. It means I want our kids to know I love them. There's nothing dubious going on between me and either of our children. People who abuse kids are as abhorrent to us as they are to any of you. That's exactly why we founded Childlight, for Christ's sake!'

Cameras flashing on all sides, silence reigned in the room except for a tentative burst of applause from someone at the back of the auditorium. For the lost boy too far from his saviour, it felt as if the throng had transformed itself into a sea of Bart and Marianna Dysons straining on their jewel-studded leashes, intent on pummelling the good-for-nothing son of a murderer into a pulp. He shook his head in an attempt to clear his mind of the old troll's ridiculous demonic hallucination. There was nothing wrong with his character, and he would take these howling predators to the ends of the Earth to prove it.

'I'd like to pose a rhetorical question to you all, please... Has any of you ever given your child a sip from your wine glass?' his wife's refined accent posed over the airwaves. 'Yes, of course you have. Has any father among us here ever seen a picture of a model in a magazine and shown it to his son? I expect you've done that too.'

Discomfort replaced the dumbstruck reticence in the front rows, accompanied by muttering and a few low-key statements of disgust.

'As parents, we're all responsible for our children's exposure to things, whether good or evil,' Lynn carried on, unable to see the audience's reactions. 'Jeff and I believe that being responsible involves providing in a safe environment for Jet and Kierney to learn as much as possible about life. That way, they can make up their minds based on actual knowledge and experience, rather than sensationalism and immature guesswork. As Jeff said, we're proud of Kierney for standing up for herself and her dad like this, despite the fact we advised her not to do it. She knows her dad's done nothing wrong.'

'And with that...' her husband chuckled, flexing his legs back to life. 'Any more questions, please?'

Not to be outdone by these radical, hippy upstarts, the more straight-laced correspondents held their line, casting further aspersions about the couple's motives and libertarian lifestyle. It appeared, however, that they were now in a slim minority, as their more broad-minded peers began to shout them down.

With a conqueror's humble smirk, Jeff stood back and let the warring parties slug it out in front of him. He wondered if his partner could hear this latest development. By the quizzical expression on her face, the mystery would need to be interpreted at a later time, once they were on their own. A roar of full-blooded proportions swelled in his throat, a sensation that had eluded him for several satisfying years.

'Come on, folks...' he cried out. 'Just because Lynn and I are public figures, does it mean we don't have the right to live a normal life as well? I can't give my daughter a kiss and a hug for getting good marks at school because I'm Jeff Diamond? Well, stuff you!'

By now, the couple's supporters had been whipped into a frenzy, and a cheer rose from the crowd.

'Hey, d'you know what?' the celebrity prodded them a little more. 'In case you've never tried it, I can highly recommend staying in touch with your kids, if you pardon the tasteless pun... I bet they're cool people to get to know. They can teach you a lot about yourself. As my exquisite better half says, we've brought our kids up to express themselves freely, whether that's with words, through art forms, sport or physically. It's all positive. It just so happens this time Kierney decided to be more flagrant about putting her point across. She's paid the price, but we're totally behind her. Are we not, angel?'

'Definitely!' his wife laughed after another pregnant pause rife with confusion. 'Kizzy underestimated the risks and went for it, and she… and we… learned a good lesson in the process. Can we call that a wrap?'

'Sure can, gorgeous. Thank you. Have a good day over there. Hurry home. I miss you.'

The fans, newly converted or original variety, whooped as the good-looking pair blew each other kisses. Cathy signalled for the couple's media agent to draw the press conference to a rapid close, and the connection with Lynn was dropped.

***

'Are you and your sis' of a mind to celebrate your dad's fiftieth?' Gerry asked, accepting a pint of draught bitter from Paragon Holdings' Chief Executive Officer.

'Hmm… We should,' Ryan mused, nodding and toasting the greying former accountant. 'Good idea. Kiz and I haven't talked about it yet. She'll be keen to do something.'

The pair had arranged to meet in London to work through a number of contracts under negotiation for new venture capital deals, some necessitating seven-digit down-payments. At twenty-four years old, the captain of the Australian cricket squad still reserved the right to call upon his father's right-hand man to oversee these complex transactions.

Fiona had jumped at the chance for a trip to Europe in the northern hemisphere spring, as long as it included a spot of shopping on Bond Street and a stopover in Paris. Her husband obliged with only minor reservations, knowing she would be entertained royally by a handful of friends with outstanding capabilities in the field of retail therapy, leaving him free to enjoy a working holiday.

'Two things I never was,' the Irishman changed the subject, opening his state-of-the-art laptop and searching for the folder containing the draft contracts.

'Oh, yeah? Which two things are these?' his best friend's son frowned.

'Shy and retiring.'

Ryan laughed. 'No. That's true. Once a workaholic, always a workaholic. We don't have to do this straightaway. Aren't you jet-lagged? Let's get some dinner first.'

'Yes, boss,' Gerry attempted a clumsy salute. 'This one's a no-go, in my opinion.'

The blond sportsman peered at the small screen, recognising the name of an Israeli company which had patented a technique for harvesting genetic material from cancer patients and re-implanting healthy stem cells into the same person. Biotechnology had become an ethical minefield early in the new millennium, and the former financial wizard devoted a large *quota* of his leisure hours to the European Commission's legal directives whenever he wasn't on the golf course.

'Palevsky Blass? Don't they have the right permits?' the younger man asked. 'Roland Blass hounds me twice daily. He's such a pushy pain in the arse, I've stopped answering the 'phone to him. I don't mind giving them the flick.'

'No, mate. Look at this...'

Gerry scrolled down a couple of pages and dragged his index finger back and forth along a set of bullet points, tracing over the words as if he were reading braille. 'Where's the governance around how they're planning to test this? It says nothing about usage restrictions. Who's to say they won't grow whole organs or something outlandish like that? It's like playing God.'

'Playing God?' Ryan repeated. 'More like beating God at his own game! If the poor guy's got cancer, he probably doesn't think God's done a particularly good job.'

'Stuff that for a game of soldiers,' his mentor grumbled. 'It's not right to interfere with genetics. It *is* playing God. You're as much of a heathen as your bloody father.'

The larrikin drained his glass and squelched it down onto a soggy towelling drip-mat, attracting the barman's attention for another round. 'That I am, to be sure. Two more, please. And proud of it. By that definition, isn't all medicine playing God? I hope you never need a pacemaker, my *venereable* friend!'

'Damned cheek! There's a big difference between fixing something that's broken and growing new human body parts.'

'Sure. I'm sorry if this offends your *Catholitude*, but the guy with cancer's probably quite in favour of growing new body parts. I agree we need to impose strict oversight, but we don't burn heretics anymore, I'm told. We give them Nobel prizes.'

Gerry whistled, slamming the lid of his computer closed and pushing it to one side like a dinner left to get cold. He should know better than to pick a fight with Jeff Diamond's son when it came to progress versus religion. The great man had persecuted his business partner's Luddite views for twenty years, agreeing to disagree on most occasions in order to preserve their friendship.

'You're an imperious bastard these days,' he teased. 'You were an impertinent upstart at four years old, and things've only got worse since.'

'You were an impertinent upstart, *sir*,' Ryan corrected his trusted adviser, emphasising the absent mark of respect. 'What do you fancy for dinner? *Sushi*? Or boiled ham and potatoes? I think we should throw these down and find somewhere with live music. Talk about Dad's birthday bash instead of boring business bollocks.'

'Ah, my admirable *alliterary* ambassador, your ambitions are my alimony. Point me in the right direction. As long as I'm back at the hotel by midnight. Us pensioners shouldn't stay out late, you know. It's not good for us to break the curfew.'

The cricketer scowled. 'What the hell are you talking about? Two pints, and you're wasted.'

The unlikely team left the pub and made for a narrow street off Leicester Square, up for trying a blues venue recommended by the women behind the bar. His younger companion noticed the retired businessman was in less of a hurry these days, even having swapped his shiny black leather dress shoes for more comfortable loafers. Perhaps he would one day take heed of his deceased buddy's advice and maximise his downtime while he was able.

Gerry Blake was a rare breed. His instinct for commercial opportunity was matched only by his gigantic personality, put to good use over a career spanning thirty years. Having seized the helm of Blake & Partners' Victorian office when his father had offered him the post as a graduation present, he had not only built the family business into one of the largest management consulting firms in Australia, but had also run the day-to-day operations of Paragon Holdings.

Like his own father before him, Ryan Diamond was fortunate to have a mentor of such high calibre, and schoolboy humour aside, he mined every last nugget of acuity from him at every opportunity. Theirs was an unspoken manly codependence, quite different to any other relationship the sportsman knew, each using the other to bridge the gulf cleaved by a legendary icon.

'What do you think Dad would've done on his big five-oh?' the Colorado-based probationary executive asked. 'If Mum'd still been around...'

His dinner guest hesitated, studying the drinks menu. 'Gone somewhere exotic, I don't doubt.'

'Like where?'

'Oh, I don't know. Somewhere starting with "New" perhaps.'

'"New"? How do you know? Did they plan something?'

'No,' Gerry chuckled. 'They used to have this thing about going to places with "New" in their name, because they went to New Zealand for his twentieth; the first birthday your mum and dad spent together. And then they were in New York for the first birthday after they got back together. I don't recollect if they ever visited any other "new" places for subsequent birthdays, but that was the original plan.'

'Oh, right! I never knew,' Ryan pursed his lips. 'That's kind of cool. Where could we go to activate that tradition again?'

The Irishman watched the young man's gaze lose focus, his mind reconstituting a fond memory or two. 'Well, New York's a no-brainer since Kizzy's there already.'

'Na. New York's too easy for both of us. It'd have to be somewhere we wouldn't normally go.'

'There's New Norcia,' the imposing fifty-three-year-old sniggered, his finger poised next to the name of an unpronounceable beer on the list.

'Isn't that in the middle of nowhere?' the cricket captain laughed. 'In Western Australia?'

'Just a bit! Bloody awful place. Fi conned me into driving there to visit a bakery at some old monastery. Three hours there and three hours back, and then we went to an inner suburb of Perth a day or so later for lunch and walked past the New Norcia Bakery *café*! What a waste of bloody time. Where else is there?'

'Newark, New Jersey?'

'Jesus, Mary and Joseph! We'll be knifed before we get out of the parking lot. No, thank you! I'd rather go back to New Norcia. Try again, Boy Wonder.'

'New Orleans? That'd be cool.'

Gerry raised his eyebrows. 'Ooh, now you're talking. That's a great suggestion.'

'Newcastle? The New South Wales or the Geordie-land version. Or Nova Scotia?'

'Clever,' the Irishman replied. 'Get the Spanish influence in. New Orleans is still doing it for me. Would Kizzy be on board?'

The next-generation Diamonds had seen little of each other over the past two years, big brother running his film-making outfit in Colorado Springs and kid sister climbing a near-vertical ladder at the United Nations, flitting between New York, Geneva and Brussels on a regular basis. Ryan guessed Kierney would always plump for celebrations at Coldwater Creek, being such a romantic chip off the old block.

'Maybe,' he mused, thanking the waiter for their drinks and a plate of *hors d'œuvres*. 'New Hampshire. New Caledonia. I'll send her a text.'

'Stuff it, man! I vote for *N'Orleans*,' the accountant thumped his fist on the edge of the table. 'Motion carried. I think it'd be *formidable*. He'd approve, I'm sure. Don't you think?'

And so the decision was made, Kierney's assent pending. Lynn would also approve, her son thought, as he composed a message on his mobile telephone. The family had spent a number of short breaks in this most un-American of American cities, soaking up the esoteric mix of Creole and French cultures, appeasing their children with talk of *voodoo* and transvestites before leaving them in the safe custody of whichever nannies were on board at the time and creeping out after dark to enjoy the vibrant nightlife.

'Hey, Uncle Gerry... Do you remember the time when we were discussing cricket fielding positions; you, me, Dad and some other dude? Someone you worked with?'

'When was that?'

'Oh, I don't know,' Ryan scoffed. 'Ages ago. When I was about thirteen. I think the other bloke's name was Johnno.'

The Diamonds' financial guru picked a chunk of sourdough out of the bread basket and tore it in half, pausing with the piece held in front of his mouth. 'Ah, Johnno... There've been a few Johnnos over the years, you idiot. Fielding positions, you say? Where were we?'

'At your club. We'd been playing snooker on a night after school. I met you and Dad there. This Johnno was a wazzock actually. He had sons my age who played cricket, and we got talking. There were other blokes there too, engaged in a bit of drunk and disorderly.'

'Drunk and disorderly?' Gerry shouted, objecting to the young man's effrontery to all present. 'Couldn't have been me, mate. And did you say "wazzock"?'

Ryan grinned. 'Yes. What's wrong with that?'

'When in Rome,' the Irishman shook his head. 'I don't think I've ever heard that word in common parlance. If it's the bloke I'm thinking of, he *was* a bit of a wazzock. John Phelan. Runs a construction company in Oakleigh or Bentleigh or thereabouts. Anyway... What of all this?'

Their main courses arrived as the band members began to file onto the stage. Too many tables were crammed into the small venue, within spitting distance of the performers, and one of the guitarists recognised the blond celebrity and made it known to his fellow musicians. Receiving a thumbs-up and a smile, everyone carried on with the jobs at hand.

'I don't know why it came into my head,' the sportsman replied. 'Meeting up with you here still feels weird to me, despite everything that's happened in the last couple of years. When I'm with you and we talk about Dad, I feel like a kid again. Like I don't know anything.'

His mentor guffawed. 'Because you don't know anything, boy! You're still green behind the gills. Everything you've achieved since you took over is a complete fluke. Was that the time when he had to take you aside and explain the birds and the bees?'

'Exactly! Yes! One of the other guys asked me what the difference was between long leg and fine leg, and Johnno yells out before I had time to answer, "It's what your dad gets to sleep with every night!"'

'Fuck me! Yes, I do remember that now. Your old man was none too happy about it, was he? Shit, yeah.'

The young man downed his beer. 'Shit, no! And then you made it ten times worse.'

'Did I?' Gerry sniggered. 'I wouldn't do that. You must have me confused with someone else. What did I do?'

'You know very well what you did... Dad pretended to laugh at first, but I knew he didn't really find it funny. He hated it when people embarrassed me or Kiz in public. He said, "Not every night, mate, unfortunately."'

The former businessman's eyes lit up, and he rushed to swallow his mouthful. 'Ha! That's right! And I said, "Does that mean there's an opening?"'

'Indeed. He was ready to knock your block off, I think,' Ryan smirked. 'He scrunched my head into his side and blocked my ear with his hand. Then he said "Excuse me? Are you seriously expecting me to answer that in front of my son? There's an opening, but you bloody well ain't the man to fill it, Blake-san. Get fucked somewhere else."'

'Blake-san,' Jeff Diamond's closest friend caught his breath. 'Christ! Haven't heard that in a while. It was bloody funny at the time.'

'Hmm… I remember being pissed off that I didn't understand what you were all laughing about. Dad got me to come with him to the bar while he bought another round of drinks. Explained the joke in private. It was a cool moment in time. He was always good like that. Always wanted me to be part of his world. That's all really.'

***

"Your Mother Never Liked Me" was released in August nineteen-ninety-one, Lynn Dyson Diamond's directorial *début*. A fast-paced comedy, the throw-away label assigned to the movie in perpetuity by her charismatic celebrity co-star's summing-up well, not entirely tongue-in-cheek.

Inspired by his challenging assimilation into the aristocratic family, the screenplay had been written for the most part with Jet and Kierney, plus the addition of one or two extra, irresistible ideas from the man himself. The collaboration had come about during a succession of long paternal absences from *Escondido*, a project the threesome threw themselves into *con gusto* for the colder autumn months.

The film was a parody, first and foremost, telling the story of a rock singer looking to quit the high-rolling life after meeting a young *divorcée*, her three children, a wealthy ex-husband and the mother-in-law from hell! Taking little responsibility for the plot, Jeff had stood in the wings while Lynn navigated the obvious sensitivities with Marianna, ready to pick up the pieces from wherever they landed.

Sparks hadn't flown however, and the couple were mollified by their latest work's apparent easy passage to acceptance. Lynn's parents appeared enchanted by the script and its underlying messages of tolerance and allowing people to prove their worthiness in spite of any superficial impressions. Having witnessed Junior and Julie's acrimonious parting and Sandy's camouflaged demise, the Dysons' former perfectionist view of the world was these days less rigid and unimpeachable.

The protagonist's character was deliciously flawed, his inner saint tempted far too easily back into the sinful substructure of showbusiness. The director gave her talented leading man plenty of latitude to stretch his long thespian legs, shooting scene after scene in single takes which had the cast and crew clutching their stomachs at his comical antics and ad-libbed expressions one minute, then dabbing their eyes in stunned silence the next.

Milos Kallidis, who played the children's father, and The Australian Elvis on steroids sparred with each other to generate some of the funniest moments of the movie. From petty jealousies arising when the star managed to sneak the two daughters backstage to meet their idols, "The Wiggles", to a furious father's failed attempt to bribe his son into lying to his mother about her new lover's transgressions, the story mirrored the fate of so many fractured families around the world.

The resultant global success was unprecedented for a film shot in and around Melbourne, putting the magic of hopping on and off city-centre trams high on the priority list for tourists, not to mention introducing some of the Victorian capital's least commercialised music venues to a whole new *clientèle*.

And with the fervour finally dying down, the last quarter of the same year saw each exalted Diamond go their separate ways once again. Jet had devoted himself like a gladiator to cricket training over the spring and had secured a place in the Australian Under Nineteens as their all-rounder, announcing himself as an accurate fast bowler and a creative batsman who could turn matches around from the middle order.

The fourteen-year-old, growing in both mental and physical strength, performed well in a team where he was the youngest by almost three years. He demonstrated still greater potential as a leader than his grandfather had projected, over and above his considerable technical command of the game, and seemed able to cope with any workload put before him.

Jeff negotiated permission from both his wife and Melbourne Academy to take Kierney to Africa while her brother revelled in school and sport. After two weeks touring feeding centres and refugee camps, privileged to be invited into some of her father's meetings, the twelve-year-old returned home disturbed by the hardship she had witnessed and determined to make reparations. Polar opposite in personality to Jet, the dark-haired girl was no less ardent and single-minded in the face of her own ambitions. She vowed to develop a personalised social justice agenda through a mixture of apocalyptic poems and songs, ranging from morbid weighty treatises to stark, black humour.

Demand for the Diamonds' documentary series continued unabated. To celebrate the new movie's blockbuster performance, having received Golden Globe and Oscar nominations, the celebrity couple devoted an entire episode to the powerful spoof. It showed how the idea had germinated after the family had been invited to dinner by Kierney's best friend's parents, during which the two fathers had shared vastly different acculturation experiences with their respective in-laws.

Fergus Loudon, a dentist in Melbourne's eastern suburbs, had migrated to Australia from Northern Ireland after qualifying. He had met his Singaporean wife in the Immigration Department, both waiting to receive their permanent residency papers. Jia En's parents were dead-set against their daughter marrying a Christian; even one who hadn't stepped onto consecrated land for a decade except for the purpose of sightseeing.

Lynn told the cameras that she and the children had enjoyed coming up with funny ideas, sharing their progress with their itinerant father every evening over the telephone, creating storyboards and swapping jokes. Jeff's contribution, as always, was to feed them the inevitable back-story.

Fifteen years of married bliss, during which he had supplied two more Dyson heirs to be flexed and moulded into champions, had only partially closed the wounds of shameful inadequacy. No-one could deny Jeff Diamond a seat at the table these days, yet an undercurrent of bitterness continued to leech from his dormant past.

'This was a real family affair,' he added, overdubbing a length of background video footage of Jet and Kierney joining their parents on stage to collect the award for Best Motion Picture.

The director, holding her husband's hand and smiling, went on to remind viewers of an reporter who had suggested the movie-going public might become confused by the zany parody clashing with their more earnest appeals against famine and hardship across the world. To prove their point, the documentary cut to the scene where the handsome celebrity had tested the television studio audience.

'So are you confused?'

'No!' came the unanimous reply.

'Thanks, guys! It's dangerous to assume anything, I admit, but we're not going to insult people's intelligence by dumbing things down to the lowest common denominator,' Jeff said. 'We can get serious with messages through comedy without offending people. It's a different lens on our mission, that's all. Topics like tolerating the disadvantaged and mentally ill, stateless and starving refugees, and exploring the futility of war are made more palatable and accessible if you expose the humorous sides.'

Another fulfilling year drew to a swift conclusion, suspended on a web of airline flight-paths and freeway jaunts. Program after program, campaign after campaign were launched by the Diamond Celebration Foundation's mighty media machine, their impact bolstered whenever possible by public appearances which their fans clamoured to see at every opportunity.

In New York, while touring to promote his own recent album, the songwriter was welcomed on stage during a concert by The Vultures to join them in performing one of the platinum-selling hits he had co-written with them. The live recording was rushed through editing and production processes and issued as a spontaneous Christmas single, hitting the Number One spot in over thirty countries within two weeks.

The couple's extraordinary capability of turning simple ideas into marketable and lucrative commodities was rubbing off on the children as if by osmosis. Like

Lynn before them, their extra-curricular schedules were stuffed to the gunwales with activities of all kinds, with precious little time to cultivate a separate social lives.

Jet's interest in the fairer sex transitioned from theory and distant fantasies to a strong desire to gain some practical experience the closer he came to his sixteenth birthday. His father thanked his lucky stars that the young buck had lasted this long as a virgin, only too aware of how his inner time-bomb would be ticking in his ear and preventing him from falling asleep.

'Do you think Jenna'd go out with me?' the teenager asked his dad while driving back to *Escondido* one Saturday lunchtime.

Jenna was Gerry and Heather's daughter; now a sophisticated, leggy sixteen-year-old with attitude to spare. A year above the young cricketer at Melbourne Academy, Lynn had heard through Celia that she had become rather a headstrong handful for her mother. By all accounts, the Blakes' accidental granddaughter bore all the hallmarks of a second Tamilla, the younger of her aunts.

It came as no revelation to the red-blooded rock star that Jet found Miss Blake attractive. Despite growing up with minimal contact with the fun-loving party animal who doubled as the Diamonds' manager, she had turned out at least three parts indomitable to one part proper. What a perfect combination for a fourteen-year-old boy on the verge of manhood; the architypal red rag to a raging bull!

'Depends if she's already going out with someone, mate. You need to tread carefully. Don't want to get done over before you even start.'

'Done over? What? Beaten up, you mean?' the youngster responded, sounding a little downhearted. 'I don't know. How do I find out?'

Sneaking a sideways glance at his passenger, Jeff read his mind and chuckled. 'No. Well, yeah. You might get beaten up, but I meant more like she'll tell you to take a running jump if she's got a boyfriend.'

'Oh,' Jet grimaced. 'Makes sense, yeah. She might like me more than him though. That's what happened with you and Mum, didn't it?'

His father grinned, stoked to be reminded of his conquest over Dean Keller, the Richmond Tigers' star forward and the man he deposed as Lynn Dyson's love interest way back in nineteen-seventy-two. He could hardly believe almost a whole generation had cycled round. The memory of the clumsy footballer being thrown out of Bart Dyson's house after a drunken stand-off remained fresh in his mind.

'You're not wrong there. Whoever he might be, Jenna's boyfriend's not likely to be a moron. You need to be prepared for her to turn you down, mate,' the kind man counselled. 'And that's OK. Sixteen for a girl's like eighteen for a bloke. She might well think you're too young. You've known each other since you were kids.'

The boy nodded. 'Hmm... True. She probably still thinks of me as a kid. If I ask her and she says no, then she'll tell everyone at school. I'll be in for a verbal whipping.'

'A verbal whipping?' Jeff echoed. 'What's that? From your mates? It's possible.'

'Fuck,' his son muttered, staring out of the window at the string of car showrooms on the Nepean Highway whizzing past as the Aston Martin gobbled the sticky late-spring bitumen. 'I've changed my mind in that case. I'm not going to ask her out. I'm not going to put myself through that sort of humiliation.'

The young man's knuckles gripped onto a file containing training notes, flicking the pages' corners idly with the ball of his thumb. The world's greatest lover glowed inside, realising his own recklessness had not been replicated in this fine, strapping sportsman. Rather, whether Lynn's influence or his own, their son had developed sufficient control over his sexual urges to apply some forethought before jumping in with both feet.

The billionnaire reached over and snatched the folder from Jet's hands and proceeded to hit him on the head with it.

'Hey! What are you doing?' the cricketer screeched. 'Keep your eyes on the road, old man! I won't be asking anyone out at this rate. My girlfriends'll be crying over my coffin.'

The rev-head lifted his right foot off the accelerator, and the black beast obeyed with a reluctant lag. 'Jesus! Shut up, you bloody idiot! If you fancy Jenna, ask her out,' he scoffed, tossing the papers back into the lad's lap. 'Be honest with yourself first. Then, when you're sure you know what you want, be honest with her. You'll know exactly what to say if you've thought about it, and she'll know you're fair dinkum.'

'Would Gerry whip me too?' the youngster wondered aloud, 'if he found out she'd said no?'

Yes, he would, the doleful father mused.

Verbal whippings had been a Blake family speciality through time immemorial. His mind had now led him to a far less pleasant place, and he pictured Gravity and Miss Irony facing off for their first jig in quite a while. It still hurt to remember the scorn heaped upon his teenaged self by all three supercilious siblings where his crush on Lynn Dyson was concerned.

To counteract the unwarranted yet unsinkable loneliness unleashed by this innocent betrayal, the lost boy cast his thoughts back to his dream girl's original circle of friends. Their lives had been simple and straightforward in comparison with his own at the same age, content to date each other with no expectation of unrequited heartbreak and little danger of polluting their privileged stock. From the outside, it had appeared a safe arrangement when he arrived on the scene, yet he now saw his son's anguish from a far different point of view.

'Yep,' he admitted. 'Gerry'd be unable to resist twisting the knife. He's always been a bastard like that. He'd have to hear about it first though, and you know he hardly ever sees Jenna. But a verbal whipping from Gerry'd be a badge of honour too. Only the best get berated by Blake-san, y'know.'

Jet laughed. 'Cool, thanks! You're right. You're right about everything, as usual. I should practise on a total stranger first.'

The driver shrugged, keeping his eyes on the road to allow the fifteen-year-old to save face. 'Up to you, mate.'

The mighty sports car slipped through the south-eastern suburbs of Brighton and Caulfield, dodging trams and weaving in and out of the dense Saturday afternoon traffic. Its famous occupants shrouded blithely *incognito*, Jeff requested and received an update on the last few weeks at school before the boy's hormones had him relapsing into another daydream.

'Jetto, are you sure you're alright?' the concerned father pressed. 'You keep travelling into outer space mid-sentence. What's on your mind? Still messed up about Jenna?'

The boy shook his head. 'No.'

'Good. So what's up? Can I help?'

'I know what you're going to say,' Jet smirked.

'Ah, yeah? What was I going to say?'

'Trust me. I'm a doctor!' both chanted in unison, embellishing the family's well-worn phrase with their evil grins.

Fortunately, the car had rolled to a standstill for a red light at a broad intersection, its limitless supply of potential energy burbling under the bonnet in anticipation of the throttle's next nudge floorward. Father and son wrestled as boisterously as their seatbelts would allow, attracting the attention of a group of teenaged girls who were halfway across the road. They screamed and pointed into the darkened cabin, recognising the pair through the tinted windscreen.

'Dad, stop!' the cricket star demanded. 'Look at them! We're making arses of ourselves. That could be my first real girlfriend over there.'

Jeff laughed at his son's alarm, straightening himself out and giving the young women a nonchalant wave. His own misspent youth was not so much of a distant memory as to render him impervious to self-consciousness, lifting a patriarchal hand to warn the pedestrians not to linger in the middle of the road.

It was indeed awkward for a fourteen-year-old to be caught behaving like a seven-year-old while seeking to appear twenty-one, he recalled. Conversely however, when one was nearing forty and sprung by a nubile audience while gallivanting like a fourteen-year-old, it was somehow restorative to picture oneself at twenty-one. Life was all about perspectives after all...

'OK, lover-boy,' the dark, sultry celebrity goaded. 'Out you get. I'll pull up over there. Take your time.'

The youngster's jaw dropped, panic hitting him when he saw his dad pointing to a nearby service road with his eyes settling on the passenger door handle. The lights turned green to break the tension, and with a defeatist sigh, the rally driver's feet tap-danced on the pedals as his left hand snapped the gearstick from first to third in a nanosecond.

The *coupé* took off like a guided missile, leaving the other vehicles in its wake as dust specks on the rear-view mirror. Worth the price of a speeding ticket every time, the rev-head turned to his son in triumph as he eased the rate of acceleration before they became airborne. Both heads tipped forward as momentum stabilised.

'Oh, my God!' Jet shouted, twisting round to watch the junction fade into the distance beyond the shimmering haze of spent fuel. 'That was awesomely fast. I broke my neck, I think.'

'Awesomely? Is that in the dictionary?'

'It's in my dictionary. Can I ask you something else, please?'

'*Bien sûr, mon ami,*' Jeff replied. '*Qu'est-ce que c'est que t'inquiète?*'

'*Est-ce qu'on dit masturbation en français?*' the teenager sniggered, putting on a sickly accent.

'*Oui, mon ami. C'est la masturbation, je crois,*' his father confirmed, slamming on the brakes again when the next set of traffic lights turned amber. '*Oh, merde alors!* We should've gone on the freeway. Is that it, mate? A question unworthy of such apprehension.'

Jet slapped the joker's shoulder, only to be knocked off balance by yet another rapid getaway. He lurched sideways this time, an irresistibly narrow gap opening up beside them to their left. The car swerved into the inside lane to dodge a slower car ahead of them and gained valuable ground in their quest for the finish line.

'You're lucky Mum's not here.'

The billionnaire cocked his head. 'I make the most of my opportunities, son. Come on. What's on your mind?'

'OK,' the teenager pulled a queasy face. 'If two people under sixteen masturbate each other, is that under-aged sex?'

'In a legal sense?'

'In any sense.'

'Well... Yep,' Jeff's head moved from side to side.

Frustrated, the Diamond firstborn failed to contain his laughter, even though this was by far the oldest trick in the family's compendium of lame dad jokes. He was in no mood to play games. Whereas his sister liked nothing more than to debate a complex issue with innumerable dimensions, Jet preferred his questions answered with a clear set of options from which he might pick.

'It makes a difference,' the intellectual continued. 'Legal sense or moral sense.'

'But why?'

Jeff abandoned his puerile capers, deciding against instigating further shenanigans in the face of such a sensitive subject. He guessed this enquiry held more than idle curiosity for his young passenger, and neither was he about to shut the boy down to save his obvious discomfort. He and Lynn had committed to full disclosure with their offspring, and thankfully, Blake-style mortification was not a technique they condoned.

'Because...' the thirty-eight-year-old continued, 'if it was a private, consensual act between two minors, then yes, it is under-aged sex, which is illegal but not, in my opinion, immoral. But if one person's much older and the other's under sixteen, then it would be all of the above: under-aged sex, illegal and immoral. It could be implied that the adult's taking advantage of the kid, if push came to shove.'

A mixture of horror and total confusion was painted on the young man's face. 'What?' he gulped. 'Say that again.'

His father laughed. 'Your conscience is telling me you already know the right answer, mate. It's illegal whether the under-aged person consented or not, because people over sixteen aren't supposed to engage in any sort of sex act with a minor. Even if both consented, only the adult can be held responsible for breaking the law. Then in the other *scenario*, both are responsible because neither has the authority to give or withhold consent.'

'Wow! That doesn't seem fair,' Jet moaned. 'If you're old enough to do it, why aren't you old enough to take responsibility?'

The superstar nodded, coaxing a little more from the willful motor now they were clear of electorates blessed with a generous police presence. 'Well might you be perturbed, like your father before you, my boy. The age-old question, in the shell of a nut,' he mimicked Gerald Blake Senior. 'Laws need to be simplified far enough to allow legislators to write them down in such a way that the majority of people will understand them. They have to draw a line in the sand somewhere, Jetto. For reasons known only to them, sixteen is the number they chose for sex.'

His son sniggered. 'But why?'

''Cause otherwise they'd have to introduce some sort of permit to regulate for public safety.'

'A permit for sex? Like a driver's licence, you mean?'

'Exactly! I guess sixteen's the threshold where statistically it's been shown most people are able to control their urges. Unlike their ability to control a motor vehicle, which clearly doesn't happen for another year.'

The schoolboy let out a cynical chuckle which startled his dad. 'That's nuts! I'd rather do the permit thing.'

'It is nuts, I agree. You'd rather take the sex test?'

'Yeah,' came a far less certain confirmation. 'No sweat.'

'Or maybe not,' the father smiled. 'Depends who the examiner is...'

'And what the pass mark is,' Jet cackled. 'Would you have to have sex with the examiner, or do they watch?'

Jeff grimaced. 'Jesus Christ! I'd rather not have those images in my head, thanks all the same. Whatever, mate... These things aren't easy to make rules around,' he found himself defending the very lawmakers he used to despise. 'They can't have a different rule for every possibility, so they need to set a bar at the level that makes most sense for the general populus, even if it pisses off almost every male teenager in the process. You're right though: by protecting all of us, it also penalises those among us who mature earlier and can accept responsibility for their own actions before the average person can. Mum and I spoke about this constantly when we were...'

'Young?' his son teased, reaching his right hand out and winding his fingers along the great man's wrinkled eye socket. 'Those were the days, eh, Dad?'

'You little bastard!' the thirty-nine-year-old cursed. 'I was going to say "first together," but it comes to the same thing. Fancy walking from here?'

'No, thanks! Keep driving. Anyway... I always think it's weird that you can legally have sex two years before you're legally allowed to watch it.'

'Now that *is* nuts!' the unapologetic upstart's *chauffeur* agreed. 'I'm with you on that, kiddo. And you know the irony therein?'

The teenager shook his head. They had reached Mount Eliza's shopping strip, requiring them to slow to a respectable pace and beep the horn at every local resident who stopped to wave and shout out their greetings. The Aston Martin coasted into a parking space outside the newsagent, its engine spluttering its disappointment as the driver pulled the key out of the ignition.

'I'm going in for ciggies. D'you want anything?'

'No, thanks. Except if you're getting ice-cream.'

Jeff chuckled at the contrary statement. 'Here we are, talking about how close you are to the age of consent, and you dare to ask me for ice-cream? No way! We've got ice-cream at home, and we can both have some there without being spotted. Call me a hypocrite... OK with you, Mister Whippy?'

The handsome songwriter slammed the door, rolling his eyes as he spied his son giving him the finger from the passenger seat. Making a swift diversion on the footpath, he ducked into the florist a couple of doors down and emerged a short time later with a dozen red roses.

'Hold these carefully, please,' he said, passing the bunch of flowers across and settling back into the driver's seat. 'All this talk of sex has got me horny beyond belief. You guys better make yourselves scarce for a couple of hours.'

'A couple of hours!' Jet cried. 'You wish! What's it worth? Anyway, carry on with the irony thing about watching R-rated films. You left me in suspense in your senile desperation.'

His father groaned. 'Mate, *gimme* a break! Senile desperation? You're good, but not that good. The irony is, going along with your lowest common denominator theory,' the font of all knowledge expounded as the car prowled up the hill towards the bayside cliffs, 'that for a large number of kids, they're watching sex in movies, *et cetera*, before they've managed to get their leg over in the real world. *¿Comprende?*'

'*¡Sí!*' the fourteen-year-old yelped. '*Comprendo!* Nerds anonymous. Jeez! My balls'll explode if I have to wait that long.'

'Fucking hell!' his father sneered, punching the boy's right shoulder. 'Not an outcome I'd endorse either. Not in my car, *s'il te plaît.*'

'So does masturbation count as a sex act?'

'Absolutely it does. How could it not?'

The cricketer blushed, making the empathetic musician cringe. What was behind these tentative questions, metred out one by agonising one? It was obvious that something was causing him considerable angst.

''Cause it's not full-on sex, even when there's two of you.'

'Full-on sex,' Jeff repeated, rolling the words around his mind for a few seconds. 'As opposed to what? Masturbating on your own? By full-on sex, you mean penetrative sex presumably.'

'S'pose so,' Jet's face turned a deeper crimson, too far in to care. 'Is it even called "masturbation" when you're doing it to the other person?'

'Not really. I know what you're getting at though,' the worldly man tested the boundaries a step further. 'I seem to remember having an argument with your sister about this too, but never mind that now. Full-on sex, to me, is all the way to orgasm.'

The boy squirmed, eyes dropping until his gaze fixed on a tiny piece of gravel in the passenger footwell. They had already driven past *Escondido*'s gates twice and were now looping round the coast road for another lap. Finding the lookout car park deserted, Jeff pulled off the road and pointed the conspicuous vehicle's nose out to sea. Seeking one's absolution from the front seat of an Aston Martin was a great deal more confronting than enclosed inside a confessional.

'It's alright, mate. There's only you and me here. Whatever's worrying you, we'll work it out before we go home.'

'Cool, thanks. I just need to know what's OK and what's not OK.'

The philosopher wound his window down and lit a cigarette. 'Sure. That's fine. Congratulations on being a good man, mate. Masturbating yourself in front of someone else or using your hand to bring someone else off is definitely a sex act. It could be construed as sexual assault on a minor.'

Again the boy's nerves made him shudder and gulp down a mouthful of saliva. 'By a minor?'

'Doesn't matter. There's a third party involved who's a minor,' the father replied, drawing quotation marks in the air around the eccentric technical term. 'They only care how old the perpetrator is when it comes time to try him or her. Or sentence him or her, more accurately. They'd go much easier on a minor assaulting another minor, but it's still an offence.'

Seeing his son nod, absorbing the mysterious body language, Jeff forced the issue. He wasn't of a mind to string this interminable *mea culpa* out any longer than necessary. He was keen to appear forgiving, especially since own passage to manhood had hardly been whiter-than-white.

What could have spooked the boy enough to want to exclude his mother from this fact-finding mission? Lynn typically offer the youngsters less mercy, given her greater emphasis on the family's position in society. Was his role now as father or as arbiter? Either way, the peacemaker vowed to listen and assist when invited, and then to represent both parties to reach settlement if required.

'What's gone wrong, Jetto? Are you in some kind of trouble?'

'I hope not,' the boy answered without hesitation. 'It's just that I was with a girl at Justin's party and we started mucking around. You know... Kissing and stuff.'

'Yep,' Jeff sniffed, grinning. 'I do know, but thanks for checking. So this girl was under sixteen? What's her name?'

The youngster smiled back. 'Yes. Rachna. She's fifteen. Indian,' he sighed. 'We went somewhere where we couldn't be seen and started feeling each other, inside our clothes. She was as keen as me, Dad. She told me she wanted to have sex.'

'Full-on sex,' again the amateur counsellor diffused the anxiety with some humour.

'I don't know,' the boy grunted. 'That's what I thought, but I didn't ask her specifically. I wasn't in the mood for a long conversation.'

This time, his father laughed aloud, hearing his own words emerge through this fearful teenager. 'Sure, mate. Know what you mean. Did she change her mind?'

'No, not really,' Jet shook his head. 'She masturbated me all the way, and I was... I had my fingers down there...'

'I get the picture,' Jeff smiled, ruffling the lad's head of blond curls. 'Cut to the chase, mate, 'cause your mum'll be pissed off if we're late for lunch.'

'Sorry. Everything was cool, then suddenly she moved backwards and ripped my hand away. She jumped up off the ground, screaming and panicking. I jumped up too, wondering what the hell had happened. I thought she'd been bitten by a spider or something.'

'Whoa! What was it then?'

'Bloody hell. I don't know. That's the point!'

'She was probably worried your fingers'd go too far.'

'What?' Jet yelped. 'What's too far? Make her come?'

The rock star raised his eyebrows, which the boy took to mean he ought to think more laterally. 'D'you know what a hymen is?'

'No.'

'It's a membrane across the vagina. Like a seal, if you like. Some cultures reckon that if a woman's hymen's broken, it means she's no longer a virgin. I reckon that's what she was afraid of.'

The youngster frowned. 'Oh, yeah. Could be. Jeez! Rachna started crying about being a virgin and saying we should never have done anything because it was illegal, and if anyone found out, we'd get a criminal record, and her parents'd kill her,' he rattled off. 'And since then, I've been scared for you and Mum. If it hit the 'papers, you know... Worse than Kiz's nightshirt thing.'

Jeff started the car and drove at a snail's pace past the primary school the children had attended, avoiding eye contact with the remorseful boy. 'OK,' he murmured. 'Thanks for thinking of us, mate. Very considerate, but it'll be fine. We'll deal with it. We'll always stand by you if it comes to anything, just like we did for Kizzy. I doubt anything'll come of it. Admirable that you came clean though. A very good sign, *hijo mío*.'

There were tears in the teenager's eyes, but he forced a smile, determined not to give in to his emotions. 'Thanks.'

'D'you know if Rachna's intending on telling anyone?' his dad asked. 'If she's Indian, she's unlikely to tell her parents. How would anyone find out if no-one saw you and neither of you tells anyone? Who is there to grass you up?'

'Yeah. No-one. I hope not, but she screamed so loud. Maybe someone in the house heard us. I nabbed Dawson, and we left straightaway. Went back to his place for the rest of the night.'

'Right! Good move! Have you spoken to Rachna since?'

'No,' Jet admitted. 'I know I should, but I don't want to. In case it all starts up again.'

His son's pain pierced the songwriter's bulletproof shell. It was so foreign for the upcoming sports legend to experience fear, and the acute protectiveness the situation stirred up compelled him to ask for the girl's telephone number so he could smooth things over on the lustful lad's behalf. This response wouldn't teach him anything however, and he imagined his beautiful best friend's scolding tone. If his own mother and father hadn't been so neglectful, this might well serve as one of those moments when he heard himself reciting wise words imparted a generation ago. As it was, his parents had not been equipped to deliver sage advice.

Jeff Diamond was not this type of parent. 'Mate, you have to catch up with her and talk it through, either by 'phone or in person. You both need to take responsibility for your actions. Face the music. That's the mature thing to do, isn't it?'

'Hmm...' Jet sunk lower in his seat.

'Speak to her. See how Rachna's feeling about it after a couple of days and explain how it stressed you out too. She may well've got over the whole thing already, and you're worrying over nothing. Don't walk away unless you both agree to. Maybe she's embarrassed about making a scene, so you can promise you won't mention it ever again. She's probably scared you'd brag about it.'

'OK,' the boy nodded. 'I knew you'd say that.'

The kind man chuckled. 'Yeah? So why didn't you already do it?'

'Oh, I expect it's because I'm weak,' Jet answered, regurgitating more of his father's own words, trotted out many times to describe his own fallibility.

'Very funny, mate. It'll clear the air. You have to do it, if only for your own peace of mind. And mine now!'

'Would you drive me there and wait 'til I come out, please?'

'Rachna's house? Sure. No worries. Just make sure I'm in Melbourne before you make any arrangements.'

Jet tensed up again. 'Are you going to tell Mum?'

'One of us needs to,' the lesson continued. 'As a pre-emptive strike, just in case she finds out some other way. You wouldn't want her to know you hid it from her.'

'Yeah, no. I don't mind.'

'She'll understand, mate. As you were at pains to remind me, we were also young once.'

'Were you? Are you sure about that? I think you only say that as a con' trick, to get us to cough up all our secrets. I don't believe you were ever young.'

The set of three-metre-high iron gates which separated the Diamonds' privacy from the local population's gawking curiosity swung their wide, inward arcs to admit the black beast. The atmosphere lightening for their return, Jeff felt a stab of regret for the implacable passage of time. Not so long ago, the children would have been happy to see two dogs galloping alongside the car, escorting them to the garage.

'You can believe whatever you want,' he dismissed the jocular dig at his advancing years. 'Let's get this baby into the warm. I'm starving. Don't know about you.'

'Mum never had under-aged sex, did she?' the young man checked, opening his door and taking care not to bang it into the side of the Caprice. 'Maybe she thinks you were wrong to have started so early.'

Jeff stared straight ahead, considering his son's question. It was off-target on this occasion, but he chose not to spoil the symmetry. It had been he who waited until after Lynn's sixteenth birthday before making plans to meet her. He hadn't wanted to encourage her to break the law, regardless of her own beliefs or the pressure he imagined her to be under.

The lad was right too, in one sense. Lynn wouldn't have dared embarrass her parents or sully her own reputation, so perhaps she did expect her children to do the same. Was this a justifiable reason to keep the incident as a secret between man and boy? At least until the situation had blown over and Jet had plucked up the courage to restore diplomatic relations with his fellow Melbourne Academy high-flyer.

'Y'know, Jetto...' the negotiator voiced his conclusion. 'There's no need to worry your mum about this until we're sure there's something to worry about. Speak to the girl who shall remain nameless. Tell me when... And hopefully it'll all just blow over.'

'Wow. Really?' the youngster gasped as if the heaviest of burdens had been lifted off his shoulders. 'That'd be great. Not that I don't want Mum to know, but I like your new plan much better.'

Jeff extended his right hand while the roller-door descended and the motor shut off with its familiar clunk. '*D'accord*. We have a deal,' he agreed, shaking a hand that seemed to grow larger every day. 'Tell you what? One good turn deserves another. If I promise to keep *stumm*, you tell Mum yourself once you've got the all-clear.'

'Shit, Dad! That's not fair!' Jet exclaimed. 'You moved the goalposts.'

'Did I? I'm the dad, mate. I can do these things. So anyway... Was it good?'

'With Rachna?'

The pair of Diamonds trudged the fifty metres between garage and *portico*, weighed down with a week's worth of laundry, sports equipment and school bags. Slotting his key in the lock, Jeff almost dropped the bunch of flowers onto the wet ground.

'Yes. With Rachna, whoever she is. Do I know who she is, by the way?'

The growing lad heaved the strap of his cricket bag higher on his shoulder and shook his head, waving at his mother, who had appeared in the doorway on the other side of the courtyard. 'Don't think so. Yeah. Fantastic, but I kind o' forgot about it pretty quickly. Paled into insignificance. Is that the expression?'

'*Cierto,*' Jeff agreed. 'Works for me! So are you ready for full-on sex now?'

Jet shrugged. 'Can I get back to you on that?'

'You may. Take your time.'

'What paled into insignificance? Hi, guys. You look guilty about something,' Lynn grinned, accepting a kiss from her son and then her husband. 'And red roses too! Definitely guilty!'

Wise Investment

The family's schedules stretched and bloated to accommodate the many elements they deemed of global importance as nineteen-ninety-one progressed at its usual clip. With Greg, one of their original drivers, deciding to retire to Queensland, they replaced him with Giang, a twenty-six-year-old Vietnamese refugee with a degree in economics and fluent in French and English, in addition to his native tongue.

Lynn and Jeff were criticised in the media for trusting an immigrant to ferry their children from place to place. Despite being annoyed by the pundits' small-minded bigotry, neither sought to take them to task, preferring not to dignify such worthless scare-mongering with a public response. As it happened, Giang fitted in well. Amused by their parents' apparent policy to only employ drivers with names beginning with "G", his charges identified with his relative youth and were fascinated by his exotic childhood and the danger he had encountered while fleeing a country decimated by war.

Kierney, the budding activist ever intrigued by the plight of migrants, often disappeared for long periods into the garage to hold the poor man hostage until he parted with every last detail of his family's harrowing southward journey. Seeing the twelve-year-old return to the house with reddened eyes and seething with outrage after the first inquisition, her parents were concerned she might stir up horrific memories best forgotten for their polite new employee. However, he insisted instead that their earnest *têtes-aux-têtes* were helpful. If anything, each time he relived an episode, its chilling terror diminished another notch. Jeff related to this paradox only too well, leaving their daughter free to cross-examine her witness as often as she saw fit.

The engine pulling the Diamond Train's ever-lengthening caravan of rolling stock ripped relentlessly through country after country, town after town, regardless of the couple's approval rating on individual issues. Mobile telephones and easier access to the Internet transformed the loneliness of travelling away from home, in major cities at least, no longer needing to rely on time-zone compatibility to get their fix of each other.

The ladies and occasional gentleman who staffed the couple's management company were constantly astounded by the diversity and sheer quantity of invitations they received, not to mention the lengths people would go to entice Australia's best-loved family to attend an event.

Case in point, the songwriter and his fellow smokers were often accosted by ardent fans during cigarette breaks, emerging from their Collins Street offices after hours of meetings and adjusting their eyes to the dazzling sunshine. On one particularly sunny day, a protest committee of eager women wearing T-shirts bearing his mugshot from a variety of concert tours surged forwards until they almost trod on his toes. Most were waving homemade banners, and all screamed and chanted his name, desperate to secure a commitment to lend his support to their cause.

'I have no clue what we're doing tonight, let alone three months from now,' he told them, handing his half-smoked cigarette to one of the administrative assistants while he scanned an enormous invitation which had been thrust into his hand. 'Detail's wasted on me, ladies. It's beyond my capability, so you'd be unwise to trust me with this.'

The women refused to budge, giggling in giddy stupefaction. Wishing neither to humiliate them in public nor to disappoint the small group of fans who had made the prestigious lobby of 333 Collins their home for the last few years, the celebrity reached into his pants pocket and produced a handheld telephone.

He chuckled at the looks of incomprehension and amazement while his thumb pressed a few buttons, being himself not yet immune to a certain wonderment at the technological inventions which had come about through Paragon Holdings' investments.

Waiting for the call to connect with the switchboard upstairs, he held the revolutionary device to his ear. 'Hang on,' Jeff pacified the crowd's impatience. 'I'll let you know if we're free. My social secretary'll put you out of your misery.'

'You mean Lynn?' one of the women called out from the row behind, swooning along with her friends. 'Is she up there? Ask her to come down!'

'Mandy, hi,' the handsome man shouted above the excitement, shaking his head. 'Lynn's away in Europe at the moment. Tennis. Yeah. Hi, Mand! I'm down on the street. Can't move for people wanting to know what Lynn and I are doing on the nineteenth of April. Can you put us out of our misery, please?'

'Oh, my God! You really do have a social secretary!' another woman laughed, causing a ripple effect of adoration.

Jeff grinned, the child inside still not immune to these moments either. 'Mandy, d'you have access to Lynn's diary too?' he asked, before turning to the group and playing along with their mirth. 'Yep. I need her permission to spend time with my wife. Protocol, y'know… That's great, Mand. Cheers. I'll be back up in a minute. *Adiós*.'

The imposing figure flipped the lid on his cigarette packet, offering it to his amused employees and the front row of the noisy throng. Following the same route, he made fire for each doting female before lighting his own. Pheromones permeated the smoke surrounding their heads, and he chanced an arrogant smirk as his dirty mind composed a series of visible thought-bubbles hovering above them.

Starting to walk over to where he had parked his car, the superstar took the throng along with him down the street. Hooked on his every move, the crowd watched him dial another number on the mobile telephone, amazed and delighted at the attention.

'Cath, hi,' Jeff snapped the handset against his right ear. 'All good. Peaceful, if a little demanding! Hey, quick one... Yeah, nineteenth April in the evening. I've been kidnapped by aliens inviting us to their spaceship for a dinner function thing in Port Melbourne. Mandy says we're available, but she wanted to make sure with you before I say yay or nay.'

A short pause sent the crowd into a flurry of conjecture. Their idol couldn't help but smile at the rows of eyes following his every move. As ever, it would be hard to decline if they had no genuine conflict on this day. People dedicated to worthy causes always went to a great deal of trouble to stage such ambushes, so who was he to let them down? The extra level of accessibility to their idols delivered in spades when their turn came to raise funds or garner support for the many charities on their list. Snubbing these women now would be bad for business, even if the couple were forced to send their apologies at a later date.

'Yeah?' he yelled into the tiny mouthpiece, finding it difficult to hear his public relations manager's reply above the traffic and the general *mêlée*. 'OK! Sounds good. Thanks heaps. Yep. Two minutes.'

The celebrity gave the assembled open mouths a thumbs-up, and an enormous cheer erupted. Before he could turn back to the group's leader to confirm their attendance, five or six pens were thrust towards his hand by anxious autograph-hunters.

'We're in, guys,' Jeff confirmed, duly signing the reverse of their invitation and fishing one of Cathy Lane's business cards out of his shirt pocket. 'Keep these and send us another one, OK? I'll ask the crew upstairs to reply as soon as they receive it. Here's the "PO" box and stuff. We've *gotta* go now. Thanks for the invitation, ladies. And for your persistence.'

Ducking out of the way to evade assault from an amorous brunette who attempted to kiss the sexy superstar on the lips, he tucked the magic walkie-talkie machine back into his pocket. Astounded that their mission had been accomplished, the women loitered on the steps before dispersing obediently and letting the great man and his gang of fellow smokers stroll unhindered towards the lifts until they had vanished from view.

The object of their adulation exhaled and sagged against the wall as the doors slid shut. Free of one onslaught, the doors had trapped him inside with another set of gaping strangers who delved into their wallets and handbags for something worthy of his signature.

What a bizarre life he led! Making people happy was easy, and it was uplifting to think of the pleasure he brought to their days simply by letting them tell him a story. As he and Lynn were known to stress in pep talks for the tireless workers at Stonebridge Music and the Diamond Celebration Foundation, they should never overlook the possibility of one small act of kindness converting into significant pledges come the next telethon.

If this was how their weird world rolled, best not knock it.

***

'I'm having an affair,' Lynn announced at the breakfast table, holding the newspaper aloft and turning it around so Jeff could see the headline and photographs.

'Again?' he moaned, giving the page a cursory glance. 'Christ Almighty! You're never bloody satisfied, woman.'

'No. Obviously not. I'm also hopeless at staying out of sight.'

The tall blonde stood up and walked over to the coffee machine to refill their mugs. She paused next to her husband, her hip dangerously close to his cheek, and bent over to plant an apologetic kiss on his damp curls. Though both stars were rarely out of the gossip columns, snagged by greedy *paparazzi* determined to concoct a fresh scandal at the faintest whiff, their lighthearted reactions masked a sickly fatigue for the children's incessant exposure to such unfounded sleaze.

Much to Kierney's amusement, her father yanked his dream girl down onto his lap and wrapped his arms around her. The youngster never tired of seeing her parents showing affection for each other, assuming no basis of truth in these spurious sightings. Her older school friends sometimes needled her about these headlines, yet she seldom contemplated the canvas of their blissful existence ever ripping under the strain of infidelity.

'Stop it, kiddies!' the girl scolded, feigning embarrassment. 'Stop that horrible slurping noise. It's putting me off my *breckie*.'

The couple pulled apart, muttering complaints about the spoil-sport. While Lynn sat down and began to butter a slice of toast, her frowning lover slid the newspaper towards him from across the table. He read with contrived interest, wondering what his sinful wife had been up to this time.

'Steve Christie?' he exclaimed, checking the indistinct blond man in the picture. 'Shit! I could almost be jealous of that. You've got good taste, angel, I have to say. Plus he's certainly heartbroken lately, with Jeanetta Keretta filing for divorce. Not that far of a stretch for you guys to get together. 'Specially for this tabloid rag.'

'Who's Jeanetta Keretta?' their daughter laughed. 'Is that his wife's name?'

Lynn smiled. 'Jan Kerrigan, *Papá* means, darling. We joke about her because she likes people to think she's from France or Italy, but she's really from somewhere near San Francisco.'

'Yeah. And she's not his wife anymore either,' Jeff added. 'She left him. Irreconcilable differences that they probably had from the start, if you ask me.'

The man in the world's most impregnable marriage flapped the newspaper pages taut and folded them with an audacious air, before letting them flop back onto the table. Steve Christie's infatuation for his co-writer and album producer was common knowledge, cultivated over a number of years and alongside two wives.

The baby-faced singer-songwriter had first married an American supermodel whose resemblance to Lynn was remarkable, only to be devastated when their relationship didn't live up to his high ideals. The newspaper article made mention of this fact, microscopic photographs of Lynn and Brittany positioned beside each other to encourage a direct comparison.

Jeff had long been a collaborator of Steve's too, and to some extent, his mentor. It was his suggestion for Steve and Jan to have a child, and he was saddened that their little girl would now spend the rest of her childhood flitting between homes and parents. The uncertainty around this estranged child's fate after break-up Number Two hurt the compassionate man far more than the aspersions of his wife's supposed affair.

'I hope you're better to him than she was,' the philosopher said with a wry smile.

'I don't know who did what,' Lynn replied. 'He never mentions her in my company. It's odd; like she never existed. He hardly talks about Jan either.'

'Yeah? Wonder why... Last time I caught up with him, she'd been beating him with household utensils.'

'Really? That's hilarious!' Kierney piped up, stuffing her homework into her school bag. 'What sort of household utensils?'

'Anything she could lay her hands on,' her dad smiled. 'At least, that's his side of the story. Who knows what goes on inside someone else's house?'

Lynn sighed, squeezing the flesh covering her lost boy's kidneys in an effort to banish his dour mood. 'Shame though. We can't all be perfect. Do you want a lift, Kizzy?'

'Oh, yes, please. That'd be great.'

While their impressionable girl-child scampered off to collect her things, the caring woman sneaked a kiss as she handed her lover the contents of an envelope she had opened moments earlier. The single, stiff piece of card was a birth announcement from Kiley Jones and her trumpeter husband.

Her perennial dark-heart read the information on the card before lifting his gaze to a pair of expectant blue eyes. 'Whoa,' he drew breath. 'That's humbling. Rhapsody Diamond Kahn.'

'I know,' Lynn agreed. 'She told me they were thinking of calling the baby Rhapsody if they had a girl. Or Rhapsa, for short, she said. But I didn't know anything about the Diamond part.'

'Oh, well... Poor kid,' Jeff smiled, gripping his wife's hand. 'She can always change it.'

The Olympian stood staring at her billionnaire rock star while he cleared the breakfast remains from the table and stacked the dishwasher. She marvelled at his insistence on perpetuating routine. Life's hum-drum activities grounded him, and he still exuded such humility in the face of all-encompassing hyperbole.

There was no trace of self-satisfied fat cat to be seen this morning. Preparing to drop their daughter at school on her way to the Sportsdrome, where she had been training since she was ten years old, Lynn Dyson saw Jeff Diamond today as no greater or lesser man than the rough and ready student for whom she had fallen hook, line and sinker almost twenty years ago.

To everyone else, her beautiful black stallion presented as a leader with the world at his feet. Inside his own home, he remained a grab-bag of insecurities held together by an unsurpassed and perennially sharpened natural intellect. Love overflowed her heart.

'Your eyes are burning a hole in my head,' he whispered, passing close enough for his breath to warm her face, 'and I like it.'

The tennis champion coughed, aware she had been daydreaming yet again. 'Good,' she smiled. 'You deserve it.'

Jeff shrugged. 'It's all down to you, angel. There'd be nothing to deserve without you. Are you guys here tonight or at *Escondido*?'

'Here,' Lynn replied, holding her hand out to Kierney, who had arrived in the hallway, ready to leave. 'You?'

'Looks like I'm here,' he nodded, following his favourite females to the lift. 'I chase women around like a puppy. It's what I do best.'

His dark-haired gipsy girl stood on tiptoes to kiss her father goodbye, squealing as his embrace closed in on her elongating frame. He did the same to his wife, hoping she might swing the car round in front of the Melbourne Academy gates and spend the morning in bed with him instead of wasting all that sweat and heavy breathing on a range of gymnasium equipment.

'Get out of here, you gorgeous pair. Leave me alone to do a decent day's work without all these distractions.'

'See you six-ish then?' Lynn checked.

'*Sí. A las seis. Bon journée, toutes les deux.*'

'And stay away from Uncle Steve, *Mamá*,' their daughter teased, watching her parents kiss one last time for good luck.

Husband and wife locked eyes, trying not to burst out laughing. This was an unexpected didactic reaction from the girl who was finding her own path through a complicated world. She hadn't been so outspoken in protecting her father's interests until now, but the remark was not out of place, given her uncompromising character.

Both Diamond children had grown up in the safety of their cliff-side paradise; a peaceful household where free expression was the order of the day and true love conquered all. Every project the family started had these fundamental values at their core, and their parents' relationship floundering on the rocks would be a catastrophe for everyone.

There but for the grace of God... The nobody from Sydney's south-west had been born less than two years before the talented Californian. What if this age gap were reversed? It had happened before, hadn't it? A shock-wave coursed through his body, a frieze revealing the lovers' transcendental, last-ditch embrace on *la Rive Gauche* in nineteen-eighty-two.

Jeff stood in the hallway until the lift doors had closed on the two women bound for the basement garage. A fleeting panic rose from his belly, wondering if he were being *naïf* to take Lynn's love for granted in these halcyon days. By some dint of fate, he had found his way to his soul-mate in time during this lifetime. This chronological sequence might well be the only reason why he wasn't the one collecting marriage and divorce certificates rather than Steve Christie. Was he doing enough to keep their grass as green as the next man's?

'Oh, yeah!' the veteran of fifteen miraculous years muttered, turning around with the intention of brewing some more coffee before settling down at the piano to give form to the latest batch of songs clogging his brain.

Lynn delighted in their life singular as much as he did. The wasting paranoia which used to plague the ancient soul in moments like this was long departed. In its place were frequent heart-to-hearts with his beautiful best friend, both airing their hopes and fears for the future and celebrating everything that had gone before. If she were looking for a way out, he was convinced the newspapers would not be first to inform him.

***

'Grandma was full of praise for you today,' Lynn reported. 'I met her for coffee this afternoon, and she told me about the charity function you guys went to the other night. She said it was tedious.'

'Oh, good,' Kierney nodded. 'Thanks! It was pretty boring, yeah. Some funny bits though, in the speeches.'

'Grandma said the same. She'd come from another similar luncheon today too, which is what prompted her to tell me, I expect. She described your manners as impeccable, so full marks.'

'Ten out of ten for yawn-stifling, *pequeñita*,' Jeff mocked. 'Thanks for sticking with it. Won't be the last tedious event you attend. You must've been pretty whacked for school the next day.'

The young lady shrugged. 'Not too bad. It was actually really nice to spend some time with Grandma on our own. We were on the same table as Mister and Missus Broom-Handle.'

'Were you now, Miss Diamond!' her mother shrieked, impersonating the high and mighty tone belonging to the former Melbourne Academy Chairman's wife. '"What with your father's reverse snobbery and your impertinent mispronunciation of our name, I've a good mind to have you expelled."'

Keith Broome-Hamilton had recently retired from the Board of Victoria's most prestigious school, amid speculation that he had been caught fraternising with young Asian boys late at night. Rumours raced round the student population like a virulent strain of gastroenteritis, taking no time at all to reach alumni past and present.

His wife, Gwendoline, was a short, dumpy woman whose hairstyle earned her the nickname of "Chairwoman Mao". She also had a reputation as one of the strictest and most old-fashioned teachers, holding on to her position by virtue of her husband's influence. All four Dyson children had disliked her in their day, and Junior and his younger sister had their cover blown in side-splittingly shrewd fashion in front of Bart and Marianna during the interval of a recent theatrical production, when Jeff had dropped a few obscure phrases from the Chinese Communist Manifesto into conversation.

Lynn and her fellow governors closed ranks around the damning publicity at first, refusing to state an opinion on public record as to whether the rumours were true or false. Privately however, they found themselves staring down the barrel of a dilemma her husband called "Fireman's Law", realising that obscuring the impropriety in the gathering smoke risked the school's name being blackened by an ember or two if the tittle-tattle were found to be true.

In the stately institution's first ever Emergency General Meeting, the directors had voted it high time for the office of Chairman to be rotated, and Mister Broome-Hamilton fell on his sword. Yet another cautionary tale for relationships conducted under the full glare of local spotlights to leave the Diamonds and the Dysons feeling beyond reproach but thankful nonetheless. They had all agreed, moreover, that waking up next to the founding father of the People's Republic every morning constituted grounds for leniency when punishing even the most perverted behaviour.

'Were they talking to each other at lunch?' Jeff asked, grimacing at his wife's shrill accusation.

'They seemed OK,' Kierney nodded. 'In public. You know how it is.'

'What's that supposed to mean, gorgeous?' the songwriter probed, her answer loaded with more than the usual dose of trainee sarcasm. 'What do we know how it is what?'

'Huh?' the girl giggled. 'I mean, you know how it is to always be nice to each other in public. Wise up, guys. Really!'

Both parents' expressions turned serious, her mother not prepared to dismiss the sweet-natured dig. 'Is something worrying you, Kizzy?'

The teenager put her knife and fork down on her plate and sighed, unsure how to respond. Over the last week or so, she had overheard several groups of students whispering about the other pieces of recent gossip circulating; those much closer to home for her and her brother.

'Come on. What's up?' Jeff asked, seeing her unease.

Kierney took a deep breath. 'I know there's nothing you can do about it,' she answered, 'but people are starting to believe you're having an affair with Steve Christie, *Mamá*. I'm getting sick of hearing all the crap that comes out of nowhere. You know, shushing their friends when I get close to them, and all the funny looks... And I know I shouldn't say anything, but I just want to jump down their throats and tell them to stop believing what they read in the 'papers.'

The celebrities exchanged shots of penitent extrasensory perception. They had learned to live with these not-so-subtle sidetracks, having been subjected to the same shifty squints and sudden silences for many years. Until now, their children's young ears had lacked the maturity to tune into *innuendo*. Time had caught up with them. It was quite clear their daughter had become the latest victim of seedy chicanery intent on spreading slanderous scuttlebutt about Australia's favourite tall poppies.

'Oh, that's terrible. I'm sorry, darling,' Lynn replied, putting her arm around the glum girl. 'It's unfair on you and Jet, I know. Bad enough for us, but at least we're the ones directly in the firing line. We deserve it, sort of, but you and Jet don't.'

'You don't deserve it,' Kierney objected.

Her mother kissed her flushed cheek. 'Thank you. But if it's starting to get you down, maybe we need to put a statement together, Jeff?'

The world-changer had stopped eating too, nauseated to see the effect their stoush with the tabloid press was having on his hard-working and sympathetic gem. These aspersions were normally his fault, with stolen photographs or eavesdropped snippets of conversations linking him to sexy star-chasers or covetous cougars.

Journalists rarely pursued his wife with the same vigour, with her stellar career as Australia's pop darling and *élite* sporting heroine, making this current *fiasco* all the more galling. Although the showman was often complicit in these various fifteen minutes of fame, Lynn didn't deserve such rough treatment, as their daughter asserted. He had been prepared to let this defamation attempt run its course until the gipsy girl's reaction caused him to stop and think twice.

'Yeah. What should we say?' he responded after a few seconds. 'And would people believe it? Like pouring oil on a naked flame...'

'That's what I mean,' Kierney groaned. 'The Broom-Handles have to sit there, surrounded by all of us wondering what's going on between them. And even though they haven't admitted to anything dodgy, we're still all thinking he's a deviant.'

Her dad frowned. 'True enough. He's certainly been slugged royally by the *journoes.*'

'So why would they believe you two if you came out and claimed there was nothing going on between *Mamá* and Steve?'

'No guarantee, angels,' the kind man agreed. 'We'd be more believable than their situation, I hope. I think if I were married to Charlie Chaplin with a sense of humour extraction, I'd most likely turn to young boys at some point.'

'*Papá*!' the student cried, unable to keep a straight face. 'That doesn't help.'

'No, it does not,' the Olympian was more controlled. 'I'd have every right to have an affair in that case, on top of all the far-fetched reasons printed about our relationship breakdowns.'

'No, you bloody well wouldn't,' the thirty-nine-year-old teased. 'It'd surprise you though, I'd bet!'

'Oh, be quiet, Don Juan. Kizzy, newspapers thrive on this kind of rubbish. It's always a fine line whether it's worth causing a fuss.'

Jeff raised his hands. 'Apologies, folks. My view is we ought to give the tabloid-buying, commercial-channel-watching public a skerrick of credit for exercising good judgement. They know we're not all cut from the same cloth. Just because one boring bigwig's up to dubious sexual proclivities, it doesn't mean we all are.'

Starting to clear away their abandoned meals, Lynn's body language let it be known that her husband needed to stop messing around. 'We know that's true,' she refuted, smiling at his defeated expression. 'But there's at least an element of truth in most rumours. You know that as well as I do.'

'Sure,' the rock star. 'OK. You're quite correct, but what can we do about it?'

'Nothing,' Kierney sighed, sorry for putting her parents in this tenuous position. 'I don't want you to do anything. I s'pose I only wanted to put it out there. And just so you know, I don't think there's any truth in the rumours. Neither does Jet, by the way.'

'Thank God for that!' her mother exclaimed from the dishwasher, where she was having trouble slotting some unobliging pieces of dirty crockery into their designated places. 'I sincerely hope not. That'd be horrific, Kizzo. Please tell me you've never thought there was…'

Jeff shot his daughter an impish look. 'You've got her on the ropes, *pequeñita*,' he stirred. 'Hit a nerve. She's worried now, I can tell.'

The twelve-year-old left the table, chasing after Lynn with the rest of the dinner *accoutrements*. She replaced the condiments in the pantry and rinsed two sauce spoons under the hot tap. Impeccable manners indeed, her father ruminated, mesmerised as the two beauties embraced at the sink. The elegant sportswoman would be horrified to find out their children were wondering if this futile hearsay contained any truth.

'You guys are so gorgeous together,' he said, joining them in their edifying cuddle and kissing them both on the forehead. 'I'll get rid of this mess. Go and do your homework, Kizzo. *Mamá* and I'll come up with a plan by the end of the evening.'

'No. I'd like to stay and help. I've nearly finished my homework.'

'Sure,' Lynn accepted the girl's assistance, more to assuage her guilt than to lighten the load. 'Thanks. We *will* try and make the story go away, I promise.'

'I know,' Kierney kissed her mother again. 'And another thing…'

'Oh-oh!' Jeff chuckled. 'Sounds ominous.'

'No! I've got a theory about good manners that I'll run by Grandma next time I see her.'

'Another theory?' the lone blonde joked, alluding to the striking similarity of her dark and broody housemates.

The clever child stamped her feet, slamming her hands on her hips in defiance. 'Yes! My theory is that eating with silver- or gold-plated cutlery and china with gold leaf makes people more refined.'

'Oh, you reckon?' her father challenged. 'Very inventive, I must say. Love your work, *pequeñita*.'

'Why not? It's like little traces of silver and gold get into our bloodstream or fall off onto our food, and we absorb the finery. Then it causes a chemical reaction in our brains that other people don't have.'

Lynn hugged their imaginative daughter. 'That's lovely,' she said. 'You should buy a thank-you card for Grandma, for inviting you to the dinner, and write your theory into it. Grandma'd love that. And Celia too. Right up their alleys.'

***

'If I'd been born a dog, I'd probably be dead by now.'

Kierney Lynn Freedom Diamond turned thirteen on the tenth of February nineteen-ninety-two within the bosom of her family. She had shocked her grandparents by beginning her birthday speech with this peculiar line, all eyes shifting to her father.

'Don't blame me!' he bleated. 'I'm as gobsmacked as the rest of you! Pray continue, Kizzy.'

Silencing Auntie Madalena's raucous cackling, Jeff listened to his daughter recite her prepared prose with confidence and sincerity. It was as if her new pair of digits had been transposed, so self-possessed and purposeful was her delivery. Even Uncle Gerry, whose supreme crowd-pleasing skills rivalled those of his commander-in-chief, conveyed his commendation with an appreciative nod to the proud parents.

The premonition which had driven her father to write a musical in his little girl's honour had become a reality right before their eyes. "Laura's Light" spun the tale of a child cloaked in an aura which brightened with each curious question, giving her the confidence she needed to succeed in a world made by and for boys.

Kierney liked nothing better than to defend the indefensible, particularly when logic and interpretation were at odds. Destined for law-making of some kind and with all her eggs in the United Nations' basket, this occasion was the party guests' first glimpse into her vocation. To her mother's dedication to excellence, her brother's head for facts and figures and her father's panoramic vision she added an uncanny knack for organising each conundrum by its universal priority.

Lynn often cited her husband's only downfall as his inability to say no, a prognosis Miss Irony forbade him to deny. Therefore, it was justice in action that bestowed this trait on his *replica minima*. Beginning her fourteenth year as the youngest Diamond, she came into her own overnight and turned her former morbid focus on unfairness to positive advantage by posing question after awkward question until a solution became apparent.

The seven-figure *bat mitzvah* gift was a pleasant but rather heavy yoke around her neck for most of the previous twelve months. As with everything else in her young life, the intelligent youngster had approached spending her gift with extreme thoughtfulness.

The exercise of dispensing a large sum of money for the greater good had enhanced his daughter's understanding of a whole host of real-world subjects that even a school of Melbourne Academy's prestige would never address. Skills such as articulating sustainable benefits, investing for the long and short terms, managing cash-flow and reserves, interest rates and foreign exchange were wolfed down by the eager student, not discounting the projects' financial returns and the many crucial social or clinical outcomes.

And if this list wasn't extensive enough, Kierney also learned a great deal about herself. She knew what was important to her and why, and how to choose between competing demands. She was in danger of overtaking her brother in business acumen, yet neither parent was bothered.

Innovation and applying history's lessons to the future were Jet's differentiators, whereas Kierney's mind held little interest in these equally valuable capabilities. He would iterate around a puzzle until he had ironed out its flaws in a series of strident, character-building failures, while his sister had the sensitivity to keep quiet and humble about her mistakes. They had been brought up to utilise each other's strengths, in true Dyson fashion, creating a dynasty wherein as many brains and hearts and hands could be applied to a task as were necessary.

The young woman's eventual, considered decision was to use the money to establish a new international charity for educating African teenagers about birth control and protecting themselves against infectious diseases. Jeff tried not to steer her toward his own natural bias, and Lynn encouraged her to weigh up the pros and cons of allocating her funds locally or overseas. In the end, after meeting a group of aid workers face-to-face while travelling with her dad, the millions of HIV-affected children facing uncertain adulthoods had swayed her heart too far to overlook.

With her indomitable financial adviser at her side, the young woman had persevered with charts and spreadsheets galore, while they all collaborated on ways to make the program self-sustaining. Once the plan was clear and achievable, she began some careful negotiations with potential partners. Coached by the best, her million dollars multiplied fivefold and then nearly tenfold, bolstered by generous donations from a number of Paragon Holdings' and Blake & Partners' key clients, not to mention Gerry himself, to which she then added more from her grandparents, Uncle Junior and her overjoyed parents of course.

A few thousand short of the magic ten-million mark in December, the young songwriter and performer enlisted the help of her musical schoolmates and arranged a concert to raise the balance. She submitted a few original songs herself, while badgering everyone else to participate. Lynn and Jeff had never been prouder of their gorgeous gipsy girl than to watch her stride to centre-stage and introduce her very own show in front of a packed and paying audience.

Nineteen-ninety-two, another Olympic year, would see the Dysons once more knuckle down to punishing training *regimes*. With huge chunks of their diaries closed off to any normal social interaction, Lynn and Jeff spirited their children off to New York for Christmas as a reward for what had been a laborious period for all.

By far the highlight of Kierney's trip was a visit to the United Nations headquarters where, with her added maturity and growing *cache* of world-changing skills, she found herself participating in meetings on a near-equal footing with the professionals, even posing a few probing questions to the field experts. She loved learning about developing countries, humanitarian and human rights initiatives and how peacemaking efforts and international law were often at loggerheads.

Sandwiched between their parents, the two Diamond children stood in awe in front of the outgoing and incoming Secretaries General. Although there were no sittings of the General Assembly or any other large councils over the holiday period, the celebrities' visit attracted sufficient attention to warrant an hour-long audience with Senor Javier Pérez de Cuéllar and the Egyptian who was about to succeed him, Boutros Boutros-Ghali.

The heirs to Paragon's empire relaxed into normal teenagers once piled into a taxi and on the way back to their hotel. They joked about how the dark-haired girl would need to call herself Kierney Kierney de Diamond if she stood a chance of ever becoming Secretary General herself. Lynn and Jeff had been impressed by both youngsters' agility as they had switched between English, Spanish and French during their conversation with the two distinguished gentlemen.

'Let me tell you something,' Jet announced to the rest of his family. 'I know I don't want to work in a place like that. Not in an office and not in the same place every day. I don't know how anyone can face such a boring career.'

'OK. That's fine, mate,' his dad had answered. 'At least you've seen it and can make a valued judgement. And I'm with you. Me neither. Not in a million years.'

'Don't make up your mind yet. You might change as you grow older,' the Olympian cautioned her son. 'I probably couldn't have pictured myself there either, at your age, but I'm sure I would've got used to the routine pretty easily.'

Jeff reached backwards for his wife's hand, which fastened to his like a magnetised clasp. 'I saved you from that fate, angel,' he said, turning round with a broad grin. 'Remember?'

'How?' both Lynn and Kierney challenged.

'Don't tell me you don't remember!'

'No, I don't,' the blonde shrugged. 'What don't I remember?'

'You know… When we were on that first flight to London together, and you set us the task of describing a normal life?'

'Oh! Yes. Of course I remember that,' the singer laughed, giving her daughter a knowing look. 'But what's that got to do with anything, my most honourable saviour?'

Her husband shook his head. 'Jeez! All these years I thought you were influencing me… Well, whatever… You remember I wrote back then that your spontaneity needed more work?'

'Yes.'

'So I set about subtly sabotaging your natural tendency for routine.'

'Oh, did you? That'd be right,' his patient wife scoffed. 'Playing God again. I really let you get away with heaps, didn't I?'

'Still do, angel,' Jeff agreed, squeezing her fingers. 'And I'm eternally grateful, as I hope you know.'

'Hey, *Papá*?' Kierney interrupted.

'*Sí, pequeñita.*'

'Why aren't you trying to sabotage my routine then?'

The intellectual turned to face the pretty twelve-year-old. This was a first-rate question. Why wasn't he? Perhaps it was because he had wanted to keep a tight hold on his dream girl, in ways that were no longer necessary after fifteen years of marriage. He had exercised excessive control in those early years out of fear that she might run away if he gave her the chance. This was the reason, without doubt, and yet he felt none of the same compulsion to clip the wings of the one who was so much an extension of himself.

'Christ! It hurts to answer that, Kizzo,' he confessed, releasing his wife's hand, discomfited by the forgotten truth. 'I probably wouldn't do it to *Mamá* now either, if we found ourselves in the same situation again. I was the Chief Behaviour Regulator back then, wasn't I, angel? Scared that if I let you do whatever you wanted, you might realise you wanted to do something other than me.'

'Chief Behaviour Regulator?' the cricketer laughed. 'You're still one of those. Only to us instead!'

'And rightly so,' Lynn interjected. 'That's different. That was a very long time ago. Absolutely everything's different these days, guys. But almost because of what *Papá* went through, we want to take care that you two choose your own path, whether that means a little push or pull now and again, or by letting you make your own mistakes. It's all part of the master plan.'

Jeff stared out of the window at the stream of traffic, a long line of yellow cabs just like theirs travelling up and down Third Avenue. He knew Lynn had bailed him out again. She always did, and he loved her all the more for it. It oughtn't to be the case however. He was a big boy now; he could deal with his children's reproofs.

So why did his beautiful best friend still feel the need to rescue him if his transformation was as supreme as she portrayed? Time and tide surely colluded in mysterious but pleasing ways. It was perfect that their daughter was cut out for a working life spent in an office day after day, just like her mother. And also perfect that the Dyson strain who sat beside him in the taxi couldn't think of anything more claustrophobic and monotonous, just like his father.

'I'd still do heaps of other things,' Kierney piped up. 'Writing songs and recording, and playing squash. I wouldn't be chained to the desk like a red-tape slave.'

Out of the corner of his left eye, the billionnaire caught the astonishment on his wife's face. He winked and received a broad smile in return. Their daughter was prone to latching onto phrases she overheard from her parents' discussions, whether driving home from the city after a busy week at school or at the apartment's dinner table. She possessed her father's innate understanding of idiom, coupled with her mum's dry, incisive situational analysis.

'Act your age, please, Kizzy,' her mother teased, hearing the driver snort. 'Red-tape slave? Where did you hear that?'

The young girl cuddled into Lynn's side, the motion of the stop-start traffic making both children drowsy. The taxi pulled up outside their understated downtown hotel, and heads turned as the famous family collected their belongings from the trunk and sprinted out of sight through the revolving doors.

That same evening, dining in their suite because they were flying out at first light the following day, all four Diamonds shared first a *Pinot Noir* before working up to a *Tempranillo*. Testing their maturing palates with different cheeses, this was only the latest in a long line of novel life lessons they were set to experience over the next few years.

Kierney didn't care much for the bitter aftertaste which felt as if it were stripping the lining of her throat. Her brother, on the other hand, acquired quite a liking for it. In fact, the alcohol had made straight for his head, as his parents had foreshadowed, and the others waited with bated breath while he grappled with the onset of drunkenness. His tongue began to trip over simple sentences and valiant attempts to cover his slip-ups. Sympathy infiltrated their *badinage*, knowing the lad hated losing control, a Dyson through and through!

'What's a *lude*?' Jet asked.

'A *lude*?' his mother parrotted. 'Past tense of loo? How do you spell it? You mean lewd, as in gesture? Indecent.'

'No. "L", "U", "D", "E", as in *prélude*. How can you have a *prélude* if there's no such thing as a *lude*?'

Jeff groaned, launching a water cracker into the air between them like a frisbee. 'Oh, bloody hilarious, mate,' he shook his head. 'Keep drinking. You'll go through it and out the other side in no time.'

'Wait, but there's interlude too,' Kierney added, keen to get in on the act. 'What's that all about?'

'Don't you start,' Lynn warned, laughing.

'Yeah. No *postlude* though,' her husband scoffed. 'Do you have a destination for this brainwave, Jetto?'

The transformative effect of alcohol on the kids' young brains was fascinating to witness, and the wise man was keen to provide them with opportunities to test themselves in a safe haven, away from prying eyes and camera lenses. The proud parents' feet wound round each other's ankles under the table, enjoying yet another precious family memory captured for posterity.

With no smart retort to contend with, Jeff continued his son's whacky line of conversation. 'There's no *postlude* because if we don't know what a *lude* is, how can we tell if we're having a *postlude*? No point inventing a word for it.'

'Ah, yeah!' the teenager agreed before his beleaguered intellect hit a snag. 'But no... Pretty clever, Dad. But not clever enough. How come there's a word for interlude then?'

'Halfway between two *ludes*?' the amused mother offered. 'You think you're in a *lude*, but you're not too sure, so you pause to see if anything changes. *Et voilà!* Interlude.'

Jeff chuckled, refilling his and Lynn's glasses with the remains of the wine. '*Exactement, mon amie.* Then you return to what you think might've been a *lude*, to see if you can recognise it. But you don't, so there's still no such thing as a *postlude*.'

'So what's a *scription*?' the cricketer challenged anew. 'Don't I get any more? Am I too drunk?'

'Jesus! Where's this going? Clearly you're not too drunk, mate, 'cause you're just as much of a weirdo without being on the sauce. What are you on about?'

'Well, I'm gruntled that there's prescription and conscription, but disgruntled that there's no such thing as *scription* to begin with.'

His sister raised her hand as if she were in class. '*Postscription* is for when you're better, and the doc' says you can stop taking the tablets.'

'What's an *interscription* then?' her brother taunted before swallowing his words. 'Oh! I know! Repeats!'

'OK! That's enough now. You're just plain ridiculous, both of you,' the Olympian laughed. 'Why don't you play us a song instead? Kizzy?'

Playing with her long waves of dark hair, the young woman fought to remain composed and graceful, their big day catching up with her. Jeff smiled at her tenacity. Even though she had consumed less than half of her second glass, its potency was affecting her unsullied brain. He had a sneaking suspicion however, given their physiological similarities, that Kierney would soon develop an inbred natural tolerance.

'Y'see how this feels?' he asked, looking from one rosy face to the other. 'All happy and like you're having fun, but a bit scary too?'

'Remember this feeling, mate,' the girl laughed, wagging her finger at her brother. 'Too much more, and you won't be able to handle it so easily.'

Lynn's jaw dropped, hearing their daughter use one of the world-changer's favourite calls-to-arms; a phrase they had adopted as a parenting tool by linking their senses to their conscience during telling moments. It was funny to hear these nuggets echoed back to them, and welcome too. Their messages were being heard, processed and understood.

'Yeah, mate. What she says!' Jeff scoffed. 'It's extremely important that you learn to control the effects of drinking. And drugs, if you ever go there… You need to recognise when enough's enough for whatever situation you're in. Too much, and you won't be able to exercise good judgement. Even though you may not think so, Jetto, you are drunk.'

'Am I?'

'Not so much now,' his mother laughed. 'You've sobered up slightly just by thinking about it. But a few minutes ago, during all that *lude* silliness, you were slurring your words and couldn't regulate how loud your voice was.'

The boy pulled a face. 'I know! It was as if my brain knew what I wanted to say, but my mouth had other ideas. It is a strange feeling. And now I already don't feel like that, after only a few minutes.'

'Yep. We recover pretty quickly if we put our minds to it,' his father nodded. 'A good trick is to inhale a few deep breaths through your nose, to get as much oxygen up there as you can. Helps flush the confusion out.'

'Hey! That's funny. Flush the confusion out,' Kierney giggled. 'Do I sound drunk too?'

'No. Not really,' Lynn answered. 'You haven't had enough, but you *are* still a bit on the silly side.'

Jet stuck his tongue out at his sister. 'You're always a bit on the silly side,' he said. 'But seriously, Dad, it's cool when you say, "Remember this feeling." It's the behaviour version of "Look out! This could get ugly!"'

The muscles in the great man's throat tightened in an instant, overjoyed to receive such a ringing endorsement. He reached across the table and skimmed his son's scalp with the fingers of his left hand, the vindication sweetened still further by his wife's heart-stopping smile.

'Absolutely, mate,' he nodded, watching both children drain their water glasses. 'That's exactly what it is. Forewarned is forearmed, otherwise known as "ugly situation alert"!'

'Like that day when I was dying for the toilet,' the cricketer continued, 'in front of all those people wanting autographs. And then, when we eventually found one, you wouldn't let me go in 'til I'd remembered what it felt like to be that desperate.'

The teacher smirked. 'Ah, yeah! I do remember that. I felt like a real shit doing it to you, but it was too good an opportunity to miss.'

'But it really worked!' his son cried out. 'I've never let myself get that desperate since then. There's no way I want to feel that panicky again. I can feel my heart racing just thinking about it.'

'Anxiety attack,' Jeff murmured. 'Yep. Sorry, mate. I'm glad it served its purpose. Cruel to be kind.'

Lynn took over, guessing how uncomfortable this would make her lost boy. 'Right, guys. So do the same with drinking. We'll let you get drunk when and where no-one's looking... and smoke or whatever... but only if you promise you'll think about what you're doing when we're not there to help you out. We'd like to be able to trust you to look after yourselves. We don't want to be the type of parents who won't let you out of our sight.'

'I promise, *Mamá*,' Kierney jumped in.

Jet gave his mother a thumbs-up. 'Cool! Not like Mags. When he's invited to a party, his mum and dad always stay for the whole thing. He hates it, and Justin says his mum and dad hate it too. They try dropping hints like they're the only parents there, but they just hang around, asking for coffee and tea when everyone else's trying to have fun.'

'So what's pot like?' the dreamy thirteen-year-old interjected.

'Pots? They're for putting flowers in, *pequeñita*. You are a bit drunk, 'cause you just cut your brother off while he was speaking,' came the father's stern voice rebuke. 'Deep breaths, remember? I'm ashamed you even want to know what pot's like.'

'Why?' Jet whined. 'Everyone knows what pot is. It's not your fault. Even Mum just said we could smoke and drink with you. So what's the difference between alcohol and weed? They're both drugs, and they're both supposed to be adults-only. Like sex.'

With the rock star burying his face in her sleeve, Lynn shook her head at the new direction their conversation had taken. 'Might've known it wouldn't take us long to get onto this seedy subject. Sex, drugs and rock'n'roll. Who wants to talk about music instead?'

'Oh, that's not fair. I thought you wanted to help us learn about being an adult?' Kierney teased. Come on... What's pot like, *Papá*?'

'Like father, like son,' the blonde singer groaned, digging the comedian to her left in the ribs. 'You tell us... What's pot like, Kizzy? Jetto?'

While the youngsters composed their own responses, they watched their bad-boy role model close his eyes and take a series of deliberate, scopious breaths, an invisible spliff pinched between thumb and middle finger. The combination of his acting ability and an outsized sensory appreciation projected his imagination like a hologram in front of his audience.

Lynn smiled at these antics, pleased the realistic display was taking place behind closed doors. She could almost taste the sweet-scented smoke as she saw him collect the warm vapour inside his mouth and nasal cavity and curl it up into his brain. His breathing became louder, touching something deep within her and filling her heart to bursting point.

After a few moments, the mime artist opened his eyes wide and then closed them again, tilting his head back and shaking his black mane. 'It's amazing,' he replied after a few seconds. 'Mellow. In my opinion, it's the only time we should be permitted to use the word "nice". Describes the feeling perfectly. A sort of peace, like you've got all this empty space in your brain to wander through.'

'Wow! That sounds awesome,' Kierney smiled.

'It is,' her dad nodded. 'Or you can just gaze around if you want. It's as if you've got all the time in the world to think deep thoughts or explore the meta-universe. It relaxes you for a while, until the drug loses its effect. But you're right, mate. It is somewhat like sex.'

'Oh, *Papá*!' Kierney exclaimed, screwing her napkin into a ball and throwing it at her dad's glazed, faraway expression.

The missile scored a direct hit, provoking her brother into launching a second volley. Jeff scrunched the napkins together and chucked them back.

'Why does everything have to be about sex?' the young girl whined. 'You two are just the same. I'm glad I don't have testicles. I'd get sick of losing my train of thought.'

The songwriter burst out laughing, the magic spell well and truly broken. He wound a long arm around the love of his life and pulled her in close, devouring the kiss on offer. The kids didn't need to know where her hand was or what it was doing to him. On second thoughts, the high from *marijuana* wasn't nearly this enjoyable!

'And your problem is?' he quipped, prising his lips away from Lynn's mouth and giving them a theatrical wipe with the back of his hand. 'Men are quite happy being inferior beings. Aren't we, Jetto?'

The boy nodded, with no real idea what this meant.

'OK! Who's the smarter?' the question-master reset the conversation, refilling everyone's wine glass from the second bottle. 'Someone who battles on through thick and thin until he or she's thought things through, or someone who shares their dilemma to reach a solution faster?'

'The one who shares,' his son answered.

'Sure, mate. Spot on, under normal circumstances. But what if a bloke realises he'd much rather picture what sensational acts his woman could be doing to him and with him, if only they weren't sharing the tough decisions? Why not leave her to work it out and present him with a plan while he savours the moment. *Tout simple, n'est-ce pas?* Everyone should focus on what they do best. We don't mind taking one for the team while you girls work stuff out for us. Make sense?'

Lynn slapped the larrikin's chest. 'Now you tell me!' she exclaimed. 'To think that all this time I've been under the impression you were focussed on solving the problem at hand.'

Jet laughed, the top-up of wine having its wicked way with him once again. 'The problem at hand! There would be a problem at hand. Especially if the woman's your teacher or something.'

'Oh, gross!' his little sister yelped. 'That's so disgusting. You shouldn't be having dirty thoughts about teachers. What if she could read your mind?'

'Ah, but they can, angel,' their father insisted. 'Teachers can always sense when their boy students have the hots for them. It's part of their training.'

His wife frowned. 'Hmm... And you should know...'

'Dessert?' Jeff declared, springing up from the table before this innocent comment was seized upon and he was forced into yet another dubious confession. 'I'll make the coffee while I'm at it. And pot, like sex, guys, will be saved for when you're sixteen or thereabouts.'

***

Back home in *Escondido* for the long Easter weekend, Lynn returned to the ground floor having wished the children a good night. She wandered in and out of every room, unable to locate her husband. Assuming he had gone to bed, depleted after his return journey from Los Angeles, something made her turn the opposite way at the foot of the stairs.

As she suspected, Jeff had ventured outside into the cool autumn air. Without switching on the exterior lights, he had spread a picnic rug out on the dewy lawn, just to the far side of the pool, and next to it sat a low pile of blankets. Barefoot, Lynn padded along the *patio*, which was cold enough to set her soles tingling. She could see the rise and fall of his chest as he lay on his back under the stars.

The songwriter's hands were fidgeting with an object she couldn't make out. What was he up to? It was too slim for a bottle of beer, and too long to be a cigar. As the stalker closed in on her target, she smiled. The mystery plaything was an action figure she thought had been retired from their son's list of favourite toys, dressed in military fatigues but thankfully unarmed.

How she loved her enigmatic free spirit! With each year that passed, their relationship assumed new and wondrous dimensions. Nowadays, too exhausted from travelling to blast out the last few weeks' worth of intellectual mayhem in the gymnasium, he took to more meditative techniques to decompress from the trials and triumphs. His crowded mind whirred and hummed and fizzed in perpetual motion, and it was as if the resultant potential energy deprived his senses. He always needed to be touching something.

Her demanding lover's inability to shut these cravings down had confounded her in the early days, before the full story had come to light. She had then accepted it as part of a complex character determined to heal, resigned to the ever-present whisky tumbler or cigarette and his constant badgering for carnal fulfilment.

In recent times however, so much more content with who he had become, and having learned between them to keep his demons and phobia at bay, many of these vices had largely been left behind. But as hard as he tried, his hands remained ever restless in the absence of other stimulation.

'Here you are,' Lynn whispered in case he was asleep. 'What are you doing out here? I thought you wanted to watch "Four Corners"?'

The nomad's eyes opened and imbibed the silhouetted female form approaching, fringed by soft moonlight. Although he could make out not much more than a shadow, he had no trouble recalling the short denim skirt and tight T-shirt which accentuated her glorious curves, and the combination of her sultry voice and the tempting image rekindled the lustful thoughts that had led him outside in the first place.

'I'm taping it. Coming to join me?'

'Of course! Good thinking,' the tall athlete smiled, crouching down beside him and tapping the toy soldier on the head. 'What are you doing with him?'

With a coy grin, Jeff straightened the foot-high figure's legs and placed the soles of his rubber boots on the rug, lifting his tiny right hand into a salute. The introduction brought back happy memories for the young parents, though long gone were the days when this kind of game was a regular occurrence. Both children had been taught the art of conversation through endless dialogue staged by their favourite toys, often extending to the night shift for hysterical acts of foreplay.

'Drill Sergeant Polymer, at your service, ma'am,' Jeff barked in his best parade-ground voice.

'At ease, Polymer,' Lynn giggled, saluting back. 'You're looking very smart, as usual. What can I do for you tonight?'

'Thank you, ma'am,' the double act replied. 'I bring an urgent dispatch from HQ.'

The ventriloquist snapped the soldier's arm to his side and sat him down, stiff-jointed legs splayed out in a manner too ungainly for a member of the fighting *élite*. Staring at the perfection of his wife's face, his eyes now adjusted to the dark, he wasn't sure if the heartbeat pounding in his eardrums was his or hers, or both in sublime syncopation.

'My mate wants to know if he can take your clothes off and spirit you off to paradise.'

'Oh, does he? Right under my husband's nose?'

The messenger chuckled. 'Yeah, well... He knows I like to watch.'

'Is that so?' she humoured them. 'I never knew that. I've got a better idea. Why don't the two of you get down to some boy-lovin', and *I'll* watch?'

Jeff stopped in his tracks, his plastic partner unwilling to entertain this counter-offensive. 'Ahem! No can do. Not tonight, Poly, old thing. The lady's got some strange ideas, eh? You trying to tell me you want a night off?'

Before Lynn could answer, the toy soldier sprang into action, his hand making straight for the neckline of her top and peeling it back to reveal the edge of a lacy bra. Squealing, she pushed him away and scratched her skin where the sharp fingertips had tickled.

'No. I'm rostered on tonight,' she assured her two suitors. 'But take your time, Sergeant Polymer, please. We've got all night.'

'Yes, ma'am. Sorry, ma'am. At your command, ma'am.'

The amused woman sat down beside her husband on the rug and dragged one of the blankets across her legs, the rest of her toasted by his body's radiating warmth. The tiny, inanimate face was presented to her waiting lips, arms outstretched. Instead of accepting his minute advances, she altered the shape of her mouth from an inviting pucker into a wide cavern and proceeded to swallow her unsuspecting lover's whole head.

'Jesus, angel!' Jeff cried out, ordering his troop into a swift withdrawal and bringing a temporary halt to their mission. 'That's just plain scary. Quite disturbing, in fact. Can we start that again?'

Laughing, Lynn shuffled across to lock lips with the alarmed brigadier, shoving his torso down onto the rug. They kissed as if there were no time to lose, eager to enjoy their intimacy after almost two weeks apart. While his hands drew the bottom hem of his wife's top upwards over her back, he felt her weight shift and heard the whoosh that was Sergeant Polymer flying across the lawn. After a couple of circuits and bumps, he crash-landed in the rhododendrons.

'Sorry, soldier,' the smiling woman gasped. 'Time's up. You've just joined the Air Force.'

Her hot-blooded partner let out a huge roar and whipped the tennis champion's body over until she was flat on her back beneath him. They were both still fully clothed, but it didn't matter. While their little gems slept upstairs and their nannies minded their own business on the other side of the house, they had as long to renew their acquaintance as the winds over Port Phillip Bay would allow.

'Are you alright?' Lynn enquired, running her hand down the side of Jeff's leg and sensing the muscles flinching. 'Your amp's turned up pretty high tonight.'

The breathless man hugged her close. 'I'm totally fine, *mi regala*,' he replied, sitting up and peeling the blouse off her lithe body. 'Just glad to be home and even gladder to be alone with you.'

His saviour smiled, unconvinced, and kissed his black jet-stone ring, wherein their four diamonds were set. She unbuttoned his shirt and slotted her hand inside to stroke the hair covering his tattooed pectoral muscle before heading down over his obliques and towards his belt.

The other, much larger pair of hands reached the buckle first, their flamboyant owner jumping to his feet to remove his suit trousers and cast them in a casual loop onto the flagstones. 'Leave your skirt on,' he hissed, dropping down to smother her again. 'Please?'

'Sure,' Lynn agreed, laughing at the intensity in his voice. 'You really have to feel everything, don't you? It still amazes me. I was thinking that earlier, when I found you out here. Every sight, every sound and touch is so important to you. I wonder how you came to be such a sensual person?'

'Who knows? And who cares, huh? As long as you like it.'

'Like it?' his wife echoed, moaning as two of his fingers sunk deep inside her. 'It's fantastic. There's no halfway with you. That's what I love so much. No wishy-washy indecision. This is how it is, baby. Take it or leave it.'

Jeff kissed her chattering mouth, the words devoured and filed away to keep his heart safe when he was next on the road. This woman was made for him, and he for her. Through the ages maybe, but most definitely in this lifetime.

They would never know why, but still not a day went by that he didn't give thanks for this mysterious gift.

Their hot-blooded tryst over in a raft of muffled gasps of adoration and rapturous moans, it wasn't long before the couple began to shiver, even under the blankets Jeff had pulled across their calming bodies.

Dampness from the sea air had descended, so the lovers decided to adjourn inside to watch the recorded documentary on the Arab-Israeli peace talks which the peacemaker had been keen to see. Waiting for the video cassette to rewind, he twisted round to face the beauty sitting on the couch, dressed in nothing but a short, silk dressing gown and a satisfied glow.

'Angel, I've got something to tell you.'

'Oh, yeah? What's that? You're not going to the Middle East?'

'No. Not soon anyway. Steve rang me.'

'Steve Christie?'

The singer's expression bore a certain unease that disconcerted her husband. *Please don't let her be hiding something*, he begged Gravity the troll, who had stirred after several months of hibernation. His fears had been chased off for an hour by their lawn *rendezvous*, but now it was crunch time. They had learned to trust each other implicitly, faced with their careers' independent orbits. Had there been one trip too many?

'Yep. The very same. He wants to meet me for a drink to discuss your future.'

Lynn sat forward, her complexion paling. 'Discuss my future?' she repeated in a high-pitched shrill. 'What for?'

'Ha! Bloody idiot, he is. I hope... He tells me you're not happy and that you want out of our marriage. We're meeting so he can issue a challenge for your hand.'

'Oh, my God! That's utterly ridiculous! Yes, he is a bloody idiot. He hasn't spoken to me about any of this. What the hell does he mean?' the thirty-six-year-old bleated. 'Are you serious? This isn't some sort of joke, is it?'

''Fraid not, angel,' he answered, hoping her indignation came from the heart. 'It's the modern equivalent of pistols at dawn, I guess. Schooners at dusk.'

The video recorder's winding mechanism clicked off, the tape returned to the beginning. The television screen flicked onto a live channel. Lynn held out her hand for the remote control, and the anxious songwriter passed it over, frightened she would set the programme running and brush the whole matter aside.

'Challenge for my hand,' she mocked, switching the television off and inviting the traveller to join her on the sofa. 'I can't believe this. It's stupid. Are you really going to meet him?'

The lost boy slid across the polished boards and pushed the coffee table away to make room for him to sit on the floor beside his wife's long, tanned legs. 'Bloody oath, I am. For two reasons: one, I don't want to believe it either, but it's real, and the subject needs addressing; and two, I'm hanging out to hear what he has to say. What his arguments are, y'know.'

'Wow! He never gives up, does he?' the record producer sighed. 'He's like you in that way. He wants something he can't have, but he won't be told no.'

Jeff let out a sarcastic laugh, the parallel germane but altogether objectionable under the circumstances. 'I s'pose I deserve that,' he admitted, 'though I wish you hadn't said it. It's your choice at the end of the day. Just because we have a piece of paper legally binding us as husband and wife, if there's somewhere else you'd rather be...'

'Stop!' Lynn shouted, leaning forward and placing both hands on his shoulders. 'Please! That's not how it is at all. I haven't done or said anything to lead him on. For God's sake! Why would I? You're the best man I could possibly have, Jeff. I'm so lucky to be with you. You've got to believe me! Look how we were tonight... I was as hungry for you as you were for me.'

'Christ! I know you were, and I do believe you,' the rock star groaned, levering himself up onto the couch and wrapping his arms around her. 'Thanks, and I'm sorry to sound like I doubt you. I don't know what I feel about this yet. I'm petrified, if I'm honest, although I have no clue why. On one hand, I trust you and know what we have has never been stronger. But on the other hand, my primitive *macho* pride's telling me to kill either him or you, or both.'

Laughing, Lynn cuddled closer and brushed her lips across his strained jawline. 'Great! That'd do the trick. Even less sophisticated than pistols at dawn,' she teased. 'Neanderthal meets Knight of the Round Table.'

Jeff leaned back and expelled a lungful of air, embarrassed by his outburst. 'You're right. Club or jousting pole. Take your pick, Stevie-baby.'

Both celebrities chuckled and moved apart to diffuse the angst from the atmosphere, flushed and overheating from the strain. At least the concern wasn't one-sided, the front-end of the pantomime horse consoled himself, searching his dream girl's eyes for the slightest shadow of doubt.

For the blonde's part, she adored her troubled soul even more for being so driven to defend their union. 'So tell me what he said on the 'phone,' she requested, hoping to lighten the mood a little.

'Not much really. I cut him off after he said you weren't happy, 'cause I was standing with a camera crew, about to start an interview. I said I'd see him tomorrow. He claims he's taking you to the US next week. I was hardly going to talk about such personal shit in front of those guys.'

'No. Course not,' his wife sighed. 'God, I'm so sorry this has happened. What a bastard! And how awkward he's making things. Anyway, you're meeting him for a drink tomorrow evening? Where? Are you sure you don't want me to come too?'

'The Lindrum,' the handsome man ran two fingers down the side of her face. 'And no. You shouldn't be there. We'll go best-of-three on the billiard table, and whoever wins gets the girl.'

Lynn shook her head. 'Hey! Please don't joke about it. This is horrible. What a change from being outside making love on the grass... One minute I wish you wouldn't put your extreme thoughts into words, and the next I'm offended you're taking it so lightly.'

Jeff's heart cleaved open at the pain this unwelcome distraction was causing them both. His beautiful best friend's charmed existence had sent few crises of conscience her way. Lynn Dyson was a prize this uncivilised *vigilante* didn't deserve, and no more or less than Steve Christie deserved her. Whomever were to receive the rejection letter in the end, the resulting storm would cause one man's world to veer off course. He was damned if it was going to be his. There would be no coming back from a catastrophe of such magnitude.

'Oh, I'm certainly not taking it lightly, angel. No way I'd be able to. You're far too important to me, and I owe it to the kids too. It'll be fine. I know who I'm up against, and I think I know where I stand with you.'

'Think you know? I hope you're a good deal more confident than that! I love you, the whole you and nothing but you, mate,' Lynn affirmed, hugging him close. 'Thank you for doing this. The kids'll be OK. They won't understand properly, and I don't want it to be tough on you. I know you care, and that makes me love you even more.'

'Shit, angel! I do bloody well care,' Jeff closed his hand around hers and kissed her wedding ring. 'I'm only joking about it because it's such a fuckin' ludicrous position to be in. I'll make it go away tomorrow, but 'til then, press "Play", and let's be done with it.'

Duel

'Hey, Dad?'

'Yeah?'

'Why hasn't anyone written "Lord Chatterley's Lover"?' Jet asked, disrupting his father's concentration as he prepared to sink the last red ball in their first game of snooker.

'What?' Jeff exclaimed, standing up and walking away from the table.

'Or Romeo and Julio?'

Leaning over to take his shot, the older man laughed and lifted his cue again. 'Julio?' he emphasised the guttural initial letter of his Spanish-speaking roots. 'Wherefore art thou, Romeo? *¡Mira, Julio! ¡Estoy aquí!* Mate, if I didn't know you better, as the honourable sportsman your grandfather brought you up to be, I'd be half-inclined to believe you were trying to put me off.'

His son shrugged. 'Hurry up, old man. Time's a-ticking.'

'Or are you coming out to me?'

Jet doubled over, his dad's second conclusion worthy of grand theatrics. 'Coming out? Think again, good buddy. Highly unlikely! But why aren't there any classic gay romance novels?'

The thirty-nine-year-old potted the red and screwed the cue ball back to an unplayable position on the baize. He saw the lad nod an admission that he would never be able to make his next shot from this spot. What was the origin of this particular line of enquiry? Regardless, he was pleased the teenager had chosen him to provide the answers.

'*Howzat!*' the musician gloated. 'Good question, mate. There are heaps, but not typically available in your average bookshop. Why d'you ask? Want to read one?'

'Not really. Just wondering, that's all. We were talking about it at school today, and I think maybe we all should. You're always saying we shouldn't only read what we're interested in. Our English Lit' teacher didn't have much of an answer.'

The two Diamond men were kicking back in the old-fashioned billiard room at the Lindrum Hotel, passing time before the planned showdown with Lynn's challenger. Jeff had spent the day in the city with his management team, catching up on paperwork after his most recent trip and meeting with a group of politicians, including the Victorian Premier, Joan Kirner.

It had been a busy day, during which the celebrity had exercised the full scope of his current business and philanthropic interests, but nothing weighed heavier on his conscience than the upcoming encounter with Steve Christie. He had requested his son steal away from school after the afternoon's lessons to help him relax with some idle pursuits, and this latest vexing question was perfect to steer his anxious brain to happier thoughts.

Jet cursed under his breath as the white ball failed to make contact with the blue he had targetted, instead bouncing off the cushion to line up his opponent's next shot for him. The proud father noticed how easily the cricketer handled failure, with no more than a few seconds of castigation, rebounding with renewed boldness.

He slapped the growing boy's back, at first attributing his mental strength to Dyson fortitude but then recognising himself too. 'Tough luck, old bean,' he impersonated the indomitable Uncle Gerry. 'It's disappointing that Mister Middlemarch didn't give you guys a decent answer. Ask Mum to ring Richard. He'll be able to tell you off the top of his head, but I guess it's because love affairs involving only one gender's still deemed unacceptable for mainstream audiences. We can't have literature challenging common decency now, can we?'

'Why not? That's exactly what I mean,' his son argued. 'Doesn't it only make things worse? It'll never be acceptable if people don't learn about how gays and lesbians live. They'll always be like freaks, so they get marginalised even further.'

Jeff nodded, lighting a cigarette and emptying his beer glass. 'Very true. I'm impressed you understand what "marginalised" means. Very impressed, in fact. There are plenty of books about great homosexual relationships, but you can't normally find them on the bestseller shelves. We've got a few at home actually: "The Picture of Dorian Gray" by Oscar Wilde and James Baldwin's "Giovanni's Room". Oh, and there's "Maurice" by E M Forster. I haven't read that one, but Mum has. Same with everything, mate. You need to know what you're looking for and where to look.'

The fourteen-year-old let out a victorious whoop as he sunk the blue ball with a fluked shot. He went to pinch a mouthful from his dad's fresh glass, which sat on the edge of the snooker table, dripping condensation onto the carpet.

Intercepted by quick reflexes and swapping the beer for orange juice in response to a casual reprimand, the young man sneered. 'Worth a try! Have you read the others?'

'Yep. Those two I mentioned, and there's also "Fried Green Tomatoes at the Whistlestop Café".'

'Fried green tomatoes? Are you kidding? What's that about?'

'It's an American lesbian novel. I can't remember who wrote it. Set at the turn of the century. Interesting read,' the songwriter smiled. 'It wasn't too long ago that it was still frowned upon to read about inter-racial relationships, but at least we're making progress on this front these days.'

'Oh, cool. Wow! They must make films about it too,' the budding director surmised.

'They do. Sure,' Jeff affirmed. 'There are underground festivals all over the world to showcase alternative films. Perhaps... Well, we can hope anyway... in ten or twenty years' time, we'll be going to the picture house on Russell Street to see gay or lesbian romantic comedies alongside straight ones.'

'Yeah. And even action movies or sci-fi. Times'll change,' the all-knowing teenager said. 'Too slow though, isn't it? What are you guys doing tonight? Is Mum in the city?'

The philosopher nodded. 'No. She will be tomorrow, I think. I'm meeting Steve Christie for a drink here in half an hour.'

'OK,' Jet responded, none the wiser as to the reason. 'That's good. Say hi to him from me. I need to be back by six-thirty. Please could I grab some money for a burger on the way to school? I forgot to come out with any, and dinner'll be over by then.'

'No money?' his father teased. 'Unlike you not to think of your stomach. Are you alright to get yourself back on your own? You'd better get two burgers, and some chips, or you'll be hungry again by bedtime.'

The sportsman smirked, receiving a pair of ten-dollar notes and a gentle kick to the shin. 'Thanks, Dad. I'll try not to get mugged on my way out of Hungry Jacks.'

The pair continued their tabletop battle, which Jeff ended up winning quite comfortably. His son was just about to pick up his jacket and prepare to leave when the door swang inwards to reveal the dapper US-Australian singer-songwriter. Clapping eyes on Diamond Junior, his swagger faltered, allowing his rival to take control of the situation from the outset.

'Mister Christie! Welcome,' he postulated. 'Perfect timing. Jetto's on his way out. What are you drinking?'

Holding out his hand, the teenager walked up to the new arrival. The family had known Steve for as long as he could remember, with now only a few centimetres' difference in their respective heights. This narrowing gap prompted a double-take from the blond musician. His host was struck by an afterthought too, pacing backwards to the bar, wondering how many people might wonder if the fair-haired Dyson Diamond was really Steve's son, especially if this latest *fiasco* hit the newspapers.

'Well, hello, Jet,' Steve greeted the student, who had donned the same school blazer he used to wear. 'My God! You're enormous! When did you get so tall?'

'This morning,' the fourteen-year-old quipped. 'And when did you get so short?'

'Mate,' the father issued a playful warning, despite wallowing in the natural, friendly way his son delivered this put-down. 'Have some respect, please. Or get out of here. One or the other.'

'Okey dokey. Sorry, Steve. I'm off,' the lad smiled, strolling back to pick up two of the three beers which had been poured by the young woman behind the counter. 'Great to see you. Who's this for?'

'Who'd *ya* think, you clown?' Jeff shook his head, toasting his own height comparison. 'Drink it fast, and without facing the bar in your normal barefaced cheek kind o' way.'

Feeling special to be included in such a manly pursuit, the teenager sculled his *middy* in a few large gulps. Slapping the empty glass onto a drenched coaster, he hugged his father and thanked him for their play-off.

The rock star held onto the boy's hand for as long as he could, knowing that asking him to hang around would be out of order. 'See *ya* Friday, son. Enjoy the rest of the week. And don't report me for sending you to school smelling of premium lager.'

Jet smacked his lips and checked the time. 'I'm sure three Whoppers with cheese'll obliterate all traces of alcohol. Have fun, guys.'

Both men watched the well-built future cricket legend depart through the hotel lobby and skip down the steps onto Flinders Street, turning right to pick up some food from Swanston Street on his way over the river to Melbourne Academy. The spring in his gait exuded happiness at being alive and growing up without a care in the world. So alien to his father at the same age, the mood was infectious, and for a minute Jeff forgot why the pair had arranged to meet.

'How's Crystal?' he opened, noticing the other songwriter also had a stupid grin on his face.

'She's good. I talked to her just last week. I can't believe that's Jet! He's almost a man.'

The billionnaire chuckled. 'Who, him? No "almost" about it, mate. He's great, and Kizzy too. So what's the go with your offer to relieve me of my wife?'

The New Yorker was caught off-guard by his long-time collaborator's jovial opening gambit. At the local's behest, he moved to a table well away from the window, the ambiance thickening with each pace. Both superstars were tired, and the empath was only too aware of their individual battles with the black dog and longstanding addictions. If anyone knew what a tall order it was to deny a fellow sufferer his basic desires, it was he.

'Have a seat, man,' Steve suggested, pointing at the chair opposite and opening his packet of cigarettes. 'Thanks for agreeing to meet. I hope you're not *gonna* have me killed.'

Jeff scoffed, accepting a light and sending a thick cloud of smoke into the air between their heads. The joke was in poor taste, but he deserved it. Both men's fathers had been linked to the underworld, although Steve's had been a white-collar criminal and never spent time in prison.

Of Scottish descent, Henry Montrose had emigrated to upstate New York as an adolescent and had built a successful business by acting as a so-called "clean middleman" between crooked sellers and equally crooked buyers. While Paul Diamond had fought dirty and with complete disregard for the law, Henry had manipulated everyone by trading kick-backs from *Mafia* hoodlums and high-ranking police officers across the north-eastern states, maintaining a much more respectable shopfront.

Somewhere along the line, Montrose had met and married an Australian woman, who over the years had grown to dislike their children growing up in such an unsuitable environment. This grievance had seen Steve and his two siblings dispatched to Melbourne, to be raised by their maternal grandparents in the respectable suburb of Camberwell. To cap it all, the Sydneysider recalled, the imported kids' private school education, as peers of Bart Dyson's progeny, was most likely funded by despicable and ill-gotten gains.

Steven Christopher Montrose was a talented musician; a pianist and a versatile singer. He had enjoyed success in many performing and recording *genres* since the Diamonds had chosen him to play a key supporting role in one of their early musical *pastiches*. A friendship with Jeff had come first, born out of shared emotional scars expunged into lyrics and melodies that clogged the pop charts throughout the nineteen-seventies and -eighties, he then enlisted Lynn as his producer-arranger for a lengthening catalogue of platinum albums.

During his final year at school, the handsome newcomer looked up to The Australian Elvis as his hero, emulating him in every way. Struggling to control a cocaine habit which threatened to derail his rise to stardom, Steve had sought out the high-rolling dark soul to whose robust frame he now lifted his glass.

In their twenties, the unlikely songwriting pair identified their showbusiness reputations' common underpinning: dependence on alcohol and other illicit substances to transport them through nights filled with horrific dreams and a dreadful, unshakable sense of worthlessness. It had been Jeff who initiated their mutual *découvrage*, spurred on by his beautiful best friend's support.

The outlet proved fortunate for Steve, who had lapped up his charismatic mentor's advice. He then turned to him again a few years later, when his father died suddenly at his Buffalo mansion. Speculation was rife that Hank Montrose had been taken out by a hit-man, but his children were told he had taken his own life.

This inconsistency had always struck the Sydneysider as odd, given the low regard in which suicide was held within the upper *echelons* of Melbourne society. Being the victim of a violent crime might have been construed as a more honourable death.

Regardless, these successful recording artists had not reunited in the Lindrum Hotel in nineteen-ninety-two for more cloudy and debauched counselling disguised as a jam session. Both lives had moved on since those times, each showered with adulation from fans and hounded by the media at every turn.

Like his dark-haired guide, the New Yorker had become a well-respected figure in the global music scene, made wealthy through the dynamite combination of his composing talent, Jeff's prolific and poetic lyrics and Lynn's skill as a record producer. The two men faced off as equals today; handsome, influential and confident.

'Killed? Nope,' the Catholic Argentinean Polish Jew sneered, offering another cigarette and menacing his lighter under his adversary's nose. 'Hadn't crossed my mind.'

Steve recoiled. 'Sure. That was a bit low. I apologise.'

'This whole fucking thing's a bit low, if you ask me. What is it you want, mate?'

Try as he might, the old soul was unable to rid his mind of the image of a tearful Lynn in his arms, set against the backdrop of Paris by night. Ever since the bizarre publicity stunt staged by this man across the table, the notion of a love triangle through the ages had only grown more vivid.

There but for the grace of God, he heard Gravity's overused refrain hissing in his ear.

In the endless loop of mental footage, the beauty who had clung to him near *la Seine* was not rugged up in tight jeans and an elegant knee-length coat, as she had been on that night. Neither was he sporting the leather jacket which was rarely off his back. Was it possible that Lynn's soul had belonged to a former incarnation of Steve Christie? Whose child had she been carrying then? And had Steve's current embodiment been visited by a similar allusion?

Inhaling, the challenger scowled. 'Your wife's too damned fine for you, Diamond. That's basically it. We've loved each other for years. You guys've been together too long, and she's bored.'

'Bored? Is that right?'

'So she told me,' Steve crowed.

'OK! Well, if it's true, she's doing a bloody good job of deceiving me,' Jeff sniffed, recalling the pleasurable evening the couple had spent on the lawn at *Escondido* just yesterday. 'What's she bored with?'

The American stubbed out his cigarette. 'She's sick of being stuck at home while you swan all over the place, making peace with people who don't want to make peace.'

'Yeah. I can well believe it,' the negotiator nodded, the suggestion that he was wasting his effort in addition to neglecting his woman annoying him more than it ought to. 'I get bloody sick of it too, but a man's *gotta* do what a man's *gotta* do. What else did Lynn tell you?'

'She's fed up of staying home, raising the kids on her own,' he added. 'She wants a new life; more luxuries without having to play second fiddle to you. She should be treated better, and she's sick of you always out drinking and getting laid whenever you want.'

The hard-working company director laughed out loud at the last few items on Steve's rehearsed list. The idea of getting laid whenever he wanted sounded so foreign to him now, closing in on his fortieth birthday and so committed to his family. He rose to his full height and picked up their empty glasses, not prepared to give his opponent the satisfaction of buying him a drink. The noise of chair legs scraping along the floorboards was engineered on purpose to drown out the preposterous statements of fantasy.

From the bar, the showman turned and raised his voice. 'Lynn told you all this?'

'Sure thing, man,' Steve shouted back. 'Many times. She doesn't have to tell me. I can see it in her eyes, and the way she opens up to me.'

The flabbergasted bartender dropped an assortment of loose change into the revered celebrity's hand, never suspecting his shift at the distinguished hotel would give rise to such high drama. Returning to their table, Jeff placed the two chilled stubbies onto the table, pushing one along on its glistening underside towards his guest.

'Tell me... From how close can you see all this?'

'Close enough.'

'From the same distance as I didn't see anything of the kind this morning?' the hostility in his voice increased.

The good-looking pop star flinched before regrouping. 'How can you be sure I haven't been at your house today while you've been in the CBD? Your bed's very comfortable, man, with your wife in it.'

'Fuck you,' the lost boy exhaled, angry that his own weakness allowed these baseless assertions to sting. 'I have no fucking idea where you've been today, but I sure as hell know you haven't been in our bed.'

Steve raised the bottle to pursed lips and chuckled. 'If I were you, I'd have cameras trained on her all day. If it's not me, it'll be someone else soon.'

'Doubtless, mate. CCTV in our own house? That'd be awesome. Lynn'd love the extra exposure. Is that why Jan left you? Or Brittany?'

'I left them.'

'Yeah,' Jeff leaped on this little nugget. 'And now she's raising your daughter on her own. What's the difference, mate? How many kids' lives do you want to screw up as part of this process? Is this some sort of payback for what you went through? If it is, then it's not worth it. Fucking someone else's life up'll never make yours any better, mate. I'm very sorry your marriages didn't work out, but there's no use taking it out on us.'

'Shit! Lynn loves me,' the American insisted. 'Quit psychoanalysing me. That garbage's all behind me now. It's got nothing to do with why I'm here. I'm in love with your wife, and we're going to be together. Crystal, Jet and Kierney'll be just fine. They're not part of this decision.'

The great man's temper was nearing boiling point, curling his fingers and digging their nails into the palm of his right hand under the table. 'This decision?' he taunted, his other hand up-ending the beer bottle into his mouth. 'So it's a done deal, is it? Are you picking Lynn up tonight? Is that the plan? Hope you're not expecting me to drop her off at your hotel! Give me a second. I'll ring and say she can start packing.'

'Cool! Why not? She belongs with me.'

The world-changer growled under his breath. It was only the sheer lunacy of their circumstance which stopped him from grabbing his former apprentice's gullet and strangling him then and there. The idea that this imbecile expected his champion of a life partner would do whatever she was told by either man was incredulous. Even if his beautiful best friend did fancy a change of scene, which was questionable at best, the length of time she would tolerate being dictated to by this arrogant pig would be ephemeral in the extreme.

'OK, mate,' he sighed. 'Let's suppose for a minute that you're right... D'you really expect me to shake your hand and say, "Go for it. She's all yours," eh?'

As these words emerged from between his locked jaws, Miss Irony appeared from nowhere, forcing him to acknowledge that he too had dominated and been indulged by Lynn throughout their whole partnership. She had admitted as much in front of her family on their tenth wedding anniversary.

A wave of nausea washed through him, and he felt the old insecurities thrashing around in his head like epileptic limbs. The devious troll must have unlocked the drawer where they had been stashed for a rainy day, stealing one too many bricks from the bottom of his host's pedestal.

Who was to say that another man couldn't make Lynn happy, as long as he was kind and loving and respectful? Steve could meet his *regala*'s every need just as well as he could. *Get a grip*, he begged. It was maddening how his damaged psyche still had the power to destroy his peace of mind.

'Look, Jeff... I'm sure you know Lynn's bummed with how things are, man. You've had her to yourself for way too long. Time to give someone else a turn.'

'Give someone else a turn?' Jeff was seething by now. 'Who or what do you think Lynn is? A fairground ride? Some toy to be passed around between us until we grow out of it? A pet dog who needs re-homing? It's your turn to show some bloody respect, Mister Christie.'

'Yeah,' the contender agreed. 'You said all those things. I didn't. But whatever you think I mean, it's the truth. We're meant to be together now. Your marriage has run its course.'

With a laconic chuckle, the swarthy rocker lifted his left hand to eye-level and drew Steve's attention to his wedding ring. 'Is that right? I'm not so sure, mate, 'cause d'you see this? This means something. In case you never quite got the hang of things, it means Lynn's my wife until she chooses not to be, and it also means she's not yours to make plans for. As long as she's wearing the smaller one of these, our course flows on.'

'Have you asked her? Lately, I mean.'

'Yep. Every fucking day, mate,' the passionate man snapped back, swapping his beer into his left hand so he could draw attention to the black jet-stone ring on the opposite middle finger. 'Every fucking day. And do you see this one too?'

His petulant songwriting partner grunted, feigning disdain for symbols of a union he considered phony and nothing more than a media construct. His body language said otherwise, Jeff noticed. Not only had the younger man's puffed-out chest deflated in the last minute or so, but his trembling left leg was causing their table to vibrate as his knee pressed against it.

'Good. These four stones represent our family. I'm sure you've heard that before. We're a unit, y'see. Everlasting. Four or none. A concept you don't seem to understand anymore, my friend. You gave your family away. I'm not about to do the same to mine.'

'You bastard, Diamond. You fucking do so! You give 'em away every time you leave 'em on their own,' Steve replied, almost lecturing. 'Your kids wouldn't miss you if you only saw them in the school vacations, just like mine.'

Jeff sprang out of his chair and hurled it backwards in disgust. Luckily, only a handful of other patrons were in the bar to witness the spectacle of two famous Melbourne musicians quarrelling. Apologising to those closest to them, the dark-haired star snatched his wallet off the table and slotted it into the inside pocket of his trusty leather jacket.

'Y'know? I've heard enough of this shit, mate,' he announced with admirable composure. 'Remember my son? Jet, his name is. You may've seen him recently. He's getting pretty tall.'

'So what?'

'So don't you ever accuse me of neglecting my family, you toe-rag. You know as well as I do what my kids mean to me.'

Steve stood up to follow his nemesis past the line of tables, derisory to the last. 'Yeah, right. Rumour has it you fuck your daughter.'

'For Christ's sake, keep your bloody voice down,' Jeff snarled, their heads closing in on each other as they left through the narrow doorway. 'Rumour has it you can't always believe what makes the news.'

'So what happens now?'

'What happens now?' the angry superstar shot back. '*Nada*'s what happens now. I'm getting on the freeway and driving home to join my wife and daughter for dinner. What d'you think's going to happen now?'

Barging through the swing doors, the American paused on the top step and stared across the street. 'We need to settle this tonight. I'm leaving for New York on Friday, and she's coming with me.'

'Fair enough,' Jeff scoffed. 'It's Lynn's decision. We can stand here and slug it out in front of all these people if you like. But at the end of the day, whatever you want or I want has fuck-all bearing on whether Lynn stays with me or goes with you. Let me ask her, and we'll get back to you. Feel free to call the house later. You know the number, don't you? Jesus Christ!'

The peacemaker took a deep breath in and then out again, trying to stave off the dizziness which threatened to tip him down the steep flight of steps and onto the footpath. Imagining the veins on the side of his head and neck prominent and pounding, his blood pressure mounting to a dangerous level, he steeled himself to shake hands with this obnoxious pretender.

'*Adiós*, mate. Have a good night.'

'May the best man win,' Steve leered, unsure whether to accept the magnanimous gesture.

Jeff's reply hung in the air as the pair parted company, laced with venom and muttered under his breath.

'No contest.'

***

'Ry?'

'Kiz?'

'Did you really ask *Papá* to teach you to smoke?'

Ryan sniggered, cupping his hands over his girlfriend's ears. 'I don't know what you're talking about.'

His sister rolled her eyes at a perplexed Savannah, who smiled back. This was the first time she had caught up with the happy couple since their pregnancy was announced, and the *trio* had conversed in Spanish all evening in honour of their father's impending sixtieth birthday.

When the pair made the original plans to commemorate the Diamond jubilee, they had decided not to involve their partners because neither had ever known the departed celebrities. The same *embargo* had applied a decade ago too, when the Blakes, the Lanes and the remaining Two of Diamonds converged on New Orleans to live it up in honour of the great man's half-century.

Going *solo* had turned out to be a wise move on Kierney's part, since she had given her former *beau* his marching orders a month before the event. While Fiona had been kind enough to commiserate on hearing the news, Gerry had doled out his customary minuscule dose of sympathy by needling her about how astute she had been to avoid ticket cancellation fees!

Twenty-twelve was the year during which Ryan's independent movie stable received five Academy Awards and seven Golden Globes. His parents had been in their early twenties when their son came into existence. Although he knew his partner had set the timer with forty as their next major milestones, he still didn't feel old enough to be a father. He hadn't been paying attention when Savannah first informed him they were expecting a baby, yet he now found the prospect surprisingly appealing.

So with the love of his life having hit it off so well with the busy diplomat on previous occasions when their paths had crossed, the film-maker had begged the others' indulgence to flex the rules. The pair had been looking forward to letting Kierney into the secret, but had held off while the United Nations special envoy flew back and forth between New York, Geneva and Brussels in an effort to broker peace in the Republic of Congo and Mali.

Like father, like daughter. It had never been otherwise, Cathy had chuckled. This was also a big year for the Lanes, with one son getting married in March and the other graduating from university in the coming November. Malcolm had convinced his wife to hand Stonebridge Music's reins over once and for all to the man she had been grooming for the job for nearly twenty years, leaving them to retire and enjoy the comfortable life Lynn Dyson and Jeff Diamond had bestowed upon them.

'Why don't you want Sava to know?' the dark-haired gipsy teased. 'Not keen on her finding out about your debauched past that never was?'

Ryan narrowed his eyes and leaned against *kitsch* velvet cushions in a booth which would keep them hidden from their fans until Gerry and Fiona arrived. He took hold of Savannah's shoulders and eased her back onto his chest, cuddling her and kissing the side of her neck. It felt right that they had returned to the city of their father's birth for this latest anniversary; Newtown, to be precise, in keeping with the eccentric tradition.

'I've got nothing to hide,' the thirty-four-year-old sneered. 'Some of us take good care of our bodies... Unlike others who shall remain nameless, also known as *pequeñita* to her friends.'

'Oh, don't say that, bro'. It's too early.'

The siblings' role reversal when it came to corporal vices had long been a source of curiosity for the media. Sport had dominated the elder's life as soon as he could run and hold a bat at the same time, and with the dedication necessary to compete at test match levels came a fixation on healthy eating and a ban on drugs of all kinds with only the rarest of exceptions.

'Sorry, Kiz. Sav's finding it hard to give up the ciggies while she's with child. That's why I didn't want her to hear. Nothing to do with my judging you for poisoning yourself. Anyway, with those genes, you're at total liberty to chain-smoke.'

'What do you mean?' the cricketer's girlfriend asked, twisting her head round. 'Which genes?'

'Blue ones,' Kierney giggled, rolling out another dad joke. '*Papá* always said he had blue genes. You know... The depression and all that. Never mind. Ry means the *post mortem* that was done on our dad after he died. His body showed no signs whatsoever that he'd been a heavy smoker and drinker all his life, and he'd taken some pretty lethal drug cocktails in his twenties too.'

'Really? Amazing!'

'Yes, it is amazing,' the athlete agreed. 'Here we are slaving every day to get ourselves in peak form for the London Olympics, and there he was at forty-four with a heart the size of a basketball and zero damage to his brain. *¡No es justo, mi amor!* You reckon, Kizzo?'

The weather had forced the restaurant's trendy diners inside, reducing the Diamonds' privacy. A flamboyant gay couple introduced themselves and were angling for an invitation to sit down and join the celebrities, complaining bitterly that the head waiter was a "mean bitch" for encouraging them to park their "sorry pink arses" elsewhere!

Channelling his father's showman tendencies and keen not to see anyone aggrieved on their account, the broad-shouldered, blond sportsman squeezed out of the booth and imposed himself on the two displaced men. Mayhem ensued, much to the women's amusement. The kid known as Jet by anyone who had grown up in the nineteen-eighties and -nineties had never been in the least bit homophobic and was now swallowed up in a swarm of screeching queens, all keen to heap love on the cricketing hero.

'Do you miss your *papá*?' Savannah asked the laughing lawyer across the table.

'Oh, yes, I do,' Kierney smiled, averting her gaze from the shenanigans. 'Do you miss yours?'

'*Realmente, no.* I don't remember him. But I do miss the idea of him.'

The dark-haired Australian frowned. 'Ry's told me a bit about your family history in Navarre. It must've been so hard with your brothers joining the separatists. Hard for your parents. I don't know much about Basque nationalists, sorry, but I've heard heaps of families were divided. Have you been back recently?'

Savannah shook her head. 'No. I don't want to go there. Ryan wants to, so he can meet my family and see the places where I grew up. But it's not a good memory for me.'

'Hey!' the rambunctious cricketer announced his return, distracting the two women from their conversation. 'Are we going to eat? Those blokes are hilarious. You see the one with the bleached hair?'

His companions turned to follow his eyes, picking out a slight man wearing a powder-blue shirt with its sleeves rolled up to reveal rather puny biceps. He was sporting a white quiff shaped with gel, the envy of any passing unicorn.

'That guy's a set designer at Fox Studios. Just started filming some TV drama about grade cricket in the 'seventies and wanted to pick my brains about where cricketers go at night after matches.'

'Country town hotels mostly,' his sister offered. 'What did you tell them? Do you even know where cricketers went for a night out in the 'seventies?'

Ryan shrugged. 'Course not! Just gave 'em a bunch of bullshit about Coogee and Bondi with the English team. Anyway, have you chosen what you're having? I'm getting malnourished here. Sav?'

The quiet Spaniard slid her menu sideways along the table until they could both read it, while the singleton opposite picked from another. Making quick decisions, they relayed their order to a waiter equipped with a handheld device which communicated their culinary choices to the kitchen before he had the chance to pour fresh glasses of wine.

'Your sister and I were talking about missing our dads,' the actress said, 'and I told her I didn't want to go home.'

'Yeah. Bit like our dad,' the young man admitted. 'He hated everything about western Sydney for years, until he'd kind of made peace with everything.'

'But what I was going to say,' Savannah continued, raising her finger to the lad's mouth to silence him, 'is that I think I'm changing my mind.'

'Really?' both Diamonds chanted before exhaling in peals of laughter.

'Yes. Must be because I'm pregnant. I want to reconnect with that place. Not the people, I don't think. And I don't know if they want to see me.'

Kierney smiled. 'I'm sure they will. Bloodlines are pretty strong, don't you think? That's why you want to go back: because you're continuing your bloodline. The pull of family's more powerful than we think.'

'Yeah,' her brother agreed. 'Isn't that why we're here too, for God's sake. You've had more to do with Sydney than I have, Kizzo. After uni', I mean... I only come here for cricket and movie *premières*, and even then it's a quick in and out. Much prefer Melbourne to Sydney.'

'Does Melbourne still feel like home to you, bro'?'

The residents of Colorado Springs locked eyes and began to giggle. It transpired they had spent some time on their flight across the Pacific Ocean discussing this very topic.

'I have to say no. How about you?'

Their fellow Green Card holder chuckled. 'I have to say no too. Apart from visiting "G" and "G" and co', I don't feel the need to go back there. It's nice to visit Brunswick Street *cafés* and the city laneways, *et cetera*, but I always imagine I'm going to bump into *Mamá* and *Papá*. Nat's coming out to New York for Thanksgiving, by the way...'

'Nat from school?' Ryan checked. '*Excelente.* How long since you've seen her? Didn't she get married?'

Kierney sat back from the table as their food was delivered. With only half an hour until Gerry and Fiona were due to arrive, the *trio* had gone straight for an *entrée* course of *anti-pasto*. Passing round the tiny bowls of sauce, the delicious aroma made them salivate after their bland airline meals.

'Yes. And divorced. She's already living with someone else. A woman.'

'A woman!' her brother's girlfriend whooped. 'That's so cool! I love stories like that.'

The sportsman laughed. 'OK! We're in the minority being straight tonight. Anyone I know?'

'*Argh!* Like you know every lesbian in Melbourne! No, I doubt it. She's a Kiwi. So you never answered me earlier... Did you ask *Papá* to teach you how to smoke?'

Savannah noticed both siblings flinch as if they had spied a wasp flying at their foreheads. This was another thing she liked about her adoptive family, along with their ability to converse in the languages of her childhood and their deep understanding of what it was like to grow up in an environment of fear and neglect. She loved that Lynn Dyson and Jeff Diamond continued to live on for these two otherwise well-grounded personalities, as if they were merely away on tour or enjoying a well-earned retirement somewhere in France.

'I did, yeah. Why?' the sportsman replied.

'Did you?' the Spaniard echoed, her eyes teasing. 'Couldn't you figure it out for yourself?'

Kierney came to her brother's defence. 'Our dad had a really alluring way of smoking... cigarettes or joints... like the smoke was lifting him to a higher plane.'

'That's right,' Ryan chuckled. 'And when I tried to smoke, all I did was cough my guts up. I didn't get what I was missing, so I asked him to teach me to enjoy it, I guess.'

'And did he?' his girlfriend asked.

'No. Not particularly. Not as well as for you, Kiz, anyway. Some of us are cut out to be clean-living and others made to fill themselves with harmful substances.'

'Did you tell him you never really liked it?' the dark-haired squash champion wondered aloud. 'He wouldn't have been bothered. Probably relieved.'

The parents-to-be flashed their eyes at each other and laughed. The talented multi-lingual actress had more than met her match in the elder Diamond *protégé*, and it was clear to the younger that he was more than agreeable to this fact. She had seen him in various stages of crush and infatuation before, and perhaps even in love once or twice. Yet as soon as she witnessed his disposition alter in the company of this expressive, waif-like creature who wore her heart on her sleeve, their natural symbiosis became abundantly evident.

Even Gerry, never normally known for his emotional radar, had remarked on their compatibility. To the lad's consternation, the family's manager had even been moved to tears, drawing a parallel with the dignified and reserved young woman who had transformed into passionate nymph after meeting a certain nineteen-year-old migrant from New South Wales.

Plus ça change, plus c'est la même chose, Kierney mused. Fate maintained its own timetable, no matter how one might try to force its hand. Was her soul-mate just around the corner? In truth, she preferred to believe fate was attuned to her need to devote a few more years to humanitarian missions before allowing love to consume her in quite the same way.

'Dad didn't care,' her brother affirmed. 'You were always enough like him that he didn't need me to be like him too. He was cool with whoever we turned into, and I hope I can be with our kids too.'

'Kids?' both women repeated.

Ryan scoffed. 'Don't sound so gobsmacked. Now there's one on the way, there's no point stopping there. Just putting you on notice, Sav!'

'*¡Díos mío!* What did your *papá* say when you asked him?'

'*Bien sûr, mon ami!*' both Diamonds chanted, their father's time-honoured response impossible to leave unspoken.

The film-maker kissed his startled partner full on the lips before answering her question. 'Well, first he checked I meant ciggies and not weed.'

'Ha!' his sister laughed. 'Did he? Even though you were only fifteen or whatever? Typical!'

'Yeah. He answered, "Only if you need me to." I stupidly asked him in front of Mum, and I saw his mind whirring while he worked out what to say. She smiled though, which we both took as approval. Then he said, "Thank Christ for that," and drew his hand across his forehead.'

'Oh, I remember now!' Kierney cried out, putting her glass down and flicking her hair over her shoulder. 'They hadn't anticipated the question. Wasn't it about the same time as the charity telethon when they found out about that poor Progeria girl?'

'Bloody hell. Yeah. It was around that time,' Ryan paled. 'God, I haven't thought about that episode for so long. I'll tell you about it later, Sav. Jeez! Takes on a whole new dimension when you're expecting a baby.'

The lawyer chastised herself for bringing this memory to the fore without more consideration of the couple's situation. 'Sorry, bro'. That was insensitive of me. Change the subject.'

Puffing out his chest, the popular sportsman smiled, shaking his head. If there was one thing he had learned from losing their parents, it was the fact that invincibility was a state of mind. Since the awful day in February nineteen-ninety-six, the time when life as the Four of Diamonds had ceased in the blink of an eye, it was a rare day when he didn't issue a prayer of gratitude at having grown up physically and emotionally irrepressible.

The siblings had survived their loss unscathed, both emerging from grief inspired to dedicate their many future successes to the world's best mother and father. The unwelcome seismic shift was never to be righted, yet the potent combination of premature independence and a desire to prolong their parents' influence had enriched their hearts and minds in ways no-one could have imagined.

'No. It's fine. I'm not worried about tempting providence or anything. Dad reckoned he got a shitload of extra brownie points from the supreme being for helping that girl. I remember so vividly what he said after she died. Do you?'

Kierney nodded, her eyes filling with tears. 'Sure do. "A wounded soul with a good heart empathises deeply with other wounded souls with good hearts." I've got it printed out and stuck on the pinboard at my desk.'

'Chapter thirty-one, paragraph eighteen!' the comic guessed, flicking through an invisible copy of "A Life Singular". Their father's autobiography was still a bestseller, languishing on millions upon millions of bookshelves all over the world, translated into most modern languages and incorporated into hundreds of high school and university English Literature courses.

'Shut up! To me, it's a much more romantic and useful way of saying, "You've got to be cruel to be kind." You can't really understand suffering until you've suffered yourself.'

'Do you think you suffered?' Savannah asked her fellow orphans. 'From your dad killing himself, I mean.'

'Yes and no,' the human rights advocate answered, smiling at her brother. 'Yes, when it first happened, obviously. But I count myself incredibly lucky to have known deep loss at such a crucial age. It's hard to express without sounding a bit heartless, and not that I'd wish anything horrible to happen to anyone...'

'Virtual reality,' Ryan interrupted, his gaze leading the others to turn around to find Gerry and Fiona walking towards their table. 'Soon people'll be able to have an immersive experience for as long as they want and then exit the program. Dial-up compassion. Hi, guys! Just in time.'

The threesome stood up to greet the ageing accountant and his wife, and the former sportsman lunged sideways to pinch a spare chair from a nearby table. He invited Fiona to slip into the booth next to his pregnant girlfriend before the lecherous Irishman could manœuvre himself into the tight spot. Kierney shuffled into the corner while their host once more fell victim to wolf-whistles from their rowdy neighbours.

'*Olá, señorita Savannah*,' Gerry's arm floated across the table, and their lips met overhead for a chaste welcome kiss. 'Or do I now say *"señora"*? Lovely to see you again. Congratulations to you both, by the way. Wonderful to hear the news. Your dad'd be so chuffed, wouldn't he, Kizzy?'

Another bittersweet twinge of regret threatened to well up in the United Nations senior lawmaker's eyes. Was she jealous that her brother had beaten her to it, or simply wistful to think their parents would never meet their grandchildren. Ryan and Savannah's newborn would start life without grandparents on either side. Yes, this must be why she was upset. Nothing to do with her own biological clock or her unspoken competitive nature...

'Oh, sure. He'd have loved to be a granddad. They both would, I'm sure. I always imagine *Mamá*'d be just like her own mum as a grandma. Quite strict but very loving and cuddly. Shame they'll be so far away.'

The elder Diamond sibling noticed a fleeting look of disapproval cross Fiona's visage. Despite the eternal lovers being gone for over fifteen years now, she continued to harbour some kind of grudge against any attempt to commune with the departed, no matter how light-hearted or harmless their allusions might be.

An occasional Roman Catholic, like her husband, perhaps the retired commercial solicitor believed in an afterlife where Lynn and Jeff Diamond spent their time entertaining heavenly *stadia* with hits of the last half-century. Did she prefer to think of Gerry's old friend, on whose watch the fortune she now spent had been accumulated, strumming his zither on God's fluffy *cumulo nimbus*? And perhaps she imagined the world's most decorated female tennis player coaching the twelve apostles to improve their first serve somewhere on the *altostratus*, adorned with wings of long, white feathers?

'What's up, Fiona?' he channeled his father's favourite tone of remonstration. 'Mum and Dad *are* going to be awesome grandparents, even from so far away. They're still great parents, aren't they, Kiz? Every day.'

Kierney sighed, not wishing to start an argument. 'It's OK, Ry. Shall we order our main courses now? *Mamá* and *Papá*'ve just finished breakfast. They're on Greenwich Mean Time at the moment, checking out the events the Queen's put on for *Papá*'s sixty-first.'

The ageing former company executive guffawed. 'That's an insane idea, my dear! You're not wrong, as the man himself would say. Puts me in mind of that Royal Variety Performance when all the performers and their *entourages* were lining up to meet the royals. You two were only little.'

'Why? What happened?' the young woman asked.

'The Master of Ceremonies was introducing "QEII" to each artist in turn, and when he said, "Ma'am, this is Jeff Diamond, the Australian singer," she waved her hand and said, "Yes, yes. One can never forget Jeff Diamond."'

'Really?' all four fellow diners exclaimed.

'Was Mum there?'

'Yes, mate,' Gerry answered. 'Auntie Liz never forgot your darling mother either. They were like old friends; talking about all things equestrian. Lynn and Princess Anne were great Olympic rivals, Fiona. But Jeff could never be doing with horses. You know all this, don't you, guys?'

Kierney smiled. 'Yes. Definitely. That's a nice story though. What would you like to drink? Red or white? *Lo siento, Sava. ¿Otro vaso de agua?*'

***

The man of the house turned the key in *Escondido*'s front door, his paranoid, fretful brain half expecting to be confronted by the demonic sights and sounds of old times. Mercifully, they failed to materialise, leaving him safe to let himself in. He still missed the exuberant canine homecoming greetings, and renewed his intention to persuade Lynn and the kids to visit the local pound while he was home this time.

Delicious smells of cooking wafted through the hallway. Hooking his jacket onto the hat-stand at the foot of the staircase and sliding his suitcases against the wall, he followed the exotic airborne concoction to an abandoned stove of simmering pots. He lifted a lid and spooned out some of the rust-coloured sauce, blowing on it before tipping it into his mouth.

Where was his pair of angels? How rude of them not to come running to the door in the manner of faithful hounds! Jeff smiled at the narcissistic thought and levered his shoes off, letting each wallop onto the marble to announce his presence to a household with better things to do. With a gentle kick to make sure they were out of the way, he strode down the corridor to the office, where he discovered mother and daughter poring over sheets of manuscript paper.

'Oh, hi!' Lynn said, looking up at her beautiful black stallion and surrendering into arms which emitted yearning from every pore. 'We didn't hear you come in. Do you want a beer or coffee?'

Her weary husband smiled, leaning over to kiss Kierney's hair as she rushed over to hug him too. '*Bonsoir*, gorgeous one and gorgeous two,' he said, slumping down onto the office chair and swivelling it from side to side to pop the fatigue out of his spine. 'A beer'd be perfect, angel. *Gracias*. What are you guys doing?'

'A beard?' his daughter giggled, tickling his unshaven face. 'It sounded like you wanted a beard, but you've already got one. *Mamá*'s helping me finish this song properly. I know how I want the chord structure, but it's eluding us.'

Jeff accepted the A3 sheet of paper he was offered, turning it ninety degrees at a time and pretending to examine the staves with a critical eye. It was concentration that eluded him right now, anxious to discover if their gipsy girl had been let into the secret about his meeting with "Uncle" Steve. He assumed Lynn wouldn't want the children to know unless there was something worth knowing. This was his wish too, and he relaxed a little, concluding instead that his empathetic understudy was only picking up on his mood.

'*¿Me has oído, Papá?*' the thirteen-year-old asked.

'*Sí. Cierto, pequeñita.* Eluding you, eh? What an excellent word. No doubt a gift from *Mamá*.'

The girl nodded, taking the manuscript paper and spreading it out on the desk. The donor of her evocative verb arrived back, juggling a stubbie and two glasses, one highball of orange juice and the second a tumbler of *Chardonnay*.

Allowing the bottle to slide downwards into her husband's waiting palm, Lynn put the other drinks onto coasters and lifted the electronic keyboard to the other side of the room. Enquiring eyes conveyed an urgent need, melting his heart. If Steve was right, and the coming days were the last throes of this marriage, he had better enjoy them to the full.

'Hey, Kizzo,' he said, seeing his daughter switch the keyboard back on to return to her sticky composition. 'D'you mind if I have a quick chat with *la mamá*, please?'

'No, OK,' the teenager shook her head. 'Course not! Are you alright? Is something wrong?'

'I'm fine, thanks, gorgeous,' Jeff lied. 'There's something important we need to talk about. Won't take long, and then we can eat. *Soy famishado.*'

'*¿Famishado?*' Kierney giggled. 'That's funny. *Soy famishado también. ¿Mamá?*'

'*¡Sí!* Me too,' the blonde agreed. 'We've been stuck in here for ages, and the smell's getting stronger and stronger. Thanks, darling. Could you give dinner a quick stir, please? We'll be out soon.'

The obedient child gathered her belongings and took them off to her bedroom, bound first for a *détour* to the kitchen. If she was concerned, she didn't show it. The hard-working celebrities often asked for some time alone after their separate days, so being requested to excuse herself was nothing out of the ordinary.

Lynn and Jeff moved to the couch, pausing in a lingering embrace before sitting down. His leg jumped several centimetres into the air when she placed her hand on his knee, startling her and causing him to writhe in pain.

'Oh, my God! Sorry. I should've guessed that would happen. How are you? Was it horrible?'

The songwriter wasn't altogether sure why, but tears bubbled in the corners of his eyes. 'Shithouse,' he admitted. 'Christ, Lynn. You are so beautiful. And seeing the two of you working on Kizzy's music is fantastic soul food, I can tell you. I don't know where to start. To be honest, I'm having trouble believing the conversation I had with wasn't part of a fucking nightmare. And the sight of you guys here, as if this is your house and I'm only visiting, somehow makes it seem all the more surreal and frightening.'

'Frightening? Why frightening? *Digame.* How come you're so tense? Have a cigarette.'

Her husband shook his head and gripped her hand. 'No, *Regala*. Thanks, but don't indulge me, please. That's partly the problem. All the things Steve was saying about the imbalance in our relationship... They're not so far from the truth.'

'What do you mean, imbalance? What was he talking about?'

'Well...' Jeff relaxed a little, leaning them both into the soft leather. 'He tells me you're bored with your life and sick of me leaving you on your own with the kids.'

'Oh, am I? OK,' the horrified woman chuckled. 'Somewhat fanciful. Did he say I told him this word-for-word?'

'Yep. Well, he did at first,' the billionnaire responded with a sly grin, 'but then he contradicted himself by saying you didn't have to tell him 'cause he could see it in your face.'

Lynn sighed, losing the taste for her wine. There was indeed a certain veracity in this statement. She had shared a few trivial confidences with the musician during their periods of collaboration, during which she might well have let slip that her husband had been away for too long this time, or mentioned the family's dinner conversation would be limited to teenaged angst and homework topics for yet another night.

It wouldn't be such a stretch of Steve's over-active Neanderthal imagination to take these passing complaints as encouragement, especially since he had declared himself head-over-heels in love with her. This was as much her fault as his, blind to other men's advances these days. It hadn't crossed her mind that he would assume she was looking for more than her perfectly imperfect lover could offer.

'Oh, I see,' she murmured. 'And that was the sole basis for him challenging you for my hand?'

It was Jeff's turn to laugh. As much as the suggestion sounded preposterous when put to him by the gorgeous creature whose body couldn't get any closer to his, Gravity and Miss Irony's cynical chorus fuelled old fears and anger to dangerous levels.

'Looks that way,' he muttered, inhaling through his nostrils and sucking his beer bottle dry. 'So it's true?'

'Well, no. Of course it's not true, Jeff. I could never be bored with you and our life, and even if I were bored, don't you think I'd at least speak to you about changing things first?'

'Yeah. Hope so anyway.'

'Hope so? That's not very fair,' the frustrated woman replied. 'I'm disappointed you said that. I hope that's just the aftermath of your meeting, and you don't really think so poorly of me.'

The tormented soul coughed. 'Sorry, angel. I don't, no.'

'He's drawing a very long bow, Jeff. I can't deny I may've given him the impression that I was sick of sleeping in an empty bed, or that you'd been away for three weeks this time, for example. Something like that...' Lynn explained, weighed down by the effect her admission was guaranteed to have on her man's disposition. 'But it was hardly an open invitation. It was always in the context of being impatient for you to get home. I never once suggested I'm sick of you leaving us on our own.'

'But are you bored with our life?'

'No way! Absolutely not. How could anyone be bored with our life? Ever since you came up with the "life singular" idea, it's been pure magic. I love you and love what we've built, not to mention our family. We have two gorgeous kids who need us to stay together, and first and foremost, I'll always love you.'

Beginning to wonder if his wife would ever reach the end of her speech, the relieved rock star leaned over and kissed her open mouth. 'OK, angel. I hear you, and it's great to hear. It's what I hoped, obviously.'

'And expected? Come on! I wouldn't show much integrity if I couldn't own up if things weren't rosy, would I?' the determined woman continued. 'And even if I were bored with you, there's no way I would've told Steve, of all people! You and I both know how he feels, and I have zero interest in leading him on. We're never on our own when we're working on his albums; there's always at least one engineer and some session guys there. We do have lunch or a coffee, just the two of us, sometimes when he's in Melbourne, but I've never once discussed the state of our relationship with him. Never have, Jeff. Honestly.'

A lone tear escaped down the negotiator's right cheek, flicked away smartly so as not to distract her. Lynn Dyson's validation was still worth a great deal to his inner child, even after sixteen years of marriage.

'Jesus! Enough already! I believe you, angel,' he croaked. 'And thank you.'

'Good,' Lynn smiled, kissing the corner of his eye and fondling the gold band on his left ring finger. 'You're welcome, and I love you. I don't want Steve Christie as a lover, nor anyone else for that matter. But what did you mean about seeing Kizzy and me working in here when you came home? You mentioned something about making what Steve said more surreal and frightening.'

'Ah, yeah... Forget it, angel,' the songwriter reassured them both. 'Just me over-reacting as usual. He was being a complete arsehole, making reference to how much better life would be for you with him, and how it was his turn to have you. What pissed me off the most was that it was his way or the highway, like you had no choice in the matter.'

'Oh, cool!' the ambitious Olympian laughed. 'There's another reason to stay well away. He's pretty old-school when it comes to the way men and women are supposed to coexist. Women exist to please men, and in return men look after them. They're not to trouble themselves with making any hard decisions. All very nineteenth-century, as you'd well understand, *mon ami ancien*.'

If it hadn't been aching before, now the confusion in Jeff's head made it thump nineteen-to-the-dozen. He was in danger of losing sight of the actual truth, what with Lynn's ardent protestations and Gravity's *Blitzkrieg* psychoanalysis of every single word she uttered in her defence. Miss Irony sat on the sidelines cheering, so loud in his ears that reason was ready to desert him.

The intellectual couldn't understand why he felt so unhinged, so distant these days from mania that interpreting his anxiety was a challenge. Plenty of other men made passes at his wife at social events or showbusiness functions, many spilling over into the press and hanging around for days or weeks. His own artful dualism caused Lynn no less suffering too, today's roles reversed more times than he cared to enumerate.

The tormented soul saw Miss Irony's wagging finger on the edge of his mind's eye. There must be more significance, some deeper meaning to the three-way script they were acting out now. If today's foolish stunt was history daring to right a prior wrong, would brushing it off have dire consequences?

What if Lynn's soul doubted his loyalty? Had he missed a payment? Was his licence to love her up for renewal? Or had they been together so long that some higher authority sought to test the strength of their commitment? Jesus! Could their extraordinary partnership-through-the-ages possibly be more than fantasy? They had both escalated this tedious incident into a *magnum opus*, so perhaps Lynn felt the same pressure. Maybe this was the reason she was driven to explain herself in such intricate detail as the number of cups of coffee she and Steve had consumed!

Fuck you, Gravity! Move on. There's nothing to see here.

Shaking his head to force his concentration back into the here and now, Jeff rewound his saviour's last sentence and its allegory. If the soul who occupied the present-day Steve Christie had been deceived and dishonoured and was out to avenge their illicit affair, no such posturing could change the past. With any luck, the happy ending to this late-twentieth-century love triangle would be an anti-climax in comparison.

'*Merci. Exactement.* Let's leave this shit behind right now, except for one thing I'd like to be different.'

The beauty felt his anxious hand crunch the tiny bones in her knuckles, educing a nostalgia which made her want to cry with joy. 'Different? About me or you?'

'Me, angel. It's all about me!' the larrikin sniggered. 'Heard that before?'

'Get on with it! I love you, you idiot.'

'Christ Almighty! I love you too. So damned much. Anyway, while Steve was criticising my keeping you under lock and key with the kids and ignoring your needs, it crossed my mind that I don't give you many choices.'

'What? I...'

'I don't, do I?' Jeff raised his eyebrows to silence her objections, thereby proving his point. 'Wait, wench! Hear me out. I tell you where I'm going and when, and off I go. Then I come back and expect you to still be here, ready to attend to my every *penchant* and proclivity, on my terms and to my timetable. In the meantime, I take it for granted that you'll look after our kids, the apartment and this house and make our life run smoothly. That's pretty much how it goes, is it not?'

Lynn threw her head back and laughed at the top of her voice. 'Jeff Diamond! Which planet are you on tonight?'

'Yours hopefully,' the tired man answered, now constricting the blood flow in both her hands. 'You've got to admit it's all a bit one-sided.'

'It's not! Do you limit my movements to the office, the kitchen and the bedroom?'

Her husband's expression indicated this idea might have significant merit and received a sharp slap on the thigh in return. 'No, but Steve did suggest I had your every move followed by cameras.'

'Again, a prospect so attractive,' the long-legged blonde joked. 'Mate, I can go anywhere, and with anyone I choose, whenever I like. If I wanted our life to be different, I'd make it so. But I don't want to. Get it? Don't want to! Just like the first night we spent together in your Richmond flat, remember?'

'Our first night?' Jeff looked bemused. 'Whoa! How could I not remember that? I like where you're taking me, but what's that got to do with anything?'

Shifting her body forwards, the thirty-six-year-old sat across her man's lap as if they were teenagers again. 'Choices,' she insisted, kissing his pouting lips. 'When I was scared to submit to you that night, when no-one in the whole world knew where I was. Remember? After we'd been sitting on the windowsill, you said if you wanted to attack me, you could.'

'Yeah. Of course I remember.'

'Well, I think you meant it as reassurance.'

'I did.'

'But it actually made me even more nervous at the time. I was, 'ow you say, shitting myself,' the sexy woman put on her best French accent.

The rock star's jaw dropped. 'Excuse me? Who gave you permission to use that kind of language around me? Shame on you! Were you though? Fuck! That's not exactly what I was aiming for.'

Lynn giggled, her hand cupping the bulge in his crotch. 'No. Turning you on, am I? Me too, by the way. But meanwhile, back at the ranch... At the same time as I was wondering if I should grab my stuff and run, you didn't look like you were about to attack me, so I figured you had my best interests at heart.'

The red-blooded male slotted his hand inside his *regala*'s low-cut blouse and slipped the tips of his fingers under the top edge of her bra, feeling her exhale and relax against him. Every single word and deed from that night was imprinted on his heart.

Replaying his inner videotape, Jeff heard himself making this benevolent yet unorthodox statement to the sixteen-year-old schoolgirl whose virtue he had despoiled not an hour earlier. Even from such a distance, it was disturbing to reflect on the harm he might have inflicted on an innocent human being if, like so many other men, he had chosen to misuse his power.

'Christ, angel, I'm still not sure where you're going with this,' he admitted, 'but thanks anyway. I sensed your fear, and it set me off too. I'd never have hurt you. I'll never hurt you, ever...'

Compassion shone from his dream girl's smile. 'I know. It's alright.'

'Cheers. But my point is that, at the same time as I was saying this to help you feel safe, I was also convinced you'd give in to me regardless. I took you for granted even then, such was my egotistical self-confidence where sex was concerned. Nothing would've got in my way.'

Wrestling herself clear of the poet's determined grip, the tennis champion sprang up and pointed to the wall clock. 'Look! We've been ages. Kizzy'll be wondering what's going on. Let's have dinner. There's no need to change anything. OK?'

'No need perhaps,' her husband shrugged, following her lead, 'but I'd like to make things more equitable. The kids are old enough not to need a full-time mother anymore, and we've got plenty of people who could do more to organise me. Have a think about it, angel. It'll be my way of thanking you for sticking with me.'

Lynn groaned. 'Sticking with you? As opposed to running away with Stevie, you mean? It was never going to happen.'

'Good. You will think about it though?'

Strong fingers closed around the songwriter's neck, their owner exasperated by this blast from the past. 'Yes, Jeff! What was that about not giving me many choices? I shall choose to think about it in my own time, but just know I'm perfectly happy the way things are. OK? Now get up and follow me.'

Batting his hand away from her face, the sportswoman yanked her apologetic anti-hero to his feet and booted him towards the door. As it opened inwards, he stood back to let her pass through ahead of him, laughing when she refused. They hadn't gone two strides down the corridor before she grabbed his hips and span him round for a hug.

'I love the way you treat me. More than anything in the world. And I love the way you are with our kids. I love how we live our life, how we set priorities, and I don't even mind the long periods apart too much, 'cause I know how good it'll be when you come home.'

The slender goddess slipped her hands around each side of her husband's waist and tucked her thumbs inside his belt, tugging his body forward to rub herself against his erection. 'Like last night, for example. I could never get tired of making love to you when you're so forceful, so exciting. You...'

'Me neither,' a breathless voice said into her open mouth. 'Tell me this again later.'

'With pleasure! You, I was about to say... Or we, rather, are doing great things for the world. It was you who taught me about important issues when all I knew was how to train for trophies and medals and how to sing cheesy pop songs.'

'Can't deny any of that,' the cheeky peacemaker quipped.

'Oh, for God's sake!' his wife sighed. 'I'm trying to be serious. Just get it into that jam-packed head of yours that I'm never going to renounce our marriage or our family for some juvenile fun. And that's all it'd be if Steve Christie and I did get together... He'd be a very poor substitute for you, Jeff Diamond. There's not much beneath the music for him. Pretty superficial. Agree?'

'*D'accord, mon amie*,' Jeff swallowed her words again. 'You're the best.'

Tired of waiting for her dinner, the animated conversation brought Kierney to the kitchen door, coming face-to-face with the lovers locked in a jaw-breaking kiss. Although this was nothing unusual, she felt a strange *frisson* of relief to see their private discussion turn out well. She gave them a childlike wave and retreated to dish up their meal.

As arranged, the telephone rang at ten o'clock that evening, in the middle of a song-swapping session in the lounge room, where all three composers took turns at the grand piano. Kierney leaped up to answer it, thinking it would be her grandmother or Jet, only to be stopped by her mum. They allowed the answering machine to intercept the call.

The couple waited until the youngster retired to bed before listening to Steve's message. It contained an ultimatum, stating his intention to go public with the story if Jeff didn't agree to a divorce. The furious misgivings which had enslaved them a few hours ago were conspicuous in their absence, neither troubled by their historic counterparts anymore.

'So why the hell were we both at Def' Con' Five?' came the philosopher's rhetorical question. 'You don't give a toss now, and neither do I really.'

'Yes, I know. Weird, isn't it? I'll ring him back in the morning, if you can wait that long,' Lynn decided. 'He's being a total idiot. Together, forever, wherever. Let's go to bed.'

Upstairs and behind closed doors, the much-anticipated *liaison* lasted beyond midnight, stretched and punctuated by more happy reminiscences from the early years. Compared and contrasted until he could take no more, Jeff invited the love of his life to choose how and where the blissful session should conclude.

Opening the French windows wide to the elements, the amorous woman lay on her stomach with her head nearest the balcony, while her man smothered her with his warmth. The bats in the trees bore witness to her euphoric screams and his triumphant roar as simultaneous climaxes ripped through them. With centuries past and present merging again, their souls' rage and regret ignited the modern-day passions.

'What?' the depleted lover cried out, rolling sideways to see the expression on his wife's face. 'What've I done now?'

Lynn chuckled. 'Nothing. Just a strange coincidence with everything that's happened in the last few days.'

'Oh, yeah? What's that?'

'Kiz asked me to tell her about our first time.'

'When? Did she overhear something?'

'No,' the athlete replied, purring as the warmth of a human blanket engulfed her. 'It was this morning, after you left. We went from period pain to sex, as you do.'

Her husband chuckled. 'Right. Doubtless. Hope it doesn't mean she's making plans to sacrifice her virginity. That *would* be too close for comfort! What did you tell her?'

'God, no! I'm sure she's nowhere near tempted yet,' the patient mother reassured him. 'I said it was slow, then fast; scary and amazing all at the same time.'

'Nice! I would've said fast then slow, given my record-breaking performance first time around,' Jeff's eyes drilled into hers. 'But I made up for it.'

'You certainly did!'

'Yeah? D'you *wanna* do it again?'

'Hmm... Yes, I do.'

***

In a deliberate, flagrant but rather obtuse show of solidarity, Lynn Dyson flew north to Japan for a short concert tour while Jeff Diamond crossed the Pacific Ocean once again to attend the Los Angeles *première* of his latest movie. Their timing was impeccable, vacating Melbourne on the morning Steve Christie went public with his vulgar play for Australia's favourite wife and mother.

Headlines in the world's tabloids signalled a death knoll for the Australians' marriage, and commercial television stations' entertainment bulletins cast myriad suppositions out into the airwaves. "DIAMONDS NOT FOREVER" adorned the front page of the Herald Sun in Victoria and the Daily Telegraph in Sydney, all claiming shock and horror that the virtuous champion should be the unfaithful one and accusing the erstwhile tearaway of pushing his luck once too many times.

The handsome celebrity made no attempt to hide from the crowd while waiting for his flight to be called, instead spreading the airline lounge's various complimentary newspapers out around him and smiling at the hurriedly constructed articles laden with puns. With Cathy Lane away on holiday with her husband and younger son, the Stonebridge Music publicity team had called his mobile telephone ten times already that morning, alarmed to receive no instructions to run a counter-story.

Still greater uproar resulted the following day, when the megastar of stage and screen rocked up in Hollywood to traverse the red carpet alone. Playing a supporting role as an evil, manic villain in a script comprising large passages of ad-libbing, the film's previews had earned him countless acting credits and made him a front-runner for an Academy Award. The evening's only dampener was the shame he bore that his part in the breaking news overshadowed the lead actors, giving him little choice but to surf through the insurmountable fervour.

Looking devastatingly *débonair* in a tuxedo and bow-tie, with his dark, wavy hair cut shorter these days, the world-changer strutted past the hordes of screeching fans. As had been the case with adverse publicity throughout his career, the scandal surrounding Steve's proclamation only served to increase the idolatry. Women of all ages threw themselves at the barriers, desperate to be the one to console him in his hour of need.

Reporters jostled with camera operators, lying in wait for juicy secrets the performer might offer in customary *nonchalance* with the many pretty starlets crossing his path. He knew this brazen affrontery would drive everyone crazy, particularly Steve Christie's Californian associates, only the tiniest bit guilty at all the gratuitous attention he was stealing from the grand ceremony.

So where was his wife? *Paparazzi* and punters alike weren't used to seeing the billionnaire couple appear separately at this type of high-falluting event. Their affinity translating into effortless glamour and understated grace, they were the *epitome* of style and sophistication; tall, well dressed and casually glued to each other, always the draw-card for international media outlets and big business. Voices called out from the crowd, and overhead cables swooped remote control cameras on the star from all angles.

The Australian Elvis remained poker-faced. 'Lynn's on tour, and I'm here to party. End of story.'

The acclaimed musician had arranged to meet up with her husband's challenger, diverting to California on her way home from Tokyo. He had given his word that their *rendezvous* would not form part of his offensive, but she hadn't believed him for a moment. Confident in the "Together, Forever, Wherever" *mantra*, the couple agreed with their management company that they would all have a little fun at the media's expense over the developing *furore*.

On the other hand, Steve Christie did not take well to the news that his bid had been unsuccessful, left in no doubt whatsoever that the property under dispute intended to remain with the reprobate whose sole purpose in life was to advance the greater good.

A security contingent traced the family's steps, still spooked by their Napoelonic throwbacks. If any truth lay behind their hunches, and Lynn's previous incarnation had been put to death after falling pregnant to Jeff's, they had better be safe than sorry. Of course, they had confessed to no such elaborate ruse to their minders, for fear of being consigned to a mental institution!

Nineteen-ninety-two's jilted lover mounted a swift retaliation, raking up as much dirt about his rival's purported indiscretions as he could and smearing it liberally. Photographs snapped of Jeff with half-naked dancers were interspersed with other distasteful morsels revealing a drug-induced orgy in which he and members of his band were supposed to have participated as recently as the previous October, which together formed a body of evidence only the most highbrow journalists could afford to ignore.

From London, where she had landed afterwards, the ostensibly neglected wife fronted the cameras again, sanguine and safe in the knowledge that any unearthed salacious gossip would not be news to her. She even allowed herself a little indecorous pride when giving the droves of television reporters an accurate and explicit glimpse into her life as Mister Larger-than-Life's spouse.

'Being married to Jeff is as exhilarating and fulfilling now as it ever was,' she argued in response to direct allegations of infidelity and her husband's well-publicised substance abuse. 'I saw past this superficial behaviour years ago, when we were just teenagers, and now the reality of who he's become is so much more than this.

'Sure, Jeff's not perfect. He'd be the first to admit it. But he is by far the best man alive today. I truly believe this. I never doubted his ambitions, especially after the childhood he had, although it's sometimes unbelievable just how much we've achieved together. I couldn't be happier, and our kids are an absolute bonus for both of us. Our life is as perfect as it can be in the context of the world we live in.'

And from his hotel room in Beverly Hills, the grateful songwriter issued a press release to thank his wife for her sincerity. He appeared relaxed, fluent, drug-free, sober and all alone, the irresistible combination which converted new fans to Team Diamond every single day. Excited about a number of new projects, he used the opportunity to spread the word about his latest social justice agenda, imagining Steve to be cursing his nemesis' barbaric audacity from his San Bernardino mansion.

The industrious lovers were determined to put this threat to their domestic bliss behind them, separated by three-and-a-half thousand kilometres yet on similar time-zones. Deflecting all attempts to drag the story out, they *spruiked* their charitable endeavours and lauded the technological gadgets streaming out of Paragon Holdings' enterprises.

When off the air, they talked for many long-distance hours and made love in remote mode, employing techniques perfected over a decade-and-a-half of independent jetsetting.

'Why does the Polish Jew in you demand to be heard so often through your material?' Lynn asked one night, she in Paris at the French Open and he in Jerusalem for Arab-Israeli peace talks. 'So much more than the Catholic Argentinean half, I mean.'

The prolific writer shrugged. 'I have no clue, angel. Some stories demand to be told. Why don't you feel compelled to create movies about your Dutch heritage?'

'True. Good question,' the Olympian replied.

'I can hardly speak ten words of Polish and not much Hebrew either,' her husband posited. 'And yet I'm trilingual in cultures I have virtually no interest in celebrating. Why is that?'

'You're asking me? What if it's to do with the origin of your tortured soul,' she offered. 'The one who was once Victor Hugo and the one who's teaching us all so much about right and wrong.'

Jeff was smitten with this idea. He switched off his bedside lamp and lay on top of the bedclothes, staring out of the window at the trees lining King George Street in Jerusalem's hotel district. Why else would he be so obsessed with passing on all this amassed wisdom if not because he had lived many times over and had incurred some sort of divine duty to his fellow humans? Hadn't he always felt hundreds of years old? What if he actually was?

'So who are *you* then?' he asked his dream girl. 'Who have you been before?'

Lynn chuckled. 'I don't know. I'm nowhere near as old as you. I've been round fewer times than you, which is why you have so much more wisdom than I do.'

'Yeah, right. Jeez, I wish you were here so I could spank you for that gross inaccuracy. I've just spent the last eight hours fending off ditzy, empty-headed entertainment industry princesses, and now you try and tell me you're not wise. I don't know why I bother talking to you sometimes...'

'Oh, poor you,' she sneered. 'I bet you had a tough night. What hardship you endure at these gigs! However did you make it back to your room alive?'

The thirty-nine-year-old rocker grunted, moving the telephone from one ear to the other as he rid himself of his suit and shirt. Travelling was so much more bearable when his wife toyed with his *ego*. With such frivolous skits, they had no problem keeping their love alive and their sex-drives under control through frequent and prolonged separations.

'And what about you then?' he volleyed. 'How many marriage proposals from Japanese chin-rests did you receive today? More than usual?'

'For God's sake! Don't be so sizeist. Good things come in small packages. Haven't you ever heard that from up where you are?'

'What things? Sounds a bit messy, if you ask me. And they would have small packages, I'm guessing. Not like...'

'Oh, that's enough. Hundreds,' the elegant superstar confirmed, 'of very tempting propositions. You sound out of breath all of a sudden. Are you sure there's nobody there?'

Her observation was right on the money. While their mouths had sparred in their usual gamesmanship when it came to who was the more popular, Jeff's right hand had set the inevitable in motion. With each upward stroke inching him closer to orgasm, his heart beat faster and his arousal impossible to disguise.

'Hey! Keep the noise down, you nympho' harlots,' the jester hissed, turning away from the receiver. 'She can hear you. Sorry about that, angel. Now what were you saying?'

'I said, "Hundreds,"' his golden-haired beauty repeated, louder this time. 'I see I'm interrupting something. Shall I ring back later?'

'No! Don't go! I'll get rid of them. Hey, ladies... Let's pick this up again later, OK? Sure. Take the shampoo with you. OK. *Sayonara.*'

The amused woman heard a thud which she deduced was a book, probably a telephone directory, being thrown at his hotel room door. 'Whatever's going on over there? Shall I call the police?'

'Ahem. All good, baby,' her husband's voice was back at full volume. 'No worries. Where did we get to? Hundreds of proposals, eh? Any interesting ones? Am I up for blunderbusses at twenty paces again?'

'Shut up,' his wife retorted. 'I'll blunder your buss if you're not careful... Are you naked?'

'Not quite.'

'Well... I am.'

Jeff moaned as his penis reacted to this latest pleasurable revelation, rocketing him close to the edge of control. He rolled over and pulled the telephone off the bedside table and onto the sheets, the vision of his exquisite lady spread out in a similar hotel room, her long, tanned limbs extended and her hair gracing a starched white pillowcase with the colour of eternal sunshine.

It was past one o'clock in the morning in Israel, and after midnight for Lynn in Paris. She would be exhausted after performing to a sell-out auditorium this evening and would have left the after-party early to share this special moment with him.

'You are amazing.'

'What? For being naked? It's actually quite easy, but thanks anyway.'

The lost boy caught his breath. 'I'm serious. Let me give you a compliment for once... I know I'm the luckiest bastard ever,' he crooned, slowing his hand until the blissful sensations trembled at fever pitch throughout his body. 'You spoil me every bloody day, and I love it so much. And I love you even more.'

'Very good,' the sultry tone of a happy woman replied. 'I love you too. I love making you happy. Preferably a little closer together than this, but that's all there is to it. I want to touch you and see how turned on you are, 'cause I am too. Where are your hands?'

Overflowing with longing, the peacemaker pressed his head back into the pillow, picturing himself in their favourite hotel around the corner from *La Sorbonne*. No matter how many times he played these erotic games with his distant goddess, there was always that period at the end of the night when he felt desolate and foresaken. Clutching the receiver to his left ear, he could hear Lynn's breathing ease off.

'Hey, angel,' he whispered. 'You need to sleep. Get off the 'phone, you gorgeous creature, and I'll see you as soon as possible.'

'Thanks,' Lynn replied. 'I am tired. Are you alright?'

'Absolutely. But before you go…' the billionnaire added. 'On the subject of former lives, can I tell you what came into my head earlier this evening?'

'You can.'

'I'm thinking you were Steve's wife before. You remember when we were in Paris with the kids, walking to the hotel, it seemed like we drifted back in time?'

The romantic heard a gasp through the telephone line. He had hit a nerve, and his heart soared. This odd experience, occurring during a fortnight of unforgettable leisure time, had unsettled them to the extent that they agreed not to speak about it for the rest of the holiday. Then once back at home, the couple had dived straight into their busy daily schedules, seldom revisiting their metaphysical retrospective.

'Wow!' his dream girl gulped. 'I haven't thought about that for so long. What do you think it was?'

Jeff sniffed. 'No idea, angel, but my mind keeps telling me there's a link between our journey through the ages and Steve's obsession with stealing you from me. I reckon he's got a prior claim on you after all.'

'What? Are you serious? Oh, my God! Do you really? Please don't ever say that to him.'

'Tell me about it!' Jeff laughed. 'No fucking way! That'd stretch the "Together, Forever, Wherever" concept too far even for my liking.'

'Oh, wow,' the intrigued woman repeated in a whisper. 'It's made me shivery all over. Are you? It's like adding "whoever" to the list. Mine too, magic-man. Let's not talk about this anymore. Half of me thinks it's healthy to have a bit of a wake-up call now and again, but the other half's sorry it ever happened.'

Candid truth leaked out between every word his wife uttered, spawning an overpowering rush of empathy in her Middle East correspondent. Lynn had nothing to feel guilty for, but he knew why she did. He felt the same way whenever a presumptuous fan brushed his arm or tried to steal a kiss. It went with the territory, and there was little point in torturing themselves any longer.

'Hey, angel,' he responded. 'Fine by me, although I'd quite like to add "whoever" to our slogan. None of this was your fault. I know that. But you're right… It's done me a good turn too, I can tell you.'

'Really? Oh, that's great. I thought it was just me.'

The world-changer laughed. 'Nope. I was getting complacent subconsciously, I reckon. It pissed me off big-time when Steve accused me of neglecting you and the kids; like throwing stones in his own glass house, *et cetera.* But it sure was an overdue kick in the priorities too, if you know what I mean...'

'Priorities?' the Olympian echoed. 'Since when've you not been able to prioritise things? Please don't think there's anything to worry about. No-one thinks you're complacent. We're all fine and keen to have everything back to normal. So have a good night, alright? Get some sleep. I love you so much.'

Smiling at her vote of confidence, Jeff prepared to sign off and resuscitate his fading lust in a *solo* performance. 'Jesus Christ, you're such a killjoy. *Merci, mon amie.* By the time we get off the 'phone, your time-zone'll have caught mine up. Sleep well, angel. I love you too.'

Man-To-Man

Kierney's thunderous irascibility reverberated through the capacious ground floor corridors as she stormed out of her father's study and tore up the stairs. Tears prickled the surface of her eyes, and she was scarcely able to hold her footing until the bedroom door slammed shut behind her.

One of her advisers at Melbourne University had disputed a funding application she and her classmates had assembled for an Eritrean irrigation project, and she had arrived home desperate for the champion of African rebirth to tear the academic's argument to shreds.

The champion of African rebirth did nothing of the kind, as it turned out. And as if he were rubbing salt into the seventeen-year-old's open wound, as soon as his reasoning followed, her error lit up like the flames outside Crown Casino after dark. She knew he hadn't meant to hurt her feelings with his honesty, yet being exposed as a greenhorn in this dusky sanctum for disobedient scholars seemed more painful than a public humiliation.

'Angel, may I come in?' Jeff's voice was coaly and restorative. 'Sometimes making mistakes is the only way to learn. There's no shame in going in tomorrow and 'fessing up to Prof' Riesling. Can I come in?'

The widower heard the bed creak, followed by a deep sigh and the sound of bare feet thudding onto the floorboards. His daughter had been giving him the silent treatment lately, which both amused him and broke his heart. They didn't have much time left together, and wasting it on infantile standoffs benefitted no-one.

Was this how he would have behaved if he had grown up in a normal family? The billionnaire pulled his fingers back from the handle, expecting it to admit him into the bohemian beatnik beauty's den, where iniquity and erudition clashed on a regular basis.

'I'm not ready to receive you,' Kierney opened the door just enough to poke her nose and pouting lips through the crack, unable to keep a straight face. 'Make an appointment.'

'I don't do appointments.'

'Well, I do. Aren't you the bloke who says it's never to late to learn?'

Her father stifled a strong desire to laugh. How sweet was the pain of being cut to the quick by one of his own sarcastic scimitars! He was confident these recent poisoned barbs of enmity were nothing more sinister than the metaphorical slingshots of an adolescent power struggle. This was no remnant of grief, for these wild and wonderful diatribes were a mutual domain. His daughter was also far more formidable and venturous when it came to the inexcusably cruel fate ahead, waxing and waning in her acceptance of something she found both objectively unjustifiable and subjectively defensible.

'Fair enough,' he reasoned. 'I was going to suggest a walk down to the river. I've been cooped up in here since lunchtime, and so's Indie.'

Kierney snatched her bedroom door open just in time to witness the wise man wince, his right hand clutching at his chest. 'Oh, OK then. Oh, my God! Is that *Mamá*?'

The teenager threw herself at his torso, and the pair embraced as their shared tension seeped into the landing carpet. With a single surplus stamp of her foot, she swivelled on her heels and retreated into her room to fetch a jacket for their evening stroll.

Father and daughter sat on the bottom step of the staircase and laced their shoes while Indie tore around in circles in the driveway outside. This sight must also have pleased their missing loved one, they agreed, after Jeff drew another sharp breath on straightening his legs and leaning over to retrieve the dog's leash from its hook.

Locking the glossy, black-painted wooden gate at the side of their rented home, the two dark Diamonds and their golden-haired canine companion strolled along the footpath for a few blocks until they reached the water's edge. The current was strong in this section of the Yarra, ready to spread its wings as it left the suburbs of the inner-north for the city and upped the pace with the estuary's finish line in view.

'You're not going to win every argument you get into, *pequeñita*,' Jeff said, hoping the past few minutes of general chatter was enough foreplay not to incite more of the youngster's wrath. 'Even if you're right.'

'I know that!' Kierney snapped back, although this time with less venom.

'Do you though? It didn't sound like it, the way you sprayed me with so many passionate expletives.'

The student frowned. 'Yeah. Sorry about that.'

'*De nada*, gorgeous,' her dad laced an arm around her shoulders and pulled her closer. 'I love tempestuous women. But pick your battles, if you know what I mean...'

'No, I don't know what you mean. Don't argue with you?'

'Of course you can argue with me! I love tempestuous women. Did I already say that?'

'*Papá!* You know you already said it. What *do* you mean then?'

The intellectual grinned. 'I mean, even if you're right, some people take time to come round. You have to remember this when you confront someone with an opinion that comes from a perspective they haven't considered before. They're probably feeling the same way you did this afternoon with Professor Riesling. You need to preserve people's dignity for as long as it takes them to admit defeat.'

Kierney giggled. 'It's not Professor Riesling. It's Rieckling. How do you expect me to take you seriously when you keep making me laugh?'

'Weakling? Fuck! Poor bastard. Now I'm doubly sure he'll have gone home to lick his wounds. It's a strong man who can withstand a *shellacking* from such a tempestuous woman.'

With a loud groan, the seventeen-year-old wrestled free of the comedian's grip and jogged after Indie, who was weaving in and out of the trees and shrubs which lined the riverbank, catching up on the day's urinary news. Jeff shoved his hands in the pockets of his leather jacket, checking the house keys hadn't fallen out of the one on the left and retrieving his cigarette packet from the other.

The lighter's spark caught the young woman's attention. Encouraging the dog to jump up and place his muddy front paws on her chest, she waited for her father to catch them up. She rubbed noses with the excitable Labrador before pushing him down.

'*Gracias*,' she said, blowing smoke into the chilling air. 'I know you're right. It's just hard to back down when I shouldn't have to back down.'

'Jesus! I know exactly what you mean. It happens every bloody day for me. And it'll be the mainstay of your career at the UN too, so you'd better get used to it.'

'I know,' Kierney moaned again. 'Will I ever be in a position to make decisions without having to convince everyone else first?'

Her father stepped back, coughing hard as he was bombarded by the *trifecta* of this precocious question, a cheerful shout from a group of runners and another ethereal message from his *regala*. 'Shit! That's classic! *Mamá* says, "Don't hold your breath." I'm sorry to be the one to break it to you, baby, but the answer's a resounding "No."'

'Never?' the ambitious teenager yelped.

'Nope. Not a chance. Unless you've found a way to become Queen of the Universe.'

'But *you* can.'

Jeff's eyes widened. '*I* can? I don't think so. And I wouldn't want to either. The world doesn't need any more dictators, Kizzo.'

'No. I'm not talking about being a dictator,' his daughter sighed, gritting her teeth. 'You know I want to make things better for everyone. Not even as UN Secretary General?'

The peacemaker held his hand out for the dejected changeling. Eager to impose himself on his adopted family's heated discussion, Indie took his master's gesture as an instruction to turn for home and inserted his slobbering muzzle into the space between the joining hands.

'Hey, mate! Back off a second,' the celebrity requested, waving to another fan who was frantic with delight at having spotted her handsome idol. 'G'day. Thank you. No, Kiz. Not even. I assure you, I haven't made a single unilateral decision of greater importance than deciding which cubicle to use in a public toilet.'

Kierney was stunned. 'That's not true. Surely not.'

'Christ! It *is* true. And it's fantastic that you want to be able to make the big decisions. Bloody fantastic, in fact. The world needs people who're prepared to stand up and take accountability. But with accountability comes the responsibility of making sure your decision isn't going to result in dire consequences, like war or civil unrest. Or other bloodshed or terrorism... You know all this. Unless you're going to stamp out democracy in the western world when you're "Sec' Gen"'.'

'No. Of course I'm not. I know I can't make unilateral decisions. It's just that some people don't know their views are plain wrong.'

Jeff offered the future leader another cigarette, the itching sensation coming from his tattoo driving him pleasantly crazy. 'Oh, I hear you, *pequeñita*. I hear you loud and clear, and I applaud your wanting to take the politics out of government. The world'll be a much better place when you do, but trying to govern unilaterally'll only bring politics front and centre. It pains me to tell you how long I held on to my obstinate rightness about everything. "Just take my fucking word for it!" I used to want to scream at people at your age. It was *la mamá* who taught me patience and tenacity, *et cetera*, and it's a damned shame she's not here for you now too.'

The *duo* turned around underneath the freeway flyover, tracking back across dewy grass until they reached Mary Street. Kierney took the leash from her father's hand and clipped it to Indie's collar, subdued and pensive. The lively dog pulled ahead, with no less energy after his run than before.

'I have you to teach me now,' she smiled, tugging to slow the dog down. 'What was it *Mamá* said that changed your mind?'

'Ah, y'know... Telling me I couldn't expect people to change quickly. Showing me how hard I resisted certain things, like when I first got this.'

The billionnaire lifted his right hand to his daughter's eye level, flexing his middle finger to draw her attention to the black jet-stone ring Lynn had given him in London; the talisman to which she had added a small, twinkling precious stone in each quadrant whenever their family supplemented its number.

'I used to fiddle with this the whole time,' he continued, twisting the stout band again and meeting resistance where it had fused to his skin. '*Mamá* teased me that I didn't always adapt as well to change as I wanted everyone else to.

Before she pointed it out, I was like you are now: champing at the bit to show people the right way, but with no-one to talk things through with and be given the space to be wrong.'

The young woman linked arms with her kindhearted mentor. They reached the junction with Barkly Avenue and laughed at having to lean into the corner as they wheeled round using Indie's added impetus. The intellectual's waggish behaviour was a surefire sign of preoccupation, thought-bubbles floating above his head and broadcast on a wavelength she had no trouble receiving.

'I'm going to be fine, *Papá*. I know what I have to do now. I never forget the things you tell me. Nor you, *Mamá*, if you're still listening. I promise I won't try to be the benevolent dictator after all.'

Jeff chuckled. 'Well, that's a relief, Madam Ong. What've you got planned for dinner?'

'What've *I* got planned? Not a whole lot. What've you got planned?'

'How about that little *sushi* place on Swan Street, opposite the sports nutrition shop Ry goes to?'

Kierney nodded. 'OK. That'd be great actually. I haven't had Japanese for ages. David doesn't like it.'

The jagged, russet roofline of the Diamonds' temporary home in Burnley South, on loan from a pair of Indian doctors taking a sabbatical from glowing careers at the Epworth Hospital, loomed overhead as Indie and his chaperones let themselves in through a gate hidden in dense hedging. They had only remarked the day before on how easily they had settled in, comparatively speaking.

Giving up *Escondido* had been tougher than Jeff expected, both despite and because of the thousands of memories secreted within. The family's peaceful *hacienda* was now boarded up, pending conversion into a recovery centre for people with severe depressive illnesses. He knew Kierney missed it on some esoteric level, as did he, although neither she nor her brother ever expressed any regret that experiences from their childhood home were consigned to photographs and videos.

'What are you writing about at the moment?' the teenager asked as they swapped their dog-walking boots for casual dining footwear.

'Drugs,' her father answered. 'Good ones and bad ones.'

'Oh. That's interesting. In which context? Are we walking or driving, by the way? I think it's started to drizzle.'

The Aston Martin cleared its throat with typical manly exhilaration, its engine raring to make mincemeat of the kilometre dash between Burnley South and Cremorne. Jeff scoffed that it might fear for its life in the Royal Place car park, keeping company with the Chargers and Ford GT models he had coveted as a youngster, before he had set out on his perilous journey to financial abundance.

November in Melbourne meant lighter evenings and intermittent cloudbursts. Force of habit prompted the superstar to remove an umbrella from the car boot in case the rain was heavier when he and Kierney left the restaurant. No matter where they dined in their hometown, his weary heart was assaulted by flashbacks to happier times, and tonight was no exception.

Richmond's three parallel thoroughfares had played significant roles in his life ever since he first moved from Sydney in January nineteen-seventy-two. From Victoria Street's endless line of Vietnamese eateries to the eclectic mix of cuisines available on Bridge Road and Swan Street, the celebrity couple had sampled most fares in the ensuing decades.

In more recent years however, with his furious workload taking him out of town so often and with Jet boarding at Melbourne Academy during the weeks, Lynn and Kierney had gravitated towards more child-friendly haunts on Lygon and Brunswick Streets while based at the city penthouse.

Foremost in Jeff's mind tonight was one of a string of final dinners he and his dream girl shared prior to her forced *exodus* from Australia, part of her parents' grand plan to exclude him from her future. Waiting to cross the road with their seventeen-year-old, it struck him that a visit to this neighbourhood had given rise to his own drunken and despondent epiphany. The young Olympian had revealed him for what he was, and he had learned something too: contrary to his own arrogant opinion, he didn't hold the monopoly on wisdom after all.

And as nineteen-ninety-six drew to its end, closing so many doors on their life singular, the names on the widower's stakeholder list were dwindling fast. The Diamond Celebration Foundation took care of the majority these days, under new management and with an independent Board of Directors.

Their son's destiny had been disclosed a few months earlier in Paris, the day before he had taken an escort to EuroDisney, and the remaining tweaks and tucks required to the gorgeous gipsy girl who now held his hand would demand his full attention in the lead-up to Gerry's wedding.

This left only the name written on the first row; that of Victoria Lynn Shannon Dyson, the same young Olympian under whose tutelage and unfaltering allegiance Jeff Diamond had reached and then surpassed his potential, time and time again.

Their two stakeholders in common had sanctioned his passage to the next life in search of a distant lighthouse. The least he could do was to equip his children well for an orphaned adulthood.

'D'you remember when we all sat down to talk about drugs *en famille*?' Jeff opened, pouring beer from a tiny can into an even tinier glass. 'You guys were thirteen and fourteen-ish, I think. We were in Barcelona on holidays.'

Kierney laughed. 'Impossible to forget! It was hilarious, that conversation; who could come up with the most ridiculous euphemism! Riding the winged donkey, strapping on my chemical armour...'

Her father frowned. 'I don't know what you're talking about, *pequeñita*. Were you high that night? I only remember giving you guys sensible, practical advice.'

'Don't give me that, you liar!' the young woman cried out, lifting her gaze to the ceiling. '*Mamá*, please send him some horrible music to tell him off.'

Jeff held his breath as if waiting for something to happen. When nothing did, he raised a triumphant eyebrow, making his dinner partner giggle. Instead of the usual *Stravisnkyesque* symphony that filled his brain whenever he imagined Lynn angry with him, he only felt a sweet stinging in his left pectoral muscle. This was a good sign, especially after the way their earlier conversation had ended. If his offspring bought into this wacky beyond-the-grave telepathy, which had started out as a means of uniting them in grief, they stood a much greater chance of keeping in touch for longer.

'Y'know, there's absolutely nothing in your *mamá*'s diaries about drugs.'

'Isn't there?' the teenager replied. 'Not even about you?'

'Well, yeah. There's heaps about me in the old days,' the former bad-boy conceded. 'More from a "What am I going to do about him?" angle.'

'And that's only from last year,' Kierney chuckled, breathing in the aromatic steam from a bowl of *katsu* curry chicken. 'Yum! This smells delicious. Yours looks good too.'

'Bloody cheek! Yeah. It's hot. Look at these whole chillies lying in wait. Trap for young players! Better not bring Gerry here. He'd blow himself up!'

The restaurant was emptying out after the first rush of after-work diners, and the celebrities had the rear half of the place to themselves. The staff faded into the background after the brand of friendly welcome which bordered on harassment, and the polite young woman tutted at the demonic cackle emanating from her father's burning mouth as he lifted his *ramen* noodles thirty centimetres above his soup to cool them down.

'It's as if it was a step too far for Lynn Dyson to put anything incriminating in writing,' the author continued, swallowing his mouthful and scooping up some more broth with the deep spoon. 'That's OK though. I totally get it.'

'Did she ever talk about what she wanted to happen to her diaries?' Kierney asked. 'She always told us to make sure not to write about things we wouldn't want anyone else to find out. I suppose we never know who might pick them up after we're gone. Maybe hundreds of years from now. Like when journalists uncover rare diaries of politicians or other famous people.'

Jeff nodded. '*Exactamente. Mamá* cared more about keeping her reputation intact than I ever did, and I understand it'd upset a whole generation of sports fans if she or you guys were associated with drugs. As Dysons, y'know.'

'Yes. I do know. Ry's obsessed with it. He'd hate to have his integrity questioned like that.'

'Sure. And you? What level of scrutiny are you prepared for?'

The prospective law student paused. 'I don't know.'

Her father lifted his empty tin of beer to the chaste and circumspect seventeen-year-old. 'Good answer. How do you define integrity?'

Kierney laughed. 'Not the way Ryan does, I'm guessing you want me to say.'

'Spot on, *pequeñita.*'

'Integrity's being true to yourself, as far as I'm concerned,' she hazarded. 'Integral. Everything's part of the whole. Is that right?'

The great man leaned back in his chair, pinching his eyes shut to stave off tears he could easily pass off as a side-effect of his spicy dinner if he chose to compromise his own integrity. Here he was, about to give his absent son a serve for placing too much emphasis on perception rather than reality, when his own primal instinct was to hide from the truth.

'Sure,' the lost boy whispered, catching his breath.

'Are you OK? What just happened, *Papá*?'

'Nothing. All good. Your definition's a bit airy-fairy for me. Try something a tad more concrete.'

The willing pupil grinned. 'Aggregate? Sand, little stones and water and whatever else is integral to making concrete. Better?'

Her father coughed, shaking his head. 'Jesus! I can almost hear myself giving Gerry's dad the shits over Sunday lunch. You are a handful, Miss Diamond. A real handful sometimes, dear.'

Kierney sipped from her glass of water, innocence personified. 'Thank you, Auntie Celia. Tell me what you think integrity is then, Mister Philomath.'

'Well,' the negotiator cocked his head. 'Since you asked... The purest form of integrity, in my not-so-humble opinion, is doing the right thing even when no-one can catch you doing the wrong thing. And that doesn't mean I always set a good example, by the way. I don't profess infallible personal integrity either, in case you're wondering.'

'Oh... Cool. I love that analogy though. See? You've taught me something else tonight. *Gracias, Papá.* Please may I have another lemon, lime and bitters?'

'You may,' the emotional man answered. 'Or, but for the small matter of three months and your brother's standard of integrity, you could even get a glass of wine and live by your own.'

'Or by *Mamá*'s standard of "Phew! None of the wines on this menu would tempt me into compromising my integrity."'

'Kierney!' her remaining parent feigned outrage. 'Was that really you, or has the devil occupied your soul? How dare you speak such blasphemy about your mother? I hope you would've said that to her face. Otherwise your own integrity's just been smashed against the rocks.'

The jubilant smile vanished from his daughter's mouth, and she let out a muted groan. 'Hmm… I don't know if I would, to be honest. Sorry. That was a mean thing to say.'

Jeff held his left hand out to his flustered dinner companion. 'You would've. Practise resilience, baby. If you're going to stand up in the highest court in the civilised world and prosecute your case, you're going to need to think on your feet. You would absolutely have said those words to your *mamá*'s face at nearly eighteen years of age, with another year of maturity up your sleeve. Wouldn't you?'

'Oh, *Papá*! I love you so much for believing in me. Wow! This is really tough, but I'm so grateful you're pushing me hard. Yes, I would've said that to *Mamá* if she were here with us tonight, just like I tease you.'

'Tease me? You don't tease me, *pequeñita*. You denude me. On a daily basis! You're going to be a fucking fantastic lawyer, by the way. *Mamá* said so.'

The young woman lifted a screwed-up paper napkin from her lap to dab the corners of her eyes. If she were destined for a successful career in human rights law, it was all her parents' doing. How on Earth had this gorgeous man, who cuddled her every night and validated her every day, turned into such an influential heavyweight with no parental guidance whatsoever? Who would her youthful soul have grown into if it had been born into a different family?

'Thanks, both of you,' the young woman said, sitting taller in her chair. 'So, you think *Mamá* didn't include any reference to drugs in her diaries so as not to dishonour the Dysons' clean sporting name?'

The grieving husband rubbed the breast pocket of his shirt again. 'Yep. Just a wee bit hypocritical, eh, angel? But is hypocrisy the same as having dubious integrity?'

'*Argh!*' Kierney used her mother's typical sign of frustration. 'Stop testing me! Yes. Why not? It's doing something you say you don't agree with, isn't it? Do as I say and not as I do. Sounds like a lack of integrity to me.'

'Another good answer, Kizzo. So if you consider your *mamá* to be a person of high integrity generally… You do, don't you?'

'Of course I do.'

Jeff raised his hand to mollify her newfound assertiveness. '*Bueno*. Hang on a sec'… Stick with me! If you think *Mamá* has integrity, is it still hypocritical to want to save you guys, or Junior, Grandpa or Anna from having to answer unhelpful questions about their deceased relative's drug use?'

'No. I s'pose not. So you don't think *Mamá* was being hypocritical after all? I was meant to defend her, wasn't I?'

Again, the teacher responded with a gentle nod. 'Yep. And you will in future. Those diaries weren't written for public consumption during her lifetime, Kiz. *Mamá* and I never shied away from answering questions honestly in the here and now. She did it to protect you guys when she could no longer protect you from intrusive *journoes* who simply want to dig up dirt. You understand the difference between slander and libel, in terms of the consequences?'

'I think so,' the student replied. 'Slander is spoken, whereas libel is written down. But that's not in terms of consequences.'

'Indeed. Slander's much easier to refute. To dismiss, even. That's why it's always prudent to understate things when you're creating a permanent record of your opinion.'

Kierney's eyes widened, smiling as the waiter cleared their table. 'Oh, my God! I know where you're going with this! With the Internet and everything being stored forever, on tape or whatever, slander and libel are turning into the same thing.'

'*Bingo*, my *s*mart-arsed child! I had the same conversation with your brother last night. I'd finished writing about Steve Christie and the way he defamed me in TV interviews when he wanted Lynn to leave me, and it occurred to me that we'd never spoken about this with you two.'

'Really? Oh, good. I can't wait to read that bit. May I?'

'*Cierto.* It needs finishing off, but you're welcome to look it over,' her father assented. 'That's how we made the idiotic episode disappear from the media. You won't remember, but the story vanished overnight.'

'How?' the curious young woman pressed.

Jeff grinned. 'Under the auspices of what's now known as the Broadcasting Services Act Nineteen-ninety-two, in brackets: Commonwealth, close brackets, your *mamá* and I managed to enlist the help of one of the Victorian Government's best legislators.'

'Don't tell me! He belonged to Gerry's club,' the mini-socialist huffed.

'No, actually. *She* went to school with *Mamá* and Michelle, so almost as bad!'

Both left-wing members of the Diamond family chuckled, unfurling another shining example of their tenuous integrity. Metaphysical pincers squeezed the superstar's inked chest, sending stinging sensations radiating out from his heart. He signalled for the bill, pulling his wallet from the back pocket of his jeans.

'I'll get this, *Papá*. It's a cheap one. Do you mind?'

'Jesus Christ, angels!' he cursed, rolling his shoulders. 'You're ganging up on me tonight. Go for it! Totally emasculate me. This is your time, *pequeñita*. Take it by the balls.'

The pair darted across the four lanes of traffic stopped at nearby lights, dodging well-meaning but zealous autograph-hunters and making for the Aston Martin and home. In the five minutes it took to reach the mock-Tudor mansion, Kierney managed to wheedle a number of non-libellous confessions of her dad's past excesses, in exchange for a couple of her own contemporary escapades.

'The important thing for me, as I've always said, is not to pass judgement on what you want to put into yourself,' the rock star told his spongelike muse. 'My experience, and *Mamá*'s too, can benefit you with the how. Drugs are far less harmful if you're careful with how you use them.'

'Respect them,' his daughter repeated some earlier advice.

Jeff nodded. 'Sure. How often, where you get 'em from, if you've got the right equipment and it's in good condition, *et cetera*. But mostly, I need to find out why you're taking whatever you're taking. And in the future, you need to promise yourself you'll know why and make sure you're satisfied with the reasons you admit to yourself before you indulge. Fair?'

'Fair enough. I promise. Apart from the odd joint, I don't have any interest in taking anything harder.'

'Yeah. I believe you. That's how your *mamá* felt too, which is precisely what I mean about knowing why. If you purely want to consume something to have a better time, that's cool. Enjoy it, then leave it behind. But if you think you ever need to take drugs to cover up some other sort of destructive emotion, like anger or unhappiness, then that's a discussion you should have with your brother. Or with a professional.'

Kierney disappeared upstairs as soon as they entered the house, tripping over Indie's dancing feet on her way. Assuming she wanted to change into more comfortable clothes for the rest of the evening, her father looped his leather jacket over the end of the bannister and slapped his thigh to attract the dog's attention.

By the time her male housemates had let themselves outside for a smoke and a sniff around the hedges, the teenager had poured two hypocritical glasses of *Tempranillo*. With the bottle tucked under her arm, she carried the wine out onto the *patio* to join them.

'Cheers, gorgeous,' her dad toasted. 'You're not going to write about this tonight, are you?'

'Very funny. Now, on the topic of Ry and I being able to say anything we like to you or *Mamá* as long as we think we have a good reason for saying it...'

'Ah, yeah? Sounds ominous.'

'Can I ask you something about Rod Germany's suicide?'

Jeff blanched. 'Fuck! D'you think you have a good reason to ask?'

The event to which Kierney referred had been a difficult chapter to articulate, given the author's stated intentions. Roderick was a Melbourne Academy student with everything going for him: loving parents, albeit quite demanding; a creative musical talent; and for a loner, a likeable personality.

One of the school counsellors had recruited the country's most outspoken advocate for childhood mental health to assist after the fourteen-year-old made a futile attempt to take his life. At the time, Jeff had hesitated to become involved with a family who prioritised religion and appearances above the irrefutable challenges faced by a sensitive child struggling to make sense of the world.

Not that the celebrity sought to shy away from the situation or wished to avoid sullying his reputation for helping those in need; he had no fear of adverse publicity. In fact, he was a master of generating his own adverse publicity! His reticence sprang from a far more controversial justification: his belief in the right to choose, whether this choice be for life or death.

The Australia of nineteen-ninety-one bore no tolerance for such progressive points of view, and another half-decade of extra maturity had moved "the lucky country" little further. His daughter's question was loaded, and they sat eyeing each other off at opposite ends of the outdoor dining table.

'Yes. I think I do.'

Jeff sighed. 'I think you do too. *Digame.*'

'*Mamá* told me you tried to tell Rod's parents about your past and your attitude to suicide, but they wouldn't listen. Is that true?'

'Yeah. I said I wasn't the right person to speak to their son, or at least they should know a bit more about me before they let him speak to me. Apparently, Rod used to harp on about me at home all the time. Mostly about music and general stuff, but I did share some background info' with him when he opened up about the way he saw life.

'Then when Rod took a walk on the wild side one night, and his dad insisted I speak to him, *Mamá* and I decided not to mention anything about choosing to die, or about forever souls or going round again; those dumb-arse things we talked about all the time in the context of our relationship but really hadn't bothered to discover if there was any basis for believing them. Y'know, *pequeñita*... Before, that shit was simply our peculiar, private joke; a way to keep reminding ourselves how much we loved each other.'

'A joke? Didn't you really believe in it then?' the young woman asked. 'Deep down?'

'Ah, yeah,' her father insisted. 'With every fibre of our beings. Absolutely. Just like we believe in it now.'

Kierney shook her head, watching his fingers disappear between the buttons of his shirt once again. 'Yes, but why do you say it's a joke? Why...'

'Shhh,' Jeff cut her off. 'I know what you're going to say: how dare you piss away life with your kids because of some sick fucking joke? Am I right?'

Turning her head to stare out over the lawn, the teenager lifted her left hand behind her neck and massaged her tingling muscles. 'Something like that.'

Indie was startled out of his post-run slumber by the sound of his master's chair scraping over the deck. The songwriter rounded the table, hands beckoning his gipsy girl to stand up, which at first she refused. On the second attempt, she rose to her feet and waited for him to sit down before climbing onto his lap.

Both Diamond children knew Rod Germany had taken his own life, and that he had made at least one other attempt prior to this. They were also aware of their dad becoming the young man's *confidant* and advocate in the intervening period. The tragedy had been announced during school assembly, and an extraordinary Board of Governors' meeting was called for the following evening. Replaying these fraught days in her mind half a decade hence, Kierney recalled the novelty of spending the night in a dormitory with a bunch of her friends because the summit had extended beyond midnight.

Less than two years after his first ineffective bid to die, with a string of chart-topping singles under his belt and a growing fan-base of all ages, the troubled musician had overdosed on a cocktail of prescription drugs; sleeping pills, painkillers and anti-anxiety medication, all swilled down with a bottle of vodka. According to newspaper reports, he had left a note crediting Jeff Diamond as his "rock" and for being the only person to take him seriously.

Questions had been asked, answers were provided. The matter was dropped and hadn't been mentioned since.

'We treated our "soul-mates through the ages" thing a bit like a joke 'cause no-one would've believed us if we hadn't,' Jeff whispered into the seventeen-year-old's ear. 'It stopped being a joke as time went by though. We kept having these weird hallucinations, like we were us one minute and then two completely different people the next, in a completely different time and place.'

'That's what *Mamá* used to say too.'

'Yeah. We normally felt it at the same time. Bloody strange at first, but after a while, we started to like it! Looked forward to it happening again even... We never really tried to analyse why it was happening, beyond a theory about finding each other in several successive lifetimes.'

Kierney leaned back into the storyteller's warm embrace as if she were eight years old again. 'It's lovely. I've always believed it too.'

'But no further than its loveliness,' the wise man reminded her. 'It's a bit like a religion. You want to believe it for the promise it brings of something to look forward to. It's irresistible, attractive... But if you pick the whole thing apart, there ain't much rhyme or reason to any of it, is there?'

'So did Rod believe it too? Is that why he decided to die?'

'Jesus, gorgeous... I can't say for sure. I wish I could, but I'd be lying. And now's not the time to start lying to you, even if it might make things easier to work through. He and I started off discussing why he wasn't happy with life and why he felt like he didn't belong.'

'And that's when you told him about your childhood,' the empathetic teenager interjected.

Her father frowned. 'Yeah. Not in much detail. First rule of being a good counsellor, *pequeñita*, is to focus on the person who needs help and not to dilute their troubled waters with your own. Or pollute them... For the person suffering, it sounds like you're belittling their problems if you can't wait to tell him, "Hey, man, I've been where you are, and look! I'm perfectly OK now, so get over yourself." That's another thing worth remembering when you're changing the world at the UN.'

'I already know that,' the young woman giggled. 'I only think you've mentioned it about four thousand times!'

'Only four thousand? Fucking hell. I'm just not trying hard enough, am I?'

'Stop it, *Papá*! I'm sorry. My fault. Carry on, please.'

'Certainly, ma'am,' the desolate man was glad she had injected a drop of mirth into the sour theme. 'Gradually, we started going through various ideas of what a happy existence might look like for him, *et cetera*, and he suddenly blurted out, "I'm too good to live in this world. People do nothing but hurt other people, and I can't bear being part of it."'

'Oh, wow! That's the opposite of how you were when you were younger, isn't it?'

Jeff nodded, reaching sideways to retrieve their wine glasses one by one. 'Absolutely. Good pick-up. I've always been driven to change things here, even when I was so fucked up that dying was the only positive idea in my brain.'

'Is that how you feel now?' Kierney asked, her body as stiff as a board.

'No. You and your brother are two very positive ideas in my brain. We've been over this, and I'm sure we'll talk about it heaps more. Let's not change the subject though, alright? I love you guys more than you know, and I hate the thought of leaving you behind.'

The graceful youngster tipped forward and slid off her father's lap. Holding out her hand, she invited him to walk around the edge of the lawn. Thrashing out the pros and cons of his forthcoming exit was not on her agenda for tonight either, so she urged him to continue.

'It was like the gates opened for Rod at that point. His eyes had life in them again, if you forgive the tasteless expression. He said, "I wasn't this unhappy in my old life, and I want to see if it's better in the next one. I'm never going to be happy in this life." Then he hugged me so tight, as if he'd won the keys to the kingdom. I couldn't argue with him. The next day, he was dead.'

'So he didn't tell you he was planning to kill himself?'

Jeff frowned. 'Not in so many words, but I had my suspicions. I'd asked him a week or so before. We talked about it, yeah. It wasn't a matter of how or why, but when.'

The fir-tree branches overhead parted to release a fruit bat whose feeding frenzy had been disturbed by the perambulating pair. Momentarily spooked, both Diamonds halted in their tracks and laughed when they identified their would-be assailant.

'Whoa!' the songwriter shouted into the dense foliage. 'You've clearly put on too much weight to be jumping out of trees, mate. A bit lacking on the defying gravity front tonight. You OK, *pequeñita*?'

'Yes. I thought it was going to land on us.'

'So did he, I reckon. Anyway... Is that what you wanted to know about Rod? Why did you bring this up?'

Kierney smiled, taking his outstretched hand and carrying on along the path, the soles of their shoes crunching the wet gravel into the sand underneath. 'Oh, I don't really know. Yes and no.'

'*Touché*, you little fox,' her father chuckled at another of his overused sayings volleyed back to him.

'But it is "Yes and no,"' she insisted. 'I read what you've written about it and wanted to hear what you considered as your part in the story. Are you worried his parents'll read too much into it when the book comes out?'

This time, Jeff was the only one to grind to a standstill. 'Am *I* worried?' he called after her. 'Kizzo. Worried for whom? Them? Or you guys?'

'Any of us.'

'No more than I am about the rest of what I've written. No less either. You know I haven't tried to glamourise all the unsavoury stuff. File the rough edges down, as your *mamá* would've said. Does it worry you?'

The pair had completed their lap of the garden, arriving at the kitchen door. Both diverted to collect the wine bottle and empty glasses, with Indie waiting patiently to be let in. Kierney grumbled as four muddy feet slipped on the tiles, leaving a pattern of paw prints worthy of an aboriginal painting in the short time it took her to grab a towel to dry him off.

'I'm not worried for us,' she replied. 'Lie down, boy. Keep still a minute! Not for me or Ryan, I mean. I s'pose I'm thinking of whether people'll blame you after the fact.'

The billionnaire shrugged, holding up the kettle. 'Tea? I'm not going to care after the fact, am I? They can blame whomever they like. It's not going to make any difference, although I apologise in advance if anything in the book ends up causing grief for you two. It's all our own work, *Mamá*'s and mine. The foreword states that quite specifically.'

'Good,' the student scoffed. 'They can sue you and *Mamá* in that case. Can people sue your estate, by the way?'

'They can try. You'll have to let me know.'

'Oh, *Papá*. That's not funny. Or fair...'

Jeff shook his head. 'Perhaps not, gorgeous. You remember Graham Winton and his silver-tongued "everyman philosophy" *glibbery*?'

'Yes. What's he got to do with this?'

'Well... I'm sorry, baby. Nothing's fair with all this, is it? I was thinking that, just as I apparently do "everyman philosophy", I'm most likely guilty of "everyman lawyering" too. I believe in natural justice, if you like. None of this complex fucking interpretation of legalese. That's a money-making piss-take, and they're welcome to it.'

The Two of Diamonds retired to the lounge room, its beamed ceilings and yellowish lighting accentuating the house's snoozy atmosphere. As they waited for their tea to cool to a drinkable temperature, the author likened himself to an old man fallen asleep in his recliner with the newspaper over his face.

'Are you writing tonight?' Kierney asked.

'Yep. Planning to. Is that alright with you? Michel de Montaigne *ce soir.*'

The canny woman gave her introverted sage a nod. '"Memory full, judgement empty." That was him, wasn't it?'

'Sure was,' Jeff confirmed. '*Bueno.* It still surprises me that you guys paid any attention to my esoteric ramblings.'

'We did! And do. Wow! Is that more rain outside? We were lucky. Look at it!'

The seventeen-year-old crossed the room to pull the heavy velvet curtains; yet another decorative feature in such stark contrast to *Escondido*'s clean, bright lines. She paused with the two edges close to her ears, peering through the gloom until her eyes adjusted well enough to see droplets dancing off the paving stones.

'Education,' her father continued. 'Knowledge *versus* information.'

'Hmm... I remember. Something about having hæmorrhoids but still having to look up what they were.'

'Jesus, you are seriously challenging my conscience today!' the intellectual shouted. 'Come and sit down. I'd like to try a few things out on you, so I know how to craft them in the book.'

His daughter skated across the polished boards in her socks, only too glad to be drawn into her parents' necromantic autobiography again. She and Indie vied for position at the storyteller's feet, he licking her chin while she fondled his jowls and behind his ears.

'Your *mamá*'s old friend, Mick Mountain, was quoted as having said, "I know one, who, when I question him what he knows, he presently calls for a book to show me, and dares not venture to tell me much, as that he has piles in his posteriors, 'til first he has consulted his dictionary, what piles and what posteriors are." And you just nailed it with your paraphrasing.'

Kierney giggled, now lying on her side, stretched out alongside her hairy companion. 'Thanks. Knowledge is doing worthwhile things with information.'

'*Exactamente, pequeñita.* And also not.'

'Also not? Not what?'

Her father looked perturbed for a moment, before inhaling and launching into another lengthy, memorised quotation. '"Nay, even the folly and impertinence of others will contribute to his instruction. By observing the graces and manners of all he sees, he will create to himself an emulation of the good, and a contempt of the bad." In other words, knowledge is also knowing when to do nothing with the information, or when the information warns you against doing something.'

'Pardon?' the teenager sniffed, ruffling the fur on Indie's back. 'Did you get that, boy?'

'You used the word "worthwhile", which, with your permission, I'm now going to plagiarise…'

The student laughed again. 'Oh, OK! I'm flattered. Wish I knew why!'

'Knowledge is acting on the information at hand, whether it encourages us or discourages us from our intended action. But my aim's to take it a step further. When we act on this knowledge judiciously rather than maliciously, we turn that knowledge into wisdom.'

Jeff took two cigarettes out of his packet and lit both with the same flame, handing one down to his spellbound child. She accepted it with a smile, swathing her conjecture in a veil of smoke. Life had so many tangents and dimensions, and who better to learn from than the man who understood them all?

'I love the idea, *Papá*, but it sounds like you mean an evil person can't be wise? I don't think they're mutually exclusive. If you're saying that, it's almost as if you're redefining what "wisdom" means.'

'Exactly right,' her father grinned, angling his hand down to knock the end of his cigarette on the edge of the ashtray. 'When I started this piece, like you, I was fighting the dilemma that "wise" and "good" can't be the same thing. However, all the synonyms I've found today for wisdom seem to come with an overlay of goodness. So for the most part, I reckon people reading the book are likely to take the same view, if that's what the word means to them.'

'But there's always one,' his daughter laughed.

The billionnaire shook his head and smiled. 'No, *pequeñita*. You're unique, but not quite that special! There's more than you who'll be cynical about it. But not as many as I'm looking for to get my point across, which is why I need another device to make sure I take everyone with me.'

Stubbing out her cigarette and exhaling to clear her lungs, Kierney rolled onto her back and slapped the floor. 'Oh,' she whined. 'I want to be the uniquest of them all. I think I've guessed what your device is.'

With nothing but Indie's quiet snoring to disturb their peace, Jeff admitted these words into his consciousness, a much healthier form of sustenance than the usual creative *stimuli*. As the weeks ticked by, a certain implied amnesty was incorporated in every conversation he shared with his children. Each new sign of self-sufficiency made his departure easier on all of them.

'Ah, yeah?' he replied, opening one eye and peering at her expectant face. 'I was hoping you'd say that.'

'Love.'

'*Sí*. Gold star. The love and wisdom *combo*'s vital for changing the world. Love begets wisdom begets love begets more wisdom begets more love… On and on, *ad infinitum, et cetera*.'

The young woman covered her mouth, a yawn slipping out unannounced. 'Sorry! I'm tired. I was up at five this morning. You didn't hear me go out, did you?'

'Nope. Why were you up at five? Couldn't sleep?'

'Oh, yeah. I could've slept for another four hours,' Kierney chuckled. 'I went running before a breakfast meeting. Stupid idea. I'm not doing it again. Sorry, *Mamá*. I've got very lazy lately.'

Her dad sniffed. 'Fuck! You and me both, baby. Sorry, angel. Go to bed then, if you want.'

'Yes, OK. In a minute. I want to know how you're going to connect your love and wisdom *combo* with turning information into knowledge. Everyone needs to know this.'

'They sure do,' Jeff answered, leaning forward on the couch with his elbows on his knees to combat a sudden dizzy spell. 'You have to apply a lens of love over every piece of information you receive before you do anything with it. What impact is this going to have on my fellow man, woman or child? What collateral damage could this inflict? As opposed to only concentrating on the good it'll do for your original target.'

'Oh, I see,' Kierney muttered. 'Because people don't think before they act. Perfect! I love it.'

'*Merci, mademoiselle.* Kind of you to say so. More than "Think before you act." Trying to get folk to think more broadly before they make decisions, like I did when I first met your grandpa. You can imagine I was itching to meet the man they call "Big D". He had a formidable reputation even back in the early 'seventies, but I didn't always agree with the way he did things. I watched and learned every time I was in his company... still do actually... but I didn't necessarily emulate him.'

The seventeen-year-old remained silent, processing her dad's confession. It had never been a secret that the pair of statesmen often didn't see eye to eye; one a staunch conservative and patriot, and the other a left-leaning global crusader. In deference to Lynn and her Dyson loyalties, he had deliberately stepped back while the Diamond grandchildren submitted themselves to demanding aristocratic duties and destinies preordained by their birthright.

As adolescents steeped in their parents' wide-ranging humanitarian agenda, Ryan and Kierney had begun to pit the purist, single-minded approach to individual or team excellence against the focus on building capacity and capability on a far greater scale. Their mother's prudent neutrality on the subject had prevented them from posing too many tough questions, for fear of seeming ungrateful for the privileges their name afforded. Nevertheless, the balance between these two polar world views had begun to shift in the months since she was taken from them.

'Are you in Melbourne tomorrow night?' Kierney asked, deciding not to open the door to another lengthy debate.

'That's the plan. I'm playing squash with Gerry before dinner. D'you and Dave want to join us?'

The willowy athlete shook her head. 'No, thanks. I'm going to the dance studio after uni'. It's the dress rehearsal for Friday's show, and I wondered if you'd come and pick me up, so you can see a sneak preview?'

'Absolutely. That'd be great. Love to, gorgeous. Good incentive not to drink too much.'

'*Excelente,*' his daughter chuckled. 'I'll text you when we're coming to the end. About ten-ish, I think.'

Jeff smiled, checking his watch and snatching up his cigarettes and lighter. 'Better get to work. Appreciate your counsel, Ms Diamond. Now go to bed. That's an order.'

Making a *détour* to the kitchen to let Indie out for one last inspection of the old house's bushy boundaries, Kierney hugged her father and kissed him goodnight. She poured herself a glass of water and collected her bag from the table at the bottom of the stairs before disappearing to the first floor.

Jeff followed the light-footed youngster, diverting to a cupboard hidden in the wood-panelled hallway. The contents of *Escondido*'s wine cellar had been transported to this house four months ago and was now severely depleted. Apart from the occasional case dropped off by their high-rolling manager, the current occupants saw no reason to augment their collection.

The writer picked out an old favourite, struggling to read the labels in the semi-darkness. Although the Henschke's "Hill of Grace" vintage bottled the year he and Lynn were married was no match for the bigger reds produced in the Barossa Valley more recently, he could rely on its *Syrah* varietal to conjure up some of their more decadent Massif Central exploits.

'Y'know what Cath told me today, angel?' he projected towards the ceiling, hearing the cupboard door's gentle click. 'They want to do a glossy coffee-table edition of our life singular, with more pictures and less adult content.'

His wife's reply was delivered before he reached the study, and he paused with the corkscrew at the ready to absorb its full impact. A symphonic *mélange* of grand proportions set his pulse racing, while the "JL" tattoo almost whistled through his skin.

'You reckon?' the widower chuckled, blowing the dust out of last night's wine glass and then polishing it with his untucked shirt-tail. 'Yep. *Moi aussi, mon amie!* I said I'd think about it. Maybe next year, eh?'

***

'I don't work any harder than a huge number of others who donate their time, energy and money to worthy causes,' Jeff assured the assembled group.

The celebrity wound up his latest press conference at the Addis Ababa Hilton. The lobby was packed with international reporters, and he and his party fought to vacate the *daïs* and check out after another trip to the Ethiopian feeding camps.

Gerry's elder sister had begged him to allow her twin daughters to visit the Diamond Celebration Foundation's facilities, hoping a few confronting encounters might inculcate a greater appreciation for their fortunate circumstances. Two weeks in an alien environment, where the height of urbanity was a hairdryer or a battery-operated music player, the spoiled pair was only just beginning to feel the magic of their host's most venerated place on Earth.

In contrast, the mellowing songwriter found this particular trip more inspiring than usual, embroiled in fiercely honest debates with two journalists whom he knew from his degenerate rock-star days in the company of Hunter S Thompson, who had died by his own gun a few years earlier. Now, with a flood of goodwill from this final engagement fresh in his mind and a few new perspectives to share with a disillusioned and suicidal Melbourne Academy student who was hanging out for his return, the former Sydneysider was ready to surrender the grumbling ingrates.

Also accompanying her boss for the first time was Cathy Lane, by now having clocked up nearly eighteen years' service for Stonebridge Music. He was grateful for her calming influence around the flighty young women. Even she had broken the bounds of discretion after one fractious evening with the double handful, remarking on how lucky he was to have children like Jet and Kierney.

Jeff had shrugged off the poorly-camouflaged compliment at first, but later chose to pass it on to Lynn during their passionate overnight telephone call. It was true, they agreed. They had reared two genuine philanthropists with an intrinsic sense of dignity, who saw the value of hard work and keeping promises.

'Thank you, ladies and gentlemen,' the superstar philanthropist continued, beaming into the array of cameras. 'The only difference is I'm a shameless self-promoter who likes the sound of his own voice. And I'm prepared to use it to stand up for the silent ones.'

The captivated throng clapped, and he urged them to stop when a round of whistling and cheering added to the adulation. 'Listen, guys. We can all do what I do. I've always been a sponge, so if I like the way someone acts or what they say, I steal it and look to improve on it. I'm not the first to tackle the world's difficult problems, and I certainly hope I'm not the last!'

Jacinta's teenagers scoffed at their chaperone as he sunk down into the hotel's threadbare sofa, having shaken his exigent *posse* off his tail after another long day of *spruiking*. Sweaty clumps of sand stuck to his unkempt mane of dark hair, blown by the sweltering wind which had buffeted through the car's open windows on their way back to the hotel. Helping out with irrigation schemes and other manual labour had rendered his jeans and shirt filthy too, even sporting a rip down one arm.

270

'God, you're covered in crap!' Megan screamed, pointing with one of the cracked fingernails she had lamented at full volume a couple of days ago. 'You need to shower and change your clothes.'

Cathy caught her gallant hero's eye and smiled, receiving a lazy wink in return. 'We all do,' she told the twins. 'Let's go and freshen up. Are you hungry?'

Rolling his sleeves up to hide the tear, Jeff exhaled. 'Oh, yeah. I heard Kareem say we're being picked up in an hour. The Oxfam guys're taking us somewhere nice, I'm reliably informed. Let's hope I can stay awake and not embarrass you any further, ladies. You eating more than rice tonight, Robyn?'

The identical girls stood up as one, their grins less forced than at the start of their holiday. They collected their wide-brimmed sunhats and turned towards the lifts, shorts bearing the scars of many hours on hot PVC car seats. The backs of their tennis shoes had been squashed flat to give their feet more air, another indication that the change in their outward appearance corroborated an inner metamorphosis.

The superstar hauled himself out of the couch's quicksand, ushering his marketing manager in front of him. With the twins far enough ahead to be out of earshot, the adults placed bets as to how long it would take them to put this experience behind them and revert to life on the North Shore. The foursome went their separate ways on the landing, agreeing to meet downstairs again in three quarters of an hour.

'You're amazing, you know,' his loyal employee cooed, pausing outside her room. 'Where do you get your energy from? I'm exhausted, and I'm only a tourist on this trip.'

'Yeah, right! Cut the sarcasm, Cath. I'm like a greyhound: manic for twenty minutes every day and then knackered for the other twenty-three hours and forty.'

The mother-of-two laughed out loud. 'I think my sons are part greyhound in that case. I know I've said it a hundred times before, but Lynn's a very lucky lady. Can I tell you what an honour it's been to travel with you?'

As Cathy turned the key, Jeff bent his head and kissed her cheek, catching the door as it swung back on its spring. 'No, you can't,' he snapped. 'See you downstairs.'

Three famine relief specialists funded by the Diamonds' charitable organisation and another two field workers from "Teachers for Peace" were waiting for the Australians when they descended, all dressed for a casual dinner. They were taken to an established colonial-style building on the outskirts of the Ethiopian capital.

Jeff had known the educators for many years, their paths intersecting during several deployments to war-zones and natural disaster locations since the non-government organisation was founded. Two of the aid agency staff, North Africans, attended British universities on DCF scholarships and had credentials coming out of their ears. The third was a guileless recent graduate who joined up straight from college in the American mid-west with an engineering degree and an extreme dose of burning ambition.

The young man took his idol's hand and shook it hard enough to dislocate his elbow, babbling about how fantastic and amazing and inspiring the charity's work in Africa was, not to mention owning a copy of every single album on Stonebridge Music's catalogue. Happy for the outpouring to sustain his flagging spirits, the musician humoured him for a minute or two, before calling a halt and steering the group outside onto the street.

Taking the lead, one of the older men rescued the bemused celebrity and his touring party and took them off in search of the restaurant. They soon found themselves turning into a quiet, leafy avenue which could have been modelled on rural England, complete with meticulously tended flowerbeds and trees trimmed to accommodate drooping telephone lines.

The twins were dolled up to the nines in honour of their repatriation, brightly made-up and doing their best to navigate the uneven terrain in high heels. Their efforts met with the American engineer's approval, drawing his attention from the charismatic rock star to the striking women. Discovering their connection with the great Jeff Diamond presented the perfect opportunity to introduce himself.

'Our uncle's his manager,' Robyn answered. 'It's the first time we've been allowed to travel with him. It's been amazing.'

Ethan nodded. 'I'm sure! Where do you live? Australia, yeah?'

'Yes. We're from Sydney,' Megan got in on the act. 'And where do you live?'

'Right here!' the engineer cried out, sweeping his hands from one side of the street to the other. 'But I'm from Portland, Oregon. It's on the west coast. I've never been to Sydney, but I hear it's great.'

Cathy followed the youngsters' every move. Keeping them out of trouble was part of her brief, a small price to pay for seeing her illustrious leader in action on one of his African escapades. When Jeff had agreed to having the twins tag along, Jacinta and her mother had begged the friendly office manager to run point. It wasn't rocket science to figure out that a roaming pair was bound to be more brazen than each could be alone.

Wondering how long it would be until he had cause to alert Kierney to the same dangers, Jeff had made sure to warn Megan and Robyn when they first arrived that two precocious fifteen-year-olds did not make a sensible thirty-year-old.

His publicity guru had chuckled at yet another priceless example of her boss' incisive, conscience-pricking wit. She stopped short of elucidating in sharp relief the number of impressional women who had fallen at the old Jeff Diamond's feet. These days, perhaps even more readily if that were possible, girls of all ages threw themselves at the new Jeff Diamond with equal abandon, yet with far more civilised consequences.

The lovable rogue, tonight dressed to kill in a crisp cream linen shirt over black pants with a million-dollar sheen, hadn't always behaved like the perfect gentleman when it came to dismissing unwanted advances. The knock-on effect of this emotional detritus, magnified ten-fold once his relationship with Lynn Dyson became the young superstar's sole focus, was the recruitment of a brigade of paid sympathisers to console the flotsam and jetsam of his social adventures.

Over dinner, the aid workers and the man who made their missions possible swapped memories of their travels through refugee camps. They had seen schools in full swing, with fresh running water spurting from wells and green shoots peeping out of fallowed soil. There were also the horrific sights of children wounded by gunfire and women wailing for babies who hadn't survived childbirth. By the sincerity in the twins' reactions, Jeff took heart that their journey hadn't been a complete waste of time.

Cathy had been moved by the scale of the charities' impact too, seeing it on the ground for the first time. Her trip report would provide a fillip to the dedicated team of project managers and fundraisers back in their Melbourne offices. A personal account brought home in amateur photographs would mean so much more to the staff than the professional presentation packs they were used to seeing.

An enjoyable dinner over, the contingent returned to their hotel. Those travelling the next morning needed to pack and catch some shut-eye before an early departure. Raging testosterone unleashed a hot-blooded affinity with the engineer from Oregon, as their host watched him bid the flirtatious but under-aged Australians goodnight. Part of him wished he hadn't given Celia and Jacinta a guarantee for their safety. What harm could befall them with this well-educated college boy? And bedding twins in such an exotic location would serve as a more-than-adequate cure for homesickness!

The absent father's mind harkened back to the confidence he shared with Jet from the previous year. Fortuitously, nothing had come of this adolescent indiscretion. So much for "boys will be boys", he smiled to himself. Watching his manager's nieces fawning over their Yankee suitor, his lifelong suspicions were confirmed that girls were equally complicit in their downfall. He vowed to tell his son that Lynn had been in on their little secret all along. It was only fair.

Robyn and Megan said goodnight to their uncle's famous friend and his assistant outside the hotel bar, unaware he would shadow them all the way to their room regardless. The two veteran field coordinators shared one more drink with their benevolent ambassador before calling it a night, leaving him and Cathy together and alone for the first time since their arrival.

'Can I ask you how things are after the Steve Christie thing? Do you mind me asking?'

Jeff managed a half-smile, alcohol and rich food having sealed his sleepy fate. 'Ah, yeah... I only mind you asking 'cause I promised Lynn I wouldn't talk about it anymore. The subject's closed between us. Mountains and molehills got interchanged temporarily, but we're all good now.'

'How humiliating for him though! Why the heck would you let Lynn go? And what gave him the idea that Lynn'd be more interested in him than you? He must've been so blinkered.'

'You'd think so,' the old soul agreed with a chuckle. 'But I totally get where he's coming from.'

The staid family woman looked alarmed. 'Do you? How come?'

'Human nature, Cath. I know what it feels like to want someone I can't have. You remember that flight I took to Singapore at a moment's notice back in 'seventy-four? The Dysons had hooked Lynn up with some poor French bloke while she was trapped at a tennis tournament.'

'Did they? Wow! I never knew that! What happened?'

'Oh, nothing in the end. Thank Christ. I'll tell you the full story another time, if you get me pissed enough. Anyway... If we want something badly enough... to obsessive proportions, I mean... our mind refuses to entertain anything but the positive outcome. Steve got too obsessed with his manufactured reality, I guess. It's over now. Things'll settle down before long.'

'If you say so! I hope you're right. You're so remarkably calm in your advancing age,' Cathy laughed. 'Sometimes I look back on the old days and remember how frazzled you were. All the time. How dissatisfied and determined to push past everything as quick as you could... Lynn and the kids have really mellowed you, and I'm so jealous of how much you do for them.'

'Cheers, but you wouldn't have used the word "mellow" to describe me when I first heard about Steve's charm offensive,' Jeff countered. 'The stupid *charade* made me pretty fuckin' angry. That's what I meant about getting confused between mountains and molehills. His rationale hit a few raw nerves, I can tell you. I feel so effing guilty about leaving Lynn and the kids alone so much. The whole damned thing was a cautionary tale.'

The sudden switch into the comedian's pronounced Hercule Poirot accent made his offsider chortle. He tipped the last of his whisky down his throat with deliberate aplomb, guessing the libidinous effect it would have on the middle-aged woman. Age had mellowed him; this much was true enough. But he wasn't dead yet. There was still some innocent fun to be had until their aeroplane touched down at Tullamarine Airport.

'Lynn's never complained to me about being left on her own,' his personal assistant promised. 'I'd tell you if she did. And she *has* told me on more than one occasion that you always give her everything she wants. That's a testimony to a happy marriage now, isn't it?'

The songwriter nodded in satisfaction. A superb commendation indeed, refined still further by its passage between two percipient women. He reached for his wallet, which was sitting on the bar in front of him, opened it and pulled out the dog-eared photograph of his beautiful best friend which had kept him company for the past twelve nights. Three years spent globetrotting in his leather jacket hadn't rendered this happy snap any less of a likeness.

'Why wouldn't I give this piece of perfection anything she wants?' he asked, turning the creased and battered picture for his marketing manager to see. 'Jesus, angel... She still has the same effect on me, no matter how many times I look at this! And just as much for what's on the inside, I'll have you know. An exquisite gift of creation who makes this extraordinary life of ours the best it could be.'

Lynn Dyson Diamond was loveliness personified, Cathy admitted. Although no longer at the absolute height of her sporting career, she remained in peak physical condition, often calling into the office after a gruelling session at the Sportsdrome, her radiance needing no cosmetic assistance. Polished elegance and sophistication never masked her natural friendliness, oozing with a simple zest for life and an unwavering devotion to those who shared it.

In her entire length of service, the forty-year-old office manager could recall not a single raised voice or jaundiced opinion expressed by the blonde superstar about the tanked-up tearaway she had married against all possible odds.

Gossip was always rife by the Stonebridge Music water cooler, with some more jaded members of staff scarcely able to believe the flawlessness of the showbusiness family's personal life. After fifteen years of marriage, what if the reason her boss travelled so much betrayed an unwillingness to tackle deeper underlying divisions?

Cathy hoped the beauty in this tiny photograph wouldn't catch her spiteful drift, born out of sheer envy that such a devastatingly handsome, red-blooded male had been sleeping a few doors down the corridor with eyes for one woman alone.

'Did you know some of the girls at work run a book?' the pillar of discretion revealed, a second gin and tonic loosening her lips after several glasses of *champagne*.

'A book, as in betting? For what?'

The longstanding employee gulped, knowing she had made a grave mistake for which she was obligated to providing an explanation. She had managed to keep her lustful thoughts to herself for a fortnight but had weakened on the closing straight. Damn her boss' compelling smile and tantalising physique!

'For when your first act of unfaithfulness comes out in public.'

'Is that right?' the grin vanished from the celebrity's mouth.

'Yes,' Cathy swallowed her words. 'I'm sorry. I shouldn't have told you. It's the alcohol talking.'

'Bloody oath, you shouldn't have told me,' Jeff frowned. 'How long's this book been running? And who do they reckon'll be first to crack, Lynn or me?'

The tipsy woman sighed. 'Gerry says there must have been times when you...'

The statuesque performer drained his whisky tumbler and levered his tall frame to a standing position, pointing to his companion's glass. 'Drink up, Cath, please. Game over.'

'Oh, no. Please don't be angry. I wish I hadn't had so much to drink. It's our last night away, and I've had such a fantastic time. I'm so sorry, Jeff. Do you want me to resign?'

Cathy was close to tears. Her employer stood back, chivalrous to the last, inviting her to walk ahead of him. Inscrutable eyes were fixed on the lift doors across the *foyer* while the publicity specialist chastised herself inwardly. Her limbs felt robotic and stiff as she tried not to stumble out of the bar, the shock of her nauseous predicament causing her to perspire. What a terrible way to end such an enlightening junket... She was sure she had ruined her professional reputation and jeopardised a valuable personal relationship with one loose-lipped, tacky *exposé*.

'Nope,' the deep, smoky baritone resonated against the back of her skull. 'Of course I don't want you to resign. I'd be incredibly *naïve* to assume our friends in the office are immune to the same scandal fever that everyone else appears to be suffering from. Although it's bloody irritating to hear it from you here, in what I thought was a somewhat convivial situation.'

'I know. I should've kept my mouth shut.'

'Quite apart from dobbing Gerry in,' the billionnaire continued. 'He should fucking well know better than to air his private voyeuristic opinions with you guys. But whatever... If the bloke wants to hang himself, Cath, he clearly doesn't need your help.'

The pair stepped out of the lift when the doors opened on the second floor. Reaching her room, the dejected woman turned to face the man she had seen go from talented drunken waster to proud husband and father. His dark, sunken eyes were so familiar, bloodshot from the exhaustion of being continually in the spotlight, and the muscles encasing his jaws rippled with tension, as if he were having trouble reining in his temper.

'Jeff, I'm really sorry,' she reiterated. 'I'll offer to resign again in the morning. You might've reconsidered by then.'

'For Christ's sake! I won't reconsider,' the great man forced a smile. 'Forget it ever happened. I'm all in favour of having fun with the troops, don't get me wrong... But just don't make it public, please? Not even to me, and especially not to Lynn. What you guys think of our business is none of our business, if you get my drift. And much as I enjoy your company, Missus Lane, it's not going to be the two of us drinking together late at night who cause some eavesdropping reporter to hit the jackpot.'

Cathy let out a nervous titter. The generous artist whom her staff adored had demonstrated once again that his *ego* was under control and that he was prepared to take a joke at his own expense. They both knew he was way out of her league, yet it was nice of him to suggest the prospect.

'Have a good night, Jeff. Thanks for being so understanding. I'll apologise to Lynn too, when we get home.'

The celebrity was flexing his heels, edging closer to his own door, and raised his left hand in a lukewarm farewell. 'Lynn doesn't need to know. She puts up with enough of my shit as it is. G'night, Cath. See you at six-thirty. I'll ring the girls and get them up in time. Sleep well.'

Maiastra

'You should see him when he arrives at a hospital or a refugee camp,' Cathy Lane waxed lyrical to her colleagues. 'People hang around him all the time. All kinds of people. And kids! Kids everywhere! They just want to sit and talk to him for hours, and he's so polite when he can't stay. He's like this unstoppable force blowing in and out of their lives.'

The mood had been tense in the taxi on the way to the airport in Addis Ababa, owing to Megan's last-minute packing for the most part. She kept them all waiting for an extra twenty minutes, overtaken by an urge to photograph surroundings that had failed to impress her until the morning of departure.

Paragon Holdings' Chairman and his marketing manager knuckled down to work during the first leg of their journey, determined to get a head-start on the media releases which Monday's newspapers would expect them to produce. The repentant woman made two attempts to re-open the discussion about her resignation, only to be quashed both times.

By the time lunch was served, there was barely any residue of the previous night's awkward parting. Cathy felt grateful that her powerful employer valued her highly enough to forgive and forget so soon. Guilty thoughts caused her heart rate to surge whenever she estimated the number of worthy candidates desperate for a job like hers.

From Jeff's perspective however, he still hadn't quite got his head around the merits of forgiveness. Instead, the lost boy ruled a line in his assistant's ledger, thereby giving the impression that all was forgotten. It came to the same thing for all intents and purposes. Catherine Patterson, as her *résumé* had cited back then, had arrived fresh from university and soon became a vital cog in Stonebridge Music's wheel of fortune. It was difficult to conceive of anyone else running the giant publishing house which now supported so many writers, musicians and performing artists.

The senior employee was ebullient and animated in her first all-hands meeting since returning to the office. Recounting their trip in minute detail, she was keen to use her extra life to inspire the team. She explained how their figurehead would respect the day's loose agenda up to a point, always deferring to the host, even though no-one was ever in any doubt as to who was in charge.

'There's nothing *prima donna* about the way Jeff works,' she said. 'Whether we were in the DCF office in town or out in the middle of nowhere, he just rolls his sleeves up and gets on with what needs doing. When I asked him if he minds doing the manual labour... and some of it's pretty gross, like unblocking drains, for example... he looked at me as if I was a complete idiot and said, "This is what control freaks do!"'

The company's headcount had grown so enormous that the circle of attentive employees ran three deep in the open area next to the kitchen; four or five in places. Everyone laughed at this last comment, none having difficulty imagining the bloke with the common touch mucking in with the volunteers, most probably leading the chorus too.

'So thank God for control freaks!' Cathy added, before sending the enraptured people back to their posts.

Later that same afternoon, who should turn up at Stonebridge Music's offices but Lynn Dyson Diamond herself. Despite her promise not to mention her *faux pas* on the couple's fidelity, the contrite woman felt compelled to make amends. She had avoided checking in with Jeff on the matter after arriving back in Melbourne, but she remained plagued by embarrassment and cringed every time the episode pushed its way to the foreground of her mind.

Cathy suggested they take a coffee break after spending an hour catching up on correspondence and synchronising the next month's diary appointments. One tall and slender, and the other not so much of either measure, the pair descended to ground level and strolled along Flinders Lane, aiming to pick a *café* at random. The usual *mêlée* of workers from nearby buildings had dispersed, given the fact that the sun was past most people's yard-arm for caffeine tolerance.

'Lynn, I just wanted to say how amazing it was to travel with Jeff,' the office manager began. 'It opened my eyes to how hard you both work when you're overseas. He's so clever on his feet, isn't he? Wherever we went, he had the crowds eating out of his hand.'

The Olympian smiled. 'Oh, great. That's good. Yes, he does know how to command a room! Thanks for saying so. We really appreciate everything you do too, by the way. Was it harrowing over there this time? I was hoping things had got better, but Jeff mentioned there are still pockets of fighting that spring up sporadically.'

'We did see heaps of injured children,' she affirmed. 'I was surprised how hard-nosed he was with some of the people there though. I never think of him as overly assertive.'

The patient woman smiled. 'Oh, he can be pretty demanding when the need arises. What are you referring to?'

'Oh, for example, when he doesn't get the information he's looking for, or it seems like people don't care enough. Like the headmaster of one of the schools... Jeff asked him about attendance figures, and it was funny to see him dance around on the defensive before admitting he didn't have them.'

'Yes,' Lynn chuckled. 'Jeff's more than capable of playing the authoritarian when he chooses. I remember once, when we were there together, he thought the water supply was contaminated. He's got very keen senses, as I'm sure you know. He couldn't convince anyone to test it, and the man in charge kept assuring him it was fine. Eventually, he found someone who could test it, and it turned out there were high levels of several trace elements and fertiliser in the camp's drinking water.'

'He always gets what he wants though,' the couple's long-time associate added.

The blonde smiled. 'Usually. He knows when to stop.'

'Does he do it to you and the kids?'

'Do what?'

'Not give up until you give in.'

The steadfast wife considered her response for a few seconds. Why had Cathy asked? It seemed a strangely invasive question from someone who was not prone to passing judgement on her superiors. Perhaps she had seen signs of Jeff's lingering vulnerability during their fortnight in Ethiopia, traits he normally managed to obscure from view. It was also most unlike her husband to let his guard down, even with someone he had known for so many years. Was he trying to get his own back for the instability she and Steve Christie had inflicted on their happiness?

'Depends what he's after,' Lynn kept her options open. 'You make it sound a bit sinister. Did Megan and Robyn push him too far or something? It's pretty hard to make him lose his rag these days, but he does find those two annoying sometimes. He calls them "the matching *mesdemoiselles*."'

The older woman laughed. 'Yes. Well, I couldn't tell them apart most of the time. He's good with them. They were a bit painful on the morning we were coming home, messing around. We cut it fine for our flight because they were acting up, so Jeff was a little exasperated by the time we finally got in the taxi.'

Lynn nodded. 'Doesn't surprise me.'

'I just wonder what it must be like to live with someone who's so driven, that's all,' Cathy continued. 'He's so passionate about everything, and he loves you so deeply, so fervently. Every time your name comes up, or one of the children's, his eyes glaze over and he loses concentration for a split-second. It's so nice to see. I wish my husband would do that even once!'

'I know,' the thirty-five-year-old agreed. 'He certainly never forgets us, that's for sure. As our 'phone bills reflect! We're very in-tune with each other.'

'Really? Don't you ever want something different from what he wants?'

The singer raised her eyebrows. 'Occasionally, but rarely on the big stuff. Is that what you were getting at? About him not giving up until I give in? He's perfectly willing to listen, if that's what you're wondering.'

'Hmm... I s'pose so,' the assistant was beginning to think she had overstepped her authority again.

'Conversations are never one-way in our house. That's one thing Jeff hates. Half the time, I think people we work with are too scared to stand up to him, but he'd much prefer to have a solid, constructive argument than to be surrounded by yes-men and -women. He can't abide brown-nosers, as I'm sure you know too!'

'Definitely!' Cathy smiled, relieved to hear all appeared well behind the Diamond family's closed doors.

Lynn ordered a second round of coffees. 'That was pretty good, don't you think?'

'Yes. Another place to add to the list on the staff noticeboard.'

'You know, I obviously can't see what other people see,' the sportswoman relaxed, stretching her long legs under the table. 'My mum always criticises me for not being stronger; not standing up for myself with Jeff. But I don't have to. She won't believe me, but it's true. Honestly, all it takes is one word, one look, one tiny hint... Life's no trial living with him anymore. It used to be tricky sometimes, when we were first married. It took us both a while to get on top of his web of addictions while he was still trying to figure himself out.'

'Oh, yes,' Cathy sighed. 'I can hardly remember those days now. I told him while we were away this time that age had mellowed him.'

'Did you? That was brave of you! How did he react? He doesn't like it when people suggest he's losing his jagged edges.'

'He was fine about it,' the star's personal assistant thought back to what had triggered the aberration she was desperate to put behind her. 'I asked him about Steve Christie and how you two were after the *fiasco* that followed. He said he'd promised you he wouldn't talk about it.'

It was Lynn's turn to fall into a sentimental trance. Discovering that her faraway husband heeded her word even with one of his closest friends held significant meaning, and again Cathy was envious. How often did two such important individuals maintain each other as their absolute priority? And therefore, she ought never to have contemplated a rift in this harmonious union.

'That's nice to hear,' the dignified musician answered. 'Actually, I don't think it's age that's mellowed him. And you're welcome to talk about this with him, by the way... We do, regularly. I think youth freaked him out. If he'd had a normal childhood, he and I both assume he'd have always been pretty chilled. He understands how life works so intimately that not much fazes him. These days are easy with Jeff and the kids. Exciting and all-consuming, but extremely natural. I feel totally loved.'

'Oh, you are totally loved,' Cathy confirmed. 'He gets your photo' out of his wallet at every opportunity, and kisses it when he talks about you. And the one of Jet and Kierney too.'

Lynn swooned, smiling and clutching her heart in jest. 'Ahh! That's so sweet! Jeff doesn't do anything for a quiet life or so I'll give him more latitude. He's not that type of person. Things are very simple in his book: there are trades, investments and *pro bono*. He puts the right amount of energy into each interaction.

'When we first knew each other, his world consisted only of trades. Everything had a price. Then we graduated to a series of investments, when we paid forward to create something bigger for the future, like Childlight or African peace and famine relief. And then for Jeff, his family's utterly *pro bono*. Making the four of us happy is a not-for-profit business as far as he's concerned, and we'll always be his highest priority. No question. He treats me and the children so well because it's all done out of love.'

A stiff breeze had whipped up while the two women explored the Diamonds' delightful world, and the air temperature had plummetted several degrees. While fishing in her purse for some cash to pay for their coffees, the celebrity's fingernails dragged a small picture of her husband out, as if not to be outdone by her hopeless romantic. It had been taken on *Escondido*'s deck without his knowledge, and showed him dreaming up a new song or mulling over the day's achievements. In side profile, he had been caught in quiet contemplation, a cigarette in one hand and a half-finished glass of red on the table.

'Oh, that's a gorgeous photo'! You guys should write all your secrets down,' the publicist suggested. 'Tips for a happy marriage. Something else you could launch via The Fellowship, seeing there are so many people who go there after their relationships break down.'

'Good idea,' Lynn replied. 'We are planning to do that actually. Jeff's already started, and I've got heaps of material. He wrote a similar outline a few years ago, just before his dad died. I don't even know what happened to it. And, while we're talking about The Fellowship, it *is* time we re-focussed more on depression. We've been meaning to speak to you about a new event.'

The pair gathered their belongings and waved to the *café*'s owner. They crossed over the narrow road and headed for the rear entrance of 333 Collins Street, the athlete's lithe legs making light work of the stone steps.

'Sure. Sounds interesting,' Cathy nodded, having to lengthen her stride to keep pace. 'That'll be fun for the team to organise. It's always so hard for me to imagine how someone so outwardly gregarious and positive can suffer from depression. Surely Jeff's not depressed nowadays? What could he possibly have to be depressed about?'

The compassionate wife checked her watch, not too keen to discuss her man's unending private battles with their employees, regardless of their tenure. 'That's a dangerous assumption, I'm afraid,' she cautioned. 'Illnesses like depression and PTSD never go away. They're made worse when you have something getting you down, but even in the happy times, they're still there lurking and ready to pounce on the slightest dip. You either have depression or you don't. There are plenty of people who experience bad things without getting depressed. And there are just as many who suffer from depression despite having nothing specific to trigger it. Jeff's in the latter camp.'

'Oh… Sorry, Lynn,' Cathy said. 'I don't understand these problems well enough.'

'And you'd better not call depression a "problem" around Jeff,' the tennis champion jumped in, grinning. 'He'd say the word "problem" sounds as if it's easily fixed, like oiling a squeaky door hinge or some household appliance on the blink.'

Laughing at the amusing analogy, the women paused their conversation while they ascended in the lift to the twelfth floor, where Stonebridge Music had shifted into more spacious accommodation. In the short journey from the lobby, Lynn had signed her autograph into six people's Filofaxes.

'I always thought depression came on when you suffer some traumatic event in your life,' the plump office manager resumed.

'Yes. It does for most people. But it's also way more complicated than that.'

'Oh, is it? I had no idea.'

'There's so many variants of depression-type illnesses,' the superstar said. 'It usually manifests itself after some sort of traumatic event, as you say, but it's more likely just a trigger for a genetic persuasion you're born with. No-one knows for sure. Chicken or egg?'

Shutting themselves into a meeting room to continue Cathy's education, Lynn smiled at the blank expression on her face. 'Jeff's theory is that all mental illness is latent inside certain people, in the same way as others are naturally musical or have another talent of some kind. What makes it so hard to manage is that once it's unleashed, there doesn't seem to be any easy method of stopping it taking hold. They have to learn to control it, and it can take ages to master.'

'So Jeff's learned to control his PTSD. Is that it?'

'Learning, he'd say,' the blonde smiled. 'It still smashes him around a bit, especially when he comes home from overseas trips. Like today, in fact. According to the research he and Sarah Friedman have been doing at MIT, it seems these latent talents often occur in groups. For example, it's pretty common for artistic people to suffer from mood-related disorders, and for sporty people to have extreme anxiety. Jeff's always argued the greater the genius, the higher the likelihood of mental illness, and it looks like he may be onto something.'

'Wow,' the couple's assistant murmured. 'That's mind-boggling. I never knew any of this. You don't suffer from one of these illnesses too, do you?'

Australia's most celebrated female sports star shook her head. 'No. But thanks for asking. I'm not a natural genius, you see. Not like Jeff. He says Dysons aren't born, they're manufactured.'

Cathy howled. 'I've heard him say that before! I never thought to ask what he meant. I thought it was just a beat-up on your dad.'

'Well, now you know! It is also a beat-up on my dad. It appears my so-called talents aren't talents at all. They were honed through years and years of repetition, and now my brain and body just follow orders. Dad agrees with him. The Dyson movement's based on taking young kids with the right physical attributes and temperament and turning them into champions. Nothing to do with natural talent. Whereas the people Jeff describes as genii have brains full of what he calls free radicals, searching for something new all the time.'

'Gosh! I'm flabbergasted,' the administrator exhaled. 'I need to read up on all this. I feel bad that I've never taken more of an interest. I've always focussed on the music and movies, *et cetera*.'

'Don't worry about it. You've had your hands full with Colin's autism. I expect you know heaps about that!' Lynn nodded, knowing her husband despaired at how few people acknowledged the more serious side of his career. 'I'd better go soon. Kierney'll be home before me at this rate. Jeff says that intelligent kids... hyperactive minds which are left unattended, like in his case in a hopeless family situation... their brain cells are much more likely to become messed up.'

'Oh! Hence The Good School!'

'No, not really. The Good School's for young leaders, which is a whole 'nother thing,' the celebrity laughed kindly. 'You know, some mornings, it still takes Jeff two hours to get out of bed?'

'No! Two hours? How come?' Cathy yelped, the penny dropping that she had scarcely penetrated the surface of her complex travelling companion's personality in the entire time she had known him. 'Jeez!'

'It's true! We've got things pretty well worked out though. If he's particularly down, we'll make early appointments because he's so committed that there's no way he'd miss them. He's too honourable and doesn't want to let people down, so that makes him get up.'

The executive assistant nodded. Here was a side of her boss she recognised. The Diamonds were nothing if not committed to their work.

'To be truthful, accepting mental illness for better or worse is one of the things that've made our marriage as strong as it is,' Lynn finished, picking up her handbag and wrapping her fingers around the door handle. 'And I mean that. It's made us delve so deeply into what makes each other tick, it's no longer a case of taking each other for granted. I think we'd be wrong not to, in a way, however. I gave up thinking that being with Jeff's too good to be true about a year after we got married. It is good and it is true.'

***

Jet was all fired up, jogging through the school gates on the Friday before his dad's bumper birthday bash. He ripped the Land Rover's cargo door open, threw in four bags and tossed his blazer on top. While his mother bemoaned another week's worth of laundry, imagining the sweat-drenched sports gear smeared with grass stains and dried mud, Kierney teased him for waving at a group of girls loitering at the entrance for their own parental pick-ups.

The family had planned fish and chips at sunset to wind down from their hectic weeks, and Melbourne's volatile weather patterns obliged with a mild evening, only the slightest of breezes in the air. Jeff had gone ahead to secure a spot at the southern end of Elwood beach, where people walking their dogs were the only passing trade. They could never be guaranteed freedom from molestation in their hometown, but sought out the more isolated locations where fans would least expect to find celebrities on a rare night off.

The lad and his classmates had attended an after-school seminar given by a Catholic priest who had been engaged to create debate around religious beliefs. He couldn't wait to tell his parents how the discussion had unearthed petty bigotry in his fellow students which he hadn't anticipated, and how those whom he thought would care less about religion had shown themselves to be outrageously opinionated.

'Excellent,' his mother smiled. 'Must've been a dynamite session. It's great to hear you being so analytical about things. This program's doing you a lot of good, Jetto.'

The boy would soon turn fifteen, edging six feet tall. His parents had witnessed a marked change in behaviour since returning to school for Year Eleven and having been made captain of the Australia A cricket team. The carefree and suggestible teenager of the previous term was fast becoming a flourishing intellectual. Like his sister, he now found himself with more questions than answers, a state which exasperated and intrigued in equal measure.

'There he is!' Kierney yelped, spotting the Aston Martin parked with its nose in some gorse bushes near the footpath. 'May I ring him, *Mamá*? To find out which bench he's on?'

Lynn reversed the Discovery into the space next-door while the young girl used her mother's mobile telephone. With the handset jammed between her shoulder and her ear, she helped her brother retrieve the piping hot paper packages and the other mandatory ingredients for their typical Australian meal: tomato sauce and cold beer.

Pouncing on the signs of a ripening mind, the Diamonds had enrolled Jet into The Good School, scarcely able to believe that one of their own offspring was now old enough to attend their mile-high brainchild. The opportunity came with a workload that had overwhelmed the fun-loving teenager initially. Yet, calling upon his Dyson drive, he tackled it with enthusiasm and soon fell under the program's spell. It had also offered a chance to try his wings without his grandfather's watchful eye trained on him daily.

Jeff rubbed his hands together, sporting a maniacal grin as he walked towards his son, who looked at him sideways. This could only mean trouble! The student overheard his sister describing his indignant attitude while on the telephone. It was over eighteen months since his Bathurst *bar mitzvah*, and the trust developed over that weekend had transformed Sorprendo the Marvellous into an enquiring mind.

Sure enough, strong hands clamped onto the boy's shoulders and jerked him into a bear-hug. 'Alright! I'm so ready for this! *Ça marche encore!*' he exclaimed.

'What's started?' Jet asked. 'You look like a lunatic.'

'Yeah? That may be because I *am* a lunatic, mate,' his father replied. 'But a very happy one. Tell us more. Word-for-word, please.'

'Word-for-word? Bloody hell! You don't ask for much,' the teenager scoffed. 'Mainly, we all said we could write a book like the Bible, 'cause it's just a collection of short stories.'

The songwriter nodded. 'We all could. Many people did.'

'Who wrote the Bible?' Kierney piped up from the other side of the picnic table, where she had been picking through hot chips absentmindedly, unable to draw her nose out of a new book. 'Should I already know that?'

'I don't know, darling. Was it attributed to anyone in particular?' her mother added to the rhetoric.

Jeff shook his head. 'They don't know for sure. There are plenty of theories, but no-one can be certain. All too long ago, I guess. That's something to investigate in your time-travel experiments, mate. Put them to some good sociological purpose.'

The science-fiction nut laughed. 'Nah. Boring. I'd rather find out what stories people are going to write in the future, and then bring them back and make money on them.'

'Jetto!' his sister cried out. 'That's stealing! Tell him he can't do that, *Papá*!'

While the cricketer's horizons were expanding along the vertical axis, assimilating the *nuances* of a spiritual awakening, Kierney had begun to pick apart the vagaries of common law. She displayed an innate grasp of donation, acquisition and remuneration, and had taken her elders to task several times recently on what constituted a possession.

'Don't panic, *pequeñita*,' her dad urged. 'Did I already tell you I was contacted by the New South Wales police yesterday?'

'No!' Jet shouted. 'What've you done?'

'Nothing, Your Honour,' the son of a double murderer sneered, raising his right hand. 'In fact, quite the opposite. The cops are putting pressure on me to turn informant.'

'So I heard. On whom?' his wife was stunned. 'What brought it on, did they tell you?'

Jeff sighed, gritting his teeth as Gravity dealt him a swift kick. 'I have no idea, angel. Jet's lecture reminded me. It's like being a priest in a confessional, although with a greater security threat. It appears my criminal past finally has some value. The cops believe the guys up there'd think I wouldn't grass 'em up.'

'Would you?' his son asked, fascinated.

'I don't know. What d'*ya* reckon, mate?'

'I reckon you wouldn't.'

Their daughter's eyebrows almost leaped off her face. 'But you should, *Papá*. They're horrible men who only care about themselves.'

This disquieting piece of news had come to light during a conference call with the security firm Gerry kept on retainer. Lynn had been alone in the city apartment at the time, none too pleased at having to revisit her husband's gangland past. The Jaworskis had vanished from their life long ago, and since Alberto had sold the thriving boxing club to a fitness franchise, Madalena was their only remaining link to western Sydney.

'That's right, Kizzy,' she said. 'We can do without thinking about all that again.'

'You know what I've always wondered...' the young girl asked.

'What's that, *pequeñita*?'

Closing her book with a pen sticking out of the top, marking her page, Kierney slipped off her chair to join the others in feeding the remains of their dinner to the seagulls. 'If Jesus rose from the dead at Easter, why don't we know what he did for the rest of his life? Where did he go?'

'He got a job at the Post Office,' her brother crowed. 'Good, stable employment. No stress.'

Lynn laughed. 'Highly blasphemous, guys, but I have no sensible answer. Isn't he supposed to have died again? Rose up to Heaven to be with God?'

'Yep,' Jeff nodded. 'Gone without a trace. Ronnie Biggs managed it too. Perhaps Jesus nicked off to a tropical paradise surrounded by nubile cocktail waitresses too. Not a bad result, all things considered. That reminds me of the time you mixed up "catechism" and "cataclysm" in front of Celia, Jetto. D'you remember? Your version of events made a lot more sense than hers.'

'Who's Ronnie Biggs?' his son warbled, attracted to the combination of crime and exotic setting.

'The Great Train Robbery, mate. A gang of English blokes held up a train carrying the day's post. Going from Glasgow to London, I think it was, in the early 'sixties. There's a film about it, so we should rent it sometime.'

'Didn't he come to Melbourne for a while?' Lynn asked. 'Before ending up in Rio? His whole family came. They lived in Doncaster, I seem to remember.'

Their conversation had come full circle, the songwriter rued. It was his own fault! He had sought to move on from his nefarious connections, only to swerve straight round to the criminal world again. Why was it that he felt no less disparaged at being asked to turn informant than when reminded of his father's iniquity.

Also interesting to note was how the billionnaire still upheld a certain loyalty to the Jaworski family who, at his behest, abandoned their aim of exacting revenge for their fathers' murders at the hands of Diamond Senior. Honour among thieves? If so, he ought to keep his side of the bargain. He didn't want to test the strength of their resolve and put his loved ones' remarkable lives at risk.

'Yeah. Think you're right, angel. Anyway, back to holier matters. Celia looked ready to blow a head gasket when you described your religious education as a cataclysm. It would've been a stroke of comic genius if you'd had half a bloody clue what you were saying!'

Both adults laughed. No wonder people were warned against discussing religion and politics at important social gatherings. It was a minefield with a couple of early teens, and was only set to worsen.

'Dad,' Jet piped up again. 'Here's something you might be interested in...'

The rock star pushed aside the pile of overdue paperwork he had opened while staking out his territory and turned to where his son was pointing. 'Ah, yeah? What's that?'

'In Chinese, the word "crisis" is made up of two characters: "danger" and "opportunity". That's clever. See? Here...'

'Hey! That *is* interesting,' the intrepid peacemaker agreed, leaning over and scanning the text book the boy was showing him. 'It's a pretty constructive way of looking at things; positive change born out of disaster. Cheers, mate. I need to work out how to incorporate that into my preachings. Err, I mean secular rants. Sorry, Celia.'

Again Jet sniggered. 'Maybe they had a Bible-writing competition on the back of a cereal packet. Send in your favourite memories of God, and we'll put it all together. Then for Part Two they said, "Send in your stories about Jesus."'

'Jetto,' his dad warned. 'We shouldn't disrespect the Bible. A lot of good's done in the name of religion, even though it's not religion that does anything *per se*. It's mostly people motivated to do good because someone's rallied them together. It just happens to have a motive based in religion.'

'Absolutely. I agree,' Lynn said. 'The same method as we used for the "Together, Forever, Wherever" campaigns. Still trying to achieve the same thing, but without the religious overtones.'

Jeff was stoked to hear his wife advocating their dream. 'However the Bible came about, and whether or not you believe its short stories are actually true stories, it's an important book in the world's history.'

'Same for all the other religious texts,' Lynn agreed, seeing their children nodded in contrition. 'The Koran, the Torah...'

'Wisden,' the irreverent comic proffered without looking up.

'Wisden?' his wife repeated. 'Isn't that the cricket annual? You used that one on me before, ages ago!'

'Yep. Sure did. And your point is? It's an important religious text for some people; for cricket tragics.'

'Yeah! For me!' Jet insisted. 'But we know the authors of Wisden at least. Not like the mish-mash of short stories in the Bible. Aren't they just guides for how to behave?'

From his position on the grass, where he had begun to read the newspaper spread out on a rug, Jeff lay down and stared at the darkening sky. His son's comments called to mind an episode from his childhood which came flooding back, demanding to be made public.

'That's so true, mate. You're spot on with that particular observation. I had the same discussion with an Anglican priest one day, at the SCG.'

Jet almost choked on his Coca-Cola. 'At the cricket? How could you dream of talking about God when there was cricket to watch? Sacrilege! You should never've been allowed to get an MCG membership after that.'

'Watch it!' the Olympian scolded their son. 'Your dad only got his MCG membership because of you!'

'Thanks, angel,' the intellectual smiled, rolling onto his side and propping himself up on one elbow. 'I must've been fifteen or so. About your age, Jetto. I went with a bunch of mates from school to the test match. It was India that year. We thrashed 'em, I seem to recall.'

'Course *ya* did,' Kierney interjected before her brother could, in a fit of innocent giggles.

'Steady...' their father frowned. 'Not everyone's a winner, remember? Whatever... We'd been drinking since we got there, and I was bored with my mates' idiotic clowning around, so I tuned in on a conversation between family members who were a few rows in front of us. One of the men turned out to be an Anglican priest, so I decided to worm my way into their *milieu*.'

'Did you? How?' his daughter asked. 'Weren't they total strangers?'

Jeff sighed, catching his wife's attentive blue eyes which were eager for the same answer. 'Sure, but that's how I was when I was your age, *pequeñita*. Didn't give a shit about what people thought. If I wanted to do something, I just did it. At first, his wife tried to shoo me away 'cause I must've looked like trouble, with a tin of beer in my hand and most likely sounding pretty much off my face.'

Lynn listened to the teenaged confession, attempting to transport herself back to the late nineteen-sixties. It wasn't hard to picture the tall, lanky teenager she had seen in photographs in the Blakes' den. How she wished she had known him then too! She would have had a deeper understanding of the metamorphosis he had undergone from reprobate manchild to world-changer *extraordinair*.

'The vicar shut his wife down,' the storyteller scoffed. 'I must've piqued his interest as a soul worth saving, or something like that.'

'You were even the Pied Piper then!' Kierney chuckled, shuffling off the bench to join to her father at ground level.

'Ah, yeah. Guess so. Hook 'em in and don't let 'em go. In those days, I never let anyone get away 'til I'd managed to extract everything I needed. I remember asking the vicar who he thought was responsible for putting the Bible together. If anyone should've known, it should be him, 'cause he must've studied theology. He couldn't come up with anything remotely convincing, so I asked him if the Bible was an account of real-life events or a work of fiction. The rest of his family didn't find my intervention at all funny, but to his credit, he was up for the debate.'

Jet chuckled. 'The cricket must've been in a lull. Was it just after lunch or something?'

'Perhaps, mate. Yeah. I think it might've been. I said I always reckoned the Bible must be based on a true story, like movies purport to be. He initially took this as heresy and started chastising me as if I were one of his Sunday-schoolers, but I didn't let up. Probably the drink, on top of my usual arsehole determination.

'He asked me which religion I identified with, so I told him my father was Jewish and my mother Catholic, but that I hadn't been brought up in either. He gave me an all-knowing, supercilious smile; the kind that middle-classed people always dole out when they realise they were right about which side of the tracks I come from.'

Conveniently, Lynn's eyes were averted when her lost boy lobbied for pity, causing a smirk to streak across his countenance. *Good on her*, he thought. She never missed a chance to coach him out of feeling sorry for himself.

'So I saw red, as I always did in response to anyone who assumed some form of superiority.'

'You don't say!' the elegant women laughed. 'I'm just trying to picture you in those days; becoming a man so far before your time. I wish I'd known you in that raw state. The real deal, without the restraint you used to put on for me.'

The redeemed musician shook his head. 'Oh, you saw me pretty raw, angel,' he countered. 'Anyway, I went for the sixty-four million dollar question.'

'What was that?' Kierney wondered.

Jeff sat cross-legged, almost trance-like in his retrospective. 'I asked him if he reckoned that men who were outwardly celibate made better "men of the cloth" than those with a normal sex life and living as conventional married couples. You should've seen his wife's face! She was disgusted; came out with all sorts of insults: "You drunken layabout"; "Dirty-minded good-for-nothing"; *blah, blah, blah*... You get what I mean.

'But I guess this bloke truly had a calling, because he cut her short again and persevered in trying to convert me. Y'know... Like Celia does. "The Lord works in mysterious ways," or "You may not think he's listening, but he's just biding his time until you really need him." Then after a few minutes, his wife told him not to bother and that I only wanted to know about sex, to which I replied, "Actually, that's not true. I already know everything I need to know about sex, thanks."'

The others laughed. Although Lynn's expression gave nothing away, her telepathic endorsement left scorch marks *en route* to her husband's heart. Far from being ashamed at having revealed a tendency so base to his children, as perhaps he ought to have been, he rolled onto his back to lose himself in the blanket of stars now twinkling above the city.

'She asked if I'd ever picked up a copy of the Bible, let alone read it.'

'You had, hadn't you?' Jet grinned.

'Yep. I wouldn't have lied, mate. I started off genuinely interested in speaking to this guy, but anger had flipped my mind by this time, and I just wanted to see how far I could rile his condescending bitch of a wife. So dual benefit! I said I hadn't read it cover to cover but I had read substantial chunks of it.'

Kierney exchanged smiles with her mother, whose frown at the green light to be disrespectful had been replaced by apparent approval.

'I bet she hadn't expected you to say "substantial chunks",' the patient woman said.

The lyricist shrugged. 'Probably not. I didn't notice any reaction. I told them that, to me, the Bible was like a code of conduct. Y' know... A set of rules, but bloody long ones! Like companies have to give their employees guidelines to avoid getting the boot. Just as you intimated earlier, Captain Marvellous.'

The teenager puffed his chest out. 'So what did the priest say to that?' he asked. 'Was he angry? The man speaking tonight was, which annoyed me.'

'Really?' Lynn replied. 'That's disappointing. Speakers at these sessions aren't supposed to be oppositional. The whole idea is to open the students' minds.'

'*Cierto*, angel. We may need to reinforce that message. But no, Jetto. My cricket-loving priest was pretty cool about it. I remember him laughing, much to his wife's disgust. And at that point, I knew I had the upper hand.'

'Wicked,' his fellow school governor muttered under her breath. 'And in one so young... Where was your respect, Diamond?'

'In my beer bottle,' he leered, pretending to raise a toast. 'So I pursued the argument, postulating that the Bible was the policy manual for belonging to the human race, from a Christian point of view, and he agreed with me. I was gobsmacked that he agreed so readily, to be honest. It was rare for someone in authority to validate my opinion. Didn't happen too often where I came from.'

Neither expecting nor receiving any sympathy from his tough crowd, the orator crunched his abdominal muscles and pulled himself up to a seated position. He could almost hear the dull roar of the Sydney Cricket Ground in the nether reaches of his memory while he began to count on his fingers.

'It went like this, guys... I even stood up, I think, to reinforce my point, arrogant arsehole that I was! I suggested there were the terms of engagement, i.e. the gospels. Pure preaching. And then the parables were case studies; *scenaria* for showing people how to interpret the gospels. Practical examples, if you like, of how to live. Making it real, and all that.'

'*Howzat!*' his son cheered. 'That's awesome! I wish you'd been there tonight. Some of us tried to say things like that, but it sounds so much better with the words you choose. I need to learn some of these killer phrases. We did say "real examples" though.'

'Cheers, mate,' Jeff accepted his son's compliment. 'The vicar asked if I felt more Catholic or more Jewish, to which I said, "Catholic as a kid but more Jewish now."'

His wife chuckled. 'Did you tell him about your *bar mitzvah*?'

'Err, no,' the larrikin smiled. 'Thought better of it.'

'And your joke about being circumcised or baptised? One of the greatest chat-up lines of all time.'

Outdoor adventures always a welcome distraction from the frenetics of his day job, this evening spent in the fresh air was emitting a most life-affirming undercurrent of love for the intrepid wanderer. 'Angel, remind me to thank you for that later... No, I didn't throw that one in either. I would've if I'd thought of it though. Damn!'

Kierney's jaw had dropped. 'What joke about being circumcised or baptised?'

'Never you mind, *pequeñita*,' her father grinned. 'Something for another day.'

Jet couldn't contain himself. He had been gifted this story a while ago, told during one of many man-to-man chats, appealing to his adolescent sense of humour.

'Ha! I know this!'

'Go on then,' Lynn shook her head in mock frustration, seeing the teenager was desperate for permission to push the bounds of decency. 'If you must.'

'When Mum asked you whether you were Catholic or Jewish, when you only just met each other... And you asked her back, "Do you mean was I baptised or circumcised?" And she said, "Which is it then?"'

Even after a few seconds' pause, Kierney was no closer to deciphering the riddle. 'So what?' What's the joke?'

The original victim of this snag of schoolboy humour dispatched to the annals of time gave her daughter a kindly smile, to which the young girl pouted.

At sixteen, she remembered the mortification of being so *naïve* in the company of her worldly boyfriend. Yet twenty years later, she was pleased their own little lady still had plenty of growing up ahead of her.

'Perfect answer, *pequeñita*,' Jeff chuckled, winking at his wife. 'You just passed the test. You don't need to know everything so soon, but finish the joke, mate. Put your sis' out of her misery.'

'The joke is, Kizzo,' the boy continued, 'that Mum didn't know what a circumcised dick looks like, compared to a normal one.'

'A normal one?' Lynn burst out laughing. 'That's funny in itself.'

Her longtime lover coughed, drawing his finger and thumb across his mouth to pinch his lips together so as not to incriminate himself. 'I'm saying nothing, guys. Except that only nice girls don't know the difference. Skanky girls southwest of Sydney certainly did, even though neither term'd mean anything to them. This question was always a good measure of a woman's character for me.'

'When you wanted to,' his son teased.

'Mate! Thanks for your support! But you're not wrong, as usual.'

'Ew!' his daughter grimaced. 'That's gross. I don't want to think about any kind of dicks. I'd better not learn what the difference is either.'

'No, indeed,' her father agreed, closing his eyes, gritting his teeth and cupping his ears with his palms. 'Stay blissfully ignorant on this score for as long as you can, eh?'

The blonde beauty moaned in commiseration. Kierney's first menstrual cycle had been a watershed for Jeff, at once proud at the onset of womanhood and terrified for her *entrée* into a battleground full of sexual predators and hormonal mind-games. Confident their thirteen-year-old was well-equipped to cope with both, she had arranged an update to the self-defence training both children had received while in primary school.

'So, Dad? What happened with the vicar? Priest? Whoever... Did you say you believed in religion?'

'I was honest, son,' the wise man responded. 'I said I didn't agree with any religion. Despite my outer mongrel appearance, I still respected people who were willing to speak to me, even if it wasn't as an equal. And he was definitely willing to speak to me by this point. I gave him the example of Paul's letters to the Corinthians. As far as I read them, Paul was an all-in preacher, telling those Corinthians they should behave. I said I thought that pretty much anyone could create a book like the Bible just by pulling together a collection of moralising tales. An anthology of self-help books fit for kids in a borstal.'

'What's a borstal?' Kierney piped up. 'A prison?'

The teacher nodded. 'Yeah. Or remand centre. Youth detention, *et cetera*. For boys under eighteen, too young to be locked up with adults. Using this word made the vicar's wife prick up her ears again. She would've thought I'd done time inside, and I didn't care to alter her opinion.'

Jeff became aware of something rub against his knee. His little girl had crept forward centimetre by centimetre while he was spinning the yarn. How very sweet it was to be a few days away from his fortieth birthday, surrounded by the people who loved him and indulged his need to merge the past with the present. He held his breath while drinking the special moment in.

'That's when I first likened the Bible to Wisden,' the father nudged his daughter's leg and heard her sigh. 'The vicar nearly crapped himself laughing. He ended up inviting me to his church to carry on the conversation the next day, which I did. And then he found me a mentor. Phil McAlpine, angel. Remember him?'

'Oh, yes. The professor at Sydney Uni'?'

'Yep. The reverend knew it wasn't appropriate for him to mentor me 'cause I wasn't a believer. He must've figured out he was facing an impossible task to try and convert me, so he introduced me to Phil, who was a retired philosophy lecturer. That's how I met John Francis too, angel. Did I tell you that? I forgot 'til just now. They studied together, and John's dad and the vicar's dad went to the same divinity school, I think. We used to meet up in The Supper Club once I was old enough to pass for eighteen.'

'Wow!' Jet exclaimed. 'Old enough to pass for eighteen? That's so cool! It's amazing how these people from your past are all strung together somehow. You're so ancient, Dad. It must be hard to remember all this stuff.'

'Effing cheek!' Jeff sneered, grabbing a magazine from his pile of post and hurling it at his son.

'Weren't they worried about being caught encouraging under-aged drinking?' his daughter asked.

'Evidently not, gorgeous! No-one cared much about that kind of thing in those days. Same as seatbelts and drink-driving. You just took your chances.'

'So all those bits of your life started from one boring day at the cricket?' Jet laughed.

'Yep,' their father affirmed, raising his left hand and pointing to each child in turn. 'And let that be a lesson to you both... Don't pass up an opportunity to do something new. You never know where it might lead.'

Lynn gave her glorious soul-mate a smile, noticing how their offspring hung on his every word. His "Pied Piper" moniker was never more apt, and the setting of tonight's lesson lent itself to his relaxed delivery. He seldom wrestled with right *versus* wrong in front of these two sponges, and yet the line between these binary states blurred constantly inside his head at other times.

'What are you going to put in your Bible, Jetto?' the thirteen-year-old asked.

Her brother sunk his chin down into his hands, elbows resting on the picnic table either side of his empty drink can. 'Oh, I don't know. Stuff about respecting others; leading by example; talking to each other. All the things you guys teach us.'

'There's nothing new in that though,' Lynn said. 'Maybe not much about talking to each other, I suppose. Why would we buy your Bible and not the original?'

''Cause it'd be chock-full of modern parables that mean something to people of the twentieth century, just like Dad told his vicar. The basics are the same, but people don't covet their neighbours' asses anymore, do they?'

'No?' the rock star laughed. 'Speak for yourself! They covet Aston Martins and beach-side mansions, if our press is anything to go by. And your *mamá*'s ass, but that's totally forgivable.'

'Jeff!' his wife's voice was shrill.

'Sorry, angel. Strike that from the record. I like your style though, mate. My personal view is that a religious user guide should be more about happiness for all. The book I started to write a while ago... Y'know, the one I gave my dad a copy of before he died.'

'Yes. I remember. It was brilliant. I was just wondering aloud to Cathy the other day about where it was.'

Jeff smiled. '*Gracias, Regala.* Not much since then. Our life singular happened to it, but it was my pretentious stab at a Bible of sorts. An ethical examination of the way individuals can make the world a better place if only they tried a bit harder.'

'Why don't you have a go, Jet?' Lynn suggested. 'I'm sure Dad'd love to give you the draft copy. You could take it to its next stage.'

'An instruction manual for happiness,' the negotiator mused, extending his beautiful best friend's train of thought. 'That's a fantastic idea. We could do it together, all four of us. Come up with a practical plan for changing the world on a macro scale. Now that *would* be a Bible worth reading!'

The cricketer frowned, wondering if his parents were setting him up. He was too young to remember the early version of this work being passed to his grandfather at the end of their one and only visit. Hearing a muffled ringtone to his left, he picked up Jeff's mobile telephone and illuminated his face with its glowing screen.

'Gerry.'

The celebrity jumped to his feet, answering his manager's call, and started off along the footpath. He gave the others a thumbs-up, making for beyond the tree-line to discuss an important matter which was not necessary for his family to hear.

'You'll have to start a new religion to launch it,' Kierney suggested to her dazed brother. 'Otherwise, how will people rally around it?'

Lynn smiled. 'That's a good point, darling. Even the greatest books need a marketing plan. I don't know if the average person was as cynical in two-thousand BC as we are now. Hold on a sec', while your dad's out of earshot...'

Seizing a golden opportunity to talk to the children alone, the schemer unveiled her secret plan for the milestone due the following Tuesday. She had booked a game of golf for first thing in the morning, to tempt him out of bed, after which Jet and Kierney were to meet them at Redhill, a short drive from their Mount Eliza hideaway on the Mornington Peninsula.

The teenagers were thrilled at being treated to a day off school. The foursome would be joined by Gerry and a few more of Jeff's closest friends for a private lunch at the hilltop winery. Thoroughly distracted, their more serious conversation was abandoned in favour of assigning gift-wrapping duties, only to be cut short again when the man himself returned.

***

Jeffrey Moreno Diamond turned forty years old on the second of June nineteen-ninety-two. He and Lynn flew to New York the weekend afterwards, honouring their sporadic tradition of celebrating his birthdays in places beginning with the word "New". The Big Apple became the default choice, as it happened, after the couple were awarded yet another honour for their contribution to world peace.

The celebrated Romanian-French novelist and philosopher, Eugène Ionesco, had dubbed the modern-day Victor Hugo "*Maiastra*", after the magical bird from Romanian folklore which foretold the future and cured the blind.

'You do cure the blind, figuratively speaking,' Lynn told her modest partner, emerging from the *en suite* in their hotel room after a furious, alcohol-fuelled and drug-assisted lovemaking session had lifted them to even higher planes. 'You teach people to see what they can't be bothered to see. That's what this award means.'

'If you say so,' Jeff sighed.

'*Mais oui. Et surtout, monsieur Ionesco le dit.*'

'*Bien sûr, mon amie.* But it's beyond belief that such luminaries are saying this kind o' shit about me. The whole weekend feels like some crazy bragging carnival. I don't know how I should behave.'

The love of his life murmured, wrapping her silk robe around her and guessing they wouldn't be settling down to sleep for some time. 'I think I know what you mean. You just need to take a step back from the front line and acknowledge we're doing great things. No point trying to pretend you're surprised about this award when every single day gives us evidence of positive change. Just accept it with deep gratitude. That's your trademark anyway, isn't it? I'm sure you'll come up with something humble and meaningful to say.'

The boy from Canley Vale kissed the back of his dream girl's neck and rolled away from the tanned and naked pleasure-dome he had enjoyed for the second time that day. She was right. There was no value in minimising their accomplishments. Although there were hundreds, if not thousands of people involved in carrying out their work, he and Lynn had instigated almost every project. She was also correct to point out his many speeches which had aroused so many people's interest in truths they previously chose to ignore, whether subconsciously or not.

'Thanks. I'll accept it for you and the kids, and for the wider DCF team. Everyone does his or her thing. Most of all you. You deserve this as much as I do. I'm just the parasitic front-man you agreed to shack up with back in 'seventy-four. Jesus Christ, that was such a good day! I'll never forget that day for as long as I live.'

'No. Me neither. Nor the time you slept for forty-three hours,' Lynn recalled with a sunny laugh. 'I remember telling Mish I didn't expect life would be so exciting living with you, when I kept coming home to find you hadn't moved.'

Sounds of snoring issued forth from the pillow behind, making the singer laugh all the more. Complaining that nothing ever changed, she turned over and planted a kiss on Jeff's lips. Still he refused to wake up. Two could play at this game... She returned to her original position, and the *duo simpatico* left each other alone to sleep for real.

Presented with a replica of Brancusi's bronze sculpture of the same name by the Guggenheim Foundation, in honour of his pivotal role in peace negotiations in Africa and elsewhere, the *Maiastra* launched his fifth decade on the verge of becoming a self-satisfied fat cat. With the other three Diamonds often by his side, the everyday hero floated from engagement to interview to conference on a surreal cushion of accomplishment and a strange but agreeable amalgam of esteem and wonder.

If the Australian celebrities had been gifted the Midas touch during the nineteen-eighties, the present day saw them exert even greater influence on a global scale and attain ever more extraordinary triumphs. Also, away from the razzle-dazzle of showbusiness, Paragon Holdings' two senior executives featured in a television documentary about the success of their venture capital empire, which topped the list of Australia's fastest-growing companies for the third year running.

'Most *musos* who get rich quick in their twenties haven't yet worked out what life's about,' Jeff explained to the interviewer. 'I was in a much better position. Firstly, I had this bloke to work everything out for me, and no finer business brain exists, let it be said. And secondly, I was never young. I didn't have a normal adolescence to speak of, so I always had a keen sense for what money can buy, and what I could or couldn't afford. Making the right choices. All that.

'So I see some of these new artists... They go out and spend their entire haul of advances and royalties in the first couple of years, on huge houses and fast cars and living the high life. And then they realise thereafter that they've been so busy enjoying the spoils of their success that they haven't created any new material to back up with. The same goes for entrepreneurs too. The trick is to balance the short- and long-term thinking. If people only focus on milking as much out of today as possible, very soon their bank accounts'll be back where they started. And what I always tell people who're struggling and looking for their big break is that, even though I detested the hardship of my teenage years, now with the benefit of hindsight, I'm grateful for what they taught me.'

Hot on the heels of his landmark commemoration, a respected Sydney producer released an unsanctioned journalistic biography of The Australian Elvis and his humble beginnings. The broadcast's researchers had tracked down a selection of Jeff Diamond's childhood acquaintances, who each painted a vivid and ofttimes controversial picture of the boy.

Lynn and the children were fascinated by this programme, aired a fortnight after the superstar's birthday. It brought home to them still further how undeniable his potential had been from a very early age. Primary school teachers, local shopkeepers and neighbours recounted story after story about the rebellious young lad and the way he astounded them all with his ingenuity and farsightedness. A common thread ran throughout however, in that no-one had projected far enough into the future to recognise how special he was.

A former music teacher from Fairfield High School told a tale which the songwriter had no trouble calling to mind upon listening to the soundtrack, blowing his wife and his manager away. Apparently, beyond the perimeter, the good-looking Stones Road renegade was notorious as someone to avoid at all costs. However, despite a reputation for surviving fist-fights unscathed and for dodging and weaving out of law enforcement's reach, a natural leader emerged as soon as he stepped onto school grounds.

The softly-spoken woman described how this tough, super-cool and altogether untouchable boy from the poorest side of town would spout insightful phrases off-the-cuff to motivate any pupil who sought to decry an upcoming event.

Jeff had the knack, said this particular spokesperson, of identifying the source of the student's recalcitrance and persuading him or her to fall into line. To supplement the teachers' glowing reports, classmates had also been tracked down. They opened up with unprompted generosity about their surprise that a kid they knew as so smart, ambitious and caring towards his fellow students could be descended from a gangland family. All the girls wanted to go out with him, and all the boys wanted to be his mate.

'As long as we were at school, that is,' the forty-year-old corrected the commentary. 'It didn't happen exactly like that, Con.'

'What do you mean?' Kierney asked.

'Oh, nothing. It was fine for me to be Mister Popular while we were at school, but if I met any of them on the street, they wouldn't acknowledge my bloody existence.'

'Two-faced,' Jet murmured, attempting to concentrate on the commentary.

'Christ Almighty!' the father interrupted, pointing at the screen. 'That's my high school headmistress. Fuck! She looks ancient now.'

'So are you,' his son teased, receiving a sharp dig in the ribs from his sister.

The stout, grey-haired woman now inhabiting the Diamonds' television looked born for the job. Forthright but fair, and quite possibly hypnotised by her successful *protégé*, Lynn and the teenagers exchanged amused glances as he listened to what the retired principal had to say.

'I first heard of Jeff Diamond from the police,' the elderly lady told the presenter. 'Two detectives paid me a visit, asking about a student who'd just started in Year Seven. I didn't know him at that stage, but remember retrieving his records and noticing a near perfect attendance record and well above average marks.

'I couldn't believe the awful description the police gave me and the exemplary records I was looking at belonged to one and the same boy. At my school, there were two types of families: the Asian immigrants who worked hard and clawed their way to a mediocre standard of living; and then there were people from other countries, typically the Middle East or southern Europe, who thought Australia owed them a living and expected everything to be handed to them on a plate without putting in any effort. Very few of the latter stood out, but Jeff was definitely one who did.'

The billionnaire shook his head but stayed silent while the old woman rambled on. In profile, he appeared troubled and irate, sitting on the edge of the couch as if ready to tackle the television and pin it to the floor if it uttered another untruth. Lynn tapped Kierney on the shoulder, motioning for her to pass the camera over.

'After the visit from the police, I asked to see this young man, and also his sister, who at that time would have been in Year Eight or Nine. To look at them, one could be forgiven for concluding they belonged to a low socio-economic family: scruffy, unkempt, and so on. Insolent expressions on their faces too. Fairly typical of the Stones Road, I might add.'

Again the Sydneysider cursed under his breath, this time sporting a wry smile. 'That's at least correct,' he confessed. 'I would've gone into her office as defiant as anything. No-one told me what to do in those days.'

'No-one tells you what to do now either,' his wife sniggered, holding her hand out for his. 'Can you remember this?'

Her beautiful black stallion scoffed, distracted by the former schoolteacher's retrospective.

'Hmm… Let me think. I questioned the girl, Madalena, first because she was older,' she explained. 'She was evasive and disinterested, and had very little to say. But her brother was completely different. Although it was obvious he didn't want his sister to give away too much information, young Jeff waited for me to address him before he spoke. He looked me directly in the eye, bold as brass, whereas his sister's attention continually flitted around the room. Whenever I asked him a question, I would get an immediate, straight-down-the-line answer.'

'Some things never change,' Jet laughed, leaning back onto his father's shins. 'No messing with you.'

'Shhh!' Lynn urged. 'Let's listen to what everyone has to say, then we can talk about it afterwards.'

'I remember that first appointment as clear as day,' the headmistress continued. 'The boy made no apology for his criminal activities. No excuses. "I do what I need to do," he told me. Then... and this I'll never forget... he said, "Don't judge the picture by its frame, Missus Anderson." Don't judge the picture by its frame. How about that from a twelve-year-old?

'From that moment on, I watched him like a hawk. He and his sister went through their father's arrest, his being sent to prison, and all the humiliation that came with it. And later on, their mother's fatal overdose. Young Jeff Diamond was in and out of trouble with the police on a regular basis. Yet in school, he was the model student.'

'It's amazing how she remembers so clearly,' Kierney's chin tilted over her shoulder.

'It is,' her dad agreed, 'although she never liked me.'

Lynn countered, smiling. 'It sounds as if she admired you though. She knows you went through a lot and did well in spite of it.'

The interview was drawing to a close. 'In all my years of teaching,' the retired woman spoke into the lens. 'In my whole teaching career, I can't think of another student who's impressed me as much as Jeff Diamond. I never met anyone else who could reason things out so creatively. He seemed to possess a sense of purpose way beyond his peers.

'There wasn't a moment's hesitation when he answered one of our questions, and never a time he wasn't prepared to do more to get what he wanted. I'm not in the least bit surprised that he went on to be who he is now. Jeff Diamond is one of life's stand-outs, and a born leader. Other students used to flock to him and would be eating out of his hand, but I don't remember him once taking advantage of anyone.'

'Oh, I don't know about that, lady,' the billionaire smirked, cocking his head. 'There'll be heaps of people who'd disagree with you on that score. I think time's made her memory kinder to me than it should've been. She and I hardly ever saw eye to eye.'

'Now, Jeff and I didn't always see eye to eye,' the show's guest repeated, as if she had overheard his adult self from *Escondido*'s sumptuous lounge room, making Lynn and the children dissolve into laughter.

'Aside from all this, he was quite the most charismatic and persuasive young man,' Missus Anderson concluded. 'All the teachers would do anything for him, especially the females. Myself included, I suppose. I wasn't immune to his charms.'

Lighting a cigarette, the film's subject cleared his throat, a little disappointed the segment had ended. He squirmed his legs out from behind his daughter's back, stood up and vacated the room, leaving the others to dissect the programme during a commercial break.

Why must everyone focus on the superficial? Didn't they feel the need for something more profound, more long-lasting? It pained the intellectual to admit he played on this predisposition as often as he criticised it. Perhaps he only had himself to blame for so many fans believing his ascendency had been fashioned more of style than of substance.

Of course Jeff made best use of his abundant magnetism to reflect life's glaring injustices back into people's lines of sigh, but this feat wasn't possible using charm alone. It worked because he understood the ways of the world so well. How? He had no idea. He just did.

And what had Lynn said in her speech during his fortieth birthday party? "I've lived my entire adult life as Jeff Diamond's angel. It doesn't get any better than this."

Stop overanalysing, advised the man in the bathroom mirror. *It's working fine. No worries, mate.*

***

'*Nnneeeeeeeaaaaaaaagggggggghhhhhh!!!!*'

The kinetic mass of a muscular, fifteen-year-old missile projected itself at full pelt towards his unsuspecting father, who was standing on the edge of the swimming pool at *Escondido*, drinking a glass of orange juice and delighting in the sunrise over Port Phillip Bay.

'*Geronimo!*' Jet cheered, seizing the sitting duck around the waist and rugby tackling him into the water.

George had driven back from the city that morning with both teenagers. They had spent Saturday morning at the Sportsdrome, training for the upcoming Olympics, before coming home for a breather *chez eux*. The sixty kilometres between South Melbourne and Mount Eliza had escaped their notice, overjoyed to find a twelve-week-old German Shepherd pup sharing their ride.

Jeff hadn't heard them arrive home, his usual lethargy besetting any early productivity. Lynn was away recording and filming in southern England, so with the house to himself, he had stayed up late writing a batch of new songs and had only recently made himself some breakfast.

The two brawny male bodies sank to the bottom of the pool, discharging a swirl of orange juice in the water. When they broke free of each other's grip and burst through the surface, Jet lurched towards the side and sprang out, scarcely able to breathe for laughing. He was chased by his father, who stopped briefly to place the now empty glass onto the table before haring after the evil boy.

Kierney appeared in the doorway, distracted by the noise drifting through her bedroom window above the *patio*. 'Hey! Whatever's going on?'

The young girl had negotiated a puppy-minding shift with the family's driver, which hadn't been too difficult a deal to strike, given the amount of energy little Bourbon had to burn. She released his collar, and the floppy-eared inquisitor scampered across the deck to inject himself into the *fracas*, still coming to grips with his own oversized feet.

With a fair idea why her brother saw fit to let off steam, she leaned against the kitchen's sliding door and watched the spunky canine battler dive head-first into the writhing heap of arms and legs which had straggled and scraped its way onto the lawn. Seeing no apparent danger in letting them carry on, she sighed and wandered back inside.

'You had a good night then?' Jeff gasped, finally able to pin his son to the ground and breathe clear air.

Kicking his feet, the youngster shuffled beyond the reach of an enthusiastic set of needle-like teeth intent on nibbling his ankles. 'Shit, yeah! Fantastic.'

The father released his grip and jumped up to his full height, catching sight of boxer shorts rendered translucent by the soaking and clinging to his pubic hair. Not a good look, he decided, peeling them clear of his skin and watching them revert to the same state immediately.

Bourbon let out a shrill yap, frustrated that the game was over. He flopped down onto the grass between the two fighters, long tongue lolling out of the side of his mouth. Jeff called him over and encouraged him to curl up beside him, not in the least bit surprised to be smothered in wet kisses instead.

Laughing at the vain attempt at puppy discipline, his son rolled over and lay gazing into the uninterrupted span of blue above. 'Well, are you going to ask me to give you a blow-by-blow commentary?'

'Not just now, no,' his father snapped, drawing the lad's attention to his manly contours under the damp and darkened silk.

The cocky teenager needed no further explanation. It was only since his own sexual awareness had reached new heights that the image of his parents engaging in similar pursuits had become somehow sordid and unpalatable. Sensing he might suffer another lapse in self-control too, he elected not to cast his mind as far back as last night's close encounter with Rebecca.

'Where's Mum?'

'Not here,' the songwriter pulled a glum face. 'Somewhere near London. Home on Tuesday *arvo*. So, without giving me any details, was it worth waiting for?'

Jet grinned and shrugged. '*No comprendo.*'

'*Muy bien.* Like that, is it?' his dad teased. 'Make up your mind! One minute you're Magnus the Magnificent, who can't wait for me to ask what a great lover you are, and the next you rescind all my access privileges. Mate, I don't need to beg for it. It's not so long since my last visit to the altar of passionate gratification that I can't picture how it works.'

The sportsman groaned, desperate beyond measure to spill the beans about his latest conquest. Lynn would have been proud of the meticulous precision with which his dad and he had planned the date, and the evening went off without a hitch. He was struck by how self-important he felt this morning, reluctant to express any thanks for assistance received, and corrected his attitude just in time.

'Ah, you poor, depraved old man... That's not fair. If you must know, yes, it was bloody awesome. Bec loved the whole box and dice, so thanks for everything.'

Nudging the snoozing dog into action, Jeff straightened his legs out in front of him, letting his right foot bump into the boy's lethargic backside not quite by accident. 'Oops, sorry, mate,' he quipped. 'Come on in. I'm *gonna* get changed, then we can make some lunch while you give me a full confession. Did you tell your sis' on the way home?'

Jet loped after his father, scooping up an unsuspecting puppy on the way. 'You reckon?'

'Ha! I wouldn't either!'

When the scheming pair of Diamonds reached the sliding doors and deposited their squirming furr-ball of excitement onto the kitchen tiles, Kierney was already preparing a meal. At first delighted to be reacquainted with their little visitor, her expression turned to disapproval as her eyes travelled upwards from four ankles covered in dark hairs slicked against damp skin.

'*Gracias, pequeñita*,' Jeff chuckled, following her gaze to his shorts. 'I know exactly what you're thinking! Jesus, you're so like your *mamá* these days.'

'What the hell were you guys doing? How come you're all wet? They're not bathers.'

'Wrong place, wrong time,' her brother shrugged. 'He peed in the pool too. Getting senile, I reckon.'

'What?' the girl exclaimed.

Jeff scowled. 'Oh, for fuck's sake! What is this? Kids ganging up on me... Not such a wise move, *mes amis*. I'm *outta* here.'

After sandwiches and snacks on the verandah, and once the fourteen-year-old managed to persuade the puppy to keep her company upstairs while she worked on school assignments, Jet opened up to his father. Both parents had rejoiced to find their son determined to make his entry into the world of multi-party sexual relations a night to remember.

The fact that the children exhibited no signs of the desperate need for supremacy that had dominated the former lost boy's early teenage years nourished his age-old soul. While neither expected their progeny to inherit his insecurities, he and his dream girl had wondered now and then whether being so open about physical love risked either turning them into sex-fiends or even putting them off completely. They needn't have worried. Despite a natural inquisitiveness, both were taking their own sweet time to choose the perfect moments, whichever side of the age of consent the transaction might take place.

And for the accumulation of supercharged genes that constituted Ryan Jeffrey Blake Dyson Diamond, the "right" age was fifteen years and three months. He and his girlfriend, already seventeen and in the year above him at school, had already been dating for a few weeks.

The Diamonds and Rebecca's parents had been friends for a number of years, regular attendees at the usual range of end-of-term functions, and her younger sister was in Kierney's *clique* too. Like history repeating itself, as Australia's darling reminded her husband, her own cosy Melbourne Academy circle had almost exclusively selected their intimate adventures from within.

With their son's incessant boasting about taking the ultimate step, Lynn and Jeff had assumed that the deed had already been done. They grew tired of waiting for him to drop a hint at some point, subtle or otherwise. Consequently, it had been a challenge to conceal their amazement when, only the previous week, he had stolen into *Escondido*'s recording studio to ask his father's advice about planning a proper romantic evening.

'D'you know if Bec's parents imagined you'd stay over?' the forty-year-old asked, kicking the *post mortem* off with an easy question.

'No, I don't,' Jet replied. 'I've been in her room heaps of times before. They've left us in the house alone together before too, so I guess they're fine with it.'

'Were you nervous?'

The teenager hesitated. 'No, not really. Well, yeah... Not too much.'

'Not as nervous as Bec,' his dad surmised. 'Did she like the rose?'

'Oh, yes. Really liked it. That was a great idea of yours, *Maiastra*.'

Jeff beamed. 'Cool! Good man. These seemingly trivial touches make a huge difference, mate. Girls love to feel special. Everyone does. Remember that.'

His son turned coy, crossing the patio to rescue a soccer ball from being blown into the pool. 'Sure. And you were right about needing to take it slowly,' he answered. 'I've never recited the nine-times table so many times in my head as I did last night!'

The songwriter laughed aloud. 'I told you! You wouldn't believe me. Naming footy players from back line to forward line worked pretty well for me.'

Jet chortled. 'At first, I didn't want to look. You know... While we were taking each other's clothes off and stuff.'

'Jesus Christ! I remember that feeling too, mate. Even after several years of practice, I was at zero self-control when your mum and I found ourselves in the same situation.'

'Really? Wow! Must've been amazing. That makes me feel better.'

'*Excelente*,' his father smiled. ''Bout as amazing as it gets, yeah. So how did you go? Bec wouldn't have been too impressed if you spent the whole time looking the other way.'

The young man huffed, a grin stretching the full width of his face. 'Hey? I didn't! I don't know... I s'pose I just got used to being able to look at her naked and stretched out in front of me. I held it together.'

'Right. Well done, captain. Mind over matter. You're your mother's son alright.'

'But it was much too quick though,' Jet complained. 'I mean, once the condom was on. I almost dropped it twice! And once I was inside her, there was no way I could slow down, and I definitely didn't have time to think about what to do for her.'

Jeff watched the ruddy-faced cricketer fidget in his seat, twirling the ball in the air in front of his face. It was prudent to bring the discussion to a close, for sure. There was no holding back the tide now, and he was filled with cheer that the blond lad's path would be sober and wholesome.

Though not for sharing at this juncture, the philosopher realised that by hitting another milestone on his own journey to personal maturity, Jet had also helped his father achieve one of his. He and his beautiful best friend had steered their son towards manhood the right way, in a normal relationship between two friends; as unlike his own experience as they had hoped.

The peacemaker lit a cigarette and stood up, extending his hand to the fifteen-year-old in an authoritative mark of respect. 'Congrats, mate. You're officially a dude now. A true *Mensch*. So when're you guys going to get it on again? You'll be able to offer more bi-lateral participation next time, believe me. Won't seem half as rushed.'

'Hope so. I need to do some homework.'

The perceptive psychologist winked. 'Sure. If you can concentrate...'

'Shut up, old man,' growled the awkward teenager, bumping his partner-in-crime hard on his way past. 'You're always one step ahead of me. And please stay out of my private life from now on.'

'No worries,' Jeff promised, banging out a dramatic chord on the outdoor table. 'Keep it up.'

Past Imperfect

'"I *am* being clear," I said to her,' Jeff recounted. 'I told her over and over, "This is not a date." But she just refused to let it go.'

The nostalgic storyteller was spinning yet another humorous dating yarn. Lynn had caught up with their son's momentous news on her return from London, and Jet had scored a second *rendezvous* with Rebecca, coming home even more elated than the first time.

'Let what go?' his son teased. 'I thought it wasn't a date.'

The graceful singer smiled as her husband gave the comic a smack across the scalp, exactly as he had done for the last ten years or more. No longer likely to taking offence or capable of jealousy, she could see how much he enjoyed imparting the gory details of his female conquests. If anything, hearing his tales and understanding the extent of his notoriety, the knowledge of having been the one to snare this swarthy sex-god made her feel all the more special.

The larrikin had been in the midst of an intricate account of an unwanted reality with someone called Patricia. Boy and girl occupied opposite ends of Fairfield High School's social spectrum, and she and her snooty group of friends looked down their noses at everyone except a certain exotic-looking male student by the name of Jeff Diamond.

'She told me her dad'd never allow her to go on a date with me. "Why not?" I asked, to which she replied, "Because you smoke and drink." "So how does your dad know I smoke and drink?" I asked her. "He doesn't," she said, "but that's what he'd say anyway."'

Once again, Lynn played "fly on the wall" in the tearaway's turbulent adolescence, where she imagined the flirtatious young woman sitting on a school lunch bench with the lanky, long-haired charmer reclined against the wall and presiding over her every sense, no doubt turned on by whatever lay below her neckline.

'You're from too far out west for my mum and dad,' the condescending teenager had continued.

'Yeah, well...' he nodded. 'That's closer to the truth.'

'You know my dad'd go mad if he knew I was with you.'

'Ah, yeah. I'm used to that as well,' the young Jeff admitted. 'But you're here, aren't you? Let's forget who we are and get on with this, eh?'

Images drifted through Lynn's mind of the mismatched students sitting in the open air and working on a project, interspersed with fond memories of their own relationship's first months. What a perfect solution it had been to combine romance with education in the precious few hours she and Jeff had had available to spend together, unnoticed in a secluded section of the State Library on Swanston Street.

'But you're not like the other boys like you,' Patricia said.

'How come?' Fairfield's brainiest student ridiculed. 'That's a defective statement, if ever I heard one. Which other boys like me am I not like?'

The leggy brunette's high-pitched titter reminded her companion of Gerry's sisters. If she was so well-to-do, why hadn't her parents sent her to a private school? She would have been best friends with Jacinta and Tamilla Blake. Watching her cover her mouth as if she had sneezed, he guessed sincerity wasn't her strong suit.

'Oh, yes!' the young woman giggled. 'That does sound a bit stupid.'

'Just a bit,' Jeff agreed.

'I meant it as a compliment.'

'OK. Thanks, I s'pose. Listen, Trish... I haven't got enough money to take girls out, so I don't go on dates. I'm not that sort of bloke, like your dad says. I just fuck every girl I can.'

'Ooh! Nice one,' Lynn scoffed, breaking out of her daydream and shooting her husband a black look. 'I hope you aren't listening too closely, guys.'

In their customary brand of comedic unison, Jet and Kierney both shook their heads before dissolving into fits of laughter. Jeff apologised to the best mother in the world and carried on with his reconstruction, returning them all to the late nineteen-sixties in western Sydney.

'I asked her why her dad was so against people from the Stones Road. I was dying to hear the reasons people gave, so I could work round them in the future. "I doubt if I'll dispute any of it," I told her, "but it's interesting to hear how people talk about shit they know fuck all about."'

The unlikely pair materialised in the Olympian's mind once more.

'Because you get into fights and cause trouble,' Patricia had responded.

'All of us?'

The teenager nodded. 'He thinks so.'

'And what do you think?'

'Me? Oh, I don't know,' she said, confused. 'You're the only one from over there I've ever talked to.'

'So come on then... What do you think?' Jeff leaned in further, well aware he was gaining ground with each exchange.

'I think you're fantastic,' Patricia wilted against the tough guy's persuasive smile. 'Talented, clever, funny…'

From *Escondido*'s sumptuous lounge room over twenty years later, his wife watched the old, young Jeff Diamond back away, playing hard to get.

'Yeah, but I still get into fights and cause trouble.'

'Still?'

'Bloody oath, I do!' Jeff couldn't help chuckling. 'For one, your dad says I do, so it must be true. And second, it is actually true. But I also work hard 'cause I want to go to uni', so there's a conundrum for you and him. Did he go to uni'?'

'Of course he did! He's a dentist.'

'Cool,' the gaunt but handsome teenager smiled, giving himself a lazy push off the table, turning round and sitting next to the erstwhile unattainable female. 'I haven't been to a dentist in *yonks*. Maybe I should make an appointment?'

'Why?'

Patricia tensed up, fumbling with the top of her pen until the clip snapped off. The rumours about gangs on the Stones Road and the unsavoury people who hung around them were well-publicised. Everyone had heard about Jeff and Madalena's murdering father too, the news of his capture, trial and life sentence common knowledge in the district.

The infamous son took pity on his classmate. She liked him a lot, he could tell. Too bad he was who he was! He pretended these small-minded points of view didn't bother him. Watching the conversation ebb and flow at his whim was entertaining at least.

'I could show your dad that troublemakers like me can also be decent and responsible. Y'know… Your brother sledges plenty of filthy language on the footy field and gets into fights every now and again.'

'Edward? Does he?'

'You bet he does,' Jeff nodded. 'He's a bloke. We all do. Just some of us know when we can get away with it.'

'All my friends fancy you like crazy,' Patricia blurted out, 'but they'd never go out with you.'

'Cool. You sure about that?'

'Why cool? Don't you want to go out with us?'

The hot-blooded male raised his eyebrows. 'All at once? Might be interesting.'

'Oh, my God, Jeff! That's not what I meant. You're disgusting!'

'Nice idea though,' he smiled, leaning across and squeezing the girl's fair-skinned forearm. 'But seriously, no. I don't want to go out with any o' you 'cause it'd be too bloody complicated. Way too many invisible barriers. I'll sneak an eyeful here and there at your classy legs and your pumped-up tits while we're working here, then go back into the *ghetto* for some primal lovin'.'

The young woman grimaced. 'Euch! That's disgusting too!'

Jeff scoffed. 'Oh, is it? I don't need to date hypocrites, Trish. We're not so different, your mob and mine.'

'Sorry,' Patricia whined. 'I like you heaps and love spending time with you. You're the best looking boy at school, by a long way. And much more mature than the rest.'

'"Cheers," I said,' the rock star whose temples were now tinged with grey winked at his dream girl, recalling how he had struggled to absorb the girl's compliment. 'So I said to her, "You want to go out with me but you won't because I'm not like you. And I don't want to go out with you but I want to fuck your brains out because you're not like me. How's that for crazy, huh?" She didn't understand, but the paradox messed with my head for days after.'

'Messed with your head? Why?' his daughter bleated. 'Trish was just another rich bitch. She wasn't worth your attention anyway.'

Even after all this time, the lost boy still considered himself on the lowest rung of society's ladder. '*Gracias, pequeñita.* It felt like a bit of a bad omen. It made me realise just how complicated it'd be to date your *mamá*. If I got this sort of response from one of the uptight princesses at my very ordinary high school, how the hell was I going to convince Lynn Dyson to go out with me?'

'But it wasn't complicated, *Papá*, was it?'

'Yes and no,' her dad blew a kiss to the stunning woman on the other side of the table and slapped his other hand against his cheek with a hollow thud. 'It had its moments.'

Kierney giggled, and her brother groaned. Each Diamond sibling was developing a distinct way of dealing with their parents' open shows of affection. With hormone levels oscillating hour by hour, romantic love and sexual chemistry presented a confusing cocktail which only augmented the complexity of growing up in the full glare of celebrity.

Scanning around the room, Jeff noticed a trace of annoyance on his wife's face, only too aware that he had pushed his luck. 'Sorry, angel. You know what I was like back then.'

'Like I am now?' their boastful son butted in.

'No, mate. You're ten times the man I was at the same age. You can say no. I couldn't.'

'Oh, come on… That's not right,' Lynn scolded, breaking her silence. 'You did say no. Don't paint yourself out to have less self-control than you did. You could easily say no to things if you wanted to. You just chose not to exercise that restraint as often as you might've.'

'Jeez! Poisonous words, Ms Dyson, yet again,' the guilty man shook his head. 'Fair enough. I deserve as much, I guess. But at the time, it certainly didn't feel like I got what I wanted, which meant I could never bring myself to say no when an opportunity arose.'

As if a penny had dropped, Kierney's objection rang out. 'But *Papá*, *Mamá*'s right. You did say no to Trish Trash, didn't you?'

The whole family laughed at this spontaneous nickname. With a modest wave, Jeff heaved himself up off the floor and joined the love of his life on the couch. *Maiastra* or not, indulgence had its limits, and he had blown them wide open in his attempt to articulate his dubious past. By rights, she ought to have turned him away, but instead she welcomed his embrace. She always had, and he trusted she always would.

'So tell us about you and Dean,' he invited.

'Dean who?' Kierney asked. 'Oh, I remember! Was Dean your boyfriend before *Papá*?'

Lynn nodded and inhaled as if taken by surprise. 'Nothing to tell.'

'Oh, I find that hard to believe,' her husband kissed her cheek and grinned. 'How could anyone go out with you and there be nothing to tell?'

'Dean might have something to tell,' Jet teased. 'Shall we ring him? Have you still got his number, Mum?'

'I absolutely do not! I haven't said more than two words to him since. Don't even hear about him these days because he retired from football. We met him at Junior's thirtieth, guys, remember?'

'Do you mean Dean Keller?' the fourteen-year-old yelped. 'Dean Keller, the old Richmond player? Oh, wow! Was he your boyfriend? I never knew that.'

Her brother wagged his finger. 'Old? The *former* Richmond player, you mean, Kizzo.'

The youngsters stuck their tongues out at each other, both shuffling closer to their parents. They had learned snippets of information about their mother's boyfriends in the span of time between the old Jeff and the new Jeff; when the starlet had left her tormented nobody to immerse herself in Californian culture, only to watch from afar as he became a global phenomenon. This was news they hadn't heard before however. Their father's magnanimous solicitation promised insights into their mother at much the same age as they were now.

'How long did you go out with Dean for?' Kierney enquired.

Lynn sighed. 'Oh, six months-ish. We didn't really go out in the formal sense. We went to school together, and all the sporty kids tended to socialise in a group who knew about the same things: training, injuries, *et cetera*. It wasn't like proper dating for me either. To begin with anyway...'

'Bit like me and Bec,' Jet interjected again, blushing at his inability to keep his mouth shut.

'Exactly like you and Bec, mate,' his father affirmed before returning to his wife's cliff-hanger. 'So what does "To begin with anyway..." mean?'

'As I said, mate... Nothing to tell,' she shrugged. 'Neither of us went on dates, but for very different reasons. I was too young. Dean used to flash his money around, which was a real turn-off for me. We did go out on dates a few times after I turned sixteen, and that brings us more or less to when I met you.'

Her son cackled. 'Shit! If you hadn't met Dad, do you think it would've lasted? Like if Dad had stayed in Sydney, I might well've been Dean Keller's kid.'

'Jesus, Jetto!' Jeff moaned. 'That's a bit of a stretch.'

'He's only joking,' the tennis champion smiled at the green monster which had taken her husband's place on the couch. 'You're no less sensitive about this as I am, see? How come it's alright to talk about your old flames when you can't handle talking about mine? I hadn't had even experimented with sex by this point!'

Jeff sniffed, feeling foolish for overreacting. 'You're right again,' he replied. 'I don't like hearing about it, regardless whether there was sex involved. Even now. I hate the thought of anyone else getting close to you.'

'But you brought the subject up!' Jet cried out.

'Yep. For several reasons, if you must know,' the impetuous rocker first held up two fingers and then a third. 'One, I wanted to test myself; and two, these discussions shouldn't be one-sided. And also, I reckon, it's because I feel guilty for making your mum sit through my lecherous parables, so I need a dose of my own medicine.'

'OK. Enough already! Let's change the subject,' Lynn slapped the contrite man's knee and scooted forward to the edge of the sofa. 'I'll make some coffee, shall I?'

'No, angel. Don't...' he urged, snaking his hand into the crook of the Olympian's elbow and trying to tempt her to relax. 'I'll get coffee while you give these guys the low-down about Dean. That way, with two of my three objectives achieved, I get to escape taking my own medicine.'

His long-suffering wife chuckled, treating the children to an exasperated expression. 'Not that you're cheating or anything... Do we let him cheat?'

Kierney frowned, her conscience torn. She half-understood this aspect of her parents' relationship, but only half. Whatever the root cause of their mother's leniency, neither child questioned why the world-changer often got away with behaviour she wouldn't have tolerated from them. It wasn't in his nature to shirk responsibility. Far from it, in fact. However, when it came to delving into the past and exposing the mental scars with which he had been saddled, Lynn invariably preferred to capitulate.

Jeff kissed her open mouth before jumping to his feet. '*Merci, mon amie.* You always let me cheat. That's not why I love you so much, but it helps. You give me strength every time you do it. OK, guys?'

'OK,' the confused girl shook her head. 'Just this once. Jetto?'

Perhaps this little diversion was all part of today's lesson, she surmised. When it came to the wellbeing of one's special someone, choices made with wisdom and love would always steer towards happiness. The more special the someone, the more one was driven to do the right thing by them. What harm could result from saving this giant of a man from destructive emotions, especially if there truly was nothing to tell? It wasn't as if he stood to gain from testing his mettle against his wife's ancient history.

Her brother couldn't care less. As a matter of fact, he wasn't interested in Dean Keller at all, having ascertained a dearth of smut and spice. Grunting his approval, the young man stood up and followed his father out of the room.

'Just you and me then, Kizzy,' Lynn smiled. 'Boys! Can't handle the pressure.'

Her daughter giggled. 'So did you love Dean?' she asked. 'Even a bit?'

'No. Definitely not. It was just for fun. And it wasn't even much fun, to tell you the truth! He wasn't very friendly. He knew Uncle Junior, and Grandpa of course, so he assumed I'd find him irresistible. Everyone else seemed to think we were made for each other, and gradually, all our other MA friends were hooked up with a person of the opposite sex. Well, except Richard Kerr and John Betts! When I look back on it, those two were so courageous.'

'Being OK with people knowing they were gay?' Kierney checked.

'Yes, but not as brave as gay guys need to be these days, I think.'

'Why not? Isn't it more acceptable now than back then?'

'True. Oh, I don't know. We were so *naïve*, almost like being in denial. I would never have bothered to find out what homosexuality was. I just thought Richard and John were more interested in music than girls. It never occurred to me when I was your age that not being attracted to girls probably meant they were attracted to boys!'

The thirteen-year-old laughed. 'That's hilarious! I don't know much about it either. I can guess how two men would have sex, but it's not something I want to think about too deeply. But then, thinking of me having sex with a boy seems kind o' weird too. And certainly two women together… How does that even work?'

Her mother smiled at the girlish rush of speculation. 'You're funny too, darling. Everything becomes clear when you need it to,' she assured. 'No point in rushing it. You'll be ready when you're ready, whether it's with male or female.'

'Ooh, no! I know it'll be male. No grey area there! Piraea and I've created a league table at school for who's hot and who's not, and there aren't any girls on our list.'

Her mother nodded. 'Right! Whatever floats your boat. It's unlike you not to have grey areas, Jeff Junior… Anyway, Dean and I did go out on a few proper dates; to the pictures mainly. We could hide there without anyone spotting us and asking for autographs. The first time we went out, he was the perfect gentleman. Didn't try and kiss me except at the very end of the date, when he delivered me back to Admin.'

'Did you want him to?' Kierney asked.

'Kiss me? Yes. Every girl wants to be kissed, I think. It makes you feel like you're not with a boy just to make him look good in front of his mates. It was always like that with Dean. He showed off something chronic when we were together around his friends. It used to annoy Uncle Junior as well.'

'Oh? Why?'

'Because he was always very protective of me,' Lynn reflected. 'Big brothers don't like to see their sisters being treated poorly, no matter how horrible they might be to them themselves.'

The dark-haired gipsy scoffed. 'Yeah! Although Jet's pretty good as big brothers go. I don't often get embarrassed in public, but he does sometimes defend me.'

'Well, that's good. I'm happy to hear this. He's a good kid. You both are.'

'So what happened with Dean after your second date?' the teenager encouraged. 'Was he less of a gentleman?'

Lynn closed her eyes for a moment, not sure whether she could remember so far back. Life before Jeff was now so immaterial that it had been archived off from her mind's database. And as if on cue, the dynamic *duo* returned with mugs of hot, aromatic coffee laced with an exotic *liqueur*, and she inhaled the steam as it was placed next to her on the side table. The drinks' purveyor stood back from the couch to assess whether it was safe for him to re-enter the conversation.

'Hmm...' his wife smiled. 'I wouldn't have used the word "gentleman", no. *Papá* doesn't want to hear this part. Shall we excuse him again?'

The pretty girl nodded. 'Yes. Go and write some songs, *Papá*. This 'ere's women's business.'

Requiring no more incentives to make himself scarce, the father lifted his mug and did as he was told. Jet remained, making himself comfortable on the other couch and pretending to read a car magazine. From time to time, as the story unfolded, Lynn saw his gaze drop back down onto a page which hadn't turned in quite a while.

'I was ready to have sex, Kizzy,' she admitted, 'but something told me I didn't want my first sexual experience to be with Dean. I wanted it to be special, and for some reason, I couldn't see it being special with him. I was too young to understand my feelings really. He was too lightweight, too silly and with not one ounce of empathy. I'd started to reading more meaty novels and sort of woke up to what life as an adult was about: politics; social issues... All the grown-up stuff your dad brings to life. I started getting a bit fed up with my friends for not being interested in the world.'

'So it was "Dump Dean for Dad Day", was it?' her son interjected, flapping the magazine on the floor as he enunciated his alliterative slogan.

'"Dump Dean for Dad Day"? Are you sure you haven't been drinking? That's absurd.'

'No, *Mamá*! It's not absurd at all,' Kierney giggled. That's exactly what happened, isn't it?'

Lynn chuckled, leaning her head to one side. 'Not exactly, but close. Dean was constantly on at me about having sex, saying he was the only one among his mates who wasn't getting laid, but I didn't give in. I was surprised he didn't dump *me*, to be honest. Most of my friends were experimenting too, but I was so much younger than them.'

'Did he love you?' her dreamy daughter asked.

'Oh, no. He said he did, but I doubt it. I'm sure he wouldn't be the first guy to say "I love you" to worm his way into a girl's undies.'

'Just like Dad!' the young man sniggered.

'No, Jet,' the singer refuted. 'Not at all like Dad in fact.'

Jet lifted his nose out of the magazine, his expression one of total disbelief. From the many tawdry anecdotes his father had divulged in recent years, he had assumed they shared the same horny motivations in their formative years.

'How come?' he whined. 'Dad couldn't wait to get into your undies. That's what he told me anyway.'

The dignified mother smiled, well and truly snookered. 'Yes, sure. Your dad was keen to have sex. Pretty obvious to everyone of course. What I mean is, he didn't tell me he loved me for the express purpose of having sex. He'd never have played that card with me, although I had no idea at the time.'

'Ahh,' Kierney swooned. 'That's so romantic. I hope the man I fall in love with's like *Papá*.'

'Yes. I hope so too, Kizzy, darling. It'd be wonderful for you. Although you mustn't count on meeting an exact copy of your *papá*. You need to work out which things are important to you, not only the characteristics you're used to seeing in him. The gallant gestures or magic words that sweep you off your feet might be completely different to whatever sweeps other people off theirs. *N'est-ce pas?*'

The dark-haired gipsy girl nodded. '*Oui. Bien sûr, maman. T'as raison. Merci.* So what happened with Dean when you kept refusing?'

'Nothing much,' Lynn replied. 'I escaped to Benloch for Christmas. Dean and I didn't see each other until after New Year, and that was only for a day out surfing in Torquay with a bunch of friends. Junior drove me there and back, and there was no way Dean would've propositioned me in front of my brother, thank God! Then I went into lock-down for the tennis at the end of January, so three more weeks went by with no more pressure. But... Oh, yes!'

'What?' both teenagers cried out, hanging off their mother's every word.

'I did go out one night during The Open with one of the other tennis players...'

Kierney sat straighter. 'Did you? Who?'

'Someone good?' her brother piped up. 'Aussie?'

'No, French. Patrice Rodriguez. You won't have heard of him. He was on the circuit and played Davis Cup for a while, but I've no idea what happened to him after that. 'Seventy-two was the first year the tournament was held at Kooyong, and all the international players were staying in digs in and around MA. It was amazing! Heaps of famous faces running round "The Tan".'

'Does *Papá* know you went out with a Frenchman?' the thirteen-year-old asked. 'He'd be impressed.'

'I don't think he does,' Lynn grinned. 'Funnily enough, Patrice was beaten in the third round by another Frenchman. We had dinner, that's all. He was very sophisticated. Not like the Aussies at all. It gave me a taste of what proper dating was like, even though I didn't like him that much.'

'And he asked you for sex too, I'm guessing,' her son's deep, adult intonation drifted across the floor.

The champion smiled at the young man who was soon to understand the suffocation which accompanied the "sporting hero" label. 'You guess right, Jetto. He was five years older than me and obviously used to getting his own way. Thankfully, he didn't press the issue. I told him I couldn't because I needed to get plenty of sleep.'

'Fool! He bought it!' Jet teased.

'Excuse me! It was true. I was on court early the next day, and his next match wasn't until the evening.'

The blond hot-shot let out an evil cackle. 'I bet if you'd had dinner with Dad that night, you wouldn't have turned him down?'

'Yes, I would,' his mother replied. 'I did turn him down a few times, I'll have you know. He was surprisingly good about it too. Even though he always paints himself as a sex maniac in those days, your dad was pretty respectful of my wishes. He understood the demands of my training schedule, and how flat-out I was with music and school. He only pushed his luck once or twice.'

Lynn lost concentration for a second, being transported back in time and recalling why her enigmatic stranger had been prepared to leave her to sleep alone during busy periods. Her heart skipped a beat or two, images of her persuasive sexual mercenary causing her to marvel at how stupid she had been to let him lead a double life when it came to meeting his physical needs. The deal had suited them both at the time, despite how unacceptable the notion seemed now. How life had changed for the star-crossed lovers!

'And did you sometimes give in?' Kierney prompted. 'To *Papá*, I mean... After you fell in love with him?'

'Oh, of course I did! I'm not made of stone, *pequeñita*!'

The young woman sighed at this loving impersonation. 'Good! That's lovely. I know I'm going to find it hard to resist spending time with someone I love, even when I have to get up early for training. Is that bad? I s'pose Grandpa'd be horrified if he heard me say things like that.'

'You're right there! He was horrified by anything to do with me and boyfriends!' her mother affirmed. 'Grandpa believed in total dedication when we were younger. He's relented a bit these days. Your father taught him that, largely.'

'Because of your big argument?' Jet asked. 'About my summer program?'

'Yes. But let's not talk about that, please.'

Kierney looked concerned. 'Which argument?'

'Nothing, darling. Never mind,' their mother waved her hand. 'So anyway... Dean didn't know I'd had dinner with Patrice, and he asked me out again on the Saturday after I'd gone back to school. He was a professional footballer by this time and studying at Melbourne Uni'. He thought he was "God's gift", raking in heaps of money and driving around in a flashy sports car like Junior's. I realised I liked him less and less each time I saw him, but my school friends all considered him a great catch. Peer pressure's a powerful thing, as I'm sure you guys already know.'

Both children nodded. Growing up in the public eye, with an extended family jam-packed with successful celebrities, Ryan and Kierney Diamond had no shortage of role models. Their parents' and grandparents' long stints on Melbourne Academy's Board of Governors maintained focus on running one's own race, empowering staff to pounce on any bullying or coercion before it had a chance to damage the students' prospects.

'So, Mum, when did Dad ask you out?' Jet asked, having dropped his Mister Cool air on the promise of more carnal references. 'Not long after term started obviously... Wasn't it during Year Twelve orientation?'

'Fifteenth of Feb',' Lynn rattled off. 'Eleven o'clock in the morning or thereabouts.'

From the warmth of the lounge room rug, Kierney sprang to her knees at the anecdote she never tired of hearing. She cherished her parents' first few hours together almost as much as they did. Lynn held out her hand, and the million-dollar girl scrambled like a toddler onto the couch and cuddled in.

'And then, once I was on the bus going back to school, I realised I needed to break up with Dean properly. When I'd said yes to *Papá*, that is,' the honourable woman recounted. 'You know... Do the decent thing. It was quite scary. I'd never had to deliver bad news to anyone before, but I knew it wasn't right to two-time someone.'

'How did you tell him?' her son asked. 'I may need some tips soon.'

'Why?' his sister yelped. 'Are you breaking up with Bec already?'

Lynn raised a finger to her mouth. 'Shhh... That's Jet's business. I 'phoned Dean, but he wasn't in. I left a message with his mum, and he rang me back later, all excited because he thought I wanted to go out with him again. Then he turned really angry when he found out I was giving him the flick.'

'Oh, that's horrible! I'd hate to have to tell someone I didn't want to see them again. Did you tell him why?' Kierney asked.

'Yes. Well, I didn't tell him I'd gone off him, if that's what you mean! I said I'd met someone else. He wouldn't accept it and kept calling me almost every day.'

'For how long?' the young man asked.

'Until I showed up at a friend's birthday party with Dad,' his mother tossed her long hair over her shoulder, eyes flashing. 'He got the message pretty fast after that. Especially when some of the other guys started teasing him that I'd had sex with his replacement! That was so embarrassing.'

'Why was it embarrassing?'

'Well, just imagine…' Lynn explained to her spellbound audience. 'I'd spent all those weeks making excuses why I didn't want to have sex with Dean, and then I jumped straight into bed with the next man I went out with.'

Both youngsters laughed. Kierney appeared somewhat shocked for a few seconds while she processed the information. Her mother sympathised, remembering with alarming clarity how overwhelmed she had felt by the significance of losing her virginity, with so many additional dimensions to adulthood than any child could fathom beforehand.

'I'm going to fetch *Papá*,' her daughter announced, shuffling forwards off the cushion. 'That's a great story, *Mamá*. I'm glad I'm not related to Dean Keller. I'd much rather be a mixture of you and *Papá*. I love being me.'

The cricketer groaned. 'Corny or what? Do you love having me as a brother too?' he jeered. 'You'd better say yes.'

'Sorry, mate,' his sister smirked, already halfway to the door. 'I'll call you.'

***

'What's with this proposal you sent over?' Jeff asked, leafing through a ring-bound document which had arrived in the morning's post. 'What am I lining your pockets with now?'

Gerry tittered. 'If only you knew, oh-master. No, but to be serious for a second… It's a tender you need to read through. Mike and I met yesterday and decided to issue an "RfP" for a round-the-clock security detail for you lot.'

'Ah, yeah? Seems a bit excessive. Why?'

'Three death threats this week alone, mate. Someone evidently thinks you're fair game, and Lion's advised us to get on top of it a-s-a-p.'

318

'Three from the same source?' Jeff sighed, juggling the car-phone from ear to ear as he navigated the midday traffic on the Nepean Highway. 'Who is it? Can they trace where they're coming from?'

The billionnaire's spirits had been flagging more than usual in the three weeks since his son's sixteenth birthday, contributing to the usual annoying downward spiral. He and Lynn were under no illusion that his persistent bouts of depression could be eliminated, yet he longed for the day when the pleasures of their life singular propelled him to heights of happiness beyond the black dog's reach.

On paper, life had never been better for the globe-trotting stars and their offspring. Paragon Holdings was about to post another year of record growth, and the company's share price had rocketed to an all-time high on the Australian Stock Exchange. Stonebridge Music had between ten and fifteen of the top-selling albums on various charts across the world, and Kierney's first full release of songs on compact disc had achieved platinum status in April.

The usual crises alternated with major breakthroughs for the Diamond Celebration Foundation's charitable endeavours, with statistics painting a brighter future for the couple's projects in North Africa than workers reported from the field. These ongoing struggles weren't reason for undue concern either, leaving the world-changer at an absolute loss as to the trigger for his latest tumble into the chasm of despair.

'Don't know, mate,' his manager answered. 'Mike's working on it. When can you come in?'

Jeff laughed. 'You're asking me? How long have you known me?'

'Ha, ha! Very funny, I'm sure. In that case, ask your lovely wife to ring me. I always get more sense out of her anyway.'

A week later, the Diamonds and the indomitable Mister Blake dined with a voluptuous South African representative from the tender's successful respondent. While Lynn and Willemien discussed upcoming tours and itineraries, the men did their best to steer their eyes from the saleswoman's ample cleavage to examine her colleagues' interpretation of the three fearsome pieces of evidence.

Sure enough, the first two letters to arrive bore the hallmarks of an organisation rather than an individual, and judging by the forthright language used, they inferred a well-informed agenda and bold though misguided goals. Despite the third note's more amateur origins, the message transcribed on the page was no less chilling.

Following his manager to the restroom while the foursome waited for their main courses to arrive, Jeff whistled. 'Jesus Christ, Gezza! As much as I don't want to take this security lark seriously, I applaud your tender evaluation process. Who is this woman? Is she for real? Brings a whole new meaning to the word "bouncer".'

'Fuck you, boss!' Gerry hooted. 'A man's *gotta* have some fun while he's keeping you and yours alive. You've got the lovely Lynn. I'll take magnificent Miena. Thank you and good night... There's a brain in that body too, in case you hadn't noticed. She did her Masters at Yale.'

The songwriter zipped up his fly and slapped his old friend's back hard enough to push his knees into the base of the urinal. 'Miena? Sure she did, mate. What in? Plastic surgery? My dick-brain doesn't function too well with airbags, so I'll leave her to you. At least she won't charge us for a hotel room!'

'Indeed! Hope not,' the lecherous executive grinned. 'Airbags? Do you reckon those puppies are fake?'

His friend shrugged, shaking his head at the disappointed look on the accountant's face. For all his years of experience wooing the female population, the affable Irishman remained remarkably ignorant of the extreme measures some took to augment their sex appeal. If love were blind, the lyricist mused as they wrung their hands beneath underpowered dryers, pure lust must deprive its victims of all their faculties.

Both coughing in an effort to curb their boyish merriment, the men returned to their table to find Lynn poring over a brochure spread out across her dinner plate. Willemien, it turned out, had been appointed to the title of Sales Director at one of the security consultancies the Diamonds had been using for a number of years and was busy explaining various recommended strategies for preserving the famous family's safety.

Jeff put his hand on his wife's shoulder, sensing a level of concern. 'Everything OK?' he asked, sitting down and peering at the glossy surface which blinded him with its reflection of the restaurant's modern, stark lighting. 'What's that?'

'Our survival kit. What to do and what not to do when handling threatening letters and items arriving in the mail.'

'Cool. Just the thing for a fun night out,' her husband quipped. 'Where do we start? Did someone check our wine hasn't been laced with strychnine?'

The elegant thirty-seven-year-old exhaled. 'Oh, shut up! Willemien's gone to a lot of trouble to scope out this program. We need to pay it more attention.'

Jeff took a large sip of the blood-red *Shiraz* and sloshed it around his teeth to make the most of its delectable bite. As usual, his guardian angel was right. It wouldn't do to stick his head in the sand on this topic. What if their children were kidnapped again? For real, this time. Or worse, he shuddered.

'Forgive me, ladies,' he directed his eyes above the heaving chest, his concentration fractured as the toe of Gerry's brogue kicked his shin under the table. 'Thanks for your assistance with all this. Lynn's much better at working with you than I am. I'm bloody hopeless and way too *blasé* about stuff we should pay attention to.'

'That's quite alright, Jeff,' Willemien replied. 'As long as enough people around you are aware of the procedures you should put in place. My organisation can only advise you. And protect you if necessary, of course. It can't stop you from living your lives as you wish.'

'Life,' the celebrity muttered, sliding his right hand across the silky fabric of his wife's skirt. 'Our life. We only have one between us. Singular in fact, isn't it, gorgeous?'

'What?' Gerry spluttered, swallowing a large mouthful of wine down in one hit. 'What are you on about now? Four lives are at stake here, mate. As your manager and your friend, I'm telling you to get a grip on how grave these matters are, or there's no point in us putting this contract in place.'

Picking up the half-empty bottle, the host topped up all four glasses before requesting a second from the *maître d'*. Their dinners having been delivered to the table with a fanfare neither star enjoyed, he was relieved when conversation switched to lighter topics while they ate. Lynn had everyone entertained with some of the ludicrous juvenile behaviour they witnessed at Jet's recent birthday party, and Gerry described his mother's latest attempt to encourage her resolutely single son into monogamy.

A troop of eager waiters cleared away the celebrity diners' empty plates and refilled their water glasses, buzzing around in the hope of picking up some juicy gossip. Their guest had become more relaxed in the company of Australia's most famous stars as the meal progressed, swapping stories of her home country's turbulent political situation with a *trio* who knew much more than she did about its inner workings.

Once the frantic table-clearing excitement had died down, Gerry resumed the night's official business, turning once more to the subject of threatening letters. The buxom security specialist posed a series of unanswerable questions to her new clients, designed to gauge the likelihood of a major incident.

Moreover, after hearing how the couple had negotiated their way out of Jeff's Ethiopian hinterland hostage episode and the extent to which they had prepared Jet and Kierney for a similar eventuality, Willemien began to sound less bullish about her company's value-adding services.

'Gez, hold your fire a minute,' Jeff interrupted after a while. 'Aren't we taking this a bit too far? We all take risks just stepping outside our houses, driving to and from work or even doing stuff around the house.'

'Mate, I know that.'

'So what makes us different from the next guy is that there may be people out there wanting to cause us deliberate harm,' the jet-setter continued, 'which is the same for anyone with an enemy.'

'That's true, Jeff,' the South African confirmed. 'The more enemies we can identify and shut down, the better your chances of not getting mixed up in anything dangerous. Surely you agree with that?'

'Oh, yes. He does,' Lynn leaped to her husband's defence, resting a hand on his twitching thigh and squeezing until the spasms ceased. 'We don't cultivate enemies if we can help it. And nor are we trying to avoid the issue. It's just very claustrophobic sometimes, and it feels like so much energy's going into preparing for a future that might never happen. Energy that could be better spent on things that are actually happening today.'

'Amen to that! *Gracias*, angel,' the philosopher acknowledged. 'I know I'm behaving badly, Willemien, and I'm sorry. But Lynn's right. We could work so hard to neutralise everyone who has a negative opinion about something we do, wasting a swag of time and money doing it, only to find one of us gets taken out in a random car accident. I'm just not sure it's worth going to the lengths you're suggesting.'

'You mean you've survived thus far, so you'll take your chances?' Gerry's voice turned surly. 'That's a bloody fatalistic way of looking at things.'

Jeff frowned. 'It's not fatalistic, mate, but it is a valid point of view,' he ventured. 'If I were to be fatalistic, which I often am... Eh, Lynn?'

The golden-haired beauty leaned against her favourite harbinger of doom and smiled. 'You are, *mon brave*.'

'*Et bien, merci encore une fois*,' the songwriter chuckled at his lover's haughty accent. 'If I were to be fatalistic, I'd simply say, "Bring it on. You want a piece of me, come and get it. Let's see how far you get." It's a numbers game at the end of the day.'

'With all due respect, Jeff, Lynn,' the security consultant disputed, 'it's not a numbers game. Companies like ours wouldn't exist if security was purely a numbers game. We're here to lessen the odds, if you like.'

So the Toorak Casanova was correct! Above the magisterial blouse which trembled as its occupant argued, there was indeed a sharp mind. The peacemaker was impressed, despite an uncontrollable urge to laugh at the image of his manager in his BMW later, grappling with her fine figure while offering to fasten her seatbelt. With any luck, he would receive a detailed report tomorrow to satisfy his curiosity.

But for now, re-energised by Gerry's predicament, the intellectual was up for a debate. 'Fair enough, Ms du Plessis. I agree to a point. You guys can lessen the odds, and we'll pay you to do so as far as reasonable. I owe that much to Lynn and my far less fatalistic friend here, and to our kids as well, of course. But if any of our numbers come up, our numbers come up.'

Jeff heard his wife take a sharp breath, doubtless due to the lack of respect he had shown this well-credentialled woman. He expected some stern words would be spoken before they reached the apartment, but he had a point to prove in the meantime.

The superstars had received death threats on numerous occasions over the years, none of which had come remotely close to fruition. The Jaworski family's intimidation had been eradicated without adverse consequences, and they had been stalked and mobbed at no end of public appearances, sometimes unable to see an exit route for the swarms of people on all sides. Once even, a four-litre can of paint had been poured over his beloved Aston Martin. These were all headaches they could do without, but was it really necessary to fine-tune their life to avoid the slim chance that someone wanted to exact grievous bodily harm?

'Y'know, I heard at your drinks the other day, Gerry… from one of the guys I was talking to… that a friend of theirs' wife and kid were killed while she walked with the stroller along the footpath, in front of a line of shops,' the songwriter recalled. 'A truck mounted the kerb out of control and pinned them to the wall. Both dead before they got to hospital. Three-year-old child. Gone. Thirty-year-old wife. Gone. Why do we think we're so worth saving? It could happen to anyone.'

Mercifully for Willemien, a waitress arrived with the dessert menu just as Jeff finished his morbid diatribe, since no-one could think of any means of discrediting it. Allowing himself a certain conceit at having silenced the expert, he remained outwardly subdued and sorrowful at this poor man's lonely plight.

Lynn's telepathic appreciation burned into his heart, as ever, reinforcing his hypothesis. Yes, the Diamonds were Very Important People on the global stage, and undeniably in the eyes of the Australian public, neither of which entitled them to special privileges when it came to surviving the aforementioned odds.

'Gerry…' his dream girl took the reins, sensing her man had said all he was prepared to say on the subject.

'Yes, Missus D?'

'We should organise a meeting with Lion to implement some of these new measures. Especially in terms of Cathy's team checking with the police weekly and ensuring our travel arrangements are kept confidential. I'm sure they do it anyway, but it's worth re-iterating.'

'Right you are, my dear,' the family's loyal manager saluted, watching his clients exchange affectionate glances. 'The voice of reason speaks. Anything else while we're at it?'

'Yes,' the patient blonde smiled. 'We shall consider a security presence for Jet and Kierney when they travel outside their normal routine. That's something we could go for, Jeff, isn't it?'

The grateful husband nodded, albeit with reluctance. Gerry's description was apt in so many ways: Lynn always cut through the messy bureaucracy and extracted sufficient emotion from these tough decisions, rendering them easier to make. Bodyguards for the teenagers while on their journeys to independence was the prudent thing to do, and never would he have it said that undue risks were taken with their lives.

'And for the two of us, at rallies and other non-ticketed events with large crowds, we should have more security personnel,' the sportswoman carried on, leafing through the coloured brochure again. 'Could you please recommend how many, Willemien?'

The South African nodded, jotting these instructions down in a tiny notebook while Gerry looked on speechless. Admiring an Olympian angel in full flight was the billionnaire's second-favourite pastime, and tonight he leaned back in his chair to watch on in awe.

'For ourselves on normal days though, I'm with Jeff. I'd much rather travel under our own steam and without any kind of *entourage* as often as possible. We'll do some more awareness training, so we can be alert to potential weirdos, but that's all. I don't want to be one of those pretentious celebrities people can't see for a three-deep layer of black suits and ear-pieces whispering to their cufflinks.'

Staggered to hear his wife back him as far as she had, the rock star turned to his right and planted a heartfelt kiss on her smiling lips. 'Well said, *Regala*,' he said, before toasting the sentiment. 'And tomorrow, we dine with the devil.'

'Fucking hell, guys,' the Irishman raised his voice, his face racked with exasperation at his clients' cavalier caprice in front of their costly consultant. 'We're trying to help you stay safe. For God's sake, at least pretend you care. We could all die tomorrow, that's perfectly true. But I'd rather not deal with the tidal wave of multi-national grief that'll drown the rest of us if you do. Imagine what'd happen if either of you should fall victim to one of your so-called weirdos?'

Jeff locked eyes with his faithful right-hand man, the buzz of an awkward silence emanating from their shocked guest. Had they strayed into "fat cat" territory, assuming a Faustian level of invincibility reserved only for the deluded? He swallowed the menacing retort which sprang to mind initially, thinking better of airing his true feelings. Instead, he looped an arm around his wife's shoulders, pulling her closer until her chair rocked sideways.

'Hey! Careful,' Lynn whispered, knowing Gerry's words had hit home. 'We do take these things seriously, but we also know it's useless trying to guard against every single possibility. It needs to balance, just like all the other ledgers you manage so well for us. We'll take this document home and give it a thorough review, and I'll ring you both in the next couple of days with our decisions. Is that OK?'

***

September nineteen-ninety-three saw the Diamonds' combined "Live on Earth" tour already deep in the planning. A year-long expedition covering over seventy cities on all continents was to be the couple's first and last tour together before giving their entire life singular over to business and charitable interests. Auditions were underway, with orchestral scores receiving an overhaul and dancers put through their supercharged choreographic paces, and a mountain of visa applications had been completed and submitted to Cathy and her assiduous team of travel agents.

'Is it my imagination, or does everything take longer to organise these days?' Jeff asked at breakfast on his dream girl's thirty-seventh birthday.

'No. Not really,' she chuckled. 'Maybe it seems that way 'cause you take more interest in the process now than you used to. Before, you'd only want to know what day you were leaving and how long the flight was, so you could pack the right amount of reading material.'

Feigning outrage, the intellectual pointed his cereal spoon at his wife's face. 'That's bullshit, ma'am! I have occasionally packed my own suitcase too. Just because it's your birthday, doesn't mean you can spread vicious rumours about me.'

'Oh, it's no rumour,' Lynn teased, clashing spoons with the man she loved so much. 'But feel free to take on more responsibility.'

With their revised security measures bedded down and both teenagers alternating between the Melbourne Academy dormitories and *Escondido*'s supervised weekend paradise, the artists revelled in tandem music-making on the grandest scale. No longer concerned about joint performances impacting their careers or compromising their individual artistic integrity, they indulged in epic duets and colourful and energetic dance routines which drove their audiences wild.

October and November rocked and rolled in a whirlwind of adulation. Their album sales shot skyward with minimal lag between concert dates and chart movements, and the DCF charities raked in millions of dollars in the period leading to the festive season. Their combined efforts reaped such tremendous rewards that the celebrity couple granted Stonebridge Music staff an extra fortnight's leave and closed the office to tie in with the school year's conclusion.

Nevertheless, there was still plenty to do before the family's trip to Northern Ireland for Christmas. Jeff had been invited to participate in the latest round of peace talks at Stormont Castle, arranged far enough in advance to realign the UK leg of the tour. When she heard this news, Kierney's best friend hurried to invite the famous foursome to her father's ancestral home in County Donegal, not for a moment expecting an acceptance!

Piraea Loudon, a promising young violinist with a flirtatious attitude and a wicked sense of humour, had been a regular weekend visitor at *Escondido* since her parents returned to the northern hemisphere for work-related reasons. She and her younger sister, Olympia, became boarders at Melbourne Academy, and her friendship with the self-sufficient Kierney had flourished with the demands of newfound maturity.

The Loudons and the Diamonds had been no more than distant acquaintances since both girls graduated to high school. Surprised to receive the invitation in the first place, Lynn was delighted when Jeff agreed to spending the holidays with virtual strangers. The introvert preferred to constrain their socialising to a minimum over Christmas, once the curtains descended on their final engagement of the season, and the exhausted quartet normally flew up to Sydney's north shore on the red-eye to hang out with the Blakes.

A bracing fifty-five degrees North was a far cry from the balmy New South Wales climate in December, yet for the well-travelled Australians, Fergus

Loudon's sprawling, aristocratic country seat on the outskirts of a town whose central precinct bore the same name proved an irresistible offer.

'Angel, may I take Captain Marvellous away for a day or two while you girls are playing Brontë sisters?' Jeff asked. 'To ride bikes and grow up? Or down, in my case.'

His wife laughed. 'Hmm… Motorbikes?'

'Yep. It'll be awesome.'

'Until it starts snowing! That'd be pretty unpleasant, and dangerous too. It gets dark at four o'clock at this time of year, remember?'

'Ah, dangerous, *schmangerous*. It won't snow,' the dark-haired hero assured her. 'I've checked the long-range forecast. It'll be raining most of the time, I reckon, which is fine. Good for Jet to learn to control the bike on slippery roads.'

'And you,' the patient mother added. 'Is he old enough?'

'Nearly. He's big enough, and that's what it takes. More than age. So is that a yes, angel, please?'

The tolerant matriarch shook her head. *That old chestnut*, she could hear her husband's telepathic transmission running with minimal interference. Since when had a Dyson ever waited to reach the right and proper age to do any activity? She had no doubt Jeff would keep their precious boy out of trouble, both with the law and with nature's exigencies.

'Why not? Nearly's better than no, I suppose. Why not? There'll certainly be an excess of oestrogen when Fergus is at work. At the moment, our last gig's on the seventeenth, so we can be done with press conferences, *et cetera*, and be in Ireland by the twentieth. That'll leave a few days for you two to disappear before Christmas Eve.'

'Cool. Very nice,' Jeff grinned and pecked her cheek. 'Thanks, gorgeous. What time do you want to set off? Can I take you somewhere for lunch if we're out on time?'

Lynn's thirty-eighth birthday coincided with the kick-off of the latest Childlight project. She had seen no point in changing their schedule for the sake of yet another hum-drum anniversary, and what better way to celebrate than by allocating their undivided attention to the launch of a new Kids' Lifeline. This new service included a national call centre run from DCF's Richmond headquarters, set up to field calls from for young people experiencing abuse or neglect. Profits from the sellout "Live on Earth" tour were funnelled into the program to recruit counsellors for anonymous assistance.

Milling around near the stage while the camera crew established their angles and flustered interns adorned presenters with lapel microphones, the proud songwriter caught sight of a vaguely familiar face a few rows back in the studio audience.

'Hey, angel,' he tapped the birthday girl on the shoulder. 'D'you recognise that bloke over there? Dark suit and red tie, across from where Tamsin's standing.'

His wife scanned the tiered seating and located the studio's set director, following her man's left-hand index finger as it tracked across until she noticed a man's shy wave. 'Who is it? Oh, my God! Is he that aerospace engineer we met at The Fellowship?'

'Yep. Think so. Come on. Let's go and say hello. We've got time. I always wondered what happened to him.'

The well-built, brown-haired man scrambled to his feet, blushing and excusing himself as he pushed past the others in his row until he reached the aisle. The show's early birds began to point and chatter, seeing the miracle-workers walking towards them.

'Brian?' Jeff held his hand out. 'Bloody hell! I thought I recognised you. How're you going, mate?'

'Hello, Jeff, Lynn,' the good-looking man replied, daring to lean forward to kiss the cheek offered by the stunning blonde celebrity. 'I'm good, thanks. And you? You guys are so amazing. This is fantastic, what you're doing. I can't believe I was there right at the beginning of all this!'

'Thanks,' the rear-end of the Diamond pantomime horse acknowledged, pleased to show off the brightly lit bank of telethon desks. 'Indeed. None of us had any idea what we were in for back then! It's been such a long time since that night in the old church hall. What's brought you here today?'

The businessman reached into his pants pocket for his wallet, removed a card and offered it to the dignified patron. Lynn deferred to her front-man, who took it, flipped it over twice and then handed it to her anyway, making the other man laugh.

'My firm made a donation,' Brian said. 'I love the work you do with all these support programs. It's awe-inspiring. We contribute to most of your events when there's spare in our budgets.'

Jeff gave the older man's upper arm a hearty slap, remembering the last time they had crossed paths. 'Cheers, mate. Thanks very much. I wish we knew before. We could've caught up much sooner. How did it work out for you back then? Not too bad, by the look of it.'

The reserved engineer smiled. 'I'm embarrassed to tell you the whole thing ended up being an over-reaction. My wife and I got back together after a year.'

'Why's that embarrassing?' the kind woman asked. 'It's a great result. And you're still together?'

'I know,' Brian agreed. 'Yes, we are, and the kids are all grown up. That drama feels like an eternity ago.'

'Good news, mate,' the erstwhile amateur psychologist nodded, trying not to draw the crowd's curiosity to what he assumed was a private matter. 'That drama, as you describe it, was a natural reaction for you at the time. I'm pleased for you, mate. We both done mighty fine!'

'Cheers, Jeff. I fought for custody of the kids through the courts. Patiently, like you suggested. I think Sharon realised I wasn't the boring idiot she thought I was after all. She decided her grass wasn't much greener with the new boyfriend and it was worth trying again to keep the family together. We still cringe whenever your "My grass is green enough" slogan comes on the TV!'

Reminded of the hackneyed expression her husband had adopted to describe his marital bliss for several years now, Lynn leaned into his steadfast but ever-grateful body. Predictably, his arm slipped around her waist, and he kissed her temple.

'*Excelente.*'

'In fact, our youngest boy's attempting The Good School's exam' for next year.'

Lynn was in top-flight diplomatic mode, much to her larrikin husband's amusement. 'Oh, is he? That's great. Hope he goes well. How old are your sons now?'

'Aaron's eighteen. He's quite a bit younger than the others; the "whoops" baby, if you know what I mean! Michael's twenty-four, and Josh is twenty-two. How old are yours now?'

'Jet's sixteen and Kierney's fourteen,' she rattled off, silencing an anxious studio hand who was trying to attract the couple's attention. 'Looks like we have to go, Jeff. Sorry, Brian. It was so good to see you again. And thanks again for supporting us.'

'You're welcome. I was hoping I'd get to talk to you for a minute. I've got you to thank for making my life work out.'

The songwriter scoffed. 'Maybe half a percent. You worked it out yourself, mate.'

'Not true. I've read all your books, and a lot of your research too. It's been very helpful to understand myself and everyone else better, so thanks heaps.'

The two prosperous businessmen gave each other a manly hug, and the superstar grabbed the engineer's hand again as he was summoned away. An elated donor made his way back to his seat while the hosts for the evening's televised launch stood in their allotted spot to headline the live cross to Channel Nine's nightly current affairs programme.

Celia Blake had been over the moon with being installed as the Kids' Lifeline's patron, in response to a request she had issued at Jeff's fortieth birthday party to become more involved with charity work. Quaking in her high heels, the elegant housewife met her favourite celebrities in the Green Room, wringing a handkerchief through nervous hands.

'Relax, Missus B,' her pseudo-son urged. 'How're you going? Just be your glorious self. No need to worry. It's all completely spontaneous, and we'll do most of the talking. You'll instinctively know what to say when the kids come on the line.'

The producer counted down from five, cameras already rolling in front of a packed audience of industry professionals and journalists. The Diamond Celebration Foundation's fortunate son opened with a chilling personal account of what it was like to be an abused and neglected child, and Lynn described how, in the first year of their relationship, she had only understood the true meaning of petrified after watching her mystery man freeze as soon as she walked away from him.

'The old Jeff used to follow me around like a puppy,' she recounted. 'Can you imagine that, compared to who he is now? It was sweet at first, but later it became very worrying. When he told me he was scared I'd never come back, I didn't have the faintest idea how serious he was. It took almost five years of stability before the confidence was there for him to be able to say, "There's always tomorrow."'

The story's protagonist nodded, preparing to take up the mantle. 'It's all true, but we're hoping things won't need to spiral down so far for this generation's kids. The new Childlight helpline's designed to stop these hellish situations causing permanent damage to children, so they don't grow up with mental health conditions which hamper everyday life.

'If they know there's someone they can talk to confidentially... anonymously if they want... it'll help them keep a level of self-esteem and stay positive in the face of adversity. Take it from me, it makes a world of difference if kids can believe in human kindness, like the compassion this beautiful creature showed me when I most needed it. Trust someone's got their back well enough to get on with their education and make friends, et cetera. All we have to do is provide the right environment for kids to repair what's been done to them, then we can stand back and watch 'em thrive. To allow them to be successful.

'And by successful, I don't mean standing up here and speaking to you like I am today. Success can be anything; merely the ability to be independent for starters... To go to school, earn their own money and to have the wherewithal to make sound choices about what to spend it on. Or success might be achieving a personal goal, such as passing an exam' or getting a part-time job. That's all it takes to set these kids on an upward trajectory instead of the death-spiral of drink, drugs, homelessness and crime.'

Jeff took a deep breath while the audience's polite ripples of applause escalated into raucous cheers as the passion evident in his speech roused its collective conscience. Most Australians were aware of fragments of his back-story, after two decades of public frankness from the charismatic rocker, and with converts like Brian as regular benefactors, he felt buoyed by the contribution DCF's efforts were making to improve lives.

In the background, telephones jingled and warbled like bathers at the most popular bird bath in town, prompting the television cameras to pan past their famous *compères* to catch a glimpse of the Kids' Lifeline call centre operators in action.

'OK! So...' the man of the moment continued, in his element with his dream girl beaming and clapping along. 'There are three words we'd like you to leave with tonight, branded on your brain; words we'd like you to associate with the Kids' Lifeline: courage, resilience and persistence.'

The three bywords which Cathy's market research team had trialled on focus groups across the country were enunciated clearly and slowly, followed by a deliberate pause during which no-one even dared breathe.

'Courage, resilience and persistence,' Lynn repeated, her eyes scanning the packed auditorium from side to side, making eye contact with as many people as possible. 'Now Jeff says he was lucky, but actually that's only part of the story. He learned how to make life work for him, and I don't mean in a sociopathic way, of course! He made his own luck by actively seeking out mentors and teachers and friends to compensate for inadequate parental guidance and a lack of money. He was able to recognise what was missing and then how to go after it; where or from whom he could get help without causing trouble.

'Many of the young people we're trying to connect with through DCF's work have no idea where to start when it comes to meeting their own needs. Most of us learn these basic life-skills by growing up in a family unit, but these kids never receive this information for free. And much less how to use the information for their own good. So through Childlight, and now the new Kids' Lifeline, we can provide some of this vital knowledge *via* these good people you see behind us.'

Lynn extended her hand to her beautiful black stallion, whose eyes shone with love and on whose broad shoulders sat the world's future. She knew, from the rough script they had drafted together, that he was about to re-emphasise his good fortune at meeting her. Yet the reverse was also true. How on Earth did she, Lynn Dyson, privileged private school girl who grew up without a care, find herself as this powerhouse's soul-mate?

'And to prove how lucky I am, look at my unbelievably gorgeous wife!' he shouted to the rafters, lifting their joined hands high in the air. 'It don't get no better than waking up next to Lynn, I can tell *ya*!'

Again, the noise generated in the studio was enough to send the sound engineer's graphic equalisers well into the red zone. The couple used its momentum to transport them over to the banks of telephones, ready to take its place on a semi-circular podium where Celia and one of their company's fundraising managers were waiting.

'Whoa! Thank you,' the orator continued, inviting his dream girl to sit down next to Gerry's mother. 'It's great to see so many of you here tonight, and thanks also to everyone watching on TV. Now here's the deal... We can't solve the scourge of mental illness overnight or stop all perpetrators of abuse, but we can sure as hell help heal the scars left behind from a traumatic childhood. We can all play a part in teaching kids ways to deal with that stuff better.'

'For example,' his partner took over, 'they say Jeff Diamond's one of the richest and most influential men in the country. However, as lucky as he undoubtedly is, there are still many mornings when he can't even get out of bed. Isn't that right?'

The new Jeff Diamond nodded, flirting with the camera as only he knew how. 'Perfectly true, angel.'

'Why get up if she's in there with you?' a man shouted from behind the cameras.

'Yeah, well. I hear *ya*, mate... What do I have to be depressed about?' the prankster let out a salacious gloat which his microphone picked up loud and clear. 'Could have something to do with it, mate! But Lynn gets up way earlier than I do, and this is a family show... I want to pass on a few more secrets tonight, before we get down to business. First, the irony for people like us is that, unlike the majority of working people whose serious activities pay for the fun parts of their lives, it's our more frivolous pursuits that pay for serious stuff like this.'

Distracted by a burst of muted laughter, Lynn and Jeff looked at each other and then at a number of heads nodding among the stage crew. 'Thanks very much,' the respected leader took a deep breath and carried on. 'Moving right along... These three attributes, courage, resilience and persistence, out of the hundreds of invaluable lessons I've learned from this picture of perfection here, have since become a *mantra* for the Diamond Celebration Foundation. Through our projects, we strive to give people, firstly, the courage to act on whatever they need to do; then secondly, the resilience to handle the setbacks when they inevitably come, so people don't give up at the first hurdle; and thirdly, persistence to keep trying, no matter what life throws at you. In other words, hone your message, respond to criticism and don't let it send you spinning out of control by using professional anti-death-spiral folks like the guys on the 'phones here.'

The vehement campaigner paused for another spontaneous show of appreciation from their captive audience, before directing the attention back to himself. 'So what kind of things happen to these kids? Who here grew up with drink and drugs in the house?'

He lifted his gaze, with a camera operator tracking every *nuance* while he picked out other willing volunteers from backstage obscurity. 'Who regularly had the police crawling around in your bedroom?'

And for a third time, Jeff's hand pointed outwards after asking each question, working to a *crescendo* to metre out his important message. 'And whose teachers and friends'd turn their backs on you if you met them outside of school?

'And who watched their brothers or sisters being abused?

'By people they knew?

'By people they should've been able to trust?'

If all eyes and ears hadn't already been on this photogenic star, they certainly were now. 'Who had to sneak out of the house to go to the library? Hands up!

'And whose dad carried a knife wherever he went and wasn't afraid to bring it out in public to pretend he was a real man? Any more hands?'

Jeff's voice croaked as a wave of emotion surged from his heart to his throat. Once more, he reached for the slender, dazzling blonde beside him.

'How many of you can say you're married to the most beautiful woman in the world?' he added, beckoning to everyone in the audience to speak of their partners in this way. 'Hands up! Who here's up for winning Australian of the Year three times? The answer is any of us can. We just need some help along the way.

'We can make things come good for these kids, just like they came so fantastically good for me. Ladies and gentlemen, please dig deep and support Kids' Lifeline. It *will* make a difference, believe me, because we can arm these guys with some basic life-skills they wouldn't otherwise have access to. It's good to be smart, and it's smart to be good. That's pretty much all they need to understand. Everything else'll take care of itself.'

The studio erupted with applause. Women screamed, and men whooped and chanted, stamping their boots on the wooden structure which held up banks of temporary seating. Telephone calls behind them had to be suspended since none of the operators could hear a thing above the triumphant acclaim.

'You can do it, guys!' the handsome songwriter continued to stir the pot. 'Courage, resilience and persistence. Living with mental health issues like depression and Post-Traumatic Stress Disorder doesn't equal "loser", but only you can isolate the symptoms from messing up the rest of your life. People might think you're a hero at school if you act tough and threatening, but there's no big win in that. It'll be short-lived. People like you and respect you far more if you treat them the same way. That's what we mean by "It's good to be smart, and it's smart to be good." This is Kids' Lifeline! Get on the 'phone, kids. You need us? We're here!'

After more eardrum-puncturing cheers, the superstars moved out of the spotlight, quietening everyone down as they went. The camera followed them into the makeshift call centre, where Jeff stopped and introduced his manager's mother. Celia Blake was a natural, helped along by some easy questions, providing her own authentic account of life with the wild boy who turned into Jeff Diamond.

'Thanks, Celia. Guys, this fantastic lady and her family were my Kids' Lifeline when I needed it most,' the grateful man proclaimed, resting his hands on the grandmother's shoulders while he sang her praises. 'Not many kids have access to free services offered by people like Celia and her husband, Gerald. I was bloody lucky and took full advantage way too often. Celia's on the 'phones tonight, and there are heaps more amazing volunteers for kids to talk to, twenty-four seven from now on.'

As Lynn turned to take up her position on the bank of desks to the rear, the telephone next to the older woman rang, making them all jump. Her husband reached down and lifted the receiver, and the microphone picked up a child's faint voice.

'Hello. This is Jeff. Who's this?'

'Don't ring back on this number,' the caller begged in a high-pitched voice that splintered through the sound system. 'I took the 'phone into the hall.'

'No worries. I won't,' the show's host promised, discerning an urgency which prickled the hairs on the back of his neck. 'Can you tell me your name, please?'

'No, but my sister's leg's broken, and she can't stop cryin'. She told me to call. She needs to go to 'ospital.'

'OK. It's good you're helping your sister out,' the superstar's eyes widened, caught on camera in an unforced real-life drama. 'How old's your sister? Are your parents in the house with you?'

Listening to dead air for a few seconds, Jeff wondered whether the child had hung up. 'Are you still there?'

A few more painful seconds of silence passed, with not a sound from the audience and crew to ease the tension. It was as if the whole world were on tenterhooks, waiting for the plot to develop. Lynn slipped into a narrow space between the two rows of desks, sweeping her hand across her man's back.

Just as everyone was ready to give up hope of hearing more, a frantic but hushed exchange could be heard, presumably between the caller and the injured sister. The pair sounded frightened, unsure of what to do. One of the stage hands whispered something about a prank call, yet instinct told the lost boy otherwise. He guessed the children hadn't expected to get this far and were now at a loss.

'It's alright, guys... We're still here.'

The negotiator's wife stared into his dark eyes, noticing the way his intonation had thinned and stretched, reminiscent of the post-nightmare horrors of old. Hooking her fingers inside his belt, she kissed his shirt sleeve and felt the heat exuding from his pores.

'You rang Kids' Lifeline, and we want to help you. If your sister needs to get to a hospital, and your parents can't take her, you need to call an ambulance. Can you call Triple Zero?'

'No!' the voice snapped back. 'My dad's downstairs. He'll hear them. What do I do? Her leg's sticking out all weird, and she can't walk. She's...'

'OK. Listen a second... What about you?' the intrigued man pressed. 'Are you hurt too? How did your sister break her leg?'

'I don't know,' the child answered.

'Yes, you do. Come on... Please tell me your name. I don't even know if you're a boy or a girl. My name's Jeff. You wanted to speak to the Childlight Kids' Lifeline, so let us help you, OK?'

'OK. But don't send the police.'

'No way. No police, I promise. Does your sister's leg hurt heaps?'

'Yeah. She broke it,' the young voice cracked, becoming more insistent. 'Casey. I'm Casey. I'm a girl. Mum's out, and Dad's downstairs watching TV. We need to get outside 'cause...'

The child burst into tears, and gasps from the audience threatened to hamper the stars' ability to decipher her strained sentences. Jeff sensed the vacuum of a hand cupping the mouthpiece at the other end of the line. Unsure whether Casey could still hear him, he tried for more information.

Looking around, the entire studio stood motionless while this live call played out, and Gravity dealt the celebrity a cynical boot to the gut. Surely no-one would accuse them of staging such a confronting exchange on air? And what if the children's father were tuned in to Channel Nine at this very moment? For once, he was grateful they were competing with the football for ratings!

'Thanks, Casey,' he said. 'You're doing great. I'm Jeff, and Lynn's with me here too. You know Lynn, don't you? Jet and Kierney's mum? Were you watching us on TV just now? If you can tell us where you live in a minute, we're going to send an ambulance with no sirens. No noise. OK?'

'Yes.'

'Is there a window near you, in your hall?'

'Yes.'

'Are you at the back of the house or the front?'

There was another pause, followed by the sound of footsteps and a clunk as the telephone hit a wall or an item of furniture. Celia let out a muffled squeak, mesmerised by the vivid setting she had fallen into on the night of her DCF *début*.

'Front,' Casey answered. 'It's not a house. It's a... He'll see the ambulance. Turn the lights off.'

'Sure. We'll ask them to leave the lights off, and no siren. That's fine, Casey. It'll be a few minutes yet anyway,' Jeff reassured her, shaking his head at the dread hanging in the air. 'Which floor are you on?'

'Four.'

'Thank you. Does your dad know your sister broke her leg?'

'*Dunno.*'

'Casey, I can't help you and your sister if you don't tell me stuff,' the patient man persisted, distracted by Celia's hand heavy on his forearm. 'Does your dad know what happened to her?'

The girl gulped. 'Yes. He doesn't like her. She's biting on socks 'cause it 'urts so much, and she says she feels like she's faintin'. Hey? Are you really Jeff Diamond?'

'Jesus,' the tormented soul cursed under his breath, moving the receiver away from his mouth and shielding it with his fingers, teardrops gathering in the corners of his eyes. 'Thanks, gorgeous. I know you're sorry. And yes, it's really me. This is very serious, Casey, and I know you're only trying to protect your sister. How did your sister break her leg?'

'She fell down stairs,' the girl answered. 'Mum and Dad's angry at her 'cause she won't stop screaming. It's all swelled up, and there's a funny lump stickin' out. It's gross. I nearly threw up when I seen it.'

Leaning forward on the semi-circular couch in front of the main call centre, Jeff sat with his elbows on his knees and the receiver clamped against his right ear. Lynn's breath was as warm and restorative as ever, and his dark brown voice sounded so unassailable whenever it cracked through the earpiece that he barely recognised it as his own. Casey's speech pattern was reminiscent of Madalena's, sending images of her bruised and beaten limbs flashing before his eyes.

'She's old, y'see. For a kid. And she can't see very good.'

'Old?' he echoed, exchanging confused glances with his wife and Celia. 'How old?'

'Thirteen.'

The superstar inhaled. 'Thirteen, eh? Cool. And you? How old are you, Casey?'

'Ten. Are you comin' to get us? She promises to stop cryin'. Sorry. Dad just wants her to die, and I don't. Can you come? Please, I mean…'

The youngster's sobs reverberated around the studio in a stark reminder as to why these services were necessary. Yet still the evil troll nagged his troubled host, insisting that someone must be playing a cruel prank, eager to expose any gullibility in the celebrity couple's desire to appear virtuous in their latest moment of glory.

'Sure. They're coming in a few minutes. Wait a sec' so I can get your address, Casey, OK? We'll help you and your sister.'

A handful of choices span around his brain, hoping his decision was the best one possible. Were they doing the right thing in diverting the course of the whole evening as it had been planned for this alarming first call? How well did he understand this young girl's situation? What atrocity had been metred out on her to result in a broken leg?

Discarded memories gatecrashed Jeff's mind like they were banished only yesterday: Madalena's tear-streaked face, her limbs thrashing and fingernails scratching at his neck and face as he dragged her out of the bedroom, chased by sweat-drenched men with their pants around their ankles.

The world-changer let the telephone receiver drop and pressed it against his thigh, private misgivings trumped by twenty years of fabricated self-belief. He beckoned to one of the Childlight supervisors to come closer.

Still the cameras rolled on. Tuning in to Lynn's courage, he read the producer's mind, responding with the subtlest of head movements. He overrode her indecision around switching the broadcast to another telethon segment. If ever there were a compelling case for launching a children's crisis line, these two girls were it, unfolding right in the Australian viewing public's lounge rooms.

'Jay, can you guys trace this call, please?'

'Already working on it, Jeff,' the technician replied. 'You'll need to keep her talking for a few more minutes.'

'Right. Thanks. No worries,' the celebrity nodded, lifting the handset back up to his ear. 'Casey, are you still there?'

'Yes. Are you Jeff Diamond?'

'Yes, I am,' he coughed, unable to hold back the tears any longer. 'Listen… We're going to try to get you and your sister out and to the hospital. We'll be very quiet, and other people'll talk to your dad. I want to meet you, Casey, and make sure you guys are alright. It'll all be fine. You OK with all that?'

'See? It *is* him!' the audience heard an excitable voice cry out. 'I told *ya*. We love *yous*, Jeff and Lynn, my sister and me. Come and meet us.'

'What's your sister's name, Casey?'

'Brooke. It's Brooke. Can you come?'

The rock star shook his head, searching for a sign that the engineers had been able to pinpoint the girls' location. A ripple of nervous laughter ran around the set, and Lynn's hand balled into a fist and pressed into her heart, transferring a much needed boost of energy to her impatient husband.

He blew her a kiss and wiped his eyes, preparing to elicit some more information from his caller. 'Hey, Casey… You know what? You're very brave. Tell Brooke she's very brave too, please. We're going to send an ambulance now. We're ready for you to tell us your address, Casey. OK?'

'He says we're brave,' the tiny voice was faded out while the supervisor wrote down the suburb, street and flat number.

He gave the strained couple a thumbs-up as a match for their trace was confirmed before disappearing to place a call with the emergency services. Jeff was primed to make a dash from the studio and jump into the nearest car, so keen was he to see the unfortunate pair to safety. He resisted the temptation however, his beautiful best friend's wise words worming into his ears above his resonating heartbeat.

'Hold on. Don't try to solve it yourself. That's exactly what this service is here for.'

Lynn was right. Childlight had been formed to arrest the decline in children's mental health. One Catholic Argentinean Polish Jew racing round to a Collingwood apartment block would not address the root cause of the problem, no matter how much better it might make him feel. Tonight's caller wasn't

Madalena or Kierney or anyone else who had meant anything to him prior to picking up the telephone. Tonight's caller was a total stranger who needed help from the authorities.

'Thanks, Casey,' he said. 'Thanks very much. We've got your address. You made a good decision for your sister. You're a very special girl.'

'Are you going to take me too?' the young girl sounded terrified. 'I don't want to be left 'ome on me own.'

'No. You won't be on your own, gorgeous. We won't split you up. Stick together, eh? We're leaving right now.'

'Good.'

'No worries,' the amateur counsellor replied, remembering how difficult it had been for him to thank an adult for unexpected acts of kindness. 'You're welcome. Where's your mum? D'you know?'

'Out,' the girl became cagey once again. 'I don't know if she's coming back.'

'Has she been hurt too? Are you OK, Casey?'

'I'm OK. I think Mum's ran away. My dad...'

Jesus Christ, Jeff thought. This was the world he had grown up in too, and it seemed so foreign to him these days. He had never been more thankful that his own children didn't have to worry about their safety in their own home. What an abhorrent state of affairs for two innocent human beings...

'You don't have to tell us straightaway,' he advised the youngster. 'I think I know what you mean. My dad used to hit us too. You'll be OK. Can you see anything out of your window?'

More sounds of shuffling feet and short, sharp breaths. A yelp came from somewhere inside the room, and Celia grimaced at the thought of Casey's sister's leg sticking out at an awkward angle.

'You are so special too, darling,' the older woman whispered in the songwriter's ear, kissing his cheek and gripping hard onto his wife's spare hand. 'You are both truly amazing.'

A half-smile broke across the man's tear-stained face. Desperate to feel his *regala*'s hand in his, he appreciated full well why she had remained in the background through this whole ordeal. This was his childhood revisited, and he had to deal with it on his own. He wanted her to bail him out more than anything. She wouldn't bail him out though. He no longer needed to be bailed out, despite what his instincts told him.

This moment was payback for all the years the lost boy had spent with no control over his destiny, taking the blame for the torture his mother and sister were forced to endure day after day. As a result of his own actions and dedication, he could turn this situation around too; the first of many cases of cruelty and neglect for their foundation's new initiative.

'I can see outside,' Casey's voice broke through. 'I can't see no ambulance but...'

'Not yet, no. It's on its way. Can you open the window?'

'Only a bit.'

'Not enough to climb out?'

'No!'

'OK. Listen, Casey, please,' Jeff summoned a more didactic tone in the hope of keeping the girl calm. 'Don't panic when they get there. Just keep an eye out and make sure your sister knows what's going to happen. The *amboes* know you're hiding from your dad, so they won't ring the doorbell. They'll need to talk to him though, but keep calm and trust them. Does that sound OK?'

'Yes!' the young girl screeched, before smothering her own voice for fear of giving the game away. 'Yes. Hurry up!'

'These guys know what they're doing,' the superstar continued, determined to pass the time with his frightened caller until the vehicle reached the premises. 'They'll make sure you get to hospital safely. No-one's going to hurt you.'

'But what about Mum?' Casey asked.

'They'll find her and help her get to the hospital too.'

In truth, the forty-one-year-old had no idea how the authorities might locate the girls' mother, particularly if their father was uncooperative. He was the master of improvisation under normal circumstances and hoped his ad-libbed version of events would be close enough to reality to preserve the miniscule amount of trust he had earned so far.

'No!' the girl yelled. 'I don't want you to find her.'

'Good girl,' he replied, pulling a face at those nearby. 'That's fine. Tell us exactly what you want, Casey. Did your mum hurt your sister?'

Jeff's ear tuned into some indistinct background noise and heard the youngster take a sharp breath.

'Oh, my God! They're 'ere! Brookey, they're here! Mum pushed her down the stairs. They don't want her anymore because... They're always hurting her. It's disgustin'. I 'ate what they do, and I 'ate them. The amb'lance is 'ere.'

'OK. Cool,' the negotiator breathed a sigh of relief, shaking his thigh muscles to rid them of the stiffness which had built up over the last fifteen minutes. 'Thanks. Listen, gorgeous... What you just told us is very important. Make sure you tell the *amboes* too. Just tell the truth. They want to help you and Brooke. Everything else can be sorted out later. D'you understand, Casey?'

'Ye... Oh, I can hear someone. Brooke, it's OK! They're comin' for us.'

His heart slamming against his ribcage, the showman waved to their producer, giving a throat-cutting sign. 'I don't want this to go to air, Kerry. Shut it off, please.'

Before the production staff had time to concoct a back-up plan, the blonde singer darted behind her husband to grab a spare microphone from one of the floor assistants. Jeff smiled, breathing a sigh of relief when a dome light illuminated red on top of a distant camera, watching his long-legged angel skipping up a short flight of steps to inject herself into another telethon call. The show was in safe hands, and he was free to go.

'Hey, Casey... Good luck. See you soon.'

An urgent, reedy voice squeezed through the telephone just as he was about to hang up. 'Jeff Diamond?'

'Yes,' he whispered.

'Love you.'

'Oh! Thank you,' The Australian Elvis responded, his eyes clenched shut. 'I love you too, Casey. And Brooke too. You're both very brave. Go and get safe now.'

The producer gesticulated for the crew to switch to the other side of the studio, where Lynn had another caller primed for their moment in the spotlight. Celia prised the receiver out of the songwriter's sweat-drenched hand and hugged his shaking frame.

Exhaling deeply and leaning back on to the desk, Jeff shook his head at the low-key round of applause. The headlines on tonight's late bulletins and tomorrow's newspapers were assured. It was hard to believe that such an luckless soap opera had been selected at random for the Childlight founders to answer. The objective of introducing Celia Blake to his loyal fan-base had been comprehensively eclipsed!

The young girls' dangerous situation was *manna* from heaven from a publicity perspective, no doubt likely to generate considerable speculation from cynical media hacks. As he watched his dream girl crossing the set towards him, he pondered the many questions they would face tomorrow and how the usual suspects might persecute them for staging such high drama for the sake of superfluous air-time.

Well accustomed to processing competing ideas at full pelt, his mind felt like it was icing over, suddenly saturated by insecurity. What were the chances of tonight's showstopper being an orchestrated hoax on someone else's part...

Lynn's eyes decried this theory however, as always translating his innermost thoughts and assuaging his fears. Few words were needed these days. Eyes pleading with hers for permission, she was reminded of a phrase he rolled out from time to time: "The quietest people often have the loudest minds." For all the fervour and hyperbole which sprang forth from Jeff Diamond's mouth, he was indeed the quietest man at his core. She needed to release him from his figurehead obligations for the night.

In full view of the studio audience, the lost boy held his arms out, and his saviour walked into them, transported back to the Sydney hotel reunion almost twenty years ago. Few words were exchanged, save his apology for spoiling the private birthday dinner which was booked at a favourite Italian restaurant.

'Go to the hospital,' Lynn instructed, pointing over her shoulder to the official who had alerted the emergency services. 'They're going to the Royal Children's under police escort. Kim's got the details, look... They'll be hanging out to see you.'

'Thanks, guys. And you, angel. Sorry to spoil the rest of our evening. Go on ahead. I'll meet you there as soon as I can,' Jeff said, smiling at the ring of adoring, supportive colleagues who indulged him over and over. 'Did the whole thing go out live, Jake?'

'Certainly did,' the show's producer confirmed. 'You were so good with her. The call rate's gone through the roof.'

No longer in the mood to reflect on their unmet schedule, the concerned man's conscience was torn. Casey and her sister would soon be in safe hands without his presence, mindful of his tendency to turn ordinary scenes into command performances.

'Go!' his wife urged, grabbing his left hand and tugging him away from the studio floor. 'The car's waiting for you. I'll stay here and take some more calls. Or do you want me to come?'

'Ah, yeah. Course I do! I need you so much, angel. Stay though. Who knows? There may be more like this one. How many kids've 'phoned in so far tonight, Kerry?'

Childlight Melbourne's General Manager was carrying a thick wad of call sheets in her hand, gathered in batches from the counsellors and volunteers. 'A fair few, Jeff. We'll go through them in detail tomorrow. Get going. With any luck they'll discharge them pretty quickly.'

'Cheers,' the celebrity sighed. 'Thought as much. Do we know what happened with the dad? We're on rocky ground here. They're his daughters, no matter how poorly he treats them.'

Kerry shook her head. 'No. Nothing's come through yet. The police went with the ambulance. They were going to talk to the parents and make sure the girls got to hospital. We have to be careful not to overstep our authority, you're right, in case the girl was making things up or whatever.'

Squeezing Lynn's body tight against his, the rock star fumbled for his cigarette packet and lighter. 'I know. Jeez,' he hissed. 'That's cool. We'll find out when we get there. C'mon then. Let's go. Celia, you'll be OK with Lynn, won't you? Sorry to abandon you for dinner. Hope the rest of the show goes well.'

Rights And Responsibilities

Celia dabbed her eyes with her handkerchief. She was both overcome with grief and glowing with pride as she read the chapter headed "Redeeming Brooke". Her part in Jeff Diamond's autobiography up until this point had been mostly passive, receiving heartfelt acknowledgement for the Blake family's role in moulding the teenaged tearaway into a man who could walk with his head held high.

'Your mum and dad were so kind to that poor little mite.'

After the first Kids' Lifeline telethon in nineteen-ninety-three, the North Sydney grandmother had been inspired to spearhead many more high-profile events for Childlight. Her role as patron had seen her graduate from a hesitant bystander, in awe of the ease with which her favourite celebrities courted the cameras and manipulated the microphones, to a proficient, businesslike interviewer and moderator who presided over charity functions the length and breadth of the country.

Kierney nodded. 'Yes. Did you know what happened with those sisters before you read it? I didn't really. Only bits of it.'

'Which sisters?' Gerald looked up from his newspaper. 'Not our two? What outlandish revelations are you reading about now?'

'No, dear,' his wife teased. 'Not this time. I'll show you later. Can I fetch anyone more coffee?'

The retired company director bowed his head again. He needed a damned good excuse to avoid opening the family's copy of "A Life Singular" and peeling time's protective layer off the hard truths therein. Celia's tearful citations of various authorial perspectives reoriented from inside out had been so shocking to digest second-hand that the elderly Irishman wavered between fascination and fright at the thought of reading them for himself.

The masterful volume was placed on the arm of an adjacent couch like a valuable heirloom while the lady of the house prepared drinks and an afternoon snack. Kierney had agreed to spend the weekend with her father's surrogate parents, although she hadn't looked forward to it, only a month into her first semester at Sydney University.

The book had been released the week before Australia Day, anticipated by press and public alike. Ryan delayed his return to Cambridge to provide his sister with a few days' moral support but then had slunk away as quickly as he could, leaving her to absorb the tumultuous praise before she too made a break northwards to New South Wales and her long-awaited degree course.

The book's glossy cover beckoned to the eighteen-year-old, its pages emitting an inaudible signal which was impossible to ignore. When the first copies arrived at Stonebridge Music and Cathy had offered to deliver one to the city apartment for her to see, she assumed her intimate knowledge of its contents would render her disinterested, or at least ambivalent to its physical manifestation. She couldn't have been more wrong!

Naturally, there had been a hardback set aside for each Diamond child, a hand-written dedication from their father inserted behind the title page. Kierney lifted the Blakes' copy, pleased to see it also contained a tailored inscription from the nobody they had helped transform into a real-life towering giant of a somebody.

Celia's bookmark was a precious heirloom in itself, embroidered in bold cross-stitch by one of her twin granddaughters a number of years ago, judging by its worn edges and frayed tassles. It marked a place three pages before the end of the chapter, and a lump rose in the young woman's throat as raised circles on the surface of the paper revealed tears that had fallen on a shared and treasured episode.

'Oh,' she let out an involuntary sigh, glancing up to see if Gerald had noticed.

He hadn't, thankfully. Kierney's heart fluttered again as the story behind the story unfolded through an elaborate suite of short paragraphs crafted to educe breathlessness, to the briefest of periods when she and Jet gained and lost a little sister. Woozy with painkillers and unable to see more than rough shapes immediately in front of her, the tiny soul had drifted away almost as soon as she had arrived.

The venom in Jeff's tone leaped out at his daughter, as it must have for countless other readers, including Celia. She noticed he had resorted to italics to emphasise the disturbing scene which confronted him and the Childlight representatives at the Royal Children's Hospital after Casey's dramatic plea on national television.

> "'*What the fuck's that?*' Kim's first response slipped out before either of us had processed what we were seeing. Sparse tufts of white hair and a pointed, elfin nose were the only features visible from a mound of hospital pillows, where an orthopædic surgeon was examining Brooke's broken leg.
>
> Another girl, whom I presumed was Casey, screamed incessantly, needing to be restrained by two nurses. Not a sound came from the body on the bed though, and as we drew nearer, I began to wonder if she was still alive.

We hung back at first, unable to pick up much of what the doctors were saying. I caught sight of two specks of anthracite, eyes like pinheads in a worn, off-white cushion of a face, vacant and baffled.

'She's old,' Casey had said. 'She's old, y'see.'

Pieces of the evening's puzzle assembled themselves in a split-second. The child's head turned to her left as if she had felt my presence, and our smiles met at the same time as her sister realised I'd arrived.

With the superhuman strength of a determined child, Casey wrestled free of her minders and ran headlong into my legs. The only thing I could do to stop myself overbalancing was to scoop her up in my arms and propel ourselves towards her ailing sister.

Pandemonium broke out – exactly what I'd hoped to avoid – and within another transient moment, the girls' father burst into the ward, with three harried police officers in hot pursuit. It was impossible to discern where his anger was directed, spraying profanities in all directions and lashing out at all and sundry.

The consulting doctor held out his hand to me and tried to introduce himself with a pronounced air of resignation, no doubt perfected after years of trauma surgery. I couldn't complete the *manœuvre* with Casey hanging off my right side, so I found Brooke's hand instead.

Brittle, bony fingers with no reflexes and no warmth.

Was she dead?

Almost, I was soon to discover."

Kierney sniffed back tears and closed the book again, hearing Celia return with a tray of rattling silverware and bone china. 'Thank you. Can I help with that?'

'No, darling. Oh, are you crying?'

'Always,' the teenager chuckled, grinding her teeth. 'I'm alright. I was reading about when *Papá* first saw Brooke, and how serene she was with all the calamity going on around her. That's just how I remember him telling us the next day, when he announced he'd be bringing her home to die with us.'

'Bringing who home to die?' Gerald chimed in. 'Are you talking about the poor little Progeria girl? That was an awful shame... Jesus, Mary and Joseph! The atrocities that go on in the world, I don't know. I'm away upstairs while you sob into your teacups, ladies.'

The sixty-year-old rose from his chair, saluted the others and tucked his folded copy of the Sydney Morning Herald under one arm. Helping himself to a slice of Victoria sponge and his coffee mug, he tutted to himself.

Celia rolled her eyes. 'Right you are, dear. He's a bit squeamish when it comes to medical procedures and that sort of thing. Sorry, Kierney. I'm covering up for him, which I vowed not to do anymore. The truth is he didn't agree with what your *papá* and *mamá* did at the time. Nor did I, although reading this now helps me to understand why they took matters into their own hands.'

'It's fine,' the gipsy girl shrugged. 'Ry and I didn't agree to begin with either. I suppose we were jealous, and so was *Mamá*. It was as if *Papá* became completely fixated on making her hopelessness bearable, and somehow the rest of us had no choice but to accept her into our family.'

Casey and Brooke's parents, as it turned out, were awaiting trial on neglect charges brought by the Family Court of Victoria. The father, an unemployed builder and longstanding drunk, turned out to be the more responsible of the pair. Their mother added a gambling addiction to her own alcoholism, no doubt with her elder daughter's unfortunate genetic disorder as the main contributing factor to her downfall.

Between them, they had systematically set about segregating Brooke from the world, removing her from school, withholding meals and keeping her shut away in the second bedroom of their two-storey Housing Commission unit. If it hadn't been for Casey, their wish might well have come true. Two years younger, she had smuggled food from the refrigerator and served it covered in fluff from her pockets to a weakening thirteen-year-old whose internal organs and eyesight were deteriorating day by dismal day.

Occasionally, as Brooke's counsellor had wheedled out of her in the last few days, Casey had even stashed unswallowed mouthfuls of her own dinner along the walls of her mouth, only to regurgitate it for her sister whenever she could escape to their room.

'We did feel sorry for her,' Kierney continued. 'Really sorry for her. She was gorgeous. So sweet, but almost like a little animal in the way she behaved. Like a kitten. Just wanted to be cuddled and told stories.'

Celia frowned. 'I suppose that's all she was capable of, poor thing. And her mummy can't have held her tight for a long while. So sad for everyone. It's no wonder she craved someone as empathetic as your amazing *papá*. Hutchinson-Gilford syndrome, wasn't it? Progeria. It must've been quite a shock arriving at Casualty and seeing what looked like a little old woman instead of a girl with a broken leg.'

'*Papá* was truly amazing, wasn't he?' the law student murmured. 'Thanks for saying so. I miss him so much, and I feel like he's already fading out of our lives.'

'Oh, no, he's not, love. He won't fade out of our lives, and neither will your wonderful *mamá*. No need to worry about that. Just look at every news programme. Not a single day goes by without some mention of their achievements, their legacy. You mustn't think that way.'

The dignified young woman couldn't help laughing.

'What's funny?' her host was surprised. 'Did I miss a joke?'

Kierney shook her head, picking up the weighty book and returning to the marked page, not too far from the end. 'No. Sorry. I just remembered something *Papá* used to say, that's all. It doesn't matter. I argued with *Papá* all the time about his plan to help us get over him. I wanted to believe him because I had no choice, basically. But I didn't believe him at all. And now, already I'm at peace with everything and even quite well adjusted to being an orphan. I feel kind o' free, which must be wrong in so many ways. Does any of this make sense?'

'No, not in the least,' Celia tried to sound light-hearted. 'I miss him impossibly too. And to be perfectly honest, my dear, I'm still rather disappointed that you and your brother... and even my own son, brought up in the ways of the Lord God Almighty, or so I thought... are so willing to let him get away with such a despicable course of action.'

'Yes, I know. I don't think it was despicable, but I know what you mean. And Gerry didn't let him get away with it,' the student replied. 'They used to have stand-up fights about it. Yelling down the 'phone at each other and all sorts! Gerry tried to make *Papá* change his mind right up until the last few hours. Please don't blame him. I know he's really upset.'

Celia's eyes dipped down into her lap, ashamed to have spoken out so candidly to a vulnerable young adult so soon after her second immense loss. She also castigated herself for thinking that Lynn would ever have deserted her children in their hour of need, imagining Bart and Marianna Dyson would share her opinion. The all-Australian couple had maintained media silence in the face of Jeff Diamond's suicide, expressing nothing but a sadness for his passing and condolences to his children and his millions of fans.

'We had ages to say goodbye,' Kierney persevered. 'Maybe his time preparing for Brooke's death taught us something too. We never spoke about it before he died. She aged right before our eyes. Pegged out, *Papá* used to say... He was adamant he'd done her a huge favour. "Pass peacefully into the next life," he told her. I think that's lovely, and it's the same thing I wished for him on New Year's Day.

'He wasn't sure if he and Brooke knew each other in a previous life, or whether there was a reason why she asked her sister to ring into Kids' Lifeline to speak to him. He took her down to the beach at *Escondido*. Oh, you read about that, didn't you? Sorry. I just love the thought of them singing together in the spray from the surf.'

With the hardback sitting between them, the photographic montage on its dust jacket reminding everyone how special the megastar *duo* had been, both women paused for a moment to gather their composure. The latter stages of Progeria was surely such a ruthless existence that even a devout Roman Catholic could understand how someone old before their time might wish to hasten their demise. However, try as she might, the mother-of-three found it implausible that a forty-three-year-old in perfect physical health would leave his children behind in this callous, self-centred way.

'Did your parents know she was so close to death when they took her into their care?' Celia asked, tight-lipped.

'I'm not sure. Probably. They spoke to her doctor, and the family was pretty grateful in the end. They just couldn't cope, I think. I felt sorry for Casey, but then *Mamá* said she'd have a more normal future if she no longer had to worry about what her parents were doing to her sister. Can you imagine watching your mum or dad treat your sister so badly and not being able to do anything about it?'

'No, I can't, darling. And I suppose that's what made the situation so difficult for your dad,' the Sydney socialite continued. 'It's beginning to sink in now. He used to have to watch his parents being cruel to your auntie, I suppose, didn't he? It must've been terrible for them both too.'

'Yeah. Exactly. *Papá* hated splitting the two girls up, but it was much the same as for Ryan and me now. He prepared us for a future without him, just like he prepared Casey and her parents for a future without Brooke.'

Kierney's voice trailed off, realising she might be straying beyond the bounds of comprehension for a mature, conservative woman who had known nothing but Christian observance and the mother-country's traditions. She didn't want Celia to ask if the revered philanthropist had brought about Brooke's death, because in truth she feared he had, although he never let on.

She remembered asking her fanciful father if he thought the frail thirteen-year-old would come back as a new person and whether it was possible to find out who, but her questions yielded no definitive answers. All she knew for sure was that he had taken the withered frame from the cot which had been set up in *Escondido*'s master suite in the middle of the night and carried her down the cliff path. There, they had sung songs and gazed out to sea until her heart stopped beating.

Lynn had ventured down to witness the final minutes, finding her husband clutching the inanimate frame to his chest, wrapped in a thick beach towel and impervious to the howling gale.

> "Go bravely to tomorrow, Brooke. Leave gently and speak kindly to all people."

The chapter's final line stood out in its simplicity. These were the words the wind carried to her mother as she reached the water's edge. The teenager recalled noticing the phrase's sagacious imprimatur while proofreading the manuscript in the author's ground-floor *atelier* overlooking the lush Burnley South lawn. She had cried anew, only minutes later, when the following page mentioned her mystic mentor's elation, claimed after liberating an innocent soul from her decomposing body.

'I remember *Mamá* saying he'd delivered Brooke to somewhere better, and he agreed. It was like he knew what he was supposed to do. Weird, isn't it? He escorted her out of this world.'

'Oh, I don't know about that,' Celia was having none of the Diamonds' romance where God's gift of life was concerned. 'I researched the Progeria condition at the time. Most children with it die in their early teens, and apparently they usually have terrible cataracts, which would account for why she couldn't see very well.'

'Yes, I know that too. She was quite clever though. Typical of an old soul, *Mamá* used to say. A bit tongue in cheek, of course!' the young woman giggled. 'They were singing "This Is The Moment" from the "Jekyll and Hyde" musical. It was her favourite song, and *Papá* loved it too. That and "Shelter", which was our family's song first and foremost, but we were happy to share it for the time it took.'

'It must have been hard for you to come to terms with,' Gerry's mother whispered. 'You were all very forgiving of him.'

'We were,' Kierney shrugged. 'He was always appreciative though. It was hopeless trying to say no to him. I learned heaps about forming persuasive arguments from *Papá*. Brooke must've left feeling very special, I think. He told her how smart she was to have figured out a way to get back to paradise much faster than the rest of us. And now he's done it too.'

***

A car dropped the Childlight crisis team and its chairman outside a staff entrance to the Royal Children's Hospital, as directed by the Emergency Department registrar. A crowd flared and frothed at the front, desperate to catch sight of their heroes and the evening's wretched stars.

The delegation managed to slip in unnoticed, yet were welcomed by a line of applauding medicos, visitors and ambulant patients. Several faces were known to the celebrity as regular Childlight volunteers, and it was no surprise to anyone that news of his very public conversation had spread like wildfire.

'That was the perfect way to handle that call,' said Andrew Alston, the on-call pædiatric psychiatrist, as he ushered the rock star and his growing *entourage* up to the orthopædic ward. 'The footage'll be included in training courses for counsellors all over the world now, I expect.'

'Yeah? Oh, well... That's good, I guess,' Jeff laughed. 'As long as appropriate royalties are channeled to DCF, I'm up for it. Cheers, mate. D'you know anything about how the girls got out of the house?'

The doctor frowned. 'Sorry, I don't. The father's here, by the way,' his reply was tentative. 'He's under police supervision. He's been drinking, but they can't prevent him from seeing his kids. Innocent until proven guilty, and all that...'

'Right. Has he seen them already?'

'No,' Alston replied. 'We've been treating the older girl, and the younger one refused to go alone. I'll warn you, she's a dreadful sight. She suffers from Progeria; looks like a cross between your granny and ET. Her leg's quite badly fractured, but that's the least of her problems. She's weak. Her bones are so brittle. She wouldn't have had to fall very heavily to sustain such an injury, poor kid. We can show you in if you come round this way. The dad won't know you're here. Prepare yourself.'

Jeff shook his head, his empty stomach churning. He had seen the occasional documentary on this awful condition which rendered children elderly and infirm. How devastating it would be to have a child with this incurable fast-ageing disorder... Although he could never condone cruelty to an innocent girl, he was filled with sympathy for Brooke's parents, not to mention even more admiration for little Casey's courage.

'Shit,' he murmured. 'Jesus Christ. No, Andrew. That's not right. The dad should see them before we do, despite what he's allegedly done. As long as he's supervised well enough, it's only fair. Has the mum turned up too?'

The lift doors opened to a bustling scene quite unaware of the unfolding melodrama. Trolleys and wheelchairs transported children from one department to the next; to pathology, to x-ray, to strange beds for the night. Past nine o'clock by the time the delegation had turned onto Royal Parade, many parents were wishing their offspring a peaceful, pain-free night and returning home for some respite from the draining hospital environment, while others prepared for yet another restless few hours on a fold-out cot at their sick child's bedside.

Subdued screams and astonished faces greeted the celebrity as his security detail brought him to a consultation room, itself protected by two uniformed police officers and another pair of fearsome-looking guards. In the midst of this colourful group stood a tattooed man of about thirty years old, muscular and heavy-set, dressed in a stretched black singlet and military-style trousers. His cropped, mousy hair and filthy scowl put Jeff on edge. Was this oaf violent towards his family or did he just look the part?

'There y'are, you bastard!' the bruiser sneered from beyond his ring of protectors. 'Who the fuck do you think you are, Jeff fucking whiter-than-white Diamond? Come over 'ere and tell it to me face.'

Undaunted, the murderer's son turned on his heels, his party switching course like a school of fish around him. Walking over to the group at a leisurely pace, he felt all eyes bore into his skull. The stocky loudmouth was being restrained, spoiling for a fight, and the former tearaway recognised the same indiscriminate hatred as had dwelled in his own father. The type of malignance which brewed inside those who knew deep down that they only had themselves to blame for the sorry state of their lives.

'Evening,' the taller, darker and infinitely more handsome man greeted the *mêlée* before his gaze alighted on the lout. 'You're Casey and Brooke's dad?'

'You know I am, *ya* bastard. And you're the interfering, filthy-rich knobhead that thinks *ya* better'an all of us.'

And so he might be, one of his wife's favourite taglines drifted through the celebrity's mind, their invisible elastic connection pinging taut while he faced into this latest battle. The media pack had forced its way into the restricted area, granting Jeff and his team another tailor-made grandstanding opportunity.

Reading the situation with professional expediency, each outlet's reporter began to capture the altercation, thereby guaranteeing the Kids' Lifeline some more positive publicity. Against his better judgement, the charity's kingpin felt sorry for the girls' father and his lack of worldliness; a bloke who had not been lucky enough to learn the art of self-respect from a guardian angel. When it came to shooting one's mouth off in public, it paid to have a sixth sense for knowing when to hold one's tongue.

The imposing celebrity span around and pointed behind him, at a row of nurses and auxilliary workers. 'Mate, d'you see these guys?' he responded, his voice raised to make his intentions heard.

The irate thug scowled.

'Well, I'm sure as hell no better than these folk. All the staff here in fact, helping kids recover from whatever... I'm only trying to simplify things for everyone. You might as well know that this interfering knobhead was just recommending they let you see your girls.'

This incongruity was plain to all within earshot, including the livid father himself. Several people gasped, and there were even a few tentative hand-claps. The mean-looking man backed down a little, shaking his arms free of the security guards' grip at the same time as the double doors through to the consultation room swang open. Three more nurses strolled out, oblivious of the confrontation being enacted like an episode of a B-grade television hospital drama until they came face to face with their favourite showbusiness idol.

Maintaining his unwavering stance opposite his rival, Jeff finished what he had to say. 'Go in and see your kids. Take responsibility for your family. Love 'em or lose 'em. One or the other, mate.'

Applause rang louder and more forceful this time. The celebrity turned back to the medical team, while the uniformed officers escorted the shorter man into a consulting room. With half his concentration directed through the open door, trusting he had made the right decision, and the other half on the surgeon's update, he discovered their mother had so far not contacted the authorities. Apparently, both parents were regularly spotted at the pokies, gambling away what little money they managed to save from the bottle shop.

'Andrew, what's likely to happen to Casey tonight, if Brooke needs to stay in?'

The psychiatrist sighed. 'I know what you're thinking, Jeff, and I don't like it any more than you do.'

'She goes home with her dad?'

'If he behaves himself with them now,' Doctor Alston nodded. 'They can't hold him. He hasn't been charged with anything. On the tape of the sister's telephone call, she quite clearly says it was her mother who pushed little Brooke down the stairs. I agree she alludes to issues with him too, but there's nothing firm to go on.'

The philanthropist grimaced. 'Yep. You're right. Casey nearly said something about her dad but stopped herself. I'm willing to bet they've been in this situation before. Did anyone check previous hospital visits?'

'Oh, yes,' a female surgical registrar butted in. 'Brooke's been a regular here all her life. She doesn't have much time left. It's such a pity the family's so bitter.'

Andrew glared at the tearful young woman. 'Only once for the younger sister. Records show she was knocked unconscious after jumping off the bed. It may not be true, of course, but that's by no means indicative of any regular abuse.'

'Or it conveniently hides it,' Jeff challenged. 'Casey was petrified their dad'd hear the ambulance arriving or the doorbell ring. Statistics show there's likely to be more to this story. What did you mean by Brooke not having much time left, Adriana?'

Checking with the psychiatrist and another white-coated gentleman who hadn't been introduced earlier, the surgeon took a deep breath. 'Brooke has Hutchinson-Gilford Syndrome, I'm afraid, Mister Diamond. Premature ageing. She's nearly fourteen, which is at the upper end of these patients' life expectancy. Her heart's failing, and she's very weak. Compounded with brittle bones that are unable to withstand the rough treatment she receives from her parents, the prognosis isn't good.'

The songwriter closed his eyes, lightheaded and nauseated by the poor girl's plight. He thought back to the desperation in Casey's voice when she called into the show, presumably accustomed to covering up her sister's condition. If the parents knew their daughter had so little time left, what possessed them to subject her to abuse? Perhaps neither girl was party to the whole truth...

'Whoa,' the superstar sighed. 'That's bloody appalling. Sounds like she shouldn't go home even if she's well enough. And what about Casey? Does she know how sick her sister is?'

'I don't know. Casey's a smart cookie. I'm sure she's wondering why we're paying them so much attention. We're concerned about sending either of them home right now. Brooke isn't speaking at all, and Casey's chucks a tantrum every time we mention her mother. Do you know what went on?'

'No. Only that she was adamant she didn't want her dad to know. Casey called into our telethon and ended up on live TV, and we sensed the panic in her voice. She said their mum pushed Brooke down the stairs. After that, it's all a bit of a blur. Shit! How could you do that to a kid who's dying in front of you? Jesus Christ!'

Jeff leaned on the counter of the nurses' station, wishing his *regala* were here to help him decide what to do for the best. The Childlight crew had landed in a genuine Catch-22 *scenario*, where a one-off plea for a child needing medical attention had evolved into a life-or-death situation. Far from returning the children to a normal, happy existence, it appeared they were dealing with a multi-faceted crisis which was unlikely to be resolved tonight.

While everyone stood staring either at each other or at the floor, the swing-doors into the emergency ward burst open again, and out marched the security detail and the girls' father. He shook his fist at the washed-out billionaire, unleashed a string of incoherent obscenities and made straight for the lift lobby, pursued by the dedicated squad of reporters. After the surgeon's news, Jeff no longer cared about exposing this odious man's behaviour on national television.

'Go with them, Kim, please, mate,' the showman requested, accepting a plastic beaker of water from Andrew Alston. 'See if he's got anything to say for himself. If he wants to talk to me, we can do it later on.'

Taking control while his boss collapsed onto a faded orange visitor's chair and swallowed cupful after cupful of the cooling liquid, DCF's program coordinator briefed the remaining media personnel to keep their distance and not to record any audio involving the children. Thirty seconds to a minute of footage would be plenty, along with a few stills to present to the sisters after their ordeal. It was important that the viewing public were afforded a hopeful image which didn't reek of self-promotion.

No sooner was the celebrity given the signal to enter the consulting rooms than a controlled but urgent alarm tone brought a battery of additional staff scurrying past him, smashing their way through another set of doors. Adriana chased them, motioning for the others to remain where they were.

'Jesus! What a night! What just happened?' Jeff turned to the doctor. 'Looks serious in there.'

'Hmm...' Andrew murmured. 'Doesn't look good. "Code Blue." Heart failure, I expect. Standard procedure. Let's sit down. Can I get you a coffee or tea?'

'I'd prefer a single malt.'

The psychiatrist laughed, fishing in his trouser pocket for some coins for the vending machine. The praises he had heard sung about Jeff Diamond by colleagues in the mental health fraternity were not exaggerated. Here was a man who didn't need to care about anything except himself in order to rake in a never-ending stream of royalties, and yet here he was in a public hospital on his wife's birthday, having profanities hurled at him from one direction and giving way to a medical emergency from another.

The two men sat side-by-side against the wall, sipping instant coffee and supplying idle commentary on the posters around the room. No-one had gone in or out of the ward for a good ten minutes, despite the bells having stopped ringing.

Jeff was about to suggest ducking outside for a cigarette when a nurse pushed the nearer half of the door open and encouraged a child with spindly legs and untidy, brown hair through the narrow gap. As soon as the youngster realised where she was being taken, the stark waiting area reverberated with excited, girlish screeches. She had a plaster cast on her left arm, but any pain was forgotten in an instant as she tore into her hero's arms.

'Casey!' the superstar shouted, standing up and holding both hands out. 'Great to see you. Are you alright? How's Brooke's leg?'

The ten-year-old was speechless, tears streaming down her cheeks and snorting back phlegm like a seasoned infantryman, all while unable to stop laughing with joy. The peculiar extra-heaviness of an emotional child relaxing against his thighs was a feeling the father hadn't experienced for a number of years, now his own daughter was far too grown up to succumb to such outbursts.

'I didn't know you hurt your arm,' he said, rubbing Casey's back to calm her. 'One leg and one arm. What a pair you guys are! How's your sister?'

The girl's eyes darted around the room, frightened but unwilling to let go of her new friend. Lifting his gaze from the straggling curls to the nurse's worried expression, he changed the subject. His blood glaciated as the realisation hit him: the activity on the other side of the doors was not being applied to a new arrival wheeled in from the next ambulance in line.

'She hasn't broken her arm,' the attendant answered, coy and nervous. 'We gave Casey a cast to match her sister's. I'm Zoe, Mister Diamond. Thanks for coming to see the girls. It's amazing, what you do.'

Jeff shook the young woman's hand. His desire to find out the older sibling's fate would have to wait. Walking the dumbstruck deadweight backwards, her feet dragging across the floor as strong hands took hold of her shoulders, he invited Zoe to sit with them.

'May I borrow your pen, please, nurse?' he grinned. 'And it's Jeff, by the way. Casey, what d'you want me to draw on your arm?'

The girl giggled. 'Oh, yeah! I *dunno*. A smiley face. And your name, like all swirly.'

The substitute parent paused, ready to click the button on the end of the ballpoint. Lynn and he had stuck firm to instilling good manners in their own children, and he hoped to jog Casey's memory. He was rewarded after a couple of seconds of confusion.

'Please.'

'Good girl,' Jeff said, sliding his right hand under her wrist and lifting the stiff limb towards him. 'All swirly? Like an autograph, you mean?'

Casey beamed. 'Yes! An autograph. Yes, please.'

There was nothing flamboyant these days about the way Australia's favourite rock star signed his name. In fact, Lynn and he often joked that their blindfold signatures were more predictable than a rubber stamp. Nevertheless, he hammed it up for the enthralled youngster, who had lost most of her inhibition and seemed to have forgotten about her sister.

Signalling to one of the reporters milling around the waiting area, the musician tried to do the same. 'Did you want to have your picture taken with Zoe and me after I've finished decorating your arm?'

'Yes! Oh, yes. What are you drawing?'

Six photographers bustled their way towards their target, all desperate to snap the lucrative scoop. With his arm around Casey's back, the magnetic personality lifted her cast to reveal a half-baked cartoon which made them all laugh.

'Wait a minute, and you'll see,' the talented artist smiled, sketching his best attempt at a caricature of himself, the nurse and their distracted patient. 'Zoe, could you find out the latest from in there while I finish this, please?'

Calling time on the photo-shoot for fear of sending the wrong message to the hospital staff, Jeff felt his mobile telephone buzz in his jacket's inside pocket. Relief surged through him when he saw his wife's name appear on the tiny screen, and he punched the green button. He wasn't surprised to find the line scratchy, her call competing with dozens of other instruments in the immediate vicinity.

It had taken Lynn and Celia longer to escape from the telethon than they expected, neither with much of an appetite for their slap-up birthday meal. So with Gerry's mother reunited with her husband in their five-star hotel on Collins Street, the rear-end of the Diamond pantomime horse had opted to reunite with her own.

On hearing this wonderful news, the billionnaire requested one of the DCF volunteers to meet the tennis champion at the main entrance and escort her to the emergency department. 'Lynn'll be here in a few minutes, Casey. That's good, isn't it? We can ask her to draw something on your arm too.'

Tiredness diluted the young girl's enthusiasm, and the patient father smiled as he watched her twisting her forearm inside the loose plaster. The accessory was obviously less than comfortable, and he guessed it would be off within a few hours.

Zoe had not yet returned with an update on Brooke's condition. As ever, Jeff feared the worst without a clear impression of what the worst might entail. If the older sister was as fragile and as close to death as Adriana had intimated, their charitable efforts ought to concentrate on the sleepy tyke who was now intent on converting his thigh into a pillow.

The other Childlight team members had dispersed during a lull in proceedings, presumably to let their families know what had become of them on this abnormal Saturday evening. The clock on the wall reported nine o'clock with a sudden click, raising a yawn from both star and off-sider at once. With Casey soon fast asleep, stretched out across three seats and with a blanket over her, Kim and his chairman also found themselves nodding off.

Before too long, their relative peace was destroyed by the arrival of one Lynn Dyson Diamond, generating as much *furore* from the press cohort as her rock star partner had done ninety minutes earlier. This particular disturbance was most welcome however, especially when she sidled in beside him and stole a chaste kiss so as not to wake the ten-year-old.

'What's happening?' she whispered, stroking the softening stubble on his chin, which showed its usual signs of tension.

Jeff shrugged. 'No idea. I can only guess something serious with Brooke, because they sent Casey out with a nurse to meet us, and then all hell broke loose. Alarm bells and rampaging *crêpe* soles at the double.'

The singer brushed a tear away from her lover's cheek. 'I spoke to a doctor outside, while he was having a cigarette.'

'Christ! Why didn't you ring me? I could murder a bloody cigarette.'

'Shhh,' Lynn smiled. 'Brooke went into cardiac arrest. They've stabilised her apparently. I thought you'd already know. Sorry.'

The philanthropist frowned. 'Yeah, well... Evidently not. We've been relegated to babysitting duties. The dad was here earlier.'

He refrained from adding any further explanation, worried the distressing information might seep into the child's dormant psyche. Telling his beautiful best friend about the confrontation with the girls' father was off limits, as were his fears for Casey's future.

'Did they tell you she has Progeria?' the downhearted man whispered.

'Progeria?' his wife repeated. 'What's that?'

'The ageing disease. Y'know... Those kids who look sixty when they're six?'

Lynn blanched. 'Oh, my God. Poor thing. So that's what Casey meant by "She's old." Wow... Did you see her?'

Jeff shook his head. 'I'd like to take her home with us if she makes it.'

'Take her home? To *Escondido*? We can't talk about this now. How can we? She's got parents of her own.'

'Yeah. I know. But it's the right thing to do.'

Having fallen out of practice at keeping their voices low to prevent their conversations from being overheard, the couple paused to check whether Kim had picked up on these precarious plans. Satisfied that he hadn't, the Olympian leaned against her benevolent black stallion and sighed. Surely this was a bridge too far, even for them?

'Is it?'

'Yep. Don't ask me why 'cause I don't know yet.'

***

'"To a brave and beautiful girl,"' Casey read, tracing each word with the tip of her index finger. '"Best wishes for a happy future. Love from Lynn, Jet and Kierney." Can Jet and Kierney sign it too? Like tomorrow?'

While the songwriter and his new friend snoozed, Lynn had composed a complementary inscription underneath the cartoon etched into the cast. 'I hope so,' she laughed. 'Otherwise it won't make sense, will it? You'll see them tomorrow, I expect.'

'Oh, yay!' the youngster exclaimed, cuddling into the friendly woman she never dreamed she would meet. 'They're so amazing. I love your fam'ly. My dad was 'ere. Did *ya* see 'im?'

'Yes, I know, darling. Jeff saw him. Was he happy you two were safe after your trip in the ambulance?'

'Where's my mum?'

Lynn flinched. 'I'm not sure. She's probably at home with your dad by now. He'll let her know you're OK. We'll try to find her in the morning, darling. Is that alright?'

Her husband had awoken to the sound of female voices, the morning blues slugging him between the eyes before anyone could divert its onslaught. Excusing himself from the array of curious bystanders, he sloped out of the building on the pretext of needing a smoke, leaving his saviour and the younger of the unfortunate sisters to get to know each other better.

'People are looking for your mummy,' a Childlight official interrupted. 'I'm sure she'll come to visit you as soon as she finds out you're in hospital. You won't be staying here for much longer anyway. Just while we make sure your sister's going to be OK.'

Ten-year-old ears pricked up at this information. 'Will we go back 'ome with Mum and Dad?'

'That's not up to us to decide,' Lynn answered. 'The counsellors and doctors need to ask you some questions. Your mum and dad too... If you really don't want to go home, you should let them know why. The important thing is to keep you safe, but if you love your mum and dad, you need to tell them that too. Don't you want to go home?'

Casey squirmed backwards like a wary animal. '*Dunno.*'

The compassionate woman was pleased her husband wasn't on hand to witness this reticence, supposing his response to this choice at a similar age would have been infinitely more forthright. Confidences shared many years later from a position of safety swam in her mind, butting up against her instinct that children were best off with their parents.

It wasn't hard to imagine this girl's argumentative streak waning in the face of authority, devoid of the powerful rhetoric applied by a certain lost boy from Canley Vale, whose youthful eloquence had painted pictures laden with local colour. He had once told his dream girl how a *trio* of aggressive policewomen had been dispatched to watch over him and Madalena while their male counterparts pounded the streets in pursuit of Paul Diamond. After abandoning their attempts to extract information, the enterprising lad had invited them to pick over the spoils of crime which littered the cramped lounge room in the vain hope of leniency.

Mercifully, methods for dealing with criminals' families had become a little more sophisticated since those days. Police officers were now used for policing, assisted by trained psychologists when it came to minding problem children.

These operations were still far from congenial however, Lynn gathered: frightened kids watching strangers pick through their belongings, with no idea what lay in store and whether they were about to be separated from their every certainty. At each new charge incurred by these prolific offenders, the continual and compounding collateral damage inflicted on innocent sons and daughters was severe. If the prospect of driving across town and being dumped in the middle of the night on a reluctant relative wasn't disturbing enough, the only alternative was an emergency foster placement, where they would end up sharing a room with other confused and suspicious children.

Lynn smiled. 'Good girl. We'll work something out. Don't worry.'

'I want 'em to be nice to Brookey,' Casey blurted out, tears brimming in her eyes. 'When I give 'er somethin' to eat, Mum gets nasty with me too. I hide stuff to give 'er later, but then she made Brooke fall down the steps outside. The other day Dad bashed my 'ead on the wall 'cause I wouldn't eat dinner. He said I only wanted to give it to Brooke, but I didn't like it. It was disgustin'. Made me feel sick.'

Jeff returned in time to catch the last few sentences of the youngster's confession. He inhaled sharply as dark clouds of repugnance festered in his gut. He faced away from the others and stared out through a narrow window to steady his nerves. All he could see was his own silhouette against the room's reflection, and all he could think of was to scoop both sisters into his arms and whisk them to a world with more love.

The Diamond Celebration Foundation had been in existence for twenty years already, and each year more cases were referred to its services than ever before. How many more Caseys and Brookes were there? Families who either remained ignorant to the help available to them or simply stuck the television on and pretended everything was normal.

By instituting the umbrella emblem under which each individual charity grew, the billionaire had set the aspirational goal of ridding the world of all abuse and neglect. He wanted this pair's pain to be over, just as he had wanted his sister's pain to be over.

And his too. He was man enough to admit this by now, wasn't he?

Why couldn't every mother be like Lynn?

The despondent expression mirrored back from the gloom echoed the same helplessness of his teenaged years. The answer to this simple question eluded him. It was a problem too complex for Jeff Diamond to fix, despite all the resources at his disposal. No matter how much money they raised or how many rousing speeches he gave, a certain percentage of the population would always be obstinate in the face of change. He was not so *naïve* to believe that good would triumph over evil once and for all.

Taking a deep breath and turning back to see his beautiful black stallion cuddling a tearful Casey, Jeff chastised himself for suspending reality. Every single day, Childlight and The Fellowship rescued victims and set them on a path to success, augmenting humanity's tally one by one. Moreover, with the exception of the Dysons and their ilk, the majority of positive social change was brought about by people like him, motivated to achieve great things by having experienced adversity.

'You're a star, Casey,' the world-changer said, sitting down next to the girl's feet and offering her a selection of chocolate bars he had purloined from the vending machine on the way back from his cigarette break. 'That's why you made that 'phone call tonight, isn't it? You were trying to protect your sister, which was a fantastic thing to do. You showed her you loved her, and she'll love you back for it every day.'

His wife nodded. 'The people at Childlight'll work hard to make sure your mum and dad don't hurt you anymore. It's wrong for them to hurt you, and each other, but we need to find out why they get so angry.'

Before the ten-year-old could process this possibility, three people in white coats emerged from the ward, one of whom was Adriana. A flustered Doctor Alston approached from the other direction simultaneously, tailed by two women dressed in jeans and matching brightly-coloured sweaters.

'Watch out!' Jeff chuckled. 'Coincidence, I think not.'

'Oh, good evening, Missus Diamond,' Andrew held his hand out. 'I missed your arrival. How are you?'

The dignified sportswoman propped Casey in an upright position on her chair and stood up to greet everyone. 'Hello. Well, thank you. Please call me Lynn. How's Brooke?'

The psychiatrist crouched down in front of the young girl and took her hands in his. 'These lovely ladies are Lauren and Kirsty. We'd like you to go with them for a moment while we speak to Mister and Missus Diamond. They're going to take you to a room with heaps of toys and things to do. And if you're ready, they can help you tell us why you rang into Kids' Lifeline tonight. Alright?'

Casey nodded, in tears again. 'Can I come back after?'

'We'll come and find you, gorgeous,' Jeff interjected. 'We won't go without saying goodbye, OK? See if Lauren and Kirsty've got a can of Coke or anything else you shouldn't be drinking at ten o'clock at night.'

The medical staff laughed at the filthy look Lynn gave her husband. In truth, they were all grateful for the showman living up to his rascal reputation. Any apprehension accompanying them into the waiting area was now well and truly diffused!

The celebrities exchanged hugs and kisses with their solemn companion, who left with the psychologists without a murmur of objection. One of the male doctors led the group to an office which was too small to accommodate them in any degree of comfort, with shelving on three walls and only four chairs. Lynn and Adriana accepted the gentlemen's offer to sit down, and Jeff's palms alighted on the Olympian's shoulders to maintain their vital connection.

By the look on Andrew's face, they were going to need every ounce of mutual support. 'Well,' he groaned. 'What a night for you, Jeff, Lynn... Firstly, thanks for putting your entertaining skills to such good use while we dealt with the emergency.'

'No worries,' the songwriter smiled.

'Now, the good news is that Brooke's still alive,' said the surgeon who had shown them in, shaking hands with their guests. 'Sorry, I forgot to introduce myself earlier. Doctor Morgan. Geoff, with a "G".'

'G'day, Geoff,' his namesake raised an eyebrow. 'We won't hold that against you. It is good news, by the way. Cheers.'

'The not-so-good news is, I'm afraid, that she won't live much longer. You've already been informed that her condition is untreatable.'

Both superstars nodded, and Lynn lifted her left hand to her shoulder, where her husband grabbed it in an instant, intertwining their fingers.

'Hutchinson-Gilford children typically pass away in their early teens. In Brooke's case, we believe she suffered a heart attack when she sustained her leg injury.'

'Oh, Jesus,' Jeff muttered.

'Yes,' Adriana added. 'It's awful. Cardiac arrest probably would've occurred in the not-too-distant future anyway, but almost certainly this event brought it on.'

'Let's hope it was an accident,' the tennis champion cautioned, tilting her head upwards to check on the quieted entertainer. 'Carry on, please. We're listening.'

'Of course. Our instruments show her arteries are still allowing sufficient blood flow to keep her breathing, but there is risk of another attack at any time. And... and this is the reason for our mad dash earlier... she also suffered a stroke during her dad's outburst. Bloody man. Please excuse my French, but what an arsehole!'

The impulsive swear-word lightened the mood somewhat, garnering nothing but recognition from the appalled visitors. Doctor Alston relayed that the girls' father, Mick Maguire, had marched into the cubicle while Brooke's leg was being examined and hurled abuse at the attendant staff. He hadn't so much as cast an eye over his daughter, according to Adriana, and it was clear she was terrified of him.

Throughout the torrid tale, Jeff's body began to feel leaden and listless. 'I'll see you and raise you, Geoff. Fucking hell. I sent him in there. Jesus fucking Christ!'

'Hey, that's enough,' his wife stood up and wrapped her arms around him. 'It's not your fault. At least he didn't lay a hand on her. You weren't to know he'd react that way. Any normal person would be anxious about their child.'

Kissing her forehead, the wise man reserved the right to blame himself even if nobody else did. Some things never changed. He urged the medical team to continue their briefing with a resigned wave.

'The mother arrived in a taxi a short time ago,' Andrew added. 'There were officers waiting for her when she returned from her night out. She's drunk, but not inebriated. The officers have agreed to be present while the child psychs talk to her and Casey, just in case she gets violent. From the brief moment I spent with her, I don't think she'll be difficult.'

'Will she and Casey go home together tonight?' Lynn asked.

'Not sure at this point. It might even be better to put them in with Brooke on a fold-up, as long as they're not too distressed by all the machines in there. That'd be my preference.'

The tormented soul released the strangle-hold he had placed on his dream girl and ran his fingers through his hair. 'You're not letting the mum stay too, are you?'

'Again, let's not rule anything out yet. Certainly not until she's sobered up and had a good shower.'

Everyone grimaced. What a sordid situation they had landed in! Jeff wondered how this September Saturday evening would have turned out for them all if the allure of prime-time television hadn't collided with two girls who were sick and tired of being mistreated.

'Tell me, Geoff or Adriana...' he thought aloud. 'Is there any likelihood of Brooke leaving here?'

'I wouldn't think so,' the young surgeon rued. 'She's on a ventilator. We'll have a better idea If she stabilises in the next day or two.'

'Sure. Thanks.'

'May we see her, please?' the blonde singer read her husband's mind. 'Is she conscious? Only if you think it's sensible.'

The songwriter's sinking spirits skyrocketed with the biggest injection of pure love he had ever felt. At the end of a harrowing evening, his satiated heart was in danger of going into its own cardiac arrest. The couple embraced in full view of the rest of the group, uninhibited and in complete harmony. Whichever impulse had compelled the old soul to act as this poor girl's sentinel into the next life, time had taught his *regala* that there was no point standing in its way.

Adriana got to her feet. 'Let me go and see.'

With no more information to relay, the doctors left the Diamonds on their own to mull over the night's misadventure and tomorrow's quandary. The legal ramifications alone were mindboggling, as were the logistics of transferring such a delicate being to *Escondido*. There was no time to waste on unnecessary bureaucracy, and nothing would happen on a Sunday.

'There are easier, much more pleasant ways to have another child,' Lynn teased, her words swallowed into a deep kiss.

The dejected man chuckled. '*Merci, mon amie*. Not much of a birthday, eh?'

'On the contrary. One hell of a birthday. Can't think of another to match it. I'm sure you'll make it up to me, kind sir.'

Both musicians soon dozed off in each other's arms, startling when the door creaked open to admit the Polish surgeon. Apologising for waking them, she proceeded to outline the next forty-eight hours for the diminutive Progeria patient.

'I feel privileged,' Adriana admitted, reduced to tears for the first time in the absence of her more senior colleagues. 'There have only been a handful of Progeria cases in Australia in the entire history of the condition. The odds are one in eight million.'

Jeff whistled. 'Shit! Eight million? No wonder her parents don't know how to deal with it. I bet they never sought any support from anyone…'

'Still no excuse,' his wife shook her head. 'If they couldn't bring themselves to love her, at least they could've given her up for adoption. They would've known she had Progeria before Casey was born, I'm guessing.'

'She would have shown symptoms, yes,' the doctor agreed. 'But it doesn't mean they recognised it as anything more than a deformity. People are stupid. I'm sorry to say that, but they are.'

The celebrities locked into each other's gaze, both raising their eyebrows and breathing deeply before bursting out laughing.

'Careful about saying that kind of thing to this man,' Lynn warned, cupping her hand over her husband's mouth. 'He's made a life's work out of disproving that theory.'

'Oh, really?'

'Yeah,' the philomath wrestled free of the sportswoman's hold. 'There are still a few downright stupid people, sure, but I prefer to believe it's a lack of information that's at the root of most ignorance. Whatever… I saw that bloody pig tonight. On this occasion, your diagnosis is most likely correct, Adriana.'

Having refused the offer of a taxi, Jeff took his dream girl's hand and ushered her through a hidden gate at the doctors' direction. It led them to an unlit pathway and on into Gatehouse Street. Picking their way around the edge of Royal Park, the couple managed to share a laugh at how distant their original birthday dinner plans now seemed. Lynn clutched onto his arm each time her heels sank into the damp grass, but neither minded one bit.

Once back on firm ground and prattling on about anything and everything, two of Australia's richest and most respected celebrities traversed the maze of Parkville and Carlton roads, past the suburbs' myriad university buildings and medical research institutions, until they reached the dazzling tree lights of Lygon Street, looking its best for the tourists as ever.

They stopped opposite the entrance of the pub where they had shared their first drink and kissed in full view of their adoring public. Only the forever lovers understood the place's significance, where a second-year Computer Science student had dared to declare his love for an untouchable sixteen-year-old by scrawling his simple message on the side of a dirty delivery truck. And here they were again, two decades later, with teenagers of their own and so many momentous achievements to show for their union.

Finally reaching their destination, Jeff held the door of a tiny Italian restaurant open and ushered his beautiful best friend inside. All heads turned, as always, and the entire staff fawned around them until they were installed at their table for two.

'Sorry to ruin your night, angel,' he said, setting his menu down and attracting a waiter's attention. 'Only three hours late. Tonight didn't turn out quite how I expected.'

'You don't say!' Lynn chided. 'And there's me thinking it'd all been laid on 'specially for me... It's absolutely fine, Jeff. Really. You're the best, and that's all there is to say.'

The modest philanthropist shook his head. '*Gracias.* You demand so little of me. You shouldn't, but you do.'

'No, I don't! I don't think so anyway.'

Her husband smiled. 'Well, it feels like it.'

'You give me everything I want.'

'*Mismo, mismo, Regala.* I love you.'

No longer hungry at the end of a most unusual evening, neither celebrity opted for dessert. Instead, they kicked back to enjoy the rest of their wine and the rarity of each other's exclusive company. Jeff waited for his relaxed companion to reach for the bottle to refill their glasses, leaning over to dip his hand into the pocket of his leather jacket, which had been draped over the backs of twenty years' worth of restaurant chairs in its globetrotting lifespan. He pulled out a square, velvet box.

Without ceremony, the romantic placed the gift next to his wife's wine glass. 'It's not a particularly auspicious event, you turning thirty-seven, but I wanted to get you something appropriate for where we are in our life singular.'

'You...' the Olympian frowned, reaching forward to accept the box from Prince Charming's fingers. 'We agreed we wouldn't buy each other anything.'

'Fine,' he chuckled, withdrawing his hand like lightning. 'I've still got the receipt.'

Growling in frustration at having nothing to give him in return, Lynn flipped the lid. Inside was a delicate pendant of two doves in flight, inset with diamonds against a replica of the emblematic "JL" symbol both had inked into their skin. She gasped at its incandescence, stroking it with her finger without removing it from the box.

'You are pure class, Lynn Dyson Diamond,' Jeff crooned, holding out his left hand for her to return the gift. 'Your face is exactly like I pictured when I came up with the idea.'

'Oh, thank you so much. It's perfect. Did you design it? It must've been expensive. So much heavier than it looks.'

Removing the necklace from its stays, the billionaire kissed it and laughed. 'Frightfully expensive, as Celia would say,' he joked. 'And you're frightfully exquisite, so it belongs with you. Are you going to put it on?'

A hush had descended on the entire restaurant while the vibrant mix of tourists and locals paused with their knives and forks aloft, a real-life celebrity drama being acted out as if no-one else were there. Australia's darling hooked her two index fingers under the gold chain and proceeded to loop the fine-spun piece of jewellery round her neck and fasten it under her hair.

'Yes, please,' she answered, feeling like a teenager again. 'But can I say something to you too?'

'Sure. If you must…'

'I have to say, whatever praise you're about to heap on me, you're still my most massive inspiration.'

Jeff inhaled, closing his eyes as his heart fought to counter the surge of emotion. ''Cause of what happened tonight?'

'Of course, but not only tonight. Every day. People gravitate towards you, *Maiastra*. Even little kids, like they already know who you are, when they have no way of knowing who you are.'

'Yeah? Thanks, but you can can the *Maiastra* bullshit. *I* don't even know who I am, in that sense.'

'I know you don't. Doesn't matter though, does it?' his wife said. 'That's part of the magic too actually. It doesn't matter to you or them. It's just important you realise how powerful you are in those situations. Thank you for this. It's so light and delicate; so beautifully "us".'

'You're welcome, angel. If you can be bothered to count them, you'll find there are forty stones. As the Queen of Minutiæ, i.e. your very good self, pointed out not so long ago, we've run thirty-seven DCF programs to match your thirty-seven years. And I tacked the others on to make it a nice, round number.'

The elegant blonde laughed. 'No, you didn't. You'd never do anything so meaningless! It's one each for Jetto, Kierney and *your* very good self.'

Jeff's eyes filled with tears, and he took a gulp of wine to disguise his reaction from their onlookers. Trust Lynn to figure it out. He hadn't expected her to know the number off the top of her head, but whyever wouldn't she? He turned to the waiter and requested their bill.

'*Correctamente*, brain-box! Thirty-nine beautiful things we've created; all vibrant, successful and necessary entities with bright futures, plus this vice-ridden work-in-progress who's still honoured to share your personal space. So thank you. You made them all possible.'

'*We* made them possible,' Lynn countered. 'You're the parasitic front-man, remember? I could hardly be the arse-end of the pantomime horse all on my own.'

'True,' Jeff raised his eyebrows at the *Pythonesque* image. 'I also wanted to tell you... Ask you, rather...'

The dark eyes of her favourite lost boy drilled into her soul, their intensity no doubt heightened by the frenetic evening. 'No, actually. Scratch that. I was right the first time. I can get away with it nowadays, I hope.'

'Get away with what?'

'I also wanted to tell you, angel, that we've reached a stage in *notre vie singulaire* that I want to last forever. Splice and loop, if you catch my drift.'

'Have you? Wow, that's fantastic! Really?'

The birthday girl's heart leaped into her mouth at this sizeable admission. Not only did her handsome suitor seldom pause to take a breath on their high-speed and multi-directional mission, becoming more industrious and audacious as each page on the calendar flipped over, but neither had he ever tempted fate by declaring himself officially happy.

It was her turn to fight back tears, gazing in awe at the stunning token of appreciation hanging around her neck. It was gratifying in the extreme to know his tremendous farsightedness could envisage an end to the quest which made him accountable for righting all past wrongs. Was this gorgeous man, rare in every sense of the word, ready to curl up by the fireside in true self-satisfied fat cat fashion?

'Yeah, really!' the showman chuckled at the shock on her face. 'It's a big deal, I know. And I might change my mind tomorrow, depending on how things go with Brooke. I just think we've got everything ticking along nicely now, so we can afford to take our foot off the pedal and coast to the finish line.'

'Coast?' Lynn feigned an objection. 'Is there a training course for that? We don't know how to coast!'

Jeff blew his wife a flamboyant kiss, interrupted by the head waiter depositing an unassuming saucer next to his right elbow. Peering at the total on the faded till receipt, he pulled two fifty-dollar notes from his wallet, turning back to his sparkling dinner companion.

'Never stop learning, angel. In my humble opinion, we've reached a sort of pinnacle beyond which there's little to be gained,' he opined, holding up the saucer to the *maître d'*. 'There's no point in going higher. We know everyone we need to know, and we've been to all the places we need to visit. Most more than once. I don't see what benefit there'd be.'

His faithful partner smiled. 'Just more of the same then... Scalability. Broaden and deepen the existing programs; make sure we're covering the biggest constituency possible with each. Is that what you mean?'

'On *yer* feet, wench!' the great man commanded, pushing his chair back and rising to his full six-feet-four-inch height.

Amused by his tone and turned on by its accompanying impish grin, the tennis champion did as she was told. Happiness was infectious, particularly when it lived in one so damaged. She let him sit his jacket onto her shoulders, its weight a comfortable early warning of the embrace she would be swept into as soon as they were clear of prying eyes.

'*Bon anniversaire, mon amie*,' Jeff whispered into her right ear. 'You're reading my mind. I can feel it.'

The superstars strolled the two kilometres back to their city apartment, responding to friendly shouts and muffled exclamations from late-night revellers.

'OK. So what's the plan?' Lynn asked.

Her husband shrugged. 'Sex first, then planning. Let's keep our priorities right.'

'Oh, for God's sake! Unless you want to hail a cab, we might as well fill in the time it'll take us to get home. For our pinnacular existence, yes, but also what's the plan for Brooke and Casey?'

'Spoilsport! You know how to bring me off the boil, don't you? I have no clue about Brooke and Casey as yet. We need to talk things over with the Childlight guys and a couple of experts on child custody laws. OK with you?'

The compassionate woman slowed their pace to a standstill and wrapped her arms around her colossus, wary of chasing his newfound happiness away. 'Of course it is. Tell me about our life feline first. I want to know what I'm in for.'

'Ah, yeah. Nothing too different. Thanks, angel. I'd like to hang here, just as we are, for a long, long time. The kids are great and pretty much self-perpetuating these days. Rather than a pinnacle, let's call it a *plateau*. Table Mountain rather than Everest, eh?'

'Sounds a bit biblical,' Lynn laughed. 'Gerald would get it in the neck from Celia if he were to suggest that.'

Jeff narrowed his eyes at her derision, knowing the observation was only a smoke-screen. This insightful Olympian had the knack of cutting him down to size whenever he suffered delusions of *grandeur*. Most of all, he loved that it still riled him.

'You clever minx,' he hissed, nipping her cheek with his front teeth and hugging her in close. 'You know what I mean. A *plateau* as far as the eye can see. As much as I'm done climbing, I'm not ready to start down the hill yet either.'

'*¡Excelente!* I'm happy to hear you say that. It marks the end of "Together, Forever, Wherever" then, I suppose, doesn't it?'

The songwriter turned in surprise, a perturbed expression on his face. 'Does it? Why? I hope you're coming to live on Table Mountain with me.'

'Of course I am, you idiot. Well...' Lynn replied, unsure of where her own thoughts were headed. 'It sounds like wherever's not on the cards any more. I don't mean in terms of not travelling and not needing our invisible elastic connection, *et cetera*. But more that wherever we are, we're always here. Us, together forever.'

Grabbing his lover's hand as he had twenty years ago, to run across Victoria Street before the next bank of cars broke away from the traffic lights, Jeff let out a huge lion's roar; magnificent, purposeful and aroused. The perfect way to arrive home, she mused.

Her man had finally conquered the desperation of his inner child and was content with who and where he was. Things could well take on a distinctly different tone in the days to come, when the realities of Brooke's circumstances were uncovered to their full extent. For the time being however, his joy was mirrored in her own heart, confident that she had helped this amazing human being attain his odyssey.

The level of devotion the soul-mates felt for each other was way beyond love, Lynn decided. Stronger than sexual desire, deeper than romantic love, with no beginning and no end. Song lyrics seeped into her head from the perfectly imperfect poet at her shoulder.

***

The following week saw a veritable assault of media coverage, with every television and radio interviewer clamouring for the Diamonds' attention and journalists from all over the world eager to scoop the next episode in Casey and Brooke's story. Way above expectations, the new Kids' Lifeline found itself inundated with sponsorship offers and applications from willing volunteers, making it the most successful program DCF had ever run.

Jeff Diamond turned up to visit the call centre to film an interview for the Australian Broadcasting Commission's "7:30 Report" to face a barrage of questions. He refused to divulge any details about the two sisters and their parents' reaction to his interference. According to the humble star, it sufficed to say that Casey's call and the ensuing *fracas* acted as a catalyst to prioritise their children a little higher in their life.

Later in the same segment, the rehabilitated sufferer spoke with genuine emotion about fans who came to his book signings and other public appearances, especially when linked to a DCF event. 'Some of them cling on to me so tightly, and some of them just can't stop crying,' he recounted. 'It's heartbreaking, but also comforting to know they've placed themselves in someone else's hands. Found something they can trust. The best results come when we do something that motivates people to step out of the darkness.

'I'll let you into a trade secret...' he continued, looking straight into the lens. 'My strategy is always to make these guys ask me to sign something, 'cause it's so hard for those in mental strife to ask for anything. It's cruel to be kind, and I hate doing it. They're normally so conditioned to hearing "No" that it's way easier not to ask in the first place.

'The occasional one walks away empty-handed, which breaks my heart. They made the effort to come but didn't move forward from the experience. And I completely get it... The *status quo*'s preferable, awful as it is, to putting themselves through the rejection of hearing another "No". I know exactly what that feels like. It's a sort of masochism. But hey, when they do ask... Man! Fireworks go off in their eyes! The look of empowerment on their faces is uplifting, and for some, that's all it takes to start the journey to recovery.'

'Would you still have done all this if you hadn't met Mum?' his son asked over dinner, once the programme had gone to air.

Jeff paused for a few seconds. 'I'd like to think some of it, but I doubt it,' he answered. 'I certainly wanted to. We talked about all kinds of ambitious projects from the get-go, didn't we, angel?'

Lynn nodded, recalling some of the early conversations during which she had first plumbed the depths of her mystery man. These memories were fresh in her mind after the pair had spent the previous evening retracing their steps under the stars over Port Philip Bay. How clear the signs of greatness had been to her, and how hard they had fought as the fearsome foursome ever since!

'I started a whole bunch of things while Mum was still in California, like "EpP" and transforming The Fellowship. But not on such a grand scale, no. And not without something to hope for either. I didn't have the strength to fight my mental state, just as I described on the TV. I wouldn't have been anywhere near as successful without you three. Or as committed. I'm damned sure about that.'

'Cool! *Gracias, Mamá*,' Kierney raised her water glass. 'Pantomime horses are the best.'

'Arse-ends thereof,' her brother reinforced, receiving a black look from his mother.

'Unlike sons thereof thereof,' Jeff mocked the boy whose vocabulary was becoming richer and more creative the more he acknowledged his growing intellect over his sporting prowess. 'We all need something to motivate us, guys. You know that already. It took a humongous incentive to motivate me out of the death spiral. Solving actual problems wasn't enough to give me the kick.

It's impossible to know who I'd have been on my own. It was all so closely wrapped up together from the beginning.'

'You would still've been huge, Jeff,' his charitable wife insisted.

'Huge?' Jet leaped on the *double-entendre*. 'Huge in what way?'

'Huge in ways you'll never understand,' his mother teased back. 'Listen to what your dad has to say, please, and stop with the gutter humour.'

The songwriter winked. 'Thanks, angel. But on the other hand, if I hadn't had such a shitty life as a kid, I might not've tried so hard to snare my dream girl as a way to climb out of the quagmire. If I'd been Lena, for example, I'd have settled. Stuck my head in the sand and suffocated. That's a whole 'nother unexplained phenomenon.'

'Hmm...' Lynn murmured. 'Don't go there either, please. It is strange though, how you two grew up to be so completely different from each other. Lena escaped the depression and the nightmares, but missed out on your drive to learn, feel and love. She does none of those things, and you got the lot. In such vast quantities. It *is* a phenomenon. Good way to describe it.'

Jeff smiled. 'One thing I know for sure... It was essential to get sleeping under control. Without your *mamá*, kiddoes, I have no effing clue how I would've done that. Up there with cooking you two, it has to be at the top of the list of things you've done to make me who I am.'

'Ew! Cooking us?' Kierney giggled. 'Sounds gross.'

Her brother grimaced, opening his mouth to change the subject. 'Hey, Mum?'

'Hey, Jet?'

'Did Dad tell you what he wants to call the band?'

The Diamond men had been in cahoots in the hour before dinner, going through the playlist for Melbourne Academy's end-of-term party, a send-off before its students joined the rest of the city for AFL Finals fever. They had convinced a number of *alumni* to form a super-group, supplementing the current crop of talented musicians.

'Not Vicki Stix and Dave Brown?' the singer replied. 'Have we been fired?'

Both teenagers laughed. Their parents had headlined at the previous year's disco' using the nicknames Stonebridge Music assignd the celebrities when they reserved tickets to events they wished to attend *incognito*. Taking turns to provide lead vocals, Lynn had featured on drums and Jeff as the rhythm guitarist. It had been a tremendous night, trotting out old favourites spiced with *risqué* versions of the several lyrics.

'Yep. Terrible reviews, I'm afraid,' the cricketer lamented. 'Sorry about that. Didn't you get the letter? Am I allowed to tell them, Dad?'

'I guess. It comes with a parental guidance warning, by the way.'

The mother blanched. 'Parental guidance? What've you come up with this time?'

'*Pseudoeffingdream.*'

'What?' Lynn and Kierney blurted at once.

'*Pseudoeffingdream!*' Jet announced at full volume. 'Why? Don't you like it? I think it's ace!'

'What does it even mean?' his sister moaned. 'The drug?'

Earlier the same month, their father had opened up about his use of hard drugs in response to a group of Scotch College Year Twelve students being caught with amphetamines. At the time, Lynn was all for being straight with their children, hoping they would be put off by the fact that the lads had been expelled on the spot and were now facing criminal charges.

Jeff shared a few articles he found on the Internet, showing how Pseudoephedrine was a common painkilling ingredient which drug pedlars boiled down in hidden locations called "meth' labs". As they had come to expect from Jet and Kierney, they had been less interested in supply and demand than hearing the rock star's first-hand knowledge.

'It's Dad's nightmares,' the sixteen-year-old claimed. 'I think it's pretty clever.'

The Olympian couldn't help laughing. '*Pseudoeffingdream,*' she repeated. 'That's truly awful! We won't get away with it in a month of Sundays. I hope you haven't sent stuff to get printed.'

'Well...' her husband laboured, hit by a sudden desire to clear their empty plates from the table.

'You haven't.'

'Haven't I?'

'Oh, please tell me you're joking. We'll get thrown off the Board. You haven't...'

Stacking the dirty cutlery and crockery into a pile, Jeff leaned over and planted a kiss on the top of his wife's head. 'I haven't. Tempting though... It'd be pretty powerful, with all that teenaged *angst* going around. It took me a while to feel sure enough of what I was doing to have sex clean and sober. I'll still talk about that, but you can rest easy Governor Dyson. Your reputation survives another term.'

Live On Earth

Brooke Teegan Maguire lay like a flaccid sack of bones in Jeff's arms, listening to the sound of gentle surf lapping onto *Escondido*'s private beach. Jet had helped carry down a whole campsite's worth of paraphernalia to make their evening special. A boom-box sat on the rug beside a fold-out, canvas chair, ready to play a tape of the thirteen-year-old's favourite songs, along with matching sports drink bottles inserted into the netting at the end of each arm.

September's weather monitors had pulled out all the stops too, with a spectacular sunset brewing in pinks and oranges on the western horizon. The cliffs would block its last half-hour, but it didn't matter. They had music to sing and books to read, and the heavy-hearted forty-one-year-old would sip ten strawfuls of lukewarm beer to his ward's measure of water.

The extraordinary turn of events had overwhelmed the young girl at first. Then, learning she was to be discharged into the Diamonds' care, she had become almost serene with happiness. Breathing for herself most of the time, an oxygen tank rolled along beside her wheelchair, bound for a side entrance of the Royal Children's Hospital.

Sisterly goodbyes had been traumatic for the adults, almost causing Jeff to pull the pin. Strangely though, Casey and Brooke appeared to take the outlandish plan in their stride. Perhaps the purity of a child's philosophy allowed them to see past traditions that put mortal existence at the height of one's spiritual desires.

As expected, second-guessing the miserable Mister and Missus Maguire's final figure hadn't been too onerous on the negotiator. The frail girl's freedom had come at a reasonable price, all things considered, gifting Jeff Diamond his third angel in a quickie settlement: a modest home near Casey's school; a few commas and zeros of cold, hard cash with no decimal points; and good behaviour bonds on their remaining daughter's behalf which would see the family's assets liquidated in the benefactors' favour upon breach.

The famous proponents of freedom, beauty, truth and love were gratified to find the Maguires had already softened their attitude to parenting. Liberated from the burden of Brooke's predicament, they had become more caring and attentive to their healthy daughter.

Tonight was the perfect night for a valediction, Lynn's magic-man had decided this morning. A contracted registered nurse, who had moved into *Escondido* to keep its newest guest as comfortable and content as possible, had calculated an expected time of death based on the rate at which Brooke's organs were breaking down.

Lynn and Jeff had advised their teenagers to arrange nights out. It was beyond the call of duty for them to watch someone pass away, regardless how propitious the outcome might seem. Over the last three days, Jet had entertained the slumberous girl with rounds of noisy computer games, and Kierney backed this up with much quieter pastimes, such as reading and sitting in on rehearsals for her new album.

The storyteller cleared his throat. 'Once upon a time,' he crooned, tracing the prominent blood vessels across the child's bald head, 'there was an angelic young woman named after a stream running down a hillside. She woke up one morning and said, "Today, I'm going to buy my favourite thing." So what did you buy, gorgeous?'

Brooke gazed up, lifting a hand under her covers. Hollow cheek bones made her eyes look smaller and darker in the half-light of dusk. Jeff sensed she was crying. Nudging the edge of the blanket aside, he was startled by the speed of her fingers as they flew towards his face and clouted him on the chin.

'Hey,' the kind man laughed, hugging her into his chest. 'Watch it! Come here and cry on my shirt. It needs a wash. What's your favourite thing in the whole world?'

Muted sobs were intermingled with giggles as the pair tipped back in the chair, so far that the girl's exposed hand now pointed towards the sky. She tried to lift her head but couldn't, so her helper twisted her further round until they could see each other's faces.

Jeff bent down and landed a kiss on the end of her narrow, beak-like nose. 'I love you, angel. Remember that. We all love you and have loved having you stay with us these last few days.'

Brooke began to cough, a feeble wheeze all she could manage. 'A rabbit.'

'A rabbit? Sure. Why not? Here, have some laughing gas, baby.'

Placing the oxygen mask over the girl's face, the songwriter heard footsteps on the wooden steps leading from the house. He hadn't asked Lynn to join them, but now she was on her way, he found the prospect of her leaving before his task was complete utterly unbearable.

'Y'see that star up there, two fingers left of the moon?'

The pale-skinned head twitched, its blue veins flattened against her scalp. In the last few minutes, Jeff had also noticed her lungs were making much less effort to breathe. It was up to him to piece together the story after all.

'That's the star I reserved for you. Brooke's destiny. Your paradise, where the ground's made of soft grass perfect for rabbits. It's sunny every day and only rains at night, to keep everything growing nicely.'

His saviour had reached the bottom step, judging by the change from *staccato* tapping on the wooden slats to the scrunch and slide over stones and salt-dried vegetation. Within another ten seconds, the beachcombers could invite her to their party.

'You'll love it there,' he declared. 'Only great kids get their own star. Kids who care about animals and like music. Lynn's coming. Can you hear her?'

Brooke jerked forward when she saw the tall athlete, seeming to panic. It made the newcomer jump. Jeff removed the youngster's oxygen mask and stroked her face as she struggled to speak. Precious little energy remained, with the morphine switch blinking its persistent message. At least her last moments would be painless.

'Hello, guys. Everything OK?'

After sharing an ephemeral kiss to boost each other's resilience, Lynn brushed her lips against Brooke's forehead. The child's temperature had dropped since leaving the house, which also corresponded with the hospital's instructions.

'Shall we turn the music up?' Jeff suggested. 'I think we should try to sing louder than the wind. We used to do this all the time when Jet and Kizzy were younger.'

'Sure. I'll do it,' his wife answered. 'The disc's nearly at the end. I'll choose another one. You like "Laura's Light", don't you, darling?'

A tiny squeak emerged from the blanket, jolting the adults from the false jollity. They joined hands, their eyes searching for the slightest doubt. Selecting the soundtrack's first power ballad, both stars prepared to perform for their singleton audience, swaying with the soaring string arrangement.

Three beltings later, Brooke began to cough despite the gas flowing into her lungs. Smiling through his dread, Jeff stretched the elastic until the mask was clear of her mouth and hooked it under her chin.

'We love you, Brookey. Thanks for coming to stay with us. You're doing really well.'

Lynn crouched down on the sand on the other side of the featherweight body. 'Do you want us to turn the music off? Is it too loud?'

The thirteen-year-old's face contorted as she mouthed the word "No", making the others laugh. They continued to sing while Jeff stepped up the dose millilitre by millilitre. He had often wondered, through his many suicidal episodes, what it might be like to be in control of one's last moments. Brooke had been most stubborn about not prolonging her suffering, keen to leave for her next destination.

'Tell me to stop if you want,' he said. 'Can you hear me?'

This time an emphatic "Yes" came from thin lips, followed by three unmistakable syllables. 'No. Don't stop.'

Exchanging forlorn glances over the girl's head, the musicians inhaled at the same time and nodded. It was time to change to her second best song of all time, "This Is The Moment", written by Leslie Bricusse and Frank Wildhorn. Lynn queued the girl's all-time favourite to play straight afterwards; a hit her husband had penned for her and then re-released when Kierney was born.

'Ready?' he checked, receiving a glimpse of a smile. 'I love you.'

'I love you too, Brooke,' came an echo through the wind.

'And at Number Two on the charts, here's Brooke Maguire with the Diamond family singers on background vocals, singing the hit from "Jekyll and Hyde". Take it away, Brooke!'

> '"This is the moment; this is the day
> When I send all my doubts and demons on their way."'

Jeff shifted his weight in the rickety camping chair until all three vocalists were facing towards the incoming tide. Unexpectedly, each verse flowed more easily than the last, consonant by consonant exorcising any lingering fears of making the wrong choice. Lynn's hand rested on his hipbone, her thumb tucked inside his belt, and as the song built into its final *crescendo*, the last vestiges of muscle control sank in the girl's antiquated body.

Without wavering from the song's metre, the baritone wove a request into the lyrics for Lynn to check Brooke's face.

'She's asleep. Unconscious,' his co-star reported.

Jeff squeezed the trigger on the second line, hoping their charge would feel nothing. 'Go bravely to tomorrow, baby. Leave gently and speak kindly to all people.'

His dream girl gulped, a sob emerging through her smile. 'Good luck, darling.'

One by one, both singers lay a last kiss on the peaceful *visage* and summoned another shot of resolve from their professional wells, hearts thumping against their ribcages. It was time to fast-forward to their paling star's Number One, and the low thrum of electric bass and rolling drums increased in volume to help them out.

> '"Your arms are my safety,
> Your smile is my sunshine,
> Your love is my shelter
> Forever, today."'

The philosopher's left hand wiped his tears away before feeling Brooke's neck for a pulse. Her expression hadn't changed for several minutes, and there had been no spasms to indicate her heart was still beating. The track eked out its last few chords and came to an unceremonious *coda*.

'She's gone,' he sighed, leaning back and letting the limp bundle relax down on his lap. 'Thanks for being here. You OK?'

'Yes. Are you?'

'Yeah. All good. It feels like we should wait here for a few minutes. Send her on her way or something.'

Lynn walked down to the water's edge, overcome with grief. Her husband heard her blow her nose and realised how much harder the task had been for her than for him. He set the vacant vessel down onto the picnic rug, its tartan pattern visible in the lamplight and far too festive for the occasion. Anxious to reclaim the special song as their own, he pressed the button on the disc player to play "Shelter" on repeat.

Standing behind his guardian angel, the old soul held her close and swayed imperceptibly, whispering words of love against her neck. By the end of the second replay, she had stopped crying and even managed to sing along.

'You're such a good man.'

'And you're the best, *Regala. Je t'adore.*'

With respects paid to both their satisfactions, Jeff sent Lynn back up to the house while he wrapped the little girl in a second, thicker blanket. He moved the rest of their belongings closer to the cliff, to keep them dry and out of the sea breeze. There were telephone calls to make and forms to sign, bringing the sad chapter to its administrative conclusion.

Escondido seemed quieter than usual, the temperature warm enough to leave the French windows open to the master bedroom's balcony and to the clear sky beyond. The couple delayed coming to bed for as long as they could, determined not to dwell on the remnants of their humanitarian act. They passed the time by discussing a recent argument between mother and daughter which had ended with a customary adolescent storm-out.

'Note to self: Lynn is always right,' the comic joked, stroking his wife's shoulder.

She sniffed. 'Try telling that to Kierney.'

'Yeah. I know. She'll get over it.'

The pair had been debating a matter which had come before the student council, and the young woman had thought the students' decision more than reasonable. The school governor voted otherwise, as did the majority of her fellow Board members.

'What do *you* think?' the sportswoman asked.

'I'm staying right out of it.'

'Hey!' she slapped his chest. 'You can't. Does that mean you agree with her?'

Jeff's chin knocked against the top of her head. 'It's not my battle.'

Lynn's grip tightened around his testicles, sending his heartbeat higher. Desire made their lovemaking fast and furious, rationalising the fact that they had broken the law. Neither truly comfortable with the risk they had taken, optimist and pessimist felt joined at the hip in so many more ways than the basest physicality.

After years of punishing himself for lives lost on his watch, from concert-goers in Chicago to an artistic idealist in Melbourne, the murderer's son felt strangely at peace. They had dispatched an elderly teenager whose life was a litany of neglect to greener pastures.

'How are you feeling now?'

'Unreal, thanks. Post-coital euphoria. You?'

'No, you idiot. Be serious! I mean about Brooke.'

The intellectual smiled, hugging his dream girl. 'Good. Uplifted, like I've done something worthy at last.'

'At last? What are you on about? You've done heaps of things worthy,' Lynn refuted.

'No. Way worthier. This is another level somehow. Unearthly. I feel somehow like I've passed some kind of test. A tick in an ethereal box!'

'Really? I'm nowhere near as disturbed as I expected to be by what we did, but I'm nowhere near as sure as you either.'

Jeff shuffled down the bed until their faces were side-by-side on the pillows. 'That's good. I'm glad, angel. Y'know, I had an epiphany while she was dying.'

'Did you? What sort of epiphany?'

'I don't know! Are there different sorts of epiphanies? And since too... That our chances of a good next life are greatly enhanced by the acquittal we're given from this one.'

'Oh. Like having a *résumé* to bring with you?'

'Yeah. Exactly! That's why we have funerals, I reckon,' the thinker expounded, hearing Lynn's breathing slow as she descended into drowsiness. 'Brooke had us two belting her favourite songs into the sky, as people who loved her and understood her worth. She wouldn't have got that if it hadn't been for Casey. A good lesson, if you ask me.'

The Olympian sighed, leaning in to kiss Jeff's lips as he spoke. 'I love you.'

'And I love you too,' the red-blooded man growled, aglow with the contentment of a job well done. 'Can I marry you next time round?'

'Hope so.'

'And the time after that?'

'Hope so.'

'And the time after that?'

'Goodnight, Jeff.'

'G'night, angel.'

***

The Diamonds were relieved to touch down at John F Kennedy Airport on the latest leg of their world tour. Half a day earlier, they had been mobbed at Heathrow's Terminal Three, on their way to Passport Control, by a vocal bunch of activists who were critical of their bi-partisan political lobbying in Africa. True to form however, Jeff's flippant responses made the following day's headlines, captured as always by the unshakable flock of press vultures.

'Isn't your support for multi-nationals moving into Kenya and Tanzania flying in the face of everything you stand for?'

'You mean, "Shouldn't we be encouraging people to be self-sufficient?"' he had shot back, a steadying hand on Lynn's shoulder. 'Fair accusation on the surface, maybe… I am the King of Sardonia after all.'

Stumped, the protesters faltered, exchanging puzzled glances. It was always risky taking a stand against Australia's highest-profile celebrities, where the weight of public opinion rendered them almost irreproachable.

'Where's Sardonia?' asked a plump woman in a parka accessorised by a colourful hand-knitted scarf.

'On the western butt-cheek of Africa, not far from the Irony Coast.'

Her body language admitting a ready defeat in the glow of her idol's sympathetic smirk, the hippy inquisitor gave an embarrassed laugh. 'Just don't turn Africa into another America. Please? Globalisation's evil.'

Customs officials had summoned security, together forming a ring around the superstars and their baggage trolleys. Determined to cut a swathe through the mob of fervent young adults and convey them to the safety of a departure lounge, they were irritated by the pair's ingratitude as they paused to drag out the troublemakers' discourse.

'It depends how you define globalisation,' the tennis champion returned. 'Addressing imbalance in global wealth and wellbeing is surely a good thing, isn't it? As long as it's coexistence rather than domination, everyone should win.'

In response to another request to move on, Jeff raised his hand to thank the group for listening. 'Absolutely. Well put. We don't want the world to turn into a hulking great homogenous vat of corporate vanilla ice-cream either, guys. The US and Europe've got their own problems with poverty and disadvantage too. We can't let them help themselves to so-called poorer nations' riches. If that's what you mean by "supporting" big business, then we're not doing anything of the kind.'

'As long as countries like Britain, America... and Australia too, while I'm at it... think their own back yards are clean and tidy, there'll always be far too many people who fly under the radar. Globalisation that concentrates on making the rich richer is no good for anyone, therefore our charities are being pains in the arse about acknowledging the rest of the population. Can we go now?'

The students all nodded, silver-tongued rhetoric taking the heat out of their argument as ever, and by the time the Diamonds touched down in New York, they were primed and loaded for their next brush with the establishment. A brief telephone call to Gerry armed them with up-to-date facts and figures, leaving them with just enough time to make love under the shower.

Departing their hotel in separate taxis, Lynn headed downtown to a *gala* event at the World Trade Centre to wow an affluent audience with a *solo* act and a seven-digit cheque, while her husband was dispatched to an uptown television studio to appear on the David Letterman Show along with one of his songwriting partners.

Stuart Fielding was promoting an album which he had recorded at *Escondido* earlier in the year, produced by the legendary musician who was otherwise engaged tonight. The handsome Scot opened the show with a song co-written with the Diamonds, before Jeff joined him and their host for an interview.

The threesome joked about both stars' history of womanising and about Stuart's much-publicised second marriage to a younger woman. To take the heat off the thirty-eight-year-old singer, his billionnaire collaborator began to talk about his "first wife".

David Letterman's eyes widened. 'Wait a minute there! Who's your first wife? I had no idea you were married before.'

Jeff grinned, scoring an invisible point with his index finger in the air. 'My first and only wife. I hope.'

His genuine reaction triggered more audible swooning and an enthusiastic round of applause from the schmalzy middle-classed crowd.

'You bet! Thanks. No great sacrifice, I assure you,' he shrugged at his fellow guest and the *compère*. 'D'you honestly think I'm going to give away perfection for the pretty young things who throw themselves at people like us? I don't know why I get so much credit for not needing temporary distractions. Have you met my first wife? I got all that dangerous living out of my system long ago.'

'Speak for yourself, you smug git. I don't think I'll ever get it out of my system,' Stuart laughed.

'Each to their own,' the Australian smiled, listening to the mounting dissent coming from female audience members. 'I'm not your judge and jury. Lynn and I intend to grow old together. Sorry to break it to all you scandalmongers out there. Boring, huh?'

'Grow old disgracefully?' their host chided.

'Ah, yeah. Lynn'll do it gracefully, I'm sure,' the former bad-boy contradicted. 'No guarantees for how I'll end up!'

Despite every attempt to cover more serious topics or to promote his lesser-known colleague's career, Jeff kept finding himself dragged back to his megastar lifestyle. Referring to his recent forty-first birthday, David asked a question he found impossible to answer.

'The most memorable thing in my life? Jeez! No way I could name only one, Dave. The whole damned thing's been a bit of a hurricane, to tell you the truth. And each year really does go by faster than the last as you get older. I never used to believe that tired old *cliché*, but I'm here to tell you it's true, ladies and gentlemen! And the funniest thing at the moment is that Lynn and I are going through, albeit second-hand, what Stu's doing first-hand. Our kids can't resist getting involved with every single new experience. The more outrageous the better. And Lynn and I are quite enjoying sitting back and living vicariously through their revelations. It's very cool! And even better when we can stop them making mistakes they don't need to make.'

'Amen to that!' Letterman chuckled. 'It's tough watching your kids grow up. You guys find that too? Did Lynn ever make any mistakes? She strikes me as someone that never put a foot wrong.'

The rock star shook his head. 'None I'm admitting to on her behalf. I've made enough for both of us!'

'She married you,' his stooge jumped in, kicking his friend's ankle with the toe of his pointed, black patent shoe.

'Quite possibly. There's still time for me to be proved wrong on that score. But seriously though, we love feeding our kids all these different experiences. We're needed less and less these days, which is a double-edged sword. On one hand, it gives us the ability to try new things ourselves, but on the other, it *is* so unbelievably tough to let go. Damned straight, Dave.'

The show's host was forced to pause to let a noisy outburst of appreciation die down. 'So I hear your good lady wife is also in the Big Apple this week.'

Jeff nodded, acknowledging the audience's respect for his better half. 'Correct. That's another benefit of Jet and Kierney becoming more self-sufficient: we get the chance to travel together much more. Lynn's doing a show on a rival channel this very minute. Sorry, sir! We're touring together for the first time, and I'm loving it. Nothing feels like a hard slog when she's around.'

Again the air pressure in the studio plunged as a large proportion of their adoring audience inhaled, followed by a collective sigh.

'Thanks,' the parasitic front-man proceeded with a theatrical aside. 'Mostly because I get her to do all the work…'

'Can I read you a notice from yesterday's 'papers, Jeff?' David asked out of the blue.

'Of course. Am I going to like it?'

'Oh, yes. I'm sure you're going to like it. It's something your wife said in an interview with our friends at NBC this morning, and I quote: "Jeff's brain... his soul too... is so big, so complex that it needs extra stimulus to make best use of itself. Hence all the drugs, drinking to excess and, of course, the big love." That's quite some testimony from your first wife! Is it good to hear?'

'Whoa! Yeah. Why the hell wouldn't it be?' the great man shoved his humility to one side to absorb the compliment about which he had been forewarned. 'That's how it feels on the inside, Dave, but it's another thing entirely to hear it on the outside. Thanks, angel. Can we talk about this man now, please?'

Letterman obliged, moving on to Stuart's new release. Quite apart from giving the younger man an opportunity to shine, it offered his mentor some welcome respite from the camera. The Aberdeen native had enjoyed three Number One hits on the Billboard charts in the preceding twelve months, with one song nominated for a Grammy award. It didn't take long for the conversation to revert to the bigger star however, relating to both studio audience and television viewers that the Scotsman had stayed at the Diamonds' clifftop *hacienda* while fine-tuning each recording.

'How was that?'

'Fantastic. It was a lot of fun.'

'He scared the dog a few times,' Jeff interjected, 'with raging conniptions when things weren't going too well; when Lynn made him do stuff over.'

Stuart nodded. 'She nearly threw me out, right enough. I can be a right prick sometimes.'

'Sometimes?' his friend scoffed.

David sniggered. 'OK. So, Jeff... How old are your kids now?'

The doting father stared into the distance, enjoying the instant images his mind projected behind his eyes. 'Hmm, let me see... Jet must be about twenty-five, I reckon. He only arrived fifteen years ago, but he's already in his mid-twenties. And Kierney's older than me these days.'

Many die-hard fans present for the evening's entertainment were not in the least surprised by this response. Their hero's predilection for playing with age-related numbers was a regular feature on the family's popular documentary series.

'It's frightening and breathtaking at the same time, being on the precipice of adulthood. I'm excited for them, starting out on a long, successful journey. And so unlike my own teenaged years that I get to hitch a free ride for a second go-round.'

'Mister Diamond, sir...' Letterman changed the subject again, shuffling through his batch of question cards. 'We hear of all these messy and very expensive celebrity divorce settlements.'

Initially taken aback, the philanthropist raised his eyebrows for the camera. He had a fair idea where thos conversation was heading.

'Ah, yeah?'

'So if you and your good lady wife were to split up, how much of a payout would you be up for?'

'What?' he snapped, fighting to regain his composure before anyone noticed. 'Are you for real?'

Jeff shouldn't have expected anything less from the prime-time Saturday night show. He *was* in the United States after all, where the superficial and material reigned supreme. He decided to to cut his interviewer some slack.

'Everything,' he replied without pretence. 'At least, I'd give her everything. I very much doubt she'd take it though.'

'You sure about that?' Stuart railed him up, as sceptical as their host.

'Two hundred percent sure. We're both more than capable of making enough money on our own, cheers, and our kids are well provided for. Regardless, money's not important to either of us. Staying together is. Sorry, Dave, but you're onto a non-starter, mate.'

A vociferous reception erupted from behind the cameras, which the handsome man acknowledged with a friendly wave. 'And anyway, our manager always says he's made our finances too complicated for us to ever get divorced. He gave a speech at one of our anniversary dinners, telling us he'd quit if we got divorced. "Someone else can sort that bloody mess out," he said. Therefore, while most couples say they stay together because of the children, we're staying together for our accountant!'

The audience burst into another round of spontaneous applause, causing David to abandon his line of questioning and move on. Here was a man who could do no wrong in the eyes of his faithful fan-base, which numbered in their multi-millions.

Did Lynn and he work on each other's records?

'Not in any official capacity,' the superstar answered, leaning back into his chair again, pleased to leave the unpalatable subject behind, 'except for the odd back line. We mainly collaborate on the writing, and Lynn'll do some early production work on mine sometimes. I never return the favour, by the way!

'And all that's about to change to some extent, with this new tour. It's a sort of swansong, I guess. Or emu-song, which doesn't bear thinking about musically. Ever heard an emu sing? Or a swan, for that matter?'

The stage crew and band groaned in true Saturday Night Live fashion. The image was amusing to those aware of the lanky native Australian flightless bird, and confused chatter broke out as the less well-travelled turned to each other for clarification.

'Just because the emu's on our national coat of arms, it doesn't mean it can sing,' Jeff added.

'OK, sure,' his host laughed. 'But that's another bombshell, if you please… What do you mean by "swansong"? Are you retiring?'

'Yes and no. *Sorta, kinda,*' he responded, drowned out by anxious objections. 'Haven't you had enough of us?'

Stuart Fielding stood up and strolled past the line of cameras, nodding his head and whipping the crowd further into a frenzy. The Sydneysider laughed, expecting his fellow guest's attempts to make fun of him would fall flat. He was not wrong.

'Thanks, everyone! You will after this tour, believe me. But no… Lynn and I've been performing off and on for a long time, and now it's time to pare back the frivolity and focus more of our attention on the meaningful stuff. We're not going to stop recording. Or writing. I have no control over when songs happen anyway…'

'So can we interpret this as you having political ambitions, now you've achieved such huge success on the world stage through music, companies and charities?' David read from his prepared script.

'Political ambitions?' Jeff repeated, rejoicing inwardly at being handed the perfect platform. 'Not sure what you mean, Dave. Everything we do has a political goal in one shape or form. In terms of running for the Australian Parliament or going into the Senate? Absolutely not. Not me anyway. Lynn'd be more suited to that…

'They deal with too many hard decisions. What I'm good at is the easy stuff, where decisions have already been made or there *is* only one sensible way to go. People tell us how they'd like their donations to be spent. It's seldom up for debate, barring the details. And I'm crap at the details too! Definitely Lynn's domain rather than mine. The problem with politics is that it consistently gets in the way of good government.'

The audience was stunned, unsure whether to believe what they were hearing. After a few awkward seconds, a ripple of laughter and a delayed round of applause broke out.

'I'd hate it, to be honest,' the tireless campaigner continued, ''cause I'm someone who likes to tell people their life can get better. If I were an MP, all I'd be able to say is, "I'll see where your idea fits in my party's agenda for the next electoral term." Not going to do anyone any good, is it? Sure, there are plenty of questions to answer about what we're doing in Africa, and about how the aid gets into the wrong hands, *et cetera.* Funding allocations often require us to stray into political swamps, and I let Lynn have her head with this special kind of people…'

The world-changer paused to let his words sink in, chuckling as his fans saw the funny side too. 'But no… Those who know me well are used to me debating the hard stuff *ad nauseam.* But if there are practical things we can do to solve problems while qualified people figure out the hard stuff, that's where I come in. I always try to resist getting involved with politics for two reasons: one, because once I did, I wouldn't be able to stop; and two, because there are way better-suited people than me who are interested in this level of mind-numbing detail.'

David Letterman stood his collection of prompt cards on end and tapped them on the surface of his desk. 'We've run clear out of time tonight,' he announced, as the band struck up the signature closing number. 'As always, it's a big deal when Jeff Diamond comes on the show. My thanks go to this week's special guest, Stuart Fielding, and to this dude here.'

Rising to his feet to accept the audience's tribute, the superstar leaned forward and shook his host's hand before turning round to do the same to his fellow musician. 'Cheers, Dave. And you too, Stu. I've got a tip for you though...' he hinted to the noisy crowd. 'Watch out for the Diamond womenfolk. They have much more moral fortitude than I do. They'll sort these politicians out. G'night!'

**

The summer months flew by in a series of long stints on the road as the Diamonds' combined caravan of love snaked its way across the giant North American continent, peppered by brief family get-togethers and meetings with Gerry, Cathy and other members of their Melbourne-based support team. Once in a while, the parents would sneak home to watch Jet play cricket for his country or to attend a particular school event. Nineteen-ninety-three was already a quarter gone by the time they all managed to catch their breath on a week's vacation enjoying Florida's amusement parks.

Having witnessed her son's teenaged lethargy surface a few times when a flight had been delayed, Lynn drew the family together while they waited in full view of the public for their turn to board. 'Let's have a little spark of enthusiasm, please,' she requested. 'Many kids don't get the chance to fly anywhere, and you're bored going on holidays. Your dad didn't get to go on a 'plane 'til he was twenty.'

Both children stood taller, impatient stares replaced with smiles. Jeff gave his wife a kiss on the cheek to reinforce her point. As usual, they were on the same wavelength.

The famous family were held up on the way home too, locked in a meeting room in the Qantas lounge during their transfer out of Singapore after the Easter break. The Blakes had joined them in Florida, along with Anna Dyson and her Canadian *fiancé*, Brandon.

Both children had knuckled down to some homework to while away the three hours of stop-over. With their elder child heading into his final year of high school and Kierney not far behind, Lynn and Jeff were amazed at how dedicated they were to achieving distinction in every examination.

'What's the difference between a customer and a client?'

'Depends who you talk to,' the songwriter replied.

His son smirked. 'Well, I'm talking to you.'

'Watch it! Enough of your cheek.'

'A customer buys a product, whereas a client buys a service,' their mother offered. 'That's the way I've always seen it anyway.'

'Yep. I can go for that,' her husband agreed. 'The difference between a prostitute and an escort.'

'What?'

The startled *trio* collapsed into laughter at Jeff's habit of bringing any conversation to a screaming halt. No matter the topic, he had a tendency to come at it from a whole different angle.

'How am I supposed to know the answer from that example?' Jet moaned.

'Oh, I reckon you've got a pretty good idea, mate. Are you buying something as a one-off transaction or as a more sophisticated experience?'

Kierney's jaw dropped. '*Papá*! Why do you always use sex to show us new concepts?'

''Cause it's easy to guess the answer, *pequeñita*. You get it, don't you? An escort asks you what you'd like and tailors her service to meet your requirements, whereas a slapper just lies there and lets you do your thing. That's a product. You use it.'

The tennis champion laughed. 'Wow! That's so funny! Using and respecting relationships. I haven't heard those terms for so long. And I think I never quite understood it properly until now.'

'Didn't you?'

'No! See? You're still teaching me things!'

Her husband gave her a heartwarming smile. 'Hey... Christ knows why this has floated into my head, but d'you remember the time when Captain Marvellous asked, "What's this for?" while sticking his finger so far into his belly-button that I expected to see a lump protruding out of his back?'

'Yes!' Lynn exclaimed, chuckling at their son's puzzled expression. 'Wow! I haven't thought about that for ages either.'

'Mate, it was one of those times when I truly didn't have enough time to go through the "Where do babies come from" conversation with you, so I told you that bellybuttons were for making us laugh. To cheer people up, y'know...'

'More lies and deception,' the cricketer replied with lighthearted scorn. 'It's a wonder we believe anything you say really, isn't it?'

Jeff raised his eyebrows, catching Kierney's eye. 'I made up this shit about if someone's sad, it means their belly-button's broken. I said the way to fix it's to tickle their tummy, and it'll make 'em laugh again.'

Mesmerised by the happy recollection, his wife sighed. 'You were so funny, Jetto. You immediately stuck your stomach out like Buddha and invited Dad to demonstrate, and you laughed so hard that you nearly fell over.'

'Hey, presto, mate!' the world-changer cried out, too far away to subject his son to more present-day embarrassment. 'One touch, and they're happy again. See? Of course, this little gem stuck *en famille* for a few years, used to good effect on you, Kiz, too!'

His daughter grinned. 'That's so cute.'

'Yeah, but it really came into its own later. Remember, angel?'

'Maybe. You need to jog my memory.'

'*Oh, avec plaisir, mon amie.* I'll do more than jog your memory, if you're lucky.'

Both teenagers voiced their disgust, which only served to goad their father on. 'You used to intercepted this one's frequent temper tantrums, like when he couldn't get one of his toys to do what he wanted or whatever... You'd tell him that getting angry wasn't going to help, and that instead, he should think about how to solve the problem.'

The Olympian nodded. 'Hmm... Didn't always work, but it was a good enough diffuser mostly.'

'Exactly,' Jeff agreed. 'But what was so gratifying was that time when Tex was here. Jet was four or so. He was staying here while your *mamá* was producing one of his early albums. Mighty pissed off about nothing, as per usual, and playing up something chronic in front of you guys. Jetto, you calmly strolled over to where he was sitting by the pool, reached over and started tickling his bare stomach.'

'Oh, my God! Did I? How awkward! Hope he doesn't remember.'

All four laughed. For all his natural flamboyance, musicianship and commanding stage presence, Tex Fletcher had always been a bigger baby than either Diamond child. Their parents regularly used his petty sulks and violent outbursts as examples of behaviour which ought not to be replicated, eliciting giggles that were hurriedly camouflaged if ever the British songwriter caught them observing him at his worst.

'He prefers not to remember,' Lynn shook her head. 'Conveniently!'

'Yeah. I nearly decked him that time,' her man continued. 'He lashed out at you, mate. Nearly sent you flying, yelling, "What the hell are you doing?" But instead of running to one of us for consolation, you weren't at all scared. It was an awesome peek into your future. You just stood your ground and shouted back, "Don't be angry with me. I was only trying to make you happy."'

'Wow!' Kierney interrupted. 'Cool, bro'. Nothing's changed there then!'

'That's right,' her mother carried on. 'We never made the connection between these two separate concepts. You did, all on your own. It was weird; probably the first time I heard my words coming out of your mouth: "Being angry might make you feel a bit better for a short time but it doesn't fix anything.'"

Earlier in the year, marking Australia Day at the end of January, a committee including the Prime Minister and Governor General had bestowed the country's highest honour to the popular and hard-working celebrity, nineteen years after winning the coveted title of "Young Australian of the Year".

Much to his in-laws' embarrassment and to the authorities' dismay at the apparent snub, Jeff had refused to accept the award unless his beautiful best friend's equal contribution was recognised, to redress the ever unequal gender balance in these awards. After additional deliberation, it was announced that two "Australians of the Year" would be honoured for the first time in the program's history.

Preparing for her part in the double-act's acceptance speech on the lawn outside Canberra's Parliament House, Lynn trawled through her meticulous records to total up the number of hours worked, telephone calls placed and received, letters and meetings organised and executed in her role as the pantomime horse's rear-end.

The resulting numbers were considerable, especially when measured alongside her string of victorious tennis tournaments, her musical achievements and raising two children from newborns to independent teenagers over the same timeframe, and it hit home to her and her front-man how dedicated she had been to their quest.

'When we get divorced,' the Olympian teased her handsome co-recipient in front of an array of dignitaries and journalists on the day of the presentation, 'we'll send this gong back and forth with the kids and the cat.'

The couple also reflected in a private moment on the negative press they had tolerated over the years, from artless do-gooders who criticised them for leaving their young children in the care of nannies and schools while they pursued their wildest dreams. Now, after snatching a fortnight's relaxation with their growing adolescents, any heartache they might have taken on board as to the validity of these vitriolic complaints soon dissipated.

At fourteen years of age and only ten centimetres shorter than her mother, Kierney was full of stoic determination. She had become an accomplished squash player as her contribution to Dyson sporting excellence, as well as a skilled musician and dancer, excelling at school and with many more friends than her introversion could countenance.

The dark-haired gipsy girl grew up preferring her parents' company to that of her peer group during her childhood but, of late, had begun to hang out with the more thoughtful and counter-culture students at Melbourne Academy. Like her father at the same age, she wanted little more than to immerse herself in challenging conversations with worldly people, soaking up every opinion and experience with a healthy degree of cynicism and a pinpoint-accurate hyperbole radar.

Conversely, Jet continued his unswerving march from conquest to conquest; a true white knight. He was developing a benevolent air worn with virile, good-humoured grace. Although bearing a closer outward resemblance to his Uncle Junior than to his father, the well-built blond had inherited the Catholic Argentinean Polish Jew's unmistakable expressive confidence.

The cricket captain held his head high wherever he went and played the parts of hero and role model with natural ease. As outgoing as his sister was quiet, the young man rarely spent time on his own. When he did however, his internal intellectual grew in stature as the months passed and was also beginning to show new signs of creativity.

Noticing how their son was constantly restless in his spare time, the musicians convinced him to form a band with his mates. This proved a successful idea in no time, when weekend after weekend, the four boys took over the function room and knocked out a number of tracks which permeated the rest of the house with a distinctive and forceful beat; so much so that Lynn arranged a trip for the friends to Los Angeles during cricket's off-season, where they would stay with another longstanding songwriting partner, Greg Marlow of The Vultures.

'To make music and chase Californian girls,' his dad announced, giving a short speech at a family dinner held for the lad's sixteenth birthday. 'One shall beget the other, no doubt. And Jeez, am I envious!'

The youngster had also been overjoyed to find an old panel van parked in the garage at *Escondido* on the morning of this same occasion. Jeff bought it as a father-son project, to work on over the winter months whenever he was home from the tour. Procured for bonding purposes in the main, the Diamond men passed many hours under the bonnet, removing engine parts and either cleaning or replacing them. Car maintenance never likely to be a necessity in his luxurious and privileged existence, all agreed it was nevertheless practical expertise worthy of learning.

The off-white bone-shaker was a nineteen-seventy-four model Holden HQ, an antonymous addition to the stable of sleek sports cars and four-wheel drives. However, the sixteen-year-old couldn't have been happier with his dad's choice, long having hankered after what they fondly called a "crumpet wagon", laden with promise for the testosterone-charged teenager.

The amateur mechanic and his sporting friends spent several Saturday afternoons trawling around car yards searching for wings, panels and doors which were in better condition, preferring not to have to sand down the rusted paintwork and beat out the dents if they could help it. Jeff engineered each session so that his son did all the manual labour, setting small goals to be achieved in his absence whenever he and Lynn needed to leave home.

Of course, the principal, covert objective wasn't overlooked either... The pair and a series of ring-ins would talk for hours in the cavernous space, swapping stories and smoking while rain and gales lashed against the garage doors and windows.

'You don't have to know everything about life in advance, guys,' Jeff told his son and Dawson Jenner during one such ravaged Sunday morning. 'Leave some things undiscovered for a while. There are heaps of things in life you're best not knowing upfront 'cause you don't *wanna* miss the taste of mystery and the buzz of anticipation.'

At long last, having secured an official learner's permit, Jet won the right to take his pride and joy out on the Mornington Peninsula's open roads. Like his mother and her siblings, neither Diamond teenager was a novice behind the wheel, having grown up driving farm vehicles on the Benloch settlement. Sitting in the passenger seat, the former nobody from Sydney's south-west was stoked to see the simple pleasure their son took in showing off the results of his manual labour. How well he remembered treasuring the independence of his first car!

'What age do people stop having sex?' the self-assured young man asked, scrunching to a halt at his mother's feet.

The lad's ego had taken a bruising during their travels, forced to brake hard to avoid a vehicle that decided to turn right into a side street at the last minute. His diversionary tactic had almost resulted in the van burying its nose into a small, red Nissan Micra driven by a sexy blonde with whom he had flirted at a traffic light only a few minutes earlier.

Keen to finish the journey on a high, Jeff directed him onto the freeway and instructed him to open the throttle as far as it would go. With minimal traffic, they watched the speedometer's shaky needle pass one hundred and thirty kilometres per hour before easing off for fear of total disintegration.

Their practice run had also offered another welcome opportunity for the inquisitive young man to extract all manner of information about the opposite sex from his father. They stopped in Frankston to pick up takeaway for lunch and drove up to Arthur's Seat to eat it while surveying the picturesque curve of the Dromana coastline below, laughing and joking about men-only topics. It was important for Jet to learn the distinction between polite conversation and the types of indecorous colloquy inappropriate in female company.

The songwriter smiled through the windscreen at his wife's wagging finger. He imagined her supposing he had put their son up to aiming for her toes.

'No idea, mate. I used to do that to Mum too. We'll let you know!'

***

On the Saturday after his final VCE examination and as a treat for securing a place at Trinity College in Cambridge, Jet was given the choice of a night out in the city or a party at home. To his parents' astonishment, the fun-loving sportsman had chosen the latter, with a *bijou* guest list consciously including his kid sister. Kierney had been as surprised as anyone to receive the invitation, wondering if he would miss her as much as she would miss him once he took up his university place so far away.

Lynn and Jeff retired to the master suite early, leaving the youngsters downstairs to enjoy the safe brand of summer freedom for which *Escondido*'s gated paradise was famous. The day's heat had risen over the bay to form volatile storm clouds that crackled with faraway lightning and thunder-claps evocative of the supreme being's indigestion.

The couple lay on top of the bed, sharing an unfinished bottle of *Rioja* and eavesdropping on the spirited but well-filtered youthful discourse bubbling up from beneath their balcony. Although amused by the chatter, they were actually hoping to be afforded a few hours' quiet time in advance of their pre-dawn departure for the airport.

With Dawson and Hitesh having to leave early to ensure their girlfriends were home by midnight, Jet and Vincenzo were eager to entertain their dates and the two younger girls, producing a succession of classic tricks to show off. Their antics reduced Jeff to fits of muffled laughter as he cuddled into his dream girl.

'Do you envy him?' Lynn asked, reaching her hand behind to stroke his penis.

'Leave me alone,' he sniffed, unable to hide his arousal and powerless to resist. 'You said we have to be up early.'

His lover laughed. 'We do, and you are.'

'Jesus, woman! Leave me alone.'

'Wow! You heat up as soon as I touch you. I love how you respond to me.'

'I know,' the arrogant man chuckled, kissing her neck. 'Your approach is having the right effects.'

'Side effects?'

'I think not. Jetto's getting quite baronial, don't *ya* think?'

Lynn turned over to face her husband. Nostalgia had been rife earlier in the evening, as the couple let the youngsters in on secrets of their own teenaged mishaps over the barbecue, preaching to a spellbound row of next-generation promise. His voice retained traces of the deep-seated joy he took from watching their children become adults, stirring a primitive pride in her too.

'Don't leave me,' came the predictable reply to her kiss.

'I won't leave you, Jeff.'

'I love how we are together,' he sighed. 'It's just so easy, so harmonious.'

The singer pressed herself against the full length of his overheating body, swallowed up by boundless affection. 'And that's exactly why I won't leave you. Do you envy Jet?'

'Ah, yeah! Brings back memories, that's all,' her husband replied, groaning in pleasure. 'I have to admit he's pretty smooth.'

'He's got the best teacher.'

Lynn and Jeff made love with the volume of lively conversation rising and falling in the background, their limbs defying the humidity to weave themselves into a languid, passionate dance. With the balcony doors open to the outside world, their undulations came and went in virtual silence. They knew Jet and Kierney would expect nothing less of their parents, but there was no point broadcasting to their visitors.

'Being a teenager was fun while it lasted, but I wouldn't choose to go back there in this lifetime,' Jeff confessed, caressing the body he worshipped. 'Would you? I never thought I'd say my forties are better than my twenties. I feel so damned good!'

'I love you,' Lynn whispered.

He kissed her lips, thrusting himself into her and enjoying the welcoming warmth. 'Don't go away. Did I ask you that before?'

'Oh, yes,' she gasped. 'A million times. Why would I want to go away?'

The party upstairs outshone its ground-floor equivalent in the tumult of sexual urgency and quixotic sentiment, cupping each other's mouths to drown their synchronised orgasms. The delirious pair must have dozed off soon afterwards because they were both in a deep sleep when their son's fist pummelled their bedroom door.

'Dad, Mum, may I come in?'

Usually the lighter sleeper, Jeff became aware of the bed rocking sideways as Lynn sprang out and grabbed her nightclothes. He did the same, still semi-conscious and bidding Jet to enter. The door flexed on its hinges to reveal the sodden frame of a panicked sixteen-year-old leaving a spreading puddle on the landing floorboards.

'Sorry to wake you up,' he coughed. 'It was my fault. Enzo's fallen and can't walk on his ankle, and the lift's not working.'

The father turned on the bedside lamp, at first not recognising an enormous silhouette backlit by the hallway light. 'What? Where were you? Which lift?'

'Did you guys go down to the beach?' his wife continued the interrogation. 'Why did you do that? Especially with the weather coming in.'

'I know. Sorry. It was stupid. We shouldn't have gone. Please could you help us get Enzo back up? I think he knocked himself out when he fell.'

'Shit, mate,' the songwriter shook his head. 'Let me get dressed. I'll ring Ross to give us a hand. Where're the others? Still down there?'

The teenager accepted his dad's offer, full of remorse at having woken the busy travellers. Luckily, the family's housekeeper hadn't yet gone to bed, and made light of the request despite the heavy rainfall tapping against the windows at either end of the telephone.

As his father put on some clothes, Jet explained that the lads and their girlfriends had decided to scale the cliffs to watch the storm come in from the Heads. He also confessed to noticing the indicator light wasn't flashing on the elevator chiselled into the rock, assuming they would be able to activate it easily enough.

'It did cross my mind that we'd have a long walk up again, but we just carried on down the steps. I'm sorry to be such an idiot, Dad.'

'Pretty bloody dumb, mate. How far along are they?'

Heaping three blankets into Jet's open arms, Lynn said she wouldn't telephone the ambulance service for half an hour since the beach was inaccessible by any other route. Thankfully, their daughter and Piraea had not joined the others in their dangerous adventure. For once, Kierney's youth had worked to her advantage, and now she would have a rare chance to thumb her nose at her brother's misfortune.

The patient mother wished the men good luck, passing Jeff a pair of torches from the laundry. She watched them cross the lawn past the tennis court where Ross Monroe, a retired army supplies officer, had arrived holding two stout planks from the shed for improvising into a stretcher if required.

The *trio* picked their way down the slippery wooden staircase, the long pieces of timber difficult to control in the wind as they turned for each new flight of steps. Sure enough, when they reached the bottom, there was no power to the lift and the door wasn't budging. It was a vain hope to think they would be able to transport the injured boy back up the easy way.

'We were running through the rock pools,' the cricketer explained. 'Pippa kept pushing Enz in the back, and he slipped and went down between two rocks. He's hurt his shoulder too, I think.'

'How long was he unconscious for?' Ross asked.

'Not long. Ten seconds or so. Maybe fifteen. No more.'

Sharing the load between them while their housekeeper trudged ahead with both flashlights, father and son exchanged no words. Jet knew exactly what he was in for when the drama had sorted itself out, and it was well-deserved. He had shown poor leadership this evening.

'The tide was coming in pretty fast,' he broke the silence. 'I hope they managed to get back towards the cliff.'

Pausing on a flat layer of eroded stone, Ross reached up to slap his boss' shoulder. 'Kids, eh?'

The father failed to see the funny side. 'What the fuck were you thinking, mate?'

'I know, Dad,' the boy whined. 'I should've known better.'

'You should.'

The rescuers rounded the modest promontory on the city side of their beach to find the three teenagers huddled together against the rock face. Soaked and freezing cold, the girls burst into tears when they realised their ordeal was nearly over.

Vincenzo's right ankle had swollen to twice its normal girth, and his shoulder jutted out at a nasty angle. He screamed as his girlfriend went to help him stand up.

'Get off me!' he cried out, lashing out with his other arm.

'Cool it, Enzo,' Jeff snarled. 'Pip was only trying to give you a hand. Can you lower your arm?'

'No!' the basketballer replied. 'It's agony. Worse than my foot.'

'Thank you for coming down,' his son's latest catch, Kate, found her manners. 'I'm sorry to ruin your early night.'

The billionnaire laughed, waving his hand. He glanced at Ross, wondering if they could figure out how to correct the dislocation before they attempted their climb. The older man shook his head as if reading the star's mind.

'Jetto,' the father started, watching his son jump to attention. 'Grab Enzo's hand. Stay sitting up, mate. We're going to pop your shoulder, OK?'

The shellshocked sixteen-year-olds obeyed the celebrity's instruction without a whimper, the girls' horrified squeals competing with howls of pain. Jeff squeezed himself between Enzo and the slimy sandstone, braced himself and eased his arms round the young man's chest.

With the lad's torso held at a forty-five-degree angle to the ground, the superstar shifted his feet, digging his heels in until he found safe purchase. 'Right. When I say, "Three," pull straight back behind you, Jetto. You up for that? Much better to fix this arm before we start back. One less variable to manage.'

'Yes, OK,' his son's deep voice sounded more confident than any of them expected, which the father took as a good sign. 'Cool. Ready, Enz? On three, but *lento, lento*. One sharp pull.'

'Ready,' the lanky Italian yelped.

The girls looked on, frightened for their friend. They held on to each other, shivering in the driving rain. Ross handed the blankets around, then stood by in case he could be of assistance, admiring his imposing employer's ingenuity as he maintained his grip on the injured boy.

'Ready?' Jeff checked again. 'On three.'

'Yep.'

'Good man. *Uno. Dos. Tres.*'

A monstrous popping noise signalled Vincenzo's right shoulder joint was back in position, cracking only a few centimetres under Jeff's ear. His stomach churned, and it took all his strength to pull against the force of his son's tug. Vincenzo let out an almighty screech, more out of fear than pain, and both girls turned their faces away.

On his dad's say-so, Jet released his friend's hand, and it flopped onto the stone almost weightless. Jeff leaned down until the lad's backside rested on solid ground again, leaning his head against the cliff-side.

'Does it feel better?' the cricket captain asked. 'Can you feel your fingers?'

The injured young man flexed his frozen digits and tried to lift his arm with a fair amount of caution. Ross gave his boss a thumbs-up sign, and Jeff shared an exaggerated sigh of relief with the others. For all his accumulated know-how on so many diverse subjects, he had never paid more than an aesthetic interest in anatomy.

'Good man. Jet, you OK too?'

The sixteen-year-old was overcome with elation, any original trepidation banished in favour of acquiring the skill of fixing a dislocated shoulder. He nodded back, springing into action. He helped himself to the remaining blanket from the ledge next to where the girls were huddled out of the breeze and handed it to his father.

Bending the stunned patient forward to shield him from the wet and cold, in case shock were to set in, the musician threaded the woollen material round the lad's back. '*Vamanos,*' he announced. 'Let's get up to the house. Good work, guys. Can you stand up, Enzo?'

By now, the tide was rippling around their shins, causing the alarmed women to squeal with each new wave. The din was deafening, sending shivers down Jeff's spine. His mind still thought of his sister every time he heard a girl scream.

Beckoning for Ross to take the strain, the athletic forty-one-year-old stood next to Vincenzo's right shoulder, wondering whether he was asking too much by levering him to his feet. The ageing soldier cupped his hands under the boy's left armpit, and the pair steadied themselves to prop him up.

'Does this hurt more or less?' Jeff asked, tightening his grip.

'No. Hardly hurts at all. That's amazing! Was it really dislocated?'

'Yep. Right. Let's see if you can hop along with us, at least as far as the steps. We'll figure out what's next once we're clear of the tide. Otherwise, we're going to be washed out into the bay, and I don't fancy a midnight swim tonight. Mate?'

The drenched kids laughed. Jet caught his father's eye, reminded of his part in these nocturnal exercises. This was his cue to take action, and he cursed himself for having to be prompted. A good learning experience, as his grandfather was known to say, even though he expected a sturdy castigation later. He marshalled the young ladies' descent off the ledge, where they had managed to stay reasonably dry, and began to lead them towards the steps.

'Jetto...' his dad called after them, pointing to the planks. 'Please could you carry those up again? We can't leave them down here.'

The cricketer scurried back, guessing this overt errand was part of his punishment. They could easily have left the wood down on the beach until the morning, but he knew his father's methods too well. Strong enough to manage the two lengths with little exertion, he soon caught up with the girls again.

Ross grinned, saying no doubt the boy would be moaning about the ridiculous request and seeking sympathy. They would both have done the same as teenagers, Jeff mused in return.

Vincenzo was unable to put any weight on his foot, which meant the men's strange three-legged race was awkward, slow and treacherous. One or other lost his footing several times and almost sent them sprawling over the rocks. After about ten minutes, they caught sight of the rest of the group standing at the bottom of the staircase, gazing upward as if they were about to climb Chimborazo.

'What are you waiting for, folks?' Jeff shouted. 'Start walking! It's not going to get any lower.'

The girls groaned and began to stomp up the first flight, followed at close quarters by his son. Ross and his employer let their patient crumple to the ground while they caught their breath and worked out how they should transport him to the top.

'Shit! Great time for the lift to be on the *fritz*. Didn't even know it was broken.'

'No. Neither did I,' the housekeeper replied, ashamed. 'I should've checked. Sorry, boss.'

'Jesus,' the superstar shook his head. 'I wasn't blaming you, mate. Since when've you been our lift maintenance guy? It's Lynn's fault.'

The senior citizen took a second to realise the celebrity was joking, so impassive was his tone. They laughed, and both drew in a sharp breath.

'Cigarette?' Jeff chuckled. 'I could murder one.'

'Me too,' Ross agreed, accepting a light and turning back to Vincenzo, who was slumped over and shaking with the pain. 'Sorry, son. We need to get you going, don't we? What's the plan of attack?'

The intellectual stared at the eight flights ahead and lit his own cigarette. The wind had whipped up, stronger and colder than before, and he could only just make out the others through the mist, already halfway up.

'OK,' he said, slapping the bannister. 'Enzo, you're going to have to go up on your bum, mate.'

The kid grizzled for effect, and a puff of smoke hanging in the damp air masked his smile. In truth, he couldn't have cared less whether his ascent was dignified or not. His ankle throbbed like an old diesel engine, and he was sopping wet and frozen.

'Ross, the steps should just about be wide enough for us to go side by side. So if you grab an elbow again, we'll lift him up a couple of steps at a time. Maybe three, if you lever yourself up by your good foot, Enz. Can you do that?'

'I'll try. I'm sorry about all this, Mister Diamond. It wasn't Jet's fault.'

'That's cool,' the respected father chuckled. 'You can drop the Mister Diamond. Where did that come from all of a sudden? Makes you sound guilty. We'll talk about whose fault it was when we're inside enjoying coffee and a whisky. Raise your arms, mate. Ready?'

The threesome had settled into a sort of rhythm by the time they rounded the second landing, and before long, they felt the tremors of another, much quicker set of footsteps. Jet had escorted their girlfriends into the house and was now returning to discharge the remainder of his duties. The rock star hoped it hadn't been at his mother's instruction.

'Hey, Dad!' the youngster yelled. 'Are you guys alright?'

'We are. Take over from Ross, please. Go on up, mate. Thanks very much for your help. We'll see you at the top.'

The housekeeper agreed. He was puffing hard, with all the bending and heaving necessary to maintain his boss' fitter pace. Vincenzo moaned and yelped every now and again while father and son mocked their poorly choreographed *Escondido* shuffle.

'Not going to do this again in a hurry, are you?' the superstar chuckled at the forlorn pair. 'Storm-chasing doesn't seem like such a bright idea now?'

'Fuck, no!' the cricketer sneered in retort. 'The ambulance is here, by the way. Mum's thinking of going into the city with it, 'cause you've got to go to the airport anyway.'

It was Jeff's turn to groan. He couldn't think of anything worse than to have to leave home at this point, with only a few hours of the night remaining. The thought of their alarm clock greeting them so soon was depressing enough. He guessed Lynn had contacted the other parents, and offering to accompany the patient was entirely the right thing to do.

'Bloody marvellous,' he muttered, heaving the sodden teenager up the next few steps. 'Are Kiz and Piraea awake too?'

'Yes,' his son confirmed. 'With "I told you so" written all over their faces.'

Vincenzo weighed in to defend his mate. 'How come? They never tried to stop us.'

'Whatever, you bunch of numb-nuts,' the songwriter said. 'We can all be geniuses after the fact. You'll learn to control these impulses after a few more of these disasters. It's called *machismo, il mio amico. Tuo papà non ti dico?*'

'Dad!' Jet cried out, embarrassed. 'Don't go all "wise man" on us now. We get it, right?'

After a few more minutes, the rescue party reached the top of the cliff, where Ross stood clutching a bundle of rain-jackets. He helped manœuvre the injured boy to his feet again, and the Diamonds took the strain, hoisting Vincenzo into the air while trying to keep him as level as possible. Two uniformed paramedics assumed control at the kitchen door and transferred him onto a trolley.

Jeff exhaled when he spied his guardian angel already dressed for departure. She held her arms out to welcome her bedraggled black stallion in from his wintry ordeal. Kierney and the Violin Vamp passed around steaming mugs of coffee.

'Thanks, *pequeñita*. Nice evening for a stroll, eh, Ross? Just what the doctor ordered on Saturday night before a long-haul flight.'

The older man smiled, slumping down onto a kitchen chair. Discreet as always, he offered no direct opinion in front of the ladies. The ambulance driver poked his head in through the door to tell them they were ready to take the patient into the city. Jeff heaved his warming body off the refrigerator, which was as far into the house as he had managed to get.

Ushering his wife ahead of him, he grimaced. 'Are we going in too?'

'Don't you want to? I rang Lou and Pippa's mum. Lou and Maria are going to meet us at the Alfred. I thought at least one of us ought to be there.'

'Ah, yeah. You're right, I s'pose. What about the girls? Are they staying here? I don't know what time it is.'

'Half-past twelve,' Lynn answered. 'Pippa's mum's fine for her to be dropped back in the morning, so she and Kate can sleep in the spare room. Kizzy's staying at Piraea's tomorrow night, so everything's arranged. It's just the boys we need to sort out, as usual.'

The tired man forced a smile and rested a heavy arm on his saviour's shoulder as they left the house, indicating his acquiescence to whatever she saw fit. Beyond the courtyard *portico*, both the ambulance and his wife's Maserati's doors stood open with their engines running.

Having confirmed their baggage was already in the car's rear compartment, the exhausted musician switched the sports car's ignition off and climbed inside the ambulance to check on their injured guest. Pain relief now kicking in, Vincenzo was now comfortable; even a little chipper after his bumpy ride up from the beach. Jeff tested his shoulder with a tentative hand, but it yielded no adverse response.

'OK?' he asked the drowsy teenager. 'We'll see you on the other side. Enjoy the trip.'

The lad chuckled. 'Thanks. Will there be sirens?'

'You've *gotta* be kidding!' the celebrity scoffed at the boy's self-importance. 'Not at this time of night. You're no emergency, mate. And no feigning a heart attack either. Got it?'

The paramedics locked the rear doors and sped away into the darkness beyond the property's electric gates, which glided back into position after the high-visibility vehicle had disappeared down the unlit country lane. Lynn took her husband's hand, flicking drips off his spray jacket with the other.

'Aren't you cold?' she asked, kissing his cheek. 'My hero...'

'Oh, don't you start,' Jeff grunted, pulling his hand back. 'I s'pose you want me to get showered and out of these clothes now. Christ Almighty, angel. The things we do for our kids.'

The couple embraced, relaxing into each other's sympathy. Kierney and Piraea were making their way to the front door just as their son came loping across the courtyard.

'Has he gone?'

'Who?' the man of the house replied, holding both arms out.

'Enzo, of course! Is he OK?'

'He's fine,' the singer answered. 'His mum and dad are meeting them at the Alfred. You guys were lucky the tide didn't come in faster. Were you frightened?'

'No.'

'No?' Jeff echoed. 'Really?'

The sportsman gritted his teeth. 'I wasn't,' he insisted. 'There wasn't enough time. Dad's a quick thinker, Mum. And I'm sorry. I'll react much faster next time.'

'I'm sure you will,' the father agreed, putting an arm around the young man's broad shoulders.

Inside, the girls were watching television in the kitchen, debating whether to go back to bed or wave the stars on their way. Sending her husband into the dining room to fetch a *liqueur* of his choosing, Lynn poured some more coffee and sat down beside her brood.

'Well... Nice one, guys!' she declared. 'No early night for us after all. What on Earth were you thinking?'

'I am sorry, Mum, Dad,' Jet murmured. 'Enz and Pippa wanted to go down, and it seemed like a good idea.'

Pulling up a stool on the opposite side of the breakfast bar, the forty-one-year-old's dark brown eyes bored into his son's. 'Did it? Since when d'you allow yourself to be so easily led?'

'Sorry, Dad. I know,' the teenager stared into his mug. 'I should've known better.'

'Yep. No argument there. We have a responsibility for each other's safety, and for our friends' safety while they're here. We went to bed leaving you in charge, mate. That means all the good decisions need to be made by you. I can understand you taking a calculated risk on your own, but this is ridiculous.'

'Did you know the lift wasn't working?' Lynn asked.

'I saw the light wasn't flashing,' the youngster admitted. 'I should've tested it. We were in too much of a hurry.'

Kierney sat in silence, listening to her brother receiving his talking-to. It would be her turn to stuff up soon enough, as she had done before. Nodding to Piraea, she collected the empty mugs from the table and slotted them into the dishwasher before turning back and stretching her arms to the ceiling.

'Bed?' her mother guessed, exhanging hugs and kisses. 'Sleep well, you two. We'll be leaving in about half an hour. Have fun tomorrow.'

'*Gracias, Mamá.* We shall. *Buenos noches, Papá.* You look so unbelievably exhausted. *Gracias por rescatarlos.*'

'*De nada, pequeñita,*' Jeff smiled. '*Buenos noches,* Kizzo, and g'night, my little *vampette.*'

Piraea was proud that her best friend's father sought to address her this way, a playful dig at to her strict gothic dress code and extravagant performing style. She stepped back after giving the Diamond parents shy pecks on the cheek to allow father and daughter to embrace with their usual enthusiasm. Kierney recoiled when she made contact with his clammy clothing, grabbing her friend's arm and shooing her towards the staircase.

'And you...' the man of the house said through clenched jaws, directing his gaze to the only child left in the room. 'Are you coming with us or staying here to wreak more havoc?'

'Staying here,' the young man responded. 'Is that OK? I'll *cadge* a lift with these guys in the morning. Or I could go on the train if there's not enough room in the Disco'.'

His mother nodded. 'There'll be plenty of room. Sort it out with Giang in the morning. Go to bed, please. Everything worked out well in the end, and you've learned some valuable lessons. Drink up, Jeff. You're freezing. We shouldn't be too long.'

The chief rescuer signalled to his wife to follow the girls. She understood there were more words to be said to their son, so made herself scarce. Jet's eyes met his, contrite and determined to repair the damaged trust.

'Take it easy with Kate,' he whispered. 'I know you haven't got what you wanted tonight, but think carefully before you go in there and wake them up again.'

The teenager nodded at the sage advice, grateful for the resumption of normal service. 'Yeah, no,' he smiled. 'If you insist. In the morning?'

'Sure,' his father scoffed, slapping the rippling muscles on the lad's back. 'Only one of them though, mate. Don't forget that's your injured mate's girlfriend in there. She's not part of the plan.'

'Dad! Jesus! Give me credit for some decency.'

'Good. In case your raging dick rules your head again. Mine always did. We *are* related, remember?'

Hold Back Time

Tex Fletcher celebrated his fiftieth at the end of January nineteen-ninety-four, throwing a lavish party for himself in Beverly Hills. After so many tragic romances, he had met the love of his life, a fashion designer by the name of Terry Maitland, who was encouraging him to mellow into his advancing years.

The mammoth "Live on Earth" tour had been making its way eastwards across the United States since the New Year, requiring Lynn to backtrack to appear on stage with the birthday boy, performing one of their biggest hits. They managed to avoid interference from Miss Piggy on this occasion. However, during the pre-show media call, both artists were asked questions about their enduring three-way partnership with Jeff Diamond.

'It's not a purely sexual attraction that people have for him,' Tex espoused.

The Olympian nodded. 'No. It's much more than that. Jeff always used to say he could tell a person's motivations just from their body language when he met them, or by the way they reacted to him. But as he honed his powers of persuasion, it matters not whether you're into men or women. Everyone's sucked in!'

'Including you?' the interviewer asked.

'Yes, of course including me,' she answered, 'but I love it. He's such an amazing man. I still love being with him every minute of every day. He's the kindest, most loving man there could ever be, even though he's wild and independently-strung sometimes.'

By the time the tour had *schlepped* across the North Atlantic to Europe, the Easter school holidays were upon them. Puberty had unleashed both children's creative juices, and they had found their voices in both literal and figurative terms. "No holds barred music" was Jeff's label for his daughter's inhibition-free performances, spliced with a tenacious social conscience and sparked by her father's lowly origins. Her hit songs were more likely to tell of children suffering abuse in silence than classic teeny-bopper fantasies, while the most disagreeable adult themes such as rape and prostitution provided the young woman with endless inspiration.

And as they had promised before the school year ended, Lynn and Jeff dispatched their son and his guitar-playing mates to California, to stay with Greg Marlow and to try their luck at some supporting gigs. It was heaven for the youngsters, who spent the days busting their chops with some of the world's best sound engineers and the nights chasing American girls all over Los Angeles.

Unlike his introspective sister, Jet found no stimulation in the solitude of spending hours alone in the studio to hone his craft. He much preferred the *camaraderie* of other musicians, a lifetime of hard-line coaching in the Dyson world leaving him fearless in the face of frank feedback.

Rare were the days when the Four of Diamonds' schedules put them in the same place at the same time in this, their busiest year by far. Snatching dinner in the city or stealing a Sunday by the seaside, the family stuck together like glue during these welcome breaks. The conversation invariably turned to adolescent capers of a carnal nature, and the forever couple subjected themselves to inquisitions in the name of parental guidance.

'I made do with temporary distractions for six years before your *mamá* and I got it on for the first time, and again during our two year hiatus,' Jeff told his insistent daughter.

'Temporary distractions?'

'Yep. That's all they were, *pequeñita*. Lynn Dyson was always going to be my permanent obsession. All the others were temporary distractions.'

'Did you know this back then?' Jet asked his mother. 'Like how Dad engineered your sex life all along?'

The tennis champion smiled. 'Not at first,' she answered. 'Bits and pieces slipped out gradually. You know what it's like when you first start dating someone who you think is special... You don't want to give too much away to begin with.'

Flickers of recognition lit up both children's faces. They were racking up their own catalogues of thrills and spills these days. As much as her father hated to admit it, even Kierney now showed more than a passing interest in the opposite sex.

'I remember when Grandpa finally accepted us as an item,' Jeff recalled, his eyes pinched shut to occupy the pleasant scene again. 'I told him we'd waited a long time to be together, and he thought I was referring to our two years apart. But that wasn't what I meant at all, was it, angel?'

'No.'

'I meant we'd waited through the ages to be together. And I still believe it to this day, however kooky you might think I am.'

'Oh,' the young woman sighed. 'That's so amazing. I don't think you're kooky.'

'Well, not too much anyway,' her brother quipped.

'Shut up, Jetto. I hope my long-lost lover's already dreaming about me somewhere. But how could you know how much you'd love *Mamá*? And how did you know she'd love you too?'

The philosopher winked at his wife. 'No bloody idea, gorgeous. And I still have no idea. Just a load of instincts and theories that could well be much more wrong than right. I'm reluctant to believe there was nothing there before we met in 'seventy-two and that I just acted on a teenaged crush. It sure felt like more. Way more.'

'But Mum didn't know you were the man of her dreams,' the sixteen-year-old teased. 'Or did you?'

Lynn shrugged. 'I don't know anymore. It's all too long ago, and I've changed so much. I certainly knew nothing about no Jeffrey Moreno Diamond, but I sure as hell liked what I found,' she reached across to where her husband's left hand sat palm-uppermost on the table. 'I had a very fixed mental picture of the sort of boyfriend I wanted, and I hadn't met anyone who came anywhere near close before. I just assumed it was because I was so young. I wasn't in a hurry though. Didn't expect to meet anyone special for years.'

'But you were wrong!' their daughter proclaimed, winding her hands in waves as if weaving a magic spell and eyeing her parents one after the other. 'You never counted on the power of old souls. *Papá* was out to get you.'

Pausing after a nip of the smooth Kentucky whiskey with which his son had presented him as a thank-you for his trip to California, Jeff smacked his lips. 'Indeed I was. This is delicious, mate. D'you want some?'

'Thought you'd never ask, old man. May I? That'd be awesome.'

'No, thanks,' Kierney turned down a taste of the viscous, rust-coloured liquid which mingled with her father's blood in significant quantity. 'Which was the first song you wrote about *Mamá*?'

'Whoa!' the rock star exclaimed. 'Kiz, I can't remember that far back.'

'Liar!' both teenagers chanted, set up as ever.

'*Gotcha*, suckers! "Feed My Pain" was one of the earliest, but it took a long time to become the song you know. I was thirteen, maybe fourteen, when I wrote it. Lena was still living in the apartment, I remember. A period of intense masturbatory activity.'

'Jeff!' his wife cried in disgust. 'We don't need to go there.'

Her handsome stallion rocked forward, nearly spilling his drink at the force of her reaction. 'Why not, angel?' he roared with laughter. 'It paints a picture, that's all. Guys, this is how it was: I was utterly effin' dependent on this perfect creature from my fantasies to keep me sane through *la abuela*'s last few months, and I used to imagine the posters on my wall were windows into your *mamá*'s world. Every time I got cocky enough to think she'd look back at me, bloody Gravity'd rise up and kick me in the goolies, saying, "Don't be so bloody ridiculous!"'

The intensity in the storyteller's tone made Lynn bite her lip. Without question, she would have wanted to look back at him, but her strict, conservative upbringing might have stopped her from acting on impulse. It made her realise how bigoted and narrow-minded she had been before this giant of a man opened her eyes, then her heart and finally her mind.

'I love "*Regala*" the best,' her dreamy voice flitted across the room. 'I always cherish the idea of you giving me to yourself. Such a powerful image. Speaks volumes to me about that time in your life.'

'I reckon "*Regala*" might've come first, now you mention it,' her husband frowned, his body of work so vast these days that he often lost track of his own chronology. 'And this is going to sound so weird...'

'What sounds so weird?' his son asked.

'Like *déjà-vu*, but not exactly.'

Lynn shivered, a chill catching her by surprise. 'What do you mean? We've had this conversation before or something? I could well believe that. We're always boring the kids to death with our reminiscences.'

'Hey! I'm not bored!' Kierney countered. 'I love these stories. What's the *déjà-vu, Papá*?'

'Christ, angel... It's damned annoying because it means I owe my sister an apology.'

'Really? What for?'

Jeff shook his head, smiling. 'D'you remember when Lena came down for our wedding? You'd gone to Benloch, and she and I spent that couple of days on our own, realising we didn't even know each other.'

'Yes,' Lynn was intrigued. 'I think so.'

'Well... She mentioned I used to call those posters of you "wanking windows", and I fervently denied it at the time.'

Jet snorted, seeing the look of disapproval on the women's faces.

'Sorry for the *crudités*, people, but it's part of the story,' the orator continued. 'I told Lena I would never have called them that. And here I am now, eighteen years later, talking about imagining you through windows from my room. I must've blocked it right out of my memory, 'cause it had a certain futility to it maybe... I never put two and two together until this very moment. Freaky, eh, don't *ya* think?'

'You must've said it then,' his son sniggered. 'Selective recall. Even you're not immune. Your integrity's fallible. Hallelujah!'

'My integrity? That's a bit steep, mate.'

'Yeah, probably. But hey? What does integrity mean to you, Mum, Dad?'

Laughing at the young man's clumsy *segue*, Jeff's insides flipped as his beautiful best friend caught his eye and smiled. These were special times, when the children felt safe enough to ask the important questions. Both sensed the profound parental privilege of being trusted to supply honest answers.

'Integrity?' Lynn echoed. 'Speaking the truth. Right versus wrong. Acting with integrity is to act according to what you believe is right. Why do you ask?'

Jet had attended a Good School lecture on the same topic earlier in the week, at which his grandfather had spoken to the class. By his sullen demeanour afterwards and the sporadic prods of conscience he had doled out in the ensuing days, it was clear the session had sparked some inner soul-searching.

'Oh, just that Grandpa talked about dedication, determination,' the lad recounted. 'All the usual "D" words, and then he started on about integrity. It was like another team game to him, or some sort of shared goal, rather than a quality any single individual has. It made me wonder what you guys think it is?'

The intellectual rolled his shoulders and pressed them into the back of his chair. Not only was this an interesting question, but it also presented a challenge in not undermining Bart Dyson's authority. Despite his own position of considerable standing in the world, his father-in-law's word continued to carry a great deal of weight in their household.

'Well... In my opinion, we need to look at integrity from different perspectives. D'you mean integrity in a thing, a concept or a person?'

'A person,' Jet ventured, his face contorted with confusion. 'Erm, no... Is a team a thing or a collection of persons? Shit, I don't know! Just answer the bloody question, alright?'

'Careful,' his mother warned.

'Regardless, I guess,' Jeff smiled. 'To me, integrity's where all the individual parts of an entity tell the same story,' Jeff hazarded. 'Nothing can be contradictory within it. Everything a person says or does should be consistent, or everyone in the team behaves the same way. Or there's integrity of a system or a process... or a book or painting, piece of music... where the whole thing lives and dies by the same principles. It's not that simple to define, mate. Didn't you like where you ended up in your own mind?'

'No. I couldn't come up with a real idea of how integrity helps anything,' the teenager shrugged. 'I mean, I know we should tell the truth and be consistent. I get that. But I also know there can be more than one version of the truth, and everyone can believe different things are true. So what exactly is integrity in that case?'

His father flicked up the top of his lighter and engulfed the end of his cigarette in its flame, exhaling then dragging hard. 'Whoa! How about you, Kizzo? What's your take?'

The youngest Diamond shook her head, with no frame of reference to draw on. She had not been party to her grandfather's speech, nor to the following discussions. All she knew was that integrity was a quality her parents deemed essential, and therefore she ought to learn its dimensions as soon as possible.

'That's fine, *pequeñita*,' Jeff paused to collect his thoughts. 'You're demonstrating integrity by admitting you don't have a view yet. I don't know if I have anything to offer either, 'cause it can mean different things to different people. I guess it's knowing what you believe in as an individual and living it accordingly. Like Mum said: it's about what you do to make sure you're prepared to justify your actions to anyone who asks. Angel, did that make any sense to you?'

'Sort of,' Lynn chuckled. 'It's not like you to struggle with definitions! An example might help. Say you made a snap decision to substitute a player because you think he's having an off-day, Jetto... But then the coach says you shouldn't leave him out. Demonstrating integrity's about having the guts to stand up for the reason why you didn't select him. Standing by your decisions, even if you suffer as a result. Or also, it could be having the courage to change your decision if you think the coach's reason's more valid than yours.'

'Not bowing to pressure?' Kierney offered, resting her chin on her hands as her elbows slipped further onto the table.

'Yeah. That's definitely part of it,' her father agreed. 'You could say *Mamá* has way more integrity than I do 'cause she doesn't change her mind anywhere near as often.'

'Oh, that's not fair,' his wife decried the world-changer's self-abnegation. 'You always believe in what you say or do at the time, even if you do change your mind. Surely we can only measure integrity at the moment in which we exercise it?'

'Or don't!' Jet laughed.

'Indeed,' the philosopher stared at his attentive offspring. 'It's complicated, guys. And life just keeps getting more complicated as you understand more about it. I hope we've brought you up with enough nous to recognise integrity in yourselves and others when you see it, although none of us is any good at defining it. Esoteric... That's what it is. Word of the day.'

'You showed integrity when you accepted your punishment for putting your friends in danger that night,' his wife took over.

The sixteen-year-old cringed. To come up with a suitable forfeit for their son's error of judgement, Lynn had solicited acquaintances local to *Escondido* to compile a list of odd jobs they wanted doing, such as gardening or other fiddly, time-consuming tasks which would try the go-getter's patience.

One neighbour had delivered a pile of clothing to June Monroe, asking whether Jet might sew their missing buttons back on, and a small business in Mount Eliza's main street had booked him for three hours to file paperwork dating back several months. Despite voicing his displeasure to all concerned, he hadn't procrastinated, completing the commissions with reluctant but well-mannered diligence.

'Hmm...' the sportsman muttered. 'Never again. Don't push it, Mother.'

Both parents laughed at the lad's demonic glare, gratified that a lesson had been well-learned. The closer their offspring came to adulthood, the more they surpassed all expectations. The Dyson way, of course, but with several facets added from their father's lineage. Being born under the patronage of Unity and Liberty, the statues atop *l'Altare della Patria* monument in Rome had infused them with New Age ideals, and both bought into the bohemian *mantra* of freedom, beauty, truth and love as if there were no conscionable alternative.

While preparing their evening meal, the family's conversation moved to the importance of tasteful attire, another subject the children had grown up with and now needed to apply to their independent social lives. Following hot on her brother's heels into the dating scene, Kierney was full of questions about how much bare flesh a woman ought to put on show.

'*Alors*,' her dad chuckled. 'If we go back to *monsieur Hugo encore une fois*, I can quote you something esoteric for you to bear in mind here too. In "*Les Mis*"', he said: "It is the quality of prudishness that the less the fortress is threatened the more the garrison is strengthened."'

'Pardon?' the young woman laughed. 'I have no idea what that means!'

'Me neither,' Lynn joined in the kids' hilarity. 'Please explain. What do fortresses and garrisons have to do with women dressing provocatively?'

'Oh, I get it,' their son piped up. 'I think, anyway... Something about girls that no-one's interested in make more of an effort to put men off?'

Jeff nodded. 'Yeah. Pretty much, mate. If you just relax and dress how you feel comfortable, *pequeñita*... like *Mamá* does... you'll get the kind of attention you're looking for.'

'Not the attention you deserve?' his wife teased. 'Spoken like a true father!'

'Hey! Hardly fair, angel. Don't accuse me of condoning the "She was asking for it" excuse. You know how fine a line that is.'

The stunning singer took a deep breath, frowning into the cupboard while she reached down four dinner plates. 'No, I wasn't accusing you of anything. It *is* a fine line, and I'm glad you said it, so I don't have to. No woman asks to be raped, but some do some pretty stupid things to encourage guys. Defend your fortress in whichever way you see fit, Kizzy, but just be aware of how single-minded some men are about having sex.'

A sticky silence descended over the kitchen table. All four Diamonds had stories to tell in this arena, yet none fancied airing them again right now. Whether it be the "tennis skirt episode" of their parents as teenagers or Kierney's own recent frantic telephone call on her way home from a school function, each understood the deeper concern channelling through these wise words.

With one hand full of cutlery, Jeff brushed his daughter's shoulder with the other. 'And the inverse is also true, particularly with the application of cocktails, eh, gorgeous?'

The teenager's elongating frame sagged into her empathetic mentor's reassurance. 'I know what you mean, *Papá*. What's that from? Is that a quote too?'

'It is now,' he smiled. 'Vintage Jeff Diamond, *circa* nineteen-ninety-four. "Beer goggles" is the ridgy-didge Ocker version, I believe.'

Jet's eyes traversed the room, searching for something to focus on. He was unsure whether to prolong the humour or button his lip. Hearing how upset his little sister had been at receiving some overwrought advances from a group of men standing outside a Russell Street pub served as a timely reminder of his own bouts of alcohol-fuelled stupidity in the presence of the fairer sex.

'So, Dad?'

'So what, Dad?'

The pair of heavyweights bumped each other's shoulders like midfielders defending a loose football, knocking into chairs and jogging the table. Lynn rushed to save the open wine bottle from toppling over, grumbling to her daughter about how much more civilised the world would be without men.

'What's with the whole thing when, if you look at a woman's neckline, or legs or whatever, she instinctively covers them up? You know... Like pulls the hem of her skirt lower.'

'And it only makes you want to look again?'

'Right! Yeah! That's like even more tempting, and I can never tell if they're doing it on purpose.'

Jeff winked at his wife. 'Trust your dick, mate. It's there for a reason. But don't act on it. Waiting's almost always the right thing to do, and you'll be rewarded for doing so because the result'll be much sweeter for both of you.'

'Wait long enough, and you'll meet sixteen vestal virgins,' the elegant blonde chided. 'Isn't that how it works? Sit down, guys, and let's change the subject while we eat.'

'Jeez, angel. I didn't mean he had to wait that long! You drive a hard bargain.'

***

Kierney turned fifteen, in February nineteen-ninety-four, releasing tumultuous flashbacks which tortured her father with his intense adolescent fears of abandonment. The preoccupation crushed his spirit, waking him up in the middle of the nights and leaving him bereft for no good reason during the days.

No matter how often Jeff put his feelings into words, for Lynn or for The Fellowship counsellors, nothing eased the anguish of watching his miniature dark-haired gipsy grow into her own, autonomous entity. Song after anguished song poured forth, and the rock star willed these lyrics to purge the inevitable from his heart, knowing he could not and would not stand in her way.

Around the same time, a new band formed in Adelaide's thriving arts scene had secured Lynn's services to produce a *début* album through persistent badgering of Cathy and showering her Stonebridge Music team with demonstration tapes. To supplement their *repertoire* of home-grown material, the Diamonds suggested they record the product of the forlorn father's poetic craft.

The resultant collection of driving, soulful tracks hit the airwaves to an absolute *avalanche* of acclaim, propelling the unknown South Australians to superstar status and broadcasting the songwriter's innermost fears to the waiting world via musical imagery subtly codified into popular songs.

In spite of this unrelenting dread, Jeff received constant reassurance that his daughter harboured no such pressing desire to claim sexual bounty. Content to stay around her loved ones and capitalise on every spare moments her parents had to lend support to her increasingly adventurous projects, she had inherited their extreme courage. Moreover, she was willing to soak up any advice and assistance she could lay her hands on.

All agreed, including the man himself, that the issue had magnified out of all proportion in her father's mind. Nonetheless, the control freak of yore had returned, hating the thought of his precious daughter being shaped by anyone beyond their tight-knit circle. Overcoming this latest mental battle required a gigantic effort, and as usual, his beautiful best friend was nearby to push things along.

'So how is it for you these days on your mount, Moses?' Lynn mocked, seeing her husband emerge from the shower no more refreshed after another sleepless night.

'Oh, very funny. You have no bloody idea.'

The tennis champion kissed his sullen mouth, dragging him back down onto the bed. 'Listen, you gorgeous conundrum,' she said. 'Kizzy's experiencing more freedom to experiment at home than she could ever legally, or even illegally, expect to find in the outside world. She still looks to us to introduce her to everything. Talk to her. She's not about to cut off diplomatic relations with her greatest influence just because she's discovered corporal pleasures. She loves you more now than ever.'

Jeff sighed. 'I know all that, angel. I can't explain this blackness. It's like Gravity's called in reinforcements, and they've seized control of my rational brain. No matter how I try to tell myself I'm over-reacting, it won't let up. I guess I want her to stay my little girl forever. I can't bring myself to accept someone like me's going to have his hands all over her. Not yet. And not ever!'

'Now, hang on a minute!' his former innocent schoolgirl objected. 'That's so hypocritical! You were quite happy for someone like you to get his hands on me at the same age. You'll turn into my dad if you're not careful.'

Rolling on top of his flagrant scrutineer and feeling her hips rise to meet his, the red-blooded lover had no defence. Images of the first few sexual encounters they shared reinforced the urgency which her proximity never failed to drive. There was a time when Lynn was every bit as *naïve* as Kierney, and when he was every bit as horny as their son. The sensation was no less sublime with the passing years; rather, its promise was more consummate fulfilment than frantic thrill. The thought filled him with wonder that a whole generation had passed.

'It shits me to admit it, but you're right,' he smiled into her kiss. 'We picked the wrong year to go on this bloody endless road-trip.'

'No, we didn't,' his wife was quick to contradict, fighting off his fevered hands. 'It's exactly the right year. Imagine how bad it'd be if you were here every day? You'd be watching her like a hawk all the damned time. It might get so tense that you end up pushing her away. Even make you fall out altogether, God forbid! Anyway, I haven't got time to do this now.'

The dark-haired Adonis flexed his arm muscles and flattened his prey onto the mattress. 'What? You've *gotta* be kidding me! You've always got time for this!' he hissed in her ear. 'And it's going to take precisely ten seconds of your valuable time at this rate. You are so unbelievably sexy, Lynn Dyson. Always were, always will be. I love how you tell it like it is and make everything sound so plausible. How could I ever disagree with you?'

Jeff's projection proved right on the money, with the breathless couple finding themselves in the shower again before too long. They dressed in a hurry and raced each other downstairs in their stockinged feet. The previous day, Jet had found out he had been accepted into Cambridge University, so the family had arranged to meet for a slap-up lunch to celebrate before the proud parents left the country for their next run of tour dates.

Kierney was dismayed by the rare display of immaturity from her mother and father, wondering what had come over them. Collecting his leather jacket from the coatstand in the hallway, her dad cupped her face in his hands and planted a huge kiss on her forehead.

'How come you don't feel like I do, angel? Why's it only me who doesn't want our kids to grow up?'

The youngster groaned. 'Oh, my God! You're not still hung up about this, are you?'

'I don't want them to grow up either,' her mother insisted. 'But grow up they shall. I suppose I'm just more resigned to it than you are. You'll get over it. Let's go, or Jet'll give up on us and go back to training.'

'Yeah. In the year twenty-nineteen maybe. I'll be ready to let you go when you turn forty, *pequeñita*. OK with you?'

'Sure, *Papá*,' she agreed. 'As long as you're happy to turn the other way and block your ears when you're sitting at the end of my bed every night.'

Lynn burst out laughing as horror spread across her husband's face. A bloodcurdling roar sent the cat scampering into the kitchen as fast as its feet could propel it across the slick tiles, and the exasperated man grabbed hold of his daughter and wrestled her into a bear-hug, refusing to let go.

'Don't tempt me,' he snarled. 'I want a ten-page questionnaire filled out by every potential boyfriend, three days in advance of any canoodling. That way, *Mamá* and I can be sure he's going to treat you right. Is that too much to ask?'

His wife chuckled, dangling Kierney's coat close enough for her to take hold. 'Hey! Don't drag me into this,' she teased. 'I'd rather not have to think about it at all. Come on. We have to go.'

The Land Rover rolled along the leafy streets between *Escondido* and the main highway into Melbourne, its three occupants engrossed in familial chit-chat all the way into the city. The cricketer's admission into Trinity College at seventeen years of age was contingent on him passing his Year Twelve examinations, but it was an enormous achievement nonetheless.

As for Lynn at the same stage of life, switching from high school in the southern hemisphere to university north of the Equator required an overlap of the pre-Christmas term. This translated into a monumental workload to tackle alongside his sporting commitments, and the hard-working parents were keen to remove all barriers to success. Their humane encouragement ought also, of course, to include pointless attempts at convincing him to restrict his extra-curricular activities.

After a lazy lunch on Southbank, tucked away in a separate dining room overlooking the brown waters of the Yarra, Jeff requested a tray of *liqueurs*. Free of the usual circle of onlookers, the children's eyes lit up when the display of brightly decorated bottles was delivered to their table. A participatory type of lesson was far more enjoyable than pure theory!

The cultured bohemian described the taste of each one while pouring measures into shot glasses, explaining their origins and ingredients. A row of twelve colourful drams were lined up, setting the teenagers' saliva glands on red alert, held back on purpose by their tormenter.

Finally, the signal came for the sampling to begin. Jet opted for the sweet coffee taste of *Tia Maria*, while his sister went straight for the malt whisky, screwing up her nose at the overpowering fumes.

'Ew! That smells of you, *Papá*,' she coughed. 'How can you like something so bitter?'

The seasoned drinker laughed, taking her glass and sculling the rest down. 'Easy!'

'If you want bitter, you should try Campari,' Lynn suggested. 'Even when you mix it with orange juice, it's still bitter.'

'Wow! Sounds good. Is there any?' Jet asked, searching the tray. 'Auntie Mary's way too sweet for me.'

His mother shook her head. 'Don't think so. Try a brandy instead.'

'Leave some experiences in reserve, mate,' the philosopher advised, pouring himself a second glass of Glayva. 'You don't have to do everything today, even though I know that feeling only too well. You've mixed it up enough to give yourselves a hangover already, which of course is all part of our master plan.'

'Great, thanks! Why does your master plan have to involve making us sick?' the cricketer laughed.

'Are you still going out with Alex?' his mother changed the subject.

'Na. She wasn't my type.'

'You mean she wouldn't put out,' the fifteen-year-old teased, giggling at the perturbed look on both men's faces.

'How do we find out what our type is?' Jet asked, downing a slug of Benedictine. 'Oh, wow! That's more like it!'

Jeff grinned. 'Your sister can tell you that. We had the same conversation only a few hours ago.'

Realising she had been the victim of retribution, Kierney frowned. Lynn smiled at her husband, watching him lean back onto the plump suede cushions which lined the booth wall. For all his boisterous indignation when it came to their children partaking in sins of the flesh, she knew these teachings gave him a major kick.

'First you need to figure out what a meaningful relationship is for you,' he mused, tilting his head to draw them into his beatnik *milieu*. 'Then you have to try it on for size and grow into it. This process can take a while, so soak it up, guys.'

Their son grimaced. 'How much of a while? That sounds like it takes too much patience.'

'If you're not prepared to get to know her before you jump into bed, or wherever, it probably means you're not ready to find your type,' his mother interjected.

Jeff nodded. 'Spot on, gorgeous. You might go back and forth between Steps One and Two a *gazillion* times before you're sure what sort of partner you want. Then once you're in the market for something longer-term, you'll start deliberately looking for someone who ticks your boxes. What my advice to you is, for what it's worth, is to make sure you look for somebody who's prepared to tell you what they need too. Sex, love... relationships in general... they've got to be for mutual benefit. Otherwise, you might as well spend your whole life having one-night stands or paying for your pleasure.'

'Yikes! Paying for sex? Why do people do that? Adults make life so complicated,' Kierney moaned, trying to follow the convoluted path. 'How is it that you guys got together without all this rigmarole, and yet you're telling us to experiment with all different kinds of partners?'

'In our case, I think *Papá* and I dashed through Steps One to Fifty-five in the space of a few hours,' Lynn smiled at her husband.

'Whoa! Guess we did. Thanks heaps,' Jeff answered, this unsolicited admission bringing tears to his eyes. 'We'll come back to that later. Hopefully, whomever you pick's already done Steps One and Two a few times already, before they find you. That way, you'll both kind of understand how to meet each other's needs. Keep it simple, huh?'

Jet shrugged. 'Try before you buy. I can go for that. Isn't that what's called fear of commitment?'

Their dad laughed. 'If you're still bouncing back and forth between Steps One and Two after twenty years, yep. Playing the field's perfectly fine at your age. Either way, you'll be lauded by some and chastised by others. Mate, Kizzy, you need to be aware that, when it comes to parading your relationships in public, whatever the man does is wrong and whatever the woman does is right. As long as you can live with these injustices, you'll be right.'

His wife's initial reaction to this complaint was one of annoyance that her man should feel so hard-done-by. Yet try as she might, no examples of the opposite being true came to light. The press were seldom critical of her, even now the tearaway she married had cemented his position on top of the world. By contrast, they only needed a whiff of Jeff Diamond scandal to splatter newspaper front pages and television gossip shows with reams of disparaging copy.

'Take as long as you need to find the right person,' Lynn suggested. 'Just because we were young when we got together, it doesn't mean you two need to be hooked up for life by the time you're twenty-five, or even thirty.'

'But, *Mamá*, you didn't try before you *buyed*,' Kierney put on a babyish tone.

'Yes, I did. It just so happened that I met my perfect man first-up, so I had to squeeze in some try-outs afterwards. What are the odds of that, I wonder?'

'Quite high when I targeted you on purpose,' the handsome rock star sniggered, throwing his son an arrogant wink.

'Maybe. But according to your rule, I hadn't done my two-step for long enough to figure out if you were my type or not, so I could easily have untargetted you.'

'Fair point,' Jeff admitted. 'Whatever, we were bloody lucky to find each other so soon. I think what I'm trying to say is that it takes a different length of time for each person to find their optimum pantomime horse partner.'

The teenagers laughed, seeing their mother shake her head at the peculiar concept none had brought to mind for quite a while.

'Your dad taught me how to recognise what I wanted in a partner,' she continued. 'That's where our luck came in, I think. Although I wouldn't call it luck really... He took me on the journey that he's taking you guys on now. I have no idea how soon I'd have found out for myself, but he certainly put me on the accelerated learning track!'

Jet nudged his father, raising his hand for a fist-bump. 'Good on *ya*, stud.'

'Why, thank you, mate.'

'Take it slowly and don't be pressured,' Lynn smiled. 'The right person'll wait for you. The trick is to know when you're ready; when you've found what you've been looking for.'

'Some people go too early, and some people never stop trying and therefore never end up buying,' the intellectual chuckled, pouring himself a deep schooner of *Rémy Martin* VSOP as a not-so-subtle hint.

'Uncle Gerry?' Kierney guessed.

Jeff nodded, toasting his daughter. 'The very same. He's the ultimate commitment-phobe. He's only interested in "hot" as the attribute of choice. Don't settle for "hot" alone, guys. It's important, don't get me wrong, but it's nowhere near the most important.'

'I know that,' Jet said, switching back to *Tia Maria* and instantly regretting it.

'Guys in their teens and early twenties overestimate the importance of sex because their hormones are raging out of control,' the Olympian added. 'And for some reason, girls underestimate it. It's a miracle evolution ever works, when we seem to be hard-wired to avoid each other.'

'No. I beg to differ, angel. It works perfectly,' her husband contradicted. 'As long as it's healthy, that antagonism serves to stop people rushing into things. Have we had enough? We should escape before they run out of alcohol.'

The Diamonds filed out of the hotel's restaurant, the younger pair light-headed and unsteady on their feet once the fresh air penetrated their brains. Their appearance on Collins Street at nine-thirty on a Thursday evening was bound to attract attention, so Jeff hailed a taxi to ferry them back to their apartment.

Within minutes, they were climbing the flight of steps up to the building's lobby and calling the lift to their sixteenth-floor sanctuary, having maintained a polite silence during the driver's tirade on electronic music and lip-syncing.

***

A few days later, with Jet sleeping in the senior school dormitory and Kierney spending the weekend at Piraea's, Lynn flew back into Tullamarine Airport a day earlier than planned, after losing the US Open women's singles semi-final to her younger sister.

Tournament organisers found it preferable to seed the pair on the same side of the draw, with the prospect of a Dyson-versus-Dyson showdown a foregone conclusion. Eliminating one invincible Australian athlete before the final allowed the other players to dream of breaking their long-running domination. These days, Anna was beating her older sibling with greater frequency, a changing of the guard which had been difficult to accept at first.

However, living with a modern-day philosopher and two teenagers who grew wiser and stronger by the day, the former champion's disappointment dissolved into a reluctant admission that she was only fulfilling her destiny by making way for the next generation. The retired gymnast was eleven years her junior. It was no wonder her body was more resilient and her hunger keener, and in truth, the elder Dyson daughter's appetite for sporting glory had been shrinking for a lot longer than her record suggested.

Lynn's original plan was to fly directly to the next "Live on Earth" tour destination, meeting her husband and their hundred-strong orchestra in Auckland, New Zealand, for three sold-out shows. Instead, with an unexpected extra forty-eight hours at their disposal, she had switched airlines for a surprise *rendezvous-à-deux* in their original love-nest.

After checking her e-mails and responding to a few missed calls, the blonde sportswoman showered and slipped into bed. Jeff was on stage at Crown Casino's *cabaret* club. The regular date since the venue's grand opening suited everyone: a chance for him to rehearse new material and initiate new band members with a docile local audience plied with dinner and drinks; a favour to Melbourne's influential entertainment industry moguls; and a brisk walk home to work off any lingering highs.

Was it the time-shift from American Eastern Daylight Time to Australian Eastern Standard Time which prevented her mind from shutting down? Lynn had no reason to doubt her rock star's fidelity, but as the clock's digits advanced past midnight, she began to doubt her own sound judgement. Theirs wouldn't be the first celebrity marriage to have survived despite a swathe of shadowy affairs and drunken orgies. Did her charismatic front-man still polish his sexual mercenary badge every now and again, surrounded by nubile groupies and ambitious backing singers?

If the body of DCF-funded research had taught her anything, it was the undeniable correlation between professional glory and sexual appetite among males. Perhaps, subconsciously, she had come here to test him…

Shortly after two o'clock in the morning, the worried woman heard the lift doors open. She inserted her bookmark between pages she had read at least five times and tuned her ears for any telltale sounds of female company. There was no noise at all initially, giving rise to a whole different sort of apprehension. Had the apartment's security been compromised?

The silence was broken, to her great relief, by a single set of footsteps across the marble tiles and the metallic clatter of keys being dropped onto the kitchen worktop. She imagined the billionnaire completing his normal ritual of stopping to contemplate the four-metre wide photograph of rain-drenched African plains which greeted visitors in their apartment's Grecian-inspired entrance hall.

Stoned and uninhibited in his own home, the superstar left the cloakroom door open while he emptied a full bladder into the toilet, repulsing his undisclosed companion. Her insecurities cast aside with contrite consolation, she couldn't help but laugh at the jumbled medley of tunes she heard him whistling and crooning as he moved about their home.

Retreating to the bathroom to put the finishing touches to her costume, the elegant athlete painted her lips to match the red of her nail varnish and the tiny *roses appliquées* scattered over her black lace nightdress. With the bedside light set to its dimmest, she lay in wait for her unsuspecting *beau*.

Jeff was halfway through his second glass of water, keen to stave off the worst of his hangover for tomorrow's fourteen-hour flight. Gazing around the kitchen, his eyes alighted on a video-cassette sitting on the table, atop a pile of crinkled newspapers. It was his birthday present from six months earlier, and he must have forgotten to put it away after his last *solo* night in their city *pied-à-terre.*

The musician lifted the case and shook it until a single card slipped out into his hand. It was much too late to watch this now, he decided, even though his drug-induced *libido* was already way ahead of him. He read the message again before kissing the handwritten lines.

"Veronica: 'Do you want this R-rated?'

Me: 'No need. Jeff's perfectly capable of R-rating it all by himself!'

All yours, *mon ami.* Lx"

Knowing the vicarious pleasure her insatiable man took from tales of the day *spa*, Lynn had enlisted a female camera operator to accompany her for an afternoon of luxurious treatments. The product of this endeavour was a twenty-minute film of edited highlights featuring a body scrub and a *Lomi Lomi* massage, complete with running commentary from the *masseuse* and the odd groan of pain or pleasure from her client.

The wall-clock said two-fifty, and the nomad had no idea when his telephone would ring to summon him to the airport. His erection nagged in his trousers, demanding attention and willing him to insert the tape and revisit the other night's stimulating journey. Squeezing his penis through the fabric and running his fingers along its elongated shaft, he was about to bend down to switch on the television when he sensed movement behind him.

'Don't. I've got a better idea.'

Pivoting round on unsteady heels, Jeff almost lost his balance with the double-whammy of abject fear closely followed by ecstasy. The cassette fell out of its cover and bounced on the rug by his left foot. He feasted his eyes on the tall, slender woman in a translucent *negligée*, with her hair curling down from its clip and her irresistible mouth smiling at his alarm.

Reaching the middle of the room before her husband had gathered his wits, the lithe blonde crouched down to retrieve the dropped video. With her left hand sliding up the leg of his pants until it found his arousal, she paused to unzip his fly and release him to her lips.

'Jesus, angel,' he murmured, threading his fingers through long, golden locks and forcing himself to name the full set of current Australian Government cabinet members before their encounter was over before it had begun. 'You are amazing. *This* is amazing.'

Her tongue making one last purposeful circle around the engorged tip, Lynn leaned back centimetre by throbbing centimetre until it hung suspended in mid-air. One hand walked upwards to stroke the tattoos on his chest as she straightened her legs, while the other undid the buttons of his shirt and eased it over his shoulders. The couple stood together in silence, moving only enough to shed each item of his clothing in turn.

'I wanted to surprise you.'

'Oh, yeah? Well, congratulations!' the songwriter gasped, kissing every piece of flesh he could find. 'Mission accomplished. Bloody hell, I'm fuckin' raging for you. Can we go to bed?'

With a ceremonious shove, the bottom half of a bespoke Yves Saint Laurent suit slithered to the floor, followed by the pair of silk boxer shorts. Many overseas concert halls now boasted full shower facilities to alleviate the need to stew through press conferences and after-parties in sweat-drenched underwear, and Jeff gave thanks that he had substituted a change of clothes for the hotel room Cathy normally stipulated in his rider.

The amorous couple padded through the lounge room and traversed the corridor into the master bedroom. The urgent atmosphere reminded them both of yesteryear, when passions overtook them to the exclusion of all else, sometimes even failing to make it to the bed. Clinging to his prized possession and pressing the soft abrasion of her lacy sheath across his genitals, the charmer paused in the doorway.

'It's been a long, long time for you and me,' he chanted, closing his eyes and nipping his saviour's neck. 'Loving you is the most important task ahead of me, and now behind me too, and I'm still addicted to you. I made this promise to you without really knowing if I could live up to it. But Christ Almighty, it's my reason for being. You can count on that, you gorgeous creature.'

Lynn gulped, frozen to the spot. She recognised the theme of this *impromptu* speech, most likely introduced as a method of delaying their mad rush to climax. These romantic phrases had been plucked from his marriage proposal, originally uttered while her engagement ring hovered between their faces in the tiny St John's Wood restaurant. Then, as now, she had cried with happiness at the significance rising high above their Spartan surroundings.

'Thank you. Me too,' the thirty-eight-year-old replied, hoping her memory was accurate.

Placing a hand on each well-honed deltoid, his fingers tracing the teddy's narrow straps, the man with the photographic memory grinned. '"No, angel," I said. "Thank *you*, a thousand times."'

'You did.'

'And I also said by loving you, I'm going to make it my life's work to understand you inside and out. To know your every wish and every aspiration, and to help you make them all come true. We fly higher than anyone's ever flown before, don't we?'

The emotional *duo* took several paces into the room, only stopping when Lynn's calves bumped into the mattress. She closed her fingers around his penis again and directed it into her mouth, but her stallion moved away, turning around and sitting beside her.

'Helpless in your arms,' he smiled, inviting her embrace and kissing her pouting lips. 'And something about hearts beating, and some other old crap I read in a copy of "Proposals for Dummies" I found tucked behind the couch.'

'Hey!' Lynn shouted, releasing the jester's boiling torso and thrusting him backwards until he was flat on his back. 'I knew it, you fraud! I never should've married you. This is the last you'll see of...'

'Oh, no, you don't!' Jeff let out a deep growl, whipping them both round until he straddled her hips, directing his erection downwards until it glanced across her concealed clitoris. 'You don't want to waste this now, do you? You can dump me tomorrow.'

Overpowered by desire at the way her unplanned arrival had been received, an orgasm thundered through the singer's body like a tidal wave. It was all her husband could do to stop himself doing the same, fumbling for the hooks in *lingerie* that had morphed into a chastity belt before his very eyes.

The poet struggled to piece together the rest of his betrothal homily, unable to conceal a laugh as the pretentious portrayal came back to him from an account he had given Gerry after the fact. 'Whoa! Wait for me. You're so hot, Lynn Dyson. So damned hot. I want to hold you forever.'

'Oh, Jeff! Me too. I love you so much. I love you, I love you, I love you.'

'I want us to learn how to touch each other differently every day,' he chuckled at the peculiar consonance they had conjured up, sliding his erection between the soaked folds of her vagina and collapsing down onto her body in bliss. 'Oh, Jesus! This feels so good. I need to breathe you in, I need to taste you and feel your energy flowing through my veins for the rest of my life.'

Barely moving, the forever friends clung together as the soliloquy transported them back to nineteen-seventy-five; before children, before billions, before *Escondido* and the Ethiopian hostage situation, before Sandy and Rod and little Brooke.

And before long, the moment of no return was upon them. Their heartbeats accelerating and their senses overflowing with pent-up raptures, they exploded into each other. With no kids, no nannies, no drivers or housekeepers to overhear their joy, the earth-moving accompaniment rang off the windows and vibrated picture frames against the walls.

'We made the vision into a reality,' Lynn whispered into her deadweight's ear. 'Four diamonds.'

'*Oui. Absoluement. Et je t'aimerai toujours.*'

'*Je t'aimerai toujours aussi*, magic-man.'

Jeff traced his fingers over the smooth contours of his soul-mate's face, breathing hard and glistening with perspiration. 'So! Once more with feeling...'

'Huh? What are you on about, you idiot?'

'Victoria Lynn Shannon Dyson Diamond…'

The Olympian giggled, settling back and gazing at the ceiling. 'Yes?'

'Marry me?'

'Oh, wow! Are you mad? How can I? I'd love to, but I'm already married to you.'

The intellectual exhaled, burying the side of his face in her pink-tinged voluptuousness. 'Well, yeah. OK. Got me on a technicality. How 'bout this then? Victoria Lynn Shannon Dyson Diamond, please don't unmarry me.'

Hugging her lost boy close, Australia's darling rejoiced in her unfathomable luck. Men like Jeff Diamond didn't come along very often, and she was the first to admit that her life would have been infinitely more dull and inferior had she never met him. Moreover, if humility and indebtedness were the by-products of deep mental scars, she and the children were unworthy beneficiaries.

'I won't,' she answered, kissing the corners of the old soul's begging eyes. 'Nothing could ever persuade me to unmarry you. Now you're sounding like Jet!'

Question asked and answered, her husband's energy levels seemed to plummet. Whether the result of drugs administered in true rock-star style, in the form of performance enhancers before the show and sweet, mellowing leaf-tips afterwards, or simply the spontaneity he craved when life returned to normal, his surrender exuded a tempered joy and a more-than-willing sobriety.

'Why do I sound like Jet?'

'You know…' Lynn smiled. 'How can you divorce someone when you didn't "vorce" them in the first place?'

The songwriter rolled onto his back, pushing his head into the pillow and groaning. 'Ah, Jeez! That's bloody awful! We'll need to coach him before he meets the Dean of Trinity 'cause he's going to get barred from "Footlights" with wit like that. But to cut to the chase, will you do me the honour of staying married to me?'

'For as long as we both shall live,' his *regala* replied. 'Of course I shall.'

'Cool! Correct answer. But anyway… Why are you here? Anna put you out?'

Lynn laughed. 'Indeed. Full marks. She was on fire. I nearly lost in straight sets.'

'Shame,' the showman grinned. 'Your loss, my gain. Cheers, Anns. You turned a good night into a sensational night. I thought I was hallucinating for a minute when I heard your voice!'

'You did look a bit gobsmacked, I must admit. I'm only here to provide you with sexual gratification, of course, my Lord. I planned to wait until you came to bed, but you were taking so long.'

A yawn curtailed the exhausted man's amusement, and his left hand swept round to gather his favourite practical joker into an avaricious embrace. 'You'd have been waiting even longer if I watched the tape. Not to mention that I'd have shot my load by the time I got to bed. Talk about pressure!'

'Oh, I'm sure you would've risen to the occasion.'

'Ha! Not so sure. I'm bloody knackered. Did you drive home?'

'From the airport? No. What in? I took a cab.'

'I mean after the massage.'

'Oh, I see!' Lynn giggled. 'That makes more sense. Yes, I did. Why? What are you talking about? I hadn't had anything to drink.'

Her husband chuckled, drowsiness closing in. 'I know. Just that you shouldn't drive in a state of detoxication.'

'What? You sanctimonious oaf! That's actually pretty funny! Driving while detoxicated. *Très drôle, mon brave.* Sleep?'

'Yep. Good idea. Just looking out for your welfare, that's all. And for my ability to get driven home when I'm next intoxicated.'

The comedian's hairy forearm constricted his captive nymph while they shared a goodnight kiss. The mood swings of old had returned for some reason, and she found them strangely comforting. If this was a side-effect of a father's angst at watching his daughter depend on him less and less, these little flashbacks to more innocent times were quite enchanting on the wide spectrum of afflictions.

'Flattery's not so far from bribery,' she scolded. 'Are you OK? Is all this sudden joking around masking something more sinister?'

'Nope. I'm fine,' Jeff answered. 'You?'

'Oh, I'm mighty fine, thank you. That's good then. You seem extra thoughtful, that's all.'

'Hmm... Maybe. Not 'specially,' he hesitated, glancing gentle kisses across the back of her neck. 'I'm tired. I want to fuck you again, like you wouldn't believe, but I don't have the energy.'

Lynn sighed. 'Then wait 'til we wake up, you poor old man.'

'Ah, Jesus, angel! Don't do that to me. You sound like Gerry this time. Now I definitely won't be able to get it up.'

Prising herself from her husband's arms, the steadfast woman turned around to look into his sleepy eyes. 'Can I tell you something you already know?'

'Guess so,' the songwriter chuckled. 'At the risk of boring me, I'll allow it. Go on.'

An athletic knee skimmed the sheet, lifting far enough to put pressure on Jeff's testicles. He backed off, smiling at his wife's raised eyebrows.

'When we moved to London, I knew I loved you but I didn't know why.'

Her beautiful black stallion inhaled, glowing inside. Memories of the long flight out of Australia to begin their life singular came flooding back into his mind, making his stomach churn and bringing tears to his eyes.

'By the time we left though, there was no doubt in my mind as to why.'

Their mouths met, new passions igniting their kiss until all thoughts of slumber were banished. They wrapped their arms around each other as if their last opportunity to touch had arrived.

'*Gracias*,' Jeff muttered, running his hand from the underside of her breast to guide her hip. 'I love you. I always knew why I loved you: you're the thing that makes me complete. I knew right from the very start. The kids are fantastic, but they're extra, angel. You I could never do without.'

Lynn struggled to free herself from the rekindled onslaught. 'Stop a minute, will you? Let me say thanks at least before you eat me alive! I feel exactly the same. *Mismo, mismo.*'

'*Bueno.* Now, where were we?'

***

'One thing's for sure, mate.'

'Hmm?' Gerry replied, busy scrolling through a spreadsheet containing Paragon Holdings' latest set of accounts. 'What's that?'

'I didn't see a return on investment for that bloody vasectomy.'

Fiona shrieked. She had been pretending to read a magazine, having left work early to meet up with her *fiancé* and his best man. With another tortuous evening of marriage-related vacillations, the old friends had made a pact to compress the dithering session at both ends by closing last month's books beforehand and adjourning to a cigar bar upon receiving a pre-agreed signal. The latter prospect was intolerable for the woman who had recently given up smoking, but her inability to mask her fascination for the former had become a standing joke.

'Jeff! That's a terrible thing to say!'

'Why?' Gerry scowled.

'Well, come on… Don't tick me off, darling. It is a terrible thing to say. I didn't even know you'd had a vasectomy.'

The widower laughed. 'Yeah. Fat lot of good it did us. Not something we shouted from the rafters, no. We didn't issue a press release.'

'Sorry,' the solicitor lowered her voice. 'I meant it wasn't Lynn's fault you wasted your money. Are you going to be much longer? We've got heaps to talk about.'

Both men groaned, then burst into fits of schoolboy titters, much to Fiona's disgust. Toni, her chief bridesmaid, was due to meet them in a hideaway bar to discuss colour schemes and other minute stylistic details which could easily have been delivered straight to their tailor. Gerry had thwarted such desirable efficiencies some months ago however, by making a few unilateral decisions, and Fiona had indicated most strongly that it was in his best interest to share each and every resolution henceforth.

'Not Lynn's fault?' her short-tempered partner blustered. 'I think *that's* a terrible thing to say, don't you?'

Jeff held his hands up to arrest the warring factions so early on in the evening. 'Cool it, mate. All good. I claimed it back from Lynn's estate, so no need to worry, Fi. I think we're about done here. Let's go and get pissed.'

Bidding the Blake & Partners receptionists a good night, their boss led his *fiancée* and the firm's most important client through the foyer and out into the lift lobby. He wrestled his tie down far enough to unbutton his shirt collar, snapping his briefcase between his knees.

The threesome left the prestigious office building by the rear doors, joining the steady stream of workers piling out onto Flinders Lane on their way to the station, local car parks or the nearest tram stop. Melburnians were accustomed to seeing the handsome superstar out walking in public, as had been the family's way since they had shot to fame in the early nineteen-seventies. These days, cries of exalted recognition had been usurped by sympathetic waves and doleful smiles.

A small group of smokers parted to let their idol and his associates pass into a dark doorway with steps leading to the basement. Once downstairs, they headed for their usual spot in the corner, far away from prying eyes.

'It shits me how grave everyone is around me, even after all this time,' Jeff sighed. 'I know I should be grateful, and I am, but if the wise guys in the entertainment press think I should be getting back to my normal self, someone ought to let everyone else know to get over it too.'

'I agree, mate,' Gerry said, refusing the waiter's offer of the wine list. 'No, thanks. We know what we're having. Two crownies for me and him, please, and a *Chardonnay* for the lady. Are you a lady tonight, my dear?'

Fiona shook her head. 'You'll never understand feminism, darling. I'm sorry we make life so complicated for you simple folk. Yes, please. The Stonier was nice last time. We'll have a bottle, please, if you can keep it at the bar for me?'

'You're in for a big night,' the best man smiled. 'Good to know. Let's open a big red in that case. D'you *wanna* choose, Gezza? I'll be back in a minute.'

While his manager selected a companion bottle of red, the songwriter disappeared into the laneway for a cigarette. By the time he returned, the happy couple was up to their elbows in ties, handkerchiefs and cummerbunds of all styles and hues. Laughing at the expression on his face, they yelled their objections when he wheeled round on his heels and made for the door again.

'What colours did you two wear at your wedding, Jeff?' Fiona asked, a pale blue tie in one hand and a crimson sash perilously close to her wine glass. 'I can't remember that far back.'

'Neither can I. Dark green, I think. Lynn took care of all that.'

'Yes. You were bottle green, and I was a sort of sludgy grey-green,' the accountant mused.

The brunette frowned. 'Sludgy grey-green? Sounds a bit drab. Have you still got them? We could re-use them as your something borrowed.'

'No doubt mine's in a drawer somewhere,' Gerry replied. 'Sounds a little weird to me. Only brides do the borrowed-and-blue thing. Doesn't apply to us too, does it?'

Jeff sighed. 'Do whatever you want, guys. It's your day, and the matter wouldn't even have surfaced if Lynn were still here. That dark red's pretty sophisticated-looking. I'm fine with anything.'

The Irishman tapped the neck of his empty beer bottle on the edge of the table. 'Another one of these, or wine? And can I just say, for the record,' he caught his breath. 'I wish Lynn could come to our big day too. Fucking travesty that she's gone. No-one's moved on, mate, to be honest. It's become like a national obsession, according to Cath. She said something very similar just yesterday.'

'Cheers,' his client inhaled and let out a long slow breath. 'I know. There was a whole talk-back show about it apparently. Anyone who does the tall poppy thing in Australia's liable to get their top cut off. It's who we turned out to be. *Malheureusement*, unfortunately.'

Tant pis, the rock star's guardian angel would have responded. Another obsolete stock phrase had fallen on monolingual ears, leaving only his "JL" tattoo to share the joke. He toasted the airwaves with an oversized goblet of *Cabernet Sauvignon*, and his friends scrambled to clink glasses.

'A few years ago, I went on record as wanting my life to be set on "repeat until fade". Well, that was then, and this is now, huh? Not quite what I had in mind at the time.'

Gerry chuckled. 'No, indeed. Weren't you going to tell us some news about your new brother?'

'Ah, yeah. So I was. In other words, quit feeling sorry for myself.'

'Yeah. That too. It's for your own good,' his old friend quipped. 'Kizzy's too soft on you.'

A call had come through to Stonebridge Music's switchboard the previous morning from a man claiming to be Jeff Diamond's brother. At first, the operator had assumed it was a prank and reeled off the company's standard script for giving people the brush-off. Of course, he had rung again. Three times in fact, until the flustered staff member resorted to transferring him to her supervisor.

'Nick Jaworski,' Jeff said through gritted teeth.

'Half-brother,' Fiona interjected.

The celebrity shook his head. 'Full brother. I'd always hoped my dad lied to me when he told me in his typically caring parental manner.'

'When was this?' Gerry asked. 'You never told me.'

'No. I only told Lynn. And the kids know now too, only since they read about it in Lynn's diaries. Not even Lena knows.'

'Jesus, Mary and Joseph,' the numbers man cursed. 'Is there no end to the secrets in your closet? Next you'll be telling me *you've* got more kiddies stashed away. What did he want? Is that why you had a vasectomy so late in the piece?'

'Eh? Don't be so fucking ridiculous!' Jeff snapped, swallowing a mouthful of wine so he wouldn't spit it all over the table. 'He wants money. Surprise, surprise. I asked him why he'd waited 'til now to come forward, but he didn't have an answer. I reckon he's read something in the 'papers about me selling stuff off.'

Fiona was flabbergasted, her bottom lip glued to her wine glass while she stared through her *fiancé*'s extraordinary client. There had been a number of leaks by indiscreet investment analysts; fires stamped out *post haste* by his management company's legal team. She knew from her own commercial law experience, supplemented by the slim pickings divulged over the dinner table, that the Diamonds' financial stockpile had been sequestered in so many far-flung places that it would be virtually impossible for the market to calculate their overall net worth.

'So when was he born, this Nick whoever-he-is?' she asked. 'Is he older or younger than you?'

'Younger, but not by much. Less than two years, as it turns out. Obvious really. Any older, and I'd have some memory of my mum being pregnant, I reckon. I'm intrigued to find out if it triggers any memories for Lena. She'd have been five or so.'

'Are you going to tell her this time?' Gerry was astonished. 'That'll be fun to watch. Poor Mad-Dog. She'll have to share the booty. How's she going to live when you halve her inheritance?'

His *fiancée* leaped out of her seat. 'What are you talking about? Who is this guy?'

'Gez, for someone who's too shit-scared to talk about death, you bring it up way too readily in front of the wrong people. Long story short, Fiona: as we were leaving the prison after taking the kids to meet him back in the early 'eighties, my arsehole of a father pulled me to one side and injected a cool, malicious one-liner: "There's another kid."'

'Oh, my God,' the upper-classed woman coughed. 'What a shock!'

'Hmm… It was for a day or so, but Lynn and I decided not to do anything about it. Wait for him to come looking for us before we let him screw up our life. We had no information about whether he knew where he came from. If not, with dad dead only a week later, no-one except the Jaworski family was likely to put two and two together.'

The Irishman scratched his head. 'Hang on! So how come your baby brother ended up with them. Didn't your pa murder two from the same mob?'

'Yep,' Jeff affirmed. 'This was ten years before the arsehole killed 'em, mate. Or thereabouts... He convinced my mum to give the new baby to Missus J as payback for some deal gone wrong. She'd found out she was pregnant too late to have an abortion, or so he said. Her cousin only had daughters and wanted a son to help run the "family business".'

The songwriter's mounting blood pressure compounded a headache he had been trying to shake off all day, annoyed with himself that he still felt so much guilt and shame for his parents' selfish irresponsibility. He would rather be umpiring an argument about wedding outfits than defending a forty-year-old human trafficking crime, not to mention the inevitable questions his manager's imprudent slip of the conscience would spawn.

'That's all I know, guys.'

'Until the other day,' Fiona egged him on. 'What claim did he make?'

'No idea yet. He wants to meet, but I haven't agreed to it.'

Like you have a choice, Gravity the troll hissed in the billionnaire's ear, causing bile to rise from his stomach. As his son had said when the news was broken to the children, it wasn't like their him to leave questions unanswered. A younger sibling made little difference to him now, but failure to reach a watertight legal agreement in the next few weeks might make life unpleasant for Jet and Kierney after he was gone.

'I'll set something up,' Gerry chuckled, seeing his client's pained expression. 'Then we'll amend your sister's contract before you take her through it.'

'You know, Fiona, don't you?' Jeff said. 'I thought I sensed some overacting earlier.'

The corporate lawyer nodded, casting a sheepish glance at her partner. 'Yes. And I'm sorry. You know how we feel about you and your lovely kids. That's why we're trying to keep you so busy with wedding preparations that you'll start to feel better without even noticing.'

The grieving husband scoffed. 'Yeah? Cheers, but good luck with that. In which case, Blake-san, I might as well tell you now that I'd like security present when Nick and I meet.'

'Roger that,' Gerry replied. 'Listen, mate. I'm...'

'No sweat. How it should've been all along, in my opinion. I'm stoked everything's out in the open. Anyway, we need to find out if he intends on bringing anyone with him. My guess is he found out from his mum on her death-bed. Mike Maynard's replacement e-mailed me to say she died while you guys were away for Melbourne Cup weekend.'

The accountant blanched. Given the direction their discourse had taken, he felt less guilty for missing one security advisory in twenty years. He had been under pressure to redress the balance for his protracted bucks' party, enjoyed in multiple instalments, and spirited his *fiancée* away on his luxury ocean-going yacht over the November long weekend.

'Apologies. I'll catch up with the guys at Lion tomorrow. Is this bloke after more than blood money?'

'Maybe. Don't know if anyone else in the family ever found out he wasn't related to them. It's essential we get everything locked down 'cause I won't be there to intervene if they come after Ry and Kiz. It'd be a cruel irony if he were to take me out with only days to spare, but I'm anxious not to spoil the plan. I can't risk damaging their mental health when we've done so well to bolster resilience up to this point.'

The pair of Irish Catholics frowned, refusing to believe the Diamond teenagers could escape unscathed from losing both parents inside twelve months. Not long ago, Fiona had boycotted events involving the handsome musician for a whole month after he had appeared on television supporting the Rational Suicide movement and its push for voluntary euthanasia legislation in Australian federal and state parliaments. He had spoken out in favour of the Northern Territory's short-lived Act, from which only four terminally-ill adults benefitted before the law was repealed.

Jeff had brushed her feeble castigations aside until the Toorak solicitor had the audacity to accuse him of inciting other vulnerable people to take drastic measures, and that if anyone other than God was to make such decisions, it should be a medical professional. He had countered by echoing the statement he had put out in nineteen-ninety-five, on official public record as saying if something were to happen to his family, he would have no hesitation in going after them.

'Our kids wouldn't,' he had stressed at the time. 'They've already formed their own views, and I totally respect that.'

Fiona sat forward in her chair, wagging a finger as if she were addressing an obsequious defendant. 'How can you be so sure Kierney fully understands such deep ethical issues. She's still very young, regardless of what you think. It's dangerous to speak so openly about suicide. What if she or Jet become suicidal after you deprive them of their happiness for a second time?'

'For a second time?' the widower cut the forthright woman off, his mind awash with Juan Antonio García's weasly features. 'It wasn't my idea to shoot their mother. Jesus Christ!'

'No, mate,' Gerry jumped in to diffuse the argument. 'That's not what she meant. Is it, Fi?'

The headstrong lawyer acquiesced. 'No. Absolutely not. I take it back. You get my point though.'

'Ah, yeah. Loud and clear. "Can I help you?" her last words were. Remember that? Can I fucking help you! "Sure," I can hear the Mediterranean rat bastard saying, in his lisping spaniel accent. "Just turn your head a little to the right so I can get a clear shot." Christ Almighty! Can we get on with what we came here for, please? Sorry, guys. I should never have distracted us onto other things.'

'Of course,' his manager rallied, pouring from the second bottle of *Shiraz* and deferring to the adamant superstar.

'Actually, no. What the hell! While we're on the subject, I don't feel any need to keep my mouth shut in front of our kids. All the evidence indicates no cause and effect whatsoever. One person talking about ending his or her life does not cause the next person to run out and swallow a few hundred pills. Doesn't work that way, Fi. Those who say I should keep my opinions to myself don't understand what it feels like to want to die. And to want to die on our own terms. It's the reverse: hearing about others doing it sustains us in a strange way. It's like we feel less alone, less freakish.'

Fiona bristled, not knowing how far she could push her *fiancé*'s closest friend in this *ad hoc* debate. 'OK. I have no reason to dispute this because I haven't seen the facts, but how can any suicide be rational? Surely, if someone's reached the point where they need to take such a desperate measure, they can't possibly still be thinking rationally.'

'Why not?' the world-changer countered. 'If I'd jumped off the West Gate Bridge in the first few weeks after Lynn's death, that would've been irrational. But I've been planning this for almost a year. With your man's help, by the time the day arrives, I'll have done everything in my power to make things straightforward for all concerned. Just because I'm grieving the loss of the only woman I ever loved doesn't mean I can't act rationally.'

'But you're grieving, as you said,' his manager butted in.

'*Na.* Means nothing, mate. You hear elderly people saying they're still grieving the loss of their husband or wife after thirty years. What about parents who lose young kids to cancer or car crashes or drugs? They'd probably say you never get over something like that. But are they incapable of making rational decisions? If anything, I think something like that... No! Fuck it. I *know* something like that puts life's perspectives into extremely sharp relief.'

As usual, the intellectual's keen wit and relentless negotiation tactics rendered his opponents battered and bruised. No doubt they would regroup, in the name of the Father, the Son and the Holy Ghost, but another cigarette break would provide welcome decompression before returning to their original agenda.

'It's also OK to say, "My work here is done,"' Jeff smiled. 'I no longer have a long list of things I want to achieve. It's up to the kids now. Their lists are out of control at the moment, and I'm certainly not going to be an obstacle for them. Suicide is a basic human right. Mark Twain's supposed to've said, "The fear of death follows from the fear of life. A man who lives fully is prepared to die at any time." No-one can accuse Lynn and me of not living our life to the full.'

'Well, hello!' Fiona laughed. 'Finally, that's something I can agree with.'

'For some, life isn't everything,' the widower lamented, flipping his lighter over and over in his left hand. 'In fact, for some, life isn't anything. Take all the disengaged young blokes who choose to go off and join cults and blow themselves up in the name of Allah, for example?'

'Aren't they promised seventy-three vestal virgins?' his manager sniggered. 'Or is it sixty-three? I never remember. Doesn't sound too bad to me, whatever a vestal virgin is and however many they have waiting in heaven for them.'

'It's a tautology, mate. Two words that mean the same thing. Virginal virgins, just in case there might be other kinds of virgins. And even if you get the full seventy-three, after a few months you're fresh out of virgins again. Pays to play the long game, don't you reckon? Beware of artificial sweeteners.'

'Artificial sweeteners?' Fiona repeated. 'What's that got to do with anything?'

The poet raised an eyebrow. 'Bribes, fake inducements. I'm off for another smoke. Lynn and I believe a human lifetime's merely one leg of an everlasting round-the-galaxy trip, and that therefore some people are suicidal 'cause their soul believes it can't do any more good as its current incarnation. In its current body, y'know... For whatever reason. You two believe in the afterlife, don't you?'

'People who commit suicide don't go to heaven,' Gerry scolded. 'Didn't the nuns teach you anything at primary school?'

'Who wants to go to heaven? For me, it's like, "Put me back in the queue, and I'll try again next time." We all make mistakes, and this one's broken.'

***

'*Mamá?*' Kierney asked into the telephone.

'*¿Sí, pequeñita?*' Lynn replied in jest. '*¿Estas OK?*'

The young woman laughed. '*Sí.* I'm fine, thanks. Are you still coming home tomorrow morning?'

'We are. Why?'

'Would it be OK if you and I went out for lunch? I mean, please could I buy you lunch somewhere in the city?'

Her mother was intrigued at their daughter's grown-up request, not normally inclined to Melbourne's social mores. 'Of course, darling,' she played along. 'That'd be great. We're going into the office straight from the airport. Cathy's got a huge pile of things for us to sign apparently.'

'No. Just you,' the teenager interrupted. 'On our own, without *Papá*. I'd really like to talk to you on your own, if that's alright. Would he mind?'

'I expect he would, knowing your *papá*,' the kind woman chuckled. 'You know how he hates missing out on things. Paranoia'll suggest we're scheming against him, but that mustn't stop you. What's on your mind?'

Kierney sighed. 'Oh. That's what I thought. I wanted to talk to you, woman to woman. About him.'

'Right! One moment, please,' Lynn put on her best receptionist's voice.

The penny had dropped. Her daughter wanted to strategise. Happy to be brought into her inner circle, the busy mother reached across the huge hotel bed to extract her diary from her bag. Leafing through it until she arrived at tomorrow, she prepared to assist their caring and increasingly self-sufficient gipsy girl.

'Thank you, ma'am,' the young woman chuckled. 'What are you doing?'

'Checking our appointments. *Papá*'s giving an interview at one-thirty. Not sure where. Southbank, probably. How long can you be out of school for? I could meet you at The Domain at one.'

'*¡Perfecto!*' Kierney confirmed. 'I've got a class at two-thirty, but that's plenty of time. I'll book a table just in case.'

Lynn smiled to herself. There would have to be a massive event taking place in Melbourne on a Wednesday lunchtime to fill this particular *café*! The extra level of formality was only one of the many ways Kierney liked to demonstrate her approaching adulthood.

'*¡Excelente!*' she chuckled. 'See you then.'

'*Gracias, Mamá.* Have a good time. Safe flight. Say hi to *Papá* for me, please.'

As arranged, the elegant celebrity installed herself at a table for two at the family's favourite among the long-established eateries opposite the Botanic Gardens, near the complex junction of tram lines where the postcode changed from South Melbourne to South Yarra and a stone's throw from Melbourne Academy's campus.

Conscious of the hushed gossip, sideways glances and jerky, stabbing fingers of her neighbours, she made sure to choose a corner table away from too many eavesdroppers. If their discussion became too private or revealing, they could always request takeaway cups for their coffees and migrate into the gardens opposite, providing the forecast showers didn't eventuate. She obscured her face with a mountain of reading collected from the office this morning. Despite these tried and tested measures, she was interrupted from time to time to sign the odd autograph or to pose with tourists who were delighted to snap the famous singing star and sporting heroine in her own locality.

Her slim, long-haired daughter breezed into the *café*, her carriage already too grown-up for her school unifirm. She too had to breach a throng of eager fans to reach her mother. Standing up to greet her, the thirty-eight-year-old smiled at the onlookers and asked for some privacy. With help from the staff, and also the unparalleled respect Melburnians had for the Dysons and the Diamonds, the pair of antithetical relatives was left alone for a peaceful luncheon.

'So!' Lynn grinned, flattening her menu across her plate and looking at the pretty girl in her school uniform. 'Woman to woman, you said. Sounds serious!'

Kierney laughed. 'Hmm... I feel like a fraud saying that. Did it sound weird?'

'Not at all! You *are* a woman, so how can you be a fraud? Unless you're in transition and this is the news you're about to give me.'

'Ew! No. Oh, my God!' the teenager's face contorted into a childlike frown. 'Nothing like that. Even harder to broach that subject. Can you imagine what *Papá*'d have to say about that?'

It was Lynn's turn to grimace. A frightening thought indeed! Poor Jeff. His ethos of open-mindedness and tolerance would be tested to the utmost by such a revelation from his precious *pequeñita*.

'Yes,' she agreed. 'Let's not go that far, please. Not in a single step anyway. We know your dad likes a challenge, but that'd be one hell of a test. Come on... Spill the beans. I'm dying to know what you want to talk about so urgently.'

'Really? I thought you'd have already guessed. Doesn't the "woman to woman" thing kind of give it away?'

A waitress arrived, gushing with over-service, a bottle of water and two high-ball tumblers. Both patrons thanked her with polite platitudes and leaned forward to fill the glasses at the same time. They laughed out loud before reining in their amusement for fear of drawing attention to themselves again. As much as their outward appearances were so unalike, the similarity in their mannerisms was as obvious as if a mirror stretched across the centre of the table, further accentuated by each favouring a different hand.

'Well, yes...' the mother admitted. 'I'm sure it's got something to do with the opposite sex. And it has to be pretty controversial, given you banished your father instead of seeking his advice. Consequential even?'

'Consequential,' Kierney rolled the unusual word round on her tongue. 'That's a great word. Super- consequential.'

A heated flush of embarrassment quietened the youngster all of a sudden, noticing a handsome male waiter on the approach with their plates of salad. Her reaction melted the older woman's heart, remembering full well how difficult it had been to verbalise such nascent and confusing thoughts.

'You're gorgeous,' Lynn said, extending her right hand over the table to squeeze her daughter's left. 'It's a good idea to be careful about letting people overhear things. You don't want to read gossip about yourself in the magazines, do you? You know... Unofficial stuff. We could eat quickly and talk over there, if you'd prefer.'

'No,' the dark-haired beauty smiled, following her mother's gaze across the road to the picnic tables. 'It's fine, thanks. You know I've been going out with Dylan for a few weeks now?'

'Yes.'

'Well... I really like him. I don't know why, but I do.'

Lynn froze with a laden fork halfway to her mouth before lowering it back to her plate. 'You don't know why? That's not like you.'

'*Mamá*, shhh! Stop being like *Papá*! I just mean he's not good-looking or anything. Not a normal boyfriend, as Nat keeps saying.'

'There's no such thing as a "normal boyfriend",' Lynn responded, drawing quotation marks in the air. 'I'm sorry. I didn't mean to put you under pressure. It's none of Nat's business whom you go out with anyway.'

'I know,' the young woman shook her head. 'Your reaction was funny, that's all. Like *Papá* travels inside you wherever you go.'

The older woman sipped her water, feeling her own insides churn a little. 'That's a lovely analogy, Kizzy. He does, I'm sure. You're not destined for normal boyfriends, I don't expect. You should look for interesting boyfriends.'

'And that's what I was going to say! I like Dylan 'cause he's funny and because he's into heaps of different things. Not like others who've asked me out, who only talk about footy and hair gel or tell crude jokes. It's like they're incapable of talking about anything else. Occasionally music, but not the kind of music I'm into.'

'And Dylan is,' her *confidante* nodded. 'He was pretty good on the piano at the apartment the other night. I could hear the two of you singing and larking about all the way from the office.'

A familiar dreamy expression washed over her daughter's face as she hurried to finish her mouthful. 'Yeah. He writes songs and poems too. Some of them are brilliant. His mum's a *muso*, so he's inherited musical genes too. But what I like about him most is that he doesn't always try to be the same as everyone else. He's happy to be his own person. We admire that in each other. Does that make sense?'

Lynn raised her glass. 'Certainly,' she replied. 'Makes perfect sense. And the fact that you two talk about deeper things also means you're a great match. But why the secrecy from *Papá*?'

The answer was already obvious, but the kind teacher was determined to give her daughter space to find the right words; a skill seldom occurring naturally in introverts, but fundamental for success in the adult world. She watched Kierney's brow furrow as she prepared her response.

'Because...' the fifteen-year-old began, 'I've always found it easy to say no to sex before, but I want to with Dylan. We've kissed heaps of times. You know, properly, like you and *Papá*. It feels really awesome and close.'

The blonde singer's eyes flashed in recognition. 'OK! I absolutely know where you're coming from with that! Always good to do things properly,' she teased. 'Sounds like you are ready for more then.'

'Oh, *Mamá*!' Kierney let out a dramatic sigh. 'Yes. I think I'm ready, and he's been pretty patient about it. Hasn't put too much pressure on me.'

'That's cool. Everybody's different, as you well know. As long as you're not only giving in because you think he's been patient for long enough.'

'No,' the teenager replied straightaway. 'I'm not. I feel so drawn to him. Don't know if I love him though...'

Lynn smiled. 'No. That doesn't surprise me. I was exactly the same. I had no clue whether my feelings were love or just the excitement of being with a handsome man. It doesn't matter anyway, darling. You don't have to fall in love with your first sexual partner.'

'You did!'

'I know. And there's no law against it either!'

Kierney fell silent again, loading another pile of salad onto her fork. Both women knew there was more at stake for their family than most who faced this significant step, with droves of do-gooders on the incessant and intrusive hunt for scandal and impropriety.

'Yes,' the tennis champion continued, reading her daughter's mind. 'You are under age, and you will need to be cautious about being spotted going in and out of places. People jump to all sorts of outlandish conclusions. You know that already. Don't stress. As long as you're private about it. Kids mature at different ages. I wasn't ready before I turned sixteen, but Jetto was, and your father definitely was!'

The youngest Diamond raised her head high again, tossing her stylish side-ponytail over her shoulder to carry on eating. 'Was he?' she giggled. 'Come to think of it, I did hear that somewhere. Thanks, *Mamá*. I am really nervous that someone'll find out. I suppose that's why I wanted to talk it over with you. I'm scared *Papá*'ll blow a gasket if I bring Dylan home to have sex, but I don't want to sneak around or even do it at his house. I want the first time to be special. You know... Like Jet's first time was. I've been looking forward to my turn for ages, but I want *Papá* to be... oh, I don't know... at least comfortable.'

'Did you want a coffee?' the sympathetic mother asked, as much to break the tension as to move the story on.

'Yes, please.'

'Well, you're right. I doubt *Papá*'d be comfortable to begin with. Way too much to expect there! But he can't kid himself for much longer. He knows it's going to happen sooner or later. For God's sake, you're Jeff Diamond's daughter! We hope you have just as fantastic a sex-life as your brother. You can't escape. It's in our genes, Miss D.'

Lynn gave the fresh-faced waiter a wave. He had been hanging around at the counter for the last five minutes, unable to take his eyes off the famous pair now the lunchtime rush was tailing off. He jumped to attention, grabbing his notepad and pushing his hair back off his face with a flirtatious air.

'Oh, jeez! What you're saying sounds like a lot of pressure!' Kierney said, once the coast was clear. 'What if I don't like it? What if somehow I missed out on those genes?'

'Now you're being silly! Of course you'll like it. We wouldn't be sitting here having this clandestine *liaison* if your body wasn't dropping these unsubtle hints. You've been displaying all the right signs for the last couple of months. I expect you'll be every bit as sex-mad as the rest of us!'

'*Mamá!*'

'What? It's true, and perfectly normal. I've seen the way you flirt with boys on your way in and out of school, and with Jet's friends, even if you don't know you're doing it. We all do. It's natural to want to attract the opposite sex. Or the same sex, if that's your thing.'

Kierney shrugged. 'No. That's not my thing. Or Dylan's thing either. So here's the question: how should I tell *Papá*? Or should I tell him at all? Should I just pick a time when you guys are out of the country and get it over with?'

'Get it over with?' her mother coughed, her mouthful of food threatening to go down the wrong way. 'I hardly think that's the way you should be looking at such an important milestone! You mustn't let *Papá*'s reactions dictate how you live your life. He'd be mortified to know you want to avoid telling him something. You guys arrange the date for whenever you want, with our help or without. Either way though, in answer to your question, you should do your dad the courtesy of telling him in advance.'

The teenager pulled another anxious face, making her mother smile. 'But how? You *gotta* help me, *Regala!*' she pleaded, doing her best impersonation of the songwriter's typical insistence. 'Will you help me, please?'

'Course I'll help you, darling. Once *Papá* knows and has enough time to work it through, he'll be absolutely fine with it all. He simply needs to adjust to the idea. He and I've been discussing your virginity frequently lately.'

'Ew!' the youngster cringed. 'Have you? That's scary. Isn't there anything you guys don't talk about?'

'Not much, no. I can tell you that *Papá* despises how parochial and old-fashioned he feels about you losing your innocence. He doesn't understand his own feelings, which is unusual for him. He's told you already, hasn't he?'

'Yes. I know,' Kierney affirmed. 'But I still don't want to hurt him, even though it's my right to have sex when and where and with whom I like.'

Signalling for their bill, Lynn chuckled. 'Indeed. Spoken like a true activist! I assure you, *Papá*'ll get over it as soon as it's happened. He likes Dylan. And once it's done, it's done. No re-sealing, as he said the other night.'

'Re-sealing? That's yuck!'

'He worries more about someone forcing himself on you.'

'Rape, you mean?'

'Well, yes. Of course rape, or any kind of sexual assault. It's a possibility, darling. Even, as we were just saying, if you were put under so much pressure to have sex that you slept with someone for the wrong reasons and then hated yourself for it. We don't want you to have any emotional scars.'

'Oh, OK. Yeah. I get it. Thanks. I am grateful, *Mamá*.'

The superstar nodded. 'That's good. I know you are. There's always such a fine balance between protecting someone you love and clipping their wings. If you're happy, *Papá*'ll be happy, Kizzy. Neither of us wants you to stop growing up. It's so hard, as a parent, to see your kids stop being kids. That's all it is.'

'Yeah,' Kierney nodded, draining the last of her *cappuccino* and setting the cup back on its saucer. 'I can understand. Well... I think so. And in a lot of ways, I don't want to stop being your kid. I like having you guys looking after me. Our family's so cosy. It'll be weird for a while, won't it, when Jet goes to Cambridge?'

Lynn paused, also more than a little saddened by this prospect. Standing up and slotting the bundle of papers into her bag, she watched her ladylike daughter put on her school blazer and flick her hair out from under the heavy fabric. Melbourne Academy's uniform policy had made a few minor concessions to contemporary fashions, with the average skirt length some twenty centimetres longer in the nineteen-nineties than in her day and ties now optional for girls in Years Eleven and Twelve.

Both children had been brought up in the Dyson tradition with regard to seemly presentation and attire, and the mother smiled to see her daughter fish an extra black hair elastic out of her left-hand pocket and check the tidiness of her ponytail in the gleaming glass of the *café*'s pastry display.

'Very smart,' she praised, placing a caring hand on the younger woman's back as they walked out onto the street. 'It's weird. Things are changing more rapidly for our family than ever before. You guys are becoming well-mannered and capable individuals, self-reliant in so many ways. That's who we brought you up to be, and *Papá* and I are so proud of you. We have no choice but to get used to it, and it'll be strange for all of us for a while. All families must go through this, I suppose.'

'S'pose so,' Kierney turned to her mother while they waited for a gap in the traffic. 'Are you OK? Are you upset about me having an adult relationship too?'

'No. I'm not upset in the way your dad is. It's a shame we can't speed life up through the nasty bits and slow it down when it's lovely, that's all. You'll understand much better when you're older. *Papá* has this theory he calls the "Hare to Tortoise" stage of life, and I'm completely in tune with it.'

'Hare to tortoise? What's that?'

'Ask him,' Lynn suggested. 'It may be a good way of breaking him in gently to your news.'

The teenager nodded, lacing her hand through the crook of her mother's arm. 'Oh, alright. Thanks, *Mamá*. I feel bad now. I only thought about *Papá* being upset, 'cause he's the one making all the noise.'

The sportswoman laughed out loud, turning heads as the pair followed a path to one of the gates into the Botanic Gardens. 'True! He does make enough ruckus for the both of us! That's the front-end of the pantomime horse's prerogative. He's got the mouth, and all I'm left with is the...'

Kierney held on tighter to her mum's arm, feigning shock that she would use this well-worn family analogy in public. 'Are you upset though?' she persisted.

'No, darling. Really. It's very romantic. An exciting time, and if anything, I'm a bit jealous. I think you've been appropriately choosy about taking this step with the right person. That's all any parent can ask. In this day and age, as Grandma would say! You're living your life on your own terms, and I admire that. Honestly.'

The young woman glowed with pride. 'Thanks very much. So how do you think I should tell *Papá*?'

'What's the time? I'll give you a lift back to school, otherwise you'll be cutting it fine. Have you got a plan for your big night?'

'Sort of... My current plan is to invite Dylan back to the apartment on Saturday night. We're going to see a film with some mates. And I remember you guys'll be in the city too, won't you?'

'This Saturday?' Lynn replied. 'Yes, we are. We've got a charity dinner to go to. Shame actually, 'cause we'll be home much later than you.'

'No!' Kierney yelped. 'It's good! It means we can be more relaxed, and you know we're there.'

'And what you're up to,' her mother chided. 'We'll make plenty of noise when we get in, so you have enough warning to *decentify* yourselves.'

The young woman giggled, clapping her hands to her cheeks. 'Ugh... Something like that. Jesus Christ!' she mimicked her father. 'Maybe I'm not ready after all.'

The elegant celebrity stood still, unthreaded their arms and gripped her baby girl's shoulders. As their eyes met and they embraced, the teenager felt like crying, unsure whether from joy or nerves. After a second or two, they straightened up and continued towards the Maserati, which was parked on the opposite side of the road to Lynch's.

A bittersweet memory flooded Lynn's brain from the very first time she and Jeff had visited this classy restaurant. A replay of "the tennis skirt episode" was the last thing she would wish for her child.

'Let's get going,' she suggested, pointing to her sports car, its pale blue pearlescent paintwork glinting in the sun.

Hand in hand, mother and daughter strolled across the newly mown grass. By the time they reached the footpath, eight or ten people had appeared from nowhere, excited to make contact with the local celebrities. It was as if they had been hiding behind trees like in a scene from a Charlie Chaplin movie. After treating each fan to another set of "As and Ps", they climbed into the car. The engine roared to life as soon as Lynn turned the key in the ignition.

'This car sounds like *Papá*,' the wistful teenager mused. 'I love you guys so much.'

'And we love you too. Your plan's a good one. I'll prepare the ground with *Papá* this afternoon. If all goes well, you can ask him to tell you his "Hare to Tortoise" theory over dinner, then *segue* neatly into what's in store for him on Saturday night. Do you think Dylan'll stay for breakfast?'

'Eek!' the young woman shrieked. 'I don't know! Should he? I hadn't thought that far ahead. Oh, my God! It'd be so awkward.'

Turning into Avoca Street, where a number of uniformed children were milling around, the famous mother grinned. 'It won't be awkward for long. I'll get *Papá* up for a run if you'd prefer. Just agree a time when it's safe for us to return to our own home. Best to limit awkward experiences to one at a time, *n'est-ce pas?*'

'*Oui, maman*,' Kierney sighed. 'Or maybe Dylan won't want to stay anyway. He's shit-scared, sorry, of meeting you guys after...'

'Post-coitally?'

'Mother!'

'Don't "Mother!" me, my girl! Get used to it. If you want to be an adult, we all have to be adults together. With any luck, we'll all be sitting round the breakfast table with grins on our faces. Welcome to paradise, Kizzo.'

The student slapped both thighs in resignation. Her mother was right. She was no different to any other person going through the embarrassment of growing up. It was either brace against the winds of change or forever remain a child, a prospect she could never entertain.

'Righty-ho!' the teenager pronounced. 'That's the plan. You're right. I have to face the consequences, embarrassing or not. Was it embarrassing for you the first time *Papá* appeared for breakfast?'

Lynn stared straight ahead as she drove, thinking back to the amazing morning at Benloch when she and Jeff entered the farmhouse kitchen on the morning after Robert McLean's twenty-first birthday party. He had worn a skin-tight, black T-shirt with "Built to Last" emblazoned across his chest.

To her daughter's delight, a giggle escaped from the driver's mouth as she remembered how her new boyfriend has been as proud as punch to have his future brother-in-law draw attention to the slogan and its portentous association. She too had been proud to show off her beautiful black stallion to those who treated her like the baby of the bunch.

'No, actually,' she responded into the expectant atmosphere, gliding into a spare parking space and pulling up the handbrake. 'It wasn't at all embarrassing. Grandma was there, talking to our friends after Rob's party. She told me a while later that she was shocked by her reaction at seeing us arrive together. She said I didn't come down to breakfast with a boy, but with a man. It was a big moment for her.'

Kierney's eyes filled with tears. 'Oh, that's so beautiful. I hope you enjoy your big moment when you see us. Will it be a big moment for you too, do you think?'

'Most definitely, gorgeous,' Lynn replied, reaching over and touching her daughter's arm. 'And then we'll make sure you're protected, just like Grandma did for me.'

'Oh, wow! Did she? Contraception, you mean? That's funny!'

'Yes. But no, I'm wrong. We'd already had that conversation by then. Another awkward one! She knew I was having sex with *Papá* before the twenty-first birthday party weekend, so I'd been taken to the doctor's to be fixed up. She and Grandpa were determined not to take any risks with anyone's reputation.'

'Shall I go on the pill too?'

'Up to you,' Lynn smiled. 'Might be a wise move if you're going to follow in our footsteps, like your bro'.'

Kierney lifted her gaze to the school gates, preparing to climb out of the low-slung vehicle. She took a deep breath in and exhaled through her mouth in a single breath, feeling dizzy.

'Are you alright?' her mother asked.

'Yeah,' the young woman turned to face the driver's seat. 'Thanks for the lift, *Mamá*. And for improving my plan. I'm excited, but it's daunting too.'

'Good. The way it should be. It's a big thing. It'd be foolish to underestimate the change this is going to have on your life. *Papá*'ll tell you the same thing, and he'll be so happy you didn't rush into it. That's his biggest fear.'

'That the moment'd be lost?'

'Yes, in a way. You know *Papá*: take stock of the significant events in your life. That notion's very important to him. And to me too. It's lovely to have a set of special memories to look back on. Not just a series of rushes of blood to the head, as he'd say. He doesn't want you to have inherited his jaundiced attitude when it comes to measuring your own worth.'

'No. I haven't. Are you giving me hints for my speech?'

Lynn shrugged. 'Not consciously, but you're welcome to my thoughts. I've earned my lunch, which is another thing our learned friend'd say. Have a good afternoon, Kizzy. We'll be in when you get home, I expect.'

After a quick kiss, Kierney heaved open the substantial car door and uncurled to her full height, spotting two of her classmates ahead. She waved as her mother steered the car around in a tight loop and passed the school's entrance at a snail's pace. Straightening her clothing, as a metaphor for her own state of mind, she lengthened her stride until she had caught up with her friends, ready to make their way to the Common Room.

***

'No, no, no, no, no, no, no!'

Jeff paced around the kitchen in their sixteenth-floor penthouse, smacking the side of his empty beer bottle in time with the desperate syllables and then thumping its base down onto a coaster. Lynn had offered him a drink the moment he had stepped out of the lift, in preparation for their daughter's news. Knowing every *nuance* of his recovering mind so well after two decades together, it was important not to keep anything of import from him for any longer than necessary.

'You have no choice,' his wife smiled, whipping the bottle off the table and supplanting a replacement into wringing hands. 'It's got to happen one day. It so happens that the one day in question is this Saturday.'

The rock star growled, wheeling round for another lap. 'But why?' he whined. 'I can't handle the image of some bloke sticking it to my daughter burned into my brain? Why can't she be one of those one in twenty asexual statistics?'

'Because that's life, mate,' his wife laughed, sensing a certain obstinate pride pulsating through the airwaves. 'You can't pick and choose which aspects of parenthood you're willing to go along with. And I know you don't want me to say this, but you were that bloke a generation ago. You didn't mind sticking it to me.'

'Oh, for fuck's sake! I wish you weren't always so bloody right.'

Jeff held out his arms, longing for his *regala* to walk into them and make everything better. Kissing away their pent-up passion, they stood locked together until she felt tears drop onto her cheeks. Brushing them away with graceful piano-player's fingers, she pulled back and stared at his tanned face from arm's length.

'Oh, you're so wonderful,' she whispered. 'I love you so much. I love how much you care about Kizzy's future, and I do understand how hard this is for you. You know it'll be fine, don't you? Dylan's a great kid, and I gather he's waited quite a while.'

Jeff exhaled through his nose, lips pursed. 'Yeah. Sure. I know all these things. Everyone's ready for action except me. You don't have to remind me. I love you too, by the way. Shit! I'm sick of waiting too, to tell you the truth. Bring it on.'

'Thank you. That's what Kiz thinks too. She actually used the phrase "get it over with." She'd like to talk to you tonight, to make sure you're comfortable.'

'Comfortable?' her husband echoed. 'How the fuck am I going to be comfortable? Sitting at the dinner table, talking trivia with the *glitterati* for the fifty-fifth time this year, while our daughter's having her hymen snapped by some spikey-haired punk rocker?'

'What?' Lynn exclaimed. 'I hope you're not going to describe her momentous occasion in that way when you speak to her? Where's *my* long-haired bohemian poet gone all of a sudden? How come our special moment was a ballet, and yet your daughter's is some primitive ritual?'

Slumping down on a kitchen chair, the songwriter rocked it backwards and yanked the love of his life onto his lap, unable to stop himself from bursting out laughing. 'Jesus Christ! That's so fuckin' fair it's unfair!' he shook his head. 'It's both. Ours was both, and theirs will be too. And both are good. Ours was a *tango* more than a ballet. That's what was going on inside me anyway... Christ Almighty, what an amazing night our first time was, angel!'

'It was,' Lynn affirmed, kissing his indignant mouth. 'Be happy for her. She's in safe hands, just like I was. Remember when you span me the line about if you wanted to attack me, you could? It's stuck with me all this time. It sent shivers down my spine, but there was no way I was going to leave. You were like thunder and lightning, Jeff Diamond. Frighteningly compelling.'

Her husband accepted the commendation despite having heard it many times. 'Cheers. You're right. I do hope Kizzo has a great time. She deserves it as much as anyone, even if she *is* perfect the way she is and way too young to be having sex.'

'That's better. *Merci, mon ami,*' Lynn stroked the side of his drying face while he took another large gulp of beer.

'Hey? D'you remember the atmosphere splintering when you told me you were a virgin?' he asked, slipping his spare hand around his lover's waist and pressing her down onto his bulging lap.

'Not like you do. I was so completely out of my depth. I didn't know whether to play along or come clean. I do remember the shock on your face, and that you seemed to stop breathing almost immediately.'

Jeff gave his wife a half-smile. 'Did I? Not surprised! Bloody hell, baby. We've had this superbly blessed life. I still can't believe how happy we are. Honestly, I can't.'

'I know what you mean,' Lynn agreed, thinking about the mid-life crisis conversation her daughter planned to initiate. 'But then again, we both still want to make each other happy, so it's meant to be. We'd have to be pretty inept to mess it up from here.'

'That's what I'm scared of for the kids, I guess,' the father frowned. 'I want them to have as special a life as we've had. Can Dylan give Kizzo what we have? I don't think so. She doesn't love him, does she?'

'She doesn't know, but neither did I at first. It won't matter. That's what we talked about over lunch. She'll fall in love whenever it happens, and then she'll have another special first encounter. Like we did when we got back together. I'd never wanted anything so much than to be with you again after so long.'

'After everyone else being such a let-down?' Jeff smirked.

'Yes,' the Olympian sneered, elongating the word to let him know she was aware how much this Freudian slip continued to stoke his *ego.* 'Whatever... Please may I borrow your daughter the next weekend we're at home?'

'Borrow my daughter? What does that mean? She's *our* daughter, so you can borrow her whenever you like.'

Lynn laughed, standing up and wandering over to a calendar pinned to a magnet on the refrigerator door. 'I'd like to take Kierney away for a girls-only weekend,' she explained. 'Shopping, lunching, a *spa* and a sly glass of shampoo. You know... Girlie things. A bit llike what you do with Jet on your bonding trips, I want to teach her the dos and don'ts of being a woman. Plant a few seeds, you know... Would your paranoia be able to withstand the stress after this weekend?'

'How should I know?' Jeff grunted, holding his hands up. 'Ask me again on Sunday. But yes, angel. Of course you should. Sounds like an amazing idea. Just don't get as wet and cold as we did on those bikes in Ireland.'

'*Exactement,*' his wife leaned over to kiss her husband's forehead. 'She's hungry for information. I can see all the questions running around behind her eyes. She wants to experience life, but from a position of prior knowledge.'

The intellectual agreed. '*T'as raison*, angel. Jet's a "jump in with both feet and ask questions later" kind o' guy, but Kizzy's different. And who better to teach someone how to be a beautiful woman than the most beautiful woman in the world herself? When d'you *wanna* do it?'

He watched the blonde temptress counting on the calendar with her finger, comparing dates with information from her inner computer to match the family's diaries. Fuelling his desires ever higher, his heart overflowed with love for the mother of his precious children. His teenaged self never would have believed how easily they would take to the demands of parenthood. However, poised on one of the most dangerous precipices his miniature would confront on her own journey, he could think of no better hands to be in.

'How about the weekend after "Alien Life" opens?' she offered, a little distracted by the scheduling complexity and unaware of the lust building in her man's loins. 'Two weeks before Jet's birthday.'

Her husband shrugged. He was hopeless at retaining such details, having learned to rely on Lynn, Cathy and the Stonebridge Music team to direct him where he needed to go. Memorising such dry and uninspiring data was an arse-end thing, he concluded, glancing at his watch and relating it to the sun's descent beyond the western side of the apartment's balcony.

'What time's Kizzy coming home?'

'About now. Are you OK?'

'No,' he scoffed.

Lynn caught his arm as he attempted to slip by her and into the hallway. 'Are you OK?' she repeated.

'I suppose so. Yep.'

Less than ten minutes later, the lift whirred in the centre of the building, bringing the fifteen-year-old home to judgement. Her mother could tell she was anxious by the way she tossed her schoolbag down next to the coat stand and kicked it into position with a low grumble. The two female Diamonds met in the lounge room doorway and gave each other a kiss.

'How is he?'

'Fine,' Lynn assured her. 'He's calm. Not even here at the moment. He said he was going to get cigarettes, but I think something's brewing.'

'Oh, God!' Kierney's eyes widened. 'What's brewing? He *is* coming back, isn't he?'

The stalwart smiled. 'Yes. I'm sure he'll come back. You two are as bad as each other. Relax. It'll be fine. He's gone to buy a chastity belt.'

'A what? What's a chastity belt?'

Stuck between the two matching nervous wrecks, the youngster's trusted adviser stared back in fun as her huge brown eyes almost popped out of their sockets in horror. 'You know...' she smiled, miming the turn of a lock. 'One of those mediæval contraptions fathers and husbands used to strap their women into, to stop them straying from the straight and narrow while they went off to war. There'll only be one key, so you better behave yourself.'

Kierney winced at the very thought of being trapped in a rusty metal cage until her father saw fit to grant her freedom. Torn between the tragedy and comedy of this situation, she sighed in frustration and managed a sweet smile for her mother.

'That's not funny, *Mamá*. How do we know he hasn't had some modern version of a chastity belt made especially for me?'

'Yes, it is funny, and yours is a ridiculous suggestion, even where your *papá*'s concerned,' the older woman countered, giving her daughter a hug. 'This is turning into a gigantic overreaction that you and he are fabricating all on your own. I sincerely hope you guys can clear the air once he comes home and everything can go back to normal around here.'

Throwing her hands up in a half-hearted truce, the fifteen-year-old turned on her heels, heaved her bag back up onto her shoulder and stomped off to her bedroom on the southern side of the apartment. Lynn felt guilty that she had laid blame at her daughter's door, since this *fiasco* wasn't of her doing. She and her father were cut of the same cloth where it came to emotional blackmail. As the only rational member of the family available, it was her duty to metre out treatment on an equal opportunity basis.

Some twenty minutes later, Jeff let himself back into the apartment building and typed his key-code on the lift panel. All was quiet when he reached the top floor. He first headed for the kitchen, but finding it empty, he wandered into the lounge room in search of his womenfolk. His stunning wife sat at the piano, refining a new song they had written over the last few days.

'Hey,' he announced, having managed to creep up close behind the musician before she turned around. 'That sounds finished. I like the bridge going into the minor.'

Lynn swang her legs over the stool to face her wandering hero. He was clutching a box of two-hundred cigarettes, two red roses and a bottle of champagne. The furrowed brow he had worn on departure had been deposited elsewhere, and in its place was a lightness in his eyes.

'You oughtn't be encouraging her to smoke,' the loving woman teased.

Her husband sniffed. 'Yeah. I know. But under-aged drinking's OK? Double standards, Ms Diamond.'

Closing the piano lid, his wife shook her head and accepted a heartfelt kiss. 'Not sure about the rose though,' she added, squeezing his arm. 'Smelling roses must be illegal somewhere.'

'Is Kiz here? Where is she?'

'In her room. I made a cruel joke about you going to pick up a chastity belt, and she stormed off in disgust.'

The father laughed, seeing that the compassionate woman regretted her actions somewhat. 'Will you give me half an hour with her and then join us, please, angel?' he asked. 'I'm going in to make peace. Wish me luck.'

'Sure. Good luck,' his beautiful best friend responded. 'And thank you.'

The corridor leading to their children's bedrooms seemed to have stretched to twice its normal length tonight. The man of the house stopped to leave his leather jacket on the bed in the master suite, along with one of the cellophane-wrapped flowers. As he passed the hallway mirror, he could have sworn he saw Bart Dyson glaring back at him. He shook the disturbing vision from his mind and knocked on Kierney's door.

'¿Kiz, puedo entrar?' he asked, finding it ajar.

'Sí, Papá. Está abierto.'

The teenager eyed the door with some trepidation as it inched inward. Her father's frame filled the entire doorway, silhouetted in the murky twilight. She slid off the bed to greet him.

'Olá. ¿A dónde fuiste?'

Jeff leaned down and kissed her flushed cheek, tension written all over her face. Their unspoken communication as powerful as ever, his eyes requested she reverse and sit back on the bed, which she did without hesitation. Leaping onto her *doona* like a little girl, she turned and followed his movements.

'These are for you,' he said, presenting the teenager with the bottle of champagne and the remaining rose. 'It's my way of telling you, "Go for your life, *pequeñita*." I'm sorry to be such a killjoy about your happiness.'

Kierney felt a lump form in her throat as she saw her father's eyes glisten in the fading evening light. She clutched the flower against her breast with one hand, unable to speak, and lay the bottle down beside her on the bedclothes. Beckoning for him to sit there too, she shuffled backwards until her back rested against the wall, still holding tight to the blood-red, smooth-stemmed symbol of love.

'*Gracias, Papá,*' she croaked. '*Te amo.*'

Stepping a couple of paces to one side, Jeff dragged an armchair forwards until it lined up with the end of his daughter's bed. If she were about to give herself to another man, perhaps he should relinquish his position as bedtime storyteller. Sitting down more heavily than he had intended, he wiped his left hand across his eyes and gathered his senses.

'*Te amo también, gorgeousita.* You look so beautiful. You're a real lady already, and Dylan's a lucky guy.'

Unable to hold in her emotions any longer, the young woman lunged forwards into her beloved *papá*'s arms, nearly sending them both flying. Laughing and crying at the same time, they embraced and struggled to right themselves before the chair tipped over.

Pushing the slight body away, Jeff urged his daughter to sit back on the bed. 'I just got off the 'phone to Gerry.'

'Oh, good. How is he?'

'He's fine, thanks,' the rock star acknowledged her good manners. 'I told him I've bought a new car.'

'Wow! I never knew you were planning to get another one,' the schoolgirl responded, curious about this sudden diversion. 'What sort?'

The showman winked. 'You don't want to talk about my new car, do you?'

'Why not?'

'I told him that, as a father whose perfect and adorable daughter's about to lose her virginity, I'm entitled to buy myself a new Aston. Wouldn't you agree?'

Kierney squirmed at first but came back fighting, wondering if she was being set up. 'Why did you tell Uncle Gerry?'

'I tell Uncle Gerry everything. He's my manager. I have to. It's in the contract.'

'Oh! Complete and utter crap, *Papá*. You can buy a car whenever you want, without having to give anyone a reason. I think you only told him because you wanted to brag about me having sex.'

Jeff denied her accusation, poker-faced. 'Cruel, baby. *Muy, muy cruel.*'

'It's not cruel. It's payback,' she grinned. 'So I'm going to cancel my date with Dylan on Saturday, just so you have to ring Gerry and cancel the order for your new Aston Martin.'

'Oh, will you now?'

'Yes!'

'*Pero, pequeñita,*' the superstar continued, 'you said yourself, not two minutes ago, that I can buy a car whenever I want.'

'*Argh!*' the feisty fifteen-year-old yelled in frustration. '*Va t'en!* I don't want to argue with you anymore. I just want you to be happy for me.'

Jeff raised both hands in front of his face, chuckling at her brazen importunity. 'I *am* happy for you. Alright, already!' he bellowed back. 'I'm not happy for me yet, but I'm sure as hell happy for you. You are so beautiful when you're angry. Of course I'm bloody happy for you. How can I not be? You're growing up and taking the leap into a world where you can wrap men round your little finger. *Buena suerte, pequeñita.* I mean it.'

The fire in Kierney's eyes subsided, and her shoulders drooped. She shuffled herself over the bedclothes until she was once more leaning on the wall, and her father followed suit, stretching himself out across the armchair.

'Thanks. I'm sorry, *Papá.* I didn't mean to shout at you.'

'Yes, you did, and it was a good challenge,' the peacemaker disputed. 'You have every right to raise your voice to me, as I have to you. And I meant it when I said you were beautiful when you're angry. Keep that fire, baby. Use it wisely, but keep it. It'll come in handy when you're Queen of the United Nations.'

'OK,' the young woman nodded, giggling at the fictitious job title. 'Thanks again. I shall. And thanks for the rose. It's very romantic. It makes me feel grown up to receive a rose and a bottle of bubbly. Is it for Saturday night?'

Jeff smiled. 'Yes. It's for Saturday night. Put it in the fridge and ask Dylan to open it. It'll help break the ice. But only have half a glass, or a glass each at most. You don't want to be drunk. It's to take just enough of the edge off so you both lose any inhibitions or fear that might stop you enjoying the moment.'

Girlish again, the teenager crawled along the mattress until she was perched on the end of her bed. 'I can't believe we're talking about this,' she whispered. 'I'm so happy. I thought I'd only be able to tell you afterwards and that you wouldn't want to hear anything about it.'

Her father closed his eyes. 'I'm not sure I will want to hear about it. While it's still hypothetical, I can still ring and cancel my new car. By the time Monday morning comes around, I'll be transferring the cash, and you'll be...'

'Wait a minute!' Kierney's spirit fired up anew. 'What'll I be? I'll still be me. I'll still be your daughter, and I'll still love you the most in the whole wide world. Nothing's going to change, *Papá.*'

'Oh, yeah? So why are you doing it?'

This was a superb question, and the youngster stopped in her tracks. Why was she doing it?

''Cause it's what people do,' the belligerent student answered. 'I'm a human being. A female human being. A male human being wants to have sex with me, and I want to have sex with him.'

Jeff cupped his hands over his ears, but his eyes stared straight ahead. The budding negotiator knew her response had met with the wise man's approval. The pair of dark-haired Diamonds faced off for several seconds before the elder broke ranks.

'What's Dylan's number?' he asked, patting his pants pockets to locate his mobile telephone.

'Why?'

'I'm going to call him. He's not eighteen yet,' the father renewed his concerned tone. 'He's still a minor. I need to protect him too.'

'Oh, bloody hell, *Papá*! You didn't make all this fuss with Jet. In fact, didn't you help him get laid the first time? Stop treating my private life like some surreal film plot.'

Jeff grinned and leaned over to kiss her forehead. 'Whatever you say, Lynn. Christ! You are truly fashioned from us both. I'm only trying to scare you. There's no way I'd interfere to that extent. Where is your *Mamá*? I told her to come and rescue me if I didn't come back after thirty minutes.'

'Rescue *you*?' Kierney cried. 'What about me?'

As if she had been listening at the door, which perhaps she had, the lady of the house rapped a rhythmic riff on her daughter's bedroom door and walked in without waiting for an invitation. She stopped in her tracks when her eyes beheld a lovely sight, transported back to nineteen-seventy-two and her tiny apartment on top of the Dyson Administration building.

Here sat her mysterious, enigmatic stranger, barefoot, relaxed and smiling, lounging in the armchair with his long legs crossed in front at the ankles. The mental picture combined with the present-day scene to steal her breath away. Though his hairstyle was much tidier these days, and his clothes well-tailored and urbane, he was benevolence and wisdom personified. She had been honoured with these qualities for such a long time that it had taken him turning his attention on their little girl to reinforce his omnipotence in her own life.

The enchanted woman must have appeared transfixed by the flashback, jolted back to reality by a wink so disarming that she almost lost her balance. Springing to his feet, her husband needed only two strides to cross the room and take his beautiful best friend's hand.

'You OK? You look like you've seen a ghost.'

'I did see a ghost,' Lynn gasped, smiling at her pair of mischievous gipsies. 'I came through the door and face-to-face with you as you were when we first met.'

'Devillishly handsome,' Jeff prompted her. 'Charming, broke...'

The fifteen-year-old giggled. 'Horny?'

'Kierney!' her mother exclaimed. 'How do you know? You weren't there.'

'As all hell,' he agreed, giving the teenager a thumbs-up. 'As all hell, baby. Speaking of which...'

'Speaking of which?' their daughter cried out. 'What are you going to say?'

The showman turned to his *regala*, eyes once more brimming with tears. 'Isn't she so beautiful when she's aroused? Almost as beautiful as her *mamá*, which is a death-defying feat in itself. I think we've reached an agreement here. Shall we adjourn to the drawing room and get shitfaced? I think we all deserve a drink.'

'To celebrate your new car,' Kierney vaulted off her bed to hug both parents.

'Yeah. Something like that,' her father grinned. 'Can't think of any other reason that's earned us a drink. Can you, *pequeñita*?'

'No, *Papá*.'

Shaking her head at the matching angelic rascals scheming together, Lynn held the door open and ushered them into the corridor. On their way to the northern side of their city home, the strength of Jeff's grip on her waist threatened to snap her in two, but she didn't mind. Their paths diverged outside the hall cupboard which doubled as the family's wine store, amid promises of undying love and scornful jeers from the embarrassed teenager.

The songwriter passed Kierney two bottles of *Shiraz*, asking her to open them and let them breathe. While she attended to this errand, he headed to the kitchen for a cold beer to kick the evening off, only to find his dream girl waiting for him with one.

'Cheers! Mmm... Smells delicious,' he said, kissing her with chilled lips. 'Can we help with anything?'

The amorous woman shook her head. 'Crawler! It's ready. You two sit down and conclude your negotiations.'

When the showman reached the lounge room, Kierney slapped the cushion next to her on the couch. He paused to pour three glasses of wine, passing her two and leaving the third on the coffee table for his wife. The volume had been turned down on the evening news, and his heavy weight landing on the soft leather caused the remote control to slip between two cushions.

Raising his hands in dismay, Jeff reclaimed his glass and reached a long arm behind her shoulders to cuddle up. 'To Saturday night,' he toasted, kissing his precious child on the temple. 'And to my new car.'

'To Saturday night and your new car. There was another question I was going to ask, *Papá*, if that's OK?'

'Ah, yeah?'

'Yeah. How do you know if people are beautiful on the inside? You always say you think *Mamá*'s even more beautiful on the inside than on the outside.'

Right on cue, the tennis champion arrived carrying a tray laden with three steaming servings of hot *chilli* noodles. With ballerina-like poise, she bent over with a straight back and lowered it to the coffee table, handing round forks and bowls.

'Thanks, *Mamá*,' Kierney said, clinking her glass with her mother's.

'Thanks, *Mamá*,' the larrikin echoed, eyes flashing in appreciation. 'Kiz was pondering how she'll recognise inner beauty.'

Lynn paused for a couple of seconds, sipping her wine. 'When someone smiles,' she answered. 'People who don't smile can't be beautiful on the inside. That's my answer, for what it's worth. Not a forced, say-cheese sort of smile. Just natural. Even the plainest person with a smile on his or her face is more attractive than the most classically good-looking supermodel who scowls all the time. Don't you think?'

'But anyone can smile,' her daughter objected, digging her fork into the spicy sauce and twisting it in a circle. 'How do you know if a smile's sincere?'

'Good observation,' Jeff acknowledged. 'You can't always tell. That's the black art of a con' man. Or woman. They suck you in; make you think they're your best buddy and then stitch you up. For me, I don't think it's always possible to detect genuine beauty 'til you've known someone for a while. You're more trusting than I am, angel. We need to trust our instincts, I guess. People who seem to care about others and not just about themselves.'

The Olympian grinned at her long-time lover, who had a tendancy to care about others way too much. 'That's good advice, darling. You always need to be wary of hidden agendas. If you're referring to Dylan though, you already know he's no con' man.'

'Hope not!' the teenager grinned. 'But to be on the safe side, I shan't let him near the priceless family heirlooms on Saturday.'

Her father scoffed. 'Heirlooms? Do we have any? This is bloody tasty, angel. Not sure *Shiraz* is the best accompaniment after all, but regardless... So ladies, have you picked your weekend of credit card abuse yet?'

'So you know how much time you've got to hock our treasures?' Lynn quipped. 'Three weeks away. I'm booking flights to Sydney for Thursday evening, coming back on Sunday afternoon. Is that alright?'

'Sure thing. Better increase your baggage allowance. For once, I'm glad not to be invited.'

Smiling at their daughter, the singer shrugged. 'You can come if you like. We'll tell you all about it. Can I just say thanks to you both for sorting whatever you sorted out out about Saturday's big event?'

'You can,' Jeff gave her a baffled look. 'And you're welcome.'

'I didn't do anything,' their daughter added, ashamed. 'I didn't buy you a rose and a bottle of champagne. You made all the concessions. All I did was argue with you.'

'Maybe,' her father replied, pointing his fork in her direction and making both women laugh. 'You listened to what I had to say. You were gracious when you thought I was stalling by talking about the new car, and you didn't give in. You stood your ground; proved you're mature enough to handle a bloke lording it over you.'

Kierney sat straighter on the couch. 'Oh! I see. Thanks.'

'Y'know, baby... There's a big difference between respect and subservience. You were respectful to me just now, but you didn't agree with me until I said something you believed in. That's an important trait, and one you'd do well to make use of in bed with your hopefully-not-too-long series of lovers.'

'*Papá!*' Kierney attempted to hide her affront. 'Thanks again for the vote of confidence, but I haven't even had one lover yet. You're already turning me into a sex maniac!'

'Like father, like daughter,' Lynn interjected. 'Another important inherited trait, if your brother's anything to go by. Anyway, we've got your birthday to arrange too, Jeff. Tell me your desires, oh-master.'

The race to his forty-second birthday had been consigned to the nether reaches of the musician's mind in recent weeks. With the fallout from Brooke's death, a number of controversial peace-keeping missions to Africa and the current set of concerts on the "Live on Earth" tour keeping them all busy, it wouldn't have troubled him to let the second of June pass by unnoticed.

He paused for a moment, recalling an idea that had occurred to him while speaking with Gerry earlier in the evening. 'D'you want to invite your parents to dinner?'

'What?' his wife's jaw dropped, her eyes travelling from husband to daughter and back again. 'Would you repeat that, please? I think I lost something in translation.'

'*J'ai dit que je voudrais inviter tes parents à dîner avec nous pour mon anniversaire, mon amie.* I need to apologise for being such an arsehole to them twenty years ago.'

The tennis champion let her fork fall into her empty bowl. 'OK... That's what I thought you said, and you don't need to do anything of the sort! That's long repaired. You weren't an arsehole anyway. Well, not much of one... You've proven yourself right and them wrong a hundred times over since then. I'll invite them if you want, but they'd be embarrassed if they found out the real reason.'

'Then that'll make three of us,' the former renegade son-of-a-double-murderer mumbled into his wine. 'Your mum told me I'd understand their objections one day if I had a daughter of my own, and she was damned right.'

'But…' Kierney mimicked her father's swashbuckling cutlery manœuvre. 'Didn't *Mamá* also tell "G" and "G" that you'd let your daughter choose whom she went out with?'

'I did say that,' Lynn nodded. 'You've got a good memory. So do you think *Papá*'s shown you he'll let you choose?'

'Yeah! Definitely. I think you'd have reacted the same no matter whom I brought home; good, clean-cut boy or headstrong, would-be rock star. Don't you?'

'To be perfectly honest, I'm not sure, but I hope so,' her dad frowned, still troubled by both extreme positions. 'We need to test the hypothesis before I can declare my parental superiority. Bring home someone like me, *pequeñita*, and then we'll find out.'

May I Borrow Your Daughter?

'Ooh, *Mamá*,' Kierney swooned, brushing the softness of a silk dress across her forearm. 'This is so nice. Feel it!'

The Diamond ladies had been shopping all afternoon on their home turf, the Paris end of Collins Street, after the Olympian had been forced to change their plans due to a last-minute speaking engagement which took priority. Leaving Jeff under the panel van at *Escondido* and Gerry supervising from afar, the women rated Melbourne's retail establishments more highly than Sydney's any day.

Consequently, having transported their many purchases home by taxi, Lynn and Kierney ensconced themselves in the apartment before the shops closed on Friday evening. They spent an hour trying on various items and comparing notes before strolling back through the grid for a slap-up meal at *Vue de Monde*.

'The trick is to minimise "Oh, my God!" and maximise "Wow!"' Lynn explained over their *entrées*, swapping voices for each reaction. 'Always dress so people have to look further to see anything interesting.'

'Men, you mean?'

Her mother sighed. 'Yes. Men mostly. Whether it's right or wrong, justified or not, people are going to judge you by the way you look. If you want them to pay attention to your many other attributes, the best way is to give them nothing to pick holes in where your appearance is concerned. And the other trick is to make sure you're comfy when you move, no matter what you're wearing. Not feeling like you need to constantly tug your neckline upwards or skirt hem down.'

'Ha! I know what that's like. Piraea always wears such short skirts to parties, and then she spends the entire time with a napkin or her jacket over her legs. She can't even stand up to get another drink or whatever.'

Lynn nodded. Her daughter's best friend was a little too immodest for her own good. She felt sorry for her parents, so far away in Ireland and unable to monitor how much flesh the sixteen-year-old revealed to the randy young men in Melbourne Academy's senior years.

'Convenient!'

'Convenient?' her daughter yelped. 'What do you mean by that?'

447

'Convenient for her bank balance perhaps...'

'Oh! Yes. Sorry!'

Her mother smiled. 'That's OK. You're tired. It's good to hear you defend your mate. And sure, there are times when you'll want to dress overtly sexily, like for friends' parties or for a special date at home. But when you're out in public, and if you want to leave people with a sophisticated impression, you need to dress according to what you want people to notice. Men... heterosexual ones, that is... can't keep their eyes off bare thighs and breasts, but seldom like to see their girlfriends flaunting them.'

Kierney chuckled. 'Sounds like chicken pieces! But I do get what you're saying.'

After a good night's sleep to rest their feet, the two unaccustomed shoppers embarked upon six more hours of self-indulgence at the Chadstone shopping centre, where discerning Melburnians went to stock up on designer labels. They mooched through Giorgio Armani and Collette Dinnegan, swooning over beautiful items which were vastly overpriced, before breaking for facials, a quick lunch and a new plan to visit some of the more affordable stores where the youngster recognised outfits worn by her school friends.

They *schlepped* the whole length of Chapel Street in South Yarra, remaining empty-handed until eleven o'clock on Sunday morning. Lynn had interspersed their *haute couture* research with pearl after pearl of wisdom. The teenager learned how to vary her make-up for each type of outing, when to wear short dresses and when long, how to carry herself in a ballgown as opposed to skin-tight jeans, and how to bend down without giving your guests too much to see.

Kierney was an avid listener, keen to study other women's tastes in the shops and ready to wrestle control of debates with overbearing sales assistants, if only to get rid of them as her mother occasionally demonstrated! She watched the slender, blonde athlete carefully, imitating her elegant mannerisms as she followed from shop to shop: the way her handbag hung behind her right arm, shielded from opportunistic thieves; the way she managed to lift her chair without scraping it along the floor as she left a table.

With the weekend drawing to a close, they ended up back at the beginning, quite deliberately, to collect Friday's alterations and to make a final stop. Harking back to a bygone era, some of the most exclusive boutiques on Collins Street remained "by appointment only", including David Keith, the Dyson family's tailor for half a century. Long since retired, the shop's original owner had sold it for a song to a *cadre* of his most loyal staff members, who saw fit to treat the Diamonds with the utmost deference, fussing around them to the point of distraction.

'Can we go home soon, please?' Kierney whispered when both assistants were out of earshot. 'I'm in danger of sinking a stiletto into Jerome's head shortly.'

'Yuck!' her mother grimaced. 'What a horrible image. Might not be such a bad idea in that case. I must say, you've done well to get this far. I didn't expect you to stay the distance. Try these things on, and we'll have something to show for your dedication when we next see *Papá*.'

The teenager obliged, contenting herself with thoughts of the evening's upcoming visit to the new Kino cinema, where they had booked to see Stephan Elliott's "The Adventures of Priscilla, Queen of the Desert". Billed as an iconic *Aussie* adventure, it promised a bizarre storyline based on a group of drag queens travelling across the outback in a bus. Despite themes inherently adult, it was unlikely to showcase anything the precocious fifteen-year-old hadn't already dissected through her parents' association with the entertainment world.

Just before five o'clock, the elegant blonde called time on their mammoth day of retail therapy. Two taxis, travelling in opposite directions, nearly collided when responding to a single wave of her authoritative hand. Not wishing to hold up traffic for too long, the pair threw their assortment of bags and boxes into the nearer boot. Once safely inside the apartment, they flopped down on the king-sized bed in the master bedroom and ripped off their shoes in a simultaneous rush of relief, turning to each other and bursting out laughing.

'Whose bloody idea was it to spend a whole day shopping?' Lynn asked. 'Riddle me this, *pequeñita*. I dare you.'

'*Papá*, your voice is different,' the teenager replied. 'I think you'll find it was your idea, angel. It was fun! Mostly anyway... And thanks for all these things. I won't have to go shopping again for at least five years.'

The superstar was pleased with her daughter's answer. For children who had been brought up with the best that money could buy, neither Jet nor Kierney was interested in buying "stuff" for the sake of it. The skill she was more intent on passing on to her tall, willowy daughter was how to wear the "stuff" she did buy to maximum effect. Her own mother had taken the trouble to pass on her immaculate taste in a similar way; sage advice never forgotten.

After a shower and a quick selection of evening apparel, the pair left the building again, to walk the five minutes round the corner to Florentino's on Bourke Street. While they strode past the lines of gaping mouths, Lynn reminisced about the night she and Jeff had dined there with Michelle and one particular boyfriend, when they had witnessed their fellow diners' short relationship unravel in quite dramatic fashion.

Kierney rippled with youthful enthusiasm, asking endless questions and analysing every angle with replenished energy reserves. The fateful Saturday night with Dylan was a huge success, and with it the guarantee that sparse detail would be conveyed to her relieved parents. Suffice to say that a second, third and fourth date had since been arranged and enjoyed, giving the young woman immense confidence and a certain triumphant air which reminded Lynn acutely of her husband.

'So are you and *Papá* alright with my baptism into the world of sex?'

'As we'll ever be,' her mother answered with a wry smile. 'There's probably always going to be some level of discomfort, simply because you're our little girl. Where did she go, that sweet little innocent mite who liked to bake cupcakes and stamp her feet a lot? Now we've got Lolita living in our midst.'

The teenager dipped her eyes and focussed on pushing food onto her fork. 'Ew! Not sure that's a good thing. Do you think I've gone too early?'

'No, darling. You're enjoying yourself, and it's lovely to see. It's entirely up to you and Dylan. Not many parents get to watch at such close quarters, so we feel privileged that you're even talking to us about it. My mum and dad certainly didn't know… or rather, didn't care to know… how often *Papá* and I spent the night together in the first few months. I was living at Admin full-time, and sometimes I wouldn't see my mum between Benloch weekends. She left me to my own devices.'

'Pretty progressive for those days,' Kierney ventured. 'I'm surprised at Grandma.'

'So was I, to be honest. Those days? You make us sound ancient! I was given heaps more freedom than most of my friends. I should thank Sandy and Anna for that. They were so much younger than Junior and me, so Mum spent her parenting hours on them rather than us. Plus, I suppose we'd proven well enough that they could trust us to get ourselves from training to school to homework, *et cetera*, without having to chase us.'

The young woman smiled. 'Worked out well for *Papá* then, didn't it? I can't imagine him waiting for you to finish your homework or making sure you were home by ten o'clock. He would've been so critical of such petty restrictions.'

'That's what he'd like you to believe!' Australia's darling laughed. 'In reality, he wouldn't have had any choice in the matter. But you're right. He got lucky. He only had me to brainwash.'

'Brainwash? Do you think he brainwashed you?'

'Absolutely he did! You know how persuasive he can be. He was much worse back then too 'cause he was so fanatical. He could talk himself into or out of anything. Your *papá* had me hypnotised from Day One.'

'In a good way though?' Kierney asked, concerned. 'I hope you fell in love with him unhypnotised. Or have you just never snapped out of the trance?'

Lynn stared into the distance, helping herself to more salad. 'Who knows, darling? I have no regrets, if that's what you mean. And if I'm in a trance, it's been the happiest, most satisfying trance ever. So frankly, my dear, I don't give a damn!'

'Good! Did you ever doubt you were with the man of your dreams?'

'Oh, yes,' her mother answered. 'Heaps of times. In the early days especially.'

'Because *Papá* was your first?'

'Yes, but not only that. It was hard work coping with your dad's erratic behaviour. He could be so "in *yer* face", as they say in downtown Ulaan Baatar. Everything had to happen right then and there. He was so fearful the moment would pass and he'd never get another chance to do whatever it was. It was pretty scary sometimes. The funny thing… and probably part of what kept me from packing it all in… was the way he was so upfront about the fact that he was coercing me into things! Like he had no control over it, which was only half true. I felt like I had to believe him, with this sort of brutal honesty. Looking back on it, those first few months were extremely stressful.'

'Did you ever want to dump him?'

'No. Never. Until I had to.'

'When you went to California?' the teenager's face fell. 'Must've been so horrible. Let's not talk about that again.'

The nostalgic musician finished her last mouthful and swilled some water around her mouth. Good idea, she thought. Some memories were painful even after two decades. No-one could deny that "the gap years", as the couple now referred to their relationship's hiatus, had played a vital role in turning them into their all-conquering selves. Jeff Diamond and Lynn Dyson were survivors on a grand scale, epitomising the very courage, resilience and persistence they instilled into young and old through their various campaigns.

'Even though it was devastating at the time, splitting up allowed me to find out if *Papá* really was the man of my dreams,' she told her daughter instead. 'It gave me the space to date other men, and I quickly found out that none was anywhere near as attractive to me as Jeff Diamond.'

The fifteen-year-old swooned. 'Maybe you were still hypnotised. *Papá* planted the seed in your head to tell you that all the other men were morons.'

'Morons?' her mum chuckled. 'I'm not sure that's fair. It doesn't give me much credit for choosing exemplary male company.'

'Sorry!' Kierney giggled. 'Yeah. That didn't sound too good, did it? I bet all your boyfriends were extra-handsome.'

'Most were, I must admit. I became super-defiant during those two years in the US. Your *papá*'s ideas about meaningless relationships had rubbed off on me. I never picked anyone with the future in mind, 'cause my heart was broken. Just made sure I had some fun. Put it that way…'

A pair of waiters swooped on the diners' empty plates, only seconds after the youngster had rested her cutlery onto her plate. Glancing at her watch, Lynn wondered if their romantic conversation had made them late for the cinema. There was plenty of time, as it turned out, so she accepted the offer of dessert menus.

The young woman's eyes widened, intrigued by these insights. 'What does it feel like when your heart's broken? Is it a real thing, a broken heart? It looks like you can still feel it.'

'Desperate,' Lynn replied without hesitation. 'Horrible, like you'll never get over it in a million years. I felt lonely for the first time in my life. In fact, it was fortunate it got broken with your dad, rather than anyone else, because he prepared us so well for what we'd go through. Thanks to his grasp on how our minds work, I was able to get on with life reasonably easily during that low time in my life. Even though we hadn't even really spent that much time together in 'seventy-two, when I was travelling almost every week and preparing for the Olympics, *Papá* completely consumed me. It was as if I did everything for him, and then when he wasn't part of my life anymore, it felt completely empty.'

'Wow,' Kierney gasped. 'Sounds unbearable. I hope I never have my heart broken.'

'You might at some stage, darling. I don't mean to wish it on you, but most people have a painful break-up or two during their life. It's all about picking yourself up and carrying on. The easier you can do that, the better.'

'How long does the desperate feeling last?'

'Depends how quickly you can pick yourself up and carry on. Everyone's different.'

The teenager persisted. 'No. For you, I mean. Not for the whole two years, I hope.'

'No. Six months or so, I s'pose. I left for Munich just before my birthday and didn't feel normal until at least the following April. And it was made worse in a way when *Papá*'s career took off like a storm. His picture was all over the place, and his music was on the radio every day. He was haunting me!'

Kierney felt tears pricking behind her eyes. She had asked her father the same set of questions not long ago, receiving similar answers. Being privy to his hair-raising accounts of addiction and self-destructive habits, she and her brother had vowed never to allow themselves to descend to depths so profound that drugs and alcohol were their only options.

'How come you didn't drink and take drugs to make yourself feel better? In California, of all places! It must've been very easy to get them.'

'Far too easy,' Lynn agreed. 'There'd be something going down at every party. I never developed a need for them, luckily. I had your grandpa's years and years of physical education and psychological *mumbo-jumbo* drummed into me, so I shied away from anything dodgy. And I definitely didn't want to become addicted, 'cause I could see the effect it was having on other people around me.'

'And on *Papá*,' her daughter added.

'Yes. It was awful seeing photos of him looking so gaunt and wasted, but in all honesty, he looked like all the other rock musicians of the time: Keith Richards and Mick Jagger, and most of the heavy metal dudes. Even some of the girls were heavily into drugs... If anything, I was the odd one out, and I tried not to think about what *Papá* might be putting into his body. Or around it, come to think of it...'

The gorgeous gipsy girl smiled. 'You mean the women?'

The women. There they were... Two innocuous words which never failed to worm their way straight into the dignified star's gut. How grateful she was for the new Jeff's continuing fidelity, and also for the sanctuary afforded by her *naivetée* while the the old Jeff flitted between her bed and his duplicitous parallel universe as a sexual mercenary. The length of their marriage bore no correlation to the amount of jealousy each felt about the other; an occupational hazard both had learned to accommodate.

Her mother nodded. 'It was crazy back then, Kizzy! There'd be some new scandal every single week concerning The Australian Elvis. The press blew every story well out of proportion. No surprise, I guess! Jeff Diamond seen at so-and-so's party with half-naked girls hanging off his arms, looking like he was enjoying himself a great deal. Actually, hearing what he was up to did help heal my broken heart quite a bit. And of course, he claims they were always designed to help me out as much as to help himself out!'

Kierney laughed at yet another typically convenient excuse. 'Did he? Bit of a stretch! Do you believe him?'

'No! It's utter bullshit, if you don't mind me saying. Except that I did manage to convince myself he'd forgotten me, which worked to a certain extent.'

A waitress brought the two ladies a dessert to share, thoroughly gluttonous and evil. They clashed their long-handled spoons together several times, each competing with the other to scoop up the tastiest morsels.

'*¡Delicioso!*' Kierney exclaimed, smacking her lips when all that remained on the plate were a few smears of syrupy sauce. 'I'm so full. Chocky overdose! But anyway, how did it feel when you finally saw *Papá* again after all that time? It must have been nerve-wracking.'

Lynn folded her napkin into rough eighths and placed it to one side, leaning forward with her elbows resting on the tablecloth. Even now, she could barely contain her emotions when she called this amazing night to mind. She had been so determined to stay away from Jeff, as her parents had commanded, only to have their latent love affair reignite of its own accord as they stood face to face once more.

'Oh, Kierney,' she moaned. 'You cannot believe how good it was to feel those arms around me again after so long. It was as if he were the only one who could turn me on. His language was rich, his voice deeper, his hands held tighter... Everything I remembered from before was a hundred times more intense. It felt like I'd come home, and *Papá* said exactly the same. Not home in the sense of a place, but much more profound.'

'Yay!' her daughter cheered. 'That sounds so amazing.'

'It was amazing, darling. Really amazing. When I spoke just now about feeling empty and heartbroken... Well, the emptiness totally vanished at that precise moment, and it's never come back.'

'*Papá* filled the void.'

Her mother grinned at the *cliché*. 'Yes, quite. No-one else could light me up the way he did, and does! Other boyfriends had been the proverbial square pegs in a round hole.'

'*Mamá*! That's rude as!' the teenager smiled, pressing her fingers to her lips in surprise that such an expression should emerge from such a flawless mouth.

'Only if you want it to be,' impish eyes flashed back. 'I'll go as far as to say that *Papá*'s shape was very irregular indeed. No-one else was going to fit in the space he left in me.'

The youngster giggled. 'Hmm... Do you still feel that way?'

'Oh, yes! Without a shadow of a doubt. We're very, very lucky, darling. Not every love is as deep as ours. Or as enduring. It doesn't matter if you're Lynn Dyson, tennis player, or Kierney, songwriter *extraordinaire*, or the lady who empties the bins in the office. It can happen to any of us. And when it does, grab it with both hands. Build your life around it. Not the other way round, like everyone'll advise you.'

'Oh, I shall. It sounds so inviting. I hope I feel that way one day.'

'I hope you do too,' Lynn replied, stroking her daughter's cheek. 'It's the best feeling ever. Makes you feel so alive, to love someone with all your heart, body and soul, and then to have them love you back the same way. It'll happen to you soon, I'm sure, because you can see the magic. You might have to wait a bit longer than we did, but there's nothing to stop you having fun while you're waiting.'

'It won't be Dylan,' the student frowned. 'I already know that. He's lovely, but he's not the man of my dreams.'

'No,' Lynn smiled, looking at her watch again, 'which is fine for now. Hey, look! It's getting late. We'd better go or we'll miss the start.'

***

Lynn and Kierney were up early on Sunday morning, heading for the Sportsdrome at first light. They had fallen into bed exhausted after the movie, waking clear-headed and ready for their final day of female togetherness. With an entertaining plot, hilarious dialogue and a cast of big-screen favourites, "Priscilla" had made a strong impression on both women.

The complex issues of discrimination against a person's gender and sexuality, together with the many ways of avoiding the drudgery of everyday life, were dissected in the gymnasium, interspersed with lessons on deportment and the wide variety of ways to wear a bra' to enhance different outfits.

Mobbed by adoring fans as they waited for their breakfasts to arrive on Clarendon Street, the celebrities bargained the ability to eat in peace by agreeing to an advance session of "As and Ps"; yet another exercise in grace and poise for the teenager. Lynn ordered their second coffees in takeaway cups, and they jumped into a taxi bound for the recording studio, where mother and daughter experimented with arrangements for a raft of new songs penned by the precocious talent.

'These are really good,' the teacher praised, picking out one of the melodies on the keyboard from a piece of crumpled manuscript paper produced from Kierney's bag. 'They're much more sophisticated than mine at your age.'

'Rubbish!' the teenager cried. 'I don't believe that. You'd already had a hit album by my age.'

Lynn shrugged. 'Not on my own. I was part of a machine. Virtually nothing was created by me in isolation. That's a big difference, Kizzy. Compared to yours, my songs were simple, formulaic and rigid. I stuck to the structure I was taught. I hardly ever contemplated breaking the rules.'

'And mine are totally unstructured,' Kierney laughed, banging out a series of loud chords while her *pro bono* sound engineer played with the levels.

Over the following three hours, lost in their creative endeavour, the pair rambled back and forth through the hand-scrawled pages. The elder taught her *protégée* how to put sufficient contours around her songs to make them more likely to seep into people's brains. In return, the younger nudged these creative boundaries whenever she could.

'You need a hook for people to latch onto,' her mother insisted, 'otherwise the song'll pass them by. Hook 'em in, and they'll like it, learn it and buy it.'

'Did you speak to *Papá* last night?' Kierney asked during a quick coffee break.

'Yeah. Well, sort of,' Lynn frowned. 'He was incoherent, to put it mildly.'

The teenager chuckled. 'Oh, was he? Oops! While the cat's away...'

'Something like that. It's always a bad sign when he tells me he loves us about twenty times in the space of five minutes.'

The teenager understood. 'Aw! At least he wasn't so drunk as to block us out completely. Who was there?'

'The Pre-modernists,' the singer said, using the nickname Jeff used for some of his longstanding band members, 'and Gerry, of course. Playing poker 'til all hours, I expect.'

Tipping her mug up to drain the last few drops of coffee, Kierney groaned. 'Sounds ugly. Glad we weren't there. Did you tell him what we did yesterday?'

Her mother shook her head. 'I started to, but then he got all tired and emotional on me, so I gave up. And I woke up to a hysterical text message this morning.'

'So did I. I wonder if it was the same as mine.'

'I certainly hope not!' Lynn raised her eyebrows. 'And that's all I'm saying.'

The *débutante* blushed. 'OK, good! I don't want to know in that case. Thanks for spending your weekend with me, *Mamá*. I know how much you've got to do before you fly out again. These've been a fantastic few days.'

Holding a hand out for her daughter's empty cup, the taskmaster instructed them to knuckle down. They returned to the sound-desk, where Lynn began to play back the song they had been working on before their break. She explained how the various tracks could be overlaid on each other, to simulate the vocals being in front of the instruments, for example.

Still distracted however, the novice songwriter grabbed her caring mentor around the waist and hugged her tightly. 'Is it OK if I don't have kids 'til I'm thirty?'

'Perfectly OK,' her mother answered. 'It's not up to me! You can have children whenever you and your partner want to. Do you think you'll get married?'

'I don't know. Should I?'

Lynn smiled. 'I can't answer that either, can I, you dag? It's your choice. Marriage seems to get less and less relevant as the years go by. It'll be two-thousand-and-nine by the time you're thirty. It's hard to guess how much more liberal society might be by then. I expect it'll be much more acceptable for children to be born out of wedlock. God, I hate that expression! I mean to *de facto* couples, or even people who don't want to be a family at all.'

Pulling a face at the antiquated term, the beautiful woman was once more spirited back to June nineteen-seventy-four and to the rushed birthday meal she and Jeff had shared atop the World Trade Center before her concert at Madison Square Garden. They had included children in their future plans for the first time, and she remembered stepping out on stage that night as a different woman.

'Yeah,' Kierney said, waving her hand in front of staring eyes. 'It sounds like warlock or hemlock. Them's the devil's words, Momma. Were you surprised *Papá* wanted to get married?'

'Oh, yes! Extremely surprised. Our year in London changed him heaps. I think he finally felt like he belonged in the world, rather than leaning on its fence and observing as an outsider. Much more respectful of tradition and happy to take part in things.'

'Why?'

'Don't know,' the thoughtful woman paused before responding. 'He just grew up, I suppose. Grew out of the childhood anger and grudges that'd kept the rest of the world at arms' length. And perhaps also because he'd had a chance to live in an older culture; came to appreciate the weight of history around him, if you like. There's one thing no-one can accuse your father of, and that's not giving things the benefit of the doubt. Oh, and Jenna forcing her way into Gerry's life certainly gave them both a wake-up call too.'

'Really? In what way?'

The thirty-eight-year-old smiled. 'There was a seismic shift in *Papá* and Gerry's relationship during that year. It almost passed us by, with the two of them on opposite sides of the world. Good thing too, I reckon, 'cause there'd have been fireworks if they'd gone through it in the same time-zone! Their friendship may not have survived as well as it did.'

Confusion spread across the young woman's face. She couldn't imagine her father and her irreverent Uncle Gerry not being the best of friends. It was all she had ever known.

'But how come? What happened?'

'Well...' her mother explained. 'Up until your dad became a superstar, it was always Gerry who'd been in charge. Or that's what he thought. Gerry, I mean. *Papá*'ll say he'd been working the puppet strings all along, but I'm not entirely convinced about that.'

'Was it because *Papá* suddenly had more money than him, and Uncle Gerry started managing it for him?'

'No,' Lynn shook her head. 'Well, yes. That's true too, but it was more to do with who held the moral high-ground. As *Papá* became more successful, and people started to listen to his opinions and not just his music, his confidence grew in leaps and bounds. Everyone began to look up to him. Important people who were nothing to do with the music business. And therefore even your good, old Gerald Blake Junior...'

'Wow!' Kierney gasped. 'I see now. That must've been a good feeling for *Papá*. And a big responsibility too.'

'*¡Exactemente, pequeñita!*' the Olympian laughed, thinking how honoured her husband would have been to hear this casual observation. 'Precisely what I'm trying to say. When Gerry found out he was going to be a dad, *Papá* agonised over what was best for this baby and tried to persuade Gerry to marry Heather so they could give their child the best start in life.'

'Ahh... That's so sweet. He's such a softie.'

'Well, no, actually!' her mother countered. 'Far from it. *Papá* gave Gerry a long lecture about thinking about someone other than himself for a change, but it also made him start thinking about our children and that he faced the same duty when you guys arrived. He had to take his own medicine.'

'Jesus Christ!' Kierney channelled her dark-haired nemesis. 'I see what you mean about seismic shift. And all for Jetto and me.'

'Indeed. And for me too. He decided that I, with my conservative parents and upbringing, and having grown up in the public eye, would rather not have bastard children, as he called them.'

'Oh, yuck,' the teenager grimaced. 'It does sound unappealing when you say it that way. I wouldn't have minded if you weren't married though.'

Lynn cocked her head, pointing to the clock. 'No? I think you might've. We haven't got much longer. I bet you always knew the kids at school whose parents weren't married.'

'Yeah. Maybe.'

'It's getting easier, slowly. But when you two were little, it was still a scandal to have a family without getting married first. It was almost more acceptable for women to be single mothers than it was to live in sin with a man.'

Kierney took a moment to consider this last sentence, grinning as the esteemed musician drew imaginary quotation marks around the expression "in sin". 'Hmm... I can see how that'd happen,' she said. 'If you're a single mum, the child most likely came along by accident, and you wanted to do the right thing. Whereas if you carry on living with the man, it's like you're not a real couple. Legally, I mean.'

'Quite so,' the older woman switched to her own mother's voice. 'Clever clogs. Even though the baby might grow up with two sensible and devoted parents, it was still seen to be a sub-standard situation for kids to grow up in back then. Still now too, to some extent. So, because *Papá* was determined our family'd never be sub-standard, like the one he'd grown up in, he decided we should get married first, like the fine, upstanding Australian citizens we claimed to be.'

'Jolly good show!' the teenager crowed. 'Three cheers for *Papá*. But he likes being married, doesn't he?'

'Yes, of course he does,' Lynn smiled. 'I think he adjusted to the idea more quickly than I did, in fact. I remember him telling me, just after he proposed, that... What were the words he used? Oh, something like he didn't want to be left in *"fiancé limbo"* for long.'

Her daughter laughed. '*"Fiancé limbo"?* That's so funny. He has a big problem with any kind of *limbo*, doesn't he? The same as before I'd had sex. He was fine before I mentioned it, then fine after it'd happened, but completely off his trolley in the *limbo* phase. I can't wait to talk to him about that.'

The tennis champion stood up to stretch her legs, twisting her spine until it clicked. The insightful teenager had clearly lost interest in the music. Her head was in the stratosphere this morning, off on an entirely different mission. She imagined her husband beaming with delight.

'You may well be onto something, Kizzy,' she nodded. 'Shall we finish up here? Is there anything else you want to do, or shall I shut everything down?'

Gazing around at the random assortment of instruments and scattered sheet music, the burgeoning hit-maker murmured a guilty apology. Her mother was unconcerned by this loss of focus, since she was like Jeff when it came to musical inspiration. Unlike the blond side of the family's strict Dyson work ethic, the two dark-haired Diamonds were powered by a much more esoteric dynamic.

'And so why are you so dead-set on having kids after you're thirty?' Lynn asked, beginning to tidy the studio for its next booking.

Kierney span round, certitude shining from her flushed face. 'Mainly because I don't want my children to spend all day in day care. I won't be able to take them to work, like you did, will I?' she reasoned. 'If I want to work at the UN, I can hardly have toddlers crawling around my feet. What would Boutros Boutros Gali say if my baby *barfed* all over his suit jacket?'

Her mother chuckled, stoked to hear an element of seriousness in the young woman's comic reply. Their offspring's ambitions were more targetted than her own at the same age, as much a product of their generation as of their high-achieving parents.

'There are alternatives,' the hard-working parent smiled. 'We're lucky we live in a country which allows women some say in our lives. As independent women who like to challenge the norms, if we lived somewhere like North Korea or Burma, we'd most likely be in prison for views above our station. How would you feel about your husband or partner being a stay-at-home dad, for example? Anything's possible.'

Kierney's eyes dropped, suddenly finding her fingernails fascinating. Lynn thought she detected some melancholy but didn't press the issue. The teenager had plenty of time to research options for childcare, so it seemed a little strange that she should be upset about them now.

'You know, *Mamá...*' she said, lifting her head and making eye contact. 'I'm not sure I even want to have kids. Is that bad?'

'Bad?' the blonde beauty echoed. 'It's not a question of good or bad. Plenty of women choose not to have children, and I'm sure some regret having them because of the demands they put on their freedom. Remember you're only fifteen, Kizzo. There's no point putting pressure on yourself to make these decisions. Only a few minutes ago, you were planning to be twice your current age before having kids. That's your whole lifetime again of thinking time! You'll probably change your mind ten times in that period.'

The teenager gasped, realising she was worrying over nothing. 'Oh, thanks! That makes me feel better. I didn't know how you'd feel. Like you'd miss out on grandkids, 'specially if Jet doesn't want them either. I feel obliged to, somehow, but don't know why. You were only a few years older than me when you had Jet, and I just can't envision devoting so much of my energy to a tiny, defenceless mini-person. It's frightening 'cause I still feel pretty defenceless myself.'

'Then stop thinking about it,' her mother laughed. 'File it away in the "Not Important Right Now" folder. You have no idea who your partner's going to be yet, so don't start making plans for a family. Just because *Papá* and I started young doesn't mean you have to too. That doesn't follow at all. I can't imagine your brother having children in his twenties, can you? What you should be concentrating on now is finding the right balance between all the various aspects of your life: school, music, boys, the UN, and the list goes on. See what I mean?'

'Yes,' the youngster sighed.

'And while you're doing all this, you'll meet a diverse cross-section of mankind who'll help you work out the type of partner you need. All while trying *not* to get pregnant!'

Kierney shrieked. 'Right! That's clear then. Just mess around for a while. Do you think Jet'll have kids?'

'I have no clue,' the singer scoffed. 'He's certainly excelling at messing around for a while. No worries there. I'm not in a hurry to be a grandma either, so please don't do it on our account.'

'Ew! Sorry. Yeah. I guess this is all a bit premature for you. You guys'll be the sexiest, coolest grandparents ever.'

***

The last six months of nineteen-ninety-four whizzed past in a whirlwind of film and album releases, racing through the last few cities on the mammoth tour and culminating in both children passing their end-of-year examinations with high distinction.

As planned, Jet moved to Cambridge in early October for his first term at university and had experienced a turbulent cycle of new emotions ranging from elation at his independence and homesickness for all people and places familiar. Above all, he reported, was a sense of empowerment at having made a fresh circle of friends and settled into a foreign country all under his own steam.

Kierney missed her brother, she was at pains to admit, even though their lives had taken quite divergent paths in recent months. She had starred in her first Hollywood movie while completing Year Eleven, alongside a slew of A-list names. The raw honesty she brought to her role drew parallels with her father's catalogue of memorable performances, attracting both rave reviews and the occasional poisoned arrow of criticism aimed at her youthful good fortune and the same accusations of nepotism as had been levelled at her brother.

Jeff and Lynn encouraged their daughter to laugh off the cynical comments, hoping her self-esteem was nowhere near as fragile as other teen stars of her generation. They were right. She faced her critics openly and with a measured maturity which prompted further comparisons with her matching forebear, going on to stamp her unique imprint on the entertainment world with a Senegalese singer-songwriter and political activist by the name of Youssouf Elhadji. Within three short weeks, their single had shot to Number One in twenty-eight countries.

Not to be outdone by his little sister, Jet also took time out from his studies to direct a science-fiction fantasy screenplay on which he had been working for several years. The resulting blockbuster film received a similar reception, earning praise for its atmosphere, story and character development, but most of all for its groundbreaking, technical cinematography.

The Four of Diamonds had learned a series of worthwhile lessons by the time another year closed in on them. Despite being a weekly boarder for several years, their elder offspring left a sizeable void whenever the doting parents came home to *Escondido*. Kierney revelled in her newfound only-child status at first and, with the whole house at her disposal, commandeered the function room for private musical experimentation. After a month or so however, this lost its novelty too.

As a consequence, the superstars increasingly found themselves at home alone during their brief stop-overs. Staying in bed late, they luxuriated in the serenity of their beach-side *hacienda*, free to make as much noise as they liked without fear of being sprung. It was like the old days again, and having only each other to focus on supplied a revitalising tonic when the final curtain fell on their tour.

To celebrate the two-way emancipation, the Diamonds released "The Boy Who Would Be King", a project the same age as their son, and one which had morphed from children's musical to serious piece of New Adult theatre. And lately, a screen adaptation too. In all formats, the *œuvre* captured grown-up hearts and childlike imaginations the world over, with its powerful messages of perseverance, fellowship and standing up for what was right.

'Yep,' Jeff told the assembled media at a press conference to mark the feature film's Australian *première*. 'Jake's character's based on our son, fondly referred to in our house as Captain Marvellous. Growing up's all about becoming confident in your own judgement. Being compassionate to those with whom you share the planet, being responsible and always ready to learn. The original idea for this movie occurred to Lynn and me at about the same time as "Laura's Light", which we made for Kierney, but some of the songs are relatively new.

'They're inspired by working in conflict zones... Africa and Eastern Europe... Y'know, macro stuff. And then coming home and focussing on what's important in the micro-world. Don't take more than you give, and all that. We all need to step back from this age of entitlement that seems to have engulfed the western world. If there's one message I want to convey with this story, that'd be it right there.'

The perfectly imperfect couple struck a more stunning pose than usual on the red carpet of the film's opening night, with Jeff proudly showing off a new *tuxedo* with the couple's well-known "JL" emblem woven through the black sheen in a most gloriously subtle statement. Lynn positively shimmered at his side in a long, strapless gown made of washed gold silk. Cameras flashed all around and fans clamoured for their attention, but as far as the forever lovers were concerned, it was as if they were taking a lazy evening stroll through their beloved hometown.

'Doesn't this woman look amazing?' the proud husband shouted into the crowd, greeted with appreciative cheers and wolf-whistles from the start of the red carpet to the glass doors leading into the Regent Theatre.

He took hold of his wife's fingers and guided her in a graceful circle to give everyone another glimpse of her radiance. His spare hand gestured upwards and downwards, following the line of her svelte figure as spotlights caught the shimmering dress.

'And you know what the best part is?' he joked with a sky wink. 'I get to take this off!'

The throng erupted in uncontrolled adulation, and Lynn rewarded the lecherous comedian's audacity with a chaste kiss. Later, when quizzed by a reporter about ambitions remaining in their life singular, Jeff was equally quick off the mark, knowing his comments would soon be winging their way from news service to gossip magazine.

'Nothing much personally,' he frowned. 'Doing what we can to help our transition well into young adults, then I want to see Australia vote in an openly gay prime minister. And maybe in a few years' time, if a few more cards fall our way, we'll see our great nation become a republic with our very own Lynn Dyson Diamond as its first president.'

The accomplished all-rounder topped off the year's triumphs with another chart-topping album featuring songs written by assorted family members. Some tracks had been laid down while on the road, whereas others had been recorded as part of the Diamonds' latest television documentary series, clowning around at Melbourne Academy with the combined junior and senior school choirs and launching a brand new charming, dark-haired teenaged heartthrob onto the scene. Ageing rock music fans could forgive Troy McGrath for styling his pop-star *persona* on a certain former dark-haired teenaged heartthrob who, despite a little greying round the edges, remained no less charming to all concerned.

The pace didn't let up at all during December, despite the great man's mysterious bolt out of the blue having caught the Australian public napping. With a collective sigh of relief to have reached the end of their busiest year yet, the globetrotting celebrities gathered at Benloch for holiday festivities with the Dysons, looking forward to a week of well-earned downtime. And as always, at the first opportunity, Lynn and Jeff left the youngsters with their cousins and stole away to Coldwater Creek to renew their mutual commitment as only they knew how.

'I need to cut Gerry loose, angel.'

'Do you? Why?' his wife asked in surprise, rolling over on their picnic rug and shielding her eyes from the sun's glare. 'Loose from what?'

'Work. Us. 'Cause he's getting older and he's never got around to living his own life. Not since the day we moved back to Melbourne from London. He'd already been making *ma vie débauchée* run smoothly before we got back together, and he's been doing the same for *notre vie singulaire* ever since, *n'est-ce pas?* It's time he started focussing on himself.'

The passionate woman reached her hand round Jeff's neck and pulled his head towards her kiss. 'You're gorgeous. Gerry does just fine at focussing on himself, you idiot! What's brought this on? Has he been having a moan? He's in love! Surely he's not trying to blame you for any regrets about not doing it sooner?'

'Nope. Nothing like that. It's more my guilt than his regret.'

'Guilt? What do you have to feel guilty about?'

The billionnaire exhaled, succumbing to the glorious shock of warm skin against cool. 'Guilt that his whole career's been dictated by mine. Like yours has. Jeez, this feels so good!'

'Then shut up and live in the moment,' his wife teased. 'Weren't you the one saying we need to switch off from everything while we're here? You know as well as I do that Gerry's built his own empire alongside ours. He'd be the first to admit he's benefitted from associating with us as much, if not more, than *vice versa*. I've never heard him complain. Have you?'

'Yeah, no. Sure,' the compassionate man chuckled, no longer able to ignore the arousing effects of his *masseuse*'s capable fingers. 'I know you're right, but it's gnawing at me nonetheless. Maybe it *is* enough for him. It's just that if he's as materially-driven as he says he is, why do I always sense jealousy when he's with us? Especially here, or when we're on holiday somewhere? It feels like he's missing out on something, and he doesn't even know what it is.'

Sitting up and wrapping her shirt over her bikini, the Olympian shivered. The contrast between the dam's freezing water and their steamy love-making had left her skin ultra-sensitive to the breeze rustling through the trees. This isolated copse of gums, willows and palms was so special for the lovers; a peaceful oasis in which to purge a year's worth of toxins built up during more than a thousand hours in the air and at least double this figure in desolate and indistinguishable hotel bedrooms.

'Are you sure you're not the one with something missing?'

The world-changer shrugged, sending his beautiful best friend's heart into orbit with a telling half-smile. Despite the odd silver hair weaving across his chest to complement those on his temples and sideburns, she found him as attractive as ever. And yet more so when his honesty shone so transparent from those pleading brown eyes.

This amazing woman knew her man well, both inside and out. All too familiar was the shameful mien which came over him whenever she saw through his *bravado*.

'I'm over it, angel,' Jeff confessed. 'For the first time in twenty years, I want to smash up my own bloody soapbox. I'm sick to death of hearing my own voice.'

'Well, I'm not,' his wife countered, cupping her hand over his mouth. 'It's a magical voice, and I'll never tire of it. But I do know what you mean. It's been one hell of a year, and next year's shaping up as no different. We'll feel better after the holidays. We need a few days' break from all the hype.'

'Maybe,' the showman didn't sound convinced. 'Hope you're right. But regardless, I'm stoked we've got to the same place at the same time. That makes it so much easier.'

Two bodies combined in mutual adoration, their hearts as synchronised as their minds. With no-one but the birds and an occasional kangaroo to observe their undulations, the Midas couple savoured every sigh and shiver in their halcyon quest.

Feeling the pressure of climax building to a runaway *crescendo*, the songwriter slowed the pace until their hips came to a standstill. It took a supreme exercise in distraction not to follow suit when the momentum shift caused his wife to cry out. An orgasm raced through her, and the pair lay in satisfied silence until the intensity had run its course.

'I'd like to move to Boston,' Lynn's eyes flashed, seizing the moment. 'Once Kizzy's at uni'.'

'Boston, Mass'?' Jeff returned the question in his best John F Kennedy accent. 'To be closer to MIT?'

Paragon Holdings' Chairman and Chief Executive Officer's logic was sound enough. The conglomerate of technology companies, supplemented by others producing groundbreaking medical devices, had grown exponentially since the mid-nineteen-seventies. They were maturing as giants in their industries, reaping the benefits of being first to market with their patented wares.

Serious money was also being made on the venture capital side, and generous dividends rendered their stock highly sought-after on international markets. The rear-end of the pantomime horse saw a need for her front-man to be part of this success, even if he held no store by it. She had discussed her husband's reticence regularly with Gerry, whose twenty-plus years of oversight had brought him no closer to comprehending the disinterest his best mate displayed for their bounteous wealth.

'Partly,' the tennis champion nodded. 'But also for a complete change of scene, now the restrictions of keeping the kids safe at *Escondido* are over. We could work the east coast cabaret circuit, from Atlantic City to the Canadian border. All through New England, and even down in Florida and the Carolinas. Pop over to San Fran for the odd night or two. No more big stadium gigs. Just intimate bars and clubs, and choosing our own timetable.'

'Whoa! Actually, that'd be so damned cool,' her astonished partner-in-crime replied. 'Although I don't buy the "complete change of scene" idea. We've spent the last year-and-a-half in a series of complete changes of scene. Unless you're moving states-side on your own...'

The stunning blonde chuckled, pretending to consider the merits of her husband's suggestion. 'Hmm... Maybe you have something there, Sigmund,' she chided, sitting up and shoving him onto the warm carpet of grass. 'I don't mean soon. After the kids are settled and don't need us any more. Even after they've had kids themselves.'

'Jesus Christ!' Jeff shouted at a covey of lemon-crested cockatoos balancing on the supple branches above. 'Grandparents? Are you seriously contemplating us being grandparents? That's more than a little scary. Bloody oath!'

Lynn laughed at his over-reaction. 'OK, calm down! It's a long way off, I agree. I think Boston'd be perfect for us. We've already said we can't see Jet or Kierney staying in *Oz* once they're working, and one of those old tenement apartments in Back Bay would be a gorgeous hideaway.'

'Hey. Now you're talking! You're not wrong there. I love that part of town,' the billionnaire mused, lifting his head to kiss her lips as they loomed overhead. 'Carry on. I'm starting to like this.'

'Good! There are so many tiny music venues where we could pare our act right down. Four- or five-piece and us; the same as we're planning for Kizzy's birthday. Have you met Gerry's Fiona yet?'

'Yeah. We both have,' Jeff grinned. 'She's one half of "Sloan and Sloan".'

Lynn pulled away. 'Really? Oh, my God! As in Greg Sloan, the solicitor? Have they split up?'

'The very same, and I couldn't possibly comment on whether they've split up or not. We'll know when we see their letterhead change to "Sloan *or* Sloan", I'm guessing.'

Laying back onto the rug, the thirty-nine-year-old beauty laughed aloud. 'That's hilarious! Well done. How long have you been waiting for an opportunity to trot that one out?'

'Yeah, well... I'd be lying if I said it was totally spontaneous. I used it on Blake-san, and he was none too amused at the time. Do you know much about her?'

'Wow, Fiona Sloan! Not really, except that she's supposed to be a bit of a ball-breaker in court. Commercial litigators, aren't they? I've only spoken to her a few times at sports things at school. One of their sons is in Kizzy's year.'

Jeff rolled over and began to pepper kisses all over the nude body he coveted. There was more to the Gerry and Fiona story than would ever be made public, which wouldn't come as much of a surprise to his worldly woman, but he didn't want to sully their perfect outing with tales of cheating and elaborate lies.

'Yep to all that. Don't expect any rumours've surfaced at school yet. Gez is thinking of asking her to move in.'

'Wow!' Lynn gasped again, her heart rate soaring in response to her husband's loving embrace. 'It must be serious. Has he ever lived with anyone before?'

'Absolutely not! Let's stop with the conjecture, eh? I want to focus on you today. I'm enjoying living in the moment, Missus Dyson, and I'd be grateful if you'd do the same.'

Kicking back after the last few concert dates leading up to Christmas, working eastwards from Australia's western-most city, the megastar couple began to convert the next phase of their life singular from dreams to schemes.

First up, they would celebrate their daughter's sixteenth birthday by way of accompanying her to New York on her second visit to the United Nations' Human Rights Council. Jeff had recently finished an album of classic story songs, recorded as duets with their original writers, a number of whom were booked for two nights of jamming at Radio City Music Hall to delight their most loyal fans.

Lynn had crafted the show's *finalé* as a surprise for their dark-haired gipsy girl, where her dad would invite her onto the stage to sing her own story song, "The Princess And The Warrior", before the whole cast joined forces for "Happy Birthday, Sweet Sixteen". It was to be the first of several coming-of-age events, anticipating Kierney's relish at finally being old enough to thumb her nose at the righteous meddlers who made it their business to comment on her every move.

'I think we should look to spend a few years in Boston after all our Aussie ambitions are under control,' the singer continued, working her man's lengthening shaft until it hardened again. 'Once all the political wrangling and power-plays have been assuaged.'

'Shit, yeah! I'm up for that, as you can see... It's an amazing idea, angel. Are we retiring?'

Shuddering as his erection slipped deep inside her yearning vagina, the sportswoman lowered herself onto his *torso* and tapped their entwined fingers on the grass. 'Oh, God. I love you so much. No. Don't you still want to retire to Paris?'

'*Mais bien sûr, mon amie,*' Jeff laughed, unable to resist such a golden opportunity.

'*Argh!* I thought it might be nice to spend the last few years of our working life over there, surrounded by prestigious seats of learning. Not to mention all the blues bars and Italian restaurants in the North End. Fantastic.'

His wife's voice trailed off in response to a vigorous thrust, and the lovers gyrated sideways until she was pinned to the ground. Her black stallion increased the pace in time with her moans, covering her face and neck with wild kisses in thanks for stimulating him with all these delicious, novel concepts. Suddenly transported back in time to their first visit to this inspirational place, he marvelled at how its natural beauty never failed to draw them closer and closer. How many grand plans had germinated from casual carnal encounters at this very spot?

'Why not?' he gasped, his hand cupping her breast and grinding into her stiff nipple to heighten the intensity. 'Halfway between MIT and the North End sounds awesome. Endless brain strain interspersed with regular forays into a nearer-by Europe. Count me in, angel. I love you so much too, and I'll follow you anywhere. You know that.'

***

'Impervious.'

'What is?' Ryan asked, without taking his eyes off the West Indian fast bowler as he turned to run in and face Australia's opening batsman. 'Oh, man! You've *gotta* try harder than that, Davey! Sorry, Bart. What was that?'

The thirty-eight-year-old retired cricketer had joined his grandfather, uncle Junior and Gerry in the members' stand at the Melbourne Cricket Ground for Day Two of the Boxing Day test. Early rain had delayed the start of play, giving the men a chance to swap news over a few beers.

With the rest of his family enjoying the peace and quiet of another Benloch holiday season, he exercised his player's privileges to invite the ebullient Irishman along, having heard he and Fiona weren't heading to Sydney for Christmas. Celia had passed away in August, joining her dearly-departed husband in the Blakes' prominent cemetery plot, and their Mosman mansion had been sold soon afterwards. With little in common with his sisters these days, Gerry considered *Cairdeas* more of an ancestral home than the North Shore.

'Impervious,' the octogenarian replied. 'The word your dad used to describe my influence on you. He said I made you impervious to adversity.'

'Did he? Wow! I wouldn't say that. Did he mean it in a good way?'

Big D coughed, catching his son and the Diamonds' former manager exchanging sly sniggers. 'What do you think? You know as well as the rest of us that Jeff seldom said anything that wasn't deliberately open to interpretation.'

'Oh, sure. Impervious, eh? Whereas he made me porous, I suppose. He was always so damned cryptic. Warner's not looking too impervious against Jerome Taylor. He'll be caught soon, flashin' it around like that.'

'He's just getting his eye in,' Gerry contradicted, retrieving his wallet from the inside pocket of his jacket. 'Hundred bucks says David Warner gets his ton. Who's in?'

Both Dyson men declined the wager, outspoken campaigners against sports betting. Ryan didn't much care for gambling either, but humoured his father's best friend. At sixty-six, and steadily putting on weight since arthritis had taken up residence in his knees and ankles, his ageing appearance had shocked the younger man this trip. It made him wonder how his parents might look now if they were still alive.

'I'll see you and raise you another hundred that Burns gets a ton and Warner doesn't, providing it doesn't rain again. Fair?'

The accountant cheered. 'You're on! That's dinner sorted for me. Thanks, boy-oh!'

'No worries,' Ryan shook his head. 'I'm sorted 'cause Grandma's cooking tonight. Philo's rapt he got to drive a ute yesterday. It's all he's talked about since he knew we were coming over. How come you're so confident anyway, Blake-san?'

'Inside information,' the joker answered, tapping his index finger on the side of his nose. 'Mister Google pointed me to a slew of expert opinion that blokes who live in the mountains of Colorado can't possibly keep up with.'

All four men laughed, turning as one at the sound of a sharp crack of willow which sent the ball flying through the air. The fielder struggled to spot the high-speed red missile on its downward trajectory, juggling it dangerously until it settled into his hands on the third attempt.

'Out!' the former captain yelled over groans from the crowd. 'Thank you kindly, Gerry. You can Google with impunity on my time any day.'

'Who caught it?' his grandfather asked, his view blocked by a man in front who had leaped to his feet when the wicket fell.

'Samuels. Wait! What the…'

But Junior was too quick, whipping the crisp, green note out of Gerry's hand before his nephew could claim it. 'Your round, I believe, Jetto. I'll get 'em in. Same again, everyone?'

Grumbling as he sat down, Ryan watched his uncle climb the steep flight of steps into the hospitality suite. He missed this style of larrikin banter, visiting Australia far less frequently these days. Savannah loved their luxurious treehouse high above Colorado Springs, his work was well-respected, and their children were doing well in the local elementary school. He loved it too, most of the time, yet moments like these never failed to remind him that rivers of mateship tended to run much deeper down-under.

'Do you remember the time Dad gave me a ridiculous, bullshit cricket coaching session in the stands down there?' the younger man turned back to Jeff Diamond's oldest friend. 'You guys'd had heaps to drink, and the sun was brutal all day. It was before I was in the main eleven. Ages ago. Do you remember?'

Adjusting his wide-brimmed Panama for today's warming rays, Gerry nodded. 'Certainly do! You came over here after school, didn't you? And we'd been here since morning tea. Did we do any work in those days? I don't recall. What's your point?'

'"As big as a West Indian's box,"' Ryan rattled off, doing his best to impersonate the deceased orator. 'We were talking about how much English footballers got paid compared to Aussie Rules players. It cracked us up. And now, whenever I see or hear about the Windies, I can't help laughing.'

The retired executive guffawed, clutching both hands to his belly. 'Holy shit! I do remember that, mate. That was twenty kilograms ago at least.'

'Twenty kilograms! You bloody idiot.'

'Put the fear of God in him,' Gerry carried on. 'He was trying to tell you how to psych out the batsman by using AFL bumping and sledging as examples. You listened carefully, obviously!'

'Yeah. Of course I did,' Paragon Holdings' Chief Executive Officer smiled. 'He almost spilled his beer... That was just as funny! "Keep the play simple and the mind-games as complex as you can," he claimed. "Set your field after you've bowled a couple of balls, as if you've got the batsman's measure already. That's the sum total of my advice, son." Pretty good, considering he never really played much cricket.'

'Oh, he did play quite a bit of cricket in his teens,' the Sydney Grammar old boy refuted. 'He used to play for us when we were a man short. Highly irregular of course, so don't go spreading it around. He was a tidy bowler, but he wasn't strong enough to be a batsman. Not at that age anyway. Way too skinny.'

Ryan smiled. 'He told me about subbing for you. I think it was during the same drunken conversation when he explained what "sixty-nine" was, and then that led on to sexually-transmitted diseases. I know I felt sick at the end of it!'

With even Bart Dyson cracking a smile, the lapsed Catholic rocked on his chair again. 'Jesus, Mary and Joseph! Yes, I remember that as well. We got a few filthy looks from people around us.'

'Much like you will here if you don't keep your voices down,' the elder statesman warned.

A drinks break had been called by the umpires down on the pitch below, bringing on the motorised sports drink bottles which had become a gimmick at every first class or test fixture. The two comics shrugged at the futility of the old man's wise words, now unable to hear themselves speak above the noise of shuffling feet and *eskies* opening and closing.

Junior returned with their drinks, pursued by a *posse* of devoted football tragics. Their grovelling ratcheted up several more notches when they noticed the recipients of the All-Australian Best and Fairest's three spare plastic pots. Even Gerry Blake was a household name in this city after shepherding Lynn and Jeff Diamond's career for so many years and helping to make Paragon Holdings such a good earner for its ordinary shareholders.

The expanded group passed the time of day for several minutes, until the West Indian players returned to their fielding positions. Once Joe Burns and Usman Khawaja had flexed their knees and found their stance again, a noble silence descended on the MCG's hallowed turf.

A healthy run-rate and some creative shots from both batsmen kept the quartet's attention fixed on the ground below, its meticulously mown outfield proving slick, perfect for boundary fours. In the ten minutes before lunch, Ryan was persecuted during each change of overs by zealous fans seeking a blow-by-blow account of Australia's performance, most of which he deflected with glib statements or the excuse of being too long away from the game.

Taking their seats in the members' dining room, Bart and Junior were content to let their fellow guests jabber on. In less than two months' time, the twentieth anniversary of Lynn's demise would be upon them. Any link to their lost loved one, no matter how crude or benign, was cause to commemorate a special person who had died a futile and premature death.

'So somehow the mindless discussion went from West Indians' cricket boxes to explaining sexual positions, via STDs and the band "Sham 69",' Gerry admitted, inviting the waiter to pour the wine. 'The look of incredulity on your face when he told you a woman would stick your cock in her mouth one day was absolutely bloody priceless!'

The father-of-two sniffed. 'Excuse me? How d'you know I'm not still waiting for that day? I'm just glad Dad cared enough to tell us what was what, even if it did take me a while to match the practice with the theory. You remember there was a video of Mum having a massage? Did he ever tell you about that?'

'Too right he did! Did you watch it?'

'Of course I bloody didn't! What sort of perverted act would that be, watching my mother naked? Why? Did you?'

'No,' the Irishman blanched, relieved the Dysons' attention had been diverted by another pair of fans. 'Sorry, mate. I know that tape brought him a lot of pleasure, both before and after she left us. I agree it should remain a sacred artefact.'

Ryan dismissed the apology. 'Yeah. Thanks. It's one of only a very few sacred artefacts, as you put it. Most appropriately, by the way... I can't think of many other pieces of footage or photos unsuitable for the public domain. Except a few homemade movies they shot of each other before we were born. I think Kiz destroyed those. She didn't want them found sometime in the future.'

'She probably got rid of the massage tape too then,' the reformed womaniser said, trying not to look too disappointed.

'No. It survived. She's got it with her in New York, under lock and key with some of the other valuables.'

'Beauty,' the family's longtime manager nodded. 'That's good. We should order, mate. What are you having?'

Ryan scanned the lunch menu to refresh his memory. 'Steak sandwich sounds good. Do you still miss them?'

'Miss them?'

'Yeah. Mum and Dad.'

'I do, sir,' Gerry responded in all sincerity. 'Not in a grieving sort of way. But I still find myself thinking about all the good and not-so-good times we shared, things they said or did... Practically every day. I expect you do too.'

'Sure do,' the younger man affirmed.

Signalling the waiter to take Bart Dyson's order first, the ageing accountant leaned over and put a hand on Ryan's shoulder. 'I asked him once, mate, when he'd been waxing on about soul-mates through the ages, whether he'd ever considered trying someone else other than Lynn.'

'Did he smack you upside the head?'

Gerry chuckled. 'No. We were in the Park Hyatt restaurant. It would've been poor form. Anyway, I'll never forget how serious he was when he answered. He said, "Maybe I did when my soul was younger, which is why we haven't always been together through time. But not now, with the wisdom of so much hindsight."'

Momentous Year

'Christ, Suzie-Anna! Life's so unbelievably sweet at this point in time,' Jeff said. 'It's like some kind of renewal of us for us, if that makes sense. Relief at still being each other's Number One fan.'

'Why? Did you think you wouldn't be?'

'Hoped not, but y'know... Sometimes parents come out the other side of parenting and realise they've evolved in totally different directions.'

The songwriter had been left to his own devices for two days between Christmas and New Year while the teenagers were staying with friends and Lynn nipped up to Sydney for some *solo* television appearances. Bored with his own company, he had driven the empty Land Rover all the way from the Mornington Peninsula to the northern-most edge of Greater Melbourne.

Since Janey, the gentle white German Shepherd cross, had been found curled up under a bush behind the tennis courts never to reawaken, the family no longer shared canine walking duties. Locking the high wooden *portico* on a desolate home, with only the haughty cat to guard *Escondido* and its blissful memories, the billionnaire felt a distinct sense of tides turning.

'I'm talking about people who didn't even know they'd stayed together for the kids,' his story continued, ''cause they never stopped to think about it.'

Suzanne laughed, stabbing her old friend's arm with a stick she had wrestled off one of her dogs. 'You guys didn't stay together for the kids. What are you on about?'

'Exactly. It crossed our minds that it might happen to us in the same way, being so busy and everything. But I'm pleased to report we're more in-tune than ever with each other's hopes and dreams. Lynn's ready to spread her wings, and I'm ready to stand aside and follow her wherever she wants to go next.'

'Are you? God! I envy you,' the kennel owner sighed. 'Doesn't surprise me though. You always knew how you wanted your life to turn out, and you got it with bells on. How many people does that happen to?'

'Yeah, I know. Tell me about it! I'm chock-full of gratitude lately. I got over my *phobia* of blokes messing with my little girl. Well, no... I'm not over it. I've learned to live with it, let's say, and now I find myself more contented than I ever thought possible.'

'Great. That's good, isn't it?'

Her adorable rogue smirked. 'So what do you want, Suze? You know I'll give you whatever you want. If you and Steve want to go on a cruise, for example, or buy a city apartment, just say the word. I have so much effing money that I wouldn't notice it.'

'Jeff!' Suzanne cried out. 'That's crazy. We couldn't do that!'

'Ah, cut the remonstrations, woman,' the showman insisted, covering her mouth and hugging her close. 'Why not? You guys've been our friends for so long, and I don't mean I want to go splashing money around in some sort of arrogant spree. It's just, in my position, giving you whatever you want is so damned easy. Tell me... Sell the kennels. Ask Steve if he'd quit *carpenting* and take you around the world. I'd love to do it.'

There were tears in both sets of eyes when the pair of Sydney natives broke apart. Jeff Diamond's generosity was never in dispute, and the suburban tradesman hadn't taken too much convincing to accept the offer of a new van or piece of workshop equipment over the years. They had even come home from a three-week holiday to find their bathrooms renovated and a painter applying the final touches to the old cottage's exterior woodwork.

'Are you serious? You've already paid for heaps, and our running costs are pretty low here.'

'Yes! I'm completely serious,' the superstar laughed at her self-conscious protestations. 'There's no way Lynn and I can spend the money we've got, and the kids're well and truly self-sufficient. The tax office gets its fair share too, so have a think about it, Suze. Think big, OK?'

Suzanne sighed, wiping her eyes with the back of her hand. 'OK. Thanks, Jeff. I'll see what Steve says. So, does Kierney still want to work at the UN?'

'Yep. She's open to international law, human rights law, humanitarian aid programs... Any of those, we expect. She's obsessed with making the world a better place on a much grander scale than I ever considered at her age. I don't think she thinks about much else, to tell you the truth.'

The pair walked across the back paddock to where a pack of assorted dogs were fighting over something deceased and rancid. Wading into the *mêlée* and tearing a selection of putrid body parts out of the winners' teeth, the musician imagined the attraction of putting her feet up on a balcony overlooking the Great Ocean Road hinterland wouldn't be far from his friend's thoughts at this present moment.

'But aren't you going against your principles?' Suzanne yelled, screwing her nose up at the stench.

The handsome man grimaced. 'Fuckin' hell, Suzie! Going against which principles?'

'You know... Pulling strings. Getting Kizzy into high places? I mean, it can't be easy to get a job at the UN.'

Jeff stopped in his tracks, eyes wide with a thunderous glare. 'I can't believe you said that,' he snarled. 'Is that what you really think? I'm twisting people's arms to give my daughter a free pass? Jesus Christ! You shouldn't believe everything you read.'

'I'm sorry,' the guilty woman grinned. 'It just sounds very cosy. She wants to work for the United Nations, and you're well connected in there. Isn't that called profiting from an unfair advantage or something?'

Suzanne's point was not without validity, the intellectual was ashamed to admit. New graduate positions were notoriously scarce at the international peace-keeping institution, and the enterprising student had baulked at serving an apprentice as a lowly intern. However, prepared for a decade of back-breaking toil to prove her worth, she knew better than most the importance of securing a role on her merits alone.

'Sure,' the philanthropist appeased Gerry's conservative ex-girlfriend. 'I see how it might look, but I'd like to think our daughter'll be the right person for whichever job she gets because she's developed some outstanding qualities. Not 'cause her parents put in a good word for her, if you know what I mean. And if they choose her for the job because she's the right person for the job *and* because she's our daughter, then that's fine too. She'll pay her way, Suzie-Anna. Kierney's no lightweight taking up a place that'd be better filled by someone else.'

Kicking a punctured football along the ground to encourage the dogs to keep moving, the kennel owner huffed in frustration. 'Oh, for God's sake! I didn't mean that. It *would* be fantastic if she got in. I know it's what she's always wanted. It's just that she probably wouldn't get a guernsey if she wasn't who she is.'

'Maybe. But the only way it'd be wrong, in my opinion, is if they only choose her because she's who she is,' Jeff countered through clenched jaws.

Nineteen-ninety-five was already up and running, full of momentous anniversaries for the family: Kierney would turn sixteen in February; then Jet eighteen in July; and in September, they were to celebrate their mother's fortieth birthday. Plans were afoot for all three occasions, none particularly extravagant, but all promising to be extra-special nonetheless.

Their firstborn repatriated The Ashes in early January, scoring three wins to England's one in his first complete season as captain of the Australian test team. With maturity well beyond his years, the likeable leader had flown home from Cambridge University's Michaelmas term with his rivals, only to stare player down with steel-blue eyes from the opposite end of the crease. The whole family, Madalena included, had settled into the Ponsford Stand on Boxing Day to watch the blond speedster bowl his right-armed cannonballs past the English batting order.

As a thank-you for their contributions to the lengthy road-trip during the "Live on Earth" tour, Lynn and Jeff treated their band members and their families to a fortnight in Acapulco over New Year, in preparation for the gruelling four-month homeward course through South-east Asia. Their fast-encroaching freedom was reinforced by Jet and Kierney deciding to stay at home, preferring to party with their cousins and friends in advance of the annual Dyson weigh-in on New Year's Day.

No-one worked as hard as the couple itself however. While their musicians were free to take in the sights, speckled through the diary between concert dates were many and varied public appearances, interviews and lectures. They had touring down to a fine art by this time, travelling with golf clubs and personal computers in a perfect mix of business and pleasure, never once tiring of each other's company.

Nineteen-ninety-five was also to mark Lynn's last year of *élite* professional sport. She was happy to hand the mantle of the Australian Open Grand Slam singles title to her younger sister for as long as she wanted it. Their elder brother had led the way the previous September, choosing to concentrate on coaching his beloved Melbourne Football Club to an elusive AFL premiership win.

The two much-loved local heroines slugged it out in the women's final, both nursing knee injuries, with the crowd perched on the edge of its seat as the lead swapped from one to the other six times. At eleven games to ten in the third set, Anna broke the defending champion's serve and held on to her slim advantage to emerge victorious after three exhausting but entertaining hours.

It seemed as if the whole of Melbourne was out at lunchtime on Collins Street to watch the champion and runner-up parade down from the Paris end in an open-topped car, displaying the glittering trophies to their proud hometown. The smile on Lynn's face was every bit as genuine as her sister's, announcing during a television interview that Junior's daughter, Jarradie, would soon be hot on their heels. Little did anyone know, but Anna was already carrying a daughter of her own.

Meanwhile, and without understanding why, Jeff was now having trouble adjusting to his gorgeous gipsy girl turning sixteen; inexplicable by this stage because the milestone he presumed to be the culprit had passed with minimal ceremony a few months earlier. Baffling also because the doting dad experienced as much elation at the thought of Kierney stepping onto the next rung on the ladder of independence as he did sadness that his miniature was growing out of him.

While his wife and sister-in-law waged war on the tennis court, Jeff took himself off to the freezing New York winter to rehearse the unveiling of his collection of intricate musical tales. For a songwriter whose recorded bibliography mostly comprised his own music, this newest departure gave him a deep sense of achievement after several experimental numbers were introduced during their world tour to an unexpected level of critical praise.

'I must be truthful,' one New York Times arts columnist wrote. 'I had my doubts he could carry these songs off. Most of us know Jeff Diamond as a rock singer; raw, loud and spectacular. These songs call for a more controlled way of singing. Subtle drama rather than shouting from the rooftops. But I couldn't have been more wrong.

'From the moment he walked on the set and became instant best buddies with a pretty cynical bunch of professionals that he'd never met, and before the first track was finished, they were eating out of his hand. As his legions of fans already know, you only have to look at him to know he's got the goods. And then, when you put a microphone in his hand and he flexes those smoky vocal cords, it's smooth like thick, rich cream. Just goes to show that when you've got this amount of courage and talent, there's no direction an artist can't take.'

Lynn and Kierney flew out to join the superstar in Greenwich Village, where he hosted a sumptuous party for the birthday girl which doubled as the album launch. He put on his bravest face in front of an array of television cameras, inviting first his wife and then his daughter onto the stage to sing with him. Through shining eyes, the captivated studio audience watched the master croon a spiced-up version of Neil Sedaka's "Happy Birthday, Sweet Sixteen".

'From now on, you ain't *gonna* be mine, so...' he sang to the beaming teenager, dancing together to a pared-down rock'n'roll rhythm. 'If I should smile in sweet surprise, it's just that you've grown up before my very eyes.'

Jeff pulled a long-stemmed tight crimson rose from inside his jacket and presented it to the young beauty, who responded with a violent hug, standing on tiptoe to plant a kiss on his lips.

Looking over at his wife for moral support, he quipped, 'I'm *gonna* be in trouble for this.'

Not to be outdone, Lynn helped her consummate performer of a husband to end the show on a high with a sophisticated scene that re-enacted their inaugural slow dance, to the strains of a recent hit they had penned together, "No More First Dances". Their performance was electrifying, and the memory it created pure magic. As the music faded and the audience was about to burst into applause, the couple timed the switch between erotic balladeers to jiving athletes for the raunchy "Life Is The Deepest River".

The following day, the *trio* of Australian chameleons arrived at the landmark United Nations building on the eastern edge of Manhattan's midtown, not far from the Fifty-ninth Street bridge made famous by Simon and Garfunkel. It may not have been every sixteen-year-old's idea of a birthday treat, but Kierney was in seventh heaven to be escorted through the maze of corridors, shaking hands with some of the world's most respected diplomats and policymakers. Ever since she advanced into double figures, the serious-minded schoolgirl had been intent on a career inside the organisation, and this fresh step was a fantastic opportunity for her to find out where she might target these aspirations.

It was hard to believe Lynn and Jeff Diamond's global profile could reach a higher pinnacle than the "Live On Earth" tour, yet New York belonged to them after their latest *schmalzy* statement. The newspapers and entertainment television programmes were wall-to-wall with inspiring stories from the

Diamonds' catalogue until well after they flew out of "JFK" on Sunday afternoon.

They headed straight home after Kierney's birthday weekend, in plenty of time for her to start her final year at Melbourne Academy. Their only stop was Sydney, where they kicked off a campaign to promote gender equality and an end to violence against women and children.

Standing on a temporary stage at the St James corner of Hyde Park, the passionate orator took the microphone, waving to quieten the crowd which had come streaming from the office blocks and shops nearby. 'I'm here to talk to you about women. It's a subject my better half says I know a lot about, but believe me, I'm still learning,' he chuckled, his gaze drifting a long way into the distance, across a colourful sea of attentive onlookers, before returning to his wife and daughter. 'D'you see these beautiful creatures here? They're the reason we're all here. These angels, and all you other beautiful creatures wherever you are.'

A long left arm swept an arc over the throng. 'There's a statistic I've seen that says twenty percent of women suffer some sort of abuse at some point in their life,' he continued. 'One in five. And if that's not bad enough, most of these acts are perpetrated by people they know. One in five's a terrifying stat', and we're here to change it. Yeah? Are we?'

With cheers ringing out around the park, Jeff exchanged admiring glances with his dream girl, trusting her thoughts were with his: lounging in the breeze with their faces to the sun high above Coldwater Creek and their decision to take a well-earned break from this endless *spruiking*. Yet here they were again, like preachers spreading the gospels of decency and common sense which ought to have been unnecessary. The evidence suggested their crusade was vital, and therefore stopping now would be next to impossible.

'I've *gotta* tell you...' the celebrity carried on, stuffing his hands into his jeans pockets. 'My own mother and sister were raped and beaten, fed drugs and alcohol repeatedly while I was growing up. By my dad, no less, and his so-called mates. Abused by their own husband and father... Shithouse, huh?'

The billionaire paused to let his words sink in, seeing face after face register horror and disgust at what had once been normal for him. 'My mum took an overdose and died 'cause after a while, she had no idea what was *gonna* happen next, where she was and even who she was. My sister did better, I guess, in that she's not a drug addict and she's still alive. But she'll never enjoy a loving relationship with anyone, man or woman, and she'll never have kids. I don't think she's even bothered to find out if she *can* have kids.'

The hurt in the superstar's sonorous but croaking voice sent shivers down everyone's spines. 'Now you can't tell me you don't think that's sad, can you?' he asked, receiving nothing but shaking heads in response. 'And wrong, yes? We've got to discourage people from inflicting harm on those who trust them. We don't recover from it. Therefore, I'm standing here today because I don't want any man to lay a finger on any woman or child I know. Or anyone, full stop!'

'Guys, there's no excuse in the world for attacking the women you live with or spend time with. No bloody excuse ever. Oh, I know sometimes we get angry. I'm no exception. Y'know, I even bought my mother drugs when I was a teenager, 'cause I couldn't stand her screaming for them at all hours of the day and night. I have no idea if I wanted to make her happy or to shut her up. Shit!'

The crowd became silent and solemn, but Jeff didn't back down. He was no longer bothered about baring his soul and giving away his more dark and intimate secrets, since he now knew he had endured his childhood for a reason. Memories which had once been too real for the messenger to articulate had morphed into some of his most useful tools of the trade. While Lynn and their children could spread the word using case studies and research, his premium asset was his ability to persuade people with actual examples.

'And I know now that I was part of the problem too, even though, at the time, I thought I was part of the solution. I know what it's like to feel under pressure from a woman. They communicate in a different way to us blokes. But hey! Get over it!' he urged the men who had swarmed around him. 'And Jeez... That unrelenting pressure can make us feel out of control, for sure. But we can and must control the anger. Nobody deserves a broken arm or a black eye. And definitely not the mental anguish that goes unnoticed. No-one deserves that, OK?'

His brooding, dark eyes ran along the rows of stunned faces, from side to side, so slowly that most people were forced to look away before he did. Lynn and Kierney stood leaning on each other, a metre or so from the edge of the stage. Their favourite man was magnificent in these moments, stirring speeches seeming to come from nowhere, eloquent and compelling in their simplicity.

'Now, Kizzy here...' he continued, 'our exquisite daughter who needs no introduction, recently turned sixteen. Can you bloody believe it? No! Nor can I!'

Jeff paused, thrown off his stride by another wave of emotion. 'Kierney's old enough for some bastard... I mean, boyfriend... to take her home, out of my sight and beyond my protection, and do all manner of things to her. Things she'll hopefully enjoy, but also there's the potential for someone to do things she won't enjoy and could harm her for the rest of her life. The same goes for anyone else's daughter. Or our sons, for that matter. Let's not have any one of us, you blokes, think we can pick on someone like her. Christ Almighty! If she were a woman in most African countries, she'd probably have two or more children by now. There's so much promise in our young women that we need to educate them and protect them in the same way we look after our boys.'

The sinking sun had dropped lower in the sky until the rooftops at the far end of the park sharpened its rays like daggers trained on the stage. Childlight's events manager had to shield his eyes to see where the Diamonds were standing, ready to take over and announce the rest of the evening's line-up. Camera shutters whirred from all angles as Jeff beckoned his wife and daughter to join him in introducing the next band.

'I love you,' he whispered to both of them, kissing each in turn. 'You're the best.'

***

Jeff stood up to welcome his son at the kitchen door as he arrived down to breakfast on his eighteenth birthday. It was six-thirty in the morning, and the Diamond clan was up early to share the cricketer's celebrations before they all headed off to their respective busy days. The young man had issued a special request to wake up at *Escondido*, and the rest of his family were only too happy to comply.

'Happy birthday, mate.'

'Thanks, Dad,' Jet replied, engaging with the outstretched hand in a complex combination of slaps, shakes and fist pumps. '*Argh!* You change it every time! Hi, Mum. Hi, Kiz.'

Kierney slid down from the breakfast bar stool and stepped forward to give the blond hulk a hug. As far as sibling relationships went, theirs was amicable enough considering how little they had in common. With the university year over in time for the British summer, it had been a snap decision to return to Melbourne to come of age, torn between pleasing his family and making sure he didn't slip too far down the run-scorer's list this early in the season.

Lynn laughed when her daughter squirmed out of his arms to avoid a sloppy kiss. 'Happy birthday, Jetto,' she echoed. 'Although I refuse to believe you're eighteen.'

Jeff shook his head, depositing two steaming mugs of coffee onto the kitchen table in front of the teenagers. 'Shit, yeah! That's it now, son. I'm not answering any more questions,' he waved a dismissive left hand. 'You're on your own now.'

'Fine by me,' the cocky student shrugged. 'Don't need you to. I know everything, as of today.'

'Excellent,' his mother grinned. 'Good to know. So what's the plan for tomorrow night?'

The dark-haired gipsy on the other side of the bench sniggered. Lynn must have overheard the lad quizzing her about his party on their way down the stairs. His choice of date depended on the level of humiliation he was likely to suffer from those who might feel the need to make a speech.

Buttering a slice of toast, a wry smile spread across the sportsman's face. 'Well... What time was I born?'

'Just after ten o'clock,' the singer answered, glancing over at her husband.

480

'Phew! Thank God for that,' Jet replied. 'I'm not quite eighteen yet. Just a few more questions, and then you're off the hook.'

'In other words, where are we going tonight?' Lynn teased. 'What time? And whom shall I bring?'

'And what do I wear? And how am I getting there?' Kierney added.

'Yeah. All that,' the young man chuckled. 'I can't be expected to remember everything. I'm only a child.'

From the far end of the kitchen table, where he was leafing through the newspaper, Jeff sniffed but failed to rise to the bait. The others looked at each other, puzzled by the uncharacteristic restraint.

'Are you alright?' his wife asked.

'Sorry. Yep. It's all somewhat surreal, angel, to tell you the truth. Only a couple more hours of childhood left before we've got ourselves a *bona fide* adult. I figured if I concentrated on reading the 'paper, time might go a bit *slowlier*.'

The corners of Lynn's mouth turned downwards in sympathy. She picked up her breakfast and went to sit beside the forlorn man, resting her hand on his while he leaned in to accept a kiss. She knew how difficult the last couple of years had been for him, as his paternal role flexed and distorted with each milestone attained.

Far less sensitivity was on offer from Jet, who lunged for his dad's shoulders and shook them hard enough to rock his chair. 'Get with the program, you old fart. You bet I'm an adult. Well, nearly... And a damned fine one I'm *gonna* be too.'

'Oh, for Christ's sake, sit down,' the songwriter barked, flicking his left hand round behind him in an attempt to catch his son where it would hurt. 'Be thankful we even find the event significant. You just wait 'til Gerry assassinates your good name tomorrow night. I hope you're ready to defend yourself.'

The birthday boy joined his parents at the table, beaming from ear to ear. He was indeed thankful, and confident that everyone knew it. Judging by the fact that no-one came to his defence, he concluded all must be well.

'Good and ready, Dad,' he nodded. 'Good and ready. So where am I going?'

'To MA,' his sister piped up, pointing over her shoulder in a westerly direction. 'It's that way.'

The first-year Cambridge undergraduate had been invited back to his old school on this notable occasion, to speak at the morning's assembly. The popular former head student had been eager for the chance to talk about his new life in the UK, at one of the world's most ancient and famous seats of learning, about his sporting exploits for Warwickshire Cricket Club and the upcoming season as defending county champions.

'Tomorrow,' Jet sneered at Kierney. 'Dumb-ass!'

Jeff coughed, amused by the descriptor seldom heard unless his wayward sister was visiting. Lynn pointed to her watch and suggested to the children that time was ticking by. Hauling lethargic teenaged bodies off their chairs, they both began to clear the table, slotting the breakfast crockery and cutlery into the dishwasher.

'We'll see you tonight at the apartment,' their mother continued. 'Tomorrow's at the yacht club in St Kilda. Seven o'clock bounce-down, so be there by six-forty-five at the latest, please. We haven't said suits or anything, but smartish.'

'Smartish,' Jet repeated, saluting. 'What does that even mean?'

'Something Grandpa would approve of,' the Olympian smiled, brushing toast crumbs from the lad's polo shirt. 'You'll be an adult by the time you choose what you're wearing, so you'll have no problem. Who's coming with you?'

'He doesn't know,' the younger sibling interjected before her brother could think of a smart response.

'Don't know? Too many to pick from?' their father enquired over his shoulder. 'That's *ma* boy!'

'I do so,' Jet countered. 'Allanah. Only she doesn't know it yet.'

The tennis champion shook her head. 'You'd better ring her on the way to school. She might have a better offer.'

The Diamond menfolk locked eyes and exhaled from puffed-out cheeks, then honoured this remark with the respect it deserved: a long, vacant stare. It was simply unthinkable for a woman to turn down such handsome, hot-blooded company. All four burst out laughing.

'Right!' Lynn exclaimed. 'I see you've inherited your father's confidence when it comes to attracting the opposite sex. I'd hate to see you disappointed at your birthday party; all single and lonely.'

'Oh, don't worry. I won't be,' the lad assured his mother with a glint in his eye. 'And neither will Allanah be disappointed.'

Jeff groaned, folding the newspaper and slapping it down onto the table. 'Jesus! For fuck's sake! That's beyond arrogant. Not even I would've said that! Not even the great Don Juan myself would've gone that far.'

'Oh, wouldn't you?' his beautiful best friend begged to differ. 'Not that you're competitive or anything?'

'Shut up, you,' he snapped. 'What would you know anyway?'

Lynn raised her eyebrows, turning to see their daughter off. 'Fair enough. I agree. What would we know, Kizzy? And what would Allanah know? We're simply pawns in the game, evidently. Let's leave the world's greatest lovers to their illusions. Get out of here, you mongrels.'

'Thanks for a great start to the day,' the birthday boy said, kissing his mother goodbye and patting the top of his dad's head. 'It's going to be a fantastic weekend. I love you guys. See you for curry on the couch.'

'Wouldn't miss it! Drive carefully,' Lynn warned. 'Make sure you turn eighteen.'

Following her brother out into the hallway, Kierney paused to kiss both parents. '*Adiós, amigos.* You sound just like *Papá, Mamá.* We shall. Please may I invite Dylan tomorrow night too?'

'Sure thing, *pequeñita*,' her father answered. 'It'll be great, all of us paired off and imagining what's in store after the party.'

'Dad!' Jet complained. 'That's gross. At breakfast time too. You should know better.'

'Yes, sir. My apologies. Now piss off and grow up.'

After belting the pair of students into the family's four-wheel drive for their journey into the city, Lynn and Jeff took a pot of fresh coffee back to their bedroom. The weather was cold and blustery outside, but the temperature under the covers soon lifted by lovers in perfect tune with each other and delighted with the way their legacy was unfolding.

The superstars lay in their licentious child-free peace, allowing the answering machine to take three calls while their bodies descended from orgasmic heaven. The telephone rang for a fourth time, and the showman threw his hands in the air when the rear-end of the billionaire pantomime horse picked up the receiver. She wrenched the pillow from under his head and let it flop down over his face, which reduced them both to fits of giggles.

Showered and dressed by ten o'clock, the couple observed a minute's silence in the recording studio for their son's majority. It was Lynn's turn to cry, struck by the reality of time passing. Her husband consoled her with a new song, made up on the fly with lyrics straight from the audacious youngster's mouth.

'Why was Kizzy so disgruntled last night?' the tennis champion asked, once the emotional moment had abated.

'She went on a date with another bloke, and it didn't go too swimmingly apparently.'

The parents had been astonished the previous week when their daughter had declared her relationship with Dylan was on the wane. The pair was well-matched on the surface, yet both parents understood her urge to satisfy a certain amount of curiosity with her many suitors.

'Oh. What was wrong with him? She was keen on him yesterday. Do you know who it was?'

'Yeah,' Jeff nodded. 'Tom Laidlaw. Sports nut; bit of a surfer dude. Know the guy I mean? He's at RMIT now.'

Lynn frowned. 'Wow! The complete opposite to Dylan, and now she's going back to him. Oh, well. Did she tell you what happened?'

'Not sure if it was the whole truth and nothing but the truth, but she said he was "cold as",' the songwriter drew quotation marks around Kierney's favourite application of a superlative dangling simile. 'Like a robot, she said.'

'Oh, yes? As compared to Dylan, who I agree's anything but robotic.'

The intellectual grimaced. 'It gets worse. According to our sweetness-and-light little girl, he made love like he was wanking.'

'OK!' his wife laughed. 'I see what you mean. Have we made her too discerning for someone so young? By being so open, I mean?'

'Maybe. There was no connection between them. She said it was like he was on autopilot, and I told her it sounds like he could do with some therapy.'

'Therapy?' Lynn sighed. 'Do you think Tom Laidlaw's struggling with something?'

A familiar tightness gathered round the songwriter's jaw, detected by his guardian angel in an instant. 'Sounds like classic fear of intimacy or low self-esteem to me. I asked her if she was game to bring it up with him.'

'He probably doesn't want to talk to her again,' his wife smiled. 'She did dump him after all.'

'Yeah. It's up to her. She said she felt guilty at the thought of Tom having gone through some kind of child abuse and agreed he deserves a shot at changing. If she's back with Dylan though... Whatever, angel. I planted the seed. It's up to Kizzo whether she does anything about it.'

Lynn wrapped her arms around the man she adored. 'If she's your daughter, she'll do something about it.'

'Yeah. Hope so. Kiz has your patience and my drive. Both kids do, I guess, but it manifests in different ways. Y'know what I mean? Jet can push others, while Kizzy pushes herself more than anyone.'

'Who does that remind you of?'

Jeff kissed his favourite high-achiever. 'Well, I can think of two likely candidates right off the bat.'

***

'Hi! Very smartish,' Lynn said, greeting Jet and Allanah as they appeared hand-in-hand in the doorway of the Royal Melbourne Yacht Squadron's main function room, located on the sea front by the famous landmark of St Kilda Pier.

'Hi, Mum, Grandma,' the birthday boy leaned in to kiss both women on the cheek, nudging his attractive girlfriend forward to copy him. 'You look amazing too. Where's Dad?'

The sportswoman held her hand up, returning to introduce the young woman before answering the question. 'Good evening, Allanah. Welcome. This is Marianna Dyson, and that's a beautiful dress! Go on inside, you two. Dad's in there somewhere. Dad, Gerry and Grandpa are comparing notes on who's going to say what, I think. Junior and the gang are in there too.'

'Happy birthday, Jet,' the stately grandmother said, admiring how well turned out the good-looking couple was. 'It's hard to believe you're eighteen already. Nice to meet you, Allanah.'

'Thank you. You too, Missus Dyson.'

Lynn rested her hand on the young lady's bare, sculpted shoulder for a few seconds. She remembered how nerve-wracking it was for her school-friends to be introduced to her legendary family members. With any luck, the previous evening spent *chez eux* would have helped Allanah to feel more relaxed around the Diamonds, leaving only the Dysons to contend with. It brought to mind the first weekend she had invited her nineteen-year-old heartthrob to Benloch, and the glaring contrast between the apparent ease he had displayed in her parents' company and the abject discomfort of the following night's nightmare; the first of a thousand or more. Neither could have predicted the incredible journey both would undertake to deliver them to their son's coming of age.

The two dignified Melbourne women watched the birthday boy and his stunning blonde date stride into the middle of the room, commanding attention from all angles.

'Makes you feel old, darling, doesn't it?' Marianna said.

'A bit,' her daughter nodded.

'He's such a fine young man. Another impressive, gentle giant. Let's hope they don't break the mould.'

'Hear, hear. He's gorgeous. We're very proud of him, Mum. And he's got a good heart underneath all the *bravado*.'

The party was soon rocking at full volume. The guest list had been kept to under a hundred but included people from all phases of the birthday boy's life: fellow pupils from primary school in Mount Eliza and from Melbourne Academy, along with a smattering of teachers; sports coaches and teammates; music tutors; and a bunch of geeks from the science-fiction club whence the script for Jet's recent movie was hatched.

Lynn and Jeff danced the night away for the second time this year, surrounded by most of their life singular's significant contributors. Kierney even managed to convince Dylan onto the dance floor, where he tried to act cool while pretending not to enjoy himself in his own, sweet, punk-cum-gothic manner. Of greater frustration to the awkward lad was the large amount of attention the sixteen-year-old garnered from several of her brother's peers. The added pressure kept the gangly teenager on his guard all evening, much to everyone's amusement.

At nine o'clock, the band stopped playing to let the proud father direct their guests' focus to the stage for Gerry's address. Jet had been given the choice of who he wanted to speak at his birthday party, and both parents had expected him to select his grandfather. He had called their bluff in the most delightful way by picking the family's trusted business manager.

Although stoked by the vote of confidence, Jeff had seen fit to give Bart Dyson a part to play. Not only was it the right thing to do, politically speaking, but it would also make Lynn happy. The sixty-three-year-old Australian icon had announced his withdrawal from the competitive sporting arena at the end of the season, and he had welcomed his son-in-law's invitation as a way of passing the *baton* to the next generation.

The Diamond *duo* stood back to watch the speeches, with Kierney at their side. Jet looked comfortable and proud on stage between his grandpa and Gerry, tossing the odd stupid grin towards his friends and responding to the good-natured heckling.

'He looks well, doesn't he?' Lynn whispered in her husband's ear. 'He has your swagger. Your sense of self.'

The charismatic rock star inhaled and kissed his wife's smiling mouth in full view of the intimate gathering. He wasn't ashamed to soak in a healthy dose of *chutzpah* on this occasion, further fuelled by how sensational his own date looked. Dressed in a low-cut, black cocktail dress which hugged her curvaceous, athletic figure, hundreds of sequins shimmering with each sway of her hips.

Her long, golden hair was pinned back to reveal a youthful but all-knowing face, and high heels accentuated her grace and poise. She had taken a leaf out of her husband's book tonight with this patent public statement: despite being the mother of an adult, she was still in the prime of her life. The tips of her piano-playing fingers brushed his thigh, sending pulses of electricity racing in all directions.

Such a cornucopia of enticing qualities rendered him especially horny, and this father of an adult didn't care who knew. Keeping one eye on the Master of Ceremonies, the grateful man ran the knuckles of his left hand along the side of his *regala*'s face.

'I want to eat you,' he hissed, making a group of Jet's friends' mothers gasp in delight.

Lynn offered him a forearm to gnaw on, but he pouted and shook his head, winking at the women in the front row. 'I wasn't going to start there.'

To a chorus of shrill whoops, the elegant blonde opened her mouth, her eyes ready to dismiss his advances, but instead gave in to another long kiss.

'Yeah. That'll do for starters.'

And to cap it all, here was their gorgeous gipsy girl, right by his side and accompanied by her own first love. The quirky, super-intelligent Dylan was the perfect boyfriend for his earnest but sultry daughter, who was not the tiniest bit interested in the glitz and glamour of the party set. Jeff put his arm around the sixteen-year-old, hoping he wasn't overstepping the mark. To his delight, she shuffled closer and allowed herself to be cuddled in close while Gerry made his speech.

'Good evening, ladies and gentlemen!'

The chatter subsided, with all eyes turning to the modest stage. The rest of the Diamond family did their best to slink into the background, their own gazes trained on the man of the moment, his grandfather and the businessman. They all stood tall, representing three generations of bold, *suave* Australian manhood.

'Thank you, thank you. It's my great pleasure to welcome you to Ryan "Jet" Diamond's eighteenth birthday party, here amongst the ancient mariners of Melbourne,' the self-assured speaker paused as muted laughter rippled around the room, followed by a polite round of applause. 'My name is Gerry Blake, for those who don't know me, and I'm chuffed to bits to be chosen to propose a toast to this strapping lad tonight, particularly amid such exalted company.'

He deferred to the elder statesman to his left, then to Lynn and Jeff lurking in the wings and also to Junior Dyson on the floor in front. 'My justification for being up here is that I've known the Jet-star since he was but a bun in the oven of the very hottest *mamma* over there...'

Gerry fashioned a salacious grin as he pointed out the woman in the black dress. The guests clapped, many of them whistling, including the birthday boy. Jeff released his grip on his human treasure trove and took a step back, making sure he cast no shadow over his beautiful best friend. His heart glowed to hear Kierney cheering for her mother too, and he raised his empty beer glass to the sophisticated blonde.

'Let's first drink to tonight's hosts, shall we?' the toastmaster ad-libbed. 'To Lynn and Jeff, who made this occasion possible, in more ways than one!'

'To Lynn and Jeff!' the chant was returned, followed by another, more robust round of applause.

Joining Kierney once again, the couple embraced, thanking everyone for their best wishes and kissing again for good measure.

Gerry coughed. 'That's quite enough of that, thank you,' he quipped, turning to slap his right hand on Jet's shoulder. 'As I said, I've known this young buck for his whole life. Since he couldn't catch a ball, in fact. From junior tennis champion to the highest wicket-taker in first-class cricket, and from head student at Melbourne Academy to Cambridge University undergrad'. Then we can throw acting and directing films in there as well... This kid's done it all already. He left the country last year to take up a place at Trinity College, and boy, did we miss him. But fear not, ye gentlefolk! You'll be pleased to know he's now terrorising sleepy Anglo-Saxon neighbourhoods and teaching the *poms* how to play cricket.'

The Irishman clasped his hands together while the audience took in the teenager's list of achievements. He shook the lad's muscular shoulder, watching him absorb his guests' appreciation with a broad smile.

'But first and foremost, he's a bloody nice bloke,' the Diamonds' manager carried on, 'which, to me, is one of the most important measures you can use as a parent. So please join me in raising your glasses as I present him with his first ever glass of champagne. To Jet Diamond! Happy eighteenth birthday, mate.'

Those on the dance floor toasted the young man's name and clapped. He accepted with pleasure, the delicate flute so tiny in his fielder's hands, feigning ignorance like a professional. The sweet smell of apples wafted into Jeff's nostrils as he leaned down to kiss his daughter's freshly-washed hair, and tears pricked behind his eyes at the thought of her own not-too-distant majority.

'Thank you, Uncle Gerry,' the cricketer responded, preparing to take a sip. 'What do I do with this?'

'Drink it!' came the doubting onlookers' refrain. 'Down in one! Down in one!'

To assist the poor, confused boy, Paragon Holdings' Chief Financial Officer tipped the base of the glass upwards until the fizz trickled down the heir's throat. The bubbles were too much for him to swallow in one go, despite not being as unused to drinking as he alleged, and he fought manfully to stem the flow.

The indomitable one relented, laughing at a hysterical Allanah. 'It wasn't too long ago we were telling you what to do with something else, but you seem to have that sorted out pretty well these days.'

This rather indiscreet remark fell somewhat flat with the older generations in the hall, yet provoked raucous jeering from various groups of school and university friends. Giggling, Kierney glanced up to her father's face and stretched as far as she could to plant a quick kiss on his chin.

Seeing her idol's emotional reaction, the affectionate young woman leaned back until her shoulders rested on his chest. '*Te amo, Papá*,' she told him. '*Felicitaciones.*'

'*Gracias, pequeñita*,' Jeff whispered in her right ear. '*Te amo también.* Who would you like to speak at your eighteenth?'

'You,' his daughter replied without hesitation.

'No. Not me,' the billionnaire buried his lips in the soft, shining crown once more. 'Can't be me.'

'OK. Nelson Mandela.'

The negotiator smiled, baulking at her audacity and hearing Lynn laugh too. 'No shit! Jeez, lady! I'll see what I can do.'

Kierney span around and hugged her beloved *papá*. He reciprocated, picking her up and twirling her round in a circle, lost in his own happiness. The main stage now belonged to his son, whose guests fell silent as he pulled a single prompt-card from his jacket pocket.

A lifetime spent in front of a line of cameras and microphones had ensured both Diamond teenagers were competent public speakers. He couldn't afford to omit anyone from his long list of stakeholders, all of whom had been assigned to his success from an early age, starting with his maternal grandparents and Uncle Junior.

As he brought the evening's formalities to a humorous close, Jet invited the rest of his immediate family centre-stage, before trying to persuade Allanah and

Dylan to join them. Neither youngster was brave enough to climb the stairs, forcing Jeff to jump down to the floor. He edged both forwards with playful prods until they had no choice but to take their places in the spotlight.

'Hold it! Don't panic, everyone! We're not going to sing,' the eighteen-year-old shouted above the whistles and applause. 'We hope you have a great night. Thanks heaps for helping me celebrate my birthday. Most of all, I'd like to thank Mum and Dad for everything they've done for Kierney and me. They're the best parents anyone could ever have. They've given us so many amazing opportunities and a real sense of purpose to constantly look for ways to make life better for everyone.'

Standing between his mother and father, Jet raised their joined hands high into the air before turning to embrace each in turn. 'Thanks again. It's good to be a man, and it's damned awesome to be me! More champagne, please!'

'Cheers, mate,' Jeff said, grabbing his son by the shoulders and hugging him in close. 'You *are* damned awesome. I'm so proud of you.'

'Thanks, Dad,' Jet replied. *'Mismo, mismo.* And you too, Mum.'

'Oh, thank you, darling,' Lynn kissed the tall package of potential energy and slipped her arm around her husband's waist. 'Well spoken. Now go and enjoy yourselves with your mates. I want to spend some quality time with this man.'

Jeff pecked her cheek. 'Me? Hey, cool! Thought you'd never ask, hot *mamma.* Can we get a room?'

His wife landed a smack on the comic's chest, pushing him away and squeezing past him to leave the stage and join her friends. Following her and Kierney down to floor level, the songwriter drank in her beauty from *stiletti* to *diamante* hair-clip.

'You are the sexiest mother of a grown man to have ever graced this Earth, and I want you so badly.'

'Thanks! Me too,' the Olympian assured him, 'but we'll have to wait. We have obligations, you realise.'

'Ah, fuck 'em,' the rowdy rebel cursed under his breath. 'You didn't say that on our wedding day.'

Reluctantly, the forever friends parted company to work the room, charging their glasses and bumping into each other on the dance floor now and then. Before long, a good portion of their older guests had departed and midnight was soon upon them, a cue for the band to finish their last set and relinquish the stage to a disc jockey for the witching hour.

Tired and all danced out, the Diamonds and the Dysons crowded round a single table, alcohol having loosened their tongues enough for the conversation to latch onto whether the next generation of cousins intended to have families of their own. As any knowledgeable social commentator might have guessed from the state of their respective marriages, Junior's children were against the idea whereas Jet and Kierney appeared quite open to it.

Allanah shied away from the question too, embarrassed and not daring to believe her *impromptu* invitation meant any more than convenience for the ex-patriate student. Dylan, on the other hand, had spent sufficient time with the straight-talking Diamonds to no longer be embarrassed when it came to full and frank discussions with this mob.

'You guys are going to be such amazing grandparents,' Kierney insisted.

'Grandparenting's dead easy, I reckon,' her dad said, winking at his mother-in-law. 'Like occasional care at school.'

Marianna coughed politely. 'Oh, is that right, dear? Just you wait!'

'Except on the occasion when they've got diarrhoea,' the birthday boy defended his grandmother.

'Sure,' Jeff acknowledged. 'Good point, mate. You wouldn't do that to us, would you?'

***

Jet Diamond's extended family could hardly believe their luck when they piled onto an empty Number Sixteen tram. They had watched one pull away from the stop while they were crossing Beaconsfield Parade from the yacht club, not expecting to see another only a minute behind.

Junior and his sons sat at the rear of the trundling vehicle, with Bart and Marianna between them and the Diamonds. Tiredness combined with a surfeit of alcohol left them all with little energy at the end of a long day, and Jarradie rested her head on her cousin's arm until the tram found its way to the Coventry Street junction and their accommodation atop the Dyson Administration building.

'When's it OK to lie, Dad?' Jet asked out of the blue.

'Ideally never,' his mum interjected. 'Why do you ask?'

The songwriter smirked. 'Circular reference, mate.'

'What?'

'Yes, I agree, bro',' Kierney frowned, trying not to jog her sleeping neighbour. 'What does "circular reference" mean?'

'It means you need to use your principles to determine when it's OK to compromise them,' Jeff supplied an equally opaque explanation, chuckling at the row of blank expressions. 'If you have a strong set of values which allow you to see the bigger picture all the time, and you don't always make decisions to suit yourself, you'll innately know when it's right to go against what your principles tell you is right.'

The eighteen-year-old tutted. 'Huh?'

His sister smiled. 'I don't understand either, *Papá*. Maybe we're too tired.'

Detecting another of her wise man's lessons coming on, Lynn had sidled away to speak to her parents before their stop. They had to finalise travel arrangements for this year's US Open tennis tournament, including renting a house large enough to accommodate the whole contingent.

'OK.' Jeff sat up. 'Here's an example... Say you're about to go into a really important exam' or go out to play a grand final match... tennis, squash, whatever... and someone gives me a message that you've been diagnosed with cancer or your favourite dog's died. Something that'll devastate you. Now, in normal circumstances, my principles tell me I should always be open and honest with my kids. Yes?'

'Yes,' all five teenagers agreed in unison.

'Well, when you ask me, "How's Fido?" or whether he went OK at the vet, should I tell you they had to put him down just before you go into the exam', match, *et cetera*? This is a great way to sober up fast, by the way.'

The kids laughed, realising their heads were indeed beginning to clear. Even Dylan, the perpetual poor traveller, perked up with the introduction of a cranial challenge.

'I see,' he mumbled.

'No,' Jet added, ''cause it'd put us in a bad frame of mind, and we wouldn't perform well.'

The philosopher drew a tick in the air, watching his pupils rock from side to side as the tram crossed two sets of tracks at Domain Interchange. '*Exactement, mon brave*. And you'd understand when I told you the bad news after you appeared victorious, wouldn't you? So you wouldn't hate me for not telling you the truth earlier. It wouldn't have been any better for you to know sooner, 'cause Fido's already dead.'

'Oh, poor Fido,' Kierney lamented to her cousin. 'Why do you always use such graphic examples?'

'You know why, *pequeñita*.'

'Yeah. To make it stick. I know, but it's still horrible.'

'So if,' Jeff continued. 'Sorry, gorgeous. What if I needed you to donate blood to save your *mamá*'s life? If I didn't tell you straightaway, I'd be a total shit because *Mamá* mightn't survive long enough, and you'd have every right to hate me for not telling you the truth in time for you to help.'

The lights of St Kilda Road flickered through the trees, the darkness of the Botanic Gardens eerie through the scratched windows. Lynn's hand settled on her husband's shoulder, prompting him to bid her parents a good night before the Dyson clan disembarked. With a handful of new passengers picked up along the popular boulevard, the remaining partygoers huddled together in an attempt to remain unnoticed.

Jet smiled, lifting his arm and wrapping it around Allanah. 'I get it. Totally.'

'No doubt, mate. And you, Kizzy?'

'Think so,' the exhausted teenager sighed, settling back into her seat after letting Jarradie out. 'I have to have confidence in my own principles, so I know when to use each one.'

'Yeah,' her brother puffed out his chest. 'If I've got one principle that's "Always tell the truth" and another saying "Don't screw up the life of someone you love," I need to know which one takes priority.'

The world-changer sat back. 'Perfect, guys. You win. Watch out! Incoming "As" and "Ps".'

Lynn and Jeff wrote themselves into the history books yet again in early August, when they were invited to pose for the annual Archibald prize for portraiture. It was the first time in more than seventy years of the prestigious Australian art competition that more than one person had featured as the subject. January's judging would tell whether the *gauche* move was fitting, as the artist herself had pronounced at the press conference.

Then as luck would have it, several worthy causes coincided to bring the family together in the UK the following month, the first being to headline a BBC documentary about peace movements around the world, to mark the fifty-year anniversary of the Hiroshima atomic bomb.

A close second was Edinburgh University's decision to bestow an honourary Doctorate on Jeff for the contribution made by Paragon Holdings to medical and biotechnical research since its inception. And the third was a desire to celebrate Lynn's fortieth as a foursome even though Jet had reserved a place at a Cambridge summer school, resulting in an early start to his middle year.

The most appealing reason, however, came in the form of a secret plan hatched by Jeff and the children with Kiley Jones to produce special orchestral arrangements of their mother's most famous chart-toppers. The theatre company which had ferried "The Black Sheep" through its tumultuous European successes, from Scandinavia to the Iberian peninsular and from Ireland to Poland, had donated its services for free to put on a tribute concert in aid of Childlight.

Life Begins At Forty

'May I practise my presentation on you, *Papá*, please?'

The student didn't wait for a reply, propping her notebook up on the piano's music stand and clearing her throat. She had a killer opening line and a dynamite closing statement. A deep inward breath yielded a voice both perspicuous and unguarded, its pitch deepening as she bolted from childhood.

Each sentence rolled off her tongue like warm Spanish hot chocolate, and the temerity of her message swirled in ominous invisible balloons beneath the ceiling. When the budding lawyer executed her final *rallentando* and delivered the speech's call-to-arms, she smiled and took a bow.

'Good enough?'

She already knew her father would be pleased, since the piece was hard-hitting and imaginative. Although seldom a day went by when she didn't draw on recollections of her parents' rallying cries, this assignment had been a challenge to construct a unique argument without precedents from the Diamonds' back catalogue.

'I guess this means I've adjusted to my new normal,' the young woman hazarded, retrieving her notes and slapping them against her thigh as she ruminated. 'You have too, I hope.'

A smoky baritone drifted around the room, echoing under the high ceiling. 'It's life, Jim, but not as we know it.'

The famous Mister Spock quotation made Kierney chuckle, lapping up her dad's irresistible half-smile. The reference came from left-field but was appropriate for her current frame of mind. She was learning to live without her mother and, for the most part, succeeding. Only the occasional memory caused grief to bubble to the surface. Today had been one of those days though; a slow start before her ingrained sense of commitment kicked in.

'I don't live without her,' Jeff read her mind. 'OK, she's not in my bed, but she's still with me. Just like she was before we met. Don't limit your thinking, *pequeñita*. Don't oversimplify.'

The teenager sighed. 'But I miss her so much.'

Her father said nothing. Instead, the composite of exquisitely sculpted features in profile continued to stare into the middle-distance. He looked worldly and handsome and enlightened. Most of all, his daughter rued, he looked marooned, cast adrift from those he loved.

'You know I miss you too. I want *Mamá* to know I still miss her every day.'

'She knows, *pequeñita. Te amamos.*'

Kierney raised the photograph to her lips and kissed it. '*Gracias. Los amo mucho mucho.* Your voice is as clear to me as if we were on the 'phone. It's amazing how powerful our minds are. You were so right. And hey! You didn't tell me you met Rasul Andrew at the end of last year.'

True to his word, Jeff had syphoned off a generous slice of "The Black Sheep" royalties in favour of the cursed rebel leader whose gang of Ethiopian freedom-fighters had kidnapped the celebrity over a decade ago. The torrid experience educed a flood of emotive lyrics from the songwriter's fearful brain while sitting in the back of a car as he was taken at gunpoint to another unknown destination.

'He wrote to Ry and me,' the teenager continued, stroking her dad's picture. 'He wanted us to know how much you changed his life and said he was very sorry to hear you'd died.'

Tears sprang into her eyes, which she blinked away. Gerry had scanned the handwritten letter when it reached him, sending it straight on to the Diamond siblings by e-mail in the hope that it would give them a lift. It had, of course.

Andrew Marjan was the name the former mercenary had taken to launch his political career, promising to renounce violence in exchange for his first sizeable cheque. His letter said he had made several attempts to meet up with the world-changer and was disappointed that his rehabilitation into a force for good hadn't appealed more to his erstwhile captor.

Kierney found this fact a little surprising too, to begin with. Jeff Diamond had always been a strong proponent of second chances. Perhaps, like her paternal grandfather, Rasul's transformation into respectable public officer was simply too implausible to buy into. Or perhaps the philanthropist's many trustworthy connections in North Africa had conveyed unpalatable truths which flew in the face of campaign *propaganda*.

'I know you granted him royalties on the proviso he didn't use it for weapons or any other sort of militant activity,' the inquisitive activist asked her favourite image. 'What did he do with it? Did you know? Should we investigate or just let it go, *Papá*?'

Feeling foolish for expecting a two-dimensional model of her hero to supply an answer, the eighteen-year-old heard her mobile telephone buzz on the table behind her. She wheeled around to pick it up, reading her brother's name on the screen. Opening the text message, a shiver ran down her spine.

"Hey Kiz. AM not worth it IMHO. You?"

'How weird!' Kierney turned back to the piano, where the breeze had blown their father's photograph along the polished wooden casing until it balanced on the very edge of the closed top-board. 'That's Ry. He's asking exactly the same question. Did you put that thought in his head?'

The slender athlete pounced to catch the paper *memento* before it fell onto the floorboards. Try as she might, she could divine no clues from the star's enigmatic expression. Rasul Andrew's fate was out of his hands now, she decided, which matched Ryan's conclusion. She composed a reply guaranteed to incite ridicule.

"Thx. *Mismo, mismo.* We were thinking about it too. Cya. K + JMD"

***

Lynn Dyson Diamond's fortieth birthday fell on a chilly Wednesday, with the family waking up in a suite at London's Savoy Hotel. Her husband had arranged for breakfast to be served in their room, and it arrived so early that Jet and Kierney had to be summoned from their rooms in pyjamas to eat it before it went cold.

'This is a wonderful birthday. About as close to self-satisfied fat cats as we're going to get,' their mother laughed, gazing across the luxurious surroundings at two tousle-headed teenagers loafing around as if their spines had turned to rubber. 'Thanks, guys. It's very special to be here together.'

Upholding the family tradition, father and daughter had each composed songs as gifts for the occasion. Their daughter's offering reduced both parents to tears, delivered as a personal dedication while sitting on the end of their bed. The electric keyboard which travelled everywhere with the couple was put through its paces, expressions of admiration coming in the shape of dramatic cadences and regular key changes.

"A Mother Is" was a compilation of the many elements of good fortune to have come the teenager's way, from grown-ups who remembered how it felt to be a child. Learning wrong from right, making dreams come true, helping her to have faith in herself and encouraging her to reach for each and every star, Kierney Lynn Freedom Diamond's promise to her parents was to walk in their footsteps and carry on their work.

The multi-million-selling artist took over, singing with a smile on his face and his heart on his sleeve. In contrast to the young woman's offering, the first of three birthday presents for the woman who had stuck by him through thick and thin was a light-hearted trip back to the early days, when a certain young man dared to believe his dream girl might look at him twice.

Never once did he take his eyes off his wife's. He told her how he had dreamed they would meet, in different leagues, and how he hoped she would be sensitive when turning him down. Even Jet, normally immune to such gushing romanticism, found himself beguiled by the sensory abrasion, not to mention the extreme gratitude expressed by his no-nonsense maternal figure.

Despite the gentle ribbing the sportsman received from the pair of dark-haired songwriters, the fact he had failed to honour his mother's special birthday with a musical gift caused the young man no great concern. He made her proud in other ways, keen to defer to a raunchy video recording which his dad planned to show; an adults-only track he had written and recorded with a new Australian hip-hop act.

Like "Cruel Game" before it, the film clip flaunted the showman's sex appeal, outclassing his younger collaborators by a considerable amount. The professional tease ensured the record jumped straight to the top of the charts on the strength of this video alone, commanding attention and willing his eager viewers to help themselves to a piece of him.

The birthday girl leaned into the man she worshipped, relishing his lips pushed hard against the side of her head, only periodically relieved the pressure by singing along. Their relationship still harboured so much passion, and this amazing artist could always surprise her with novel ways to express his feelings for her.

'Oh, Jeff! That's so amazing,' she said, lifting her head and kissing his waiting mouth. 'Makes me feel like I'm sixteen again. I love you so much. I love all of you so much. This is a great birthday breakfast. And what a year we're having, between us!'

One last present remained. A plain envelope was tendered by its humble donor, who adopted the deferential manner of a Chinese businessman exchanging business cards: face uppermost to the recipient in a mark of respect.

With a simple reciprocal nod, Lynn accepted the item inscribed with her name, wondering why the forty-three-year-old wore such a wry grin. 'What's this?' she asked.

'Open it,' he replied, winking at the children.

Jet and Kierney were full of smiles too, clearly in on the joke. At the same time however, their mother detected a little awkwardness, which only added to the intrigue. Looking from one to the other, no further clues were forthcoming, so she slid her fingernail under the corner of the envelope's flap and tore it open. Inside was a sheet of paper sporting an official typeface.

'Looks like an invoice,' she quipped, unfolding the single page. 'You didn't buy me something big, did you?'

Her husband almost choked on his coffee, slamming the cup back on its saucer before it spilled everywhere. Both teenagers burst out laughing, bending double when their mother's confusion became still more apparent.

Jeff shook his head and sighed, wiping his mouth and slapping his son's shoulder at the same time. 'No, angel. I'm afraid not.'

Jet was neither able to defend nor belittle his father, so pained was he by irreverent mirth. Kierney had also turned aside to compose herself, finally gathering her composure and urging her mother to read on.

'What on Earth's so funny?' Lynn smiled in mock frustration. 'You guys obviously know what this is.'

'Affirmative,' her son spat, gritting his teeth. 'Read it. Go on!'

The singer unfolded the sheet of paper and scanned it line by line. After a few eternal seconds, amazement spread across her face. She stood up and crossed the room to where an accommodating lap beckoned. The pair kissed and wound their arms around each other.

'Thank you so much, Jeff. This is absolutely something big!' she affirmed, turning to the children open-mouthed. 'And in many ways, I'll have you know. I never expected you'd do this, but it's wonderful. Not your everyday birthday *prezzie*!'

Ecstatic at his wife's reaction, the forty-three-year-old kissed her again. 'You're most welcome. Keeping it secret was a difficult logistical exercise. I made the appointment for as soon as you left, when you were away last month, 'cause I needed a few days to recover. You would've been a tad suspicious if you'd come home and I didn't want to have sex.'

Kierney cringed. '*Papá*! Too much information.'

'You're not wrong about that,' Lynn chuckled, jumping to her feet and making her son laugh again. 'Unheard of! Did it hurt, by the way?'

Jeff coughed, puffing his chest out. 'Bloody oath it did! No pain, no gain, kiddies.'

'But you haven't gained anything,' his daughter countered.

'True,' the comic shrugged. 'Collectively we shall though. It was only sore for a few days, but there was one time when you squeezed in just the wrong spot, angel. A real case of mind-over-matter for me not to lose my erection.'

'Jeez, Dad!' Jet yelped. 'Do we have to talk about this?'

'Yep,' Jeff's eyes glinted, scowling at the memory of a sharp pain which had shot through him at the least opportune moment. 'You didn't even notice, baby, so I manœuvred us around just as you licked your lips in that superbly on-turning way you do. I was like "Priorities, mate," and then it was all on in such a bloody rush that I was forced to slow things down.'

Both parents watched the cricketer squirm. Now kneeling at her husband's feet, Lynn frowned too. She was uncomfortable on the children's behalf, although they were old enough to visualise their father's predicament. It was a comical and generous yarn to pass on to these new entrants, and his unselfish gift was gladly received.

'I don't even know how a vasectomy works,' she confessed.

'Don't *ya*?' Jeff snapped and lunged towards their son, grabbing hold of his hips and wrestling him to the floor. 'Here! Let me demonstrate using this willing volunteer.'

Hearing her brother's bleated objections, Kierney screamed and ran away. The lad cupped both hands over his genitals, plenty strong enough these days to overpower his father. The antics subsided in a heap of sniggering, panting manhood, and the sound level in the elegant hotel suite returned to a breathless kind of normal.

'The pamphlet's in my top drawer,' the intellectual answered his curious lover. 'I didn't watch while they hacked at my scrotum, and no-one gave me a video.'

'Thank God!' Lynn screeched. 'I can just imagine you wrapping that up as my birthday present!'

Her husband laughed. 'Damn! Wish I'd thought of it actually. It would've been gold! Anyway, you don't need to know how it works. Just *that* it works. Hence the certificate.'

'How do they test if it worked?' their daughter asked, picking up the clinic's paperwork.

The eighteen-year-old cackled. 'How do you think, sis'? He sat in a room full of girlie magazines for ten minutes with a cup and his hand, and "Hey presto!"'

'Jetto!' Lynn scolded, feeling sorry for the embarrassed young woman. 'That's definitely too much information. And how do *you* know? Have you been donating to the sperm bank to earn some spare cash?'

It was Kierney's turn to laugh. 'Oh, my God! That's all the world needs: hundreds of little Jets running around. How revolting!'

'Enough, guys,' their mum warned. 'We're straying off topic now.'

'Agreed. Let's not discuss my astounding 'nads any longer. All's good down there, and you can throw away the pills forever, angel. No fear of any more Jets and Kierneys running around and costing us money.'

'Oh,' the corners of his wife's mouth dipped. 'Sounds quite sad when you put it that way.'

Jeff stood up, throwing his arms in the air. 'What? Now you tell me!' he scoffed. 'OK, I'll get unsnipped. Make up your mind, woman. Thought you'd be pleased to be able to bonk away to your heart's content for the rest of our life. Together, forever, wherever and whenever...'

The showman laced his hands through two layers of satin *lingerie* until they rested on his dream girl's hip bones. She followed suit, slotting her thumbs inside the elasticated waistband of his boxers. Listening to both children clearing their throats and muttering to each other, they kissed as if nothing else existed.

'Well, as nice as it sounds, maybe not quite whenever. I am certainly very grateful. Just wait 'til I tell Michelle you gave me a vasectomy for my birthday. She'll be gobsmacked! Let's move on now. Change the subject. Thanks, everyone, for such a great start to the day.'

'Oh, well, Kizzy,' Jet sighed. 'Now we know the truth. That's all we are to them: the undesirable and expensive consequences of bonking. Might've known.'

Kierney rejected her brother's needling. 'Oh, shut up. Subject's closed, Jetto, didn't you hear? *Mamá*, do you want to know what we're doing today?'

'Yes, I do, darling,' Lynn smiled, accepting a refill of coffee. 'Something you can't wait to tell me, by the look of you. The weeks of conspiring didn't go unnoticed.'

'Yes. It's amazing. Can I tell *Mamá* now, please, *Papá*?'

Jeff shrugged. 'Someone's got to break it to her. Might as well be you, *pequeñita*.'

'*Gracias muchas*,' the youngster gasped. 'On Saturday we're putting on a show for you, made up of all your biggest hits and favourite songs.'

Australia's highest-selling female artist gulped, not sure she understood. 'Wow!' she replied. 'Where's this?'

'Drury Lane,' Jet answered, eager to be part of the action. 'Twenty-five platinum years and fortieth birthday party rolled into one.'

Jeff's heart flipped when his beautiful best friend sought his confirmation with the same steady, inquisitive stare which had bewitched him since their original trip to the theatre, a long, long time ago. He leaned forward and kissed her again, saying nothing. He didn't need to. Their children were more than thriving, and he was confident that the coming days would unfold quite perfectly for the love of his life.

'There's a rehearsal today,' Kierney continued. 'Kiley and James Howard are here. James is conducting on Saturday, and we've all got parts to play. We're doing the Act One *Finalé* of "The Black Sheep" as an *oratorio*.'

Lynn was speechless, holding on to the edge of the television cabinet as if she might faint. This was a much more lavish celebration than she had expected her family to arrange, given their usual preference for understated affairs. She already had a picture of the magnificent *Vieille Dame* of London's West End decked out with a mixture of eighteenth century splendour and high-tech' wizardry. Kierney was correct; this show would be amazing indeed.

'So!' the chief conspirator stood up and held a hand out to his flabbergasted partner. 'Get lost, kids. We've got to get moving, now the *chat*'s out of the *sac*, 'ow you say.'

The teenagers disappeared groaning rudely, one to each side of the large suite. Before either had time to undress and step into the shower, The Beatles' "All My Loving" came blaring through the air. Kierney threw her bathrobe round her shoulders again, drawing it across her body and creeping back into the lounge.

As she guessed, her parents were dancing. The way she saw things, being an expensive consequence of bonking wasn't such a bad thing after all!

That evening, at dinner in a secluded Thai restaurant in Soho, the family toasted Lynn's birthday once again. The sixteen-year-old secreted some wine into a tumbler and raised it with the adults round the table. The day's rehearsals had gone well, with the unannounced appearance from the *doyenne* of modern-day musical theatre herself spurring on soloists and assembled company alike to help the show exceed all expectations.

The performance would be recorded for worldwide television relay and also in video and audio formats for general sale. All proceeds from screening the live event were to be directed to the Diamond Celebration Foundation, with ongoing royalties slated for new day centres for mental health patients in each country.

Dinner conversation soon turned to dating, these days a standard agenda item for the close family. Jet and Kierney seldom forfeited an opportunity to seek parallels from their parents' own teen adventures. The sportsman bemoaned the difficulty of meeting potential girlfriends in the face of such a punishing training schedule, and then also that he wasn't interested in the female students who were attracted to his famous name.

'That's why it was a relief to come home for my birthday and meet up with Allanah again,' the Cambridge undergraduate confessed. 'She knows me for just being me. Not the Aussie cricket captain, you know... The girls I meet in town are always so stupidly starstruck and flirtatious, and they spend the whole time sucking up to me. Now I know what it's like when you say people always want to talk *about* you at parties, Dad, not *with* you.'

Jeff and Lynn both nodded, only too familiar with this concept. This was one of many facts of life that the globetrotting magnates had ceased to notice, but it resonated with them nevertheless, especially now their boy was suffering the same fate.

'Dating's ninety percent perception,' the billionnaire told his exasperated son.

'And ten percent contraception,' Kierney added, much to everyone's amusement.

Her mother agreed. 'Well, that's true enough. Hopefully more than ten percent.'

Jeff winked in his daughter's direction, appreciating her quick wit. 'Perception's situational, though, mate. Turn the situation to your advantage. Sometimes, way back when, I'd meet a girl on a bus or in the street, on the way out on Saturday night, and she wouldn't even make eye contact with me.'

'Yeah? Why not?' the blond charmer asked. 'Because of where you were? I don't understand what "situational" means in that sense.'

'I beg to differ,' his father scoffed. 'You hit the nail on the head earlier. "Because of where we were" is exactly what I mean by "situational". I knew this one girl, for example… Sorry to bring this up, angel, but it's just to illustrate a point.'

Lynn sighed, smiling at the inevitability of her capitulation in her husband's eyes. 'It's fine. After all these years, I've come to almost look forward to hearing your dating stories. It's so long ago; almost like it was in another life.'

'Cool,' the ladies' man replied, still amazed that his dream girl accepted his extended hand so magnanimously after the discomfiture he had put her through in those early days. 'I knew this particular woman was from the hoity-toity suburb of Glebe. She'd clearly figured out that if I was already on the bus, I must've been from somewhere further west.'

His vexed miniature frowned. 'So you were automatically no good in her eyes?'

'Pretty much. She and her friends would do their best to avoid me, like I was some kind of predator. And yet I'd meet the same girl in the bar or nightclub later the same night, and she'd be all over me.'

'Because she was off her head?' Jet asked, chuckling.

'Yeah. Often enough, mate. But also because, when you're inside the club, it's as if everyone loses their real identity. Like the cover charge admits you into a parallel universe where you can all do anything you want, and with whomever you want. Then you leave, go home and everyone's records are wiped clean and all unfavourable alliances are forgotten.

'I remember it became a bit of a fucked-up sport for me and one of my mates. We'd pick out the "nice girls" and try to sit with them on the train. They'd eye us up, surreptitiously, as if they thought we couldn't see them, but then they'd get up and move to a few seats further down the carriage. Or sometimes, they'd even get off and swap carriages.'

'So did you do the same thing at the next station?' Kierney hazarded, fascinated by the idea of her *papá* in his wild youth, on the prowl for unattainable *mademoiselles*.

'*¡Exactamente, pequeñita!* Sometimes we'd let a couple of stations go by, just to keep 'em guessing. Up the *ante* a bit, y'know. The sense of the chase, and all that hormonal surge crap. Nuts really, but it gave us a rush. A game, that's all.'

'A cruel game,' Jet's booming voice interrupted, echoing strains of one of his father's most successful songs.

'Indeed so, *mon brave*,' Jeff raised his wine glass, leaning into his dream girl to soak up the moment's inspiration. 'Regardless, I remember getting pretty damned friendly with those girls at the club, to the extent that I was ready to move on…'

'If you know what I mean,' Lynn finished her husband's sentence, looking to him for confirmation.

'*Mamá!*' Kierney grinned. 'You're not meant to like this conversation. And it's your birthday as well.'

'Oh, I don't mind, darling. Your *papá*'s sex life before we were together doesn't upset me anymore.'

'No? So it must be the sex-life since you got together you can't stand!' Jet sneered, nudging his sister's arm.

His father shook his head. 'Oh, very funny, mate. Like *you're* the world's greatest lover... Two-minute noodles are named after you.'

Both women laughed, quite accustomed to the red-blooded males going head-to-head over their respective prowess in the bedroom. The Sydney-born Casanova had genuine competition these days, and watching him oscillate between pride and jealousy was an enchanting pastime.

'Yeah, right,' the eighteen-year-old hissed, tapping the base of his empty wine glass on the table. 'Get on with the story.'

'Get on with the story? Why? You're hardly interested in my pathetic attempts at winning over classy women, are you?' his father chastised, refilling everyone's glasses. 'But seeing this was primarily for your benefit in the first place, if you remember...'

The strapping, blond student copped a dig in the ribs from his sister. 'My humble apologies, Father,' he said with due aplomb. 'Pray continue, if you please.'

'Listen to you! You've been in England for far too long,' Lynn teased. 'The cricket season better hurry up and get started or you're going to implode with all this Elizabethan blood and thunder.'

Her husband chuckled. 'Well said, angel!. I'll drink to that. Think I might barrack for the Kiwis this year.'

'Dad? Don't you dare! Bloody sacrilege!' Jet cried, casting his arms out to both sides. 'Where's your loyalty? Grandpa'll hear about this, you no-good Diamond boy.'

'Oh, fuck you, *Sorprendo* the Marvellous,' his father murmured through gritted teeth, surveying the congenial setting and pointing a wavering finger at the ungrateful reprobate. 'D'*ya wanna* hear the rest of the story or not?'

'Yes, *Papá*. We do,' Kierney leaped to her feet in desperation. 'Shut your trap, you two-minute noodle.'

The quartet dissolved into fits of laughter at the bizarre image which sprang to their collective consciousness. The light-hearted digression had served to anæsthetise them from the dire and shameful impacts of the intellectual's aphorism.

'OK!' he proclaimed, regaining the upper hand with a majesterial wave. 'Where was I? Why was I even telling this story?'

The others were taken aback, so caught up in levity that none could help the chief storyteller out. The temporary lapse in concentration served to cement their solidarity rather than isolate them, a phenomenon not lost on anyone.

'More wine, people?' Lynn offered, lifting the bottle a centimetre off the ground before resting it back down on its coaster. 'You were in the middle of a lesson on how perception could be situational.'

'Was I? Oh, yeah. Cheers, *Regala*. So there I was, having fucked Princess Snooty in a quiet corner of the club, and all I wanted at that point was to go somewhere and get blind drunk and smoke some dope. But she attached herself to me with superglue. A bit like you were saying, mate. I didn't remember promising to stay with her forever...'

'Which you'd never do,' Kierney gave voice to her father's unspoken thoughts.

'Which I'd never have done until...' the ecstatic middle-aged man echoed, wincing at the surreal indignity of his own teenaged proclivities materialising from his daughter's lips. 'Christ! This is so damned weird! Where did our life go, angel? I want the last twenty years all over again. Is it too early to lodge a request for my next birthday? Rewind and repeat, *s'il te plaît*?'

Lynn crossed the room to acknowledge her husband's submission, leaning over to kiss his seductive mouth just as a tear trickled down his left cheek. 'I wish I could,' she said, lifting her lips to the corner of his eye. 'Groundhog decades. That'd be my request too.'

'Hey, Kiz!' Jet exclaimed. 'We're going to get a brother and sister. Grouse!'

'Oh, be quiet,' Kierney scolded again. 'Please finish your story, *Papá*. I want to know how things turned out with Princess Snooty.'

'Sure, angel,' the imp grinned, turning back to his wife and winking. 'Although that's not a bad idea, mate. How about getting pregnant to start your fifth decade, gorgeous?'

Lynn sighed. 'How exactly? You're shooting cubic zirconia now, remember?'

'Ah, yeah! Fuck, that's funny! Oh, well. I'll get it reversed.'

'I don't think so, Jeff. Two's quite enough. Your turn to stay home too.'

'Hmm... Maybe you're right. Can we keep practising at least? Please?'

The youngsters were laughing hard at their parents' frivolous altercation. As much as they loved each new slice of independence bestowed upon them, there was still nothing quite like being *en famille* for these special occasions. Having grown up with two speculative old souls, soaking up their good fortune came as second nature by now.

'Yes, alright,' Lynn agreed with mock resignation. 'Practice makes perfect. We must be close to our ten thousand hours by now. Anyway, come on... Get to the punch line before they spoil it by asking us if we want dessert.'

'*Excelente,*' the showman whistled, tapping the fingers of both hands on the surface of the table and scanning the restaurant for the nearest waiter. 'Dessert? No way! Let's get the bill.'

Kierney yelped. 'No! For God's sake, finish the bloody story! Tell us how you got rid of the limpet.'

Jeff laughed, sliding his chair back and swirling the remainder of his wine around the glass. 'The limpet in question,' he repeated, eyes fixed on the glinting crystal goblet. 'I bought her another drink and probed her motives. I told her it was me and my mate she'd seen on the train, and she confirmed she knew all along. So I asked her why she'd hooked up with me at the club and how come she was perfectly happy to be seen with me now, when they'd played up like such bitches earlier. Very sheepish she became! Well... As sheepish as a girl can be after seven or eight cocktails, I guess.'

'As sheepish as a lopsided lamb?' his son offered.

'Maybe,' the father growled. 'That was a pretty pathetic effort, mate. Not up to your usual standard. I can't come up with anything better though. Sheepish as a shameful shag...'

The others groaned, losing patience with the storyteller's stalling tactics.

'She told me, predictably, that they thought we looked dangerous and that we scared them, which kind o' pissed me off because she was in a much more dangerous situation at that very moment than on the train. Y'know, in the dark and with none of her friends around.'

'Oh, wow. Did you point this out to her?' his wife asked, already sure of the answer.

'Sure did. Would you expect anything else?'

'No,' the beauty smiled. 'Just checkin'. You gave me that talk once too.'

Jet startled. 'Really? When were you as sheepish as a shameful shag?'

'Many times,' his mother chuckled. 'I was as dense as a drowning dog, more like. That was for sure. It still makes me shiver, thinking about that night when I was so vulnerable.'

The songwriter inhaled, the heady recollection serving up similar tremors for him. 'Yep,' he said. 'If we'd met when you were a couple of years older, I doubt if you'd have been any different, angel. I never would've admitted it at the time, but you and I were playing out the same scenario.'

'Not really,' Lynn disputed. 'I didn't try to avoid you when you asked me out. My friends tried to persuade me not to say yes, but I didn't care.'

'Exactly,' her longtime lover cocked his head. 'They were older than you. My case *resteth.*'

The Olympian conceded. 'S'pose it does, yes. But you're right, whatever age I was, I would likely have steered clear of you on a train on a Saturday night. Without knowing who you really were.'

'Absolutely,' Jeff blew his beautiful best friend a conciliatory kiss. 'Proves my point, Jetto, eh? It's all about perception. If you want to change someone's perception, sometimes you need to change the circumstances you find yourselves in.'

The young man nodded, the evening's improper sermon having delivered its lesson in a round-about way. His mobile telephone bleeped to signal the arrival of a text message, and he turned the screen to face his father. It revealed a suitably saucy sentence from one of his many female admirers, and the pair tittered like guilty schoolboys.

'So what happened?' Kierney persisted, sticking her index finger into her mouth in disgust at the superficial flirtation. 'How does the story end?'

The boy from Canley Vale shook his head. 'Not much else happened, *pequeñita*. We finished our drinks and went our separate ways. Then I saw her at the bus station about three hours later, getting the night bus home. Shoes looped around their wrists and giggling their posh little heads off.'

'Did she ignore you?' Lynn hazarded a guess.

'That she did! She was well aware of where I came from. And back in the outside world, girls from the Leichhardt area didn't mix with boys from further up-river. My mate and I sat right behind them, to see if we could attract their attention. She snuck a few sly looks my way, but nothing more.'

'I bet you stared her down,' Kierney added, relishing an opportunity to wield her vindictive streak. 'Who do you think you are?'

'Shit, yeah!' her dad nodded, pulling his forever girl close in to his side as if he would never let her go. 'For a while I did, but I was pretty well off my face by then too. The game lost its importance by that stage of the night, gorgeous, and now it's just a story to illustrate one of life's injustices. I've got the best there is, so who cares about all them stuck-up Sydney slappers?'

A new lyric was already bursting to escape the romantic's overactive mind by the time the family had reached their hotel rooms. With Jet and Kierney secure behind their own "Do Not Disturb" signs, he hauled the keyboard onto his aching lap and began to craft a suitable melody while the birthday girl disappeared into the bathroom.

The chorus tumbled out of his mouth as if being chased by something evil, and it left him winded and perturbed. His mind jammed with a tumult of poignant themes. Celebrating mid-life milestones and watching the generation they had created begin their adult lives weighed heavily on the great man's conscience.

How fickle and ungrateful was the human psyche, the poet mused. Was some sort of perverse survival instinct turning him from hare to tortoise at life's tipping point? Or were his kind of people simply never satisfied? Perhaps those souls who delivered their successors to a greater quest than their own were the only ones to prevail through centuries' worth of brief fragments of time. "*La Lutte*", as the great Victor Hugo prognosticated during his own middle-age. The Struggle.

The French master's latest reincarnation heard the shower jet stop and pondered the colour of *lingerie* to which his stunning bedfellow might soon treat him. Imagining his lonely soul taking up residence in the baby his parents hadn't wanted and were never likely to understand, an even greater Jeff Diamond gave thanks for the life he had battled the odds to create. What a life it was! And how he hoped it would never end...

Determined to shake this inescapable melancholy, the king of the blues turned the keyboard off and readied a disc in the CD player for the moment when the bathroom door opened. The first few chords of Leonard Cohen's "Dance Me To The End Of Love" began to drift through the airwaves, and with a swill of water to cleanse his tar-coated palette, the chameleon's *aura* shone the vibrant scarlet of revolution. His saviour would work everything out. She always did. Two sides of the same coin, the soul-mates were so different on the outside yet intrinsically and inextricably conjugated through the ages.

'That sounded good. What was it?' Lynn asked, searing blue eyes flashing towards the keyboard through long eyelashes.

'An electric piano,' her husband teased. 'Still is actually. Jesus! You look blazing hot! Come here, you fox!'

Veering round to scurry back into the bathroom, the blonde sportswoman groaned as she always did. '*Argh!* Mister Cohen, please start again when my husband's got his act together.'

'Hey! I'm trying to pay you a compliment,' the comic whined, grabbing for her hand. 'Let's dance, and I'll play it to you later. Happy birthday, *mi regala ultima*. I love you more than ever. More than more than ever in fact. Each passing hour, day, minute, second, nano-... '

'Stop! I get it!' Lynn spun on her heels, letting her satin bathrobe fall to the floor to reveal nothing but the slimmest of black G-strings. 'I love you too, and I love your choice of song. I'm dying to hear what you were playing. It sounded amazing.'

'Thanks, but not yet,' Jeff repented, gathering the irresistible form into an embrace and imbibing its glorious perfection through all five senses. 'Just so you know, I'm holding you to your promise forever and ever. Keep practising, you said. And I fully intend to.'

The no-good street kid from Sydney's west, who had lived with a death-wish for as long as he could remember, now found himself desperate to arrest the passage of time and even to re-live it. How much of this magnificent life singular remained at his and Lynn's disposal?

Another twenty years? Forty?

Would things stay this wonderful forever? He was beginning to believe they could.

***

'Olá, Lena. Es Jeff. ¿Donde estás?'

The celebrity did his best to contain his wrath on the off-chance his sister had a good reason for standing his daughter up. It was late November, and he and Lynn were in Cambridge, Massachusetts, for Paragon Holdings' Annual General Meeting. The conglomerate's Chairman and Chief Executive Officer had been interrupted during the preliminary Board session by his mobile telephone vibrating in his pants pocket.

While Gerry delivered his financial report, Jeff glanced at the screen under the table to find a text message from Kierney. With a deep sigh, he nudged Lynn's arm, not wishing to draw too much attention away from his eminent money-man. The two original directors had instilled a tradition over the years of strict *étiquette* for matters of corporate governance, no doubt influenced by the Dyson dynasty. This consideration extended to the use of the very mobile telephony they had been instrumental in introducing, in large part because of the deep responsibility they felt towards ensuring the companies' world-changing endeavours resulted in no more social opportunity cost than necessary.

Their children understood the drill too. They knew better than to disturb their parents during important meetings, and they would only resort to SMS messages if something needed urgent attention or to prompt them to listen to earlier voicemails.

Peering at the tiny glowing square lit up in the palm of her husband's hand, the mother frowned. It was unlike their independent daughter to cry wolf. Fortunately, the CFO's agenda item was metered out in less than its allotted time and passed with a unanimous vote, giving Jeff an opportunity to suspend proceedings. He rested his hands on the table and rolled his chair backwards with difficulty over the thick-pile carpet.

'Ladies and gentlemen,' he announced. 'Do you mind if we take a quick, fifteen-minute break? We'll resume after coffee. Thanks, everyone.'

The grand function room emptied except for venue staff jostling in the opposite direction to refill water jugs and serve afternoon tea. The billionaire walked over to the window, looking out over the Charles River, and his wife and their long-suffering manager watched with interest while he replayed Kierney's voicemail.

'Coffee?' Lynn mouthed to the statuesque figure dressed in full big-end-of-town attire, before turning to offer an explanation to Gerry. 'Message from Kizzy. She's in Sydney at a uni' open day, and she's supposed to be meeting up with Auntie Lena for dinner. I bet she hasn't turned up.'

The accountant nodded, understanding the implications adequately enough. The western suburbs' wild woman who, despite bearing a striking physical resemblance, possessed none of her brother's natural social graces or sense of obligation to her fellow human beings. He walked past on his way to the toilets, slapping the frustrated man on the shoulder in a gesture of moral support.

Ending the call with a promise to fix the problem and a loving farewell, the songwriter shook his head and muttered under his breath. Gripping the rim of his china coffee cup in his right hand, his deft left thumb scrolled through a growing list of numbers until he reached the one he had bestowed upon his erratic elder sister. He slurped a mouthful of the strong brew and smiled at his dream girl, sharing slim expectations that Madalena would bother to learn how to use it.

To the couple's grateful surprise, a familiar shrill warble returned his greeting after only a few rings. '¡Olá, chico!'

Gritting his teeth and emitting a low growl, the former street kid rose up inside his sophisticated, new-age shell in retaliation for his sister's carefree demeanour. The surreal and exalted world he now inhabited still had the power to paralyse him, even after years of fame and fortune.

Here he stood, in a room decorated with original works of art, the finest mahogany panelling on the walls and a combination of polished black marble tiles and plush carpet on the floor, in the company of several of the planet's greatest technological brains and his own brilliant senior executives.

And there his sister was, yelling into her handset as if it were a tin can on the end of a long piece of string, still rooted in the same outer suburban jungle and calling him by his childhood nickname.

'Have you forgotten something, Lena?'

'What?'

'Jesus! We only talked about this yesterday.'

'What?'

'What?' the angry man sought to jog his sister's memory. 'Your niece is currently sitting outside your apartment building, waiting to take you for something to eat. Remember? She rang me and left a message while I was in a meeting. Have you checked your 'phone for a missed call?'

'Holy shit! Kiz!' came a retort which at least came with a twinge of guilt. 'Oh, yeah. I did forget, chico. Fuck! What time is it?'

Lynn returned holding out her husband's next caffeine fix, which he accepted with a frustrated smile. She put her fingers in her ears to let him know that Madalena's expletives were audible from the other side of the world.

'Time you were at home, Lena, like we arranged,' Jeff hissed, rolling his eyes. 'Kierney's waiting in the library. Where are you now?'

Finding her auntie's apartment empty, the resourceful sixteen-year-old had made the most of the delay by researching student accommodation. She had flown to Sydney to check out the university where she hoped to study the following year. Her choice to spend the night in Fairfield had presented her parents with a dilemma, a neat halfway point between the mollycoddling she would receive at the Blakes' and the rude anonymity of a hotel.

Lynn and Jeff were hesitant to sanction their daughter's plan at first, knowing how unreliable Madalena could be. They only relented once the independent teenager proved she had sufficient contingencies up her sleeve. Gerry's twin nieces had passed their driving tests and were only too happy to collect their pseudo-cousin from the airport and take her shopping prior to the dinner she had booked with her wayward look-alike.

However, as Kierney's message informed her parents today, her aunt's home had been empty when the girls had arrived, and Robyn couldn't wait around because she was rostered on at her waitressing job. Having circled the block a couple of times on foot, the youngest Diamond had ducked into the public library as a refuge from well-meaning fans and the locality's unsavoury characters.

'I went to that new shoppin' centre to see what it's like,' Jeff's sister confessed. 'Sorry, *chico*. OK? I'm goin' 'ome now.'

'*Gracias*. For fuck's sake, she's sixteen, Lena.'

'Yeah, and she can survive on 'er own. She's not dumb.'

Jeff exhaled. 'Oh, sure. She can survive on her own while surrounded by decent people. I'd rather she didn't have to hang around Fairfield on her own too long, 'specially seeing as you two only made this arrangement last week.'

'Yeah, alright.'

'No, it's not alright,' the superstar snarled. 'I can't believe you forgot, Lena. Your niece wants to spend time with you. She doesn't like the fact that she hardly knows you, so I think it's great she wants to get to know you better. And so should you. Yeah?'

A stifled grunt pushed through the telephone's earpiece, adding to the caller's rancour. 'She's a woman now, Lena. Treat her with a bit more respect. *¿Por favor?*'

'Shit, *chico*. Yeah, yeah, OK,' Madalena mumbled. 'You're so fuckin' angry all the time. We're getting' dinner out, aren't we? I ain't cookin'. What does she *wanna* see me for anyways?'

'I don't know. You'll have to ask her. Does there have to be a reason? You're family. You should want to get to know her too. She wants to learn about being a woman.'

'Oh, right,' the former prostitute sounded nonplussed.

Although Christ knows what she can learn from you, Jeff contemplated, swallowing the rest of his coffee and placing the delicate vessel back onto its saucer. Truth be told, he was ecstatic that Kierney had chosen to explore life from each and every angle. His sister's world was about as obtuse an angle from Melbourne Academy, Sydney University and the United Nations as there could be.

'So, Lena,' the celebrity Chairman watched his fellow Board members file back into the room and take their seats. 'Please get there as soon as you can, OK? Lynn'll give Kizzy a ring to say you'll be there soon. Meet her in the library, please?'

'What *libery*? I don't know where no *libery* is.'

Jeff's shoulders drooped. He inhaled to regain his composure and waved to the assembly, requesting their patience for a minute or so longer. Levering himself up from the uncomfortable position he adopted during the interruption, propped on the edge of the massive function-room table and with one foot wedged against the wall. He beckoned for his wife to follow him outside into the corridor to finish their mercy mission.

'*Digame...* How long've you lived in Fairfield, Lena?' the songwriter scoffed. 'The library's next to the council offices. It's been there for at least forty years. Corner of Kenyon and Barbara Streets, by the traffic lights. D'you know where I mean?'

Lynn ran sympathetic fingers all the way from her husband's shoulder to his right hand, sending electric currents buzzing between them. Smiling at the lecherous response this educed, she stepped away to dial their daughter's number.

'Oh, yeah,' a light bulb finally flashed on in Madalena's brain. 'I know. That's only round the fuckin' corner from my flat. OK. I'll meet 'er there.'

'Cool,' Jeff sighed. 'Oh, and Lena, before you go... Would you 'phone Jet too, please? Some time over the next few days? He won "Young Australian of the Year". It'd be nice if you rang him to congratulate him.'

'"Australian of the Year"?' Madalena shrieked. 'What's that? What did he do?'

'"*Young* Australian of the Year",' the frustrated father emphasised. 'Lynn won it too, twenty years ago. It means his country thinks he's a good person, Auntie Lena. He helped us win The Ashes back this year.'

'Ashes? You mean cricket? I 'ate cricket, *fa* fuck's sake. So bloody boring!'

'Right,' Jeff scoffed, knowing how little his sister knew about most sports. 'I can understand that, but the award's for more than just cricket. It's for the way he behaves. He's a good leader, like his *mamá*. He won "Young Australian of the Year" because he sets a good example for the rest of us. You get that, surely?'

An unwieldy vacuum hung in the narrow channel of air between the telephone and the songwriter's ear. It ought to come as no surprise after such a rough start in life that this artless kept woman should have no idea about the value of role models and national recognition. They meant nothing to those who subsisted outside mainstream society. He, of anyone, should know this already.

'Whatever, *chica*. *No importa*. But will you ring him, please? He can tell you how he's doing at uni'. How many girls he's slept with, *et cetera*.

Remember he's nine hours behind you in the UK, so don't ring him in the middle of the night. About six or seven in the evening your time'd be best.'

'OK,' the celebrity's older sister agreed. 'I'm gettin' off the bus now. Goin' to the *libery*.'

Australia's most influential man voiced another round of counterfeit gratitude which was punished by a swift kick in the guts from Gravity the troll. As ever, he was overwhelmed with sympathy for his clueless sister by the time he terminated the call. Although she drove him crazy whenever their paths crossed and gave scant thanks for the creature comforts he supplied, her outlook had not shifted far from their common fractured beginnings. Unlike his…

Pausing before returning to his Board, the decorated philanthropist listened to his wife chatting to their precious and outrageously ambitious daughter. Life's pre-destined generational shift had come full circle. The graceful, sixteen-year-old child star and budding tennis champion, whose defences he had infiltrated with such obstinacy and arrogance, stood elegant and masterful beside him as partner, lover, parent and fellow world-changer. Both twice lauded with the nation's highest honours, they had now raised a son for the same challenge.

Kierney wouldn't be far behind either. Humbled by his children's achievements, Jeff Diamond felt an sudden sense of impotence collide with outright exultation, disorienting him as he resumed the meeting's agenda. Images of Lynn Dyson in her Melbourne Academy uniform, force-feeding him orange juice and mopping up the sweat of his nightmares, flashed in front of his eyes while he did his best to concentrate on his Chief Scientist's description of the companies' latest and greatest patents.

How on Earth had this vice-ridden nobody from the seedy side of life, whose sister hadn't even registered the location of her nearest library, ever ventured so far from home? And what sort of divine intervention had bequeathed him a guardian angel to share the journey, along with another two wonderful travelling companions?

Hauling himself back into the present moment, Paragon Holdings' kingpin caught the eye of his right-hand man, both drawing breath at a slide projected on the screen. Nineteen-ninety-five had been the company's most lucrative year since incorporation. Their teams had channeled a record amount of investment funds into most business lines, and a large number of innovative incubations were now approaching market-readiness.

Jeff nodded to his financial whizz-kid before switching sides to where his wife sat, her eyes also glued to the presentation. As usual, their telepathy penetrated deeply enough to turn her head. They had always been on the same wavelength, and these days little effort was required to second-guess each other. With a wink and one of his best half-smiles, the boy from Canley Vale deferred to the successful venture capitalist and champion of peace who was once more in complete control.

***

Ryan woke with a start, forcing his eyes open and tuning into a high-pitched sound that felt loud enough to burst his eardrums. What was that? Had it been part of his dream, or did it come from somewhere in the apartment? In his drowsy confusion, he couldn't remember turning the security system on before they had gone to bed.

The thirty-year-old adjusted to his surroundings after a second or two, his attention alighting on his sleeping girlfriend, whose face was contorted with fear. Her limbs jerked under the sheet as if she were mid-way through an epileptic fit, and her breathing was shallow and irregular.

Gripped by a curious elation, the cricketer leaned across to his right, only to be assaulted by a wailing banshee which launched itself out of Savannah's body. Their heads collided, felling both onto the pillows in a combination of fright and pain. Rubbing his forehead and chuckling at the bizarre situation, his amusement soon turned to alarm when he wondered if their high-impact encounter had knocked his companion out.

'Sava? *¿Estas OK?*'

A moment of respite saw the woman's chest levitate from the mattress, narrowly avoiding a repeat performance, whipping her neck and head after it in a blind panic. She screamed at the top of her voice, doubled over and catapulted her hands out in front of her, pushing an invisible adversary away with superhuman strength before sagging like a sack of potatoes.

'Hey,' he shouted, trying to bundle the unruly mess into his arms. '*Es bien. Es bien. ¡Calmate!* I've got you. Wake up. You're having a nightmare. Wake up, babe.'

He rocked the rigid body from side to side, caressing the back of his girlfriend's right hand with his thumb and pressing his lips against the sweat-drenched skin on her neck. Little by little, her screams became whimpers and then long, desperate sighs, until she relaxed and faded against his warm, muscular *torso*. Sensing the worst was over, he traced his fingers along her arm and squeezed her more tightly.

But it was too soon. Ryan realised his mistake straightaway, not surprised to find the whole process beginning again. Backing off, his mind flooded with a powerful feeling of recompense which made total sense despite the commotion.

Savannah's limbs froze in a split-second, and another bloodcurdling screech ripped through the bedroom. Her eyes were open this time, now aware of where she was and whom she was with. Stumbling, the unsettled guest shot out of her lover's bed, through the door and into the hallway.

'Oh, my God! Oh, my God!'

Ryan chose not to follow her. Graphic descriptions of the many nocturnal disturbances his mother had endured in the early days with her mystery man had educated him in how to deal with night terrors and troubled minds. He was taking his first practical examination today. No doubt, there would be times when he may begrudge missing out on his usual solid six hours, but his heart felt as resolute as Lynn's had been.

The door of the apartment's second bathroom slammed shut with the American actress inside. The sportsman could only imagine her distress at having embarrassed herself with a new boyfriend and not familiar enough with Melbourne to leave. It had taken weeks for his father to pluck up sufficient courage to spend a whole night with his dream girl, unwilling to divulge his debilitating frailty and risk scaring her off.

The atrocities to which this gorgeous woman had been subjected in her hometown on the border of France and Spain, where families suffered persecution at the hands of other families purely as a result of their surnames. Country people who could trace their genealogy all the way back to its Basque origins ruled roughshod over their Spanish neighbours, sparking small-scale territorial battles reminiscent of a bygone era.

To begin with, the Australian had laughed along with his fascinating muse about the mediæval connotations. Yet the more he discovered about the violence that had been perpetrated against the women and defenceless elderly residents of the village, the more he bit his tongue before uttering the words "rape" and "pillage" in jest.

Savannah's stories drew several parallels with western Sydney in the middle of the previous century, where his father and aunt had been subjected to untold gangland horrors as children. With these experiences to draw on, Ryan had won her over more easily than expected on their first date, able to relate to her with a level of empathy she hadn't received from other men. In consequence, although stilted initially, sex between them had transcended normal tentative *préludes* and found fiery depths neither lover had felt before.

Thanks to their parents' determination to understand the causes and effects of mental illness, the Diamond children had learned by osmosis; sometimes even as unwitting participants of experiments most dangerous. The traumatised teenager and his golden girl had been engulfed by the cyclone of depression and anxiety throughout their marriage and had thereby grown into authoritative figures who never shied away from publicising the successes and failures of their gradual enlightenment to countless sufferers.

The movie-maker slid off the mattress and put on his pyjama trousers. Melbourne's weather this December was warmer than average, and the apartment's windows had remained closed after he switched off the air-conditioning. He pushed the bedroom window wide open and drew the cool breeze into his lungs.

'Savannah,' he knocked twice on the bathroom door. 'May I come in?'

'No. You can't see me. *Déjame sola.* Go back to bed, please.'

The dark-haired European export sat on the edge of the bath, trembling and sobbing into a towel. This wasn't how she hoped her first trip to Australia would go. She could scarcely believe her luck when this special man had asked her home with him for the tenth anniversary of Jeff Diamond's passing. He was the best thing to have ever happened to her, and she didn't want to ruin her chances by revealing her true self so soon.

She loved his heart-stopping grin and how his cool confidence seemed so effortless. She guessed he must have a lot of money; she didn't know how much, but it was bound to be more than enough. She also loved the cheeky way he asked her for personal information, implying that it mattered not what her answer might be as long as she shared it with him.

Savannah had plunged headlong into love's viscous morass. She and the cocky blond cricketer had met while standing in line for burgers at Los Angeles airport, where he had waited until she finished a telephone call to ask her which language she was speaking. His suggestion of "a *Catalán* dialect" had impressed her no end. Even her fellow Spaniards could seldom distinguish between pure *Catalán* and *Euskara*, the dialect she had learned as a child to please her stepfather.

The pair had been checked in on separate flights: she off to New York for a Broadway show audition; and he transitting from his home in the mountains above Denver to Australia at the start of the new southern-hemisphere season. Ryan Diamond was a household name across the US these days, with his uncanny knack of identifying outstanding arthouse movie scripts and turning them into mainstream Box Office bestsellers.

The twenty-seven-year-old didn't even know cricket was a sport, and the blank look on her face had made the handsome charmer smile when he explained that he was on his way to train with the national squad. His gentle hint that cricket was a quaint, old English game sent her mind to croquet instead, thus making him the butt of his own humour. Keen to prolong their encounter, he invited her to his table to eat their food, entertaining her with tall tales and plenty of compliments. An hour passed in a flash, and the butterflies in her stomach died a thousand deaths when he announced his flight was ready for boarding.

The dashing celebrity more than made up for her disappointment by asking for her telephone number and promising to call her from Melbourne. She had been evasive when he asked where she lived, but the mystery was solved a few seconds later when he described out-of-work actors as "couch-surfers". His sensitive mix of courtly manners and devil-may-care informality freed her insecurities enough to admit to being of no fixed abode.

Her heart sunk into her stomach tonight too. Was she about to lose this fun-loving friend with benefits who had flown to see her in New York the moment his schedule had allowed? He had wined her and dined her at an eclectic Greenwich Village restaurant before asking to spend the night together in a Park Avenue hotel. This was the stuff of schoolgirl dreams, a real-life fairy tale, and the humble actor could easily become used to such treatment!

Savannah had rejected his first move with vociferous regret, then rejoiced in astonishment when he agreed to surf her couch instead, where they drank her flatmate's beer and talked until dawn. It was his insurance policy, the larrikin had laughed. This way, she would have no grounds to refuse his invitation a second time…

So a full-blown romance had begun, boosting airline profits and racking up exorbitant telephone bills. With only sporadic work, the actor initially felt guilty that her perfect gentleman paid for everything. Her conviction soon waned however, when he replied that he was happy to foot the bill for selfish reasons, otherwise they would never be able to see each other. His candour left her reeling in delight, and his outlay scored dividends several times over.

With "A Life Singular" still in most bookstores' Top Ten nearly a decade after publication, Jeff Diamond's childhood demons were common knowledge. At first, Savannah was hesitant to divulge too many details of her own, and it had been her boyfriend's compassionate sister who had encouraged her to speak up.

Since these first few exploratory conversations, the nightmares had been frequent and intense. The troubled young woman had caught herself in time, waking before the screams transferred from relived past to the present day. Doing her best to meditate her heart-rate lower, she had lain awake for the rest of the night in fear of succumbing to a second round. Being half Dyson, Ryan had of course slept right through the disturbances. Until tonight, that was…

'It's fine, Sav. Let me come in. I want to see if you're alright. You know my dad had what you've got. PTSD, *et cetera*. I understand what's going on.'

No response came from behind the door, only muffled crying. 'Or I could go across and ask Kierney to sit with you. She wouldn't mind. Can I come in, please? My head hurts too. We could make each other feel better!'

Hearing what he thought was a giggle, the movie director twisted the handle and pushed the door open a few centimetres. With no objections this time, he slinked through the narrow gap and held his hands out for a hug.

The tear-stained face was a picture, not knowing whether to smile or ward him off. The vision left Paragon Holdings' precocious Chief Executive speechless and annoyed by his obvious arousal. He leaned on the vanity unit, caught in an earth-shattering moment of clarity.

'Will you stay with me forever?' he blurted out.

'What?' his girlfriend's eyes flashed in dismay.

'I mean, I know you don't want to get married. And neither do I, particularly…' he continued. 'But I know I want to spend the rest of my life with you.'

Savannah gulped. 'Why?'

'Because I love you heaps, and you're everything I ever wanted.'

'Am I? You're joking!'

'I'm not!' Ryan yelped. 'I've never been more serious in my life. You love me, don't you? It certainly feels like you do…'

'*¡Sí!*' the flabbergasted woman burst into tears, almost overbalancing into the bathtub in shock. 'Tell me you're not joking. Sure, I love you, but I don't want you to hurt me.'

The cricketer lunged forward to catch his invaluable find before she slipped, strong enough to raise her off her feet and into his embrace in one smooth lift. Their mouths closing in on a deep kiss, his hands gripped under her bottom as she wound her legs around his body and came to rest on his hips.

'I'll never hurt you, Sava,' the smitten Australian promised. 'I don't make a habit of chatting up women in airport food courts. There's not usually any point. But I knew you were The One as soon as I heard you speaking to your sister.'

Ryan walked back into the bedroom, still with his tearful burden wrapped around him. His eyes begged her to believe. Leaning over the bed, he lowered her down and dropped on top of her, his full erection pressing into her abdomen. Instinctively, Savannah reached down to wind her fingers around it, and he let out a decadent moan.

'Ah, that's so good. And that's another reason, you see? Sex is awesome together, isn't it?'

'*Sí,*' the Mediterranean sprite chuckled. '*Te amo, Ryo. Te amo.*'

'*Te amo también,*' the joyful man assured. 'So will you? Live with me *para siempre*?'

His sensitive girlfriend kissed his cheek, writhing in pleasure. The son of the world's greatest lovers paused in his quest to topple his parents from their pedestal and rolled to one side, placing a large palm on her belly.

'And I want to have kids and grandkids and everything with you. *¿Qué dices? ¿Suena bien?*'

'*¡Suena fantástico! ¡Sí!* I love you *mucho, mucho! ¡Y gracias mucho, mucho!*'

Ryan kissed his forever girl. '*No. ¡Gracias a tigo!* I told my dad before he died that I wanted to fall in love with someone who spoke Spanish and who lived with mental scars because I'd know how to help her. I saw how Mum helped him cope with his PTSD, so... though I say it myself... I'm perfectly qualified to help you.'

Savannah frowned. 'But I don't want my nightmares to be why you love me.'

'Oh, they're not. Look at my giant cock!' the comedian teased. 'I love you because you're smart and beautiful and I'm crazy about you. Plus, you're funny and you know how to stand up to me.'

'But I don't speak Spanish,' his girlfriend countered again, giggling at his pathetic countenance.

Ryan scoffed and leaned in to kiss her pouting lips. 'Oh, for God's sake! Why are you making this so difficult? *Basque Catalán*'s close enough, even though I have no idea what you're talking about most of the time. Lucky I'm good at filling in the blanks with body language cues. If you smile, I nod; if you frown, I shake my head. That's good enough for me! I love you heaps and heaps, Sava.'

'So that only leaves my mental scars. Are you sure you're not going to get sick of my psycho' shit?'

'Oh, stop arguing with me. My mum never got sick of my dad's psycho' shit. They said it made their relationship stronger. Closer or whatever... Do you want to spend our lives together or not? And please say yes!'

'OK. Yes, of course I do!' Savannah croaked as her emotions overtook her again. 'But you can't change your mind.'

'I won't. You're perfect for me, and I hope I can be perfect for you. I can't say I think I know you from a former life, like Mum and Dad claimed. The whole soul-mates thing, you know. I still don't know if I believe in all that mystical reincarnation. My overly-romantic sister does, but I need scientific proof.'

The showbusiness newcomer pulled a face. 'Maybe someone'll make a scientific discovery about it. Maybe you? You're the one who told me there's so many unknowns in science.'

Ryan nodded. 'Wow! Yeah. You've got a point there. You're more intelligent than you look!'

'Asshole!' the indignant Spaniard howled, spanking his bare buttock as hard as she could. '¡Aí! That was meant to hurt you, but it only hurt me!'

'Come here! You're so gorgeous when you're annoyed. All I know is I felt connected with you from the moment we started chatting. That's good enough for me. Now can we consummate our engagement not to be married? Or do you plan to test me first by finishing your nightmare?'

***

'*Papá*, are you ready?' Kierney called up from the bottom of the stairs, not knowing how far away he was.

Lynn had sent their daughter back into the house to hasten the remaining passenger's arrival while she loaded a sleepy Jet into the Discovery. The workhorse four-wheel drive was packed and primed to depart, taking the Diamond family to Benloch to share another New Year with the Dysons.

The last quarter of nineteen-ninety-five had skipped along at a steady canter, breaking into a gallop in the lead-up to Christmas. Jeff had inveigled the world's collective consciousness once again in November, when The Fellowship ran a special event called "A Pension of Poppies and PTSD", run to mark Remembrance Day and to draw attention to the large numbers of returning defence force personnel plagued with debilitating psychological conditions.

Fresh from this successful fundraising drive, he and his beautiful best friend assembled a muddle of musicians for a cut-down tour of regional Australia, thrilling audiences of all ages in country pubs and sports ovals far away from the nation's capital cities. The performers turned the volume up and down to deliver restyled renditions of each hit song, from rip-roaring rock ballads to slick dance numbers, keeping the entertainment-starved locals on their feet and yelling for more.

Kierney said goodbye to Melbourne Academy in style after achieving the highest score among her contemporaries for her Victorian Certificate of Education. This assured her the pick of the world's blue-riband tertiary seats of learning. Her heart still favoured Sydney University however, with its copycat iconic red sandstone quadrangle complete with lead-light windows and galleried staircase.

The willowy sixteen-year-old was in great demand these days, pursued by myriad suitors. In spite of her father's careful teasing that she should spread her wings while they were supple enough to make a quick getaway, the geeky Dylan had so far survived. Unruffled by his long line of competitors, the lad's only concessions to hip and trendy were a shorter haircut and a new pair of sunglasses which he constantly left behind when shifting from place to place.

The perils and pitfalls of youth, the intellectual rued. He had been no less confident at the same age in his ability to woo the opposite sex, a distinction now emulated by his son! As much as Kierney preferred cerebral qualities over their corporal counterparts, life was all about the body beautiful for the cricketing star. No doubt both would drift to a more balanced set of criteria as their world view matured.

How fortunate had Jeff been to find his soul-mate so soon! Together, he and Lynn had grown up and out; absorbing each other's strengths and shoring up their respective weaknesses. Age had dulled neither her radiance nor her allure, no matter how many bright young things threw themselves at his feet. And yet more miraculous, it appeared that the odd grey hair and crow's foot had done nothing to dampen the beauty's desire for her black stallion's unique brand of eternal love.

Knowing his wife was keen to hit the road to beat the northbound traffic, the old soul stared into the mirror while his left hand fished around on the dressing-table for his rings. Having spent the morning preparing Jet's panel van for imminent sale, he had taken them off before climbing into the shower.

The songwriter exhaled, twisting his wedding ring home and kissing it. '*Veinte años*,' he muttered to his reflection. 'Jesus Christ! Where did they go?'

'*Papá*, where are you?' Kierney's plaintive cry floated up the stairs.

Twenty-three years elapsed, give or take. Time enough to turn a lithe nymph with boundless positivity into a leather-clad *diva* whose vocal talent matched her dazzling allure. A master of reinvention, Lynn Dyson the child-star had grown into Lynn Dyson Diamond the sophisticated headline act in a series of purposeful furlongs ridden in parallel with her husband's own rise to superstardom.

It boggled Jeff's mind to realise how cleverly his wife divided her time in so many ways, steering his peace-mongering endeavours at every weird and wonderful turn while raising two children, staying at peak Olympic fitness and managing her own stellar showbusiness career. And, if this list wasn't outstanding enough, these accomplishments had all been orchestrated despite an undercurrent of fickle public opinion, his own oscillating temperament and countless other exigences.

The world-changer stared at the four identical diamonds inset into his black jet-stone ring, poised to twist it back onto the middle finger of his right hand. Lynn had designed it for him with the help of a cloistered German in London. He gulped as his heart filled and rose in his throat.

This had been his first ever piece of jewellery, other than his watch, which didn't count due to its utility. He cherished it for the amazing future it had foreshadowed in nineteen-seventy-five and had epitomised since their daughter was born. The fabulous foursome had met each challenge head-on and prevailed through the abundant application of love and wisdom, their partnership's failsafe magic ingredients.

'Here you are!' Kierney panted, having raced up the stairs. 'Didn't you hear me? *Mamá*'s waiting to go. Are you OK? What's wrong?'

The teenager squealed as her father wrapped her up into a bear-hug and lifted her feet off the floor. She struggled to be let down, too grown up for such shenanigans these days. Her wish was granted, and the pair slumped down on the bed, breathless and all smiles.

'Nothing could possibly be wrong, *pequeñita*. I was caught in an "Is this really happening?" moment.'

'Is what really happening? Going to the farm for New Year? Don't you want to go?'

Jeff laughed out loud. 'Well, you may be onto something there, Miss Freud! I've never wanted to go, honestly speaking, so no change there in twenty years.'

'Oh, I see,' his daughter giggled. 'Your anniversary. That was a bit blonde of me. Sorry!'

As the songwriter went to scold the sixteen-year-old for resorting to a stereotypical *cliché*, the fair-haired side of the family sounded the Land Rover's horn in three short but nagging bursts. The Mediterranean *duo* grinned at each other and stood to attention.

'You go on down,' the nostalgic man urged. 'Apologise for me, please, and I'll be there in two minutes. I promise.'

Standing on tiptoes to kiss his chin, unusually clean-shaven for a day of leisure, Kierney agreed and turned to leave. 'No longer, or it'll be no sex for you, *monsieur Vingt Anes.*'

'Twenty donkeys?' Jeff shouted after her. 'Thanks a lot! Your babelfish needs new batteries.'

'Just hurry up!' came the young woman's mirthful response. 'No nookie for you!'

The man of the house was still chuckling when the front door slammed closed after his miniature. He wheeled around to collect the remainder of his things, catching sight of the four shining stones again. Lynn must have polished his rings this morning, he smiled. She never missed a trick, attending to needs he didn't even know he had.

Influenced by the many hundreds of people who had moved in and out of their life singular over the last two decades, the lovers had remained each other's highest priority throughout. They had changed a lot during this time, of course. It would have been impossible to maintain the *status quo* with so much turbulence in their kaleidoscopic worlds. The philosopher gave himself and his guardian angel a metaphysical gold star for their longevity and fidelity.

These qualities could also be extended to other significant people: Michelle, for example, who had been Lynn's closest friend since primary school; and Gerry, the indomitable businessman with whom he had vied for supremacy on the rugby field for the first time as teenagers and had gone on to create an unrivalled corporate empire.

Indeed, their eternal *karma* appeared to be rubbing off on the affable accountant. Only a few weeks ago, he had made a stunning declaration, claiming he had fallen in love with one half of a prominent Melbourne commercial law partnership. The rock star wondered whether the other half was quite as comfortable with this arrangement, yet wished his old mate well nonetheless. He was secretly hoping Paragon Holdings' Chief Financial Officer might follow his Chairman's lead and promote one of the bright young things they had earmarked as a potential successor before the employees' brilliance and youth ended up elsewhere.

The line-up of both stars' musical *entourages* remained largely static too, Jeff augmented his mental stocktake. With the increasing number of indulgent double-headed gigs they had staged in recent years, the edges were blurring between "his" and "hers" band members, outfitters and make-up artists, engineers and roadies. Economies of scale, as his wife had joked with Cathy Lane at the expense of his social conscience. He was in no position to defend anyone. As was typical for the billionnaire who, neglectful of all financial matters, he had no idea how many people were on Stonebridge Music's payroll.

Phew! That must be at least one minute already. He had better get a move-on, or Kierney's prediction would come true. The philosopher threaded his watch over his right hand, the daydream now associating his jet-stone ring with arriving in London's winter wonderland.

The watch clasp snapped into place, and he wriggled the substantial timepiece on his wrist, deep in thought. How excited the couple had been to escape to the United Kingdom together and to be in control of their own destinies! And then, when the slush dried in time for spring, there came the joy of his Scottish marriage proposal. He had been so nervous that day. *No. Make that utterly terrified!* He needn't have been though, since his dream girl was up for the challenge.

Lynn had elevated her raging colt from hell-on-wheels into a rational, deep-thinking and respected global identity. Could he have transformed himself on his own without her by his side? She always insisted he would, but the notion was farcical to the middle-aged stallion. No way on Earth could he have become so adept at evaluating the objective with the subjective, no matter how well he understood the theories he peddled.

Dismissing the dogged, notorious partners-in-crime who threatened his inner peace for so long, Gravity the Troll and Miss Irony, his obedient mind switched with ease to a delightful image of Lynn's rounded abdomen, with their son brewing inside. Christ, she had hated being pregnant! Even more so while carrying Kierney, since the second time around delivered less in terms of innocent anticipation to counteract the encumbrance during the summer heat.

If bearing children was a chore for the tennis champion, rearing them thereafter had been an illuminative awakening. The reformed tearaway had taken to it too, without doubt, but his dream girl rejoiced in every layer of motherhood. From the simplicity of tiny babies to their battering rams of independence, no other aspect of their life singular had exceeded expectations by such a margin.

Now that Kierney was straining at the leash, and with her brother already roaming free, what would the next chapter of Jeff Diamond's odyssey reveal? The forever couple had flicked through the coming months' calendar entries the previous evening, marvelling at the number of appointments which had been entered more than two years in advance.

The coming year was pegged as a time of role reversal for the successful pair. Free to set her own goals again, the Diamond pantomime horse was to undergo major surgery to give its rear-end pole position. Lynn planned to enter federal politics, aiming for a Senate seat in the nineteen-ninety-eight election. This revelation was not yet public knowledge beyond their immediate circle of advisers, but the legalities were in progress to establish a political agenda without allegiance to either of the two main parties.

Aiming to court anonymity as he headed towards his fifties, the prospective senator's parasitic front-man had begun to ease his foot off the pedal. Together, he and the ambitious Olympian had deleted his next promotional tour from the electronic diary they shared with Cathy and her team, assuming his legions of fans would need no encouragement to buy a copy of his forthcoming album whether he went on the road or not. This way, he could concentrate on more gratifying tasks, presiding over international peace talks and chaperoning his gipsy girl as she hurled herself into a precipitate adulthood.

Jeff stepped into the wardrobe out of pure habit to pull his leather jacket off its hanger. Kierney's footsteps on the stairs jogged him out of the daydream, and he changed his mind. He wouldn't need it this weekend, with temperatures forecast to soar into the high thirties. In fact, he was working up to consigning the treasured article to a dark corner once and for all. It had earned its retirement many times over, to the extent that his dream girl had even given up teasing him about holding onto it for so long.

His current excuse, not that he should need one, was that the travel-weary coat had become a substitute handbag in these days of women's equality. It was no longer acceptable for a man who called himself a feminist to depend on his wife to carry his wallet, mobile telephone and cigarette packets.

'*Papá*! Your two minutes are up. *Mamá* says we're leaving with or without you!'

'An idle threat indeed,' the showman muttered, giving the young woman a sheepish grin. 'As if, angel...'

Not only was his Don Juan alter-ego confident Lynn wouldn't relish spending their special day and night alone, but at the exhilarating speeds he tended to drive in his desire to let off steam, the Aston Martin would have no trouble overtaking the cuboid mammoth before they ran out of freeway, even with up to half an hour's head-start. Channelling the tearaway of his bygone days, it wasn't too much of a stretch to imagine the chase to be worth it. His devoted saviour unleashing her bridled displeasure on his helpless, exposed and wanton body would be a treat to behold, anniversary or no anniversary!

As the great man turned to answer his daughter's call, his eyes were drawn to the mirror in the *en suite* bathroom. A message was waiting for him, delicious in its intimacy, smeared in long-hand using a rich shade of burgundy lipstick. He pushed the door open to take a closer look, enthralled by the delicious fate it advertised upon their arrival in Benloch, awaiting him at the mercy of the brazen minx concealed beneath his *regala*'s sophisticated exterior.

Surely his movements weren't quite so easy to predict, even after twenty years together! How did his soul-mate know he would return to the bedroom before locking up and setting the alarm?

'Yeah, gorgeous. I'm right there.'

The gilt and guilty cylinder sat open and misshapen on the marble vanity, discarded among its casual conspirators. Colours for every mood and season, painting an angel into a temptress for him alone. There would be no further transgressions or delay tactics today. This woman deserved the very best, and to her ultimate good fortune, his sole mission was to deliver the same.

The wordsmith chose his weapon, twisted the barrel and took aim. Lynn's anniversary wish begged a response from her gallant nobleman.

D'accord. Avec grand plaisir.
Je t'aime, mon amie.

End of Part Six

If you enjoyed reading this book, please take the time to tell your friends and leave a review on Amazon and Goodreads.

The final book in the series, "A Life After", is scheduled for release in June 2018. Full details can be found at http://lorrainepestell.com.

So their handbook for life was complete. Not a cast-iron guarantee, but a good start for anyone looking for answers. The rest was up to its readers to make their own life singular. Jeff Diamond sealed the envelope on his manuscript, content that he had fully accounted for the life that had brought him to where he was today. Alone.

Lynn would be pleased with the way their autobiography had turned out, complete with a carefully selected set of photographs and proof-read from cover to cover by their gorgeous daughter.

It was now time to finish things off properly, and this began by acknowledging the mate who had stood by Jeff for almost thirty years. Gerry Blake had been his squash partner, his manager, his drinking buddy and his best man through the whole incredible journey, in so many ways his alter-ego. He was getting married for the first time at forty-seven years old, no doubt spooked by what had happened to his old friend.

The thankful millionnaire and the ghost living inside his heart were determined to give Gerry and his new wife the very best send-off, before continuing on their own quest for reunion. Would they find a way to be together again? And how would the kids know to keep telling their singular story?